⇾A MODERN GRAPHIC RETELLING OF *THE SECRET GARDEN*⇽

The Secret Garden
on 81st Street

A MODERN GRAPHIC RETELLING OF *THE SECRET GARDEN*

The Secret Garden on 81st Street

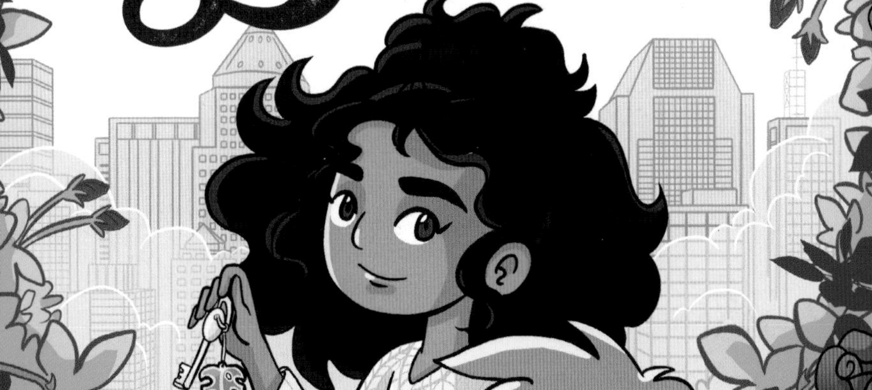

L B

Little, Brown and Company
New York Boston

BY IVY NOELLE WEIR • ILLUSTRATED BY AMBER PADILLA

About This Book

This book was edited by Rachel Poloski and designed by Ching N. Chan. The production was supervised by Bernadette Flinn, and the production editor was Lindsay Walter-Greaney. The text was set in Chalkboard, and the display type is Creative Vintage.

Little, Brown and Company
Hachette Book Group
1290 Avenue of the Americas, New York, NY 10104
Visit us at LBYR.com

First Edition: September 2021

Little, Brown and Company is a division of Hachette Book Group, Inc.
The Little, Brown name and logo are trademarks of Hachette Book Group, Inc.

The publisher is not responsible for websites (or their content) that are not owned by the publisher.

Library of Congress Cataloging-in-Publication Data
Names: Weir, Ivy Noelle, author. | Padilla, Amber, artist.
| Burnett, Frances Hodgson, 1849-1924. Secret garden.
Title: The secret garden on 81st street : a modern retelling of The secret garden / story by Ivy Noelle Weir ; art by Amber Padilla.
Description: First edition. | New York : Little, Brown and Company, 2021.
| Summary: "Entitled loner Mary Lennox moves to her uncle's house in New York when her parents pass and makes friends for the first time, who help her restore her uncle's abandoned rooftop garden, teaching her to grieve and grow." —Provided by publisher.
Identifiers: LCCN 2020019856 (print) | LCCN 2020019857 (ebook)
| ISBN 9780316459655 (hardcover) | ISBN 9780316459709 (paperback)
| ISBN 9780316459686 (ebook) | ISBN 9780316459693 (ebook other)
Subjects: LCSH: Graphic novels. | CYAC: Graphic novels.
| Grief—Fiction. | Gardens—Fiction. | Friendship—Fiction.
Classification: LCC PZ7.7.W399 Se 2021 (print)
| LCC PZ7.7.W399 (ebook) | DDC 741.5/973—dc23
LC record available at https://lccn.loc.gov/2020019856

ISBNs: 978-0-316-45965-5 (hardcover), 978-0-316-45970-9 (paperback), 978-0-316-45968-6 (ebook), 978-0-316-45967-9 (ebook), 978-0-316-45966-2 (ebook)

PRINTED IN CHINA

1010

Hardcover: 10 9 8 7 6 5 4 3 2 1

Paperback: 10 9 8 7 6 5 4 3 2 1

For my mom, who taught me that sometimes the best place to find peace is digging in the dirt. –Weir

To my grandma Marcella, who gave me a little plot of land in our backyard so I could plant wildflowers and make my own Secret Garden. –Padilla

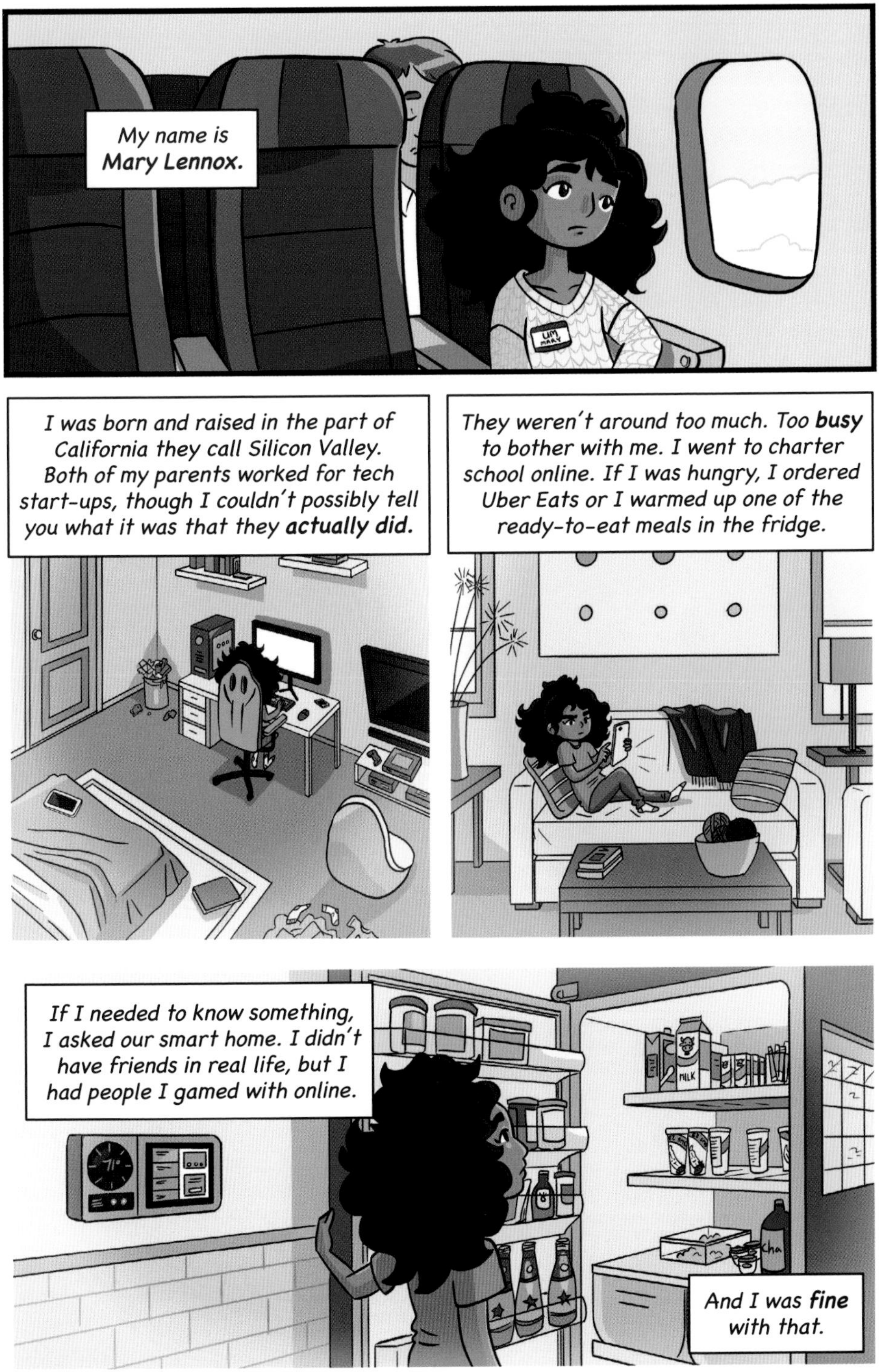
My name is **Mary Lennox.**
I was born and raised in the part of California they call Silicon Valley. Both of my parents worked for tech start-ups, though I couldn't possibly tell you what it was that they **actually did.**
They weren't around too much. Too **busy** to bother with me. I went to charter school online. If I was hungry, I ordered Uber Eats or I warmed up one of the ready-to-eat meals in the fridge.
If I needed to know something, I asked our smart home. I didn't have friends in real life, but I had people I gamed with online.
MILK
And I was **fine** with that.

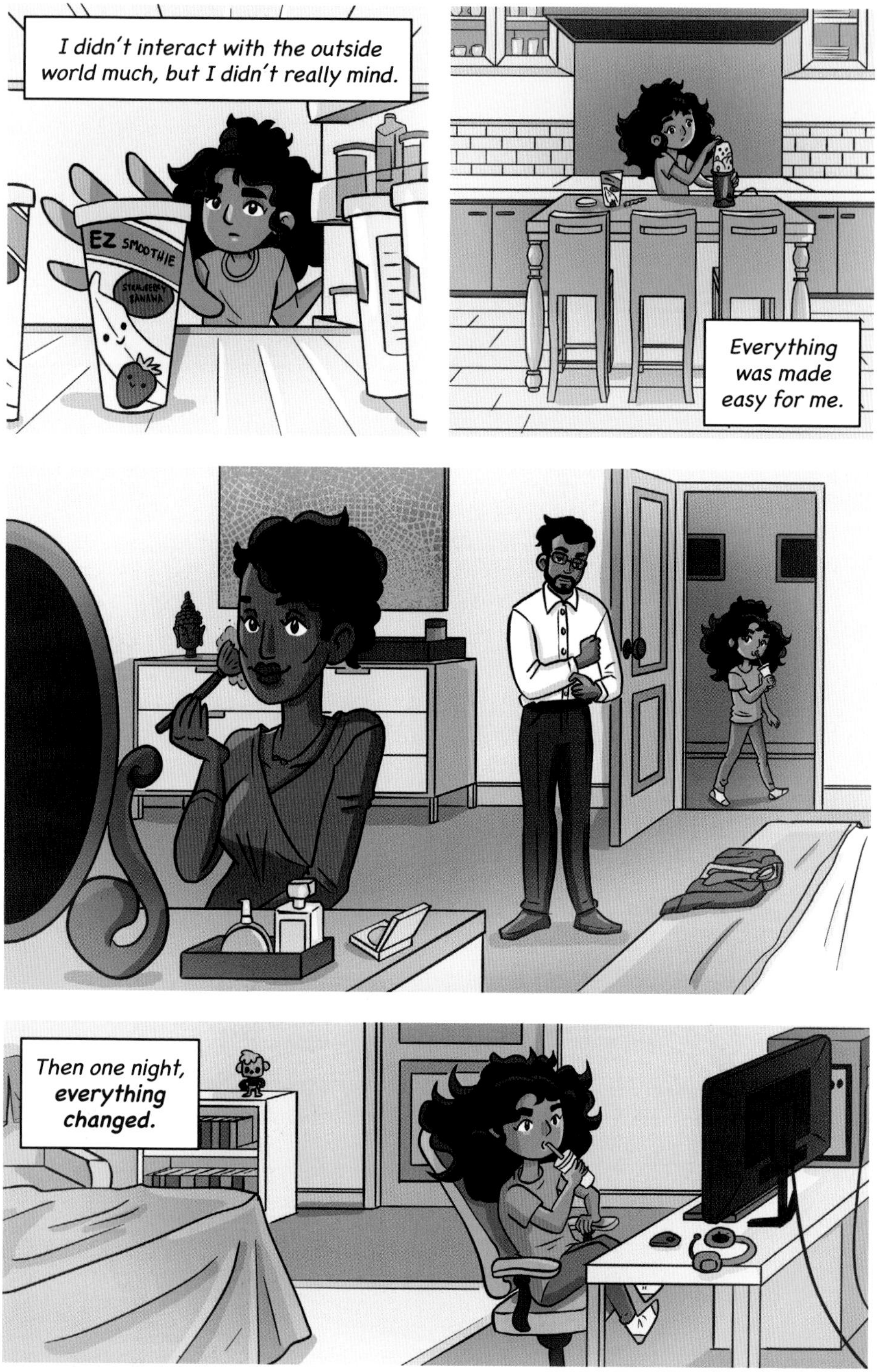
I didn't interact with the outside world much, but I didn't really mind.
EZ SMOOTHIE
STRAWBERRY BANANA
Everything was made easy for me.
Then one night, **everything changed.**

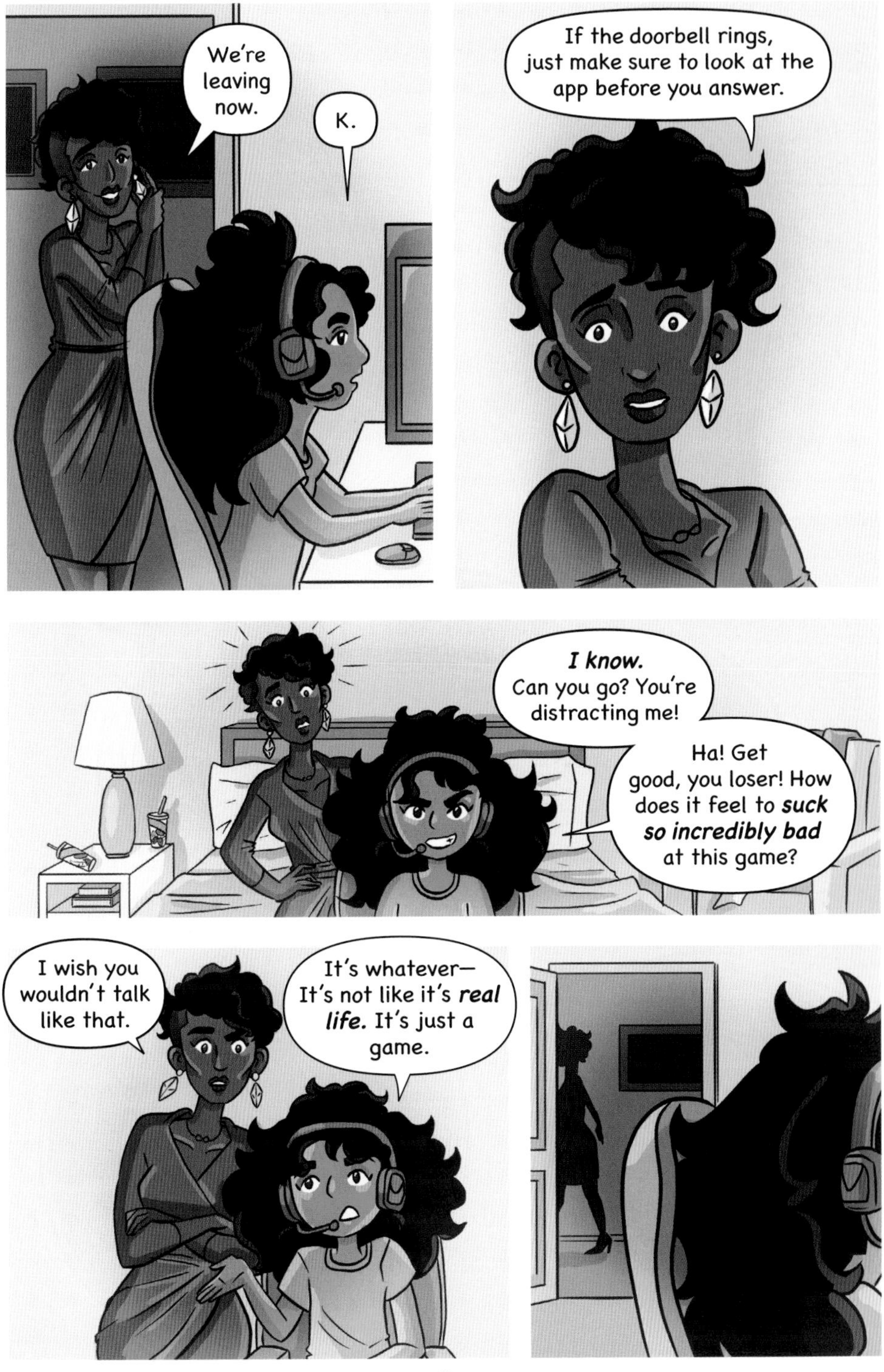
We're leaving now.
K.
If the doorbell rings, just make sure to look at the app before you answer.
I know. Can you go? You're distracting me!
Ha! Get good, you loser! How does it feel to ***suck so incredibly bad*** at this game?
I wish you wouldn't talk like that.
It's whatever— It's not like it's ***real life.*** It's just a game.

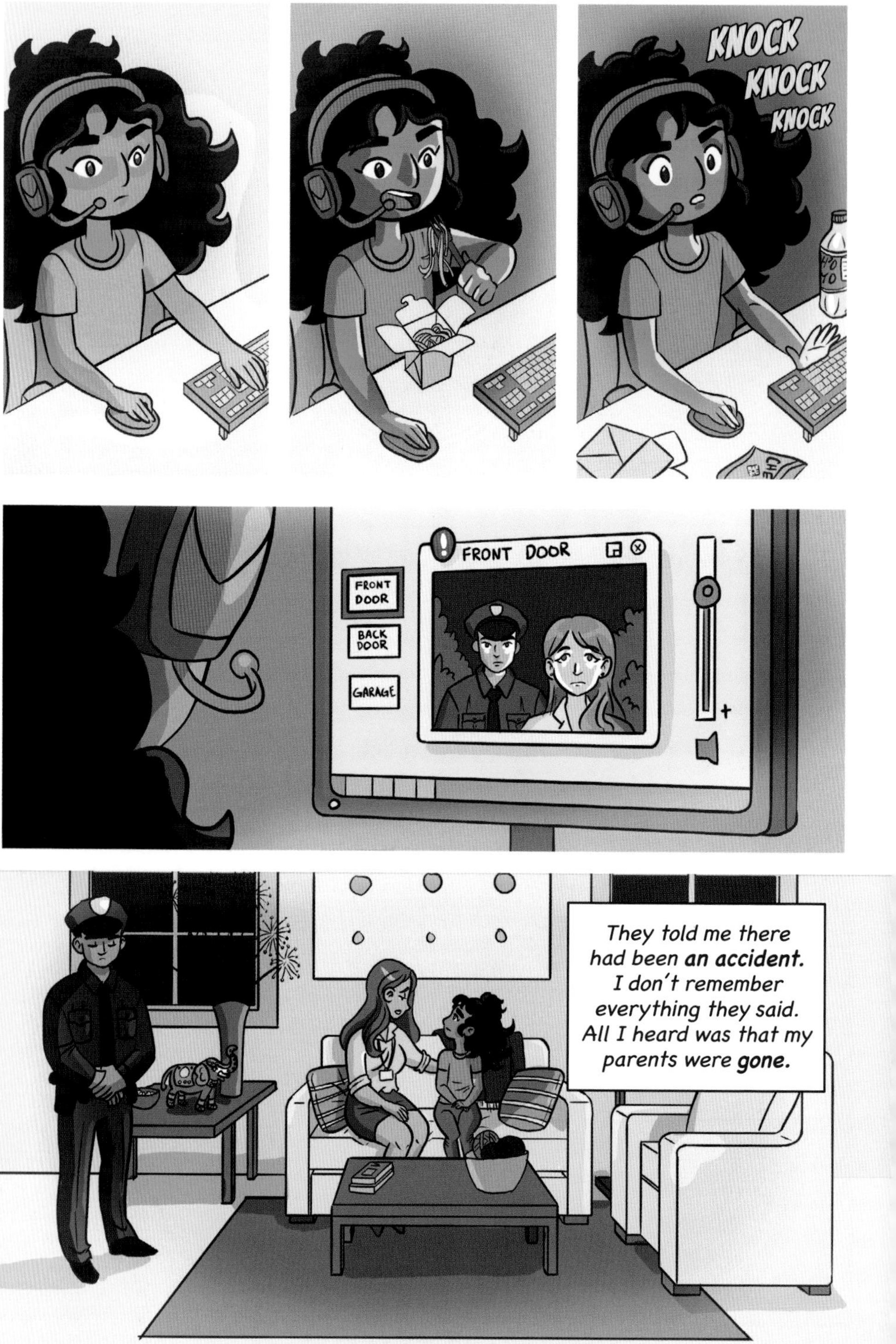
KNOCK
KNOCK
KNOCK
FRONT DOOR
FRONT DOOR
BACK DOOR
GARAGE
They told me there had been **an accident.** I don't remember everything they said. All I heard was that my parents were **gone.**

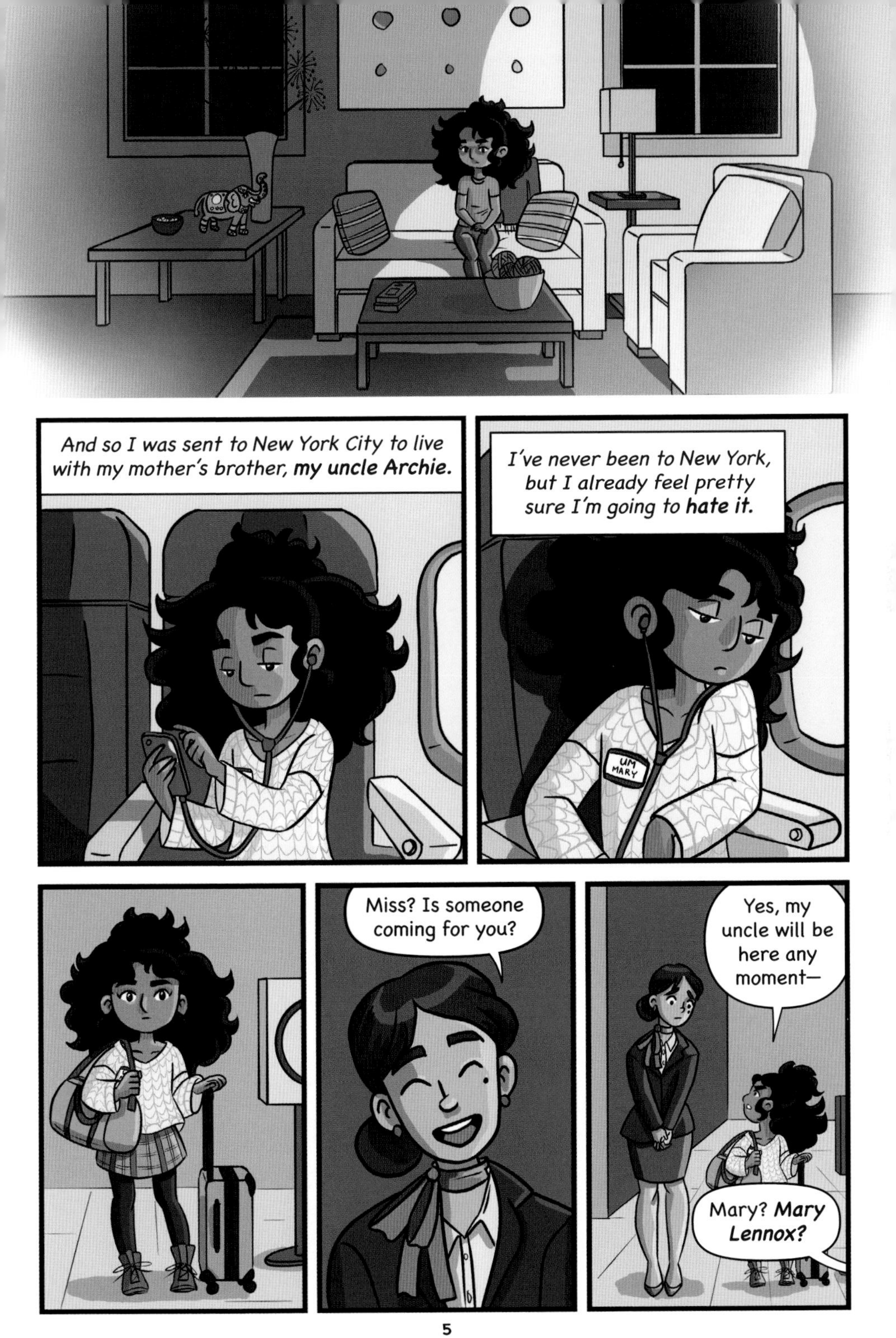
And so I was sent to New York City to live with my mother's brother, **my uncle Archie.**
I've never been to New York, but I already feel pretty sure I'm going to **hate it.**
UM MARY
Miss? Is someone coming for you?
Yes, my uncle will be here any moment—
Mary? **Mary Lennox?**

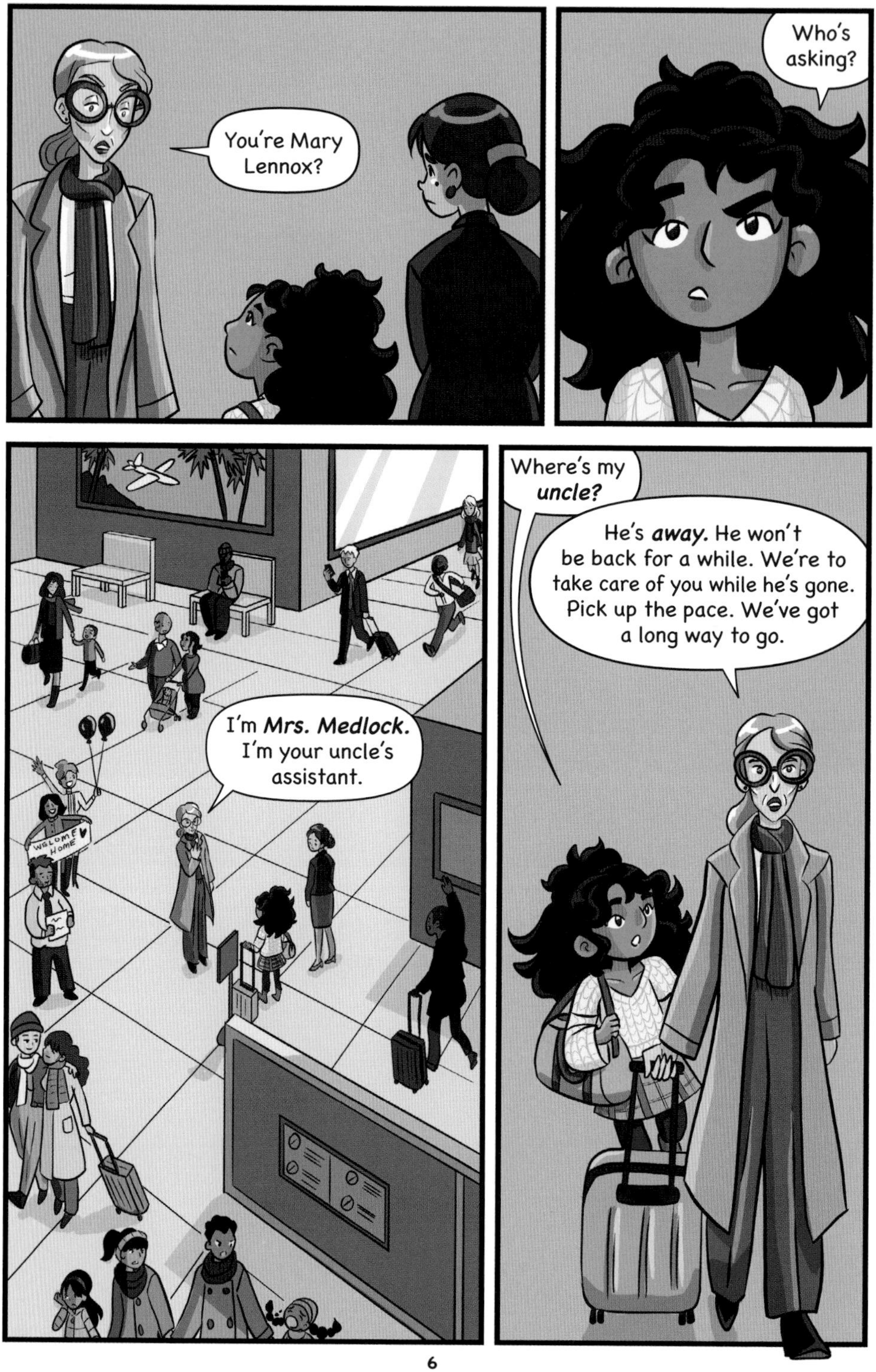

You're Mary Lennox?
Who's asking?
I'm **Mrs. Medlock.** I'm your uncle's assistant.
WELCOME HOME
Where's my **uncle?**
He's **away.** He won't be back for a while. We're to take care of you while he's gone. Pick up the pace. We've got a long way to go.

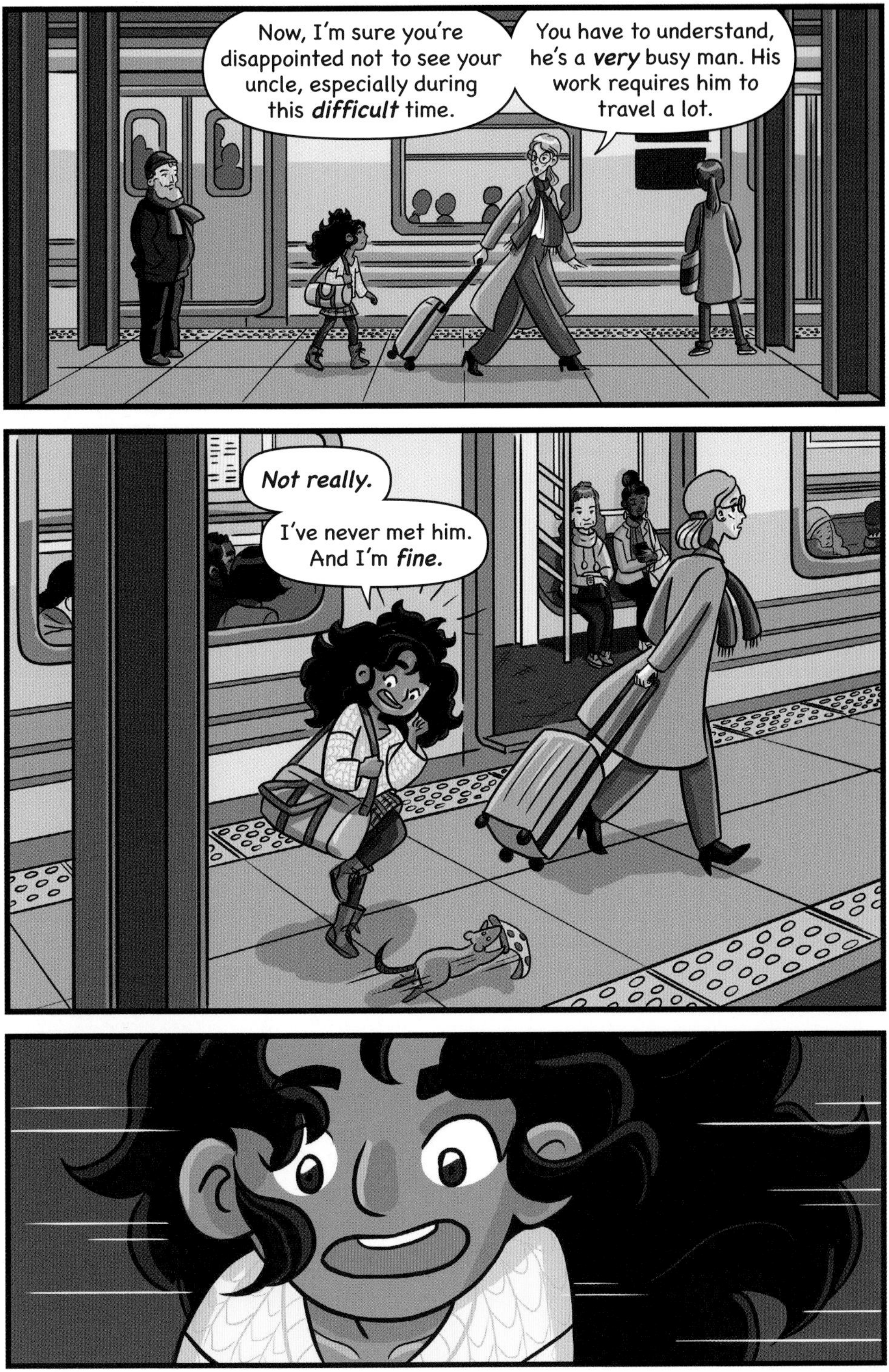
Now, I'm sure you're disappointed not to see your uncle, especially during this *difficult* time.
You have to understand, he's a *very* busy man. His work requires him to travel a lot.
Not really.
I've never met him. And I'm *fine.*

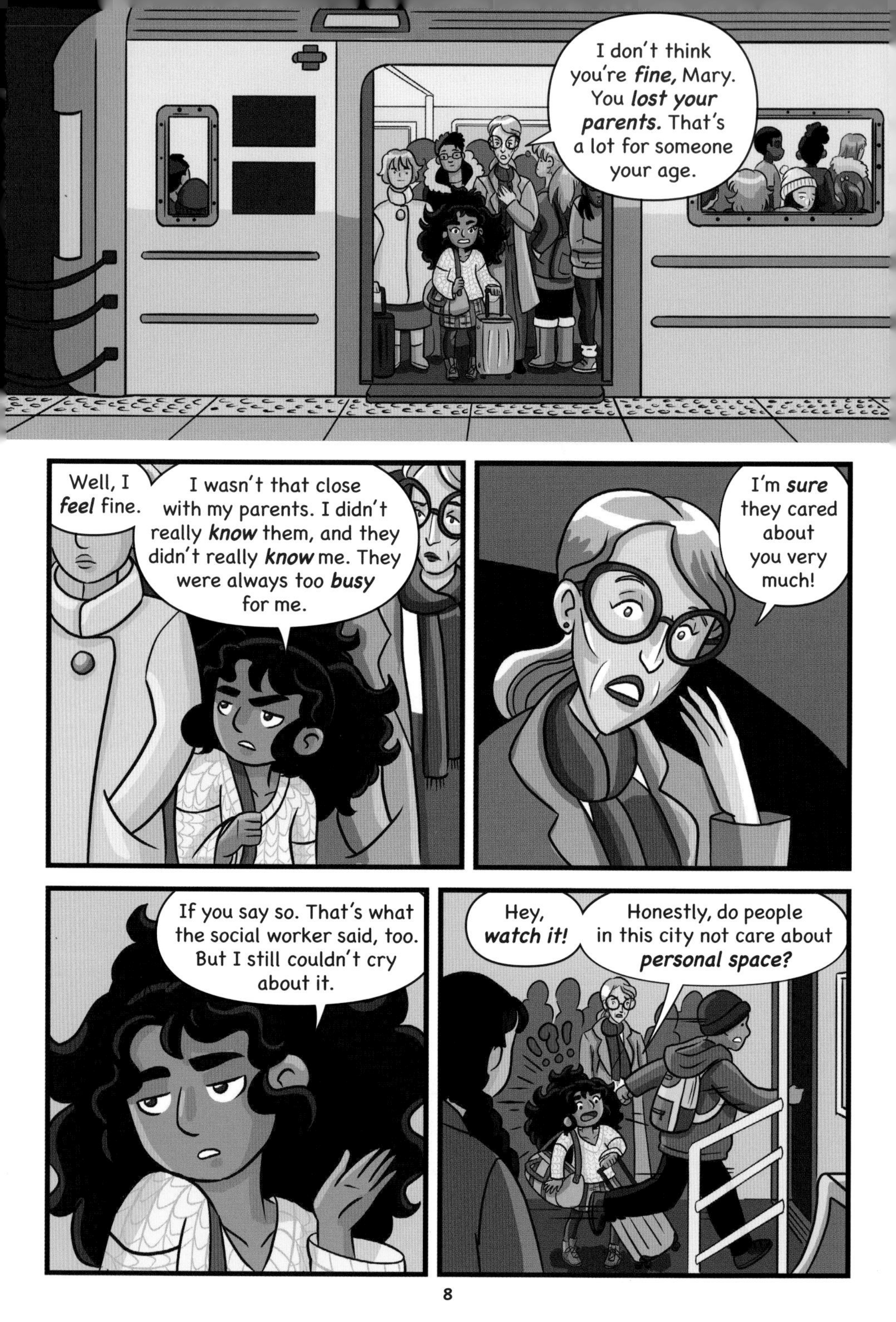
I don't think you're ***fine,*** Mary. You ***lost your parents.*** That's a lot for someone your age.
Well, I ***feel*** fine.
I wasn't that close with my parents. I didn't really ***know*** them, and they didn't really ***know*** me. They were always too ***busy*** for me.
I'm ***sure*** they cared about you very much!
If you say so. That's what the social worker said, too. But I still couldn't cry about it.
Hey, ***watch it!***
Honestly, do people in this city not care about ***personal space?***

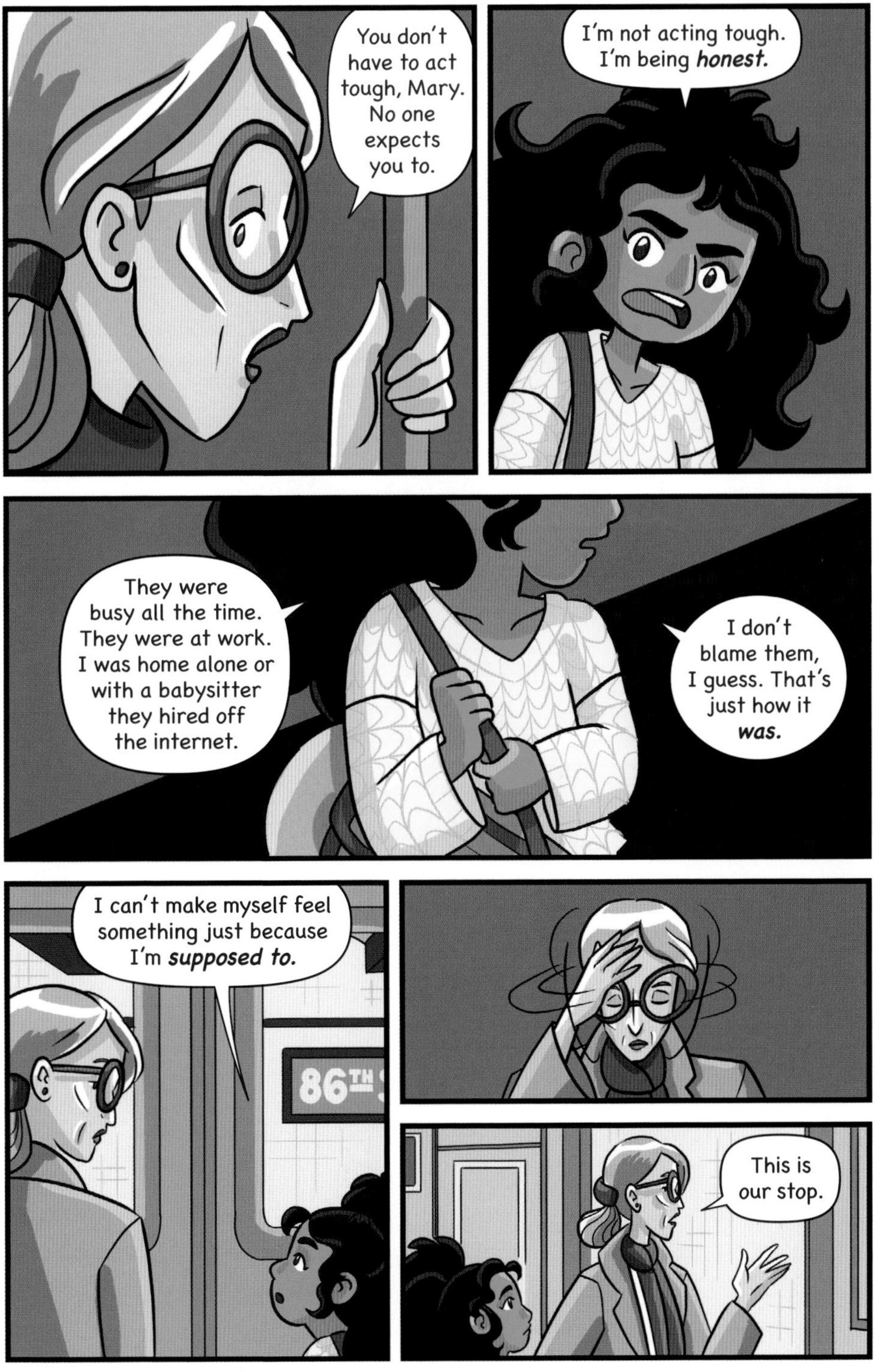
You don't have to act tough, Mary. No one expects you to.
I'm not acting tough. I'm being ***honest.***
They were busy all the time. They were at work. I was home alone or with a babysitter they hired off the internet.
I don't blame them, I guess. That's just how it ***was.***
I can't make myself feel something just because I'm ***supposed to.***
86TH
This is our stop.

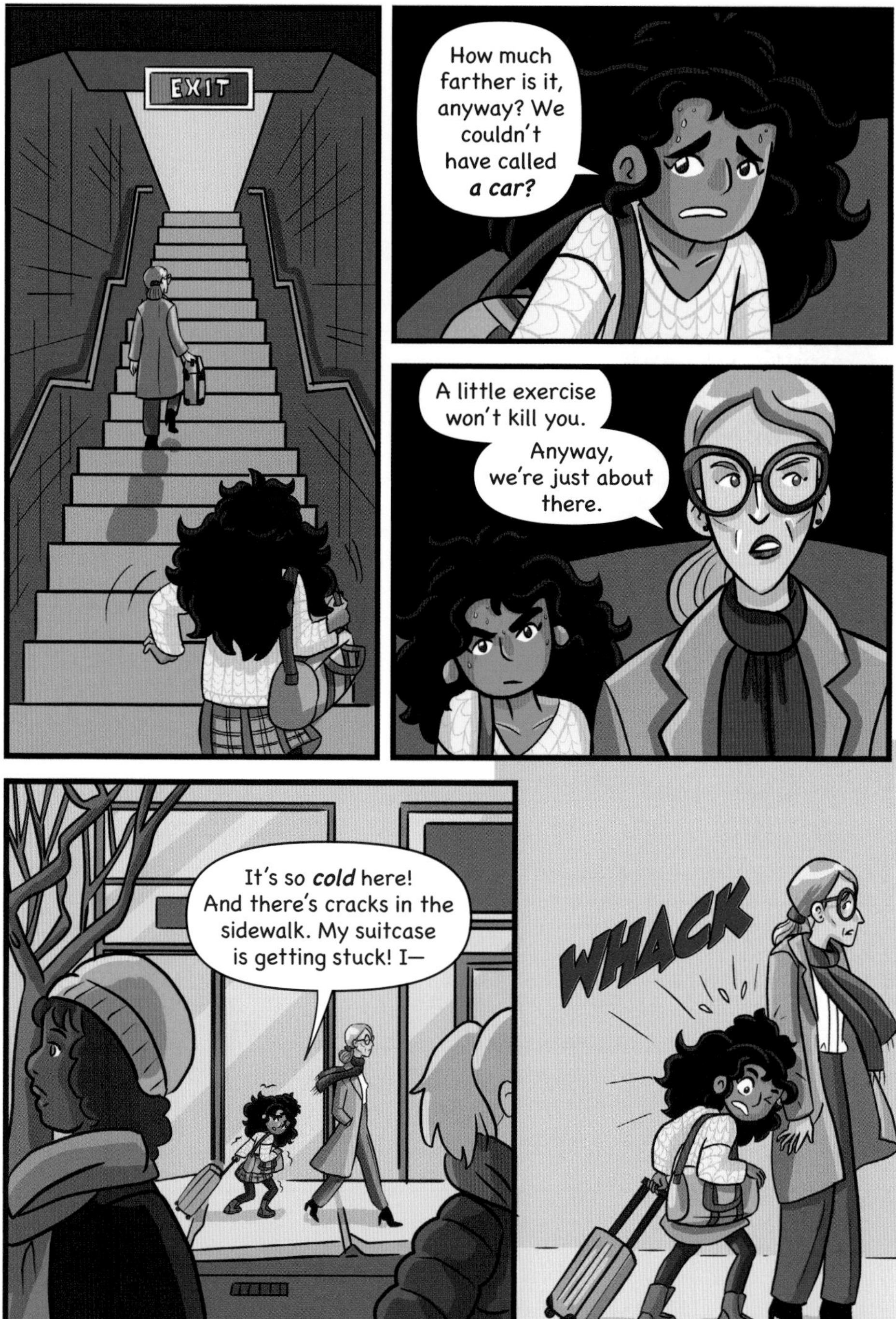
EXIT
How much farther is it, anyway? We couldn't have called *a car?*
A little exercise won't kill you.
Anyway, we're just about there.
It's so *cold* here! And there's cracks in the sidewalk. My suitcase is getting stuck! I—
WHACK

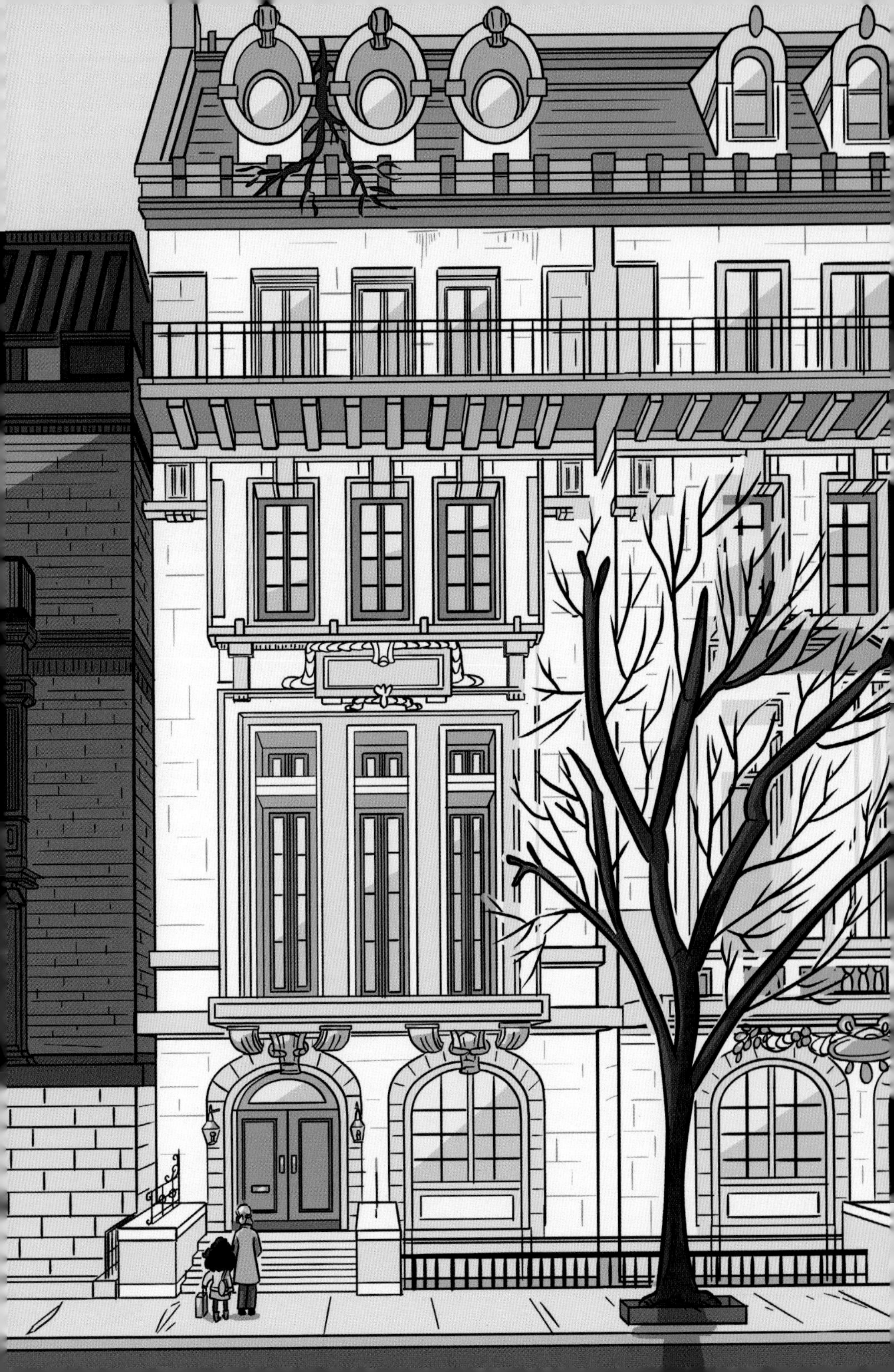

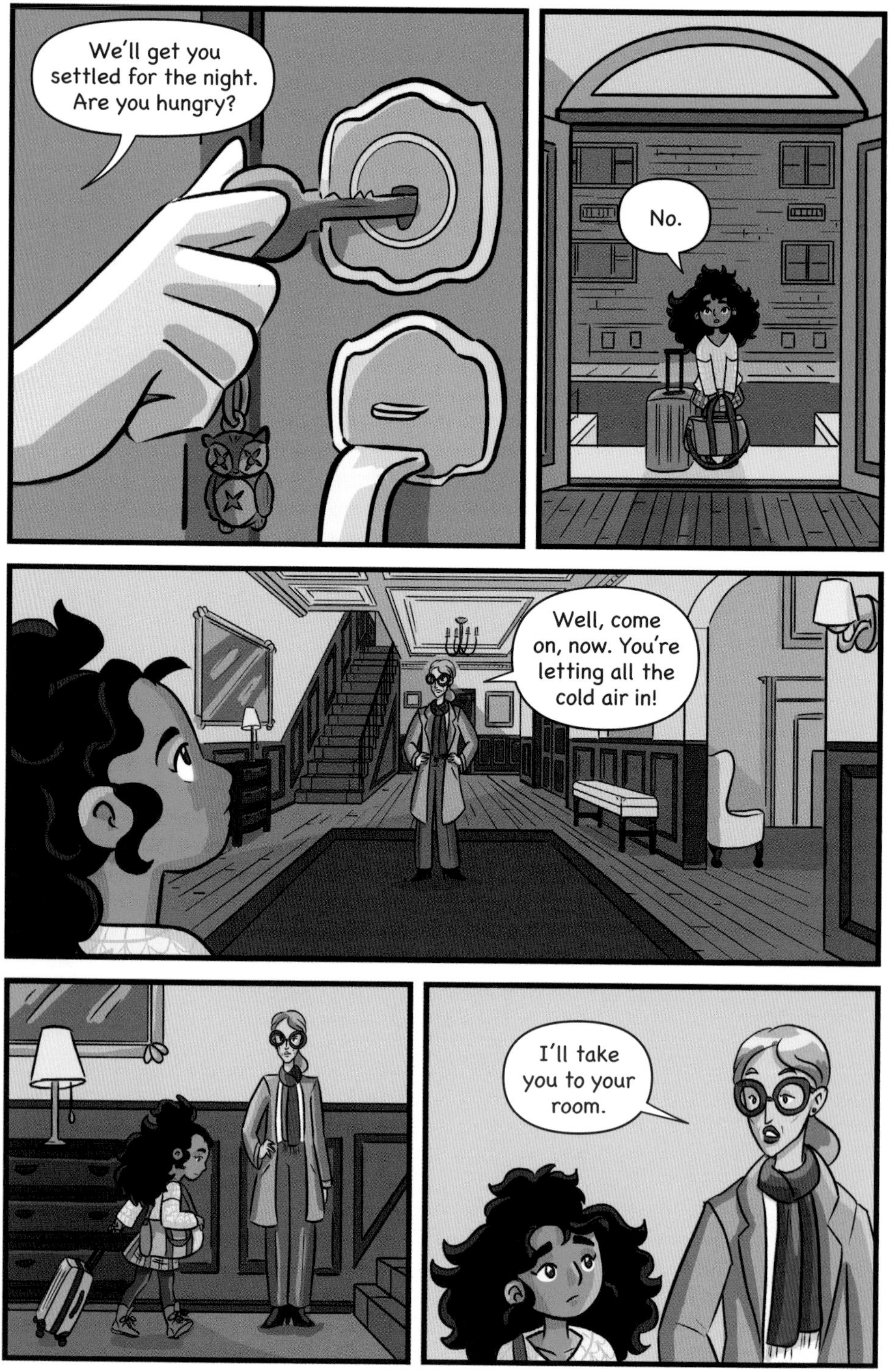
We'll get you settled for the night. Are you hungry?
No.
Well, come on, now. You're letting all the cold air in!
I'll take you to your room.

Here we are, then.

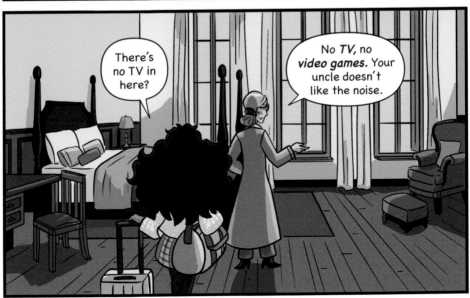

There's no TV in here?

No *TV*, no *video games.* Your uncle doesn't like the noise.

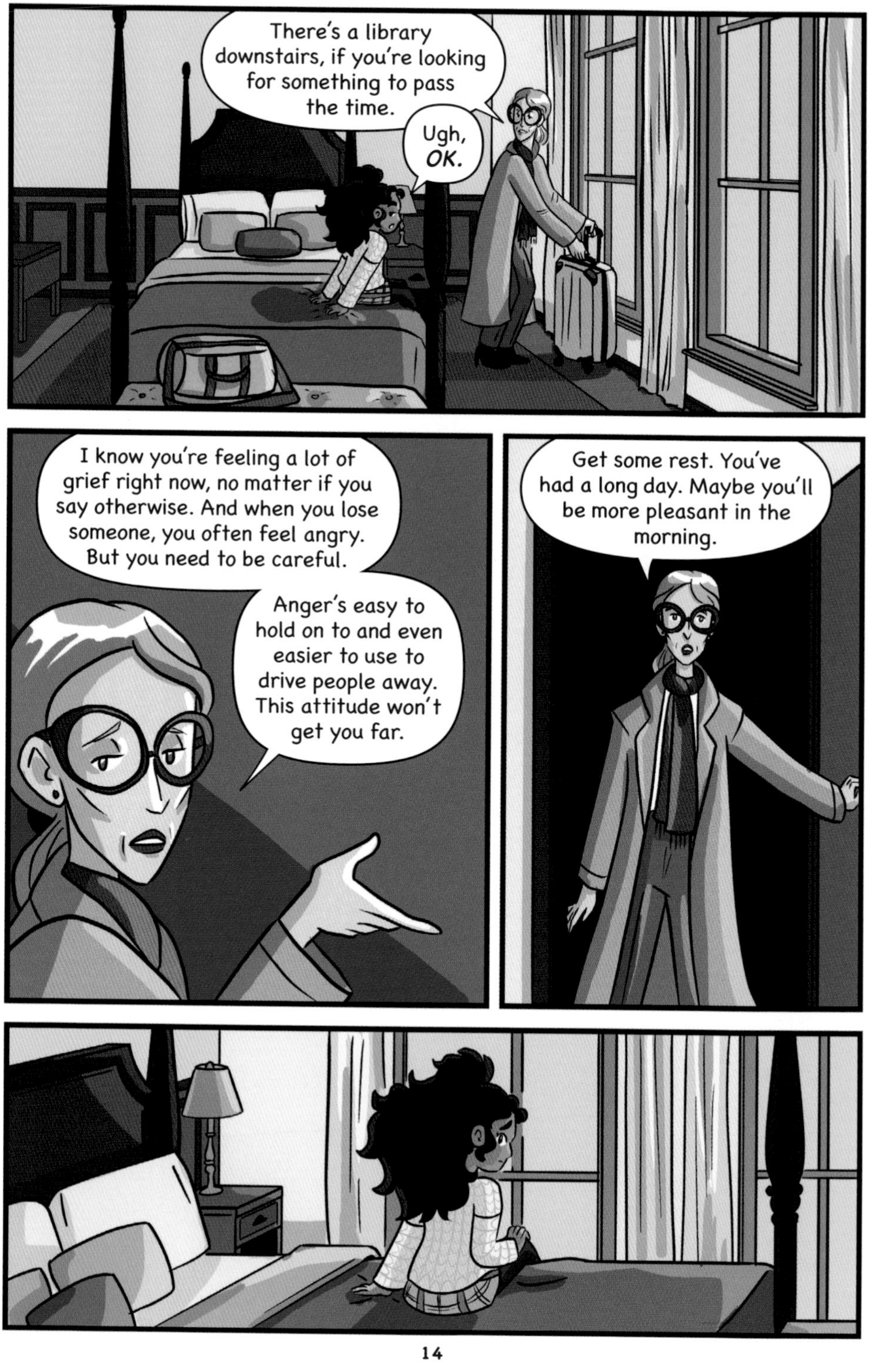
There's a library downstairs, if you're looking for something to pass the time.
Ugh, *OK.*
I know you're feeling a lot of grief right now, no matter if you say otherwise. And when you lose someone, you often feel angry. But you need to be careful.
Anger's easy to hold on to and even easier to use to drive people away. This attitude won't get you far.
Get some rest. You've had a long day. Maybe you'll be more pleasant in the morning.

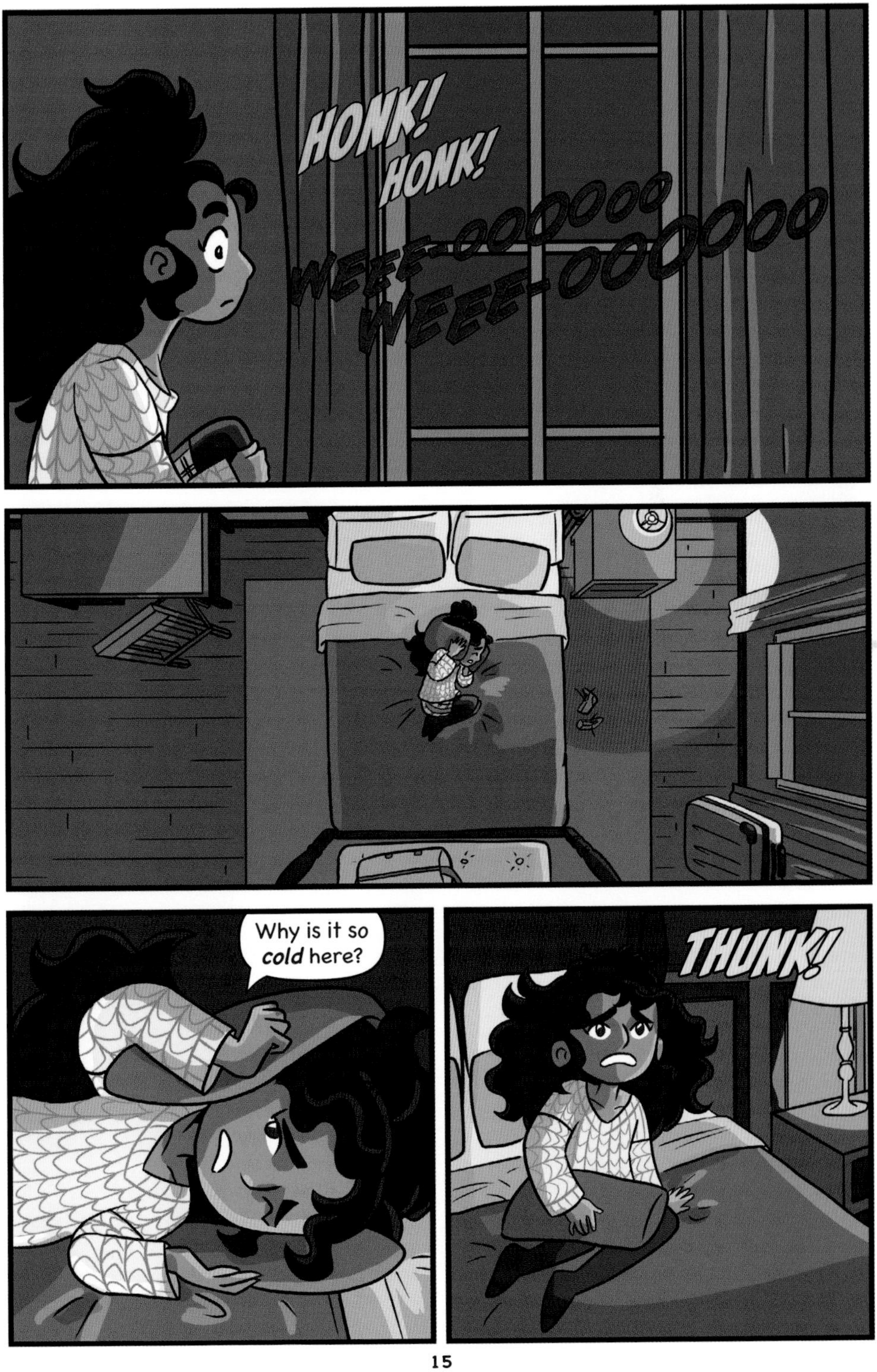
HONK!
HONK!
WEEE-OOOOOOO
WEEE-OOOOOOO
Why is it so *cold* here?
THUNK!

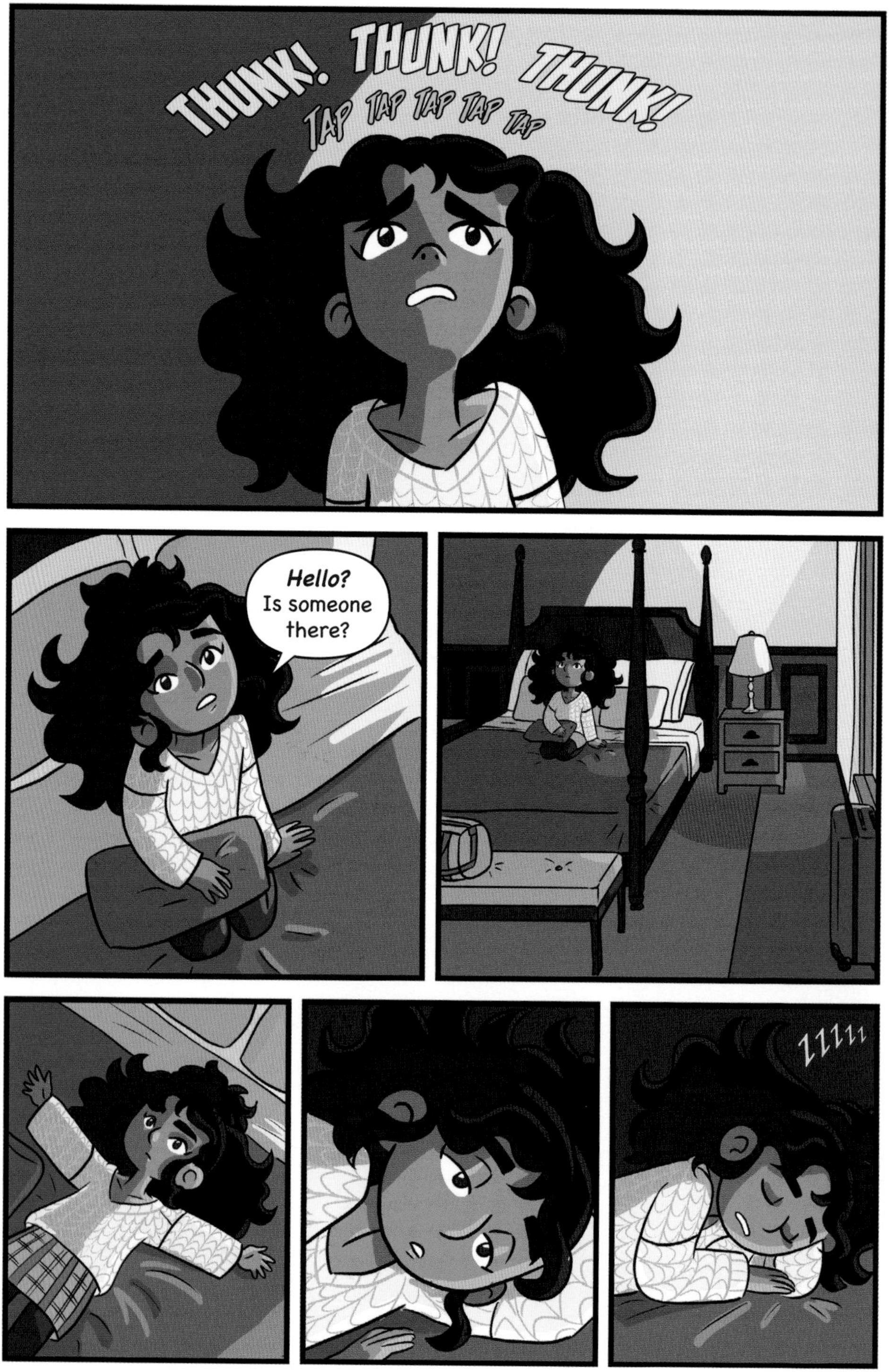
THUNK! THUNK! THUNK!
TAP TAP TAP TAP TAP
Hello? Is someone there?
ZZZZZ

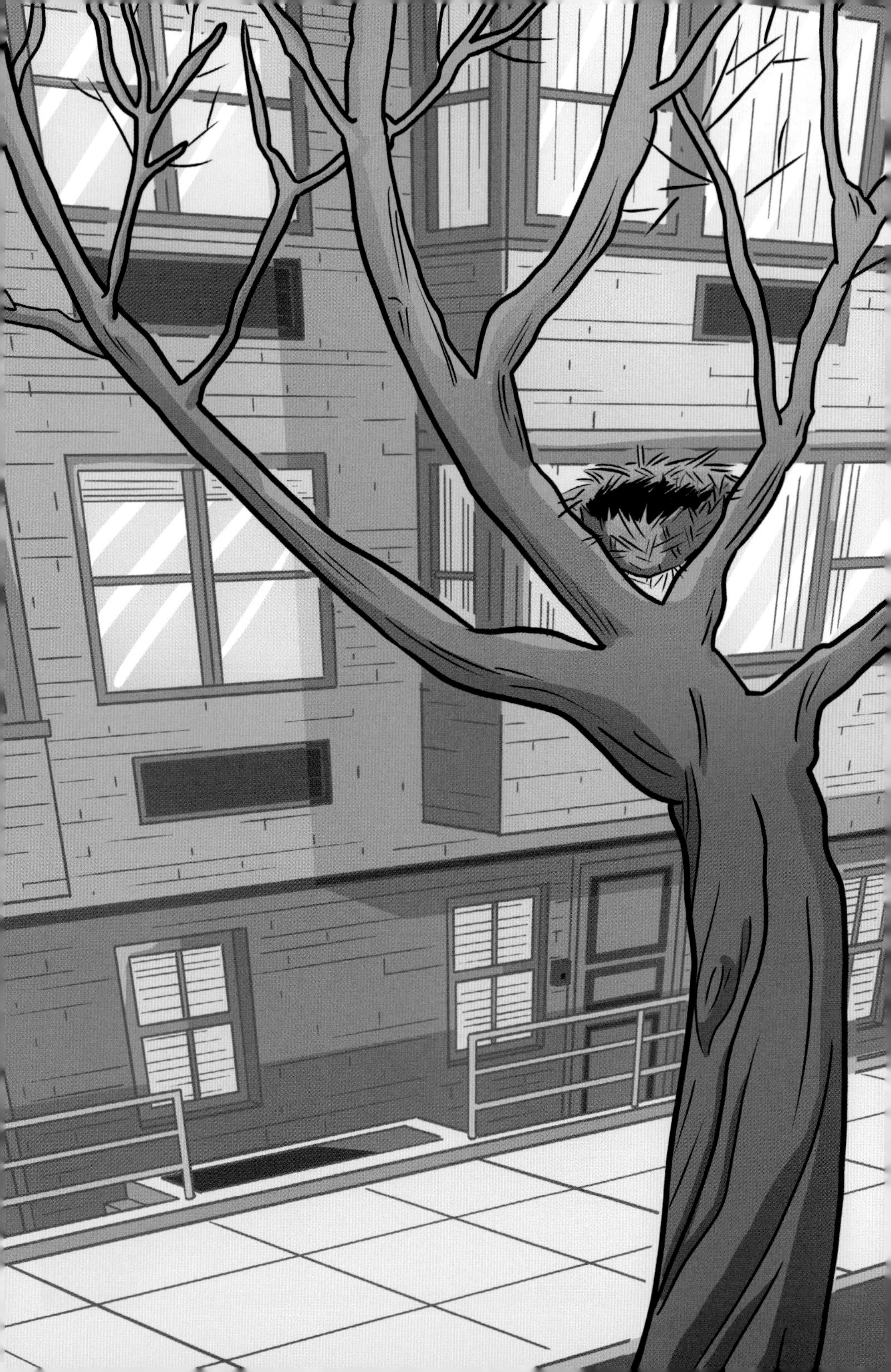

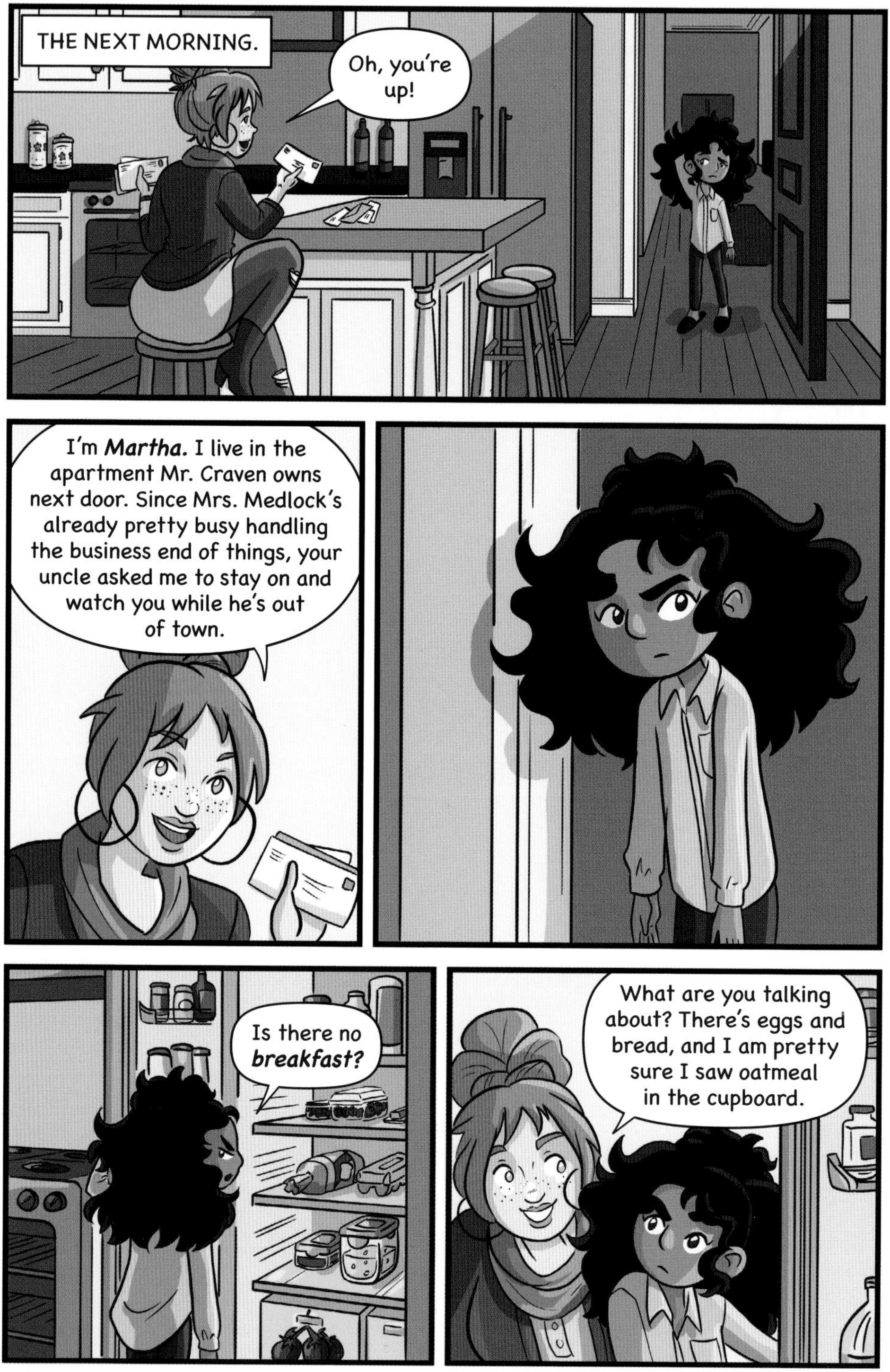
THE NEXT MORNING.
Oh, you're up!
I'm *Martha.* I live in the apartment Mr. Craven owns next door. Since Mrs. Medlock's already pretty busy handling the business end of things, your uncle asked me to stay on and watch you while he's out of town.
Is there no *breakfast?*
What are you talking about? There's eggs and bread, and I am pretty sure I saw oatmeal in the cupboard.

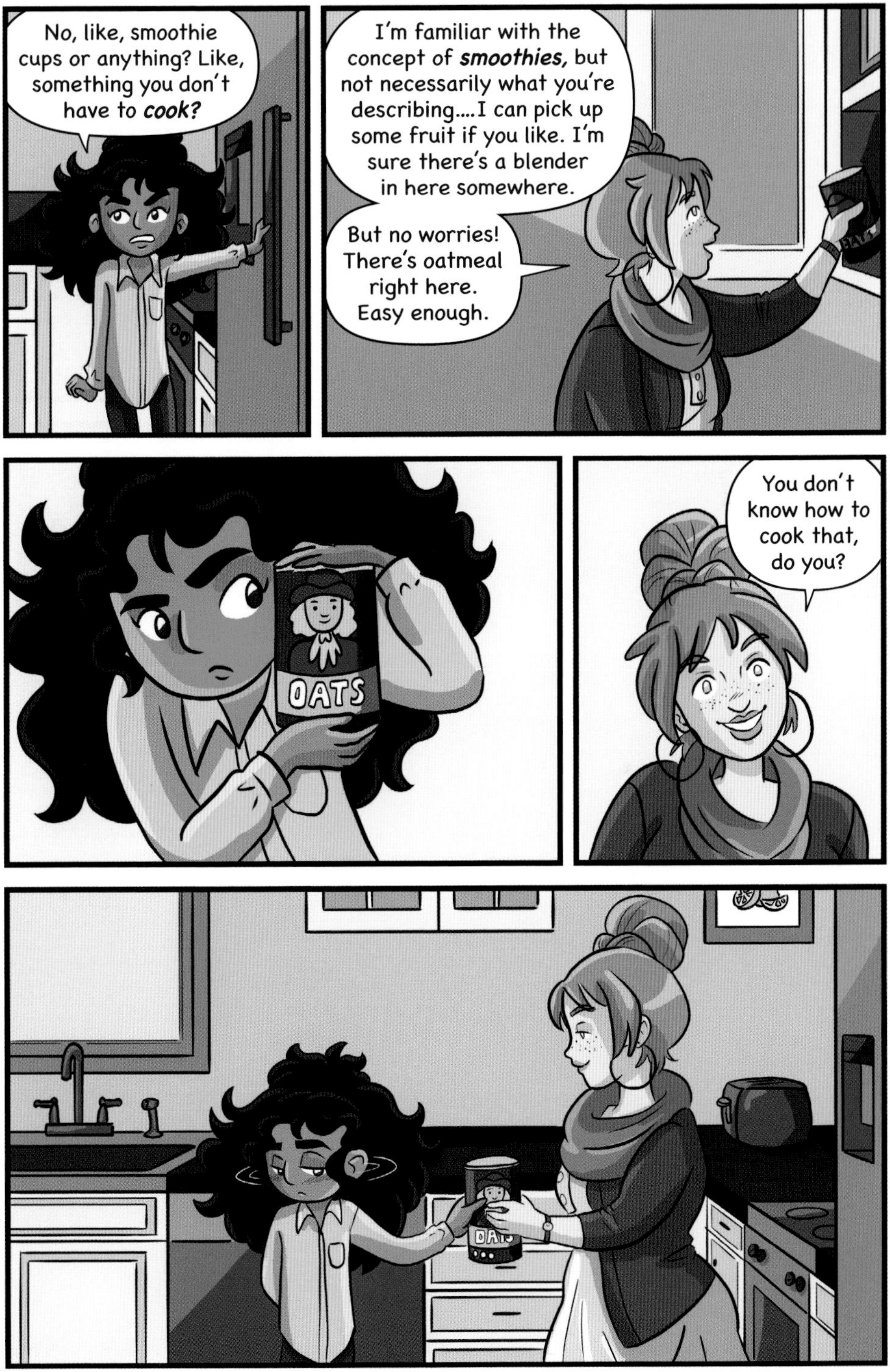
No, like, smoothie cups or anything? Like, something you don't have to *cook?*
I'm familiar with the concept of *smoothies,* but not necessarily what you're describing....I can pick up some fruit if you like. I'm sure there's a blender in here somewhere.
But no worries! There's oatmeal right here. Easy enough.
OATS
You don't know how to cook that, do you?
OATS

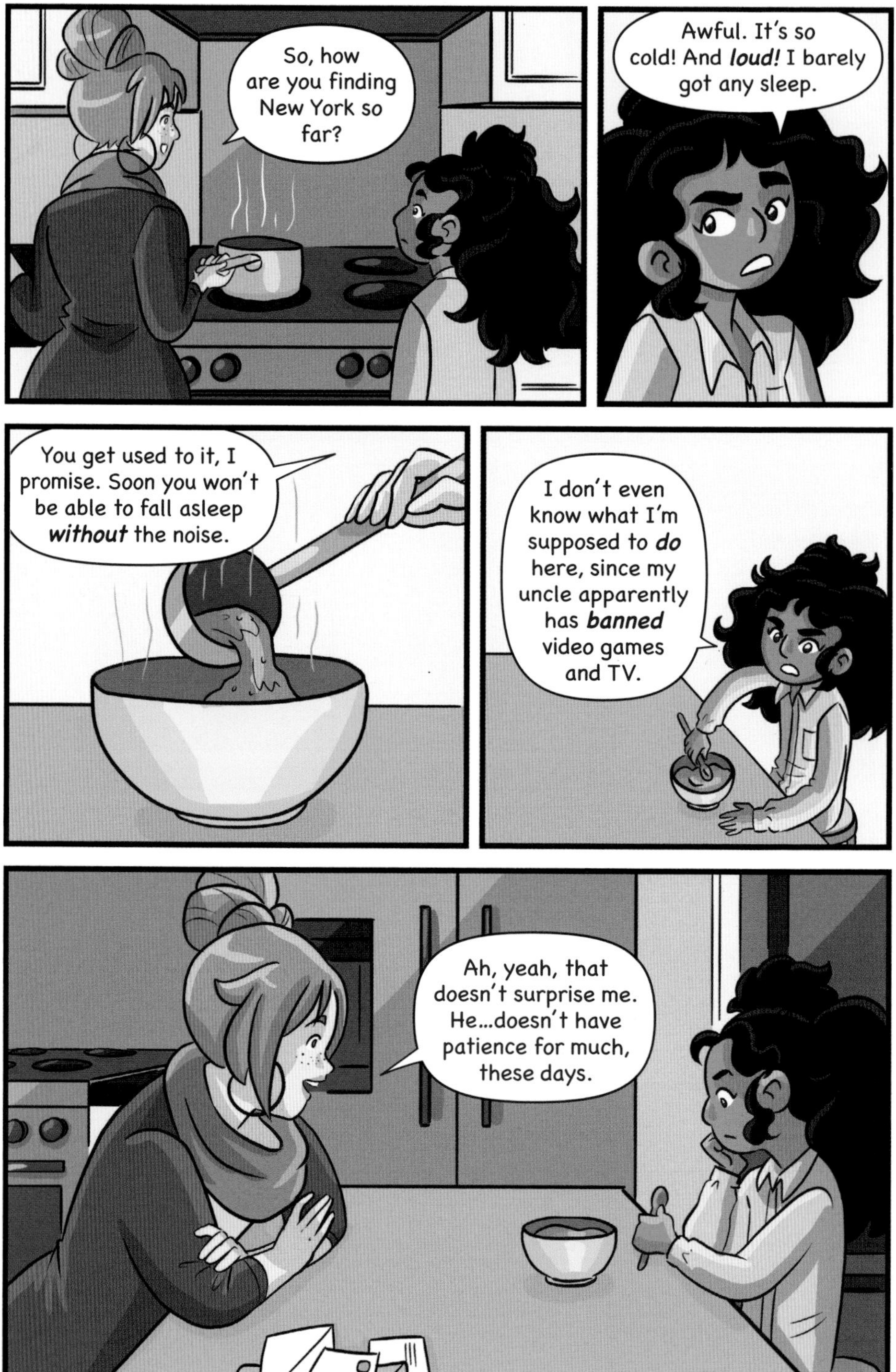
So, how are you finding New York so far?
Awful. It's so cold! And ***loud!*** I barely got any sleep.
You get used to it, I promise. Soon you won't be able to fall asleep ***without*** the noise.
I don't even know what I'm supposed to ***do*** here, since my uncle apparently has ***banned*** video games and TV.
Ah, yeah, that doesn't surprise me. He...doesn't have patience for much, these days.

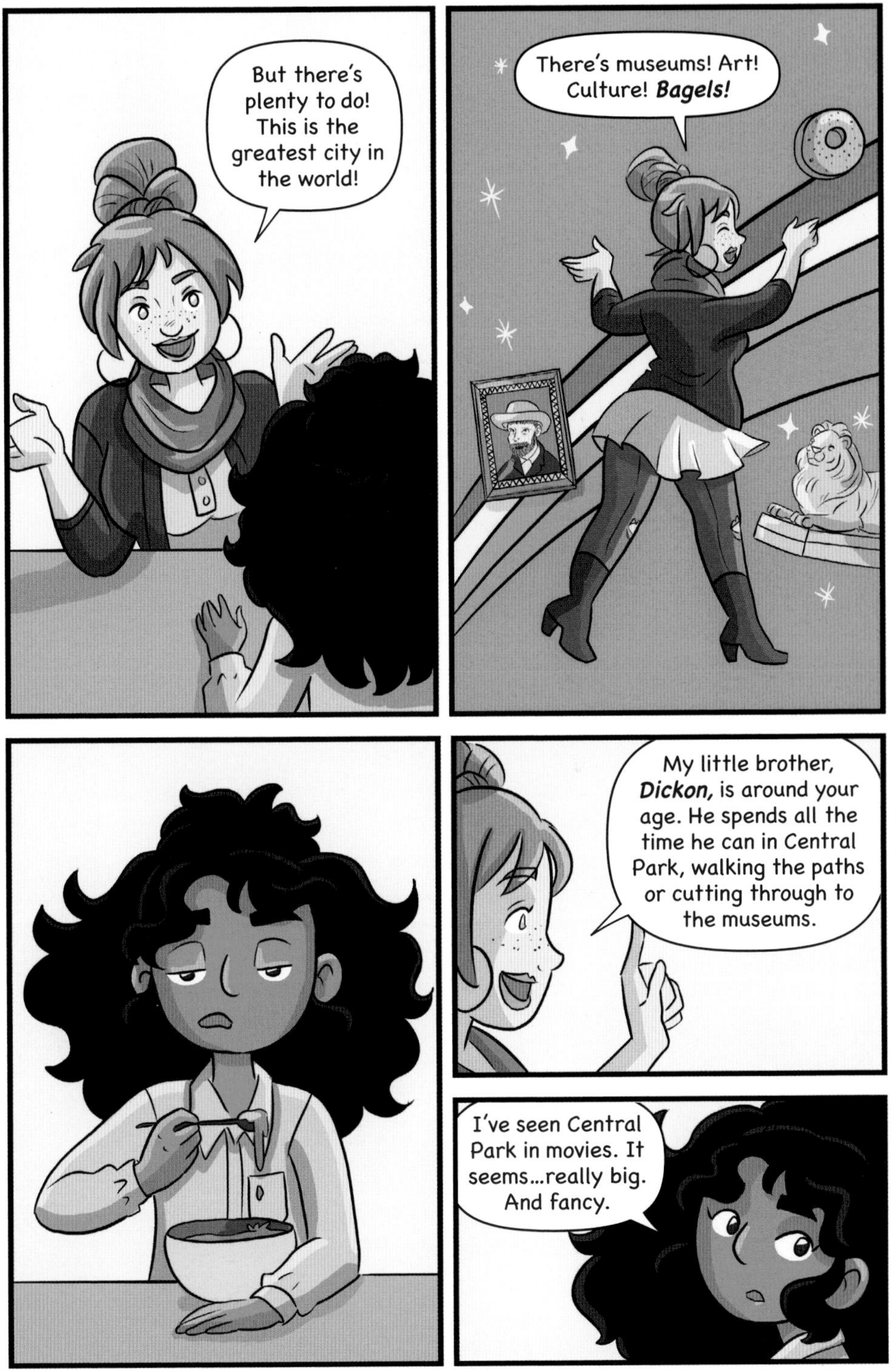
But there's plenty to do! This is the greatest city in the world!
There's museums! Art! Culture! ***Bagels!***
My little brother, ***Dickon,*** is around your age. He spends all the time he can in Central Park, walking the paths or cutting through to the museums.
I've seen Central Park in movies. It seems...really big. And fancy.

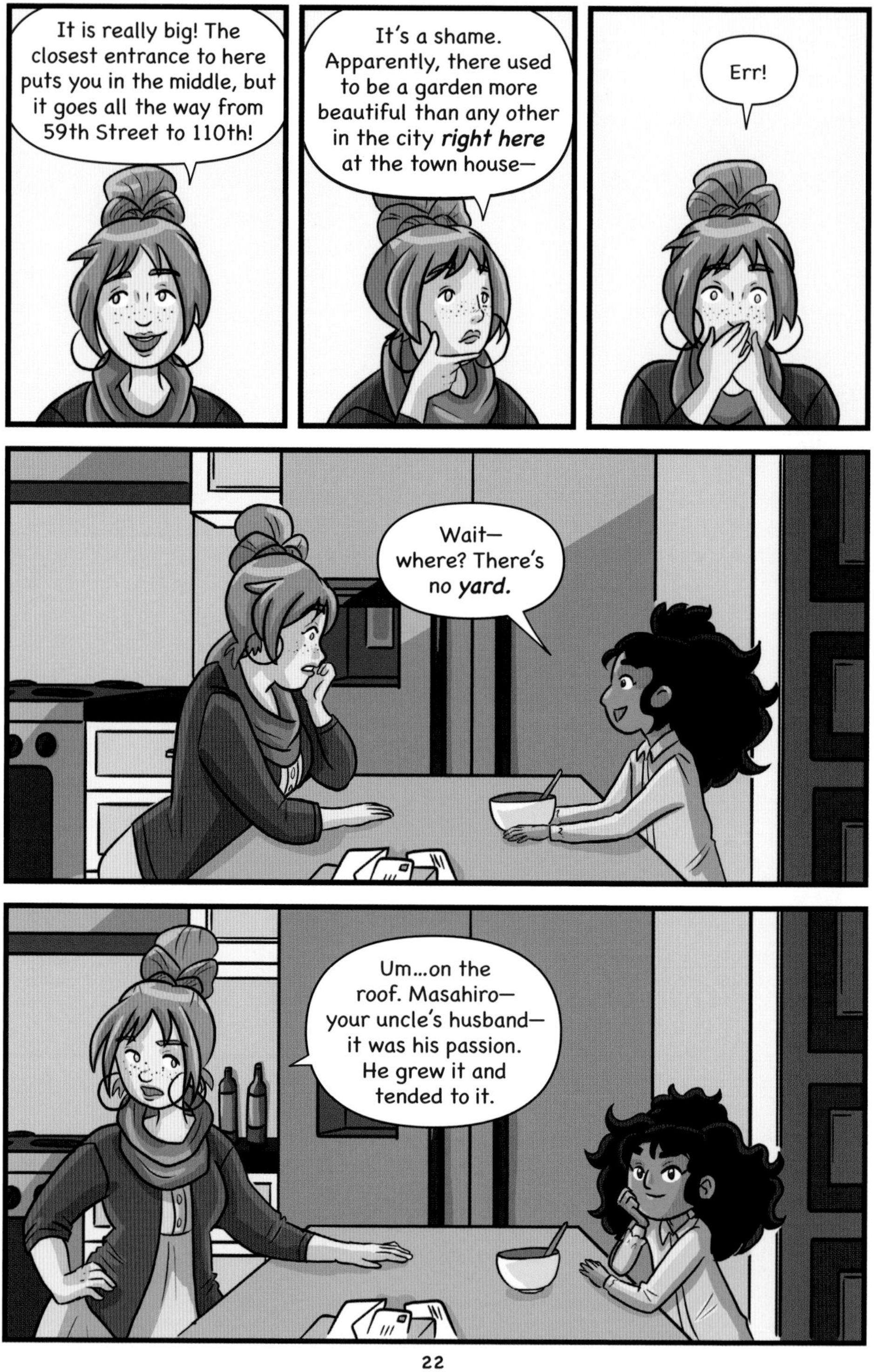
It is really big! The closest entrance to here puts you in the middle, but it goes all the way from 59th Street to 110th!
It's a shame. Apparently, there used to be a garden more beautiful than any other in the city *right here* at the town house—
Err!
Wait—where? There's no *yard.*
Um...on the roof. Masahiro—your uncle's husband—it was his passion. He grew it and tended to it.

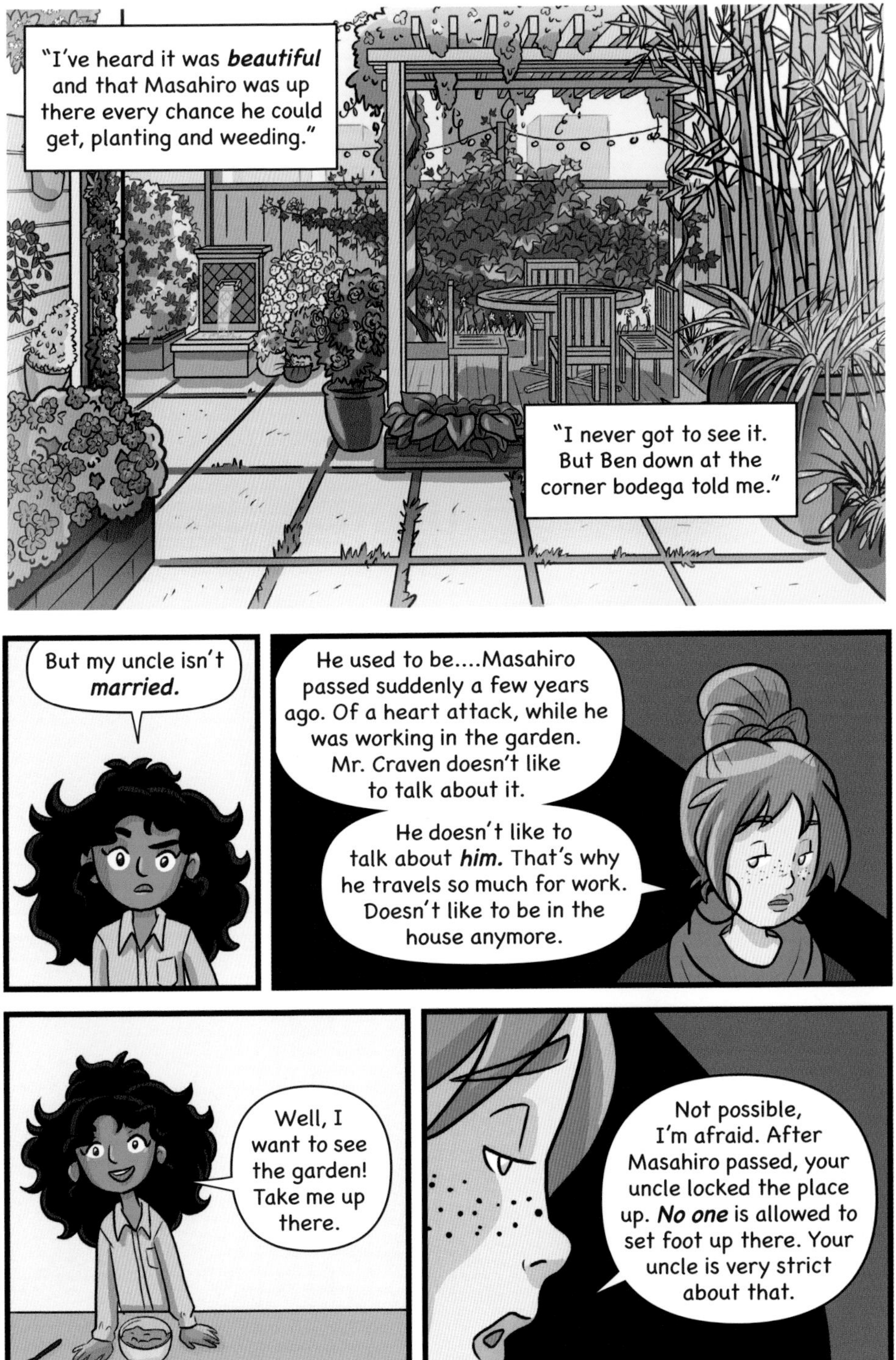
"I've heard it was beautiful and that Masahiro was up there every chance he could get, planting and weeding."
"I never got to see it. But Ben down at the corner bodega told me."
But my uncle isn't married.
He used to be....Masahiro passed suddenly a few years ago. Of a heart attack, while he was working in the garden. Mr. Craven doesn't like to talk about it.
He doesn't like to talk about him. That's why he travels so much for work. Doesn't like to be in the house anymore.
Well, I want to see the garden! Take me up there.
Not possible, I'm afraid. After Masahiro passed, your uncle locked the place up. No one is allowed to set foot up there. Your uncle is very strict about that.

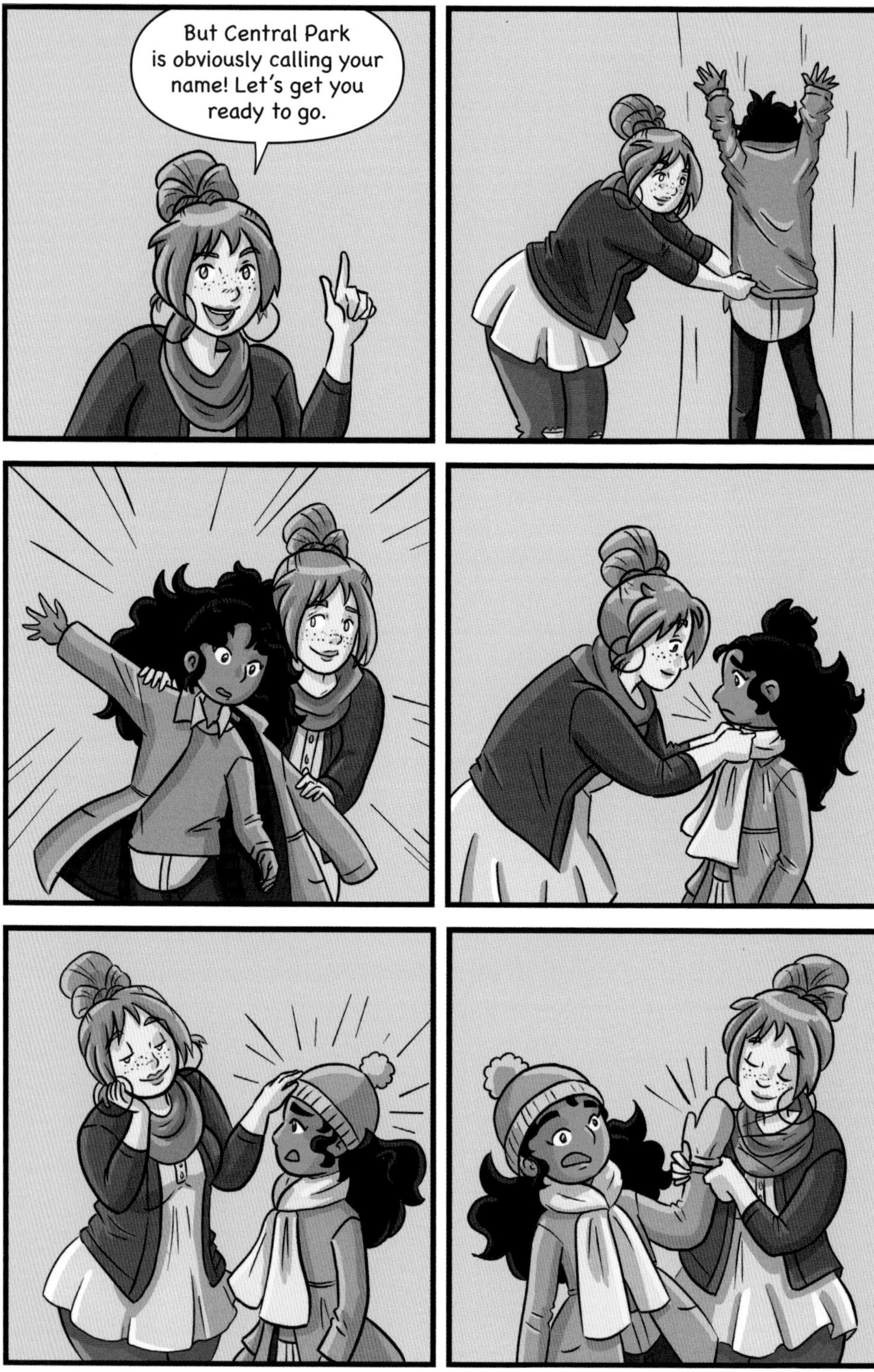
But Central Park is obviously calling your name! Let's get you ready to go.

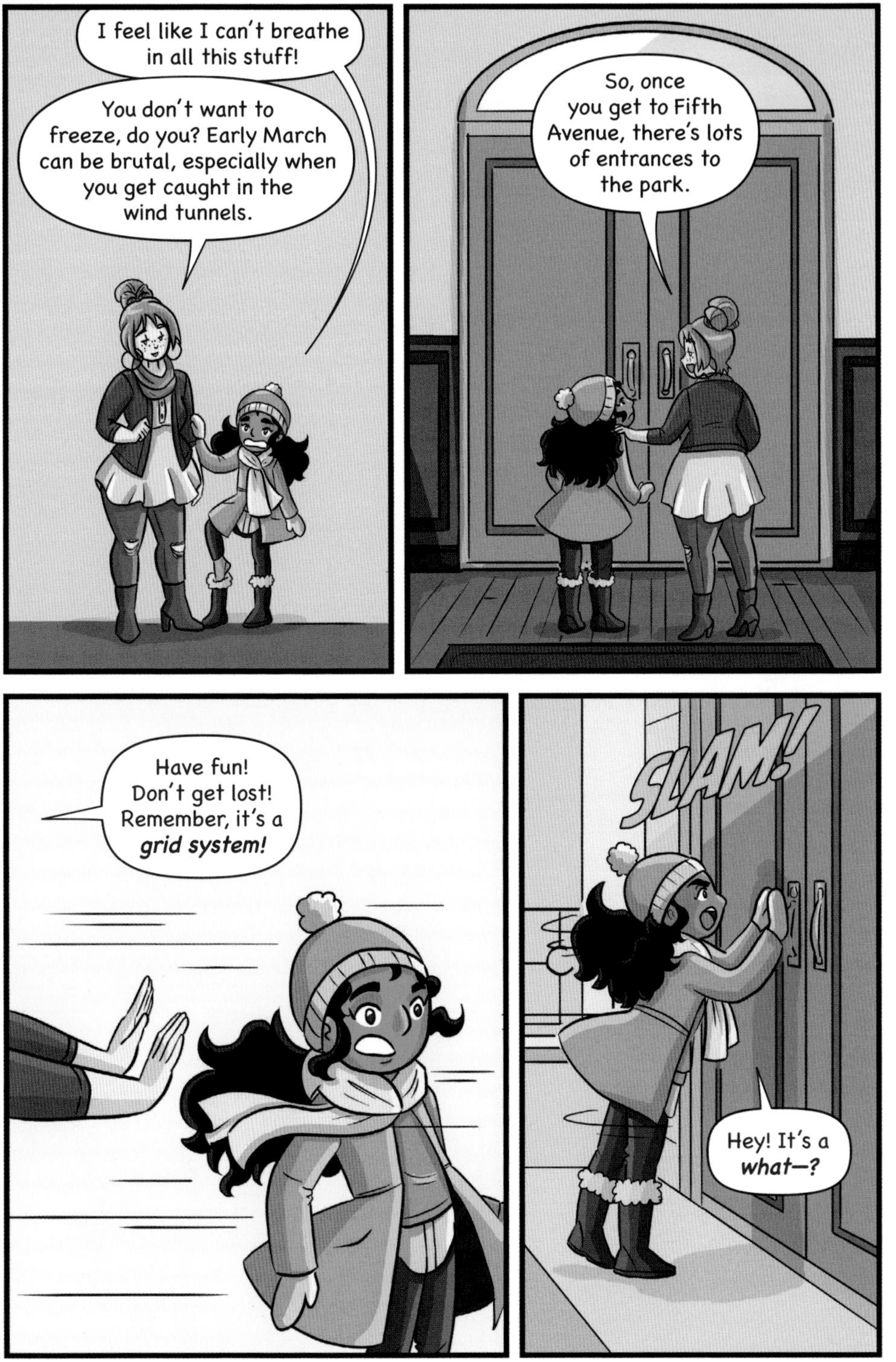
I feel like I can't breathe in all this stuff!
You don't want to freeze, do you? Early March can be brutal, especially when you get caught in the wind tunnels.
So, once you get to Fifth Avenue, there's lots of entrances to the park.
Have fun! Don't get lost! Remember, it's a *grid system!*
SLAM!
Hey! It's a *what—?*

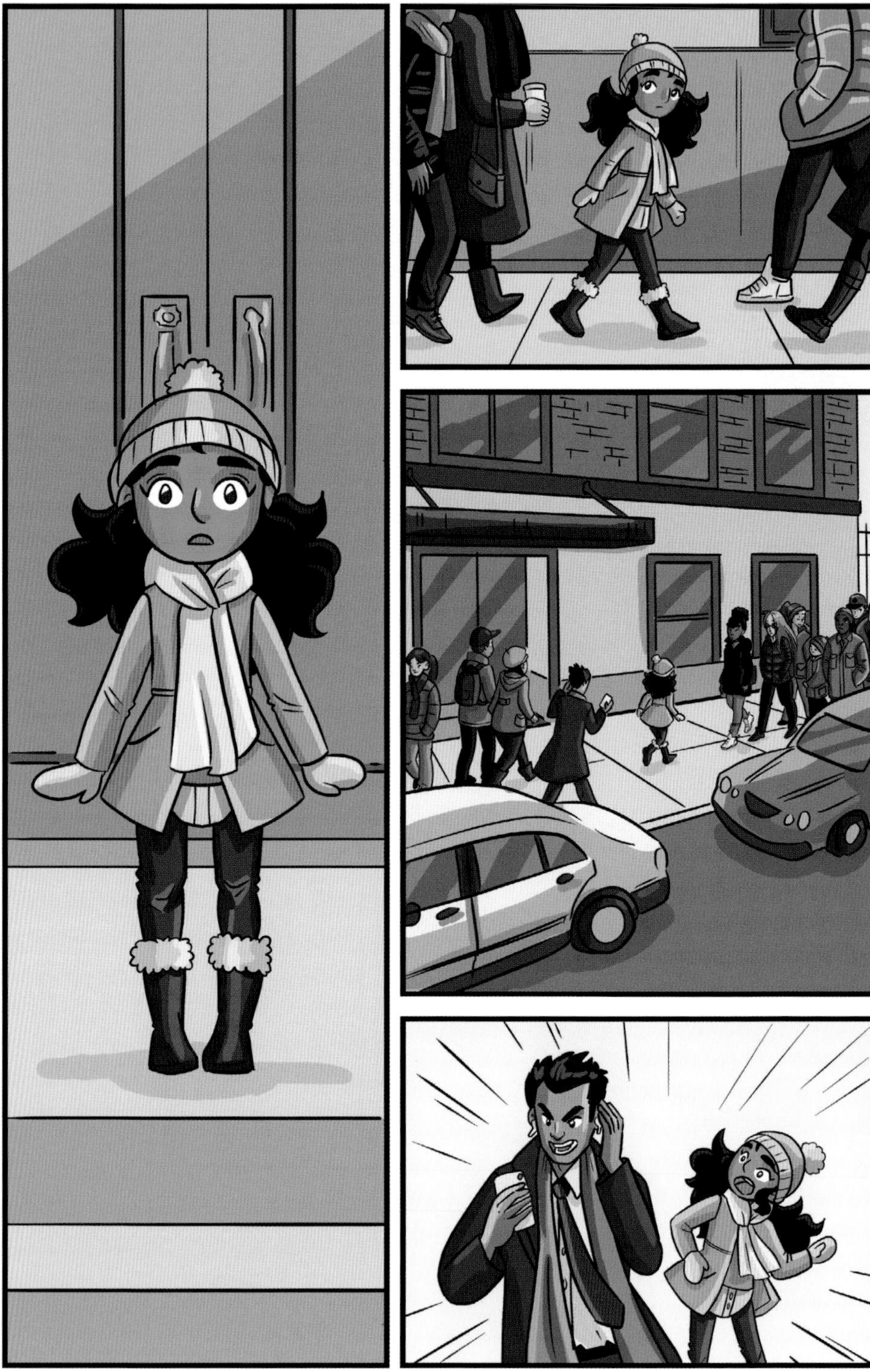

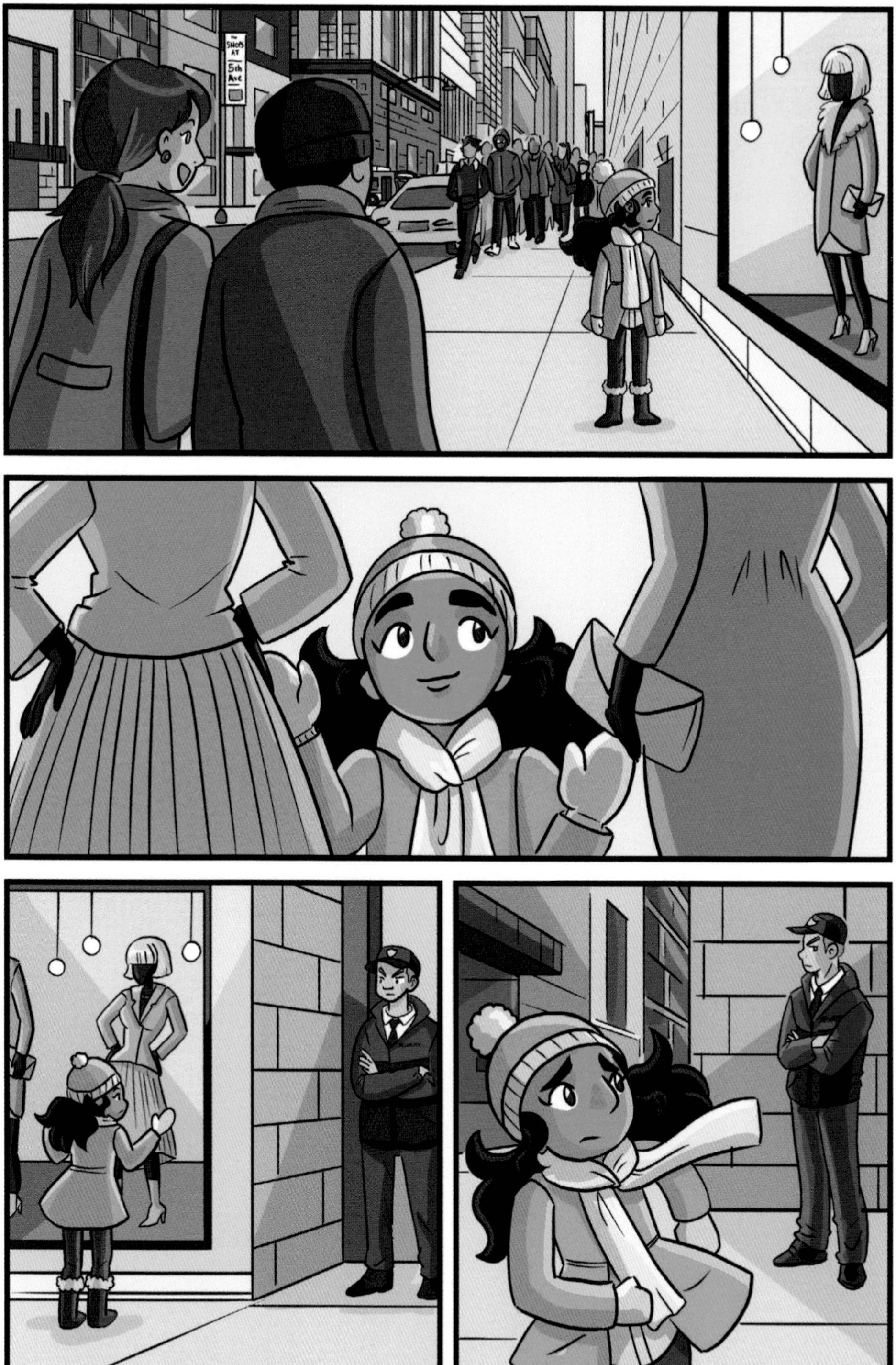
SHOPS AT
5th Ave

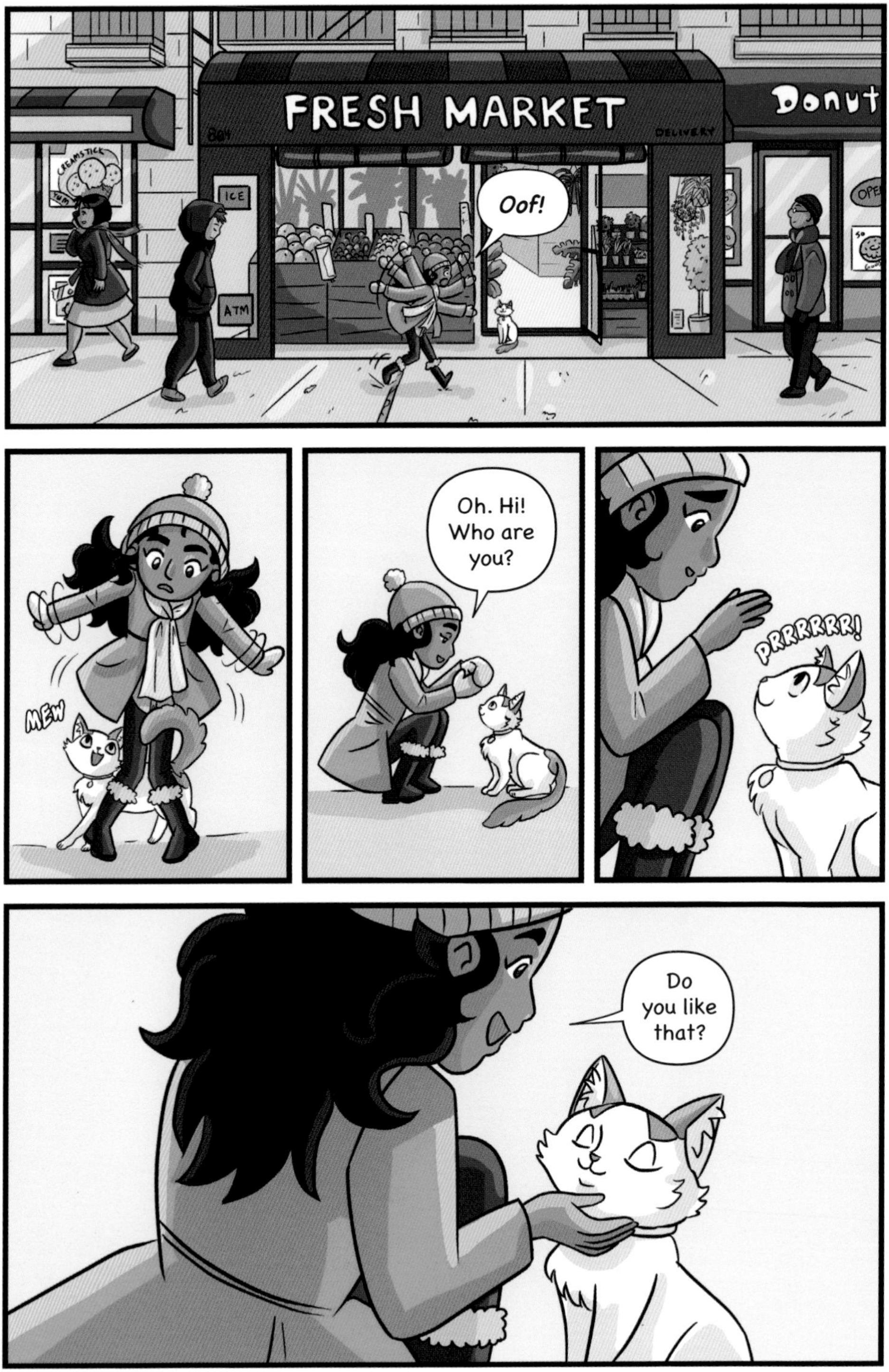
FRESH MARKET
Donut
CREAMSTICK
ICE
ATM
DELIVERY
Oof!
MEW
Oh. Hi! Who are you?
PRRRRRR!
Do you like that?

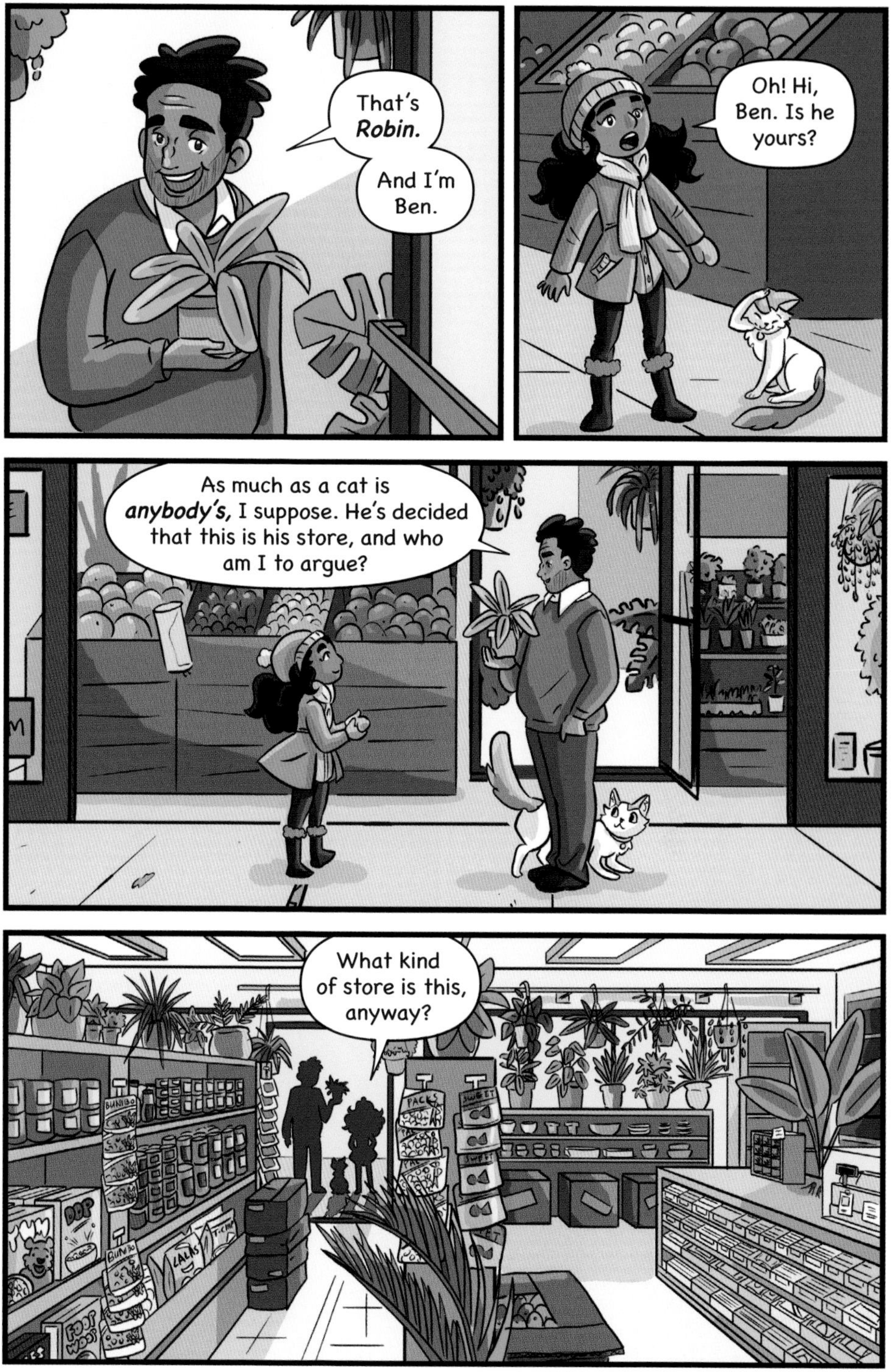
That's *Robin.*
And I'm Ben.
Oh! Hi, Ben. Is he yours?
As much as a cat is *anybody's,* I suppose. He's decided that this is his store, and who am I to argue?
What kind of store is this, anyway?

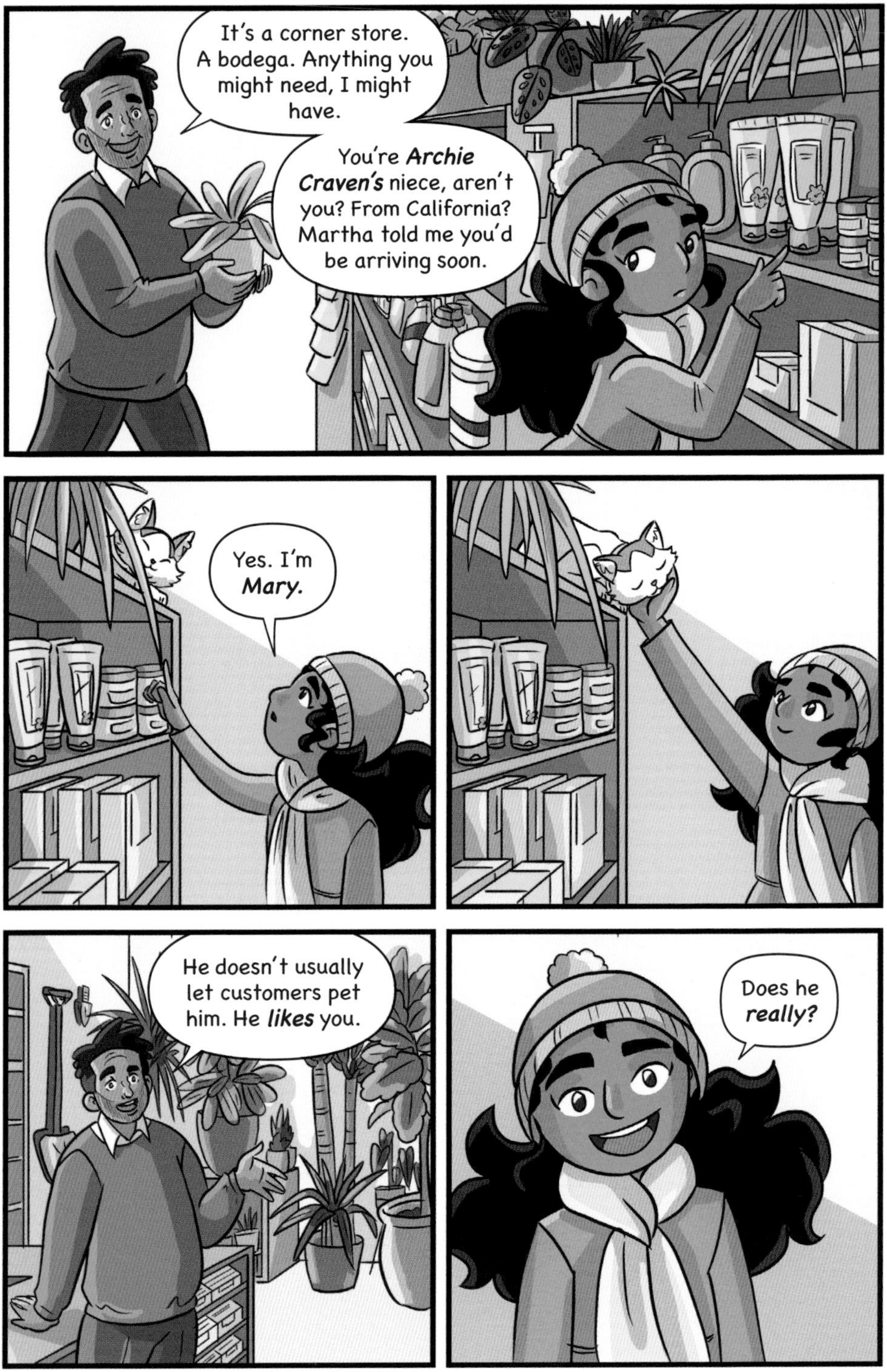
It's a corner store. A bodega. Anything you might need, I might have.
You're **Archie Craven's** niece, aren't you? From California? Martha told me you'd be arriving soon.
Yes. I'm **Mary.**
He doesn't usually let customers pet him. He ***likes*** you.
Does he ***really?***

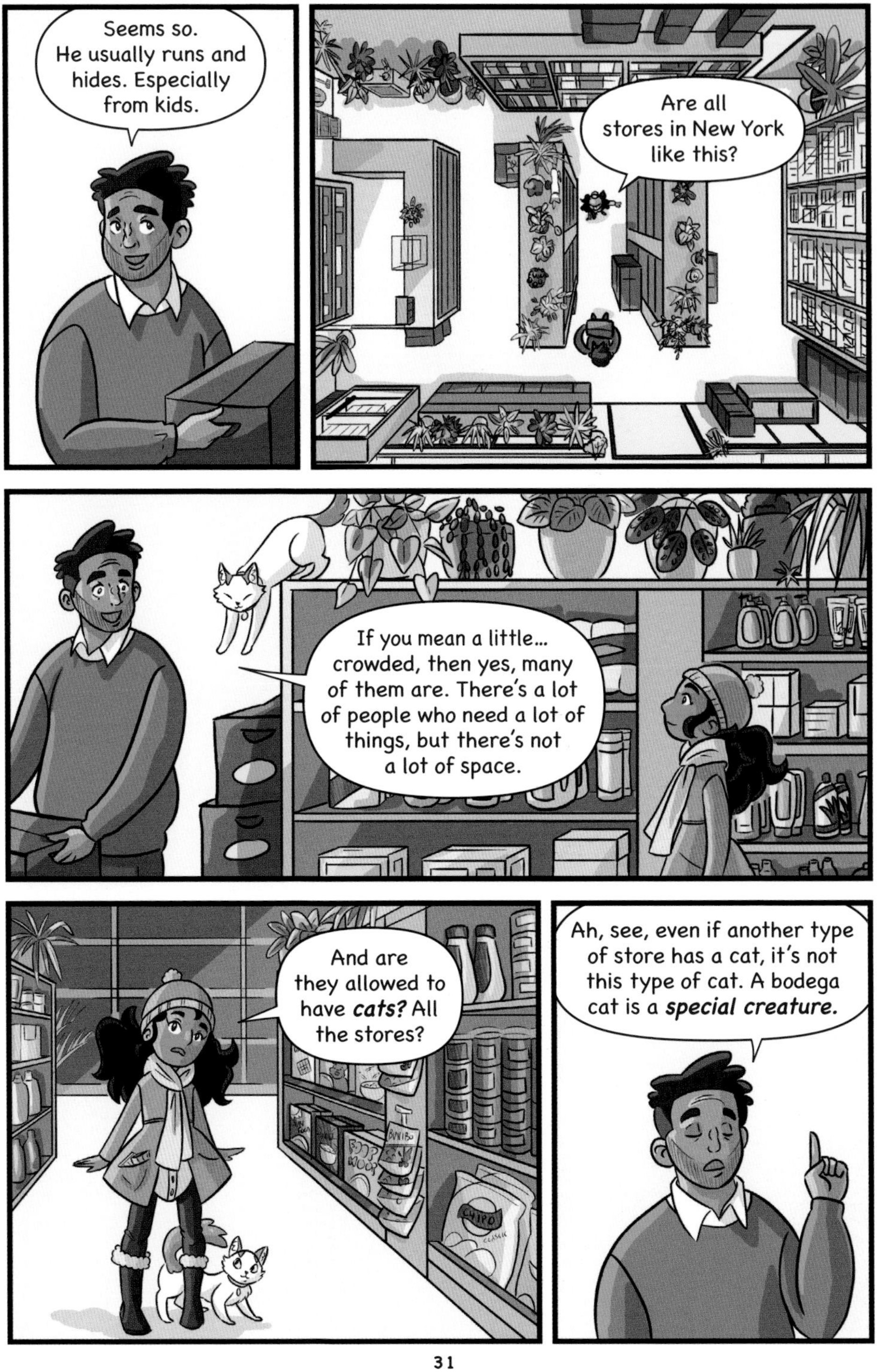
Seems so. He usually runs and hides. Especially from kids.
Are all stores in New York like this?
If you mean a little... crowded, then yes, many of them are. There's a lot of people who need a lot of things, but there's not a lot of space.
And are they allowed to have *cats?* All the stores?
Ah, see, even if another type of store has a cat, it's not this type of cat. A bodega cat is a ***special creature.***

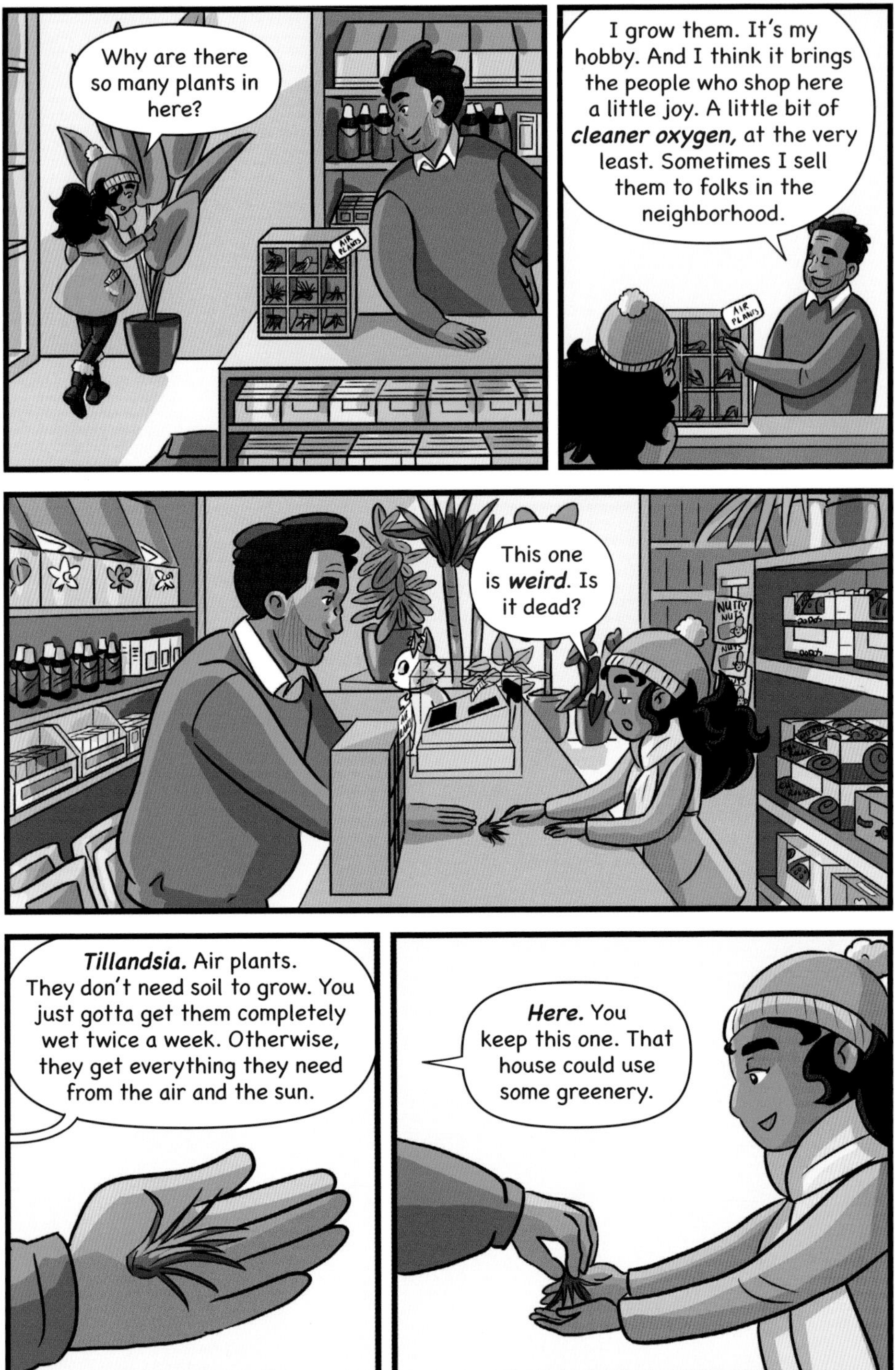
Why are there so many plants in here?
AIR PLANTS
I grow them. It's my hobby. And I think it brings the people who shop here a little joy. A little bit of ***cleaner oxygen,*** at the very least. Sometimes I sell them to folks in the neighborhood.
This one is ***weird***. Is it dead?
Tillandsia. Air plants. They don't need soil to grow. You just gotta get them completely wet twice a week. Otherwise, they get everything they need from the air and the sun.
Here. You keep this one. That house could use some greenery.

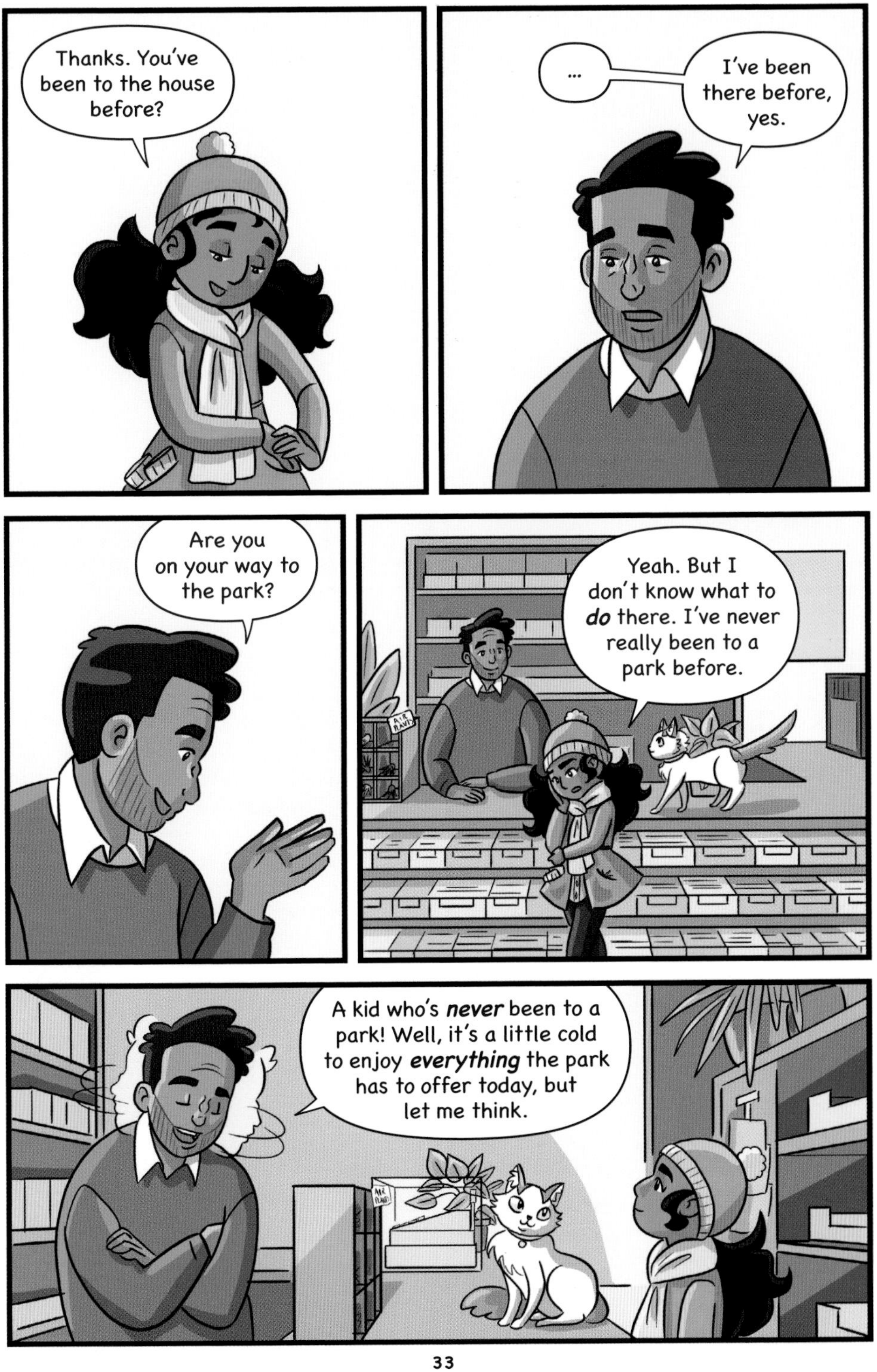
Thanks. You've been to the house before?
...
I've been there before, yes.
Are you on your way to the park?
Yeah. But I don't know what to *do* there. I've never really been to a park before.
A kid who's ***never*** been to a park! Well, it's a little cold to enjoy ***everything*** the park has to offer today, but let me think.

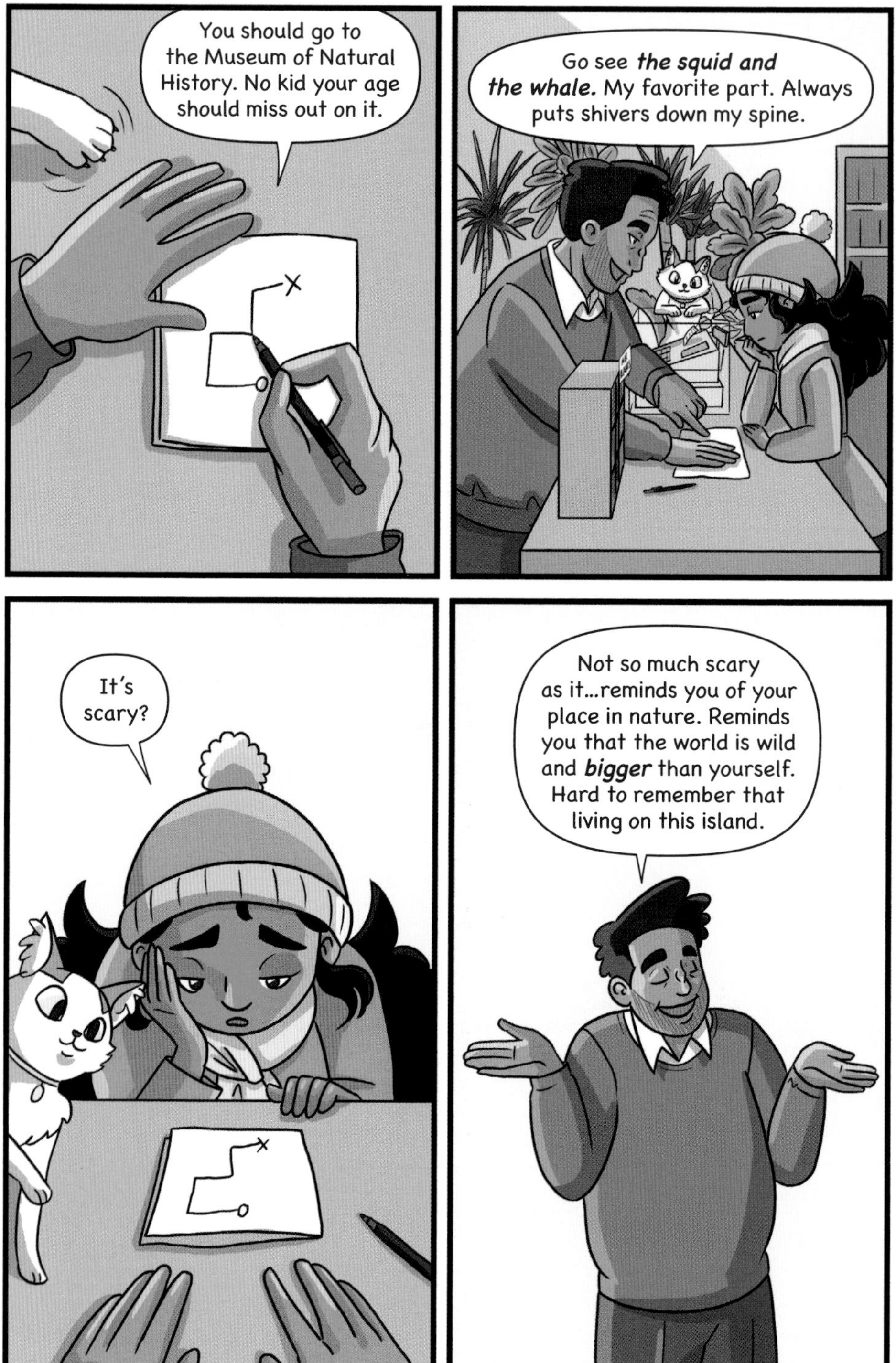
You should go to the Museum of Natural History. No kid your age should miss out on it.
Go see ***the squid and the whale.*** My favorite part. Always puts shivers down my spine.
It's scary?
Not so much scary as it...reminds you of your place in nature. Reminds you that the world is wild and ***bigger*** than yourself. Hard to remember that living on this island.

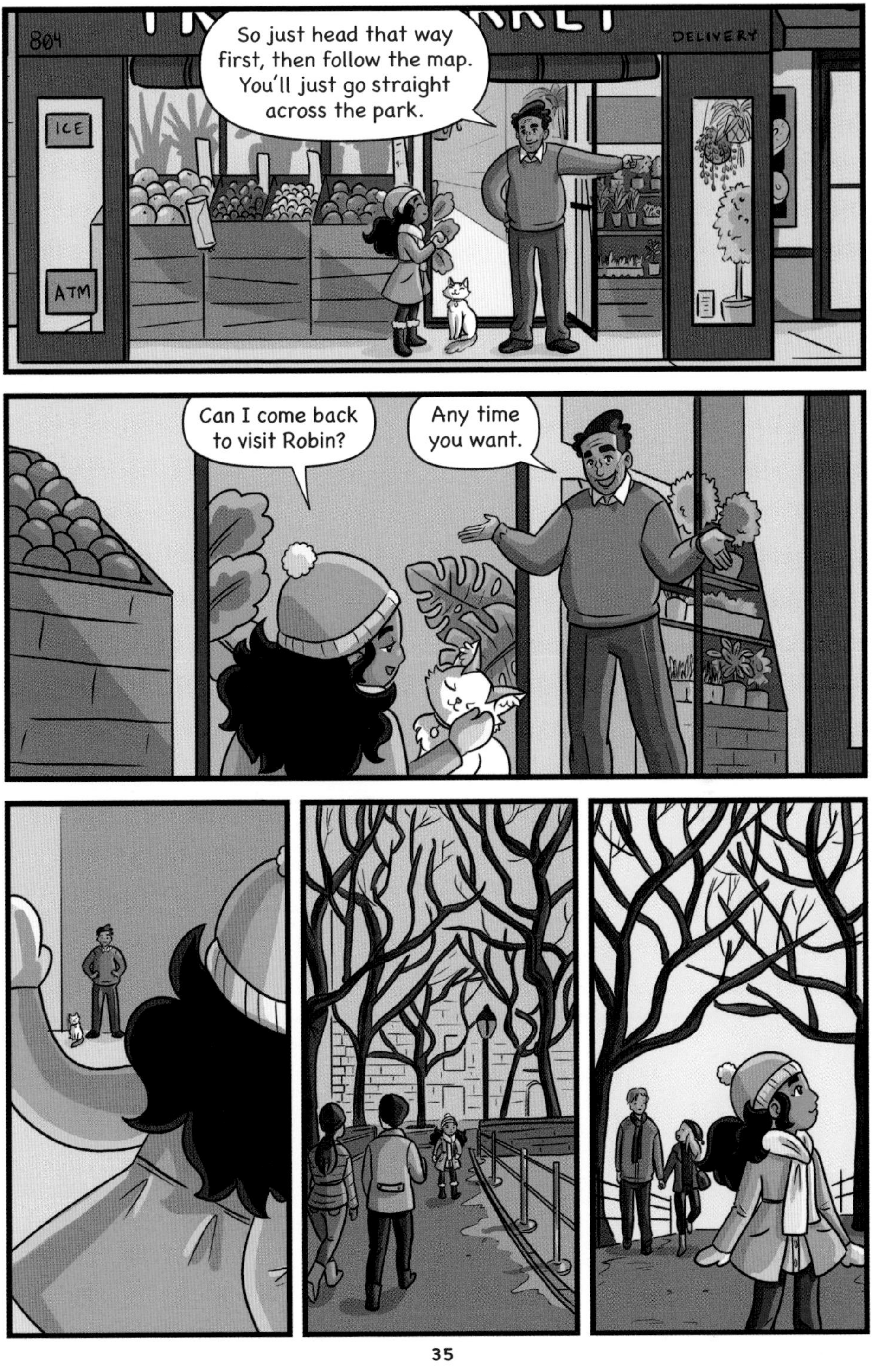
804
ICE
ATM
DELIVERY
So just head that way first, then follow the map. You'll just go straight across the park.
Can I come back to visit Robin?
Any time you want.

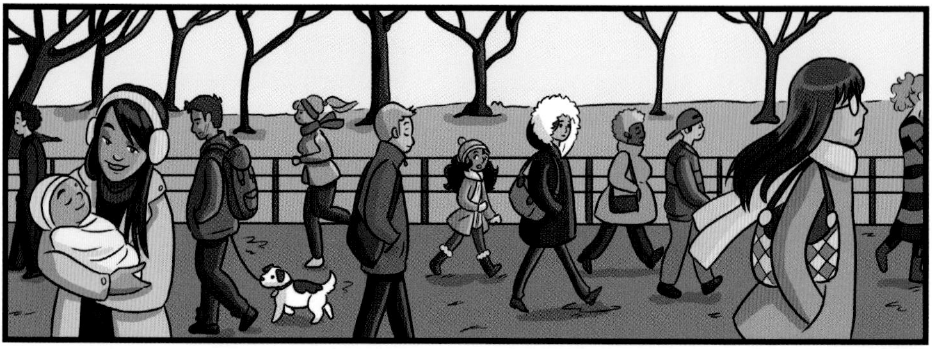
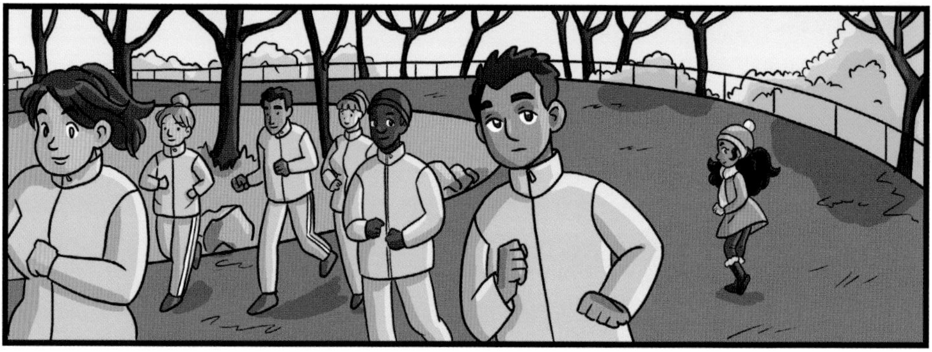
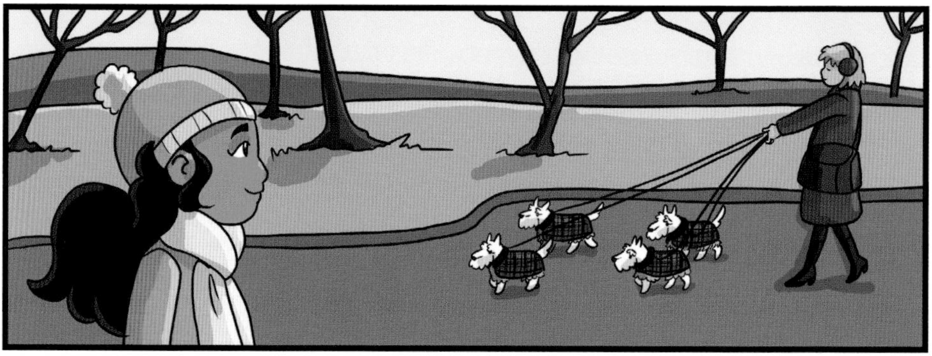
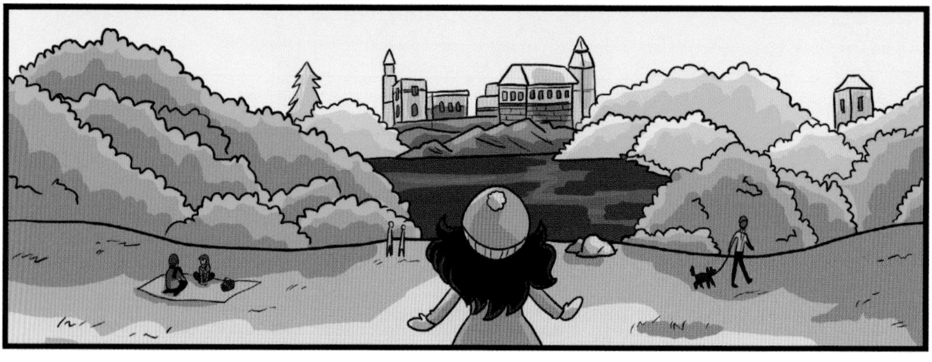

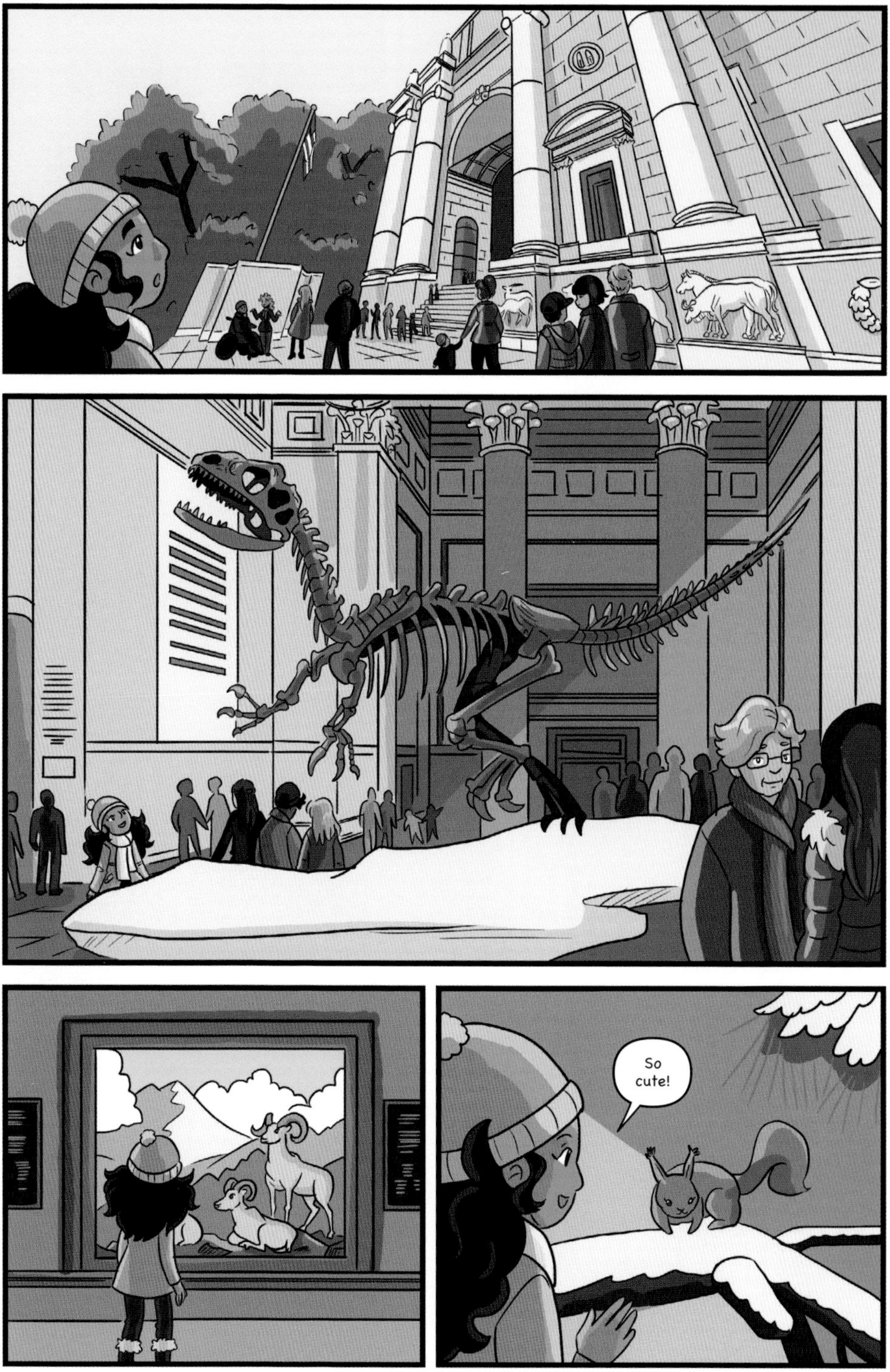
So cute!

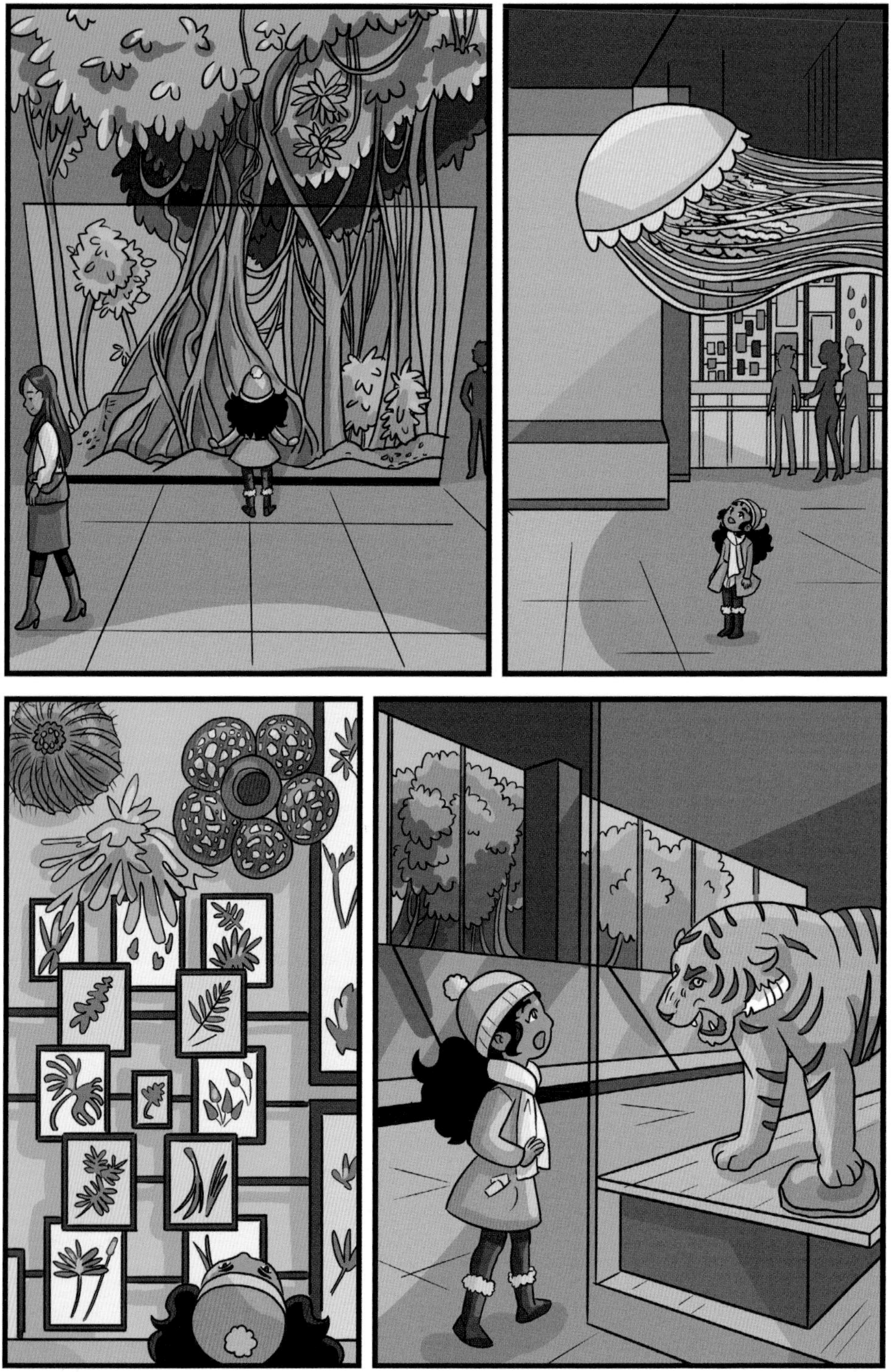

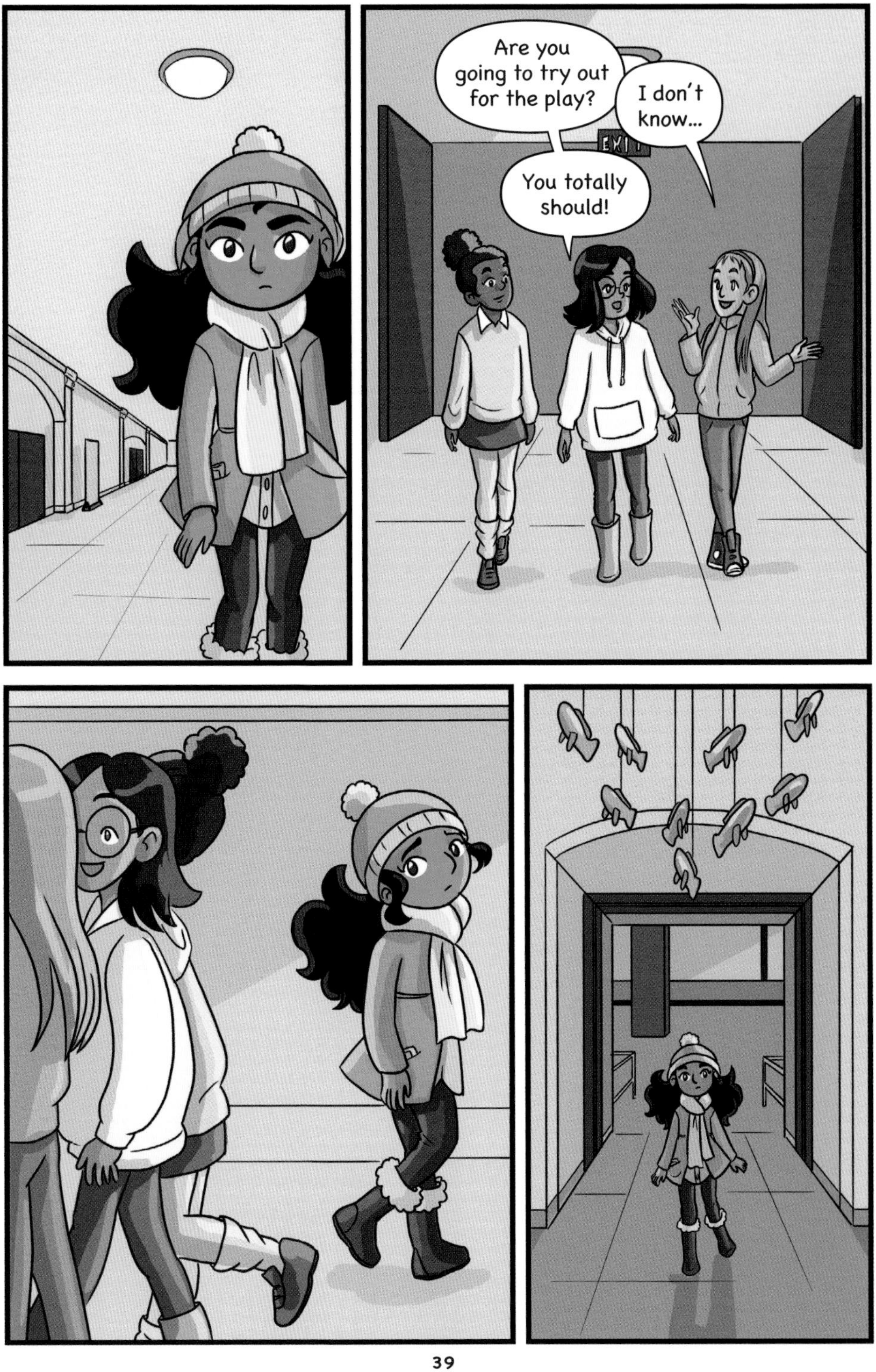
Are you going to try out for the play?
I don't know...
You totally should!

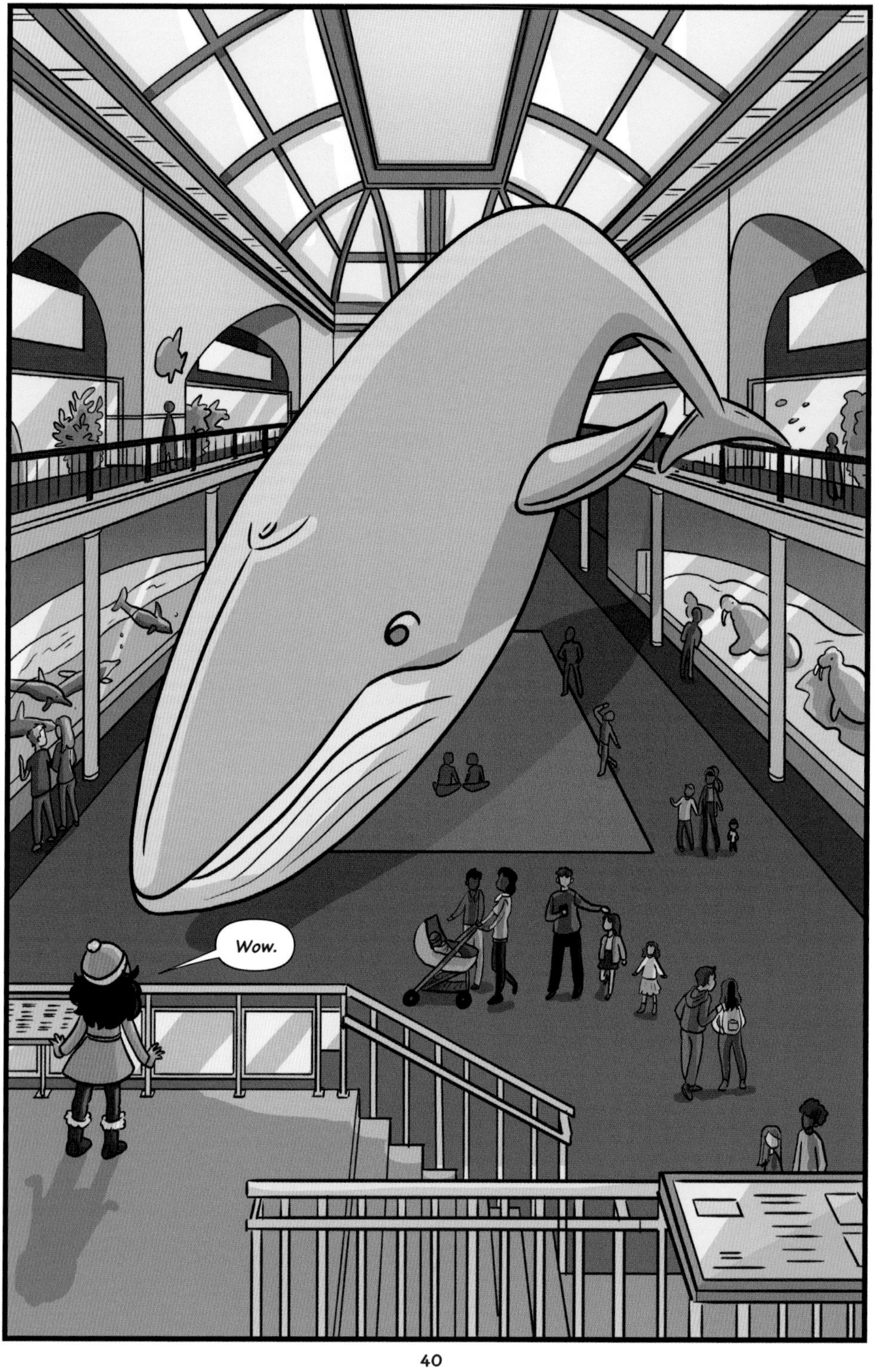
Wow.

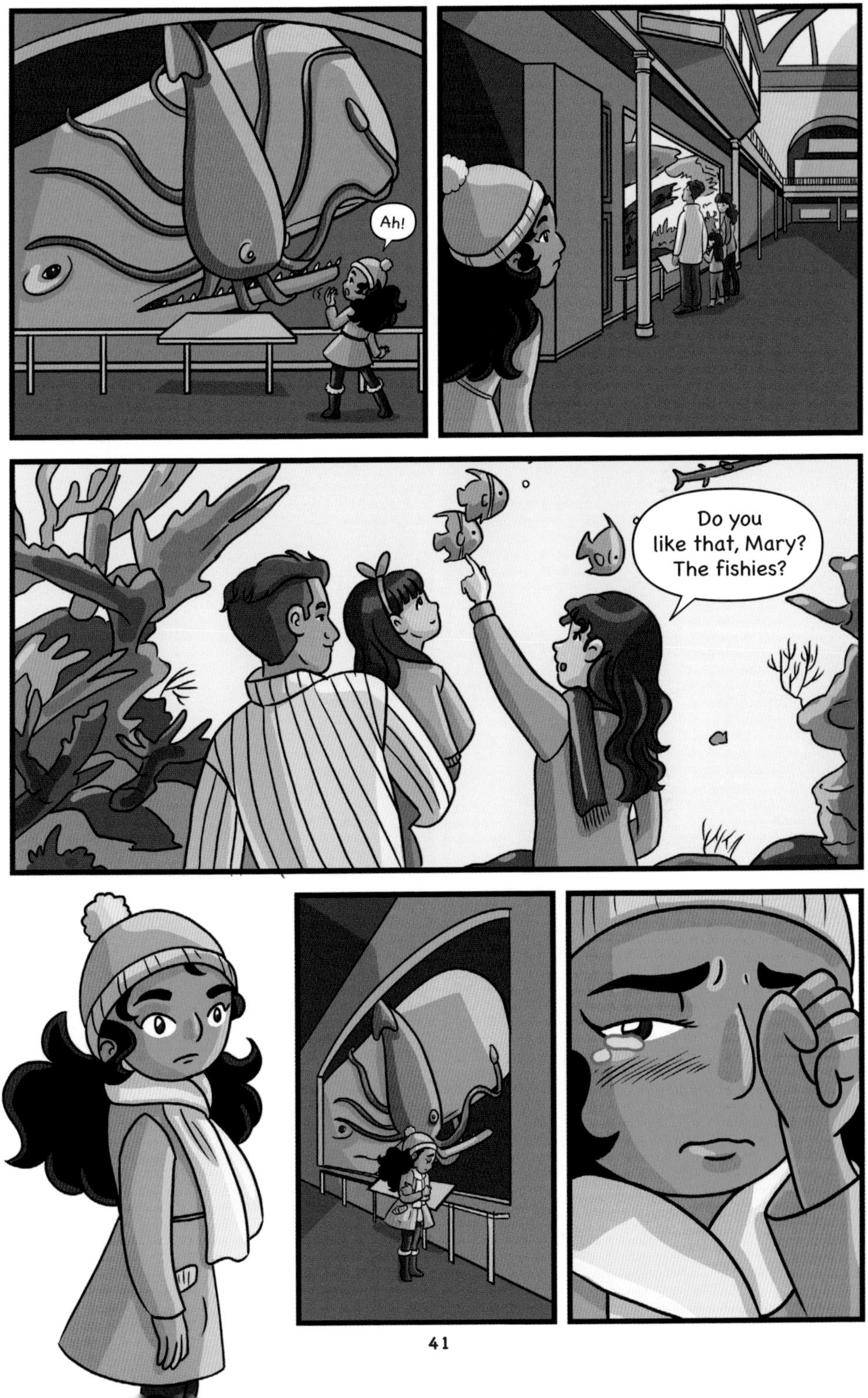
Ah!
Do you like that, Mary? The fishies?

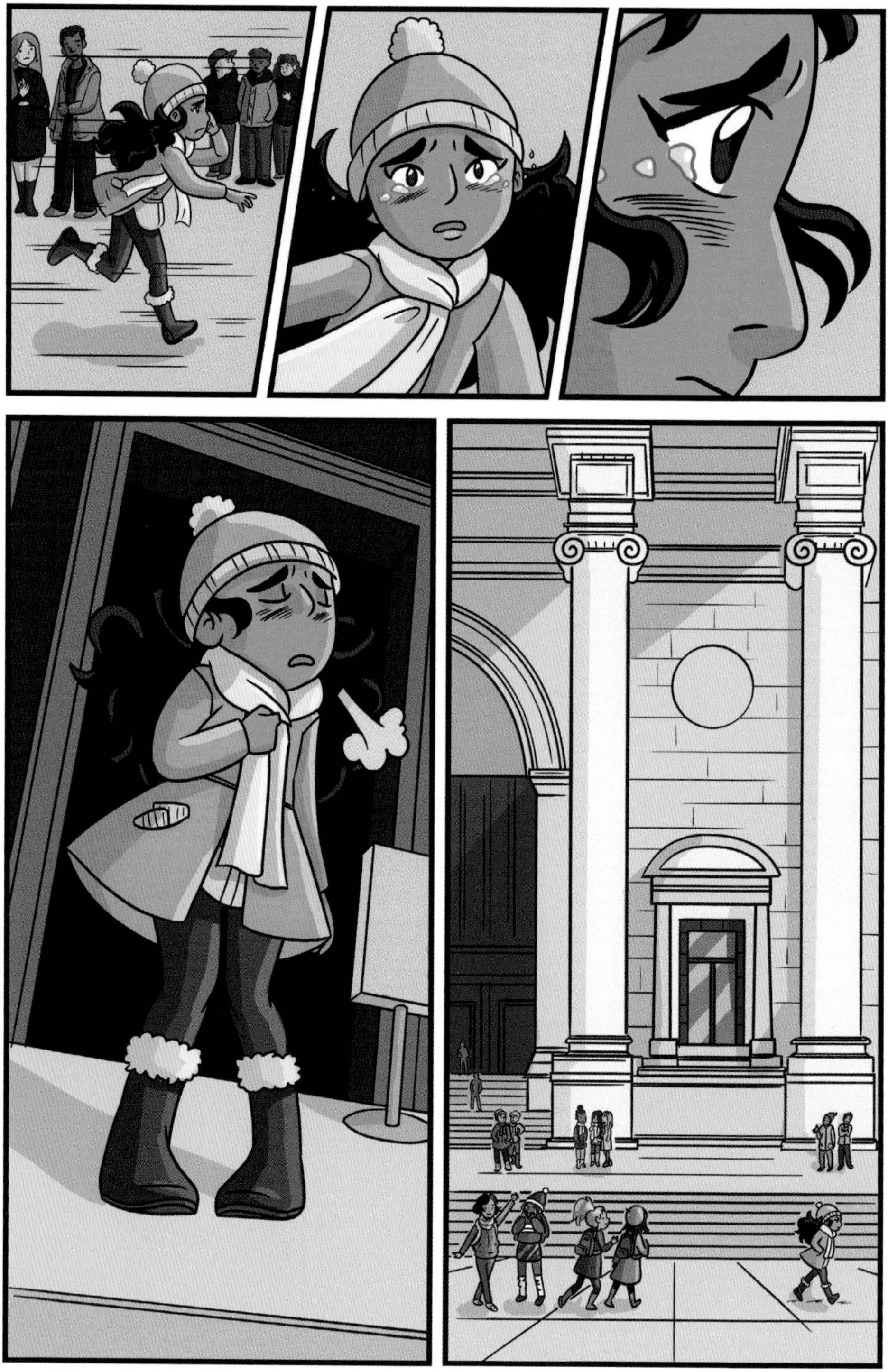

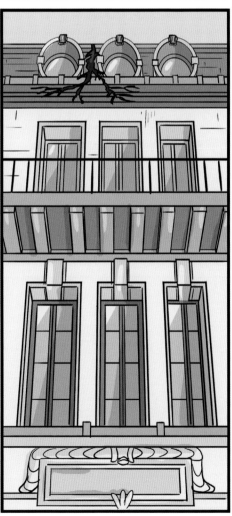

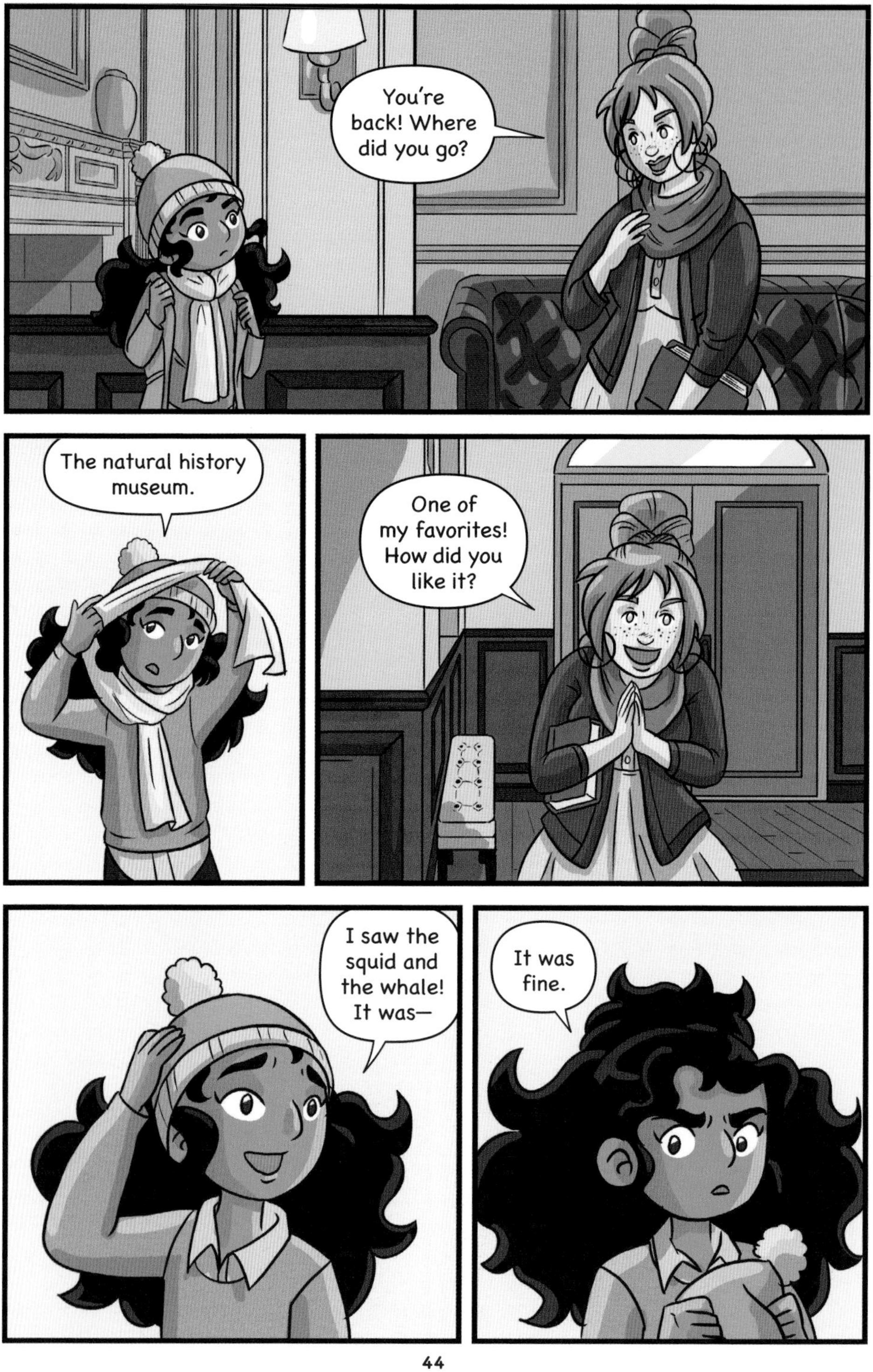
You're back! Where did you go?
The natural history museum.
One of my favorites! How did you like it?
I saw the squid and the whale! It was—
It was fine.

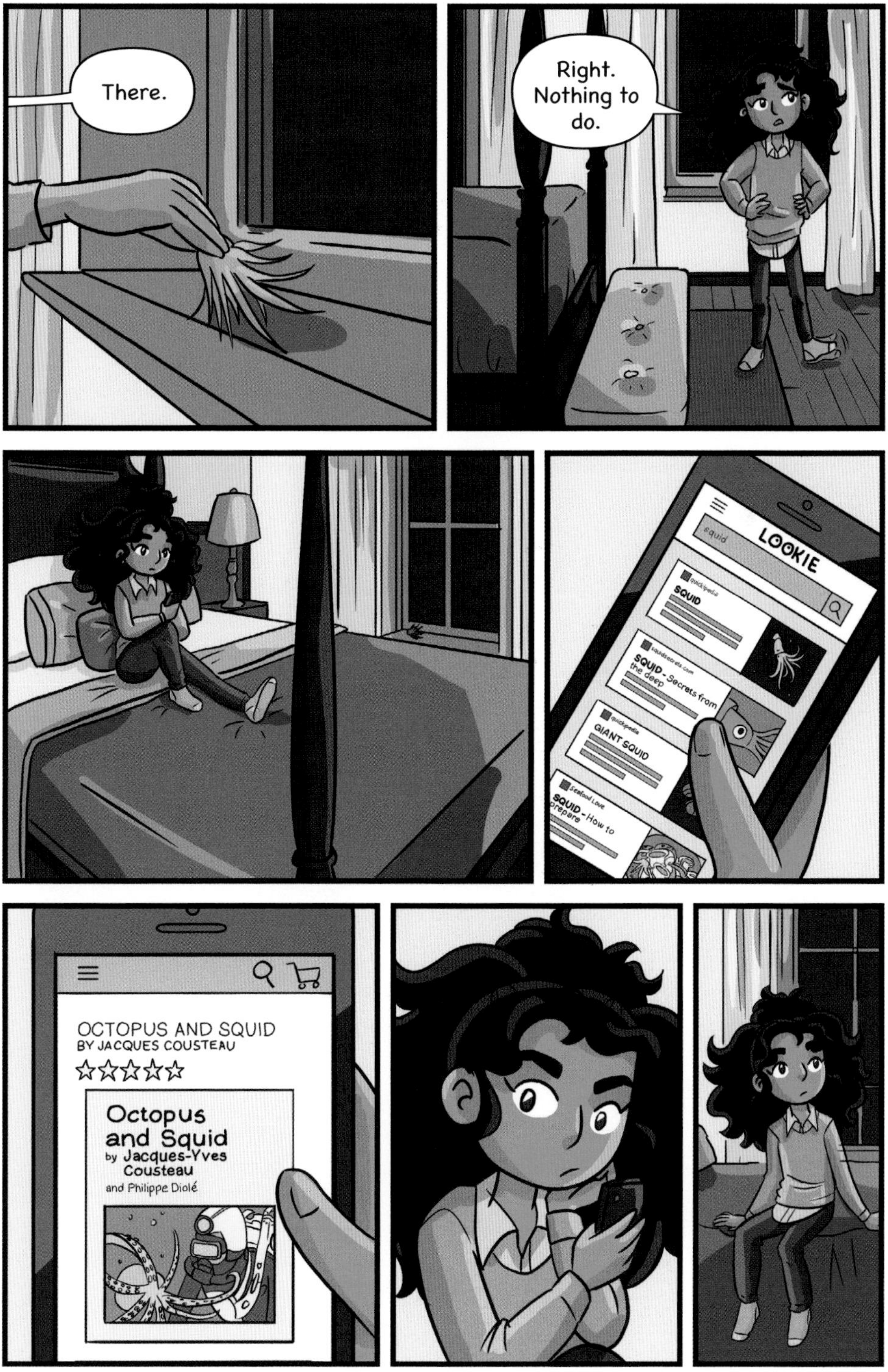
There.
Right. Nothing to do.
LOOKIE
squid
quickipedia
SQUID
squidsecrets.com
SQUID - Secrets from the deep
quickipedia
GIANT SQUID
Seafood Love
SQUID - How to prepare
OCTOPUS AND SQUID
BY JACQUES COUSTEAU
Octopus and Squid
by Jacques-Yves Cousteau
and Philippe Diolé

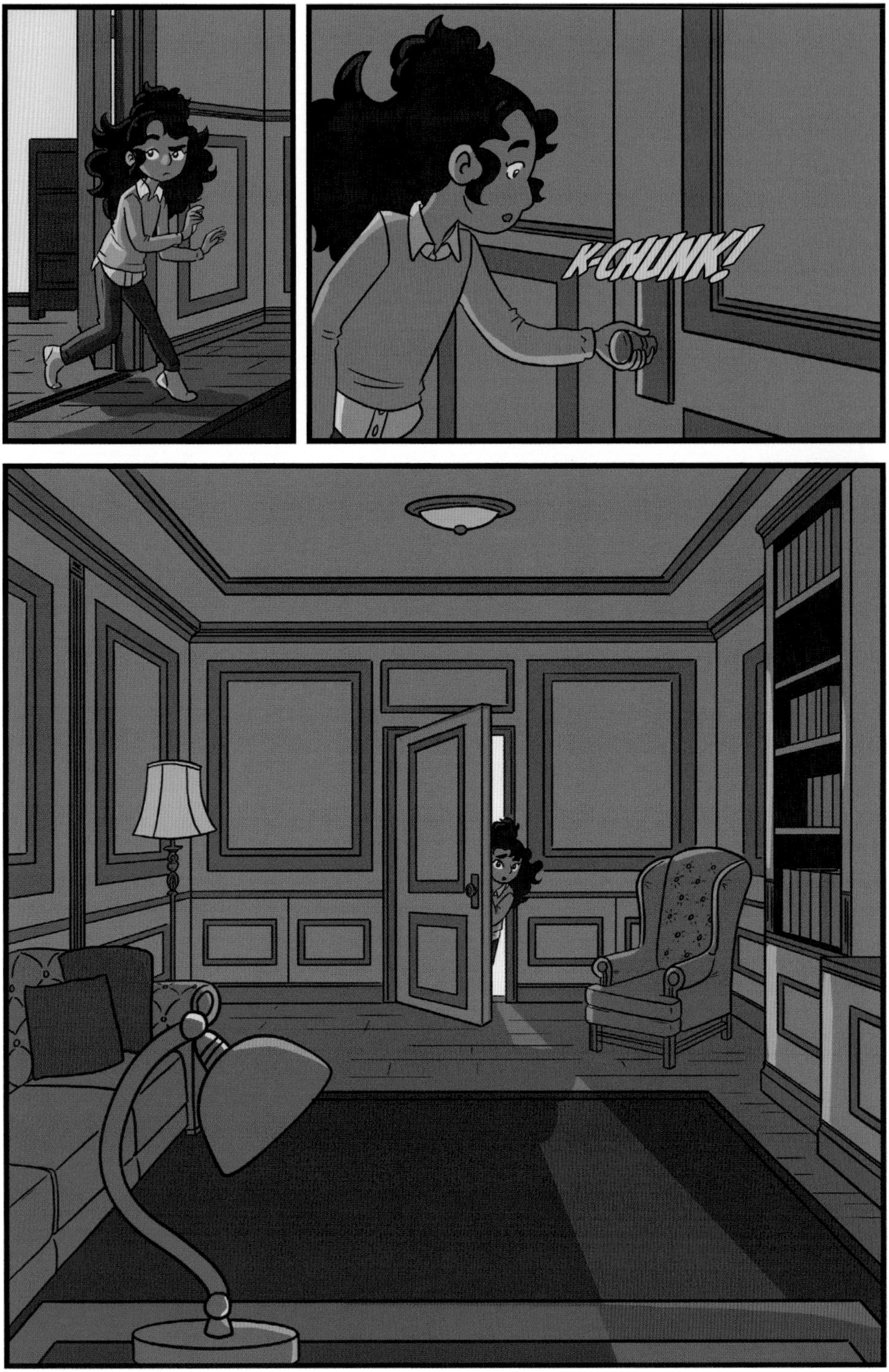
K-CHUNK!

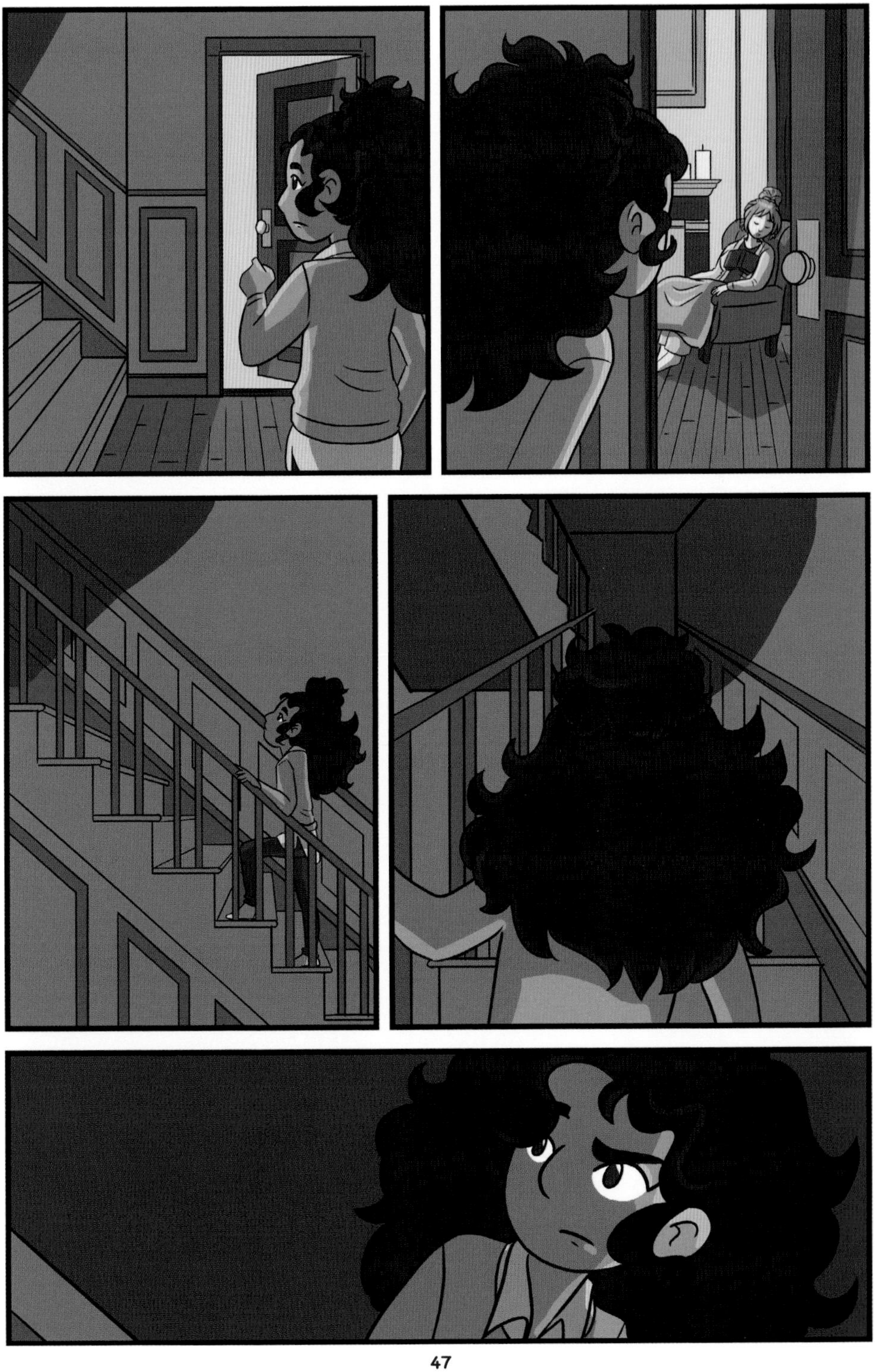

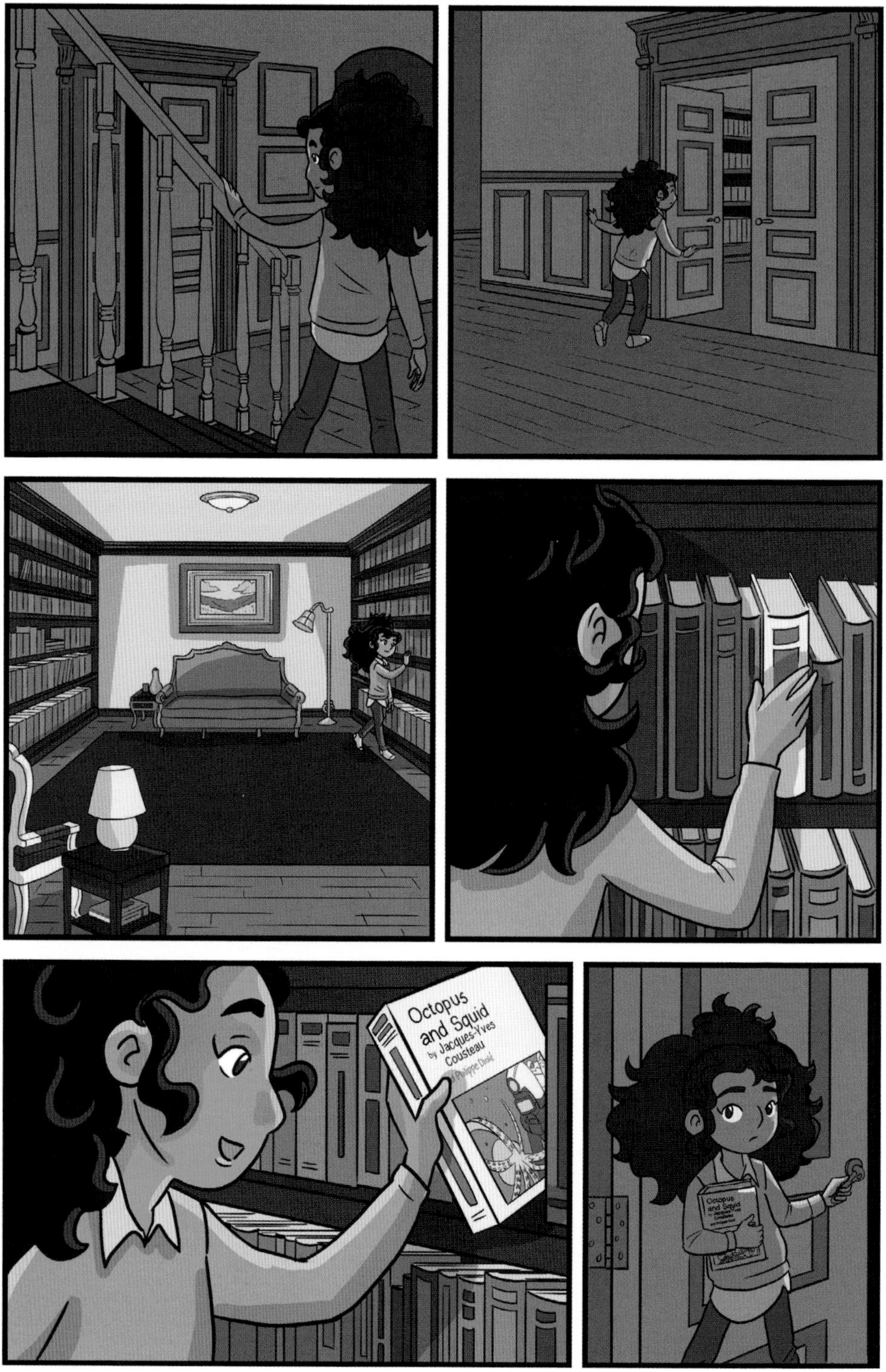
Octopus and Squid
by Jacques-Yves Cousteau
Philippe Diolé
Octopus and Squid

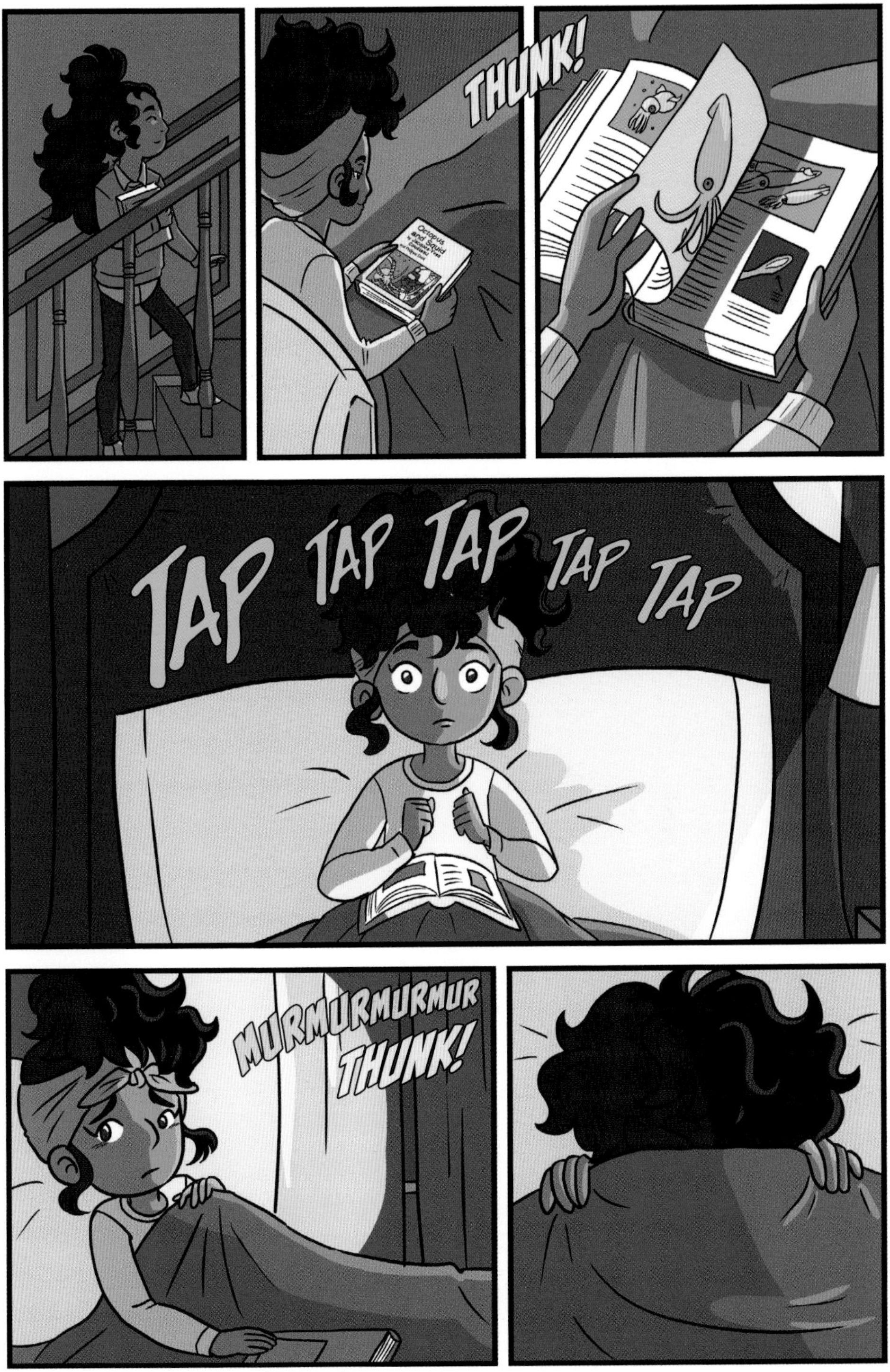
THUNK!
Octopus and Squid
TAP TAP TAP TAP TAP
MURMURMURMUR
THUNK!

INBOX | Starred | Sent | Drafts | Spam

NEW MESSAGE

TO: archibald_craven@craveninc.com
FROM: medlock_cravenhousehold@craveninc.com

SUBJECT: Mary's Arrival

Archie,

Your niece has arrived safely and is settling in. The girl's gone through a terrible ordeal, one that you are, of course, yourself familiar with, but it hasn't done much for what I suspect is an already poor attitude. She turns her nose up at most of the food that's offered and gives most answers in one-word replies. Still, Martha tries her best. You know how she is: relentlessly cheerful.

Have you given any thought to Mary's plans for school in the fall? If you are still considering boarding schools, I can begin to gather information to have ready when you return.

Best regards,
Constance

SEND

Household finance

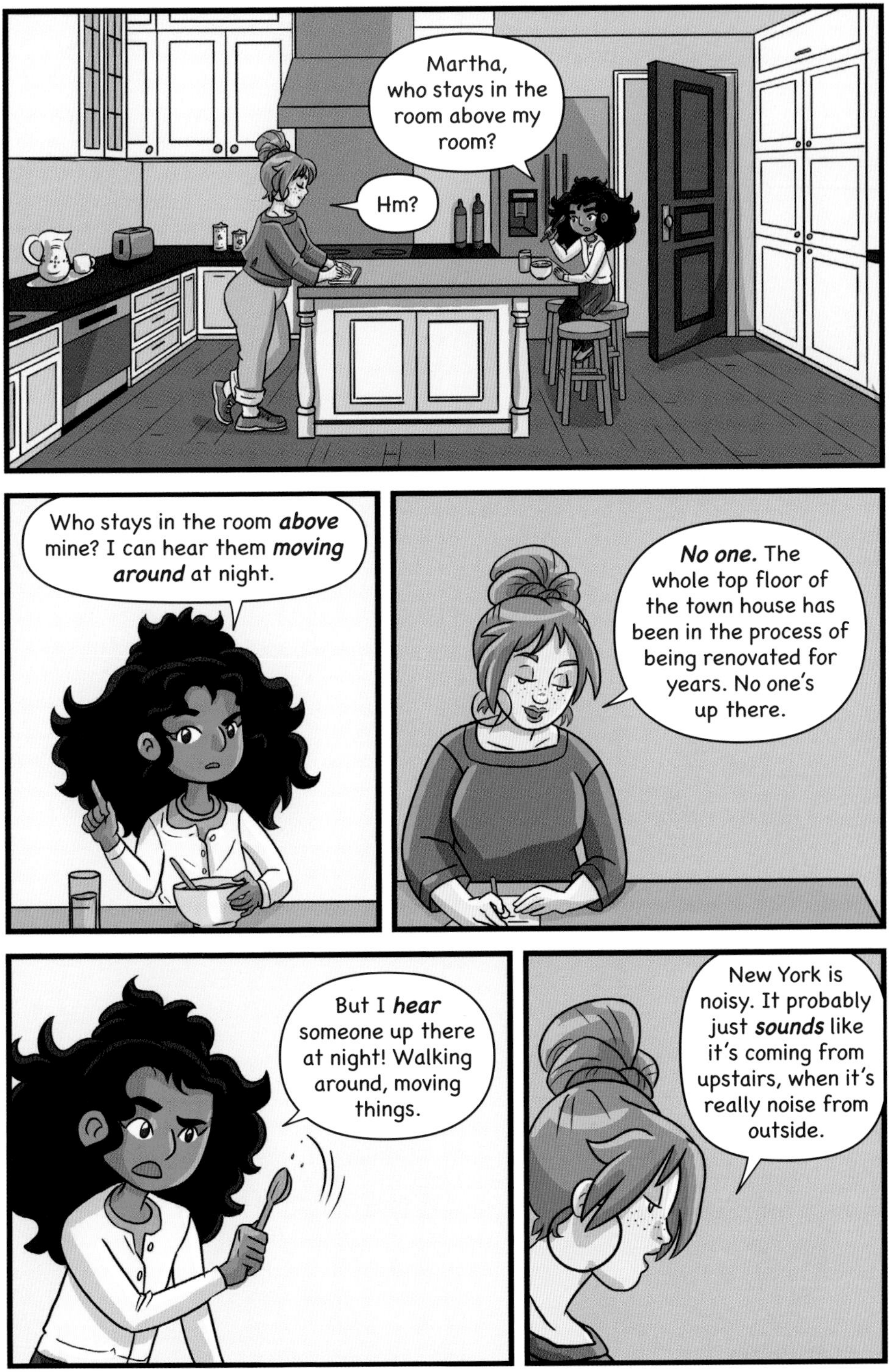
Martha, who stays in the room above my room?
Hm?
Who stays in the room *above* mine? I can hear them *moving around* at night.
No one. The whole top floor of the town house has been in the process of being renovated for years. No one's up there.
But I *hear* someone up there at night! Walking around, moving things.
New York is noisy. It probably just *sounds* like it's coming from upstairs, when it's really noise from outside.

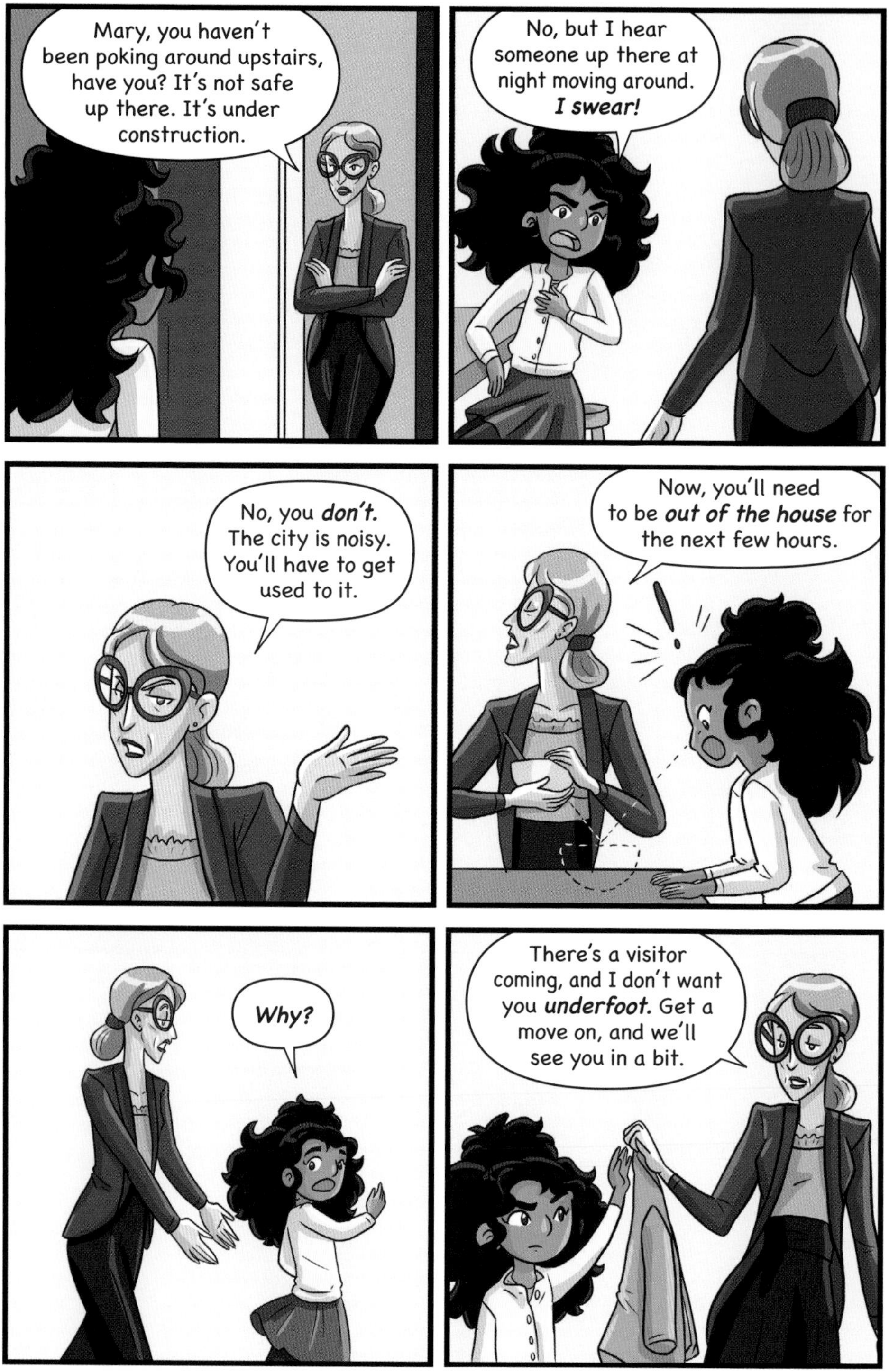
Mary, you haven't been poking around upstairs, have you? It's not safe up there. It's under construction.
No, but I hear someone up there at night moving around. ***I swear!***
No, you ***don't.*** The city is noisy. You'll have to get used to it.
Now, you'll need to be ***out of the house*** for the next few hours.
!
Why?
There's a visitor coming, and I don't want you ***underfoot.*** Get a move on, and we'll see you in a bit.

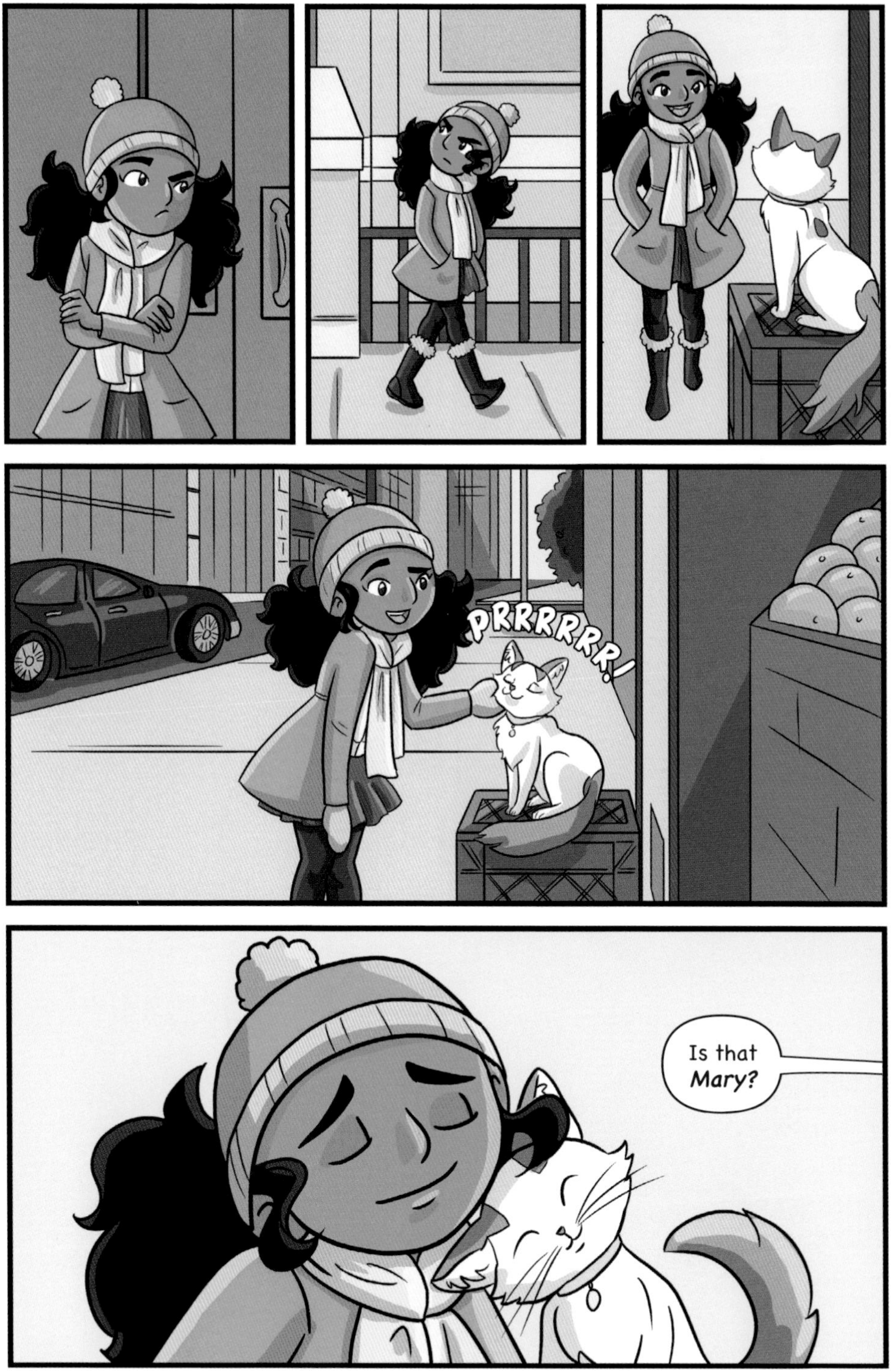
PRRRRRRR!
Is that Mary?

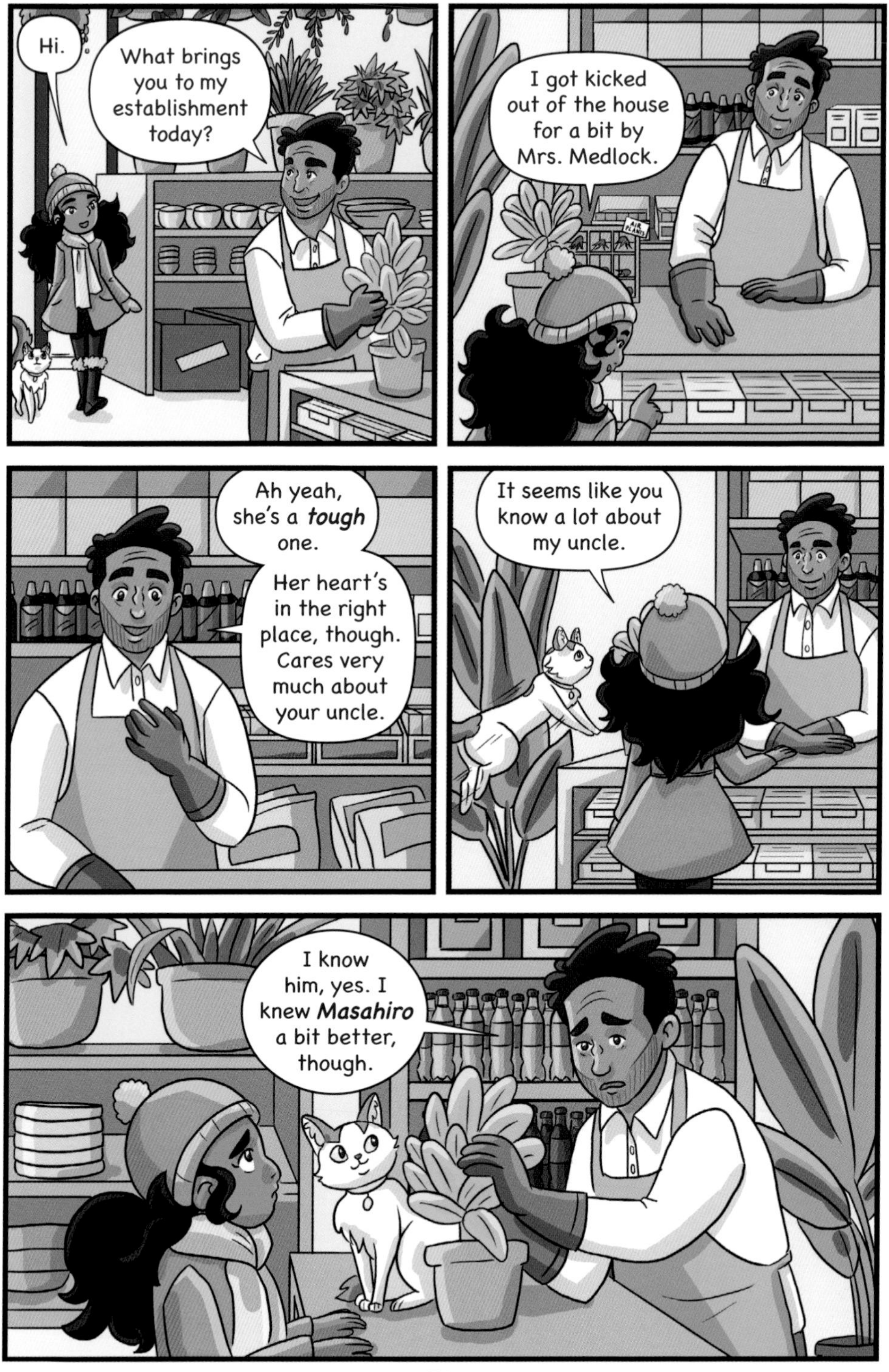
Hi.
What brings you to my establishment today?
I got kicked out of the house for a bit by Mrs. Medlock.
AIR PLANTS
Ah yeah, she's a *tough* one.
Her heart's in the right place, though. Cares very much about your uncle.
It seems like you know a lot about my uncle.
I know him, yes. I knew *Masahiro* a bit better, though.

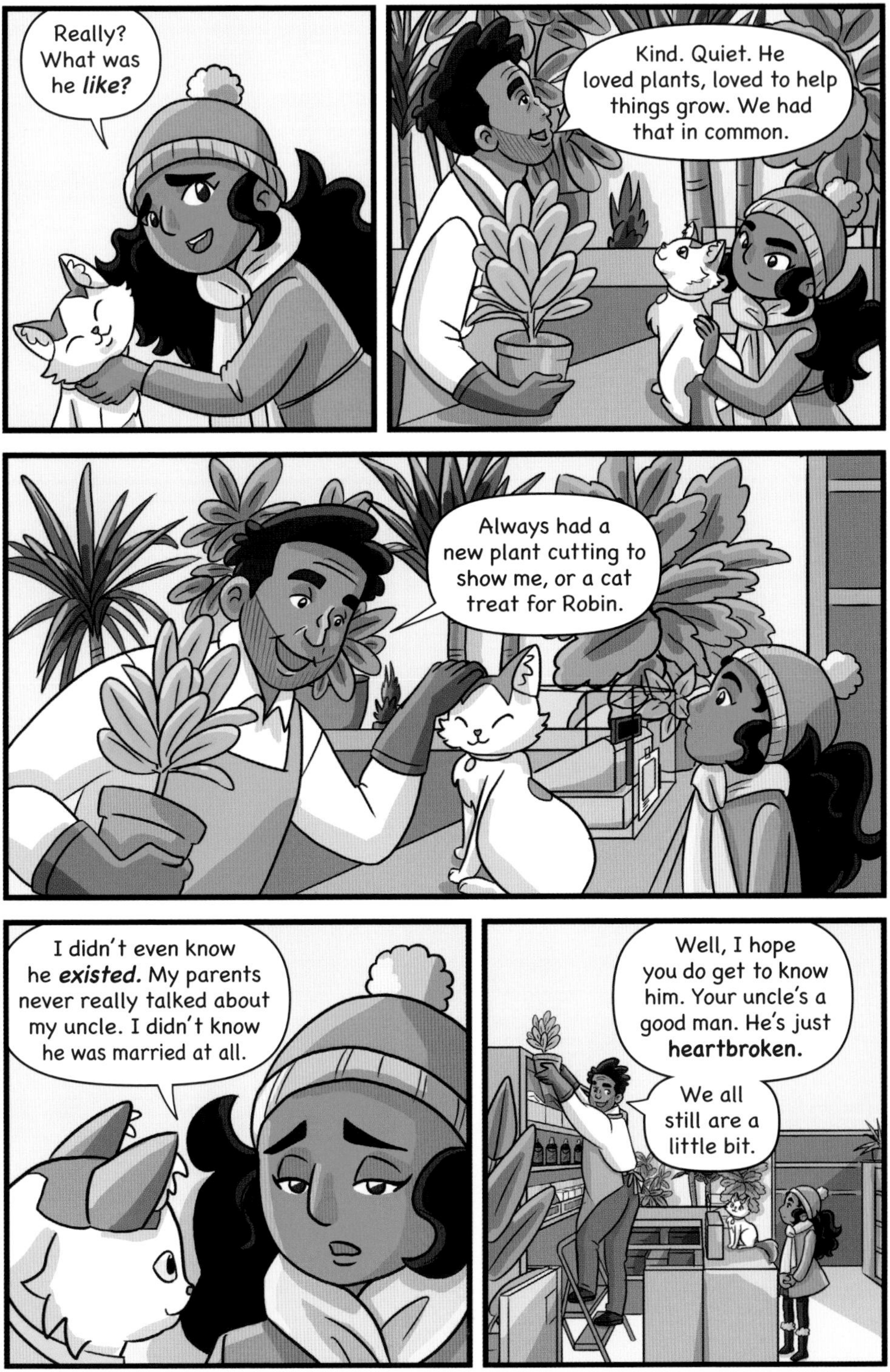
Really? What was he *like?*
Kind. Quiet. He loved plants, loved to help things grow. We had that in common.
Always had a new plant cutting to show me, or a cat treat for Robin.
I didn't even know he *existed.* My parents never really talked about my uncle. I didn't know he was married at all.
Well, I hope you do get to know him. Your uncle's a good man. He's just **heartbroken.**
We all still are a little bit.

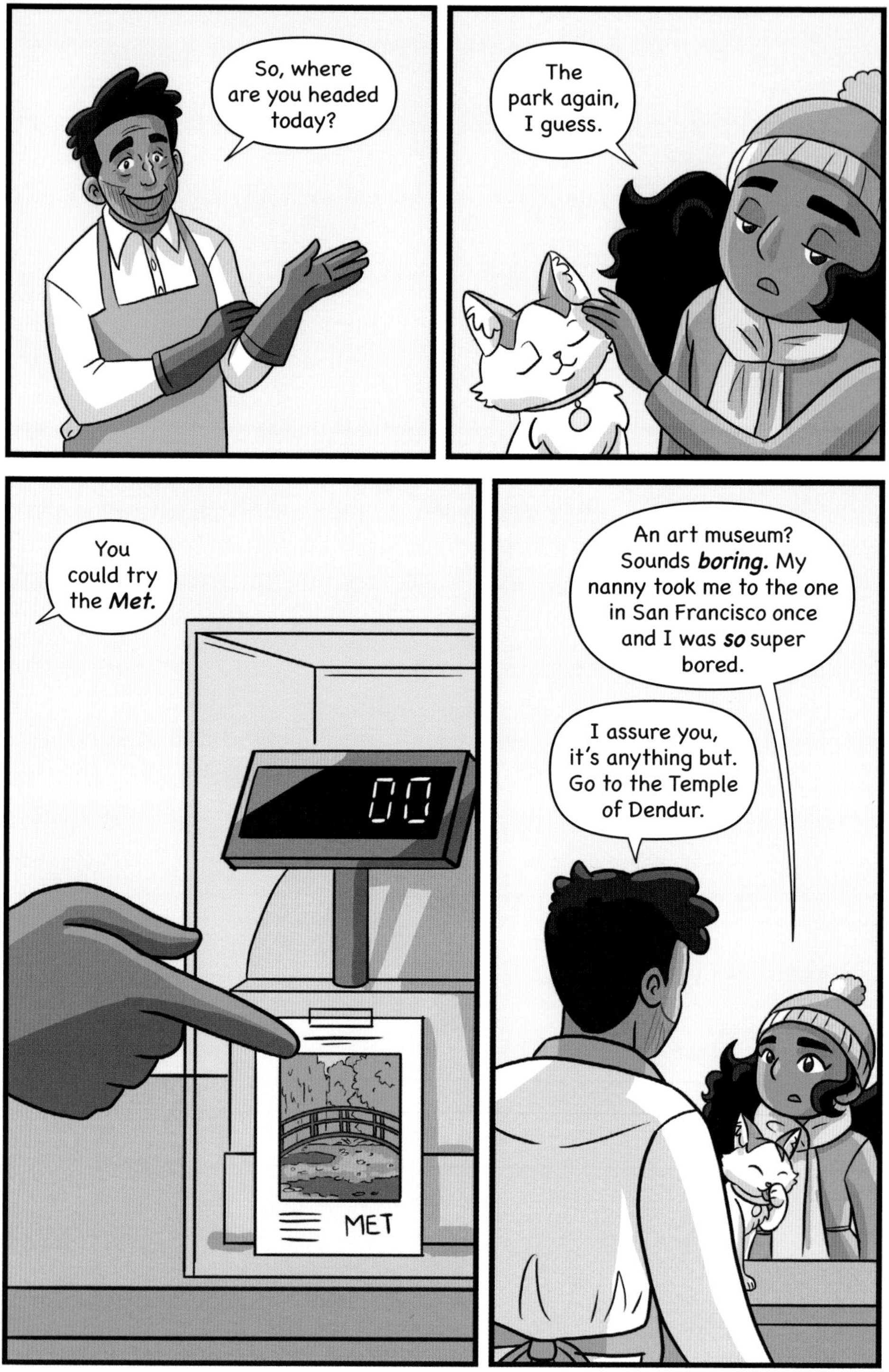
So, where are you headed today?
The park again, I guess.
You could try the *Met.*
MET
An art museum? Sounds ***boring.*** My nanny took me to the one in San Francisco once and I was ***so*** super bored.
I assure you, it's anything but. Go to the Temple of Dendur.

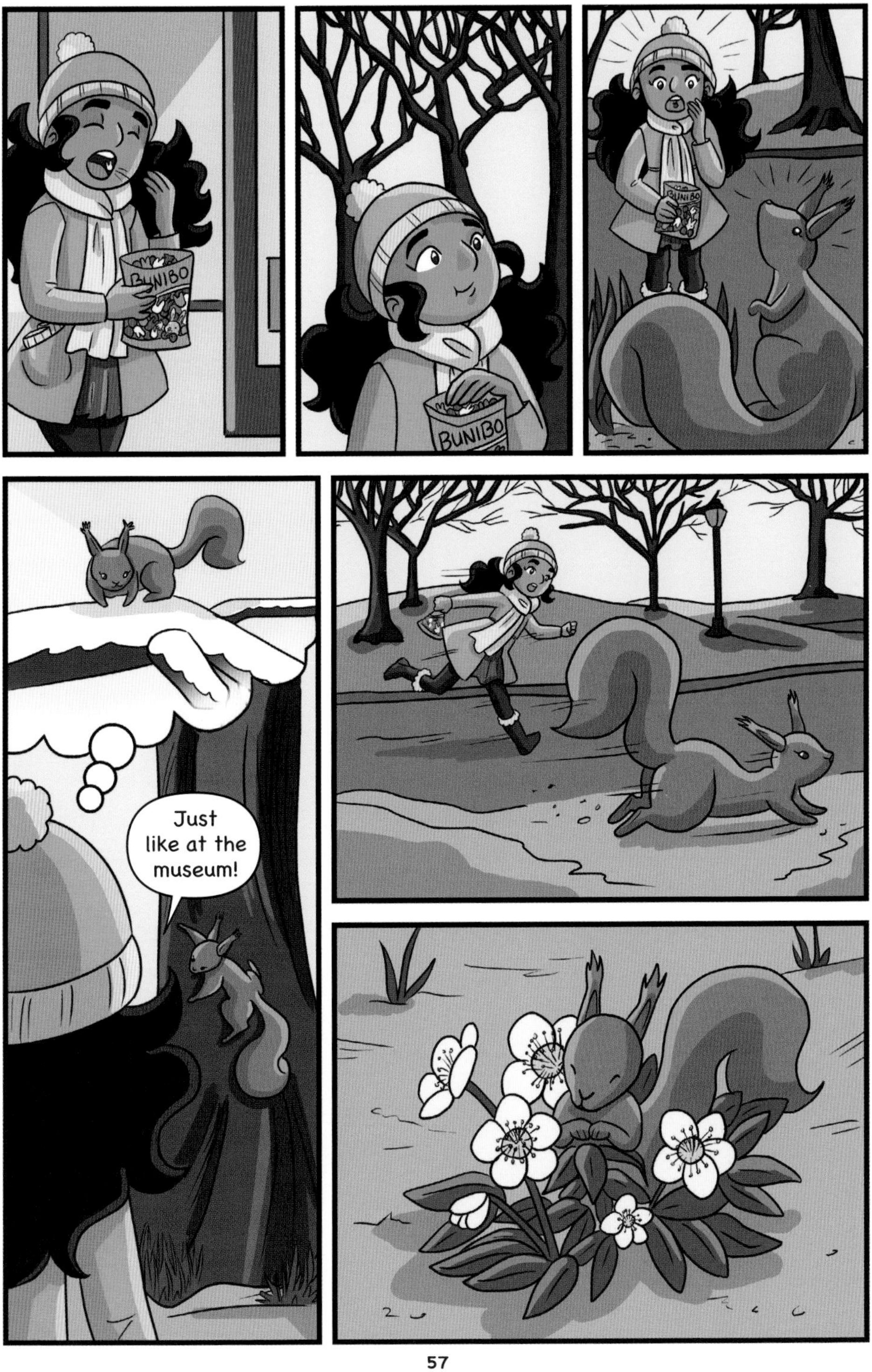
BUNIBO
BUNIBO
Just like at the museum!

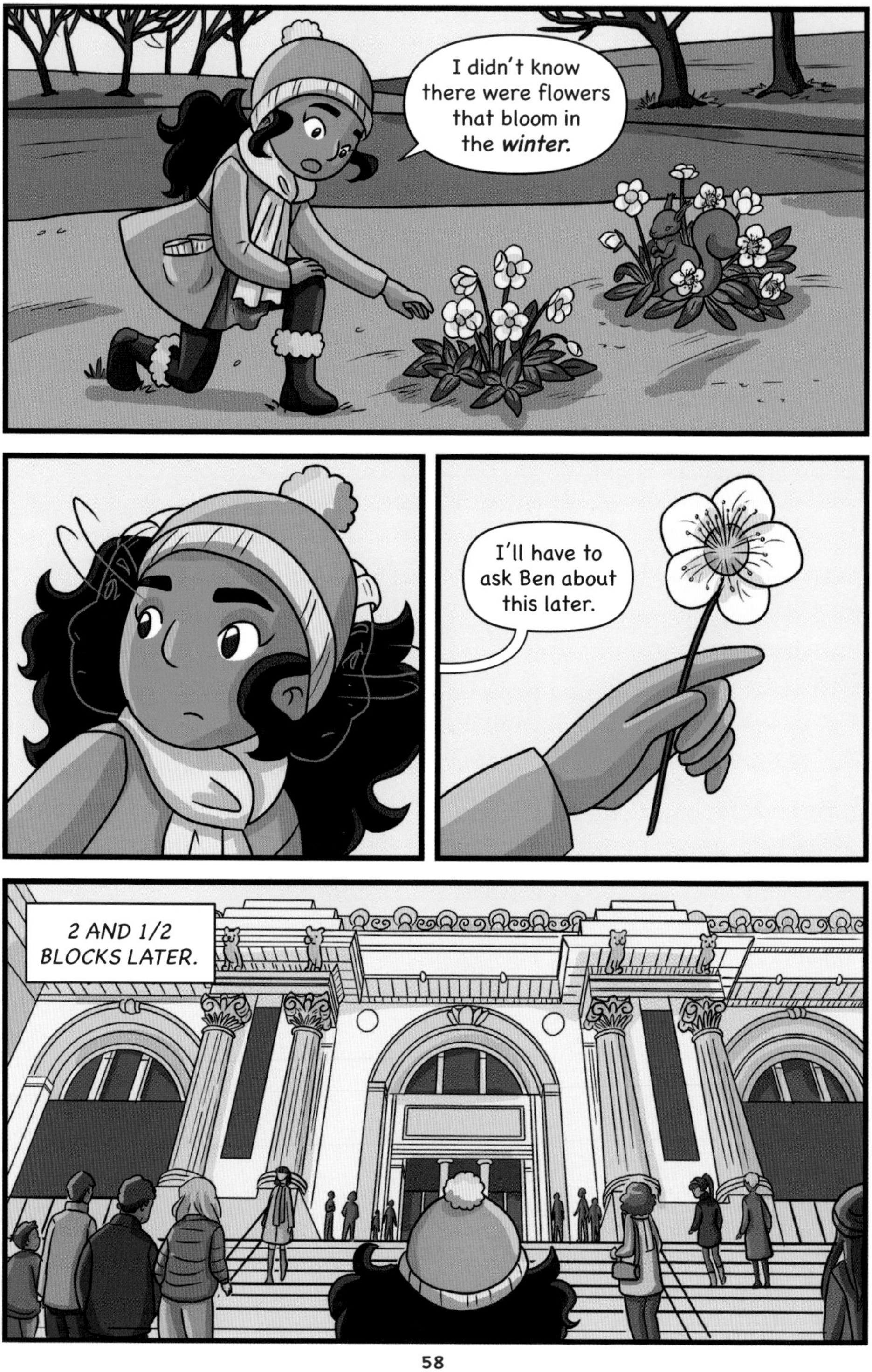

I didn't know there were flowers that bloom in the *winter.*
I'll have to ask Ben about this later.
2 AND 1/2 BLOCKS LATER.

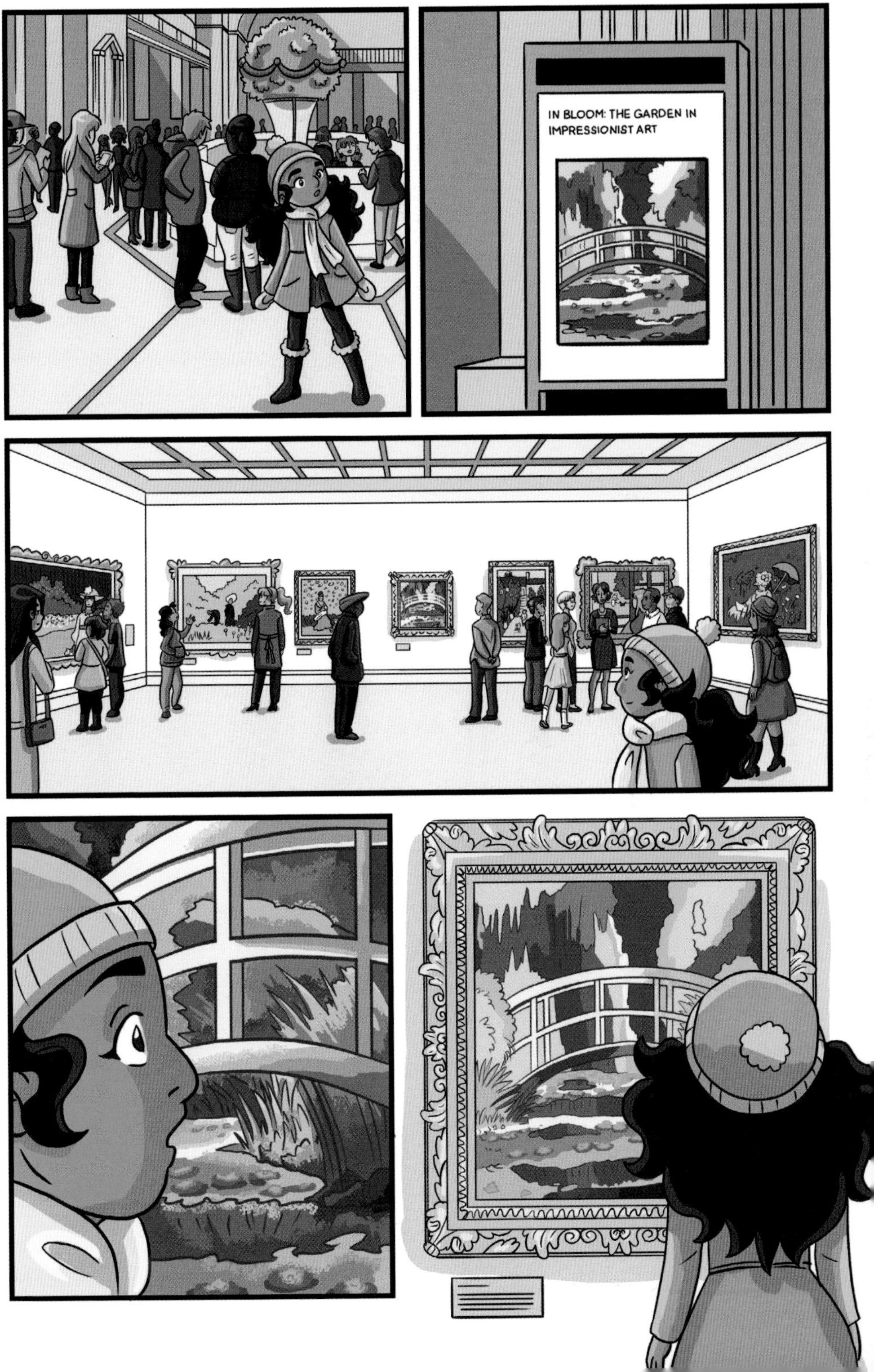
IN BLOOM: THE GARDEN IN
IMPRESSIONIST ART

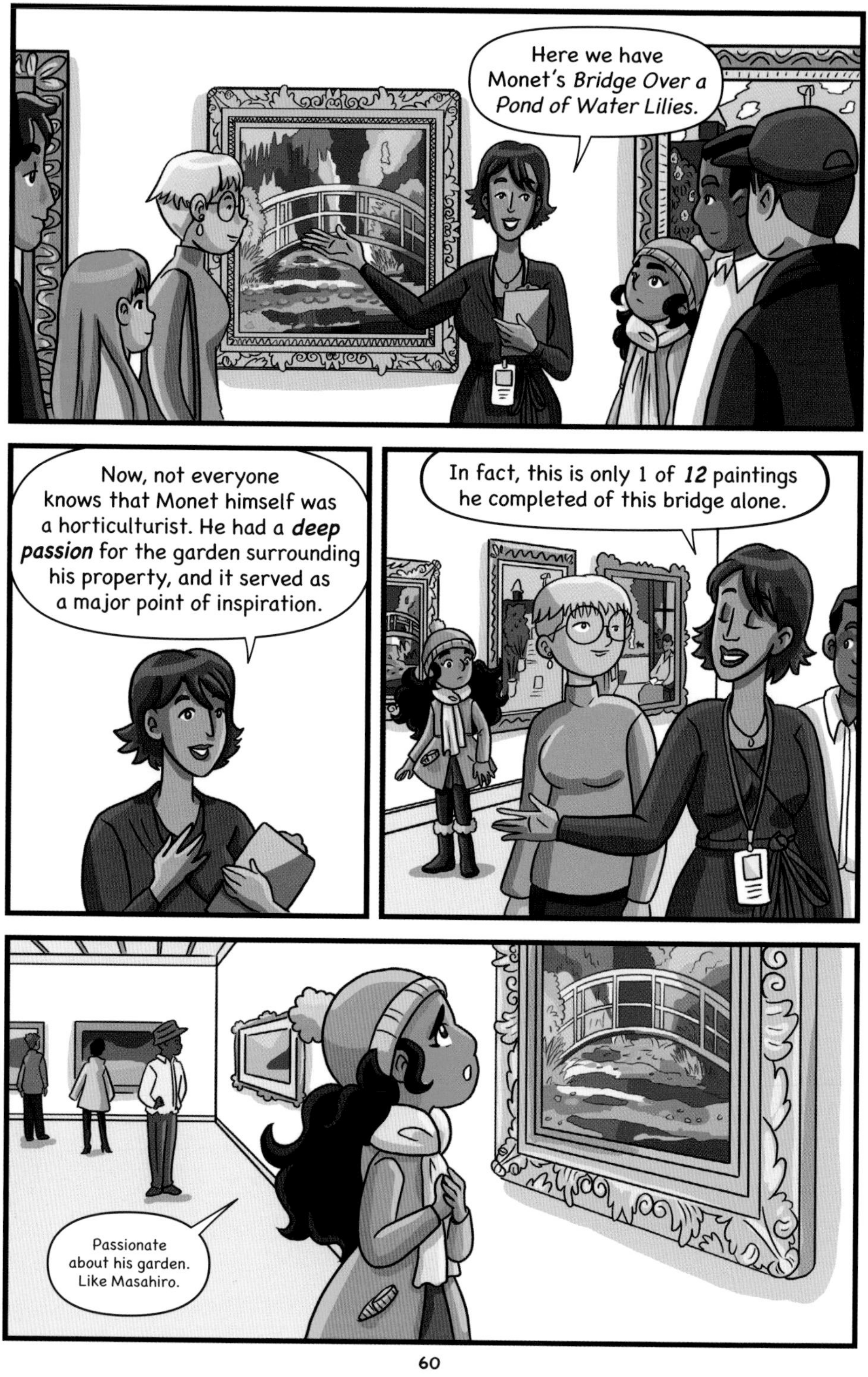
Here we have Monet's *Bridge Over a Pond of Water Lilies.*
Now, not everyone knows that Monet himself was a horticulturist. He had a ***deep passion*** for the garden surrounding his property, and it served as a major point of inspiration.
In fact, this is only 1 of ***12*** paintings he completed of this bridge alone.
Passionate about his garden. Like Masahiro.

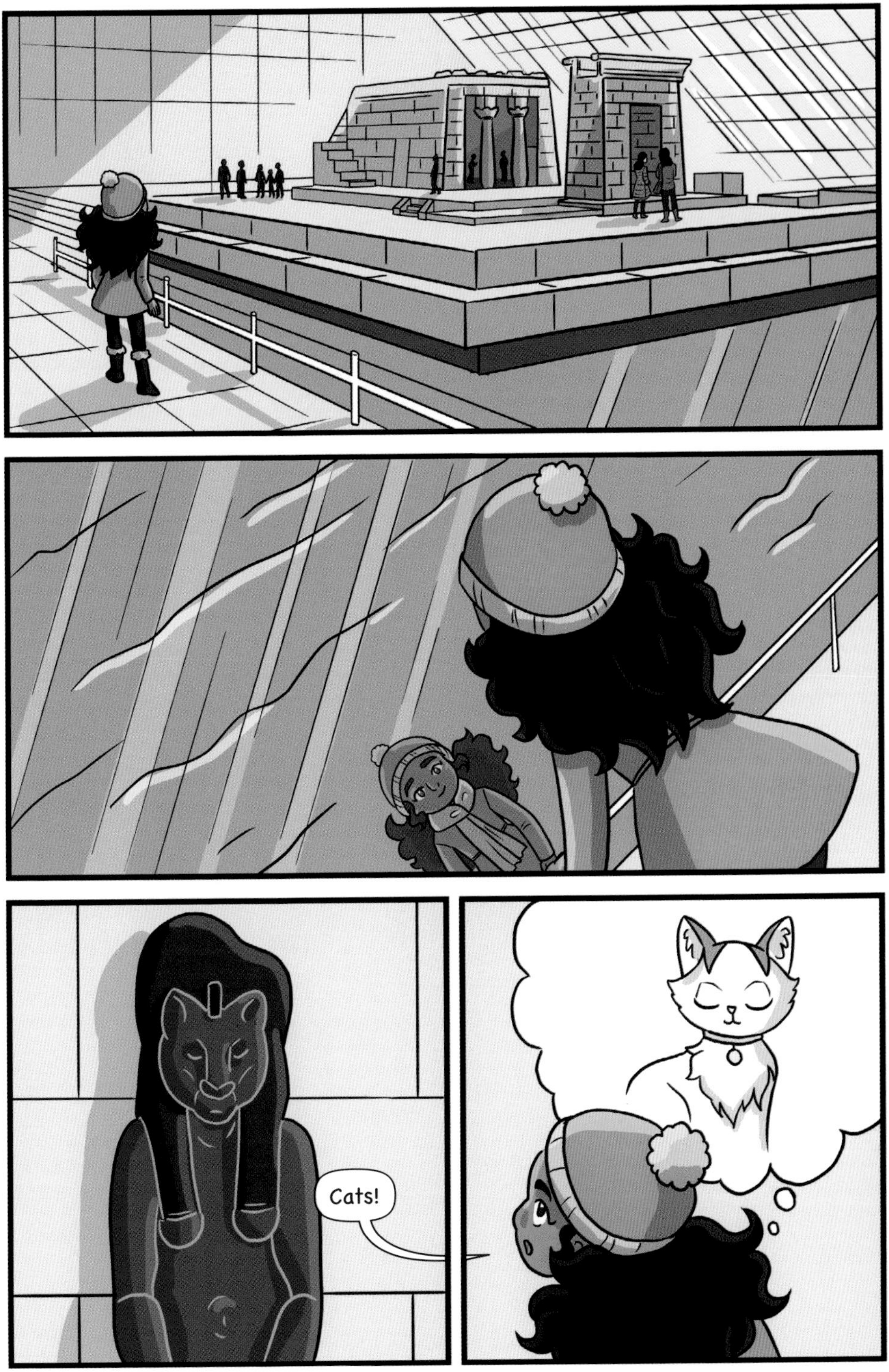
Cats!

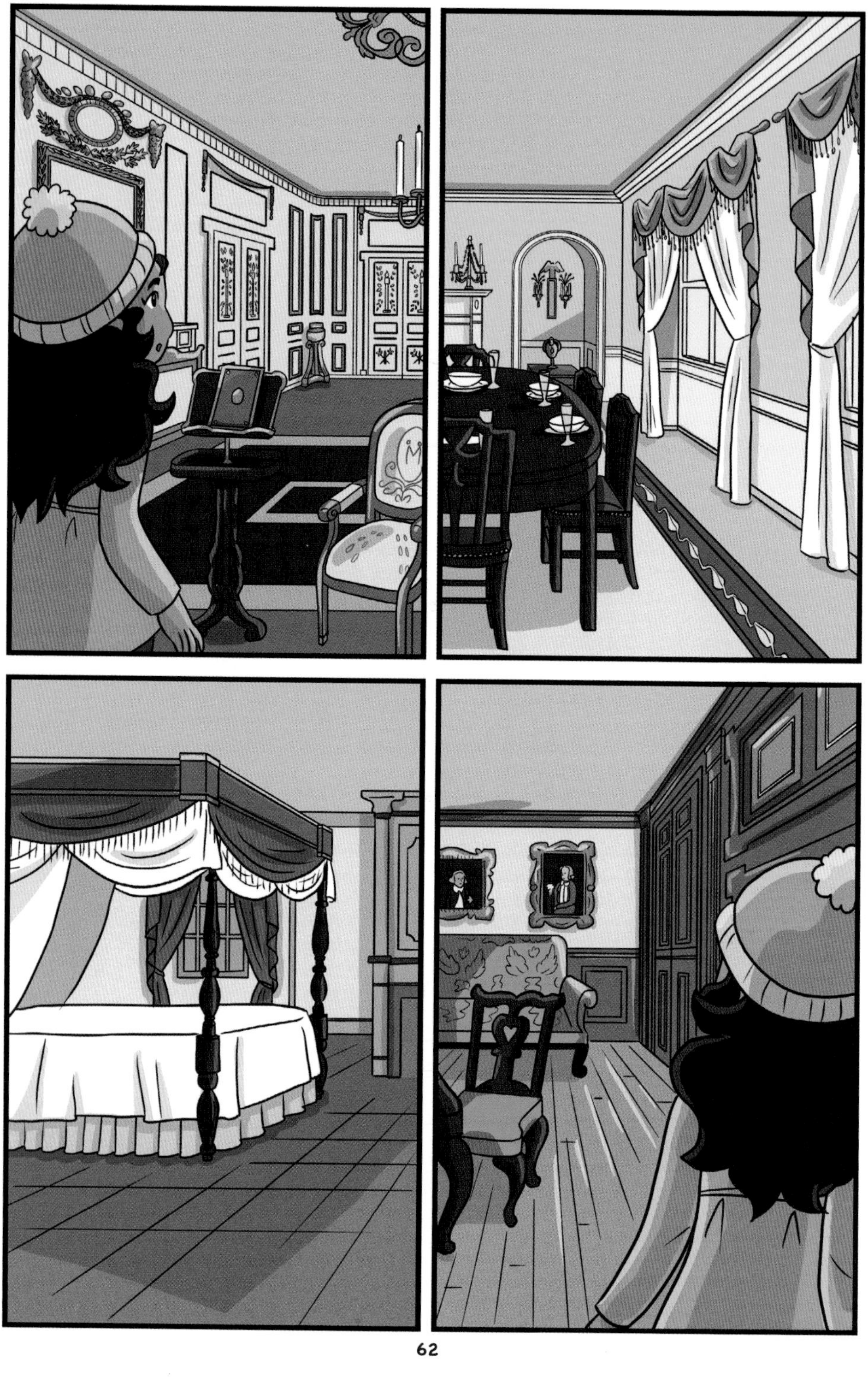

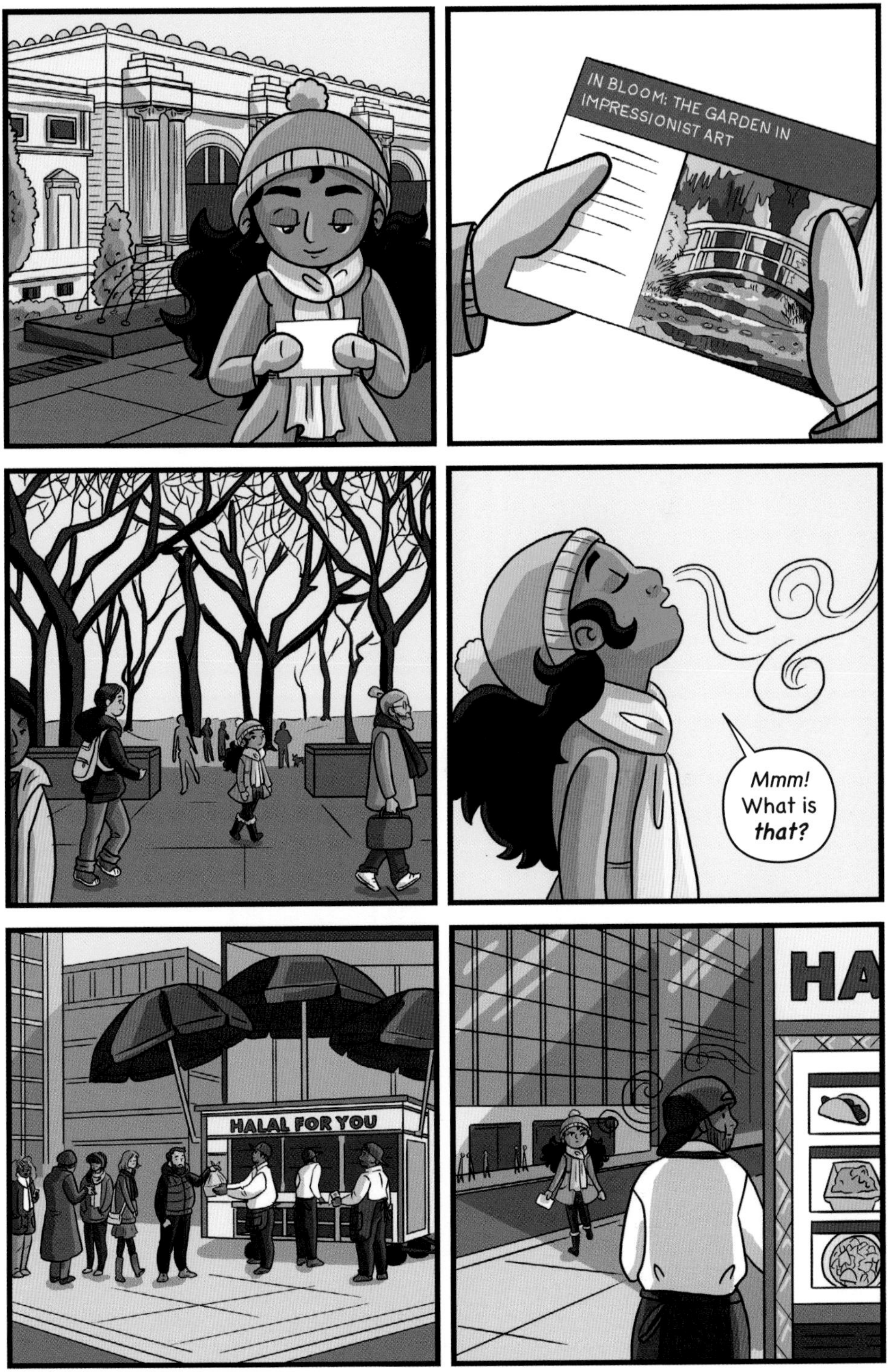
IN BLOOM: THE GARDEN IN IMPRESSIONIST ART
Mmm! What is *that?*
HALAL FOR YOU
HA

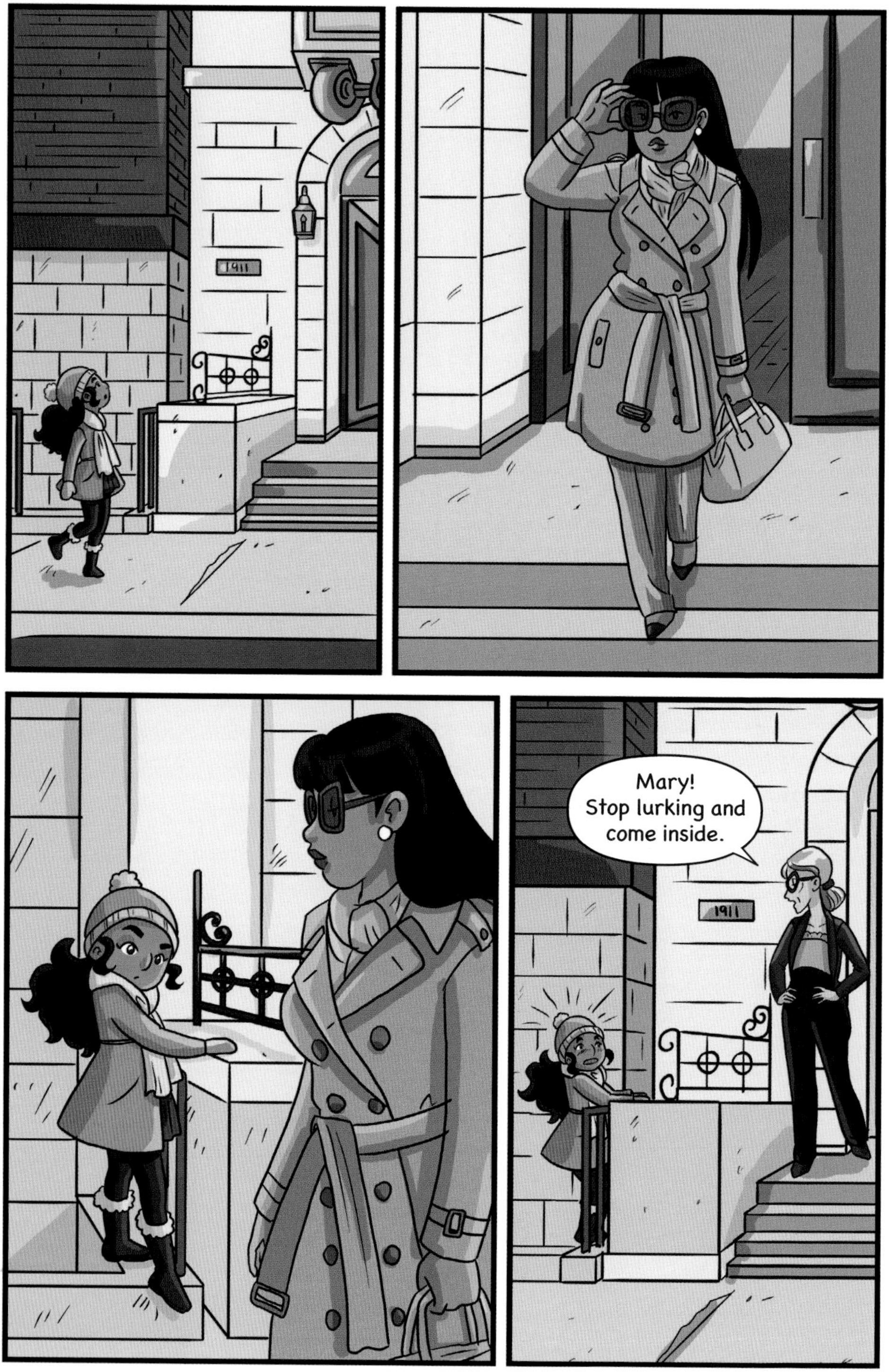
1911
1911
Mary!
Stop lurking and
come inside.

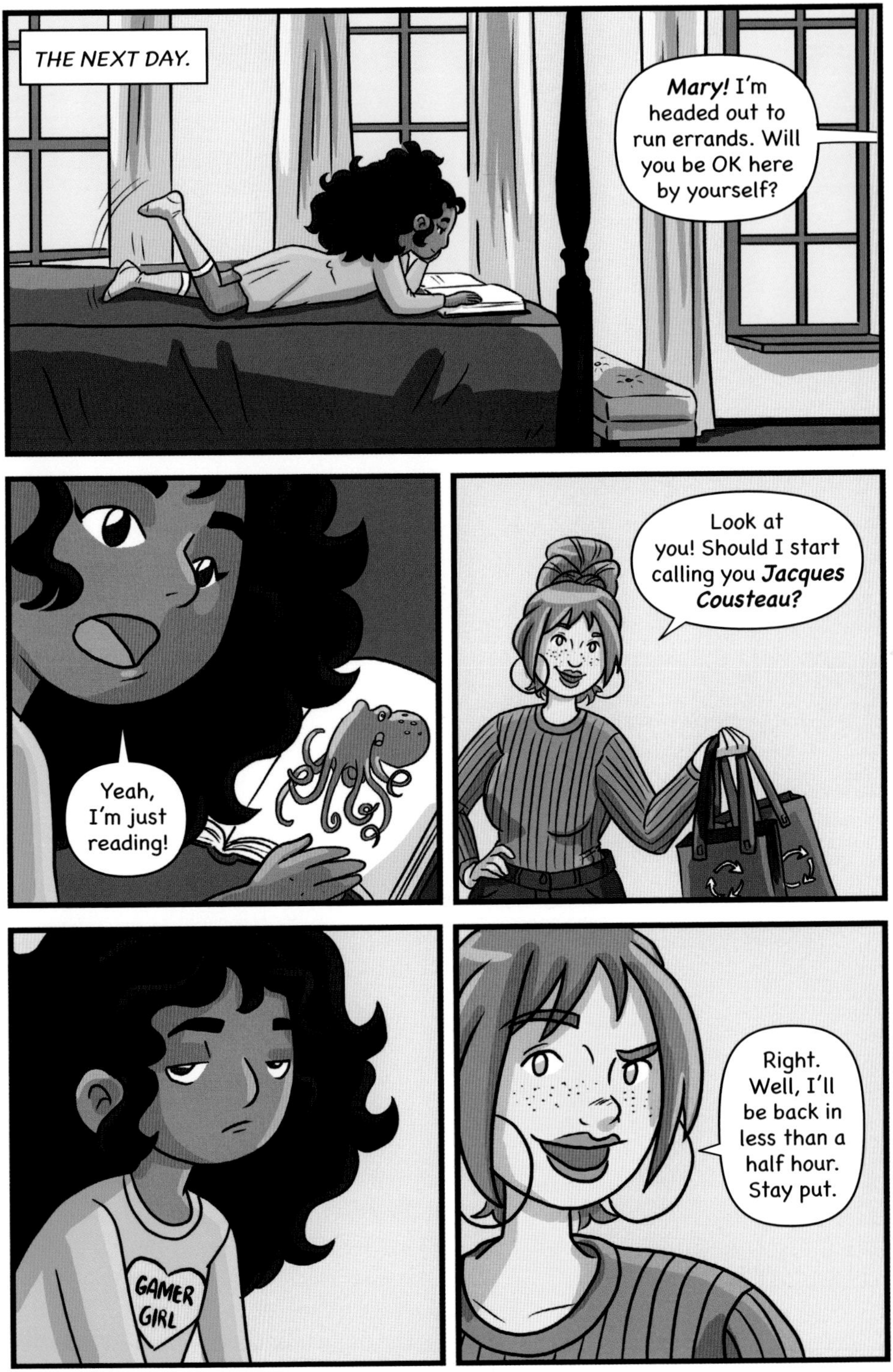
THE NEXT DAY.
Mary! I'm headed out to run errands. Will you be OK here by yourself?
Yeah, I'm just reading!
Look at you! Should I start calling you Jacques Cousteau?
GAMER GIRL
Right. Well, I'll be back in less than a half hour. Stay put.

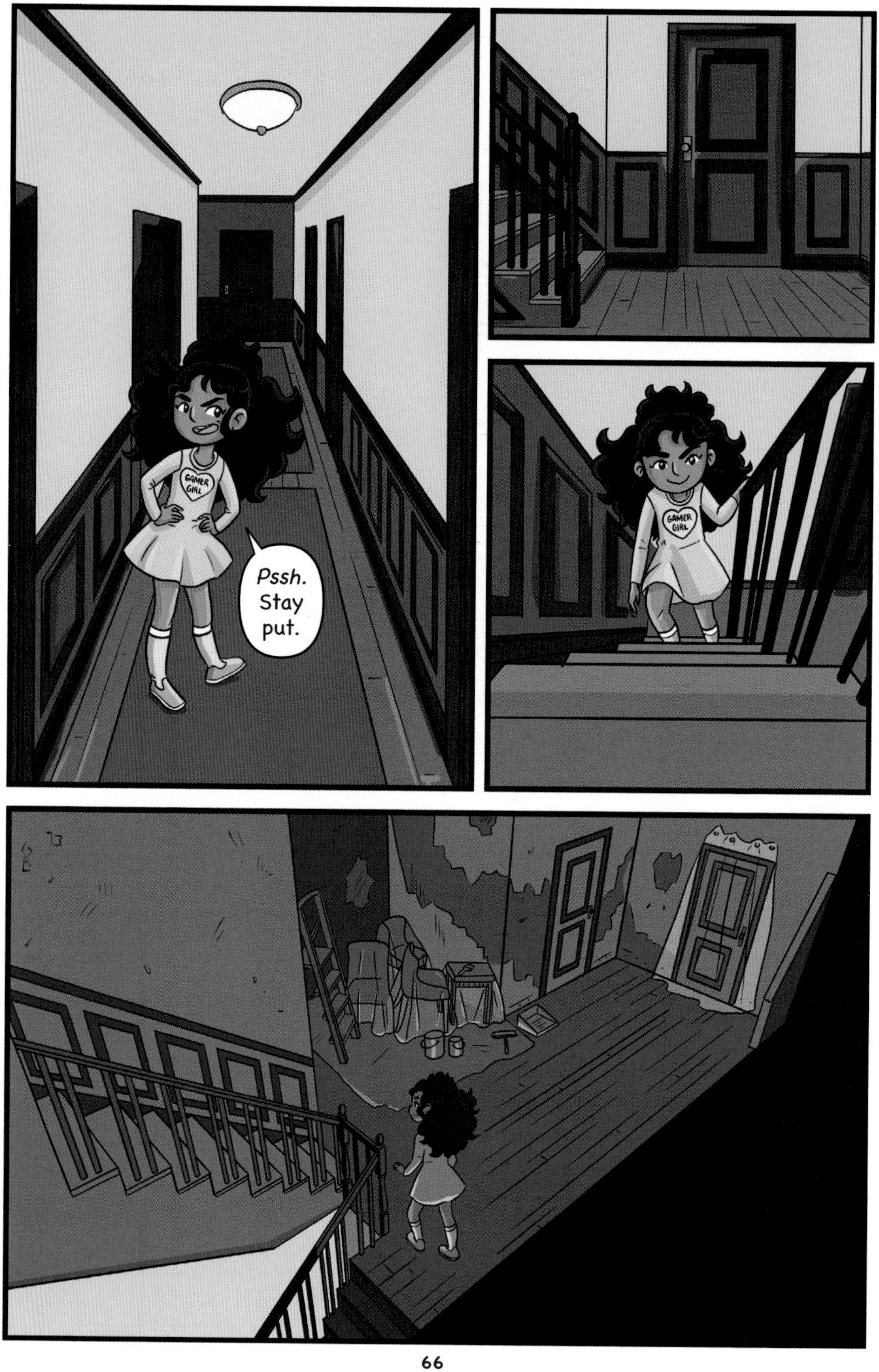
GAMER GIRL
Pssh. Stay put.
GAMER GIRL

This must be the door to the roof.

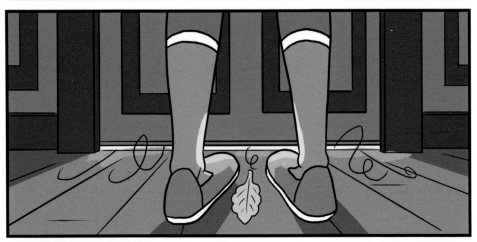

THUMP!

Hello?

THUNK!
TIKKA-TIKKA-TIKKA

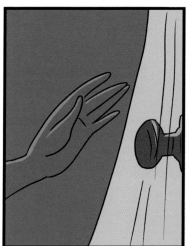

Mary? I'm back! Come eat lunch!

LATER.

Here.

What's this?

It's for the subway. I put some money on it, and if you want, we can take your first ride together.

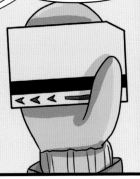

Just thought you might want to have access to more than the museums up here. Wouldn't want to miss out on the MoMA, right?

Thank you.

Sooo...

OK, we'll go right now.

Great—I mean, OK. If *you* want.

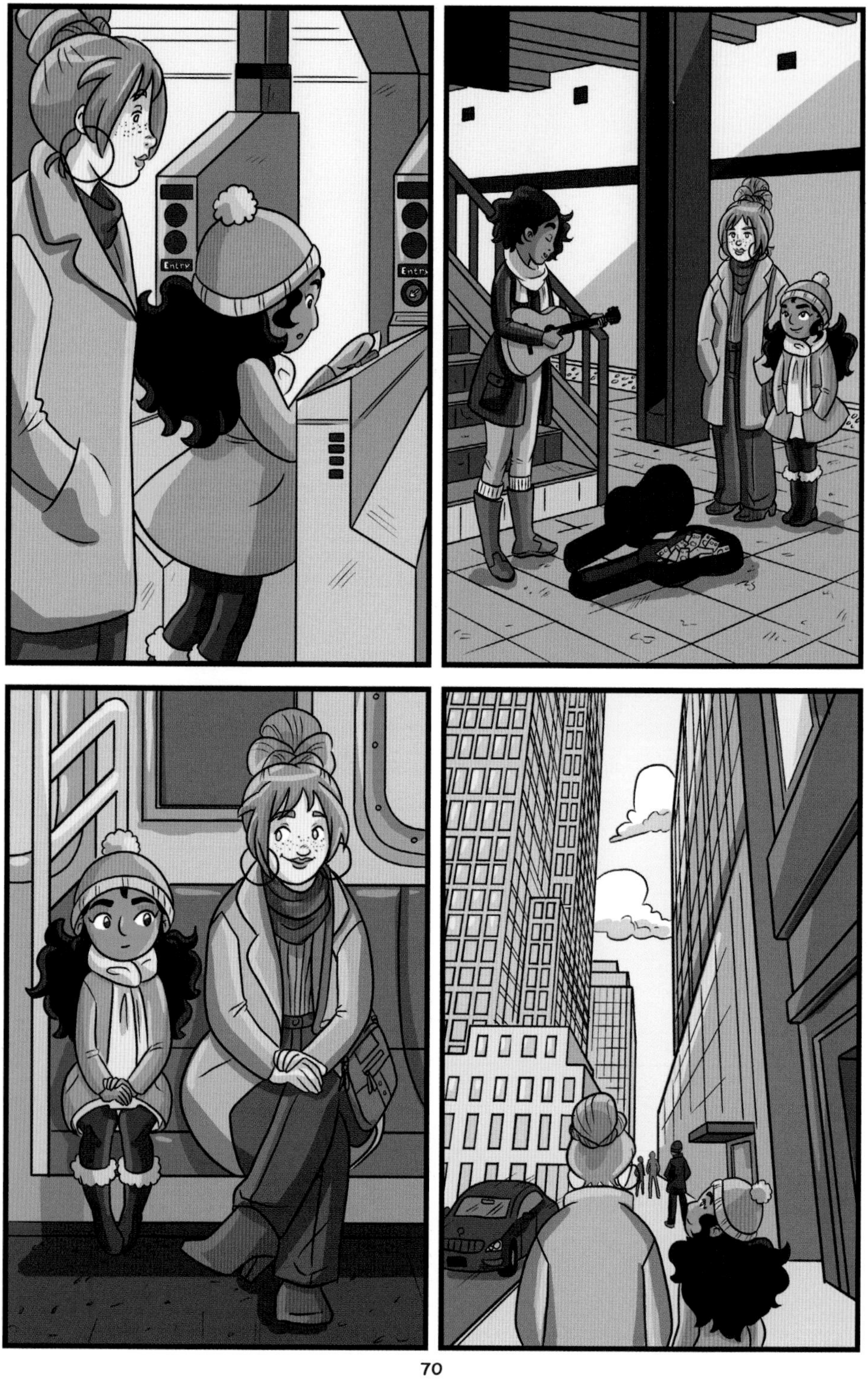
Entry
Entry

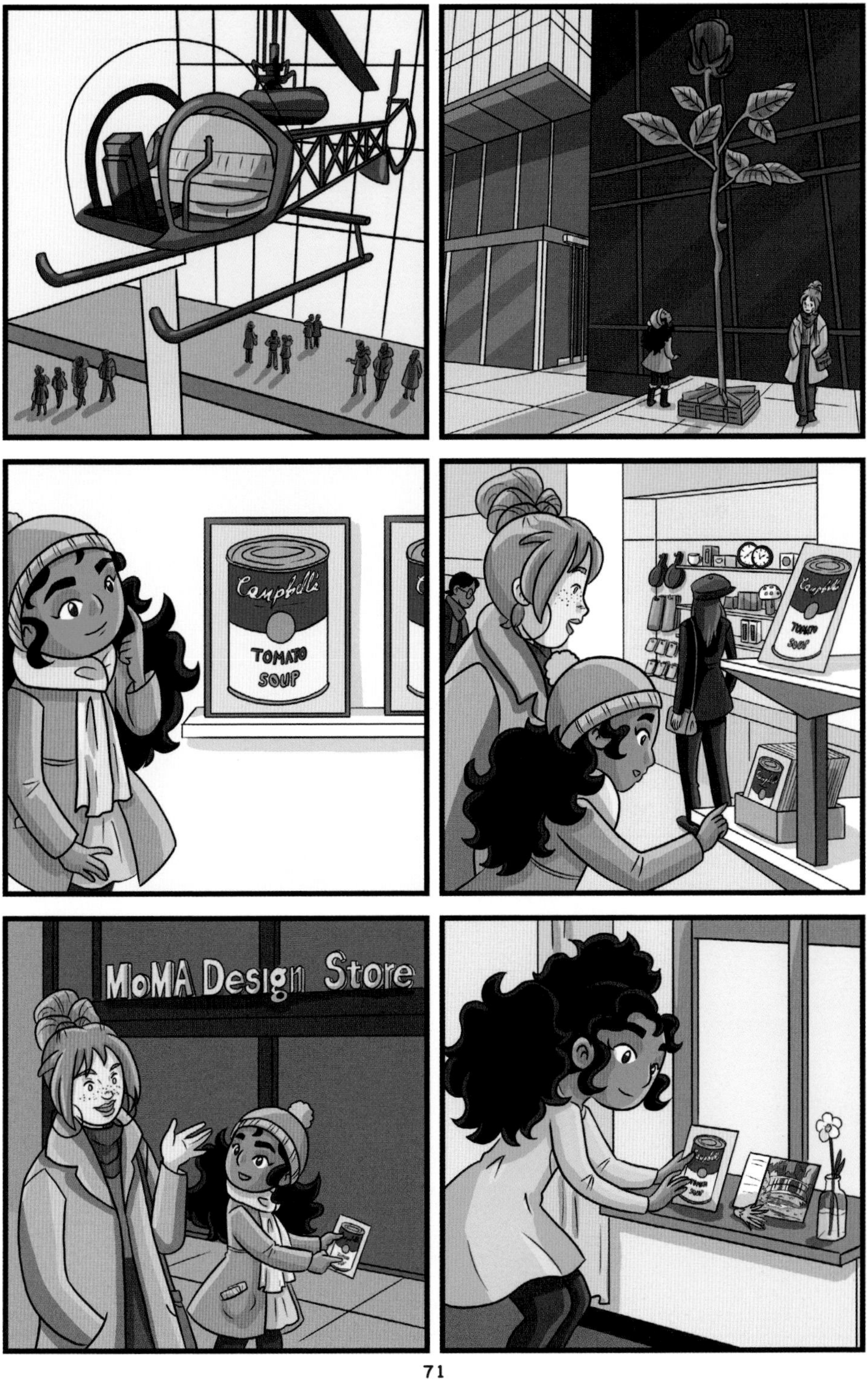
Campbell's
TOMATO
SOUP
MoMA Design Store

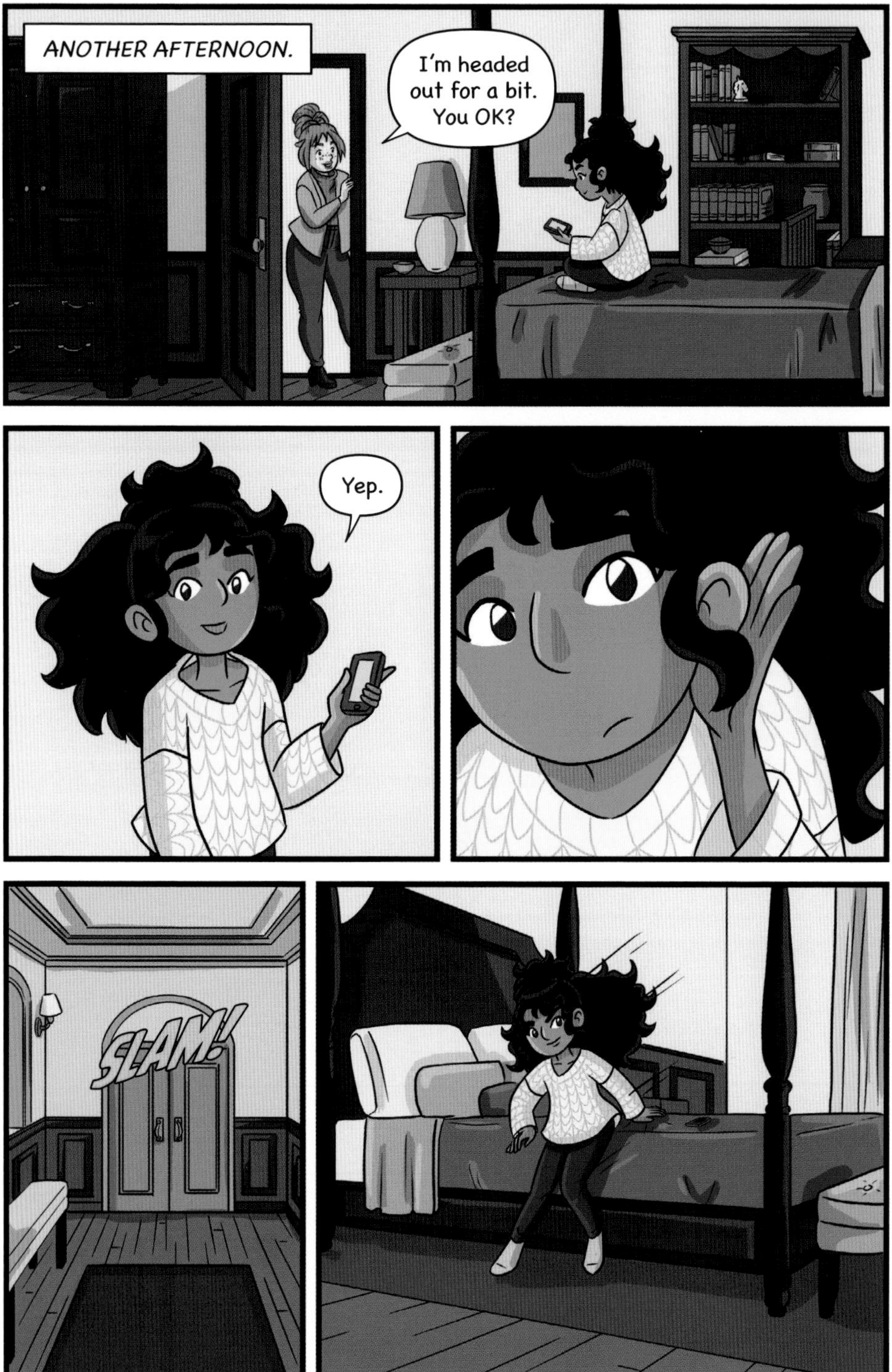
ANOTHER AFTERNOON.
I'm headed out for a bit. You OK?
Yep.
SLAM!

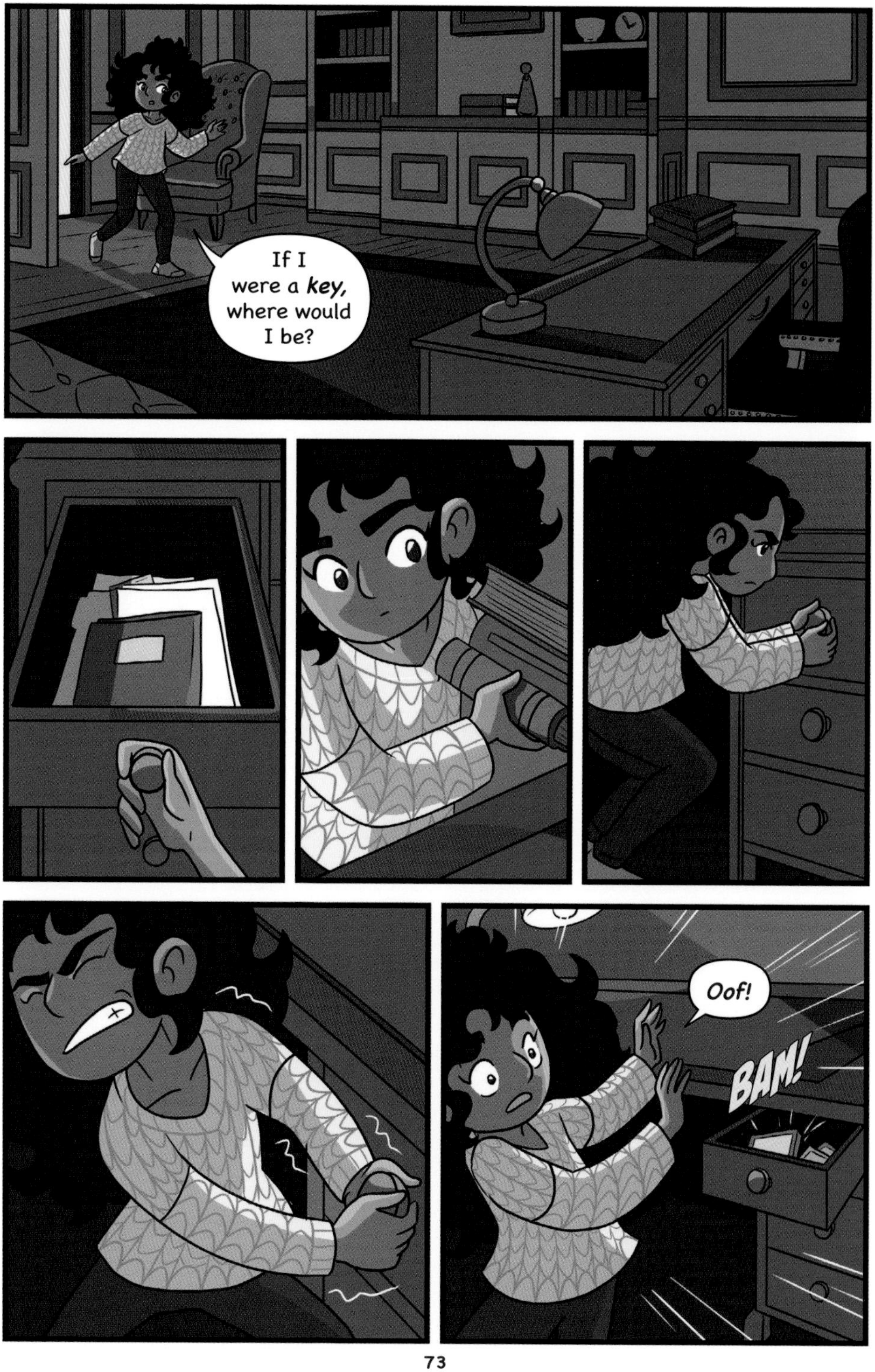

If I were a *key,* where would I be?
Oof!
BAM!

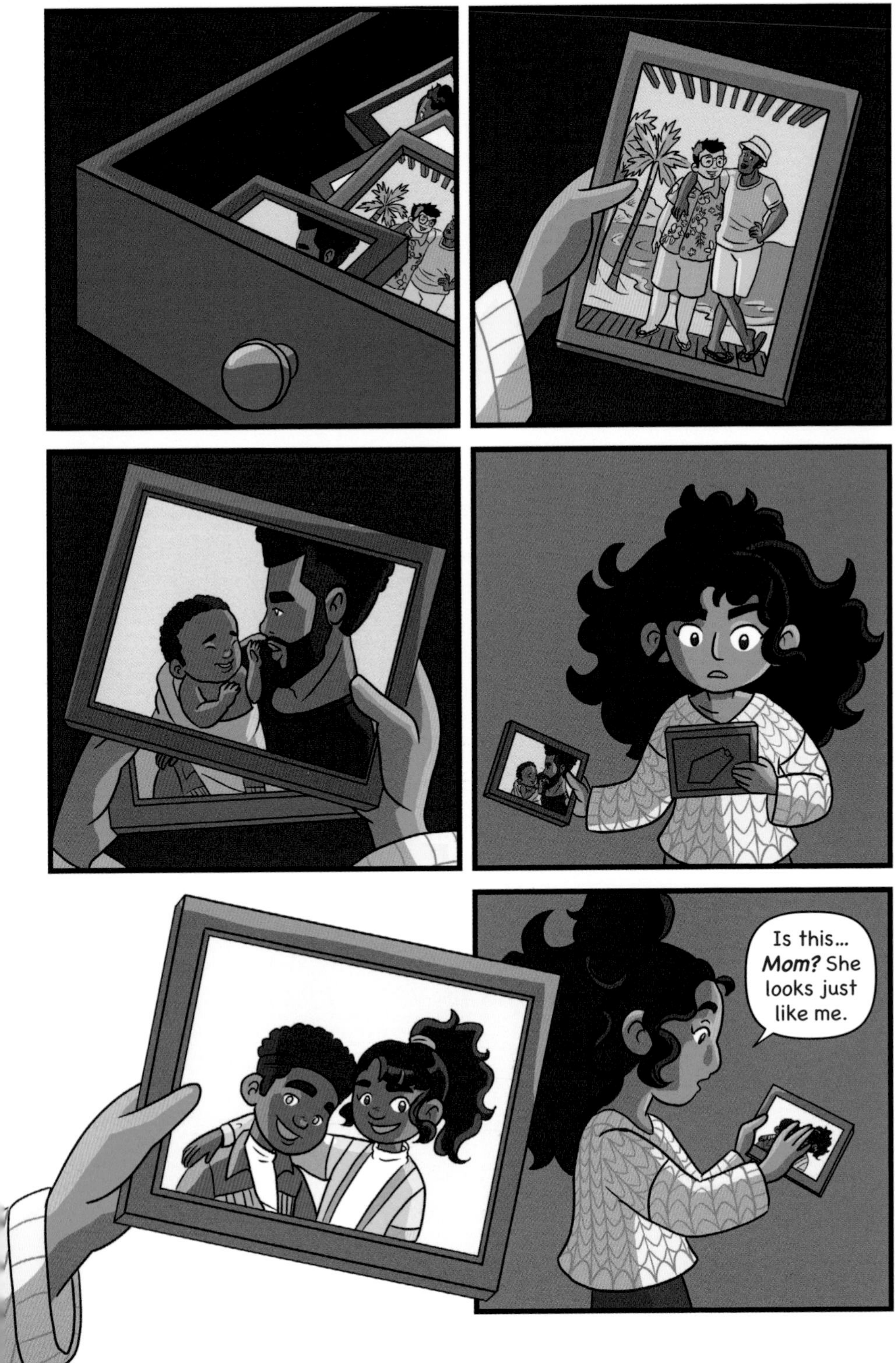
Is this... Mom? She looks just like me.

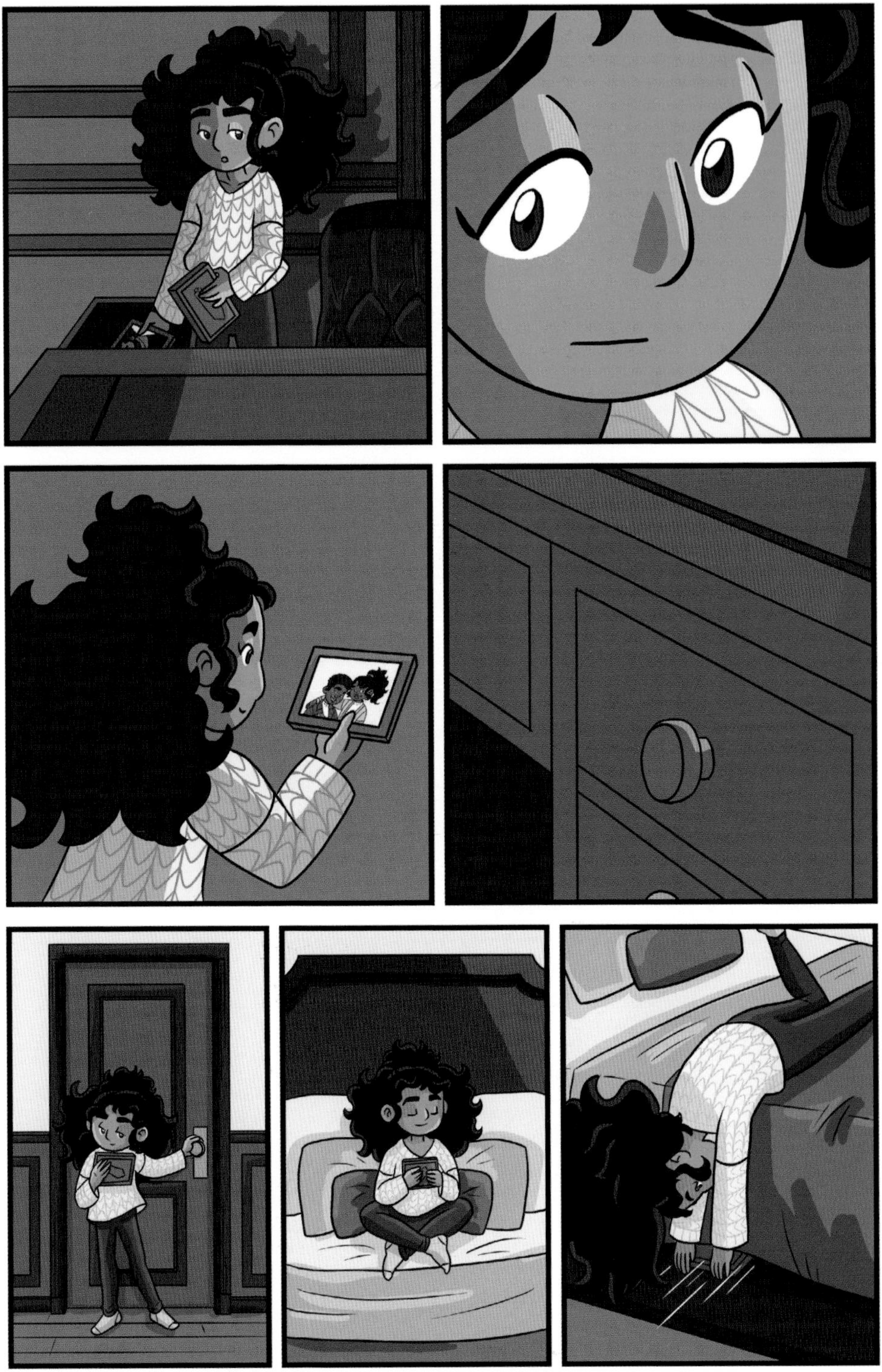

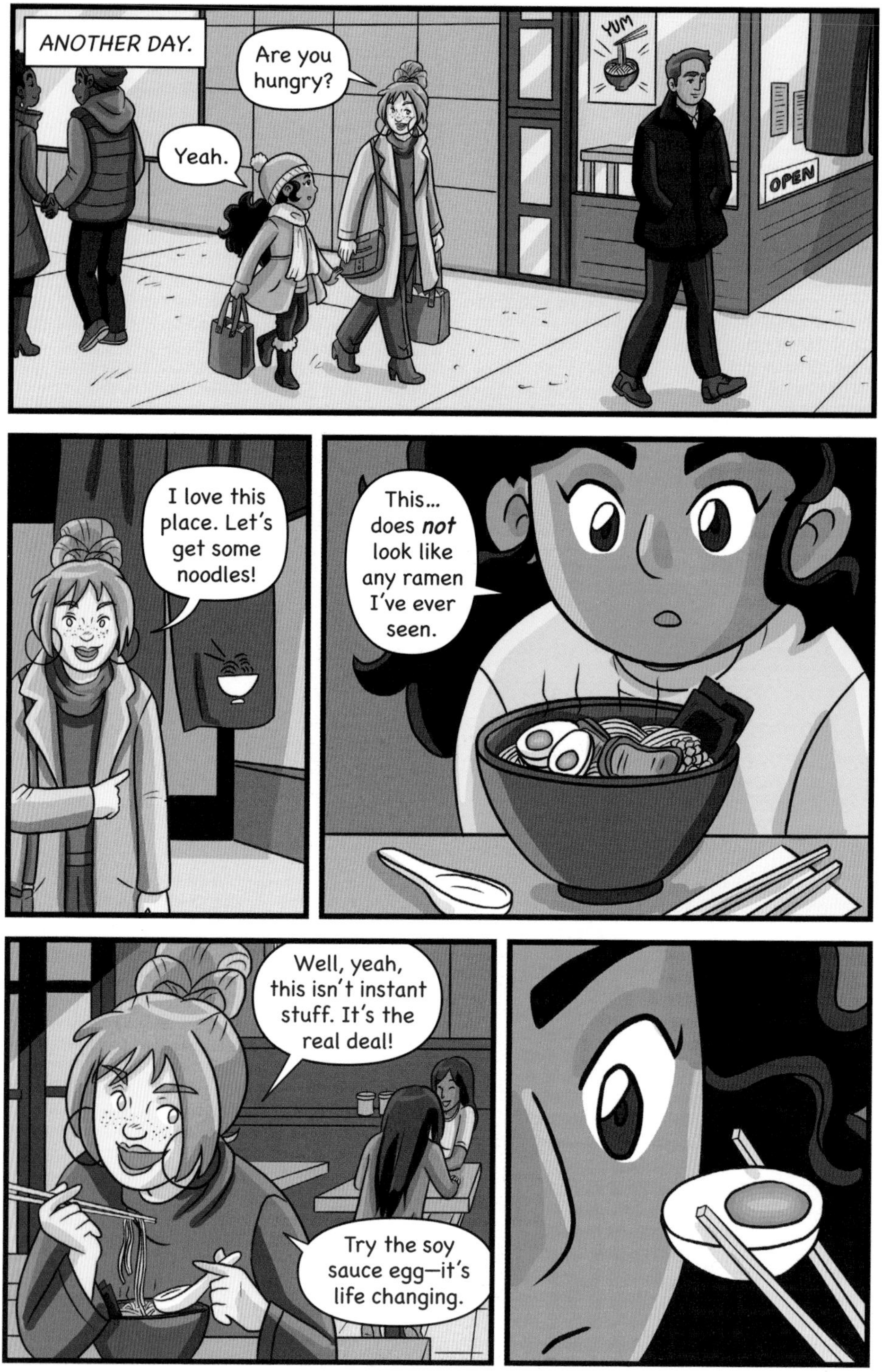
ANOTHER DAY.
YUM
Are you hungry?
Yeah.
OPEN
I love this place. Let's get some noodles!
This... does *not* look like any ramen I've ever seen.
Well, yeah, this isn't instant stuff. It's the real deal!
Try the soy sauce egg—it's life changing.

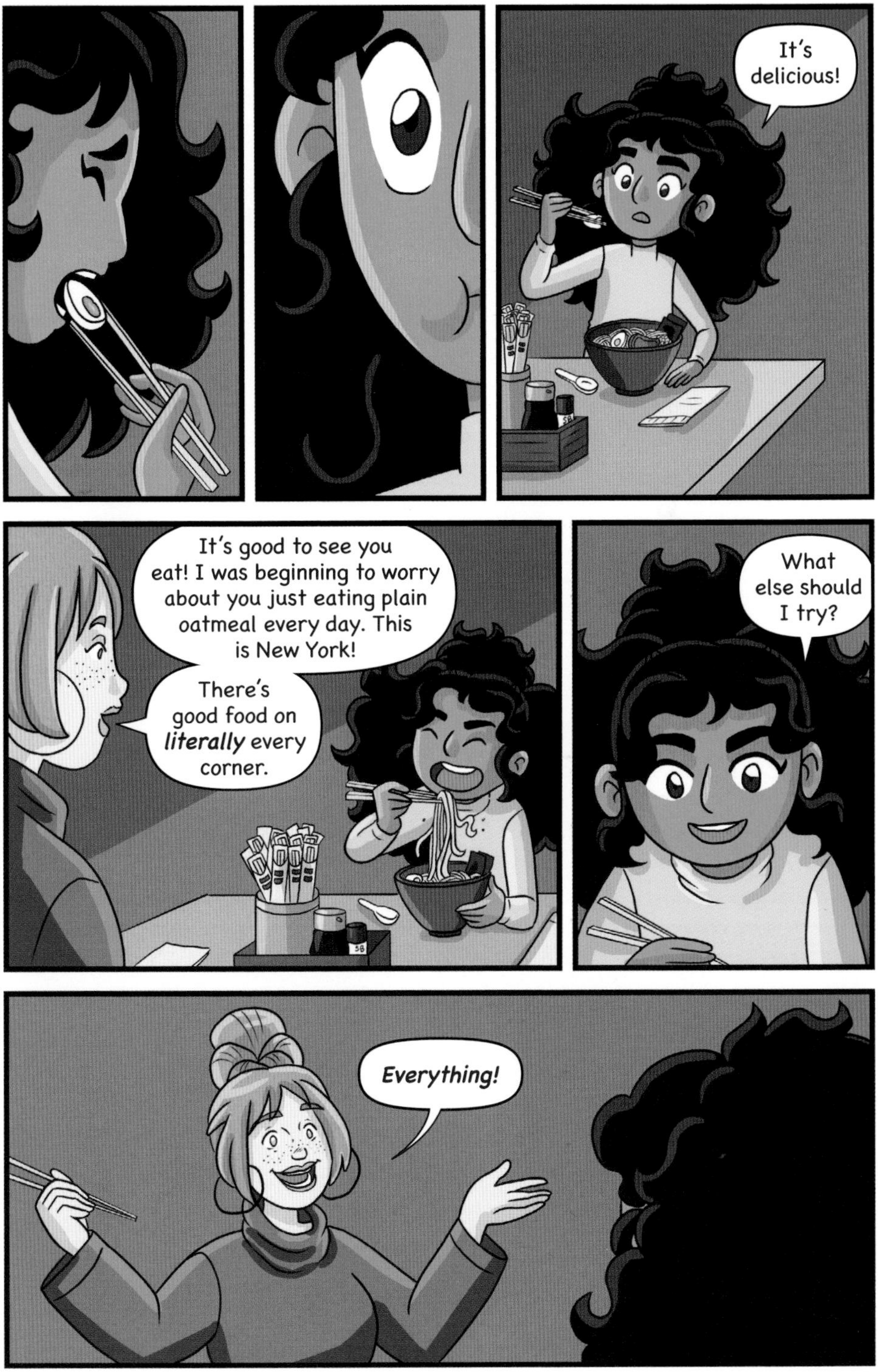
It's delicious!
It's good to see you eat! I was beginning to worry about you just eating plain oatmeal every day. This is New York!
There's good food on *literally* every corner.
What else should I try?
Everything!

OPEN
ALL BAGELS
SPECIAL
BAGEL,
CREAME
CHEESE
&
LOX
$5

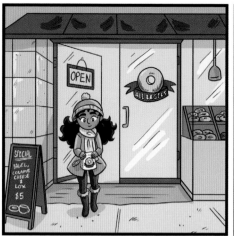

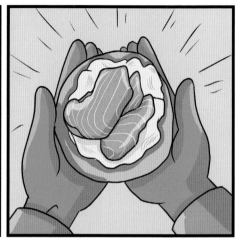

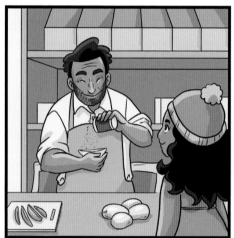

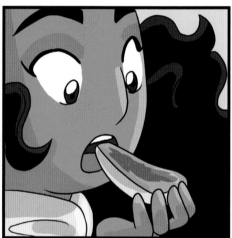

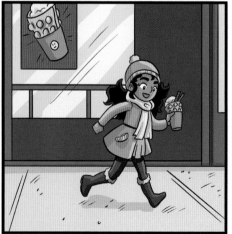

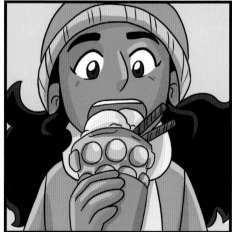

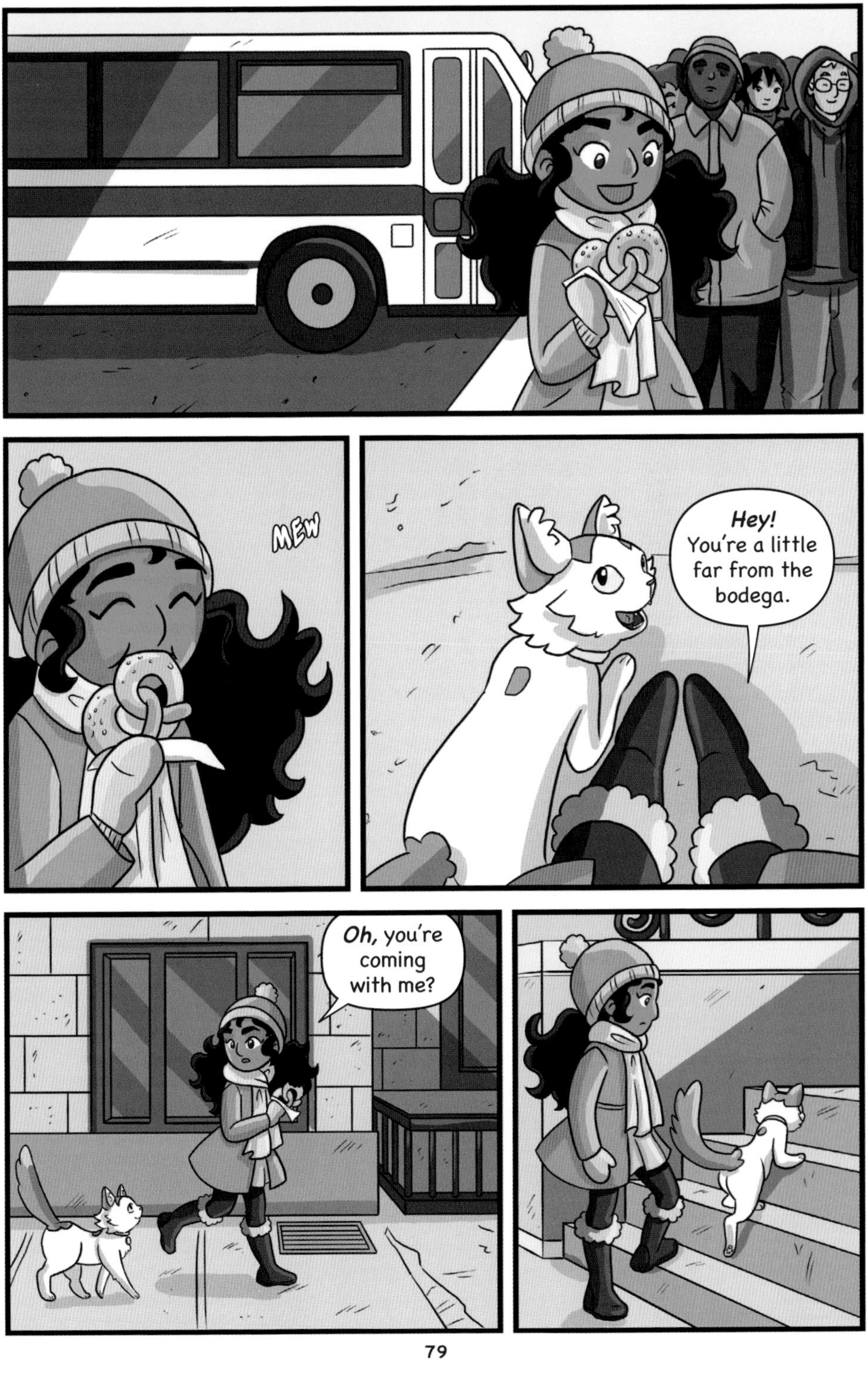
MEW
Hey! You're a little far from the bodega.
Oh, you're coming with me?

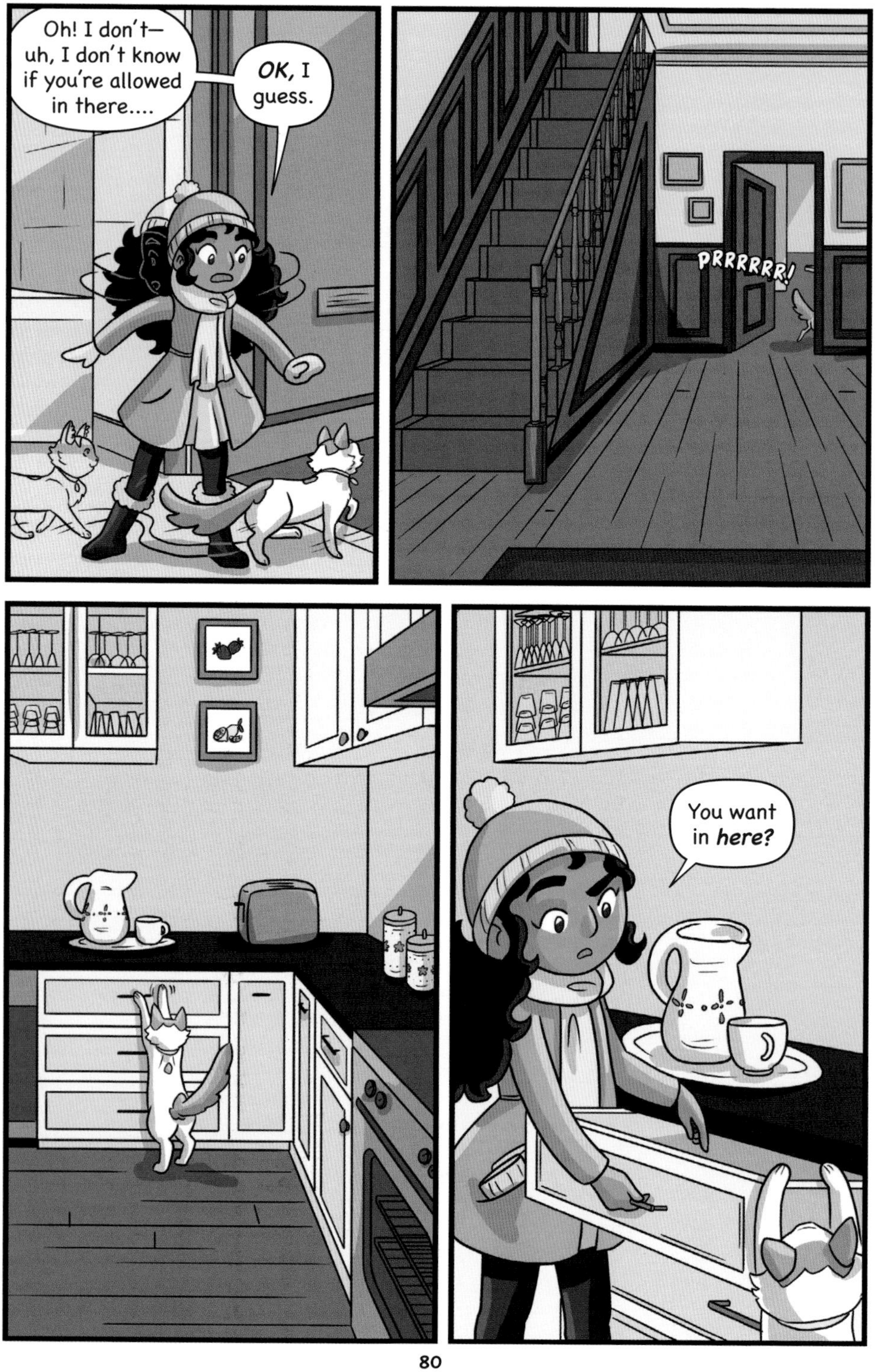
Oh! I don't—
uh, I don't know
if you're allowed
in there....
OK, I
guess.
PRRRRRR!
You want
in *here?*

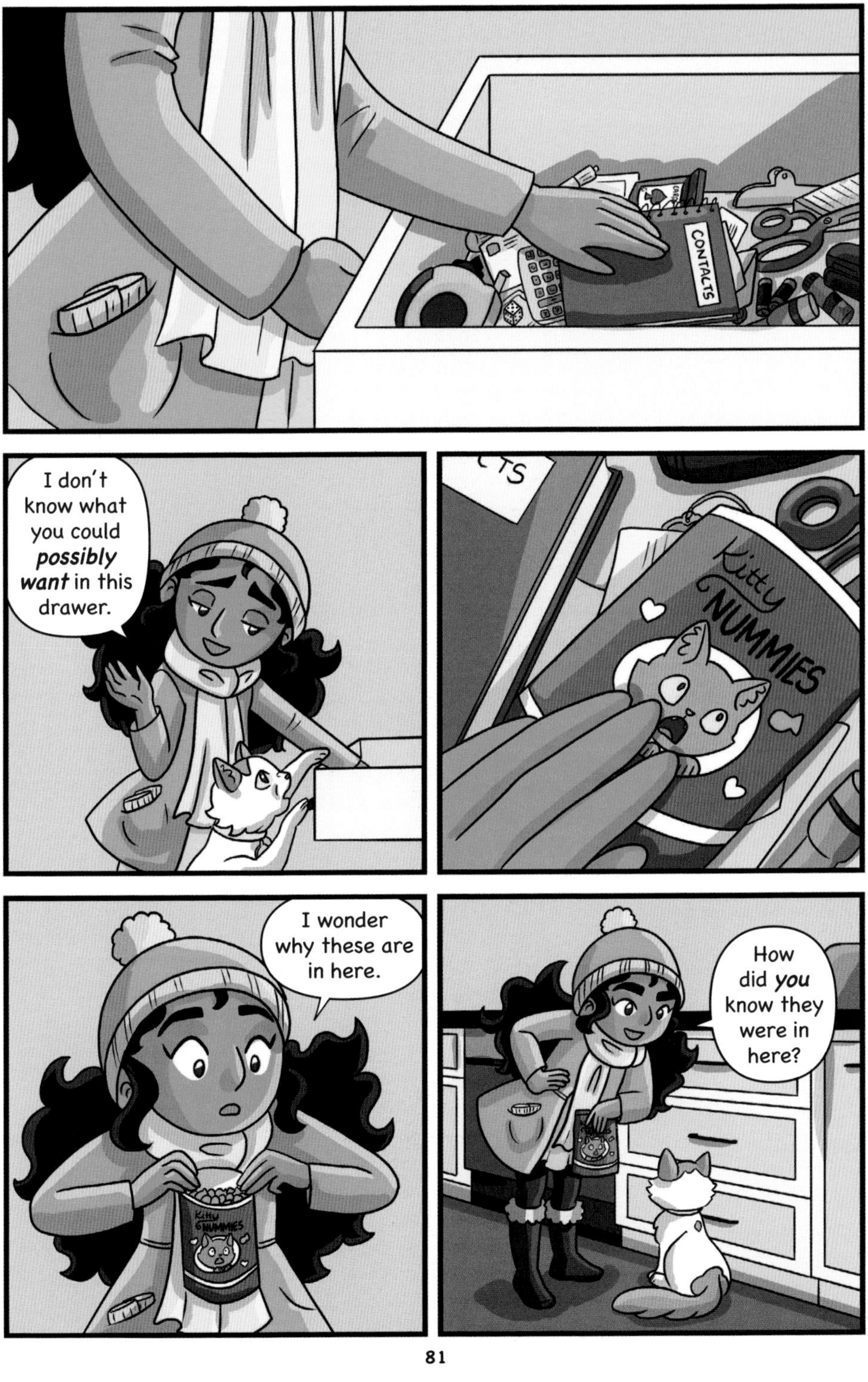
CONTACTS
I don't know what you could *possibly want* in this drawer.
CTS
Kitty NUMMIES
I wonder why these are in here.
Kitty NUMMIES
How did *you* know they were in here?

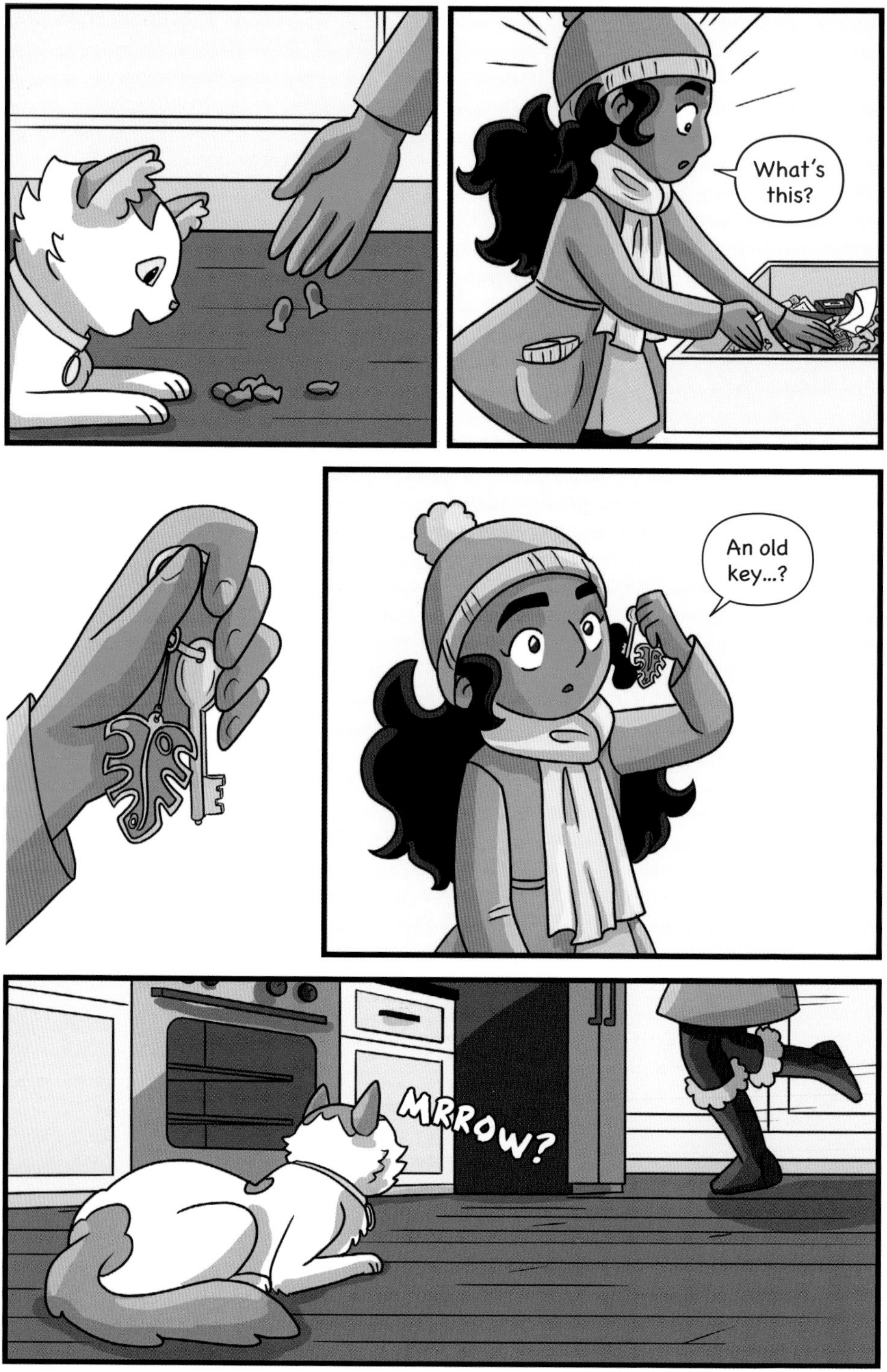
What's this?
An old key...?
MRROW?

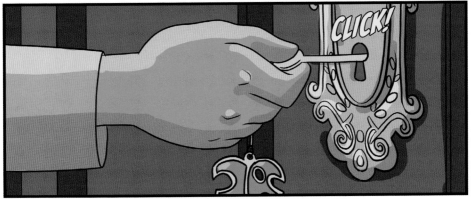

CLICK!

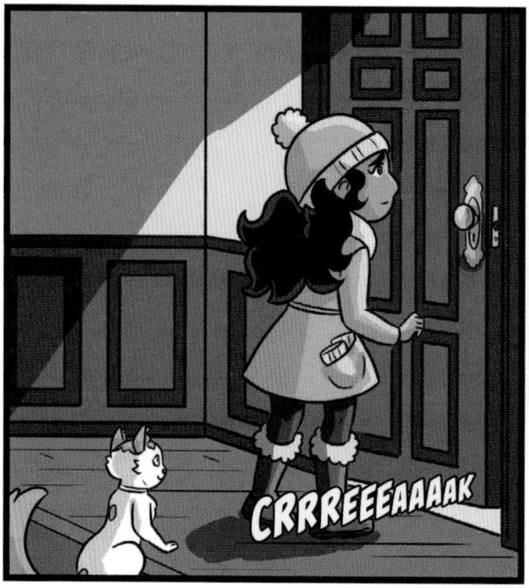
CRRREEEAAAAK
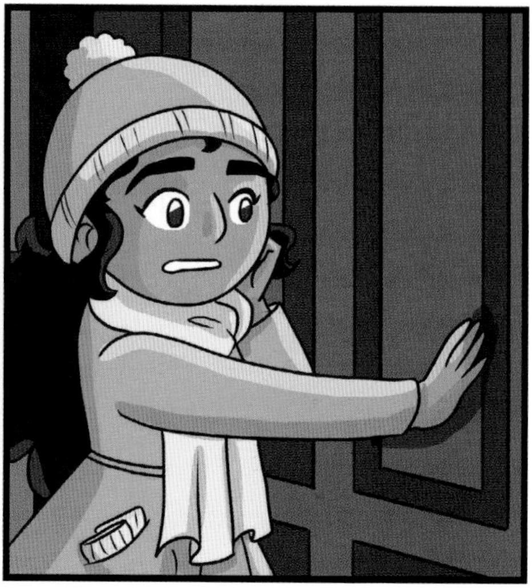
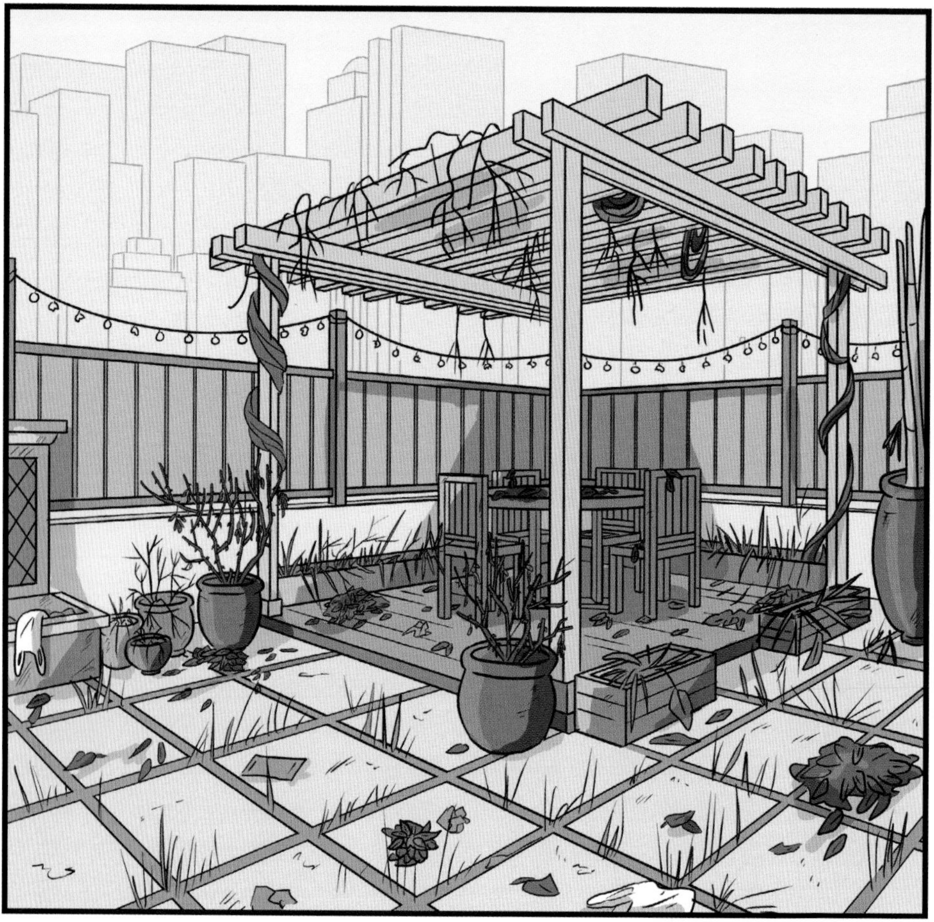

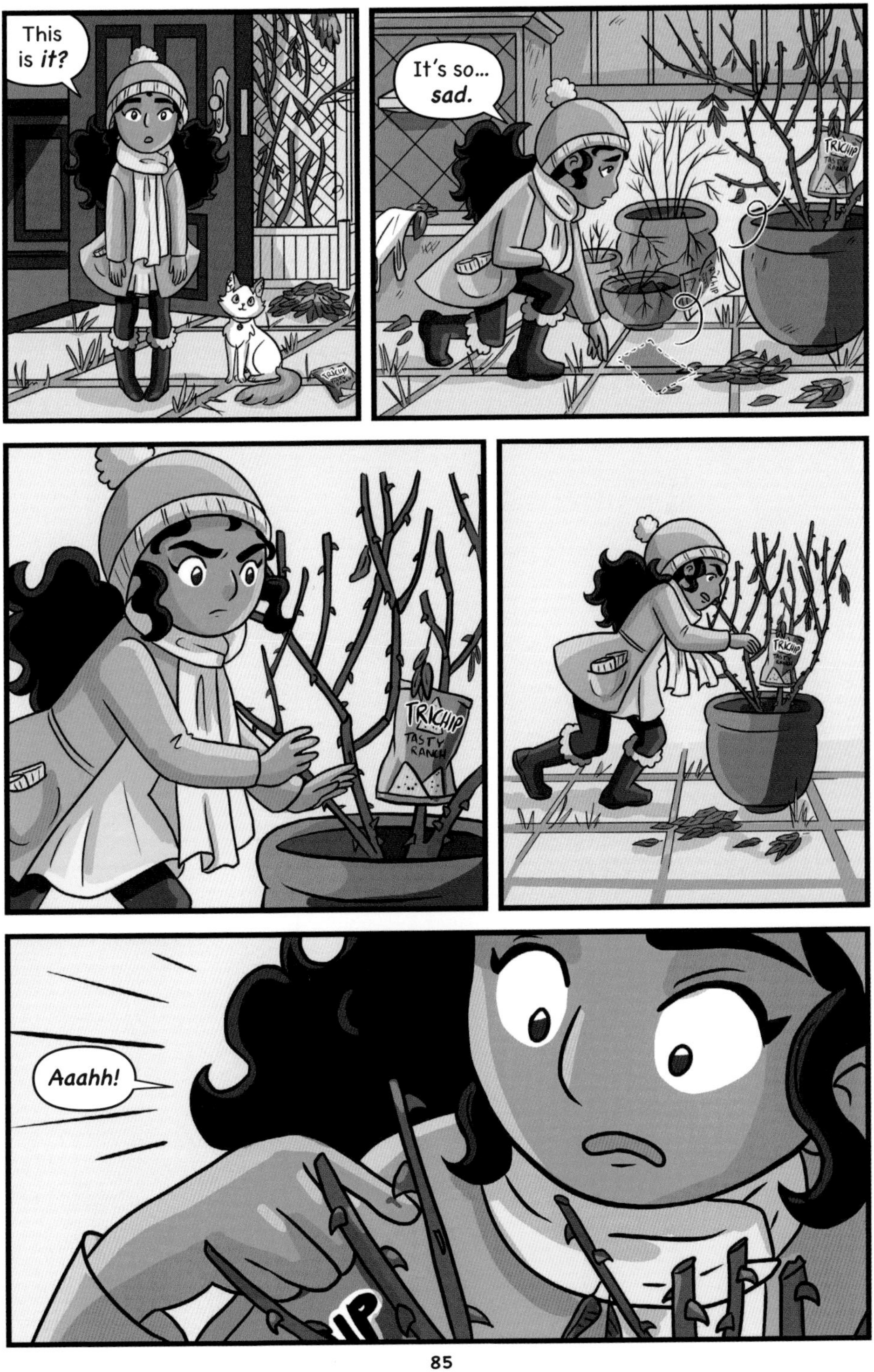
This is *it?*
TRICHIP
It's so... **sad.**
TRICHIP
TRICHIP TASTY RANCH
TRICHIP
Aaahh!

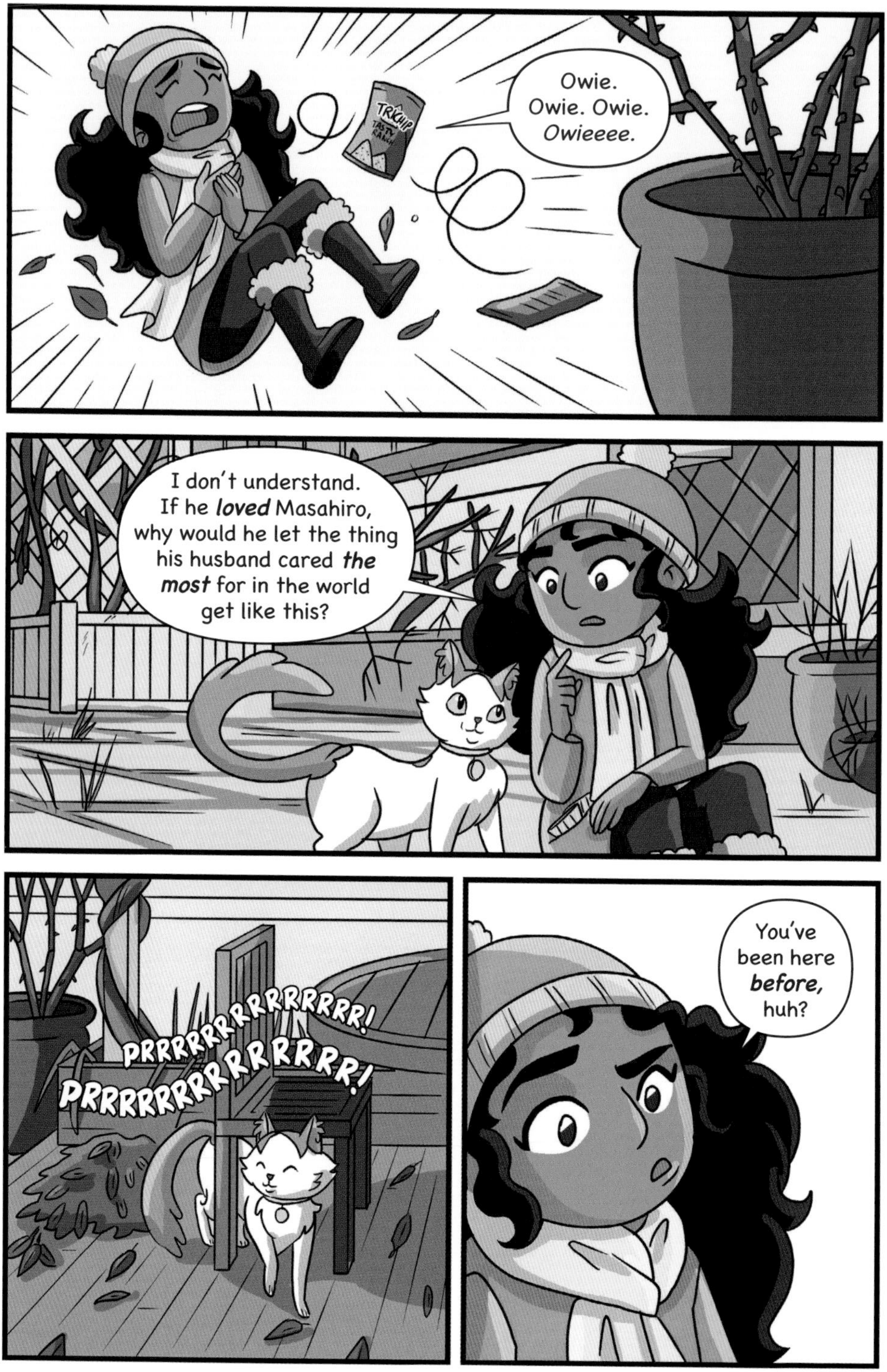

TRKCHIP
Owie. Owie. Owie. Owieeee.
I don't understand. If he *loved* Masahiro, why would he let the thing his husband cared ***the most*** for in the world get like this?
PRRRRRRRRRRRRRR!
PRRRRRRRRRRRRRR!
You've been here ***before,*** huh?

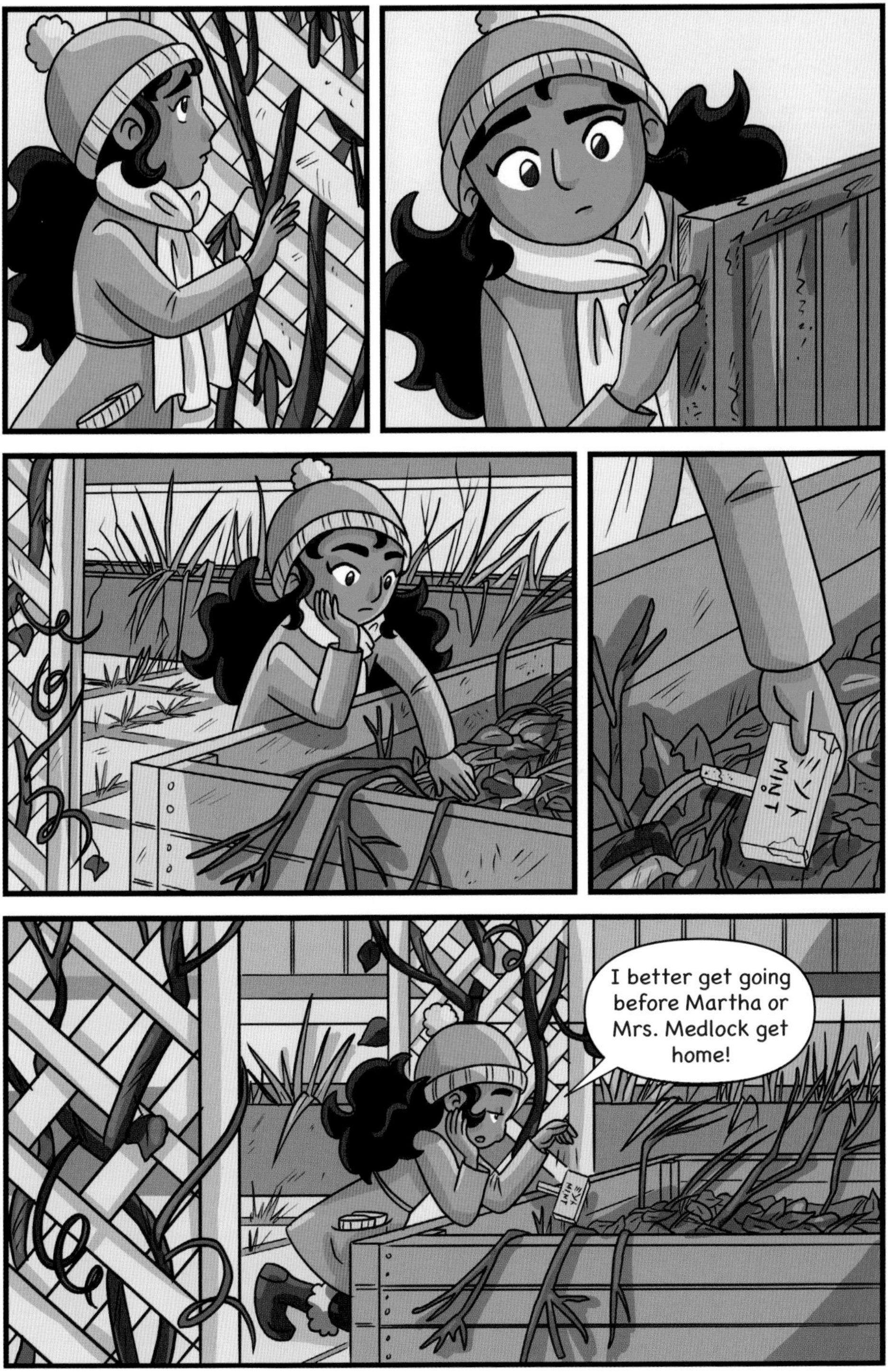
MINT
I better get going before Martha or Mrs. Medlock get home!

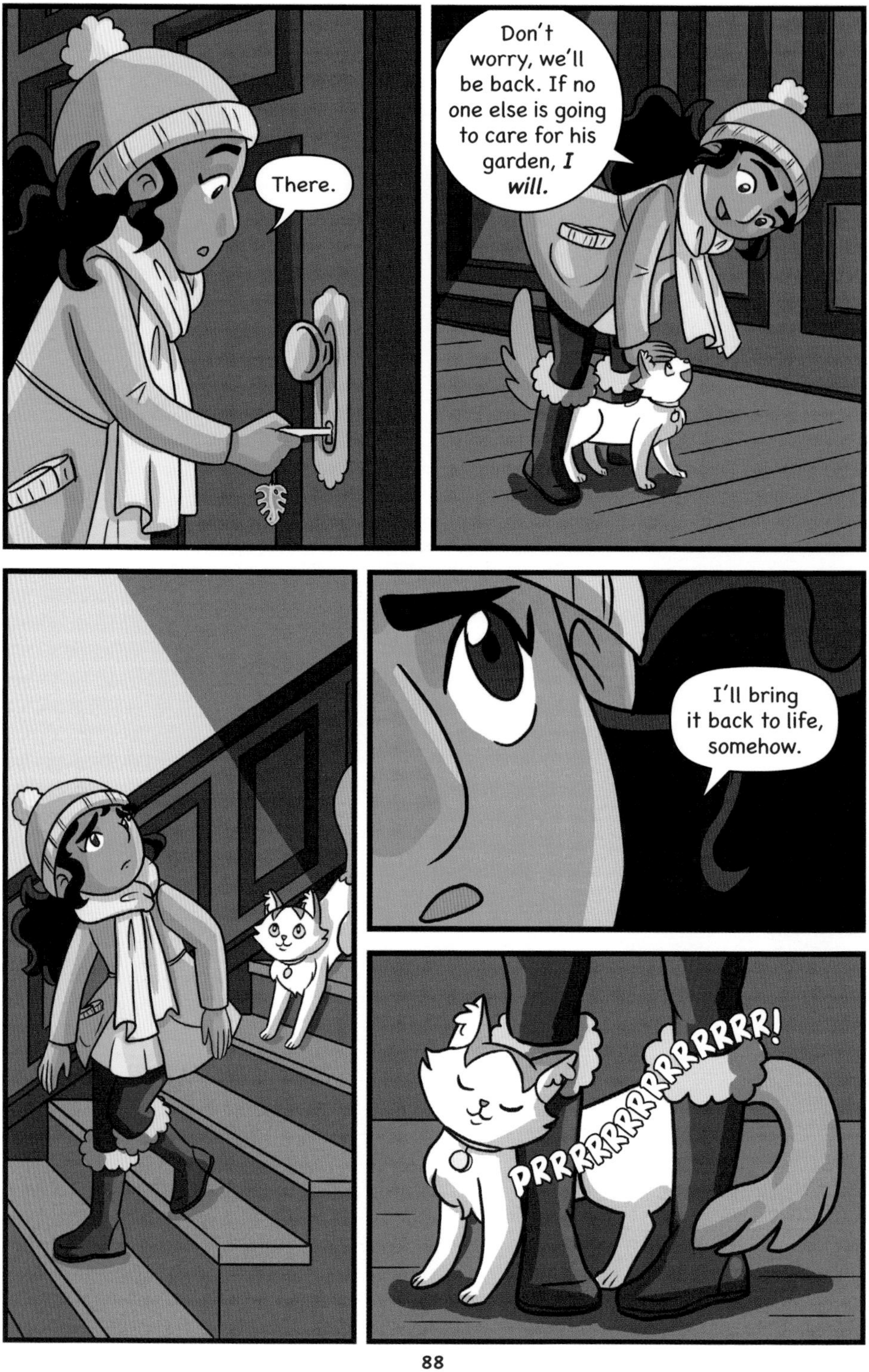
There.
Don't worry, we'll be back. If no one else is going to care for his garden, *I will.*
I'll bring it back to life, somehow.
PRRRRRRRRRRRRRRR!

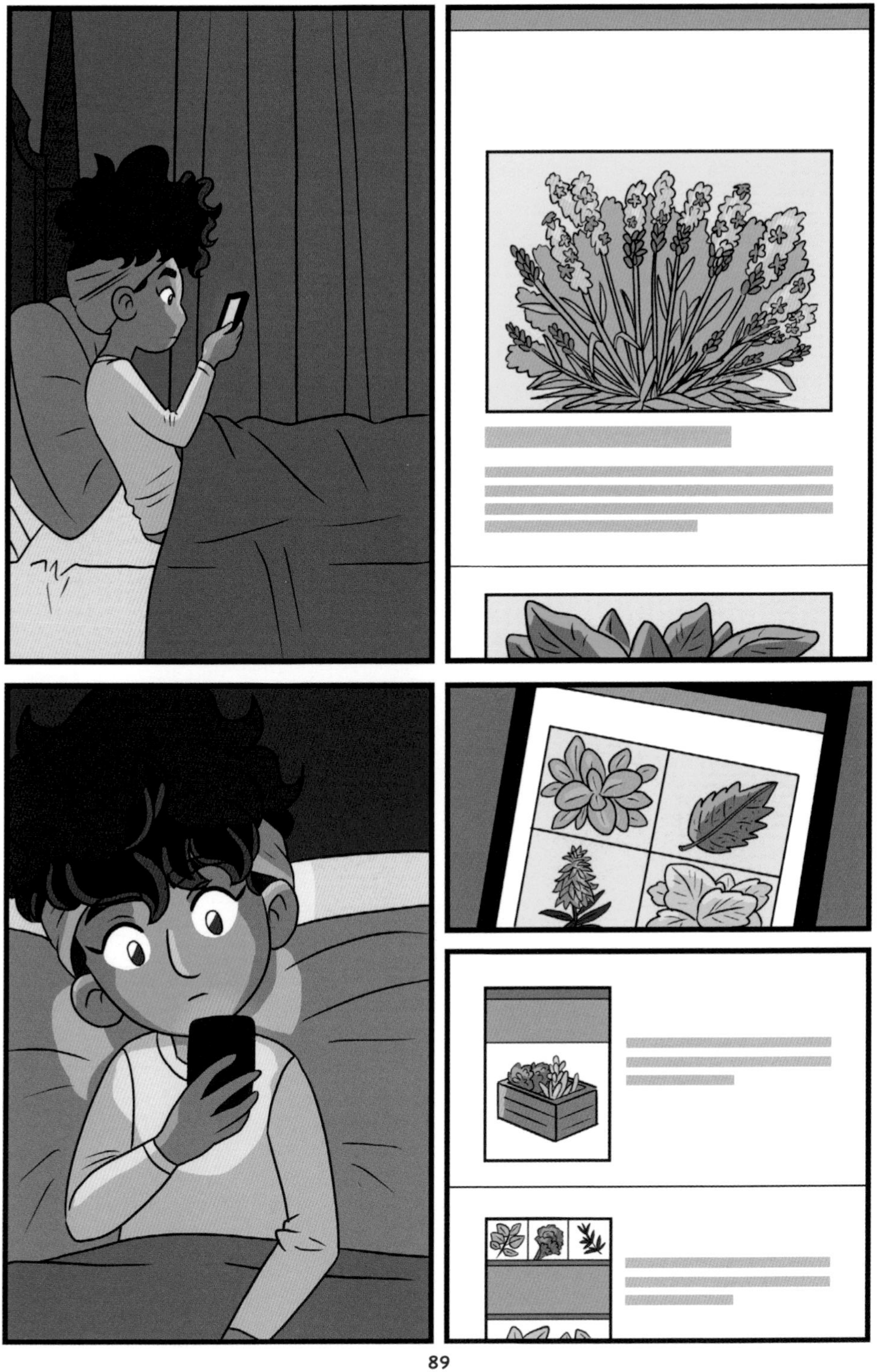

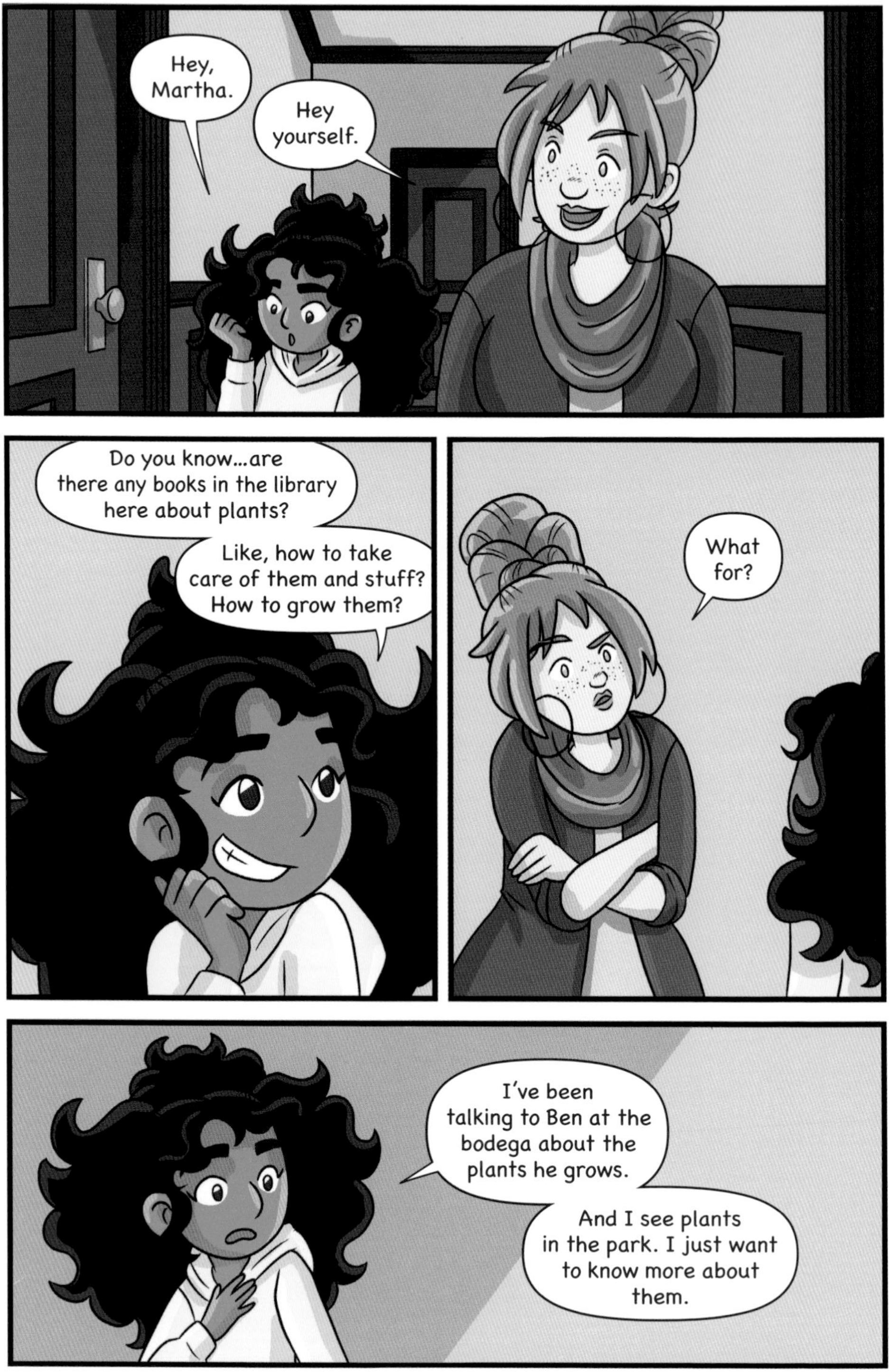
Hey, Martha.
Hey yourself.
Do you know...are there any books in the library here about plants?
Like, how to take care of them and stuff? How to grow them?
What for?
I've been talking to Ben at the bodega about the plants he grows.
And I see plants in the park. I just want to know more about them.

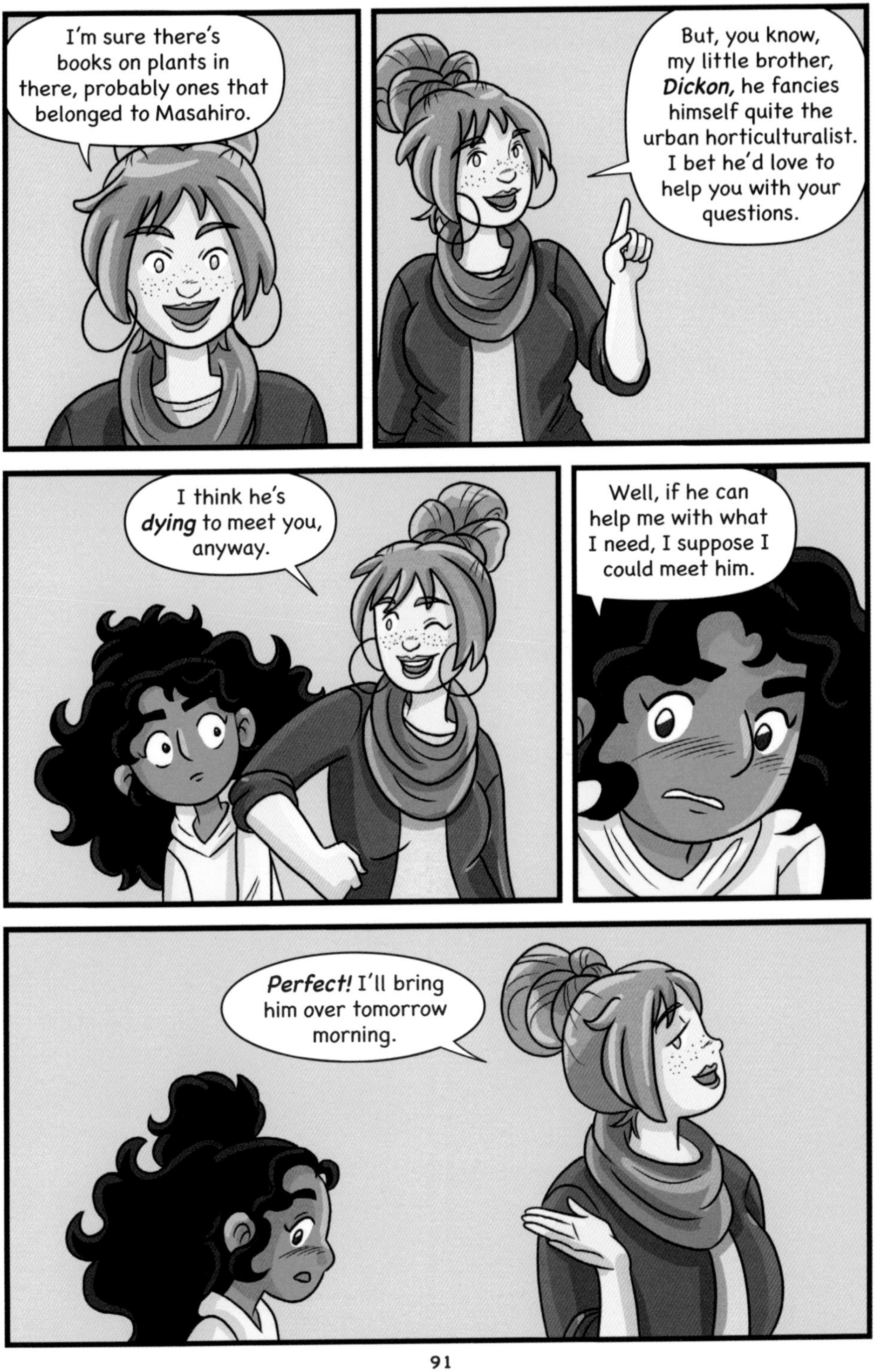
I'm sure there's books on plants in there, probably ones that belonged to Masahiro.
But, you know, my little brother, **Dickon,** he fancies himself quite the urban horticulturalist. I bet he'd love to help you with your questions.
I think he's *dying* to meet you, anyway.
Well, if he can help me with what I need, I suppose I could meet him.
Perfect! I'll bring him over tomorrow morning.

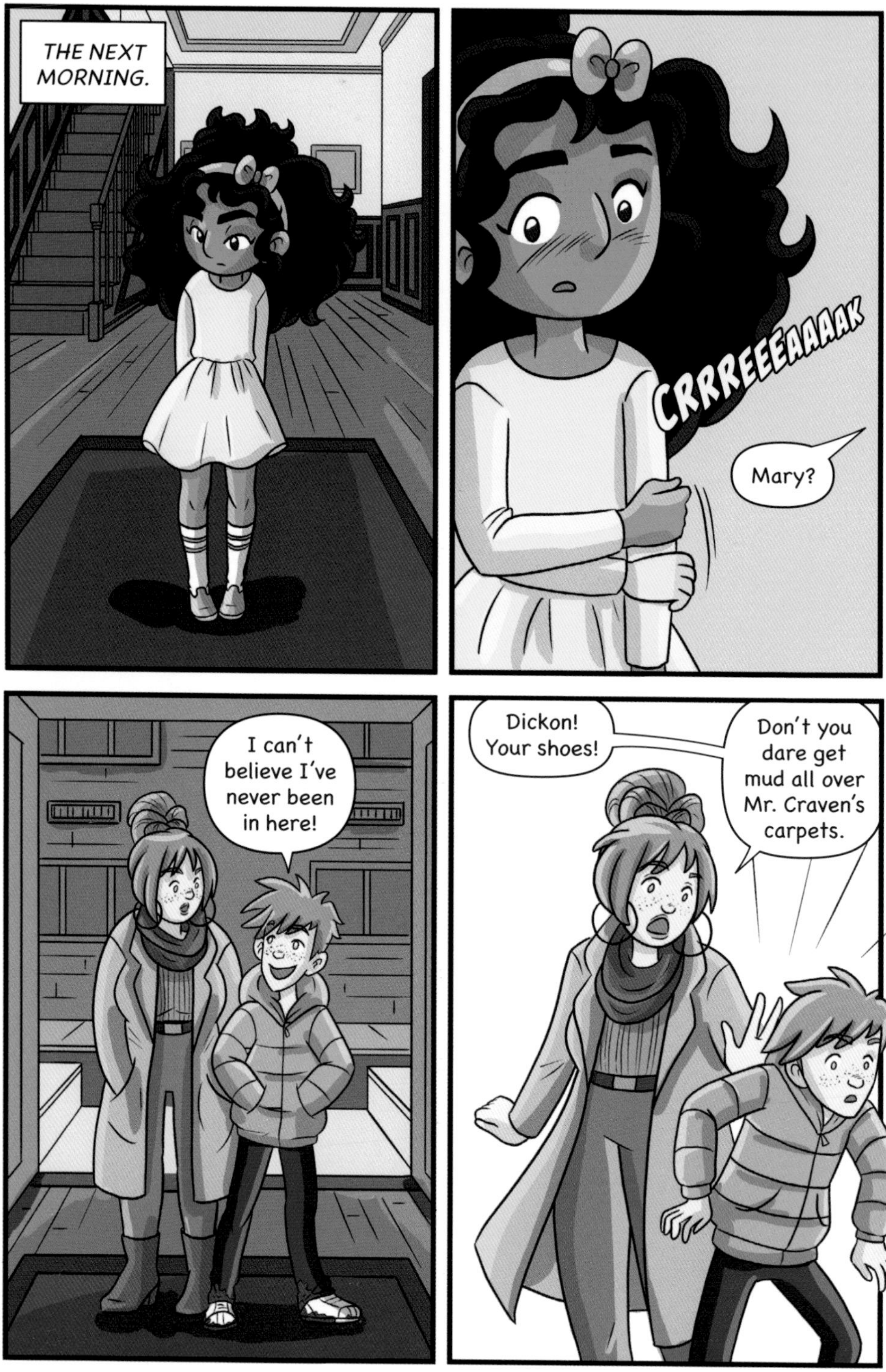
THE NEXT MORNING.
CRRREEEAAAAK
Mary?
I can't believe I've never been in here!
Dickon! Your shoes!
Don't you dare get mud all over Mr. Craven's carpets.

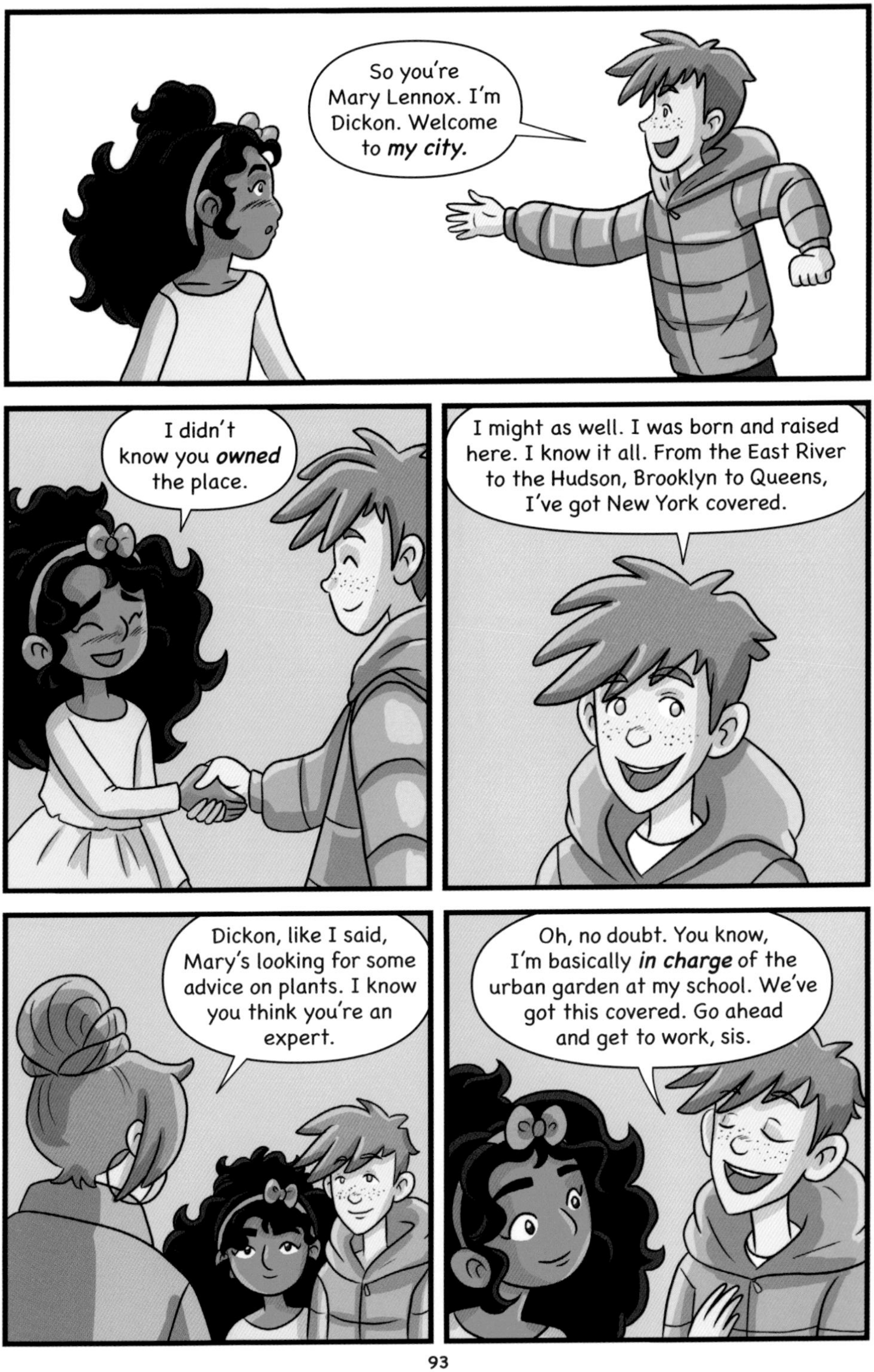

So you're Mary Lennox. I'm Dickon. Welcome to *my city.*
I didn't know you *owned* the place.
I might as well. I was born and raised here. I know it all. From the East River to the Hudson, Brooklyn to Queens, I've got New York covered.
Dickon, like I said, Mary's looking for some advice on plants. I know you think you're an expert.
Oh, no doubt. You know, I'm basically *in charge* of the urban garden at my school. We've got this covered. Go ahead and get to work, sis.

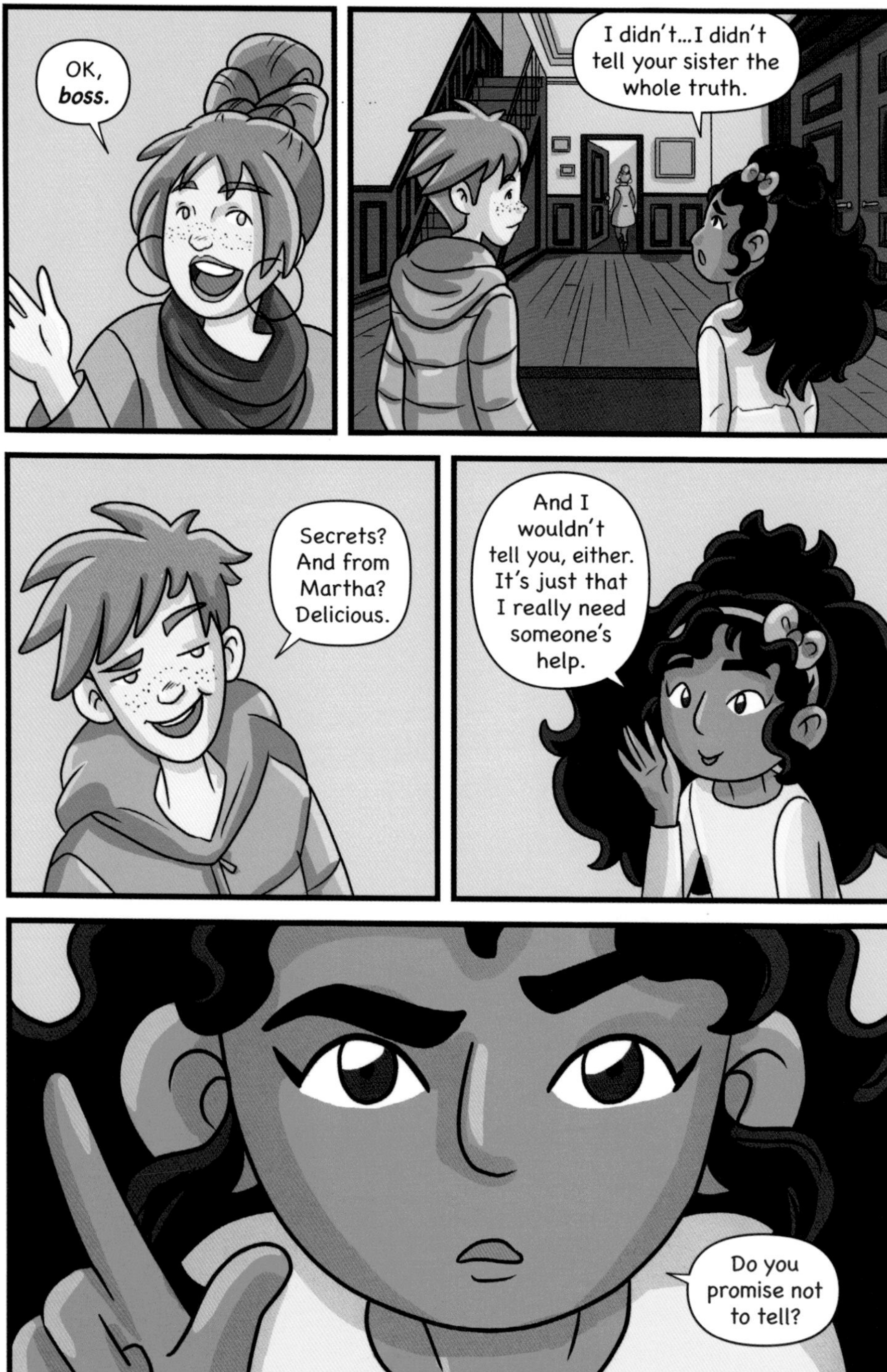
OK, *boss.*
I didn't...I didn't tell your sister the whole truth.
Secrets? And from Martha? Delicious.
And I wouldn't tell you, either. It's just that I really need someone's help.
Do you promise not to tell?

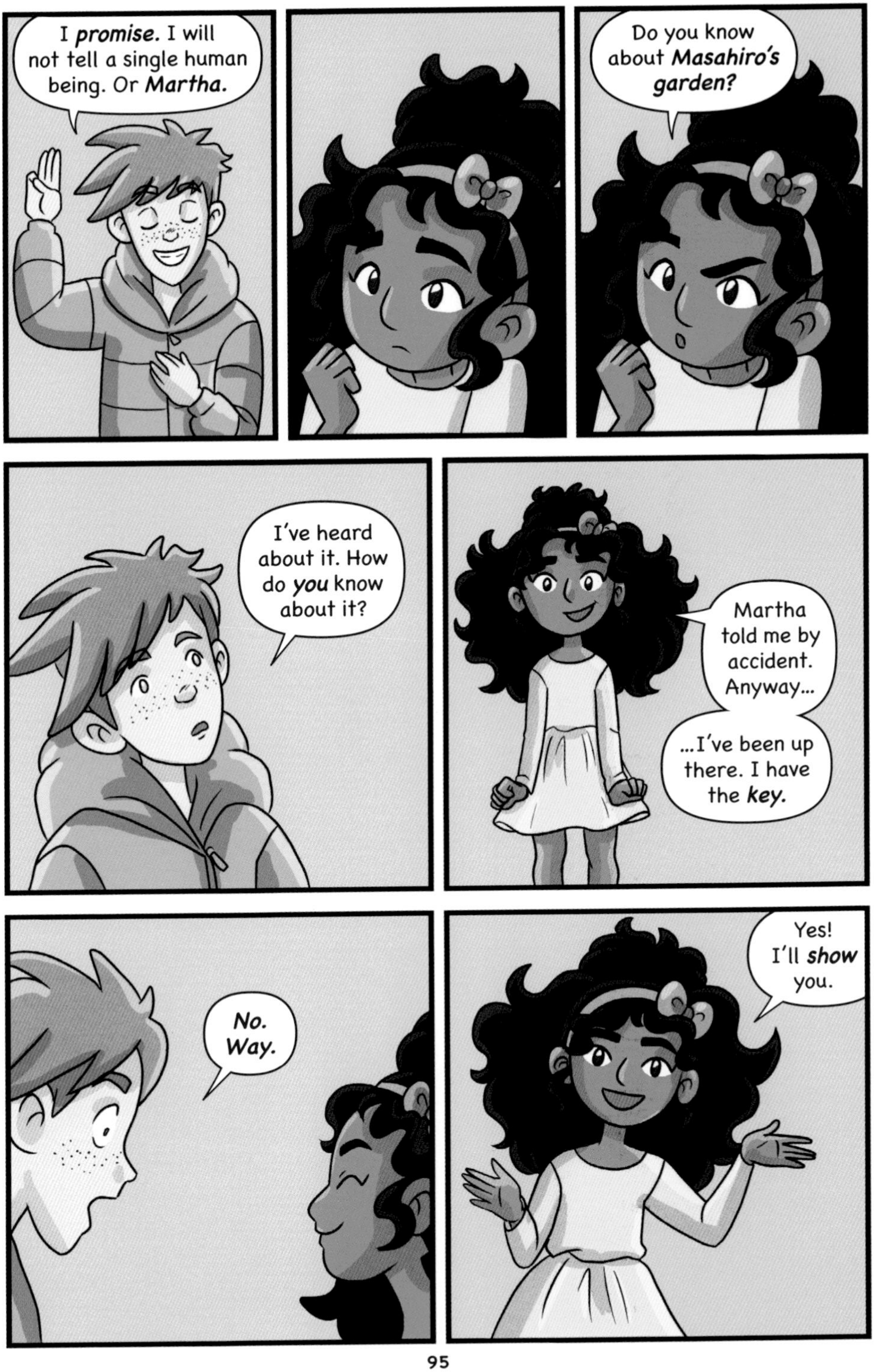
I *promise.* I will not tell a single human being. Or *Martha.*
Do you know about *Masahiro's garden?*
I've heard about it. How do *you* know about it?
Martha told me by accident. Anyway...
...I've been up there. I have the *key.*
No. Way.
Yes! I'll *show* you.

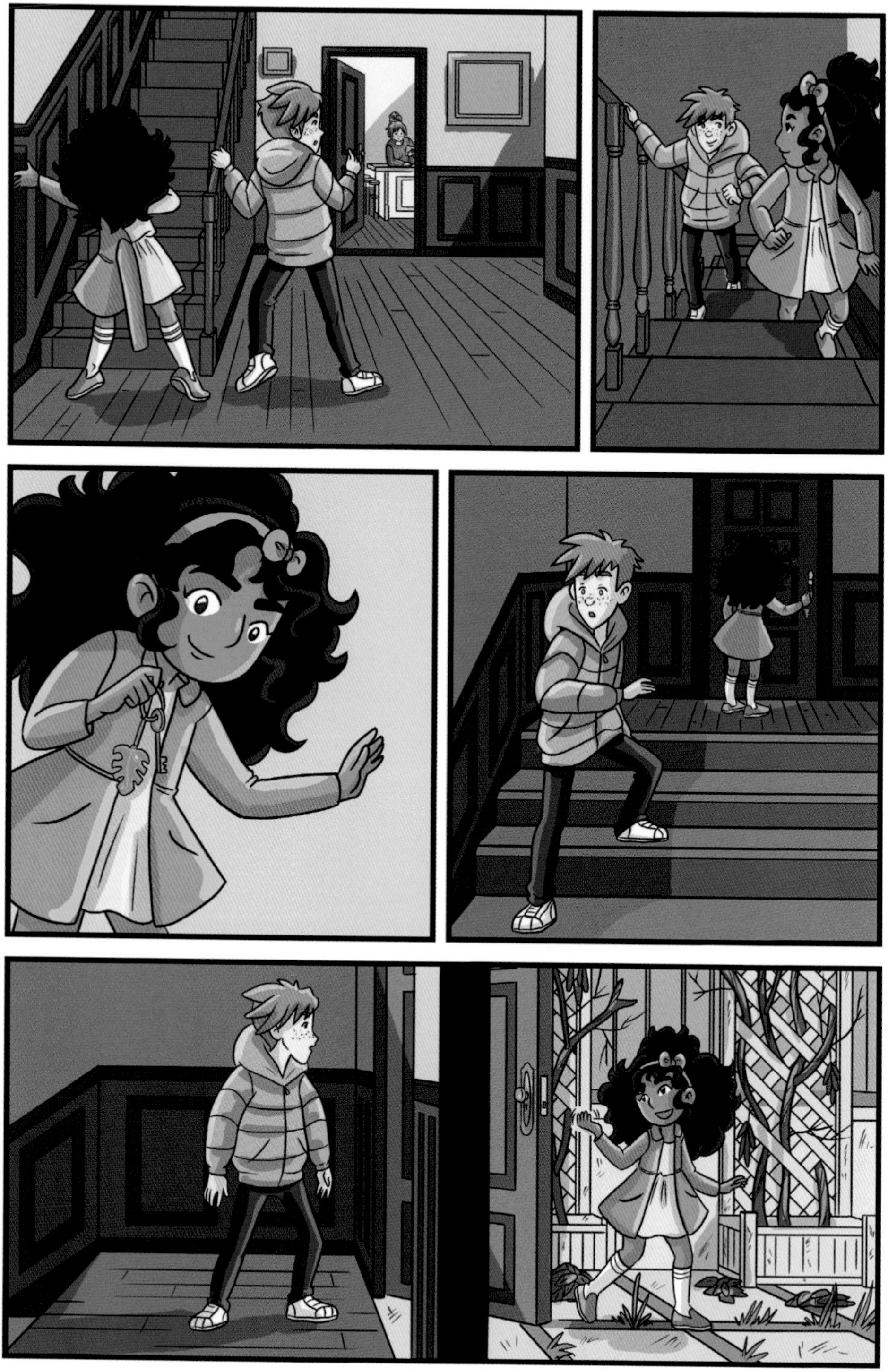

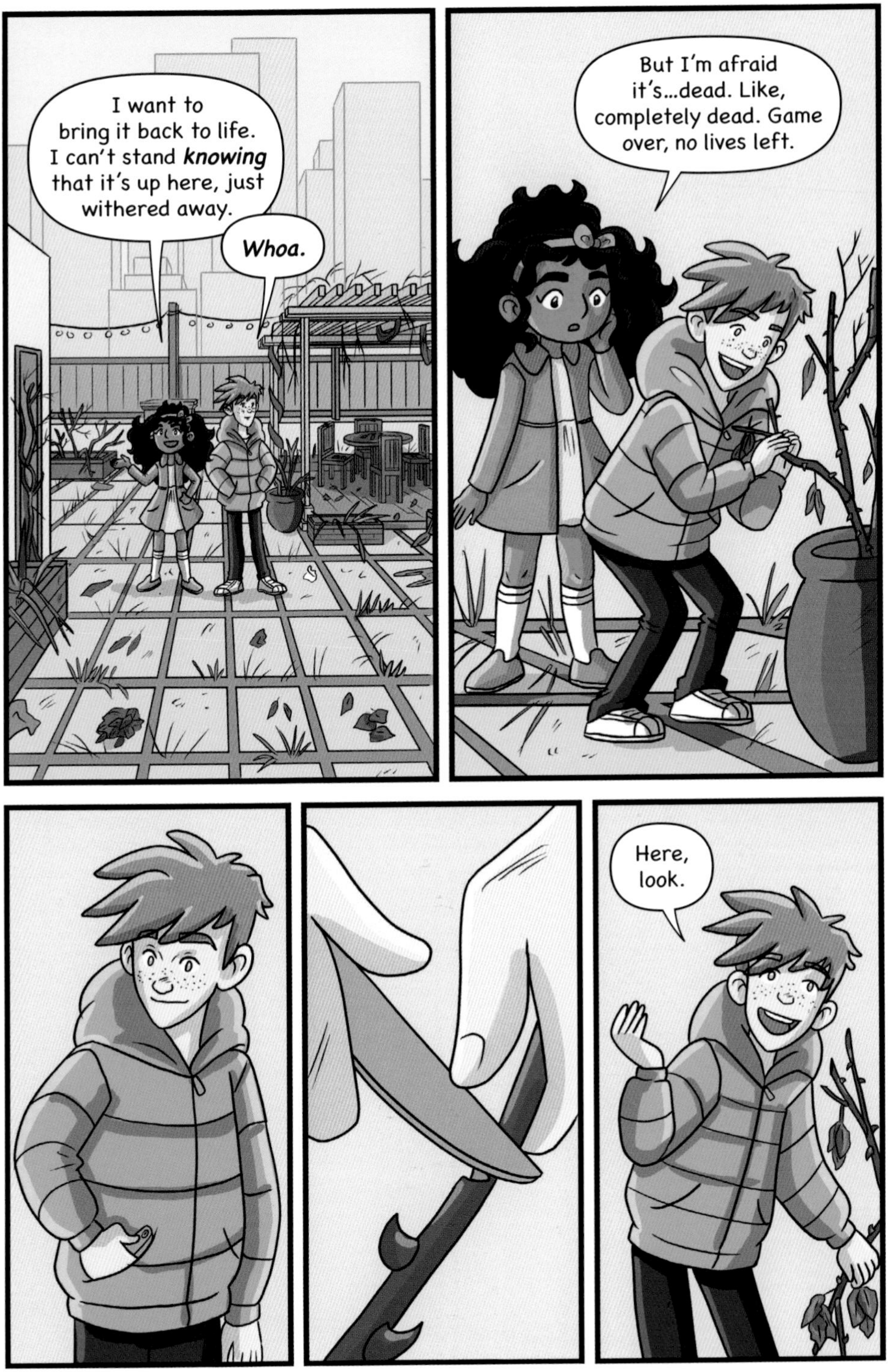
I want to bring it back to life. I can't stand ***knowing*** that it's up here, just withered away.
Whoa.
But I'm afraid it's...dead. Like, completely dead. Game over, no lives left.
Here, look.

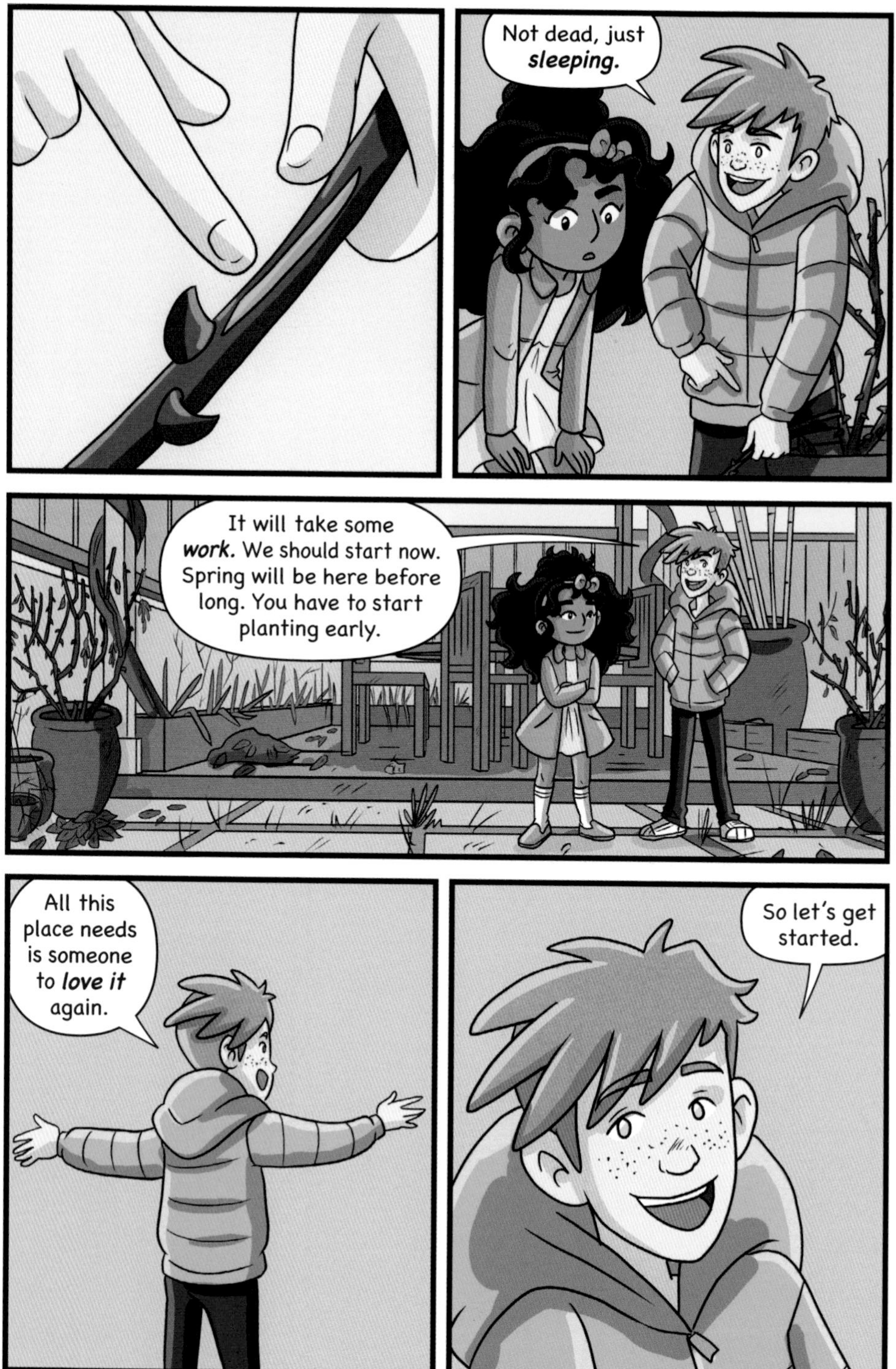
Not dead, just ***sleeping.***
It will take some ***work.*** We should start now. Spring will be here before long. You have to start planting early.
All this place needs is someone to ***love it*** again.
So let's get started.

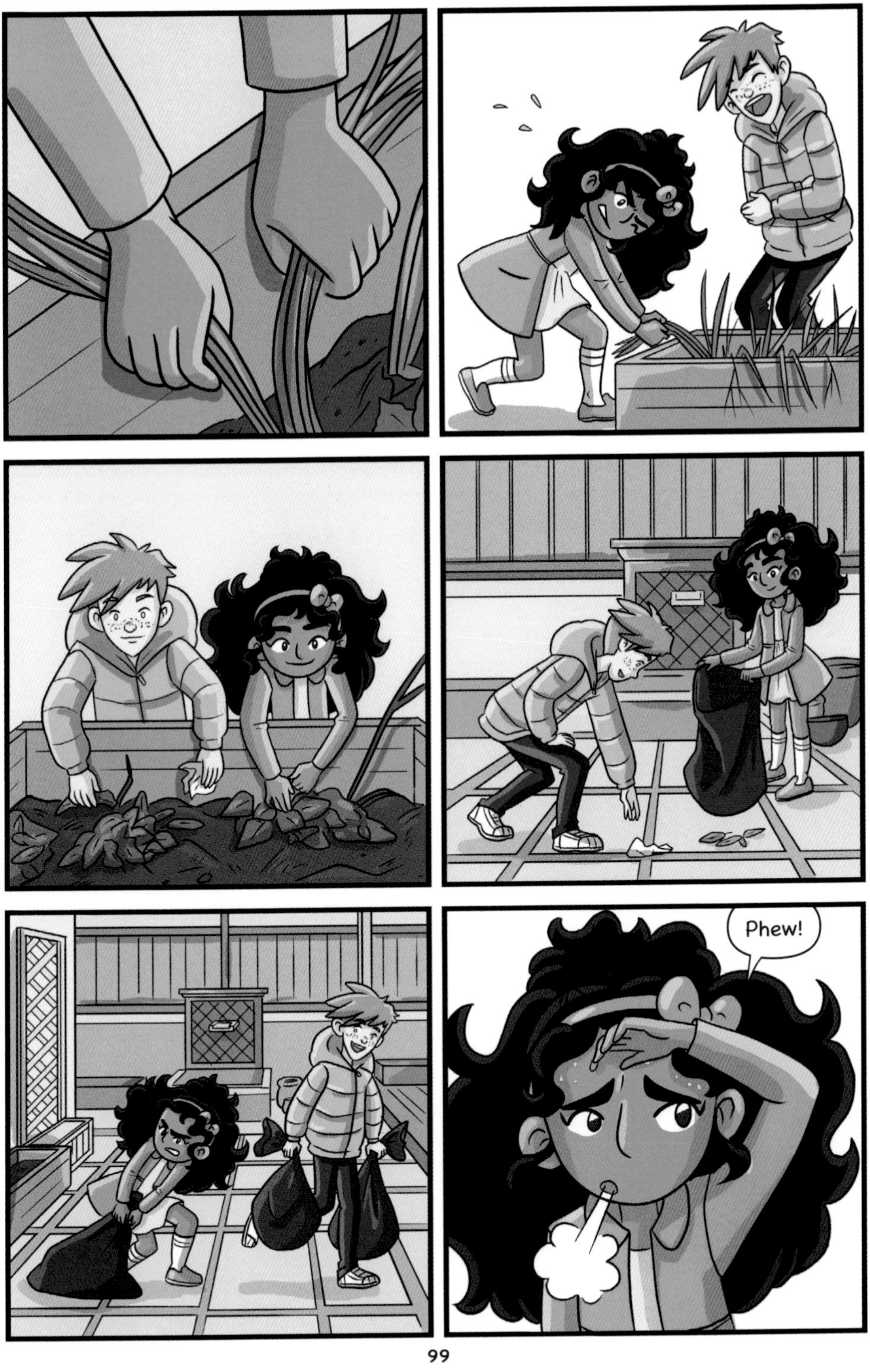
Phew!

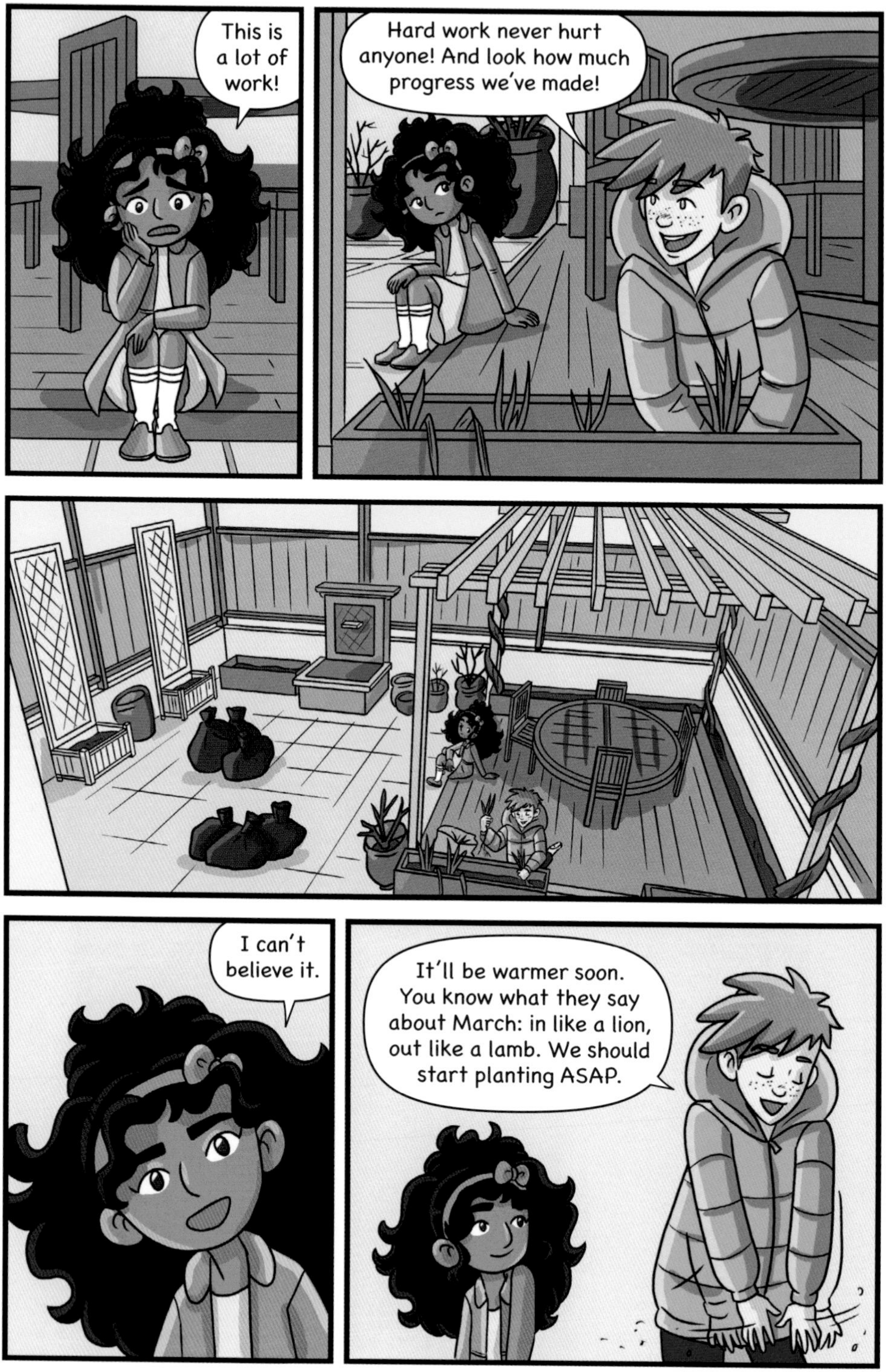
This is a lot of work!
Hard work never hurt anyone! And look how much progress we've made!
I can't believe it.
It'll be warmer soon. You know what they say about March: in like a lion, out like a lamb. We should start planting ASAP.

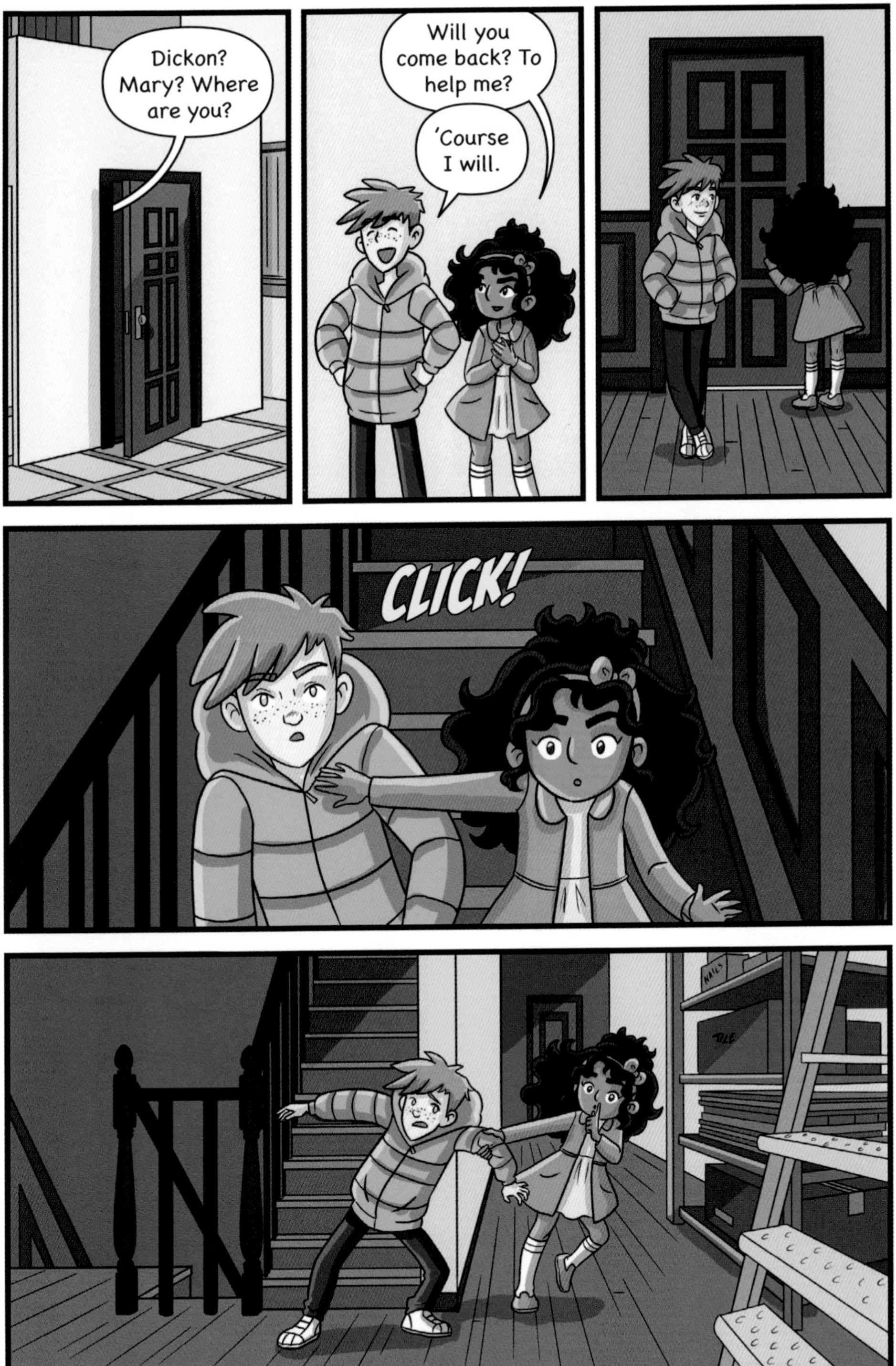
Dickon? Mary? Where are you?
Will you come back? To help me?
'Course I will.
CLICK!

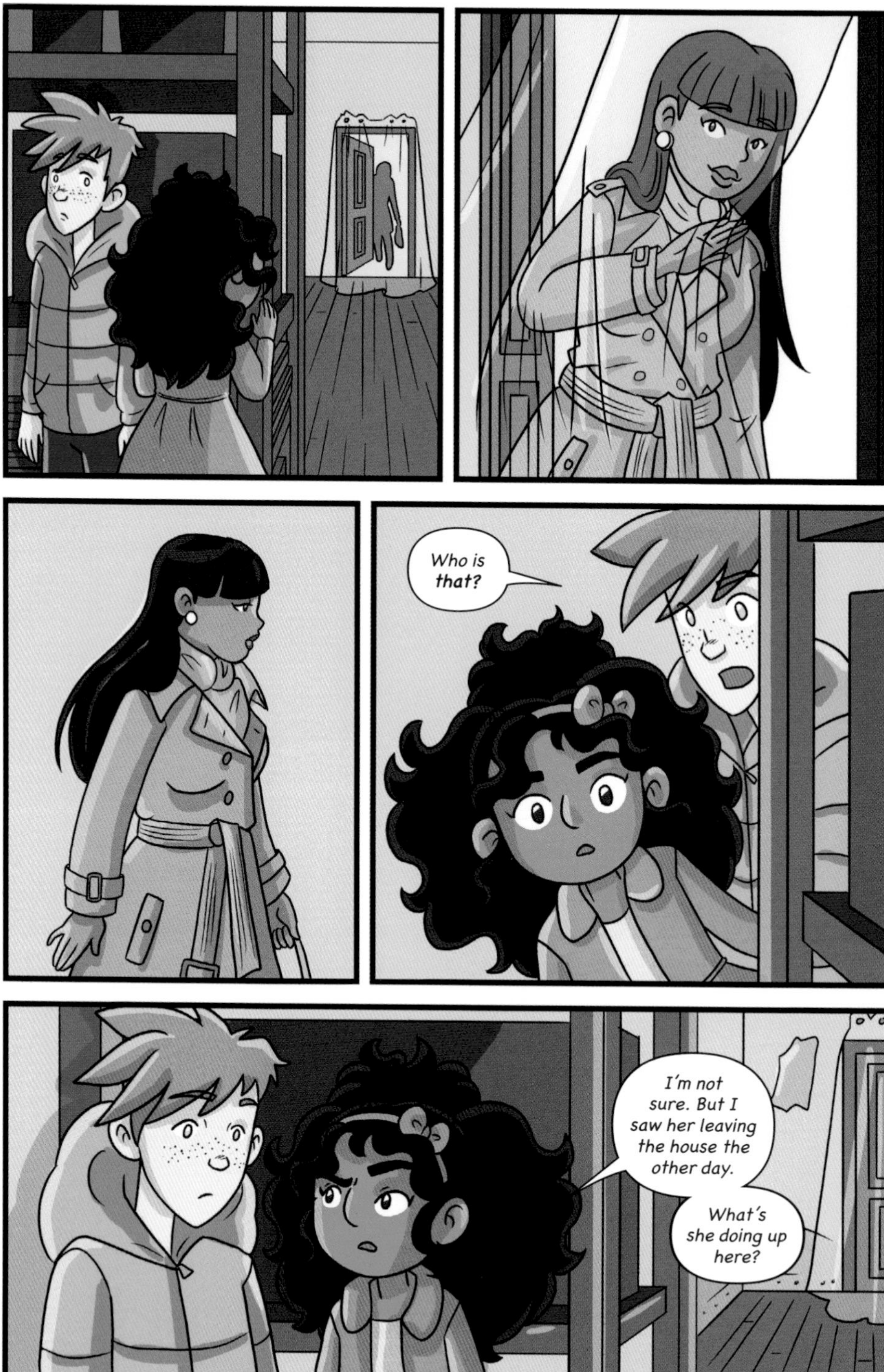
Who is that?
I'm not sure. But I saw her leaving the house the other day.
What's she doing up here?

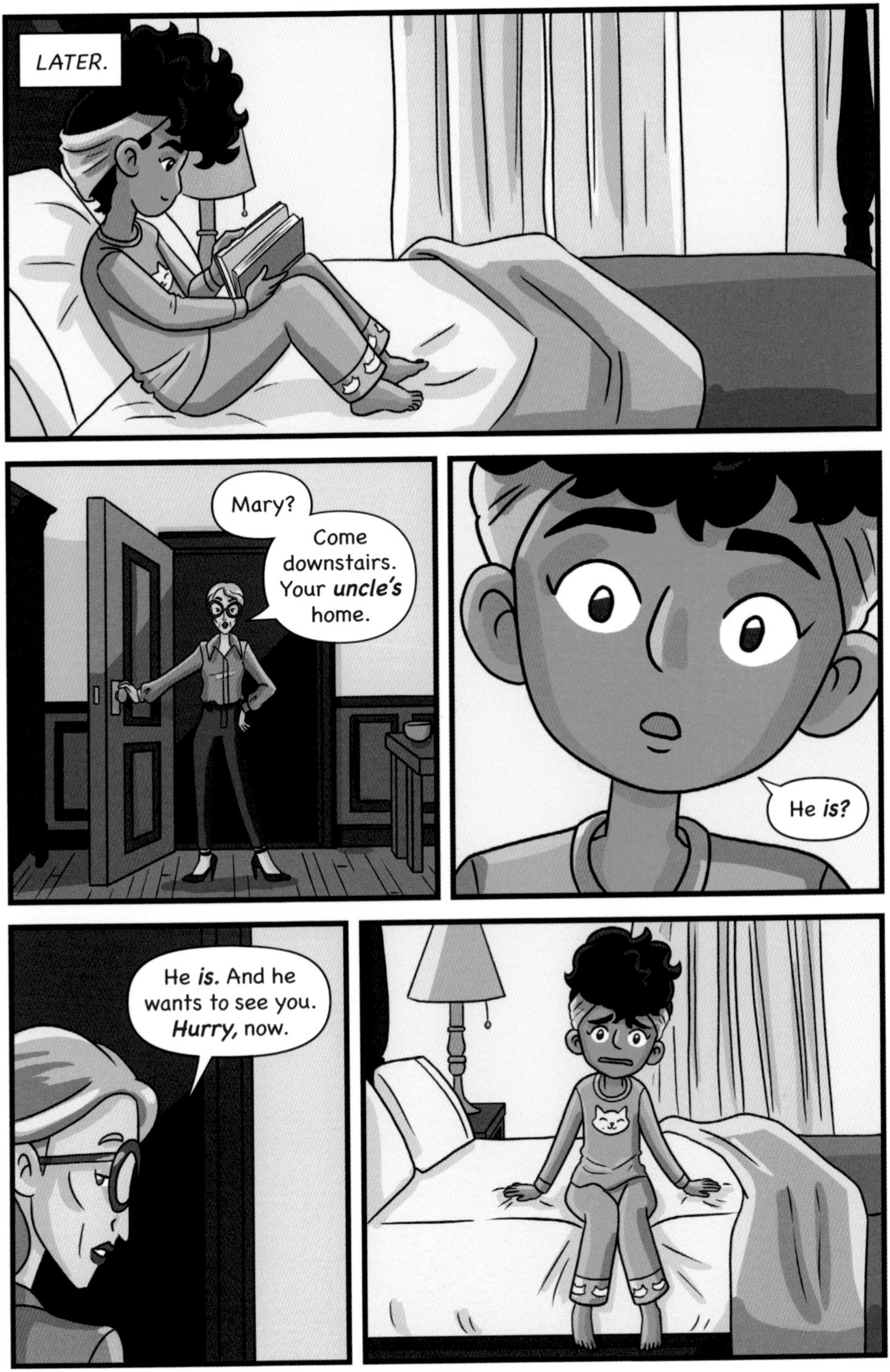
LATER.
Mary?
Come downstairs. Your *uncle's* home.
He *is?*
He *is.* And he wants to see you. *Hurry,* now.

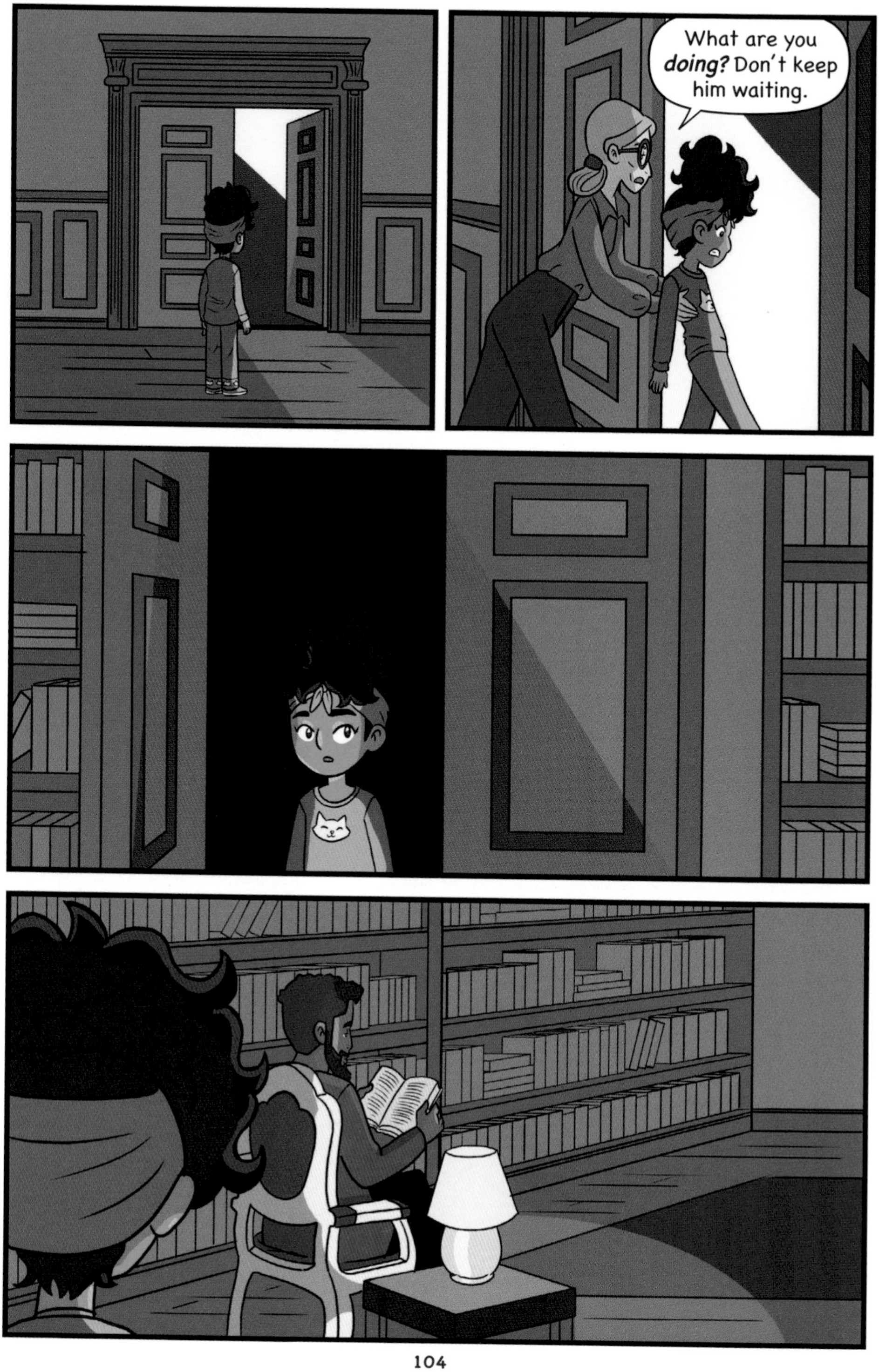
What are you *doing?* Don't keep him waiting.

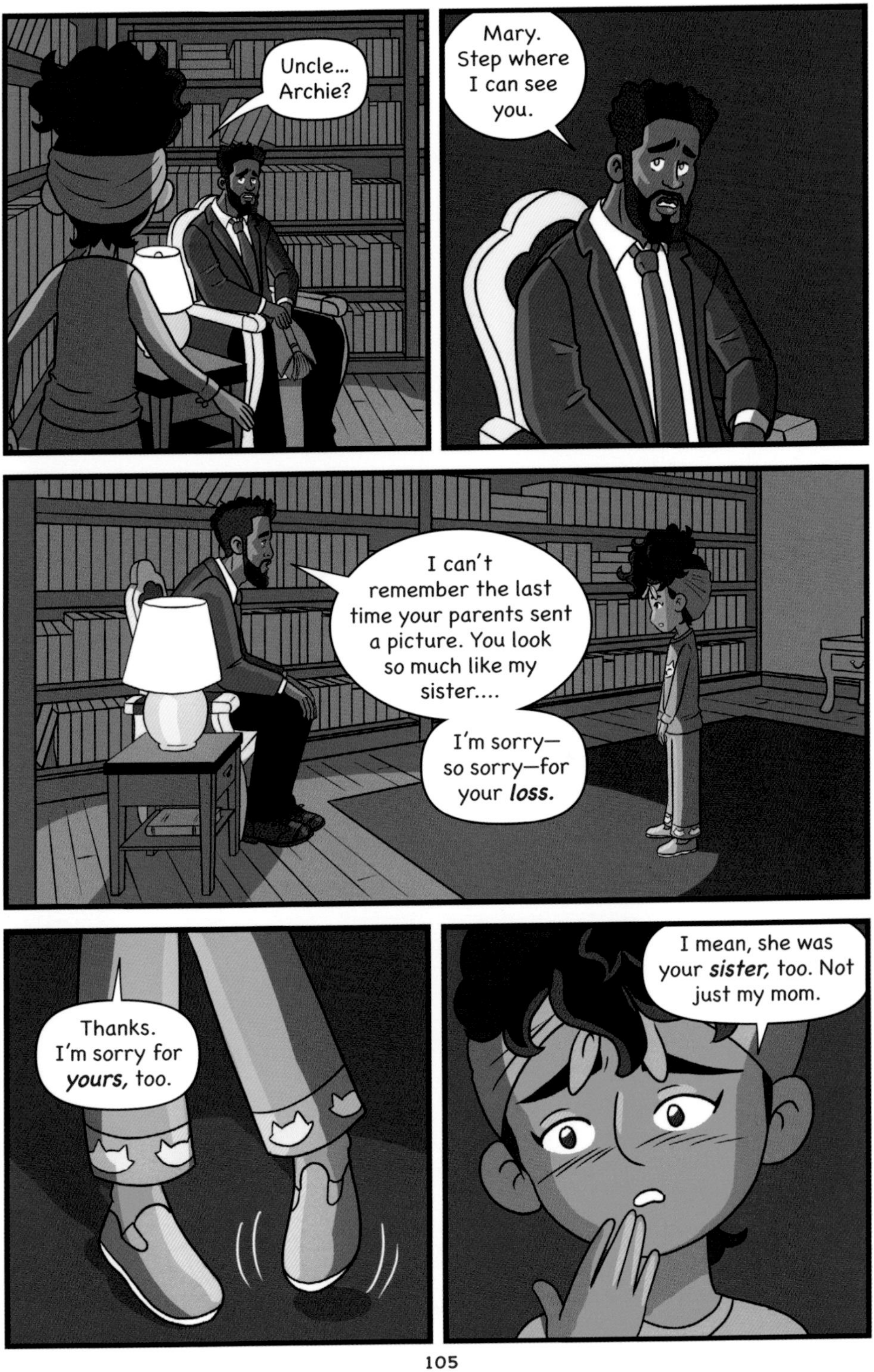
Uncle... Archie?
Mary. Step where I can see you.
I can't remember the last time your parents sent a picture. You look so much like my sister....
I'm sorry—so sorry—for your **loss.**
Thanks. I'm sorry for ***yours,*** too.
I mean, she was your ***sister,*** too. Not just my mom.

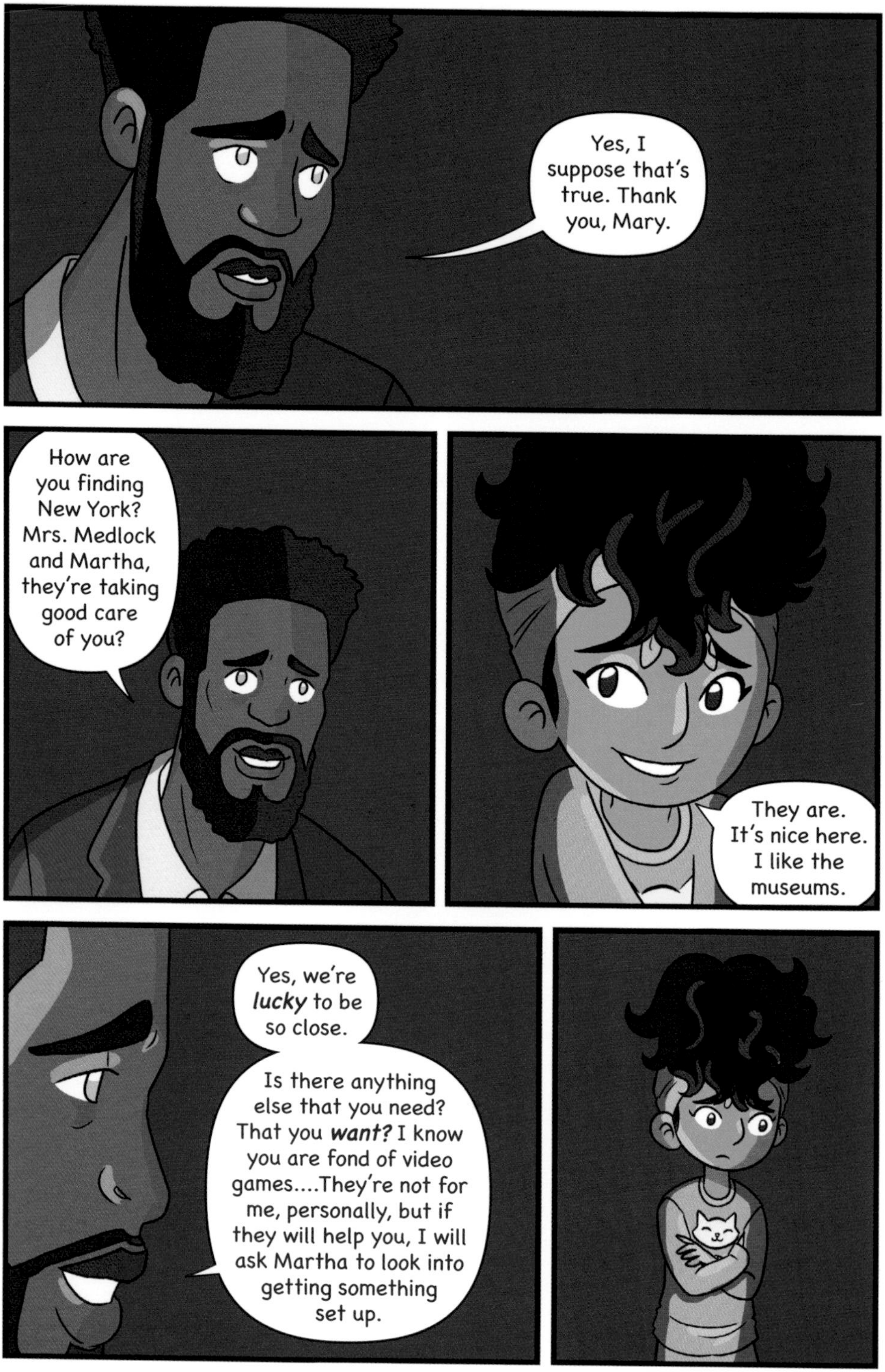
Yes, I suppose that's true. Thank you, Mary.
How are you finding New York? Mrs. Medlock and Martha, they're taking good care of you?
They are. It's nice here. I like the museums.
Yes, we're *lucky* to be so close.
Is there anything else that you need? That you *want?* I know you are fond of video games....They're not for me, personally, but if they will help you, I will ask Martha to look into getting something set up.

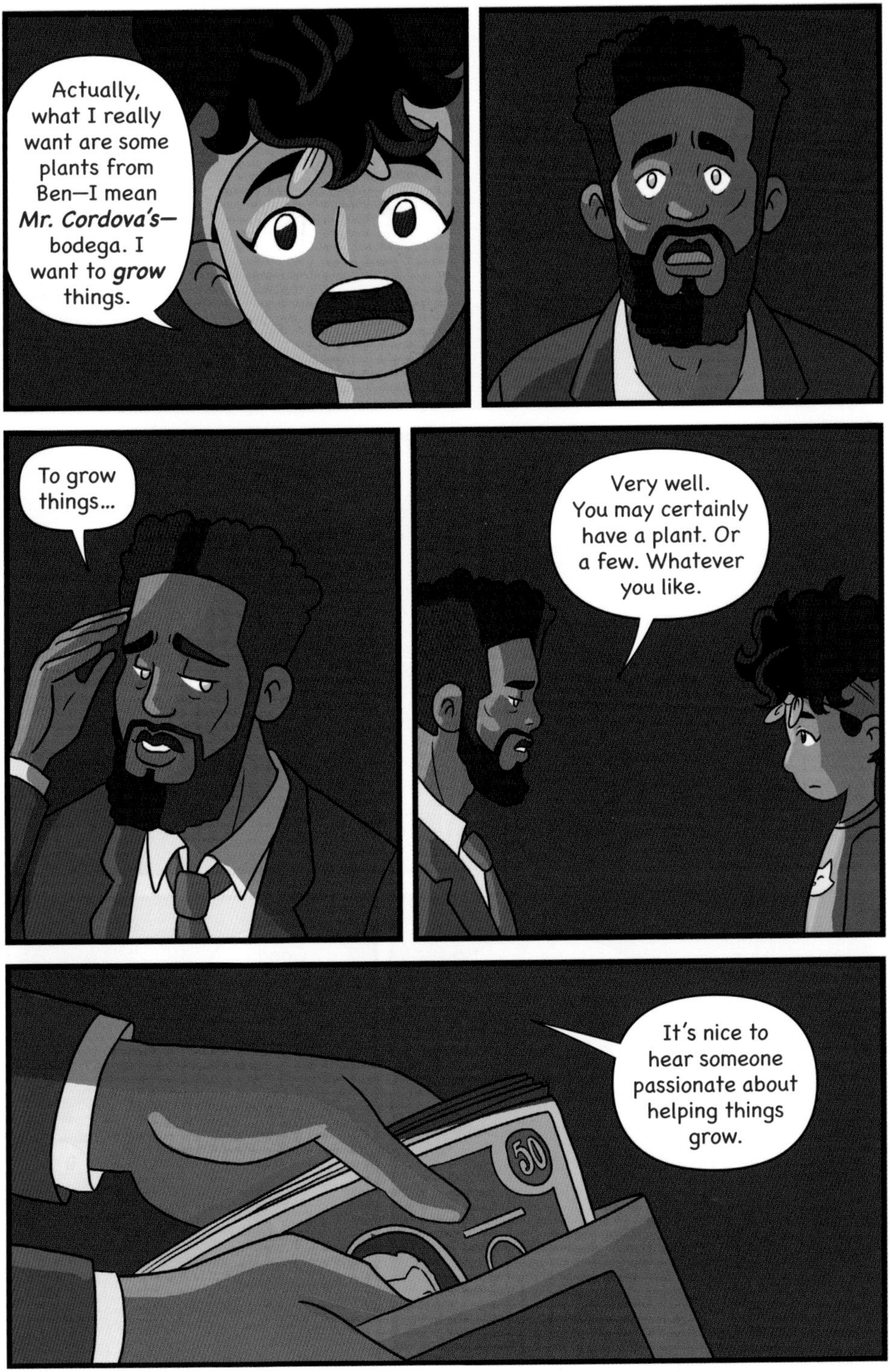
Actually, what I really want are some plants from Ben—I mean *Mr. Cordova's*—bodega. I want to ***grow*** things.
To grow things...
Very well. You may certainly have a plant. Or a few. Whatever you like.
It's nice to hear someone passionate about helping things grow.
50

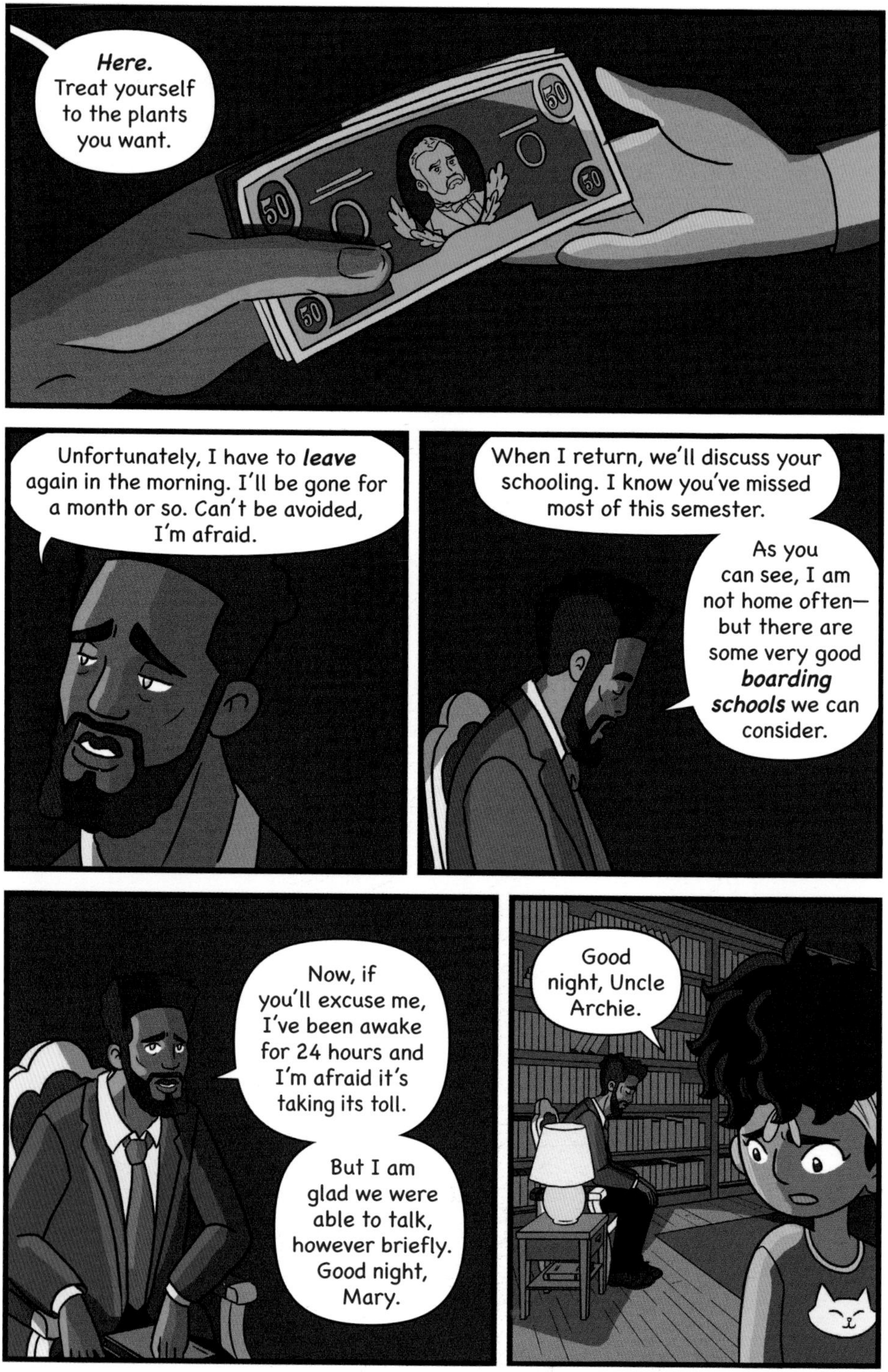
Here.
Treat yourself to the plants you want.
Unfortunately, I have to *leave* again in the morning. I'll be gone for a month or so. Can't be avoided, I'm afraid.
When I return, we'll discuss your schooling. I know you've missed most of this semester.
As you can see, I am not home often— but there are some very good *boarding schools* we can consider.
Now, if you'll excuse me, I've been awake for 24 hours and I'm afraid it's taking its toll.
But I am glad we were able to talk, however briefly. Good night, Mary.
Good night, Uncle Archie.

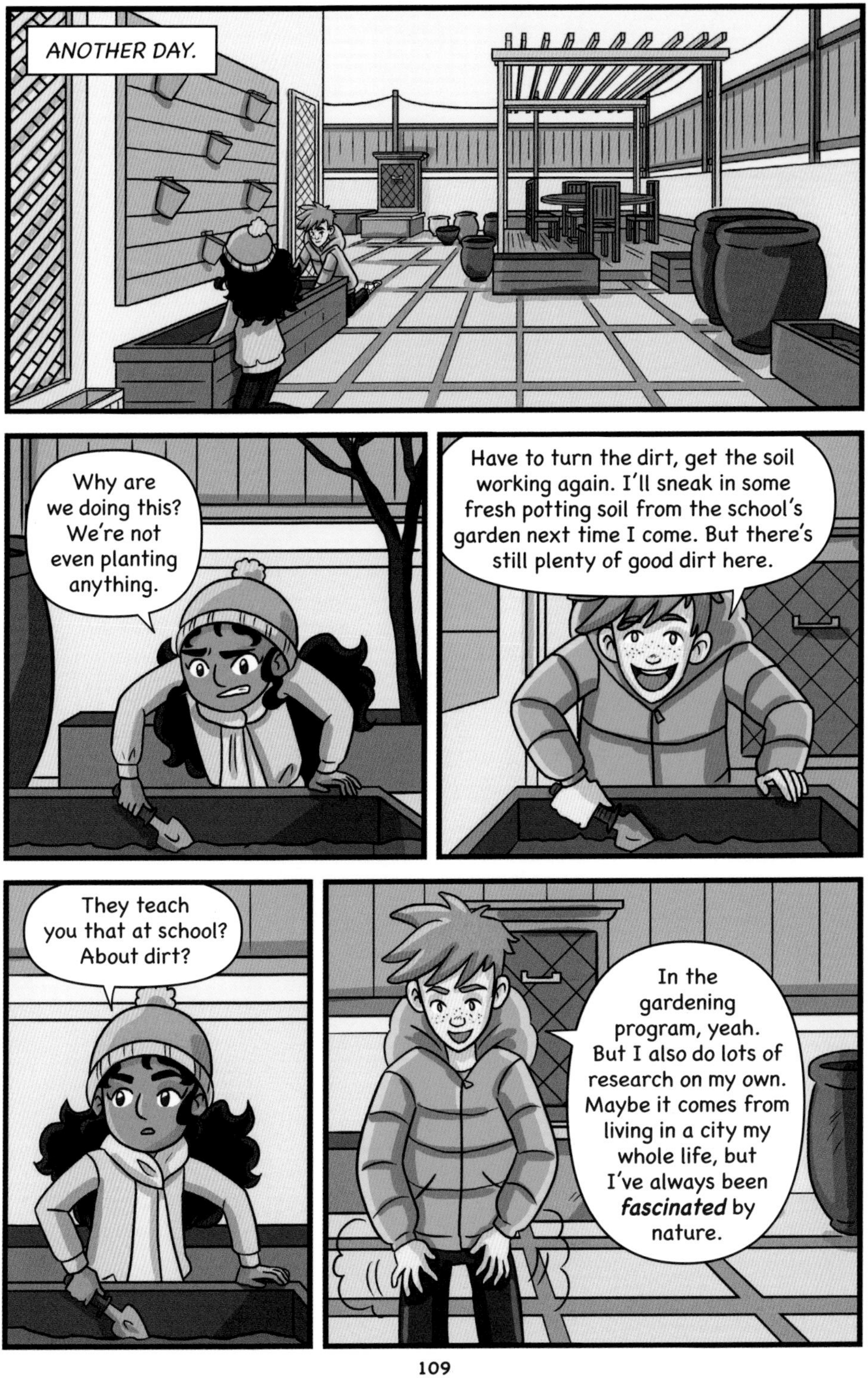
ANOTHER DAY.
Why are we doing this? We're not even planting anything.
Have to turn the dirt, get the soil working again. I'll sneak in some fresh potting soil from the school's garden next time I come. But there's still plenty of good dirt here.
They teach you that at school? About dirt?
In the gardening program, yeah. But I also do lots of research on my own. Maybe it comes from living in a city my whole life, but I've always been *fascinated* by nature.

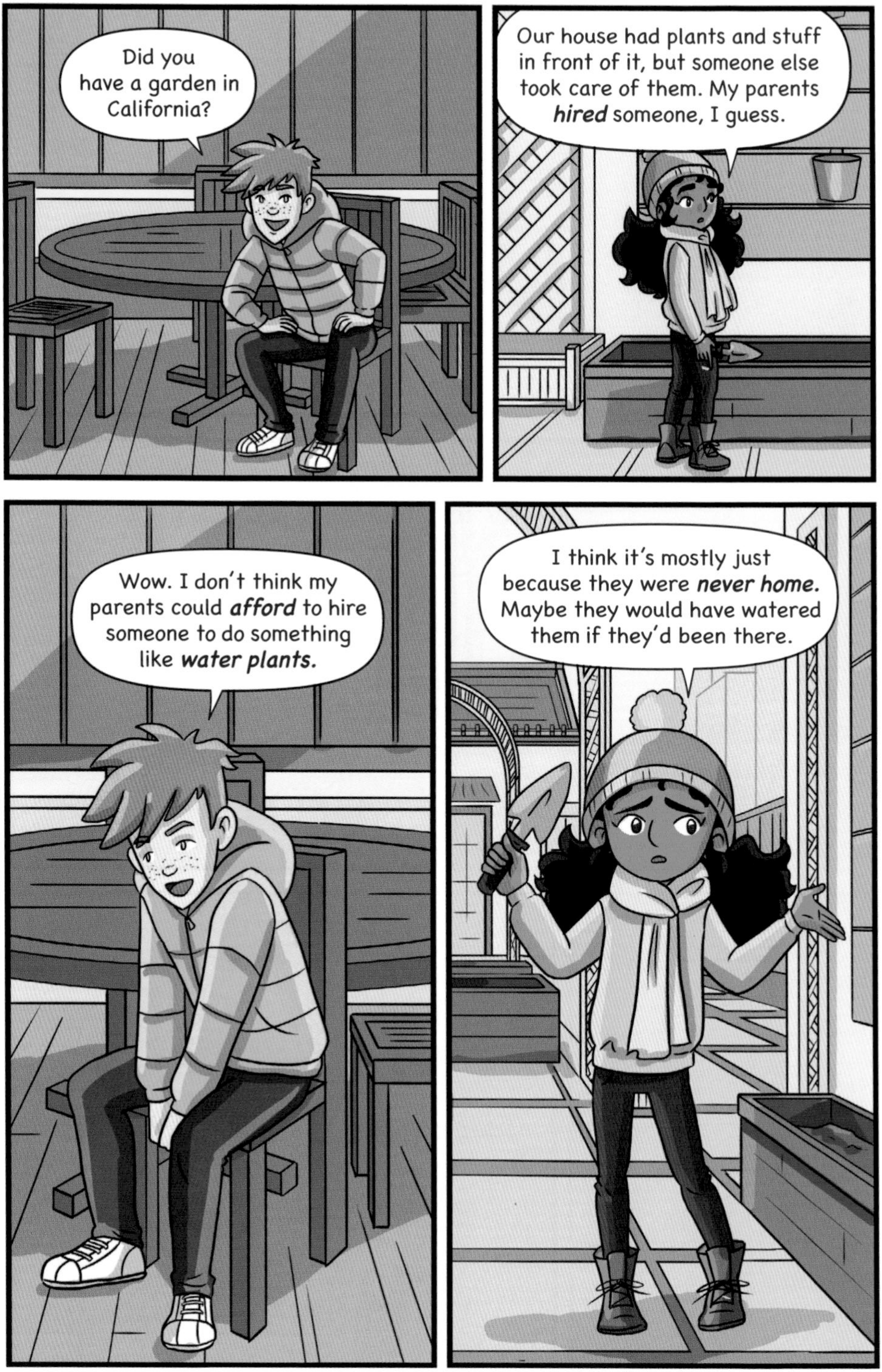
Did you have a garden in California?
Our house had plants and stuff in front of it, but someone else took care of them. My parents *hired* someone, I guess.
Wow. I don't think my parents could *afford* to hire someone to do something like *water plants.*
I think it's mostly just because they were *never home.* Maybe they would have watered them if they'd been there.

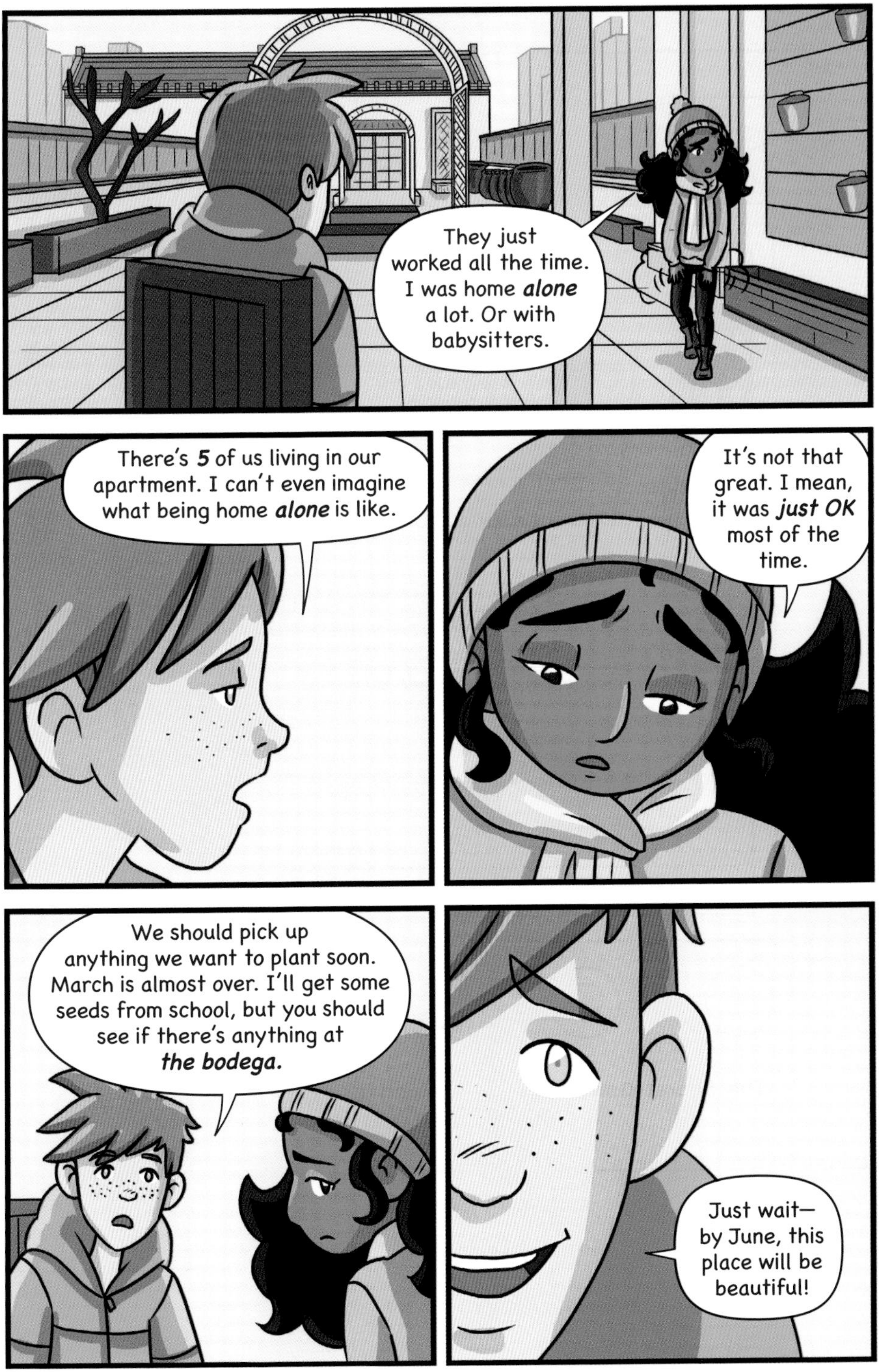
They just worked all the time. I was home *alone* a lot. Or with babysitters.
There's **5** of us living in our apartment. I can't even imagine what being home *alone* is like.
It's not that great. I mean, it was *just OK* most of the time.
We should pick up anything we want to plant soon. March is almost over. I'll get some seeds from school, but you should see if there's anything at *the bodega.*
Just wait— by June, this place will be beautiful!

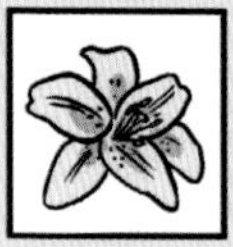

The_Secret_Garden

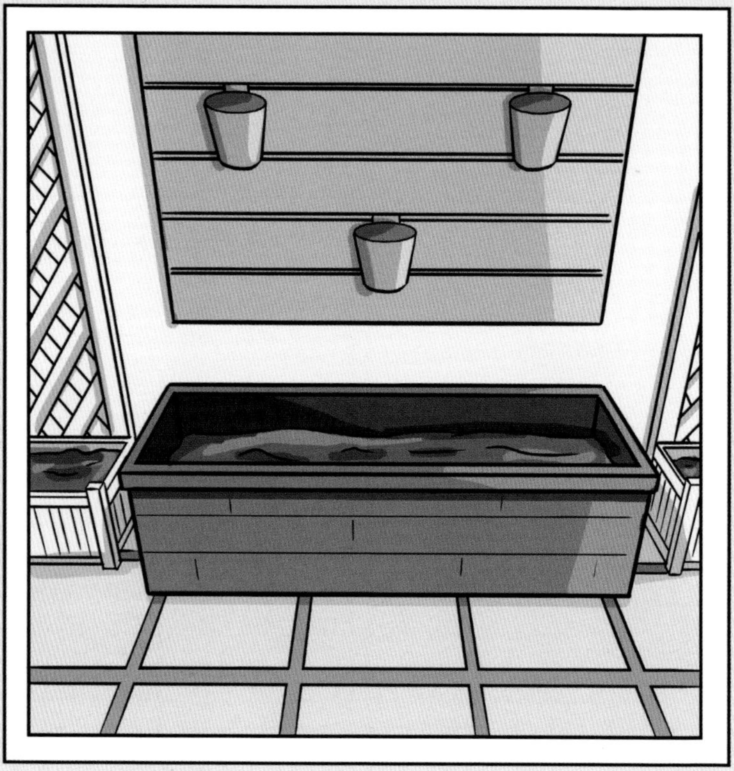

The_Secret_Garden Doesn't look like much yet...but just you wait!

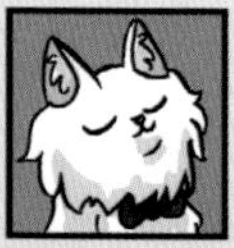

The_Cultured_Cat

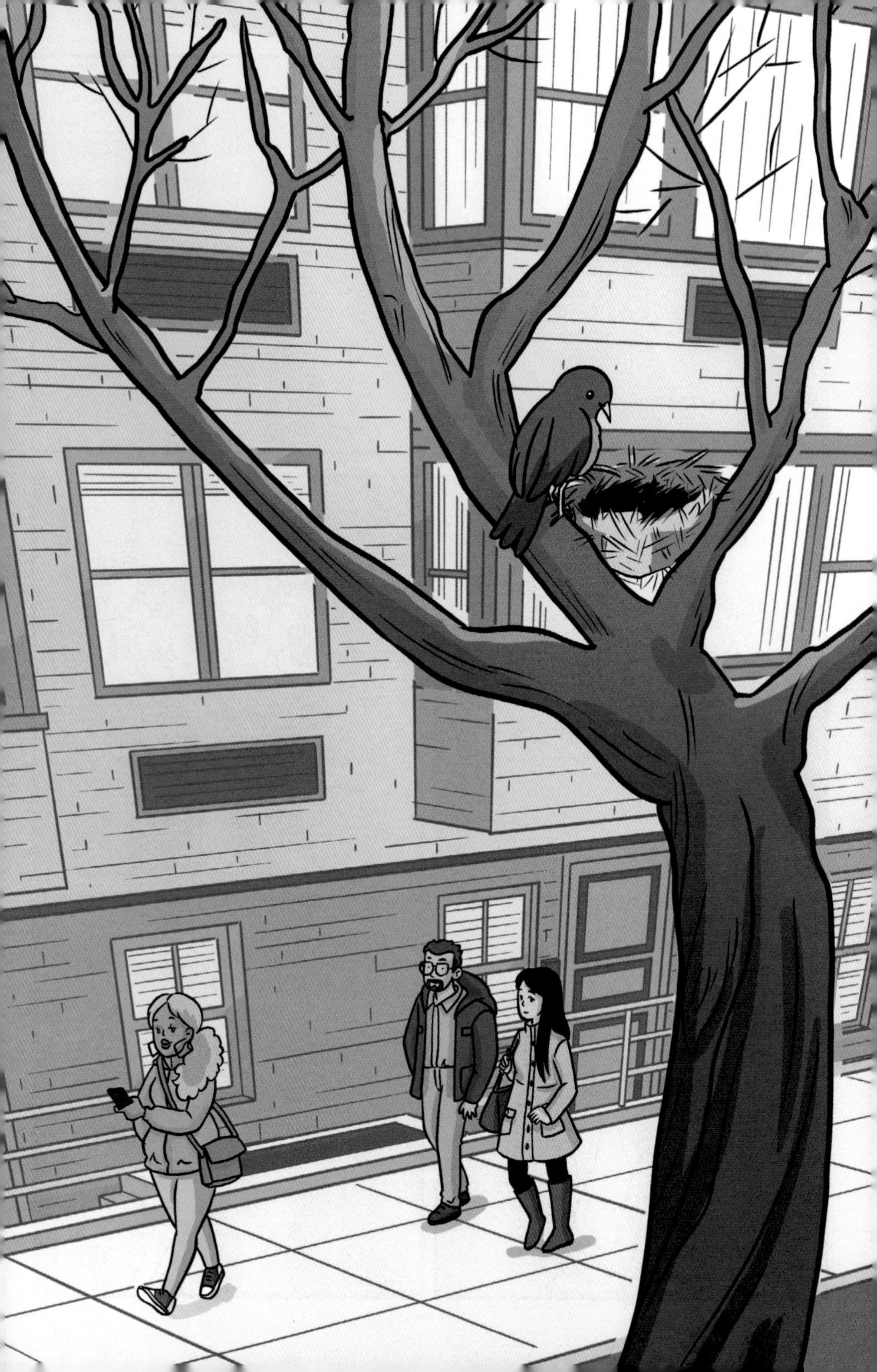

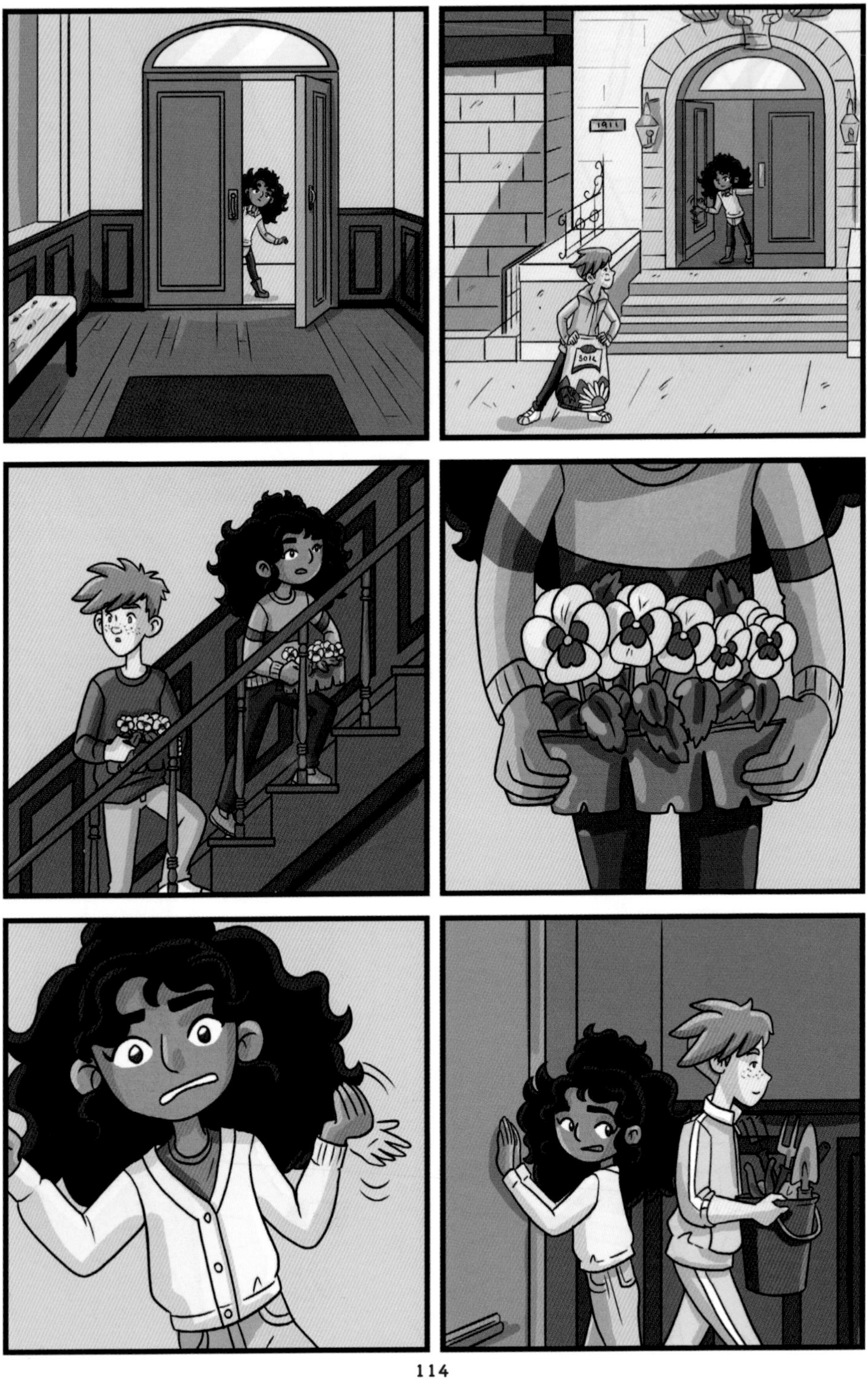
1911
SOIL

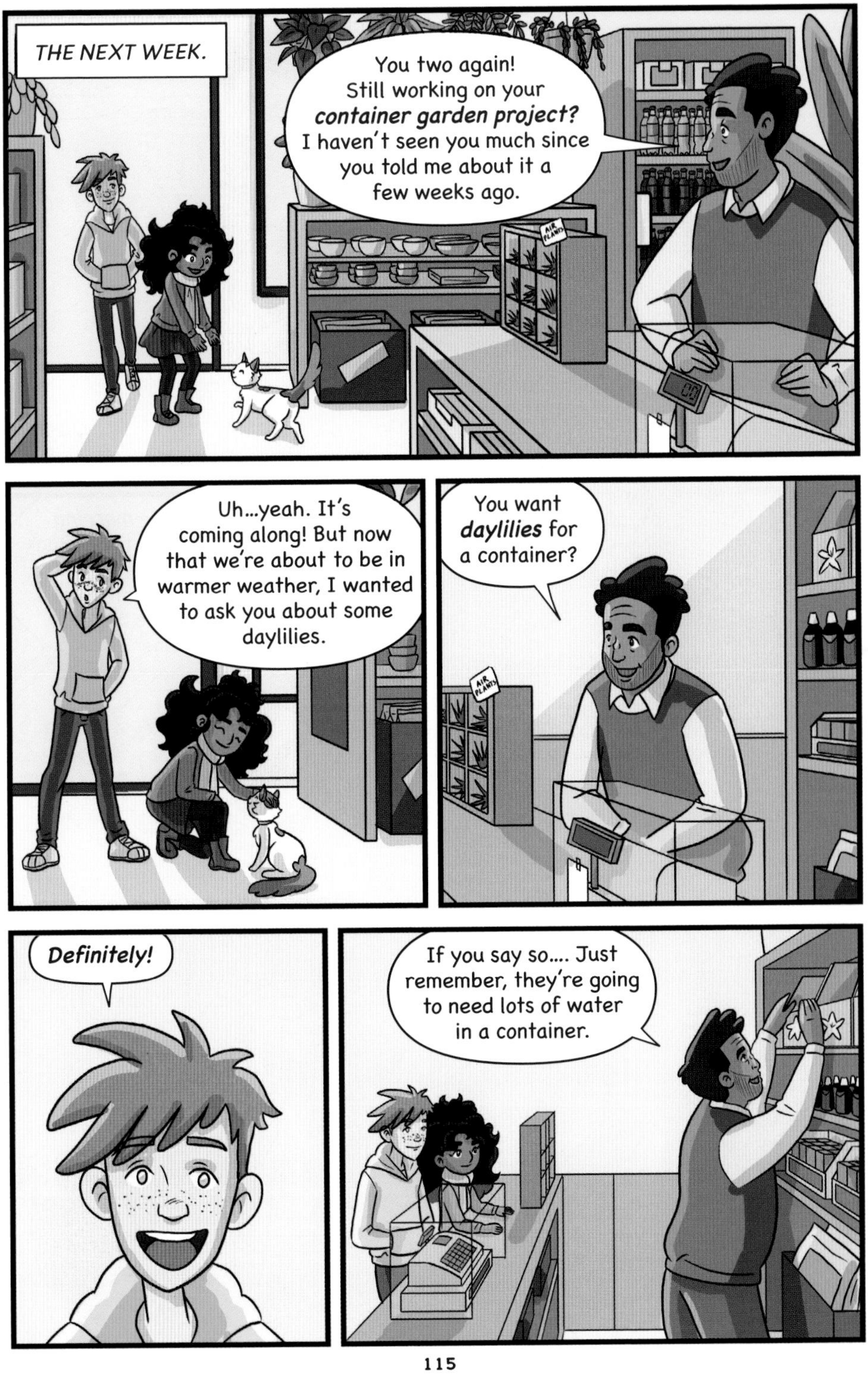
THE NEXT WEEK.
You two again! Still working on your *container garden project?* I haven't seen you much since you told me about it a few weeks ago.
AIR PLANTS
Uh...yeah. It's coming along! But now that we're about to be in warmer weather, I wanted to ask you about some daylilies.
You want *daylilies* for a container?
AIR PLANTS
Definitely!
If you say so.... Just remember, they're going to need lots of water in a container.

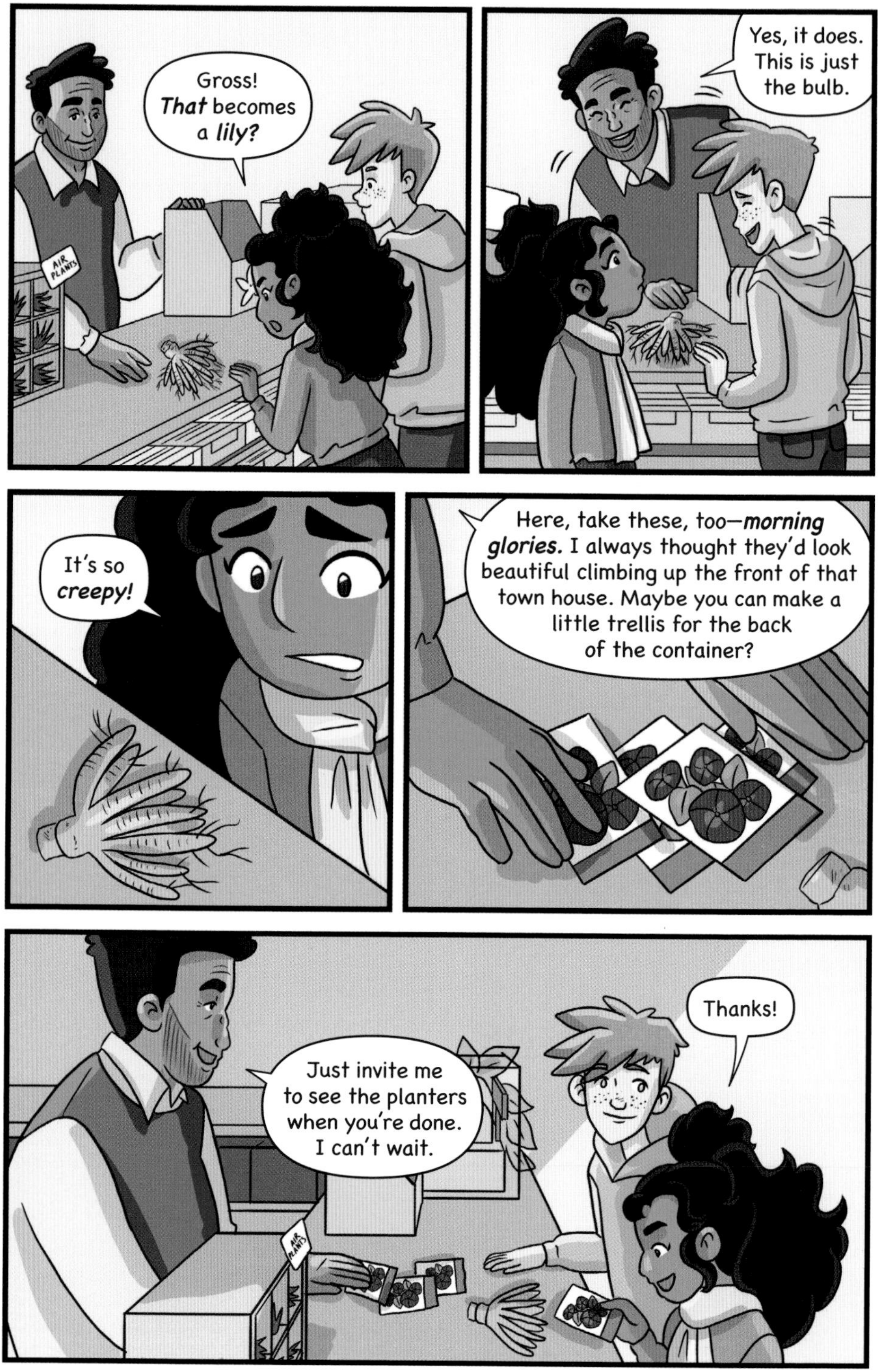
Gross! *That* becomes a *lily?*
Yes, it does. This is just the bulb.
AIR PLANTS
It's so *creepy!*
Here, take these, too—***morning glories.*** I always thought they'd look beautiful climbing up the front of that town house. Maybe you can make a little trellis for the back of the container?
Thanks!
Just invite me to see the planters when you're done. I can't wait.
AIR PLANTS

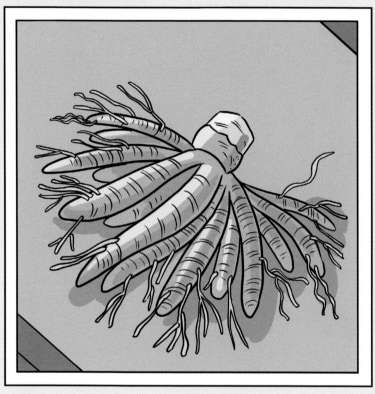

The_Secret_Garden Hard to believe it, but this ugly little thing turns into a beautiful lily! Once it sprouts, it needs plenty of hot sun. The flowers will be the most intense shade of yellow!

PrettyCoolDog

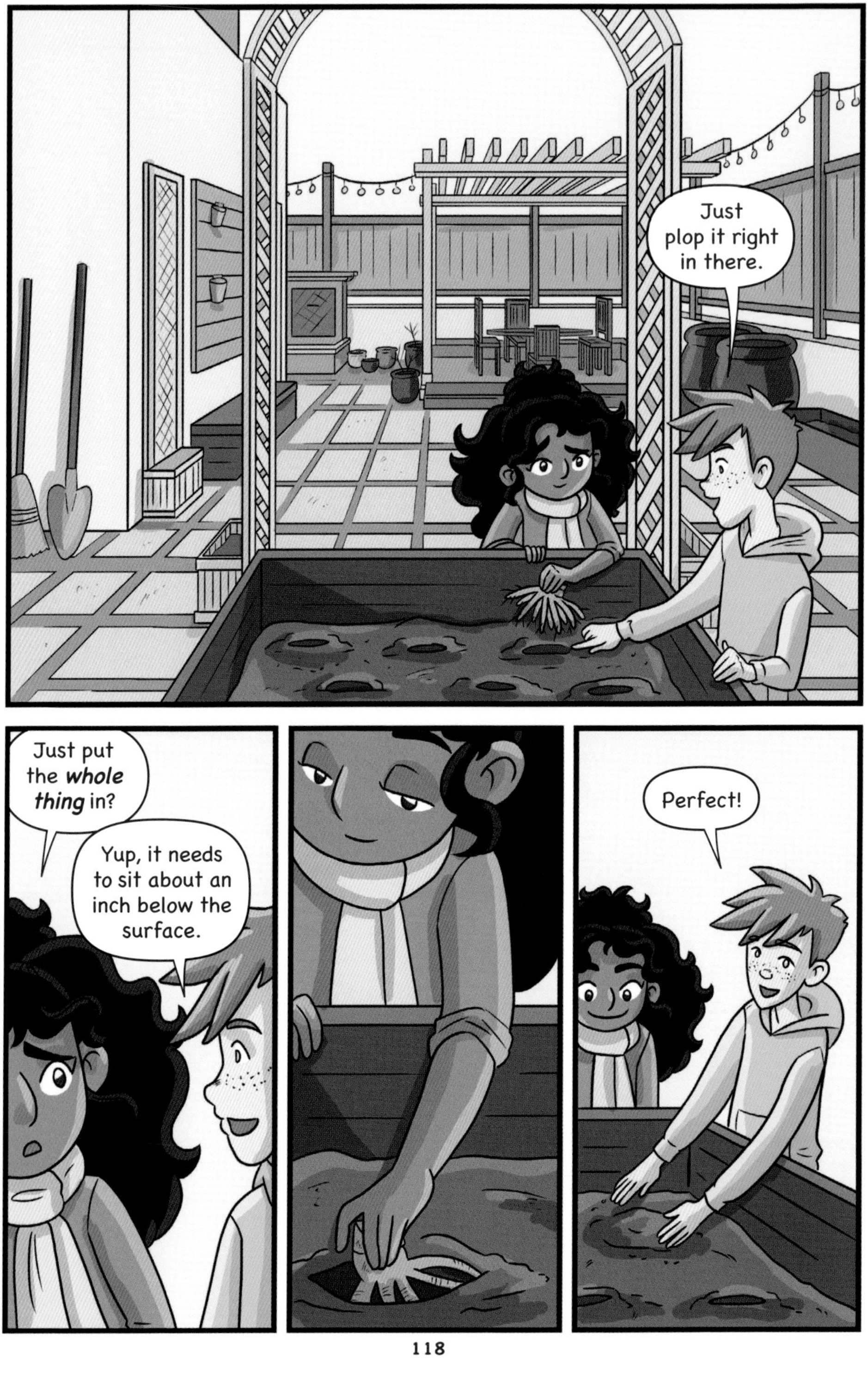
Just plop it right in there.
Just put the *whole thing* in?
Yup, it needs to sit about an inch below the surface.
Perfect!

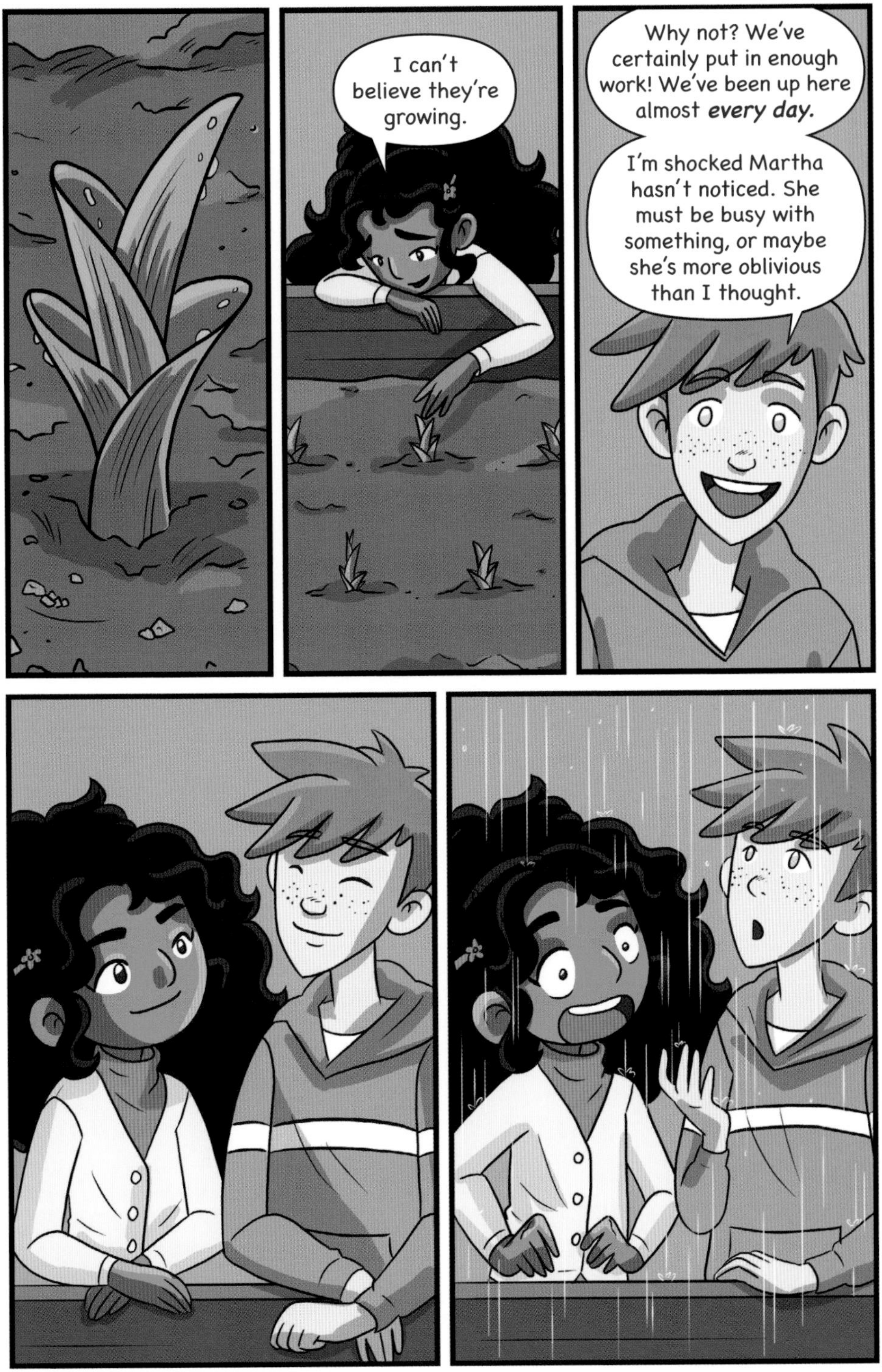
I can't believe they're growing.
Why not? We've certainly put in enough work! We've been up here almost *every day.*
I'm shocked Martha hasn't noticed. She must be busy with something, or maybe she's more oblivious than I thought.

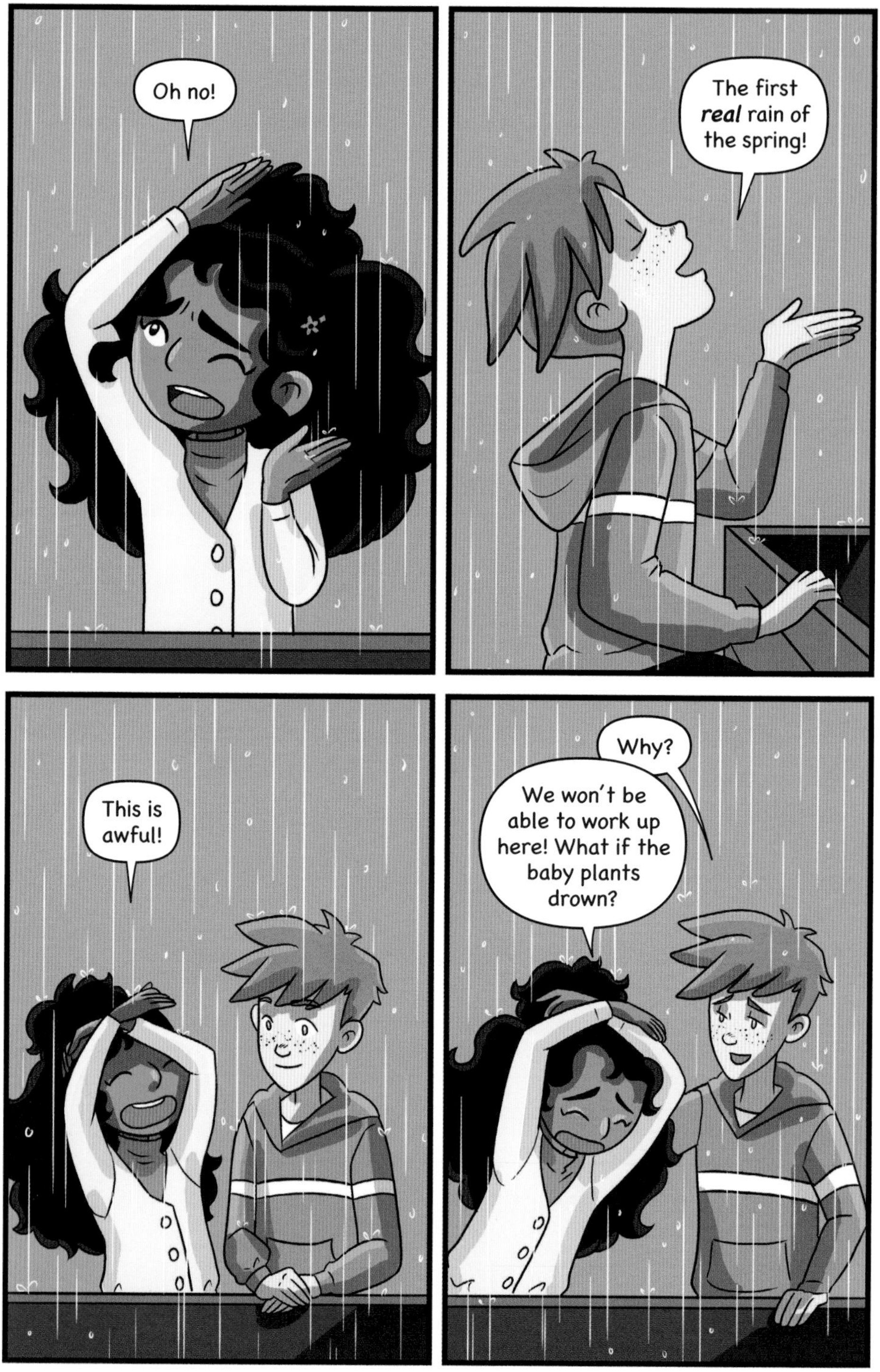
Oh no!
The first *real* rain of the spring!
This is awful!
Why?
We won't be able to work up here! What if the baby plants drown?

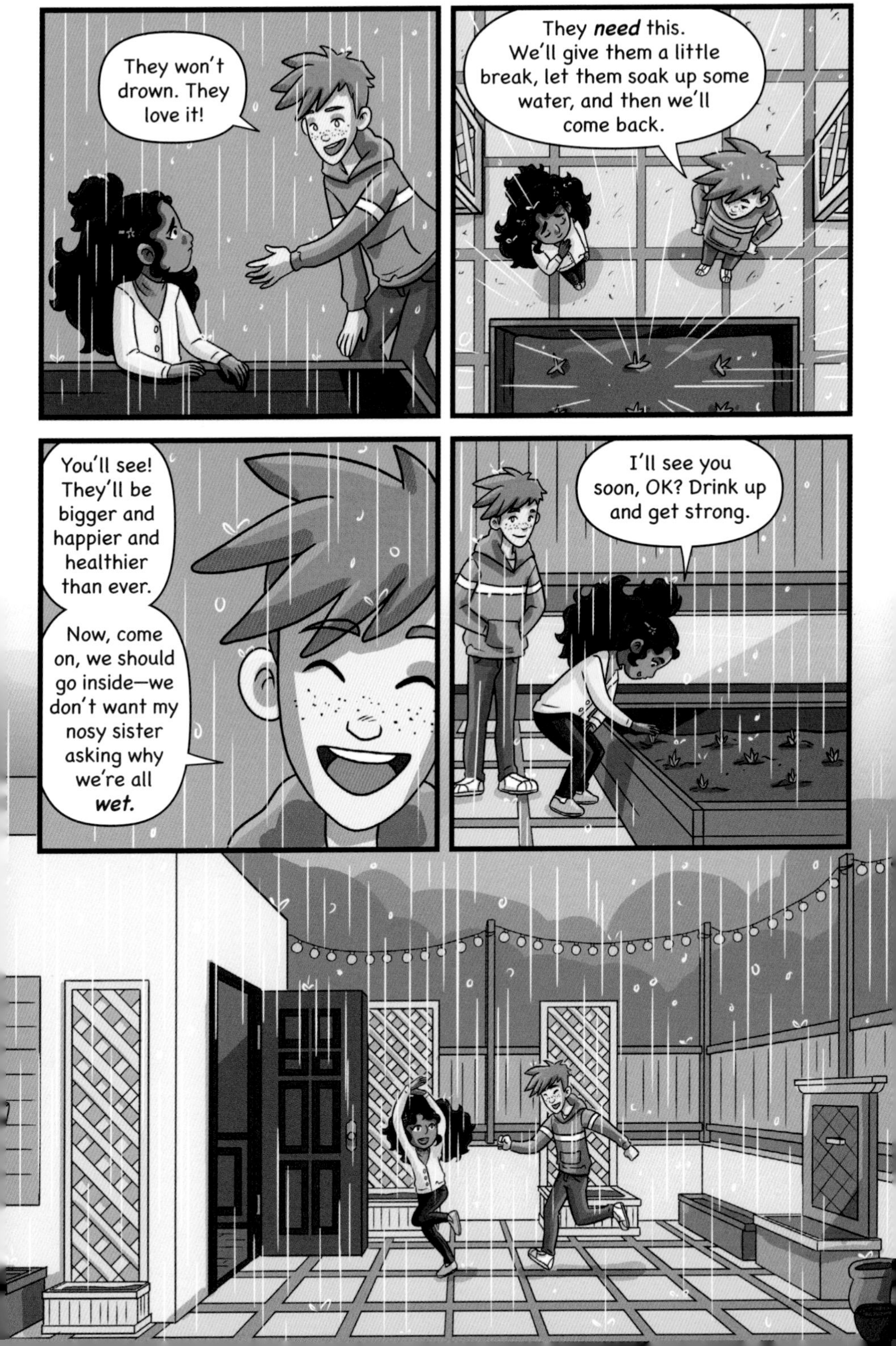
They won't drown. They love it!
They *need* this. We'll give them a little break, let them soak up some water, and then we'll come back.
You'll see! They'll be bigger and happier and healthier than ever.
Now, come on, we should go inside—we don't want my nosy sister asking why we're all ***wet.***
I'll see you soon, OK? Drink up and get strong.

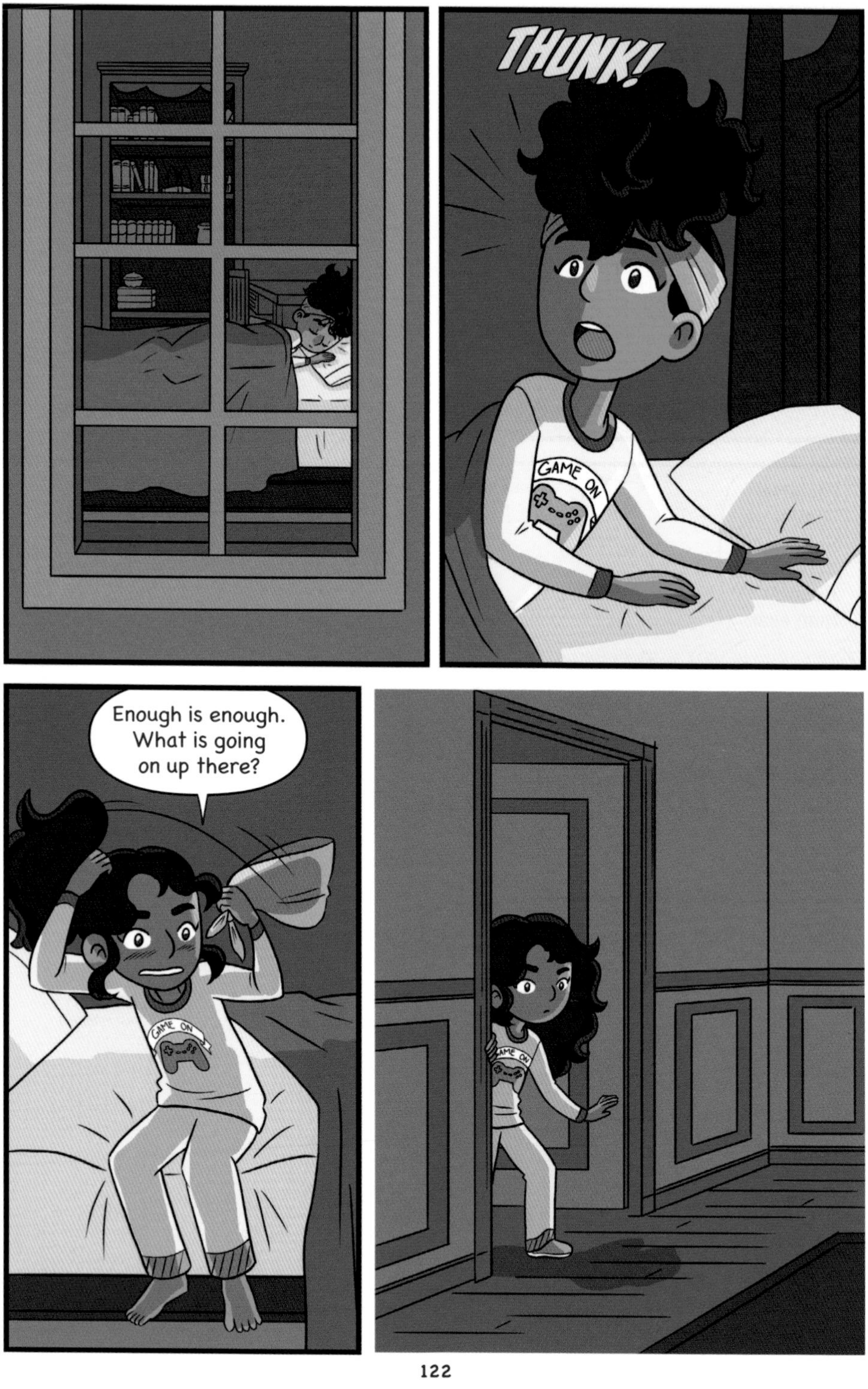
THUNK!
GAME ON
Enough is enough. What is going on up there?
GAME ON
GAME ON

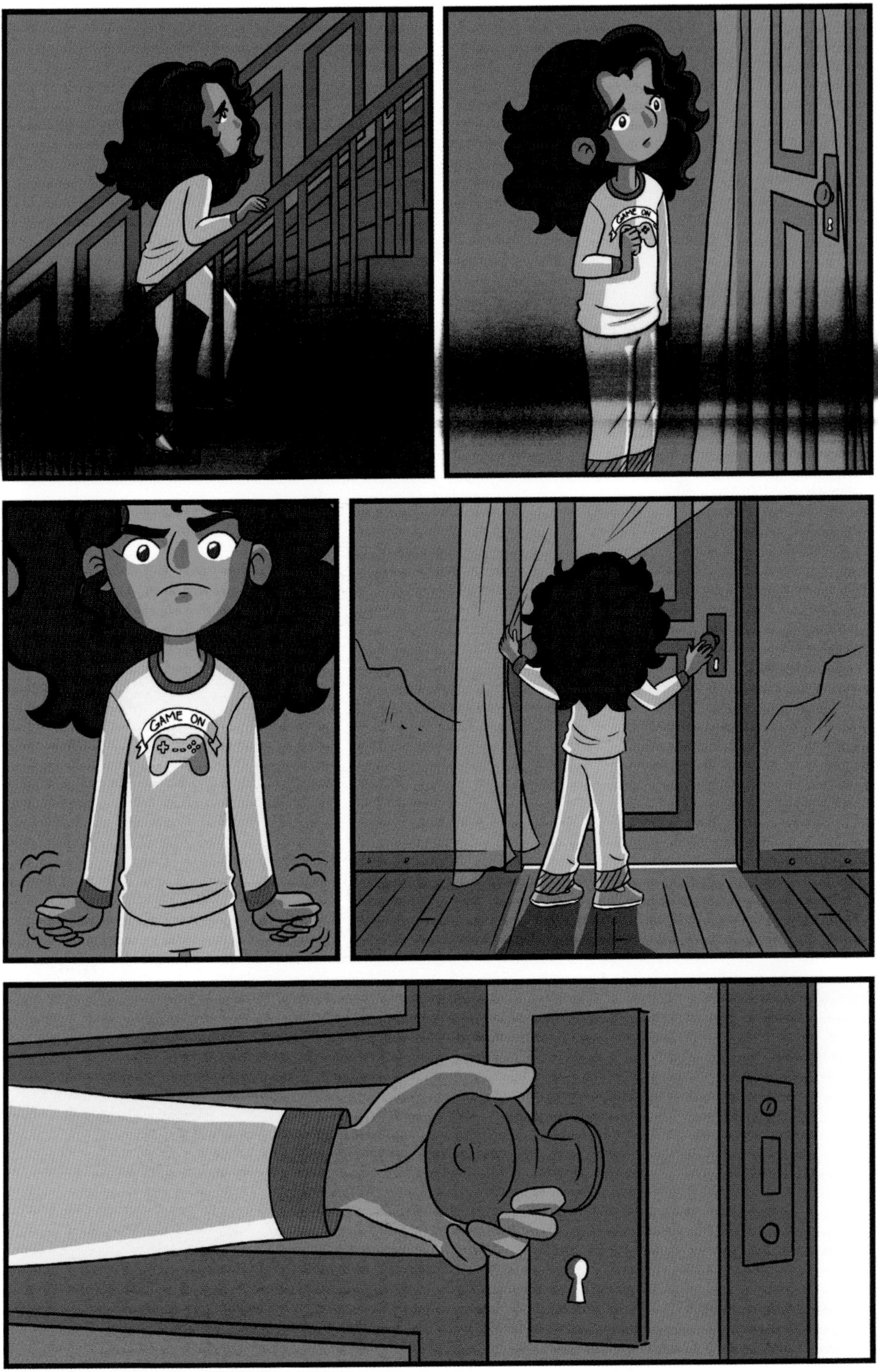
GAME ON

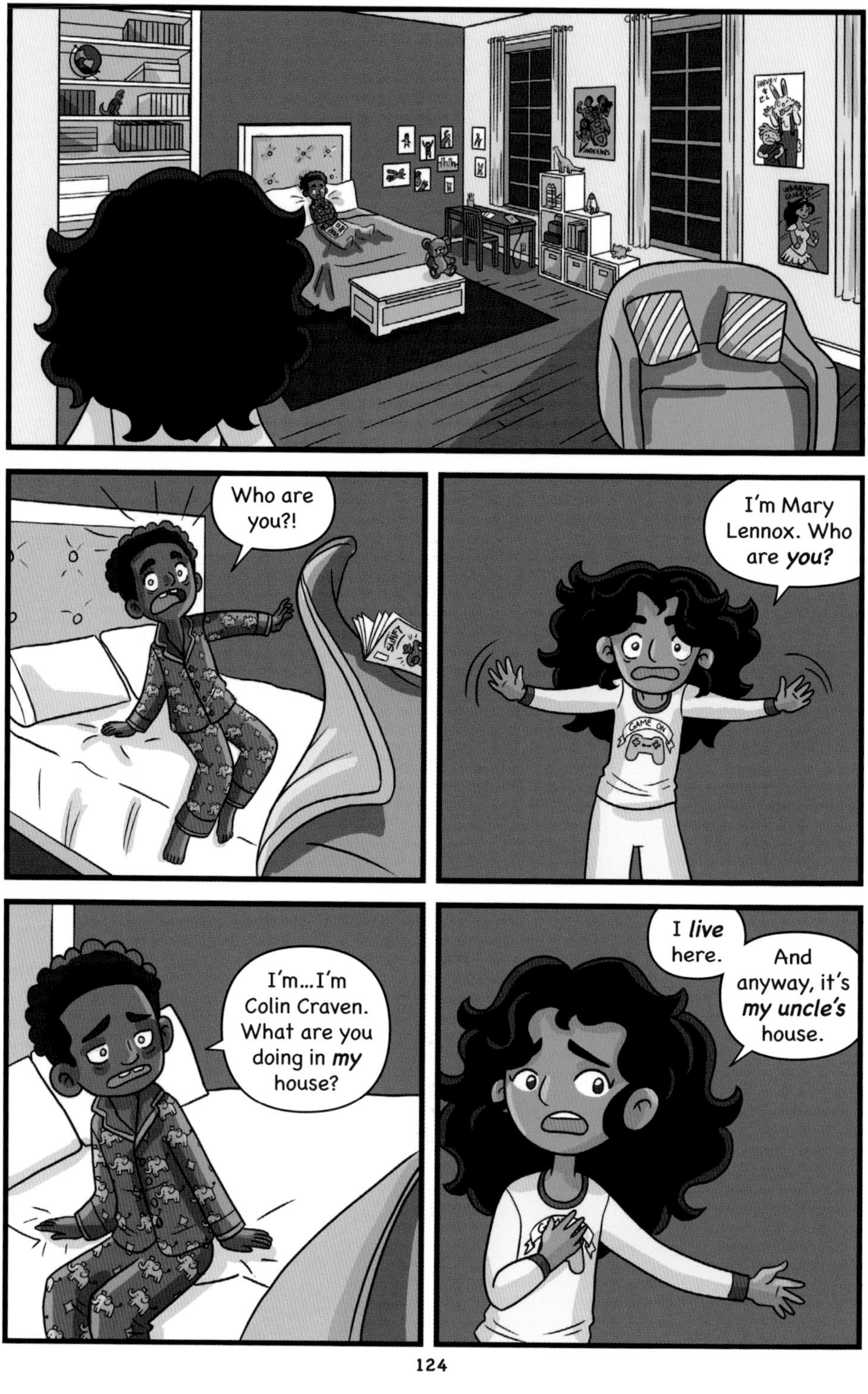
Who are you?!
I'm Mary Lennox. Who are *you?*
GAME ON
I'm...I'm Colin Craven. What are you doing in *my* house?
I *live* here.
And anyway, it's *my uncle's* house.

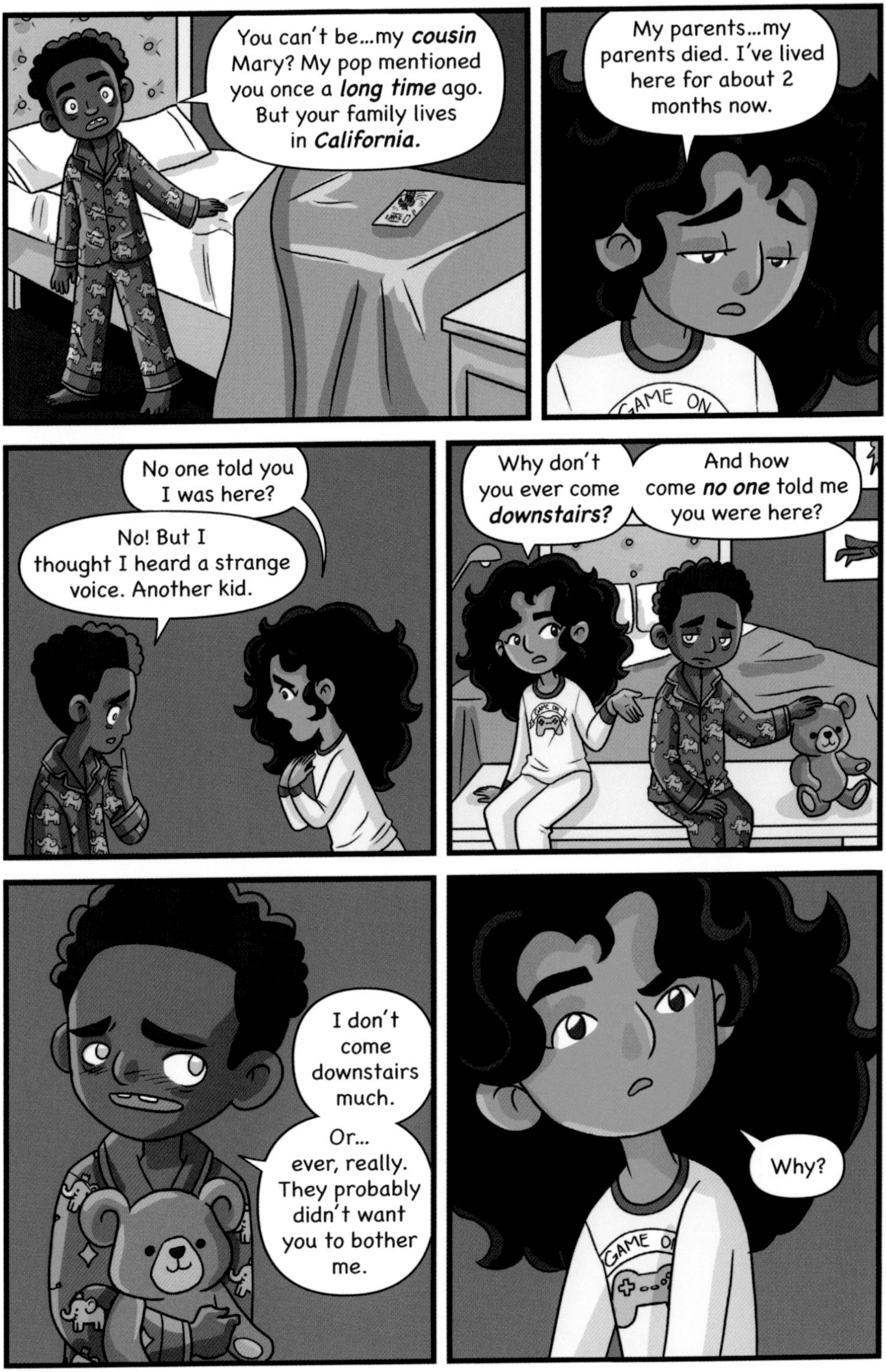
You can't be...my *cousin* Mary? My pop mentioned you once a *long time* ago. But your family lives in *California.*
My parents...my parents died. I've lived here for about 2 months now.
GAME ON
No one told you I was here?
No! But I thought I heard a strange voice. Another kid.
Why don't you ever come *downstairs?*
And how come *no one* told me you were here?
I don't come downstairs much.
Or... ever, really. They probably didn't want you to bother me.
Why?
GAME ON

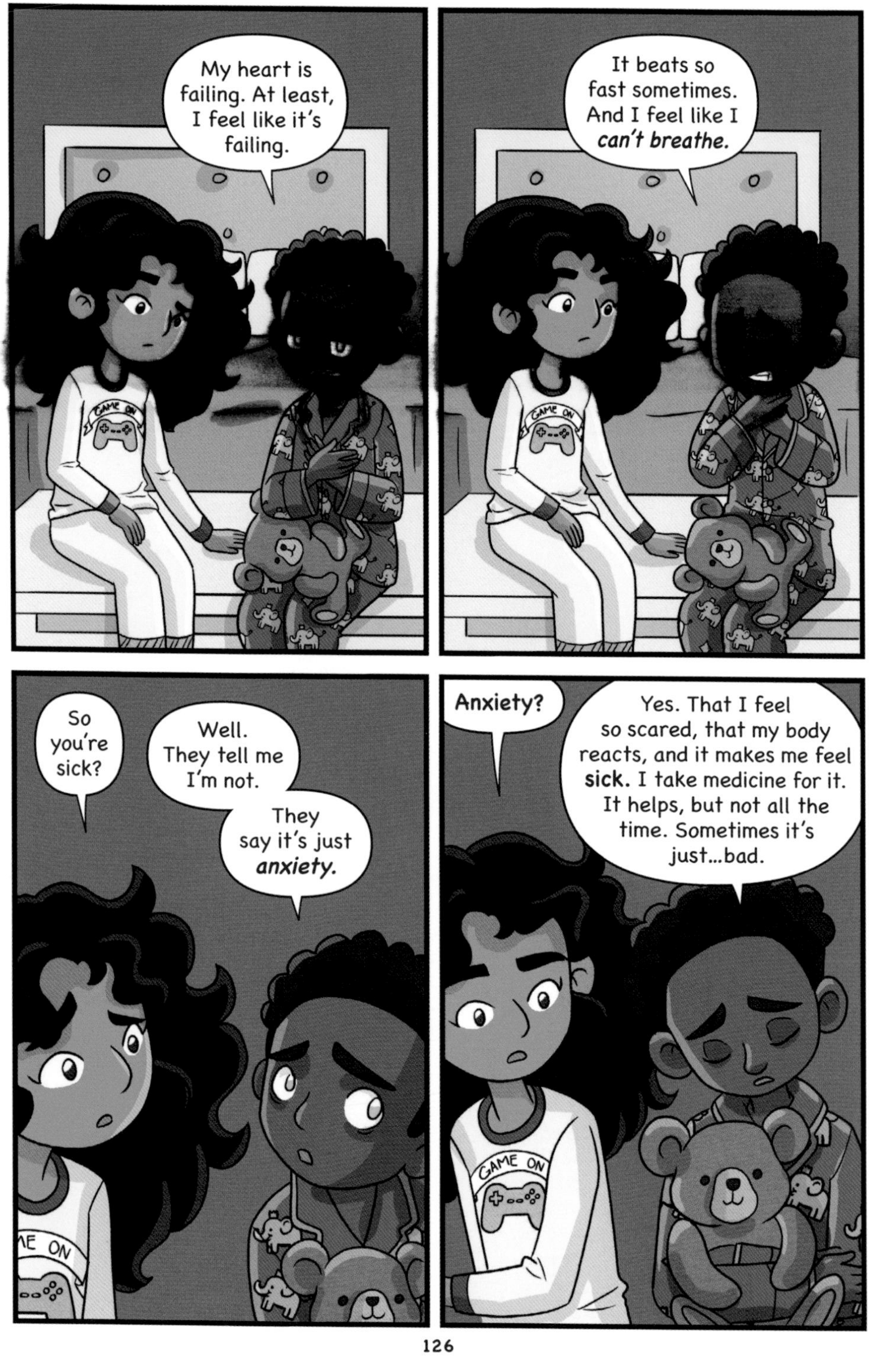
My heart is failing. At least, I feel like it's failing.
It beats so fast sometimes. And I feel like I *can't breathe.*
So you're sick?
Well. They tell me I'm not.
They say it's just *anxiety.*
Anxiety?
Yes. That I feel so scared, that my body reacts, and it makes me feel **sick.** I take medicine for it. It helps, but not all the time. Sometimes it's just...bad.

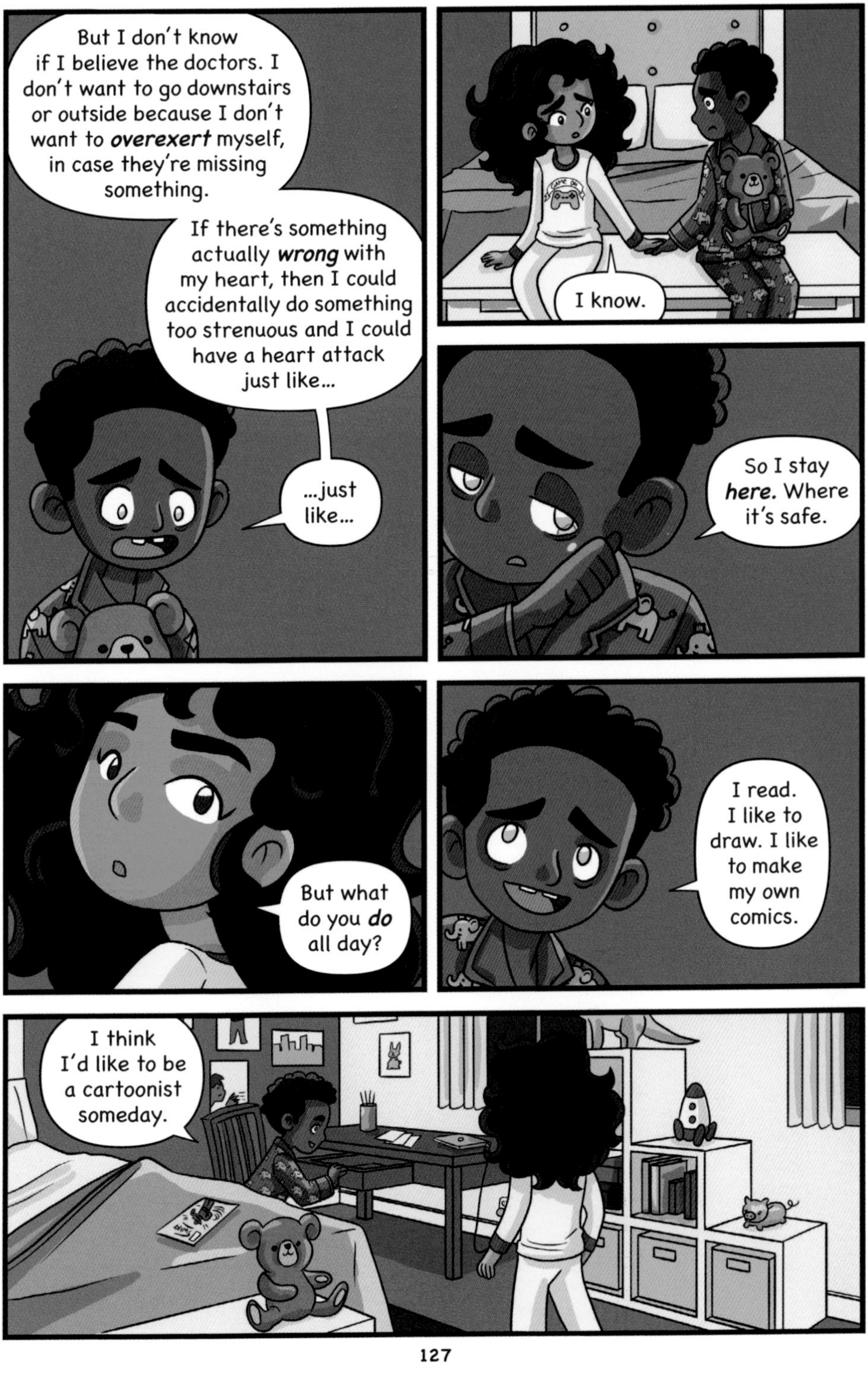

But I don't know if I believe the doctors. I don't want to go downstairs or outside because I don't want to *overexert* myself, in case they're missing something.
If there's something actually *wrong* with my heart, then I could accidentally do something too strenuous and I could have a heart attack just like...
...just like...
I know.
So I stay *here.* Where it's safe.
But what do you *do* all day?
I read. I like to draw. I like to make my own comics.
I think I'd like to be a cartoonist someday.

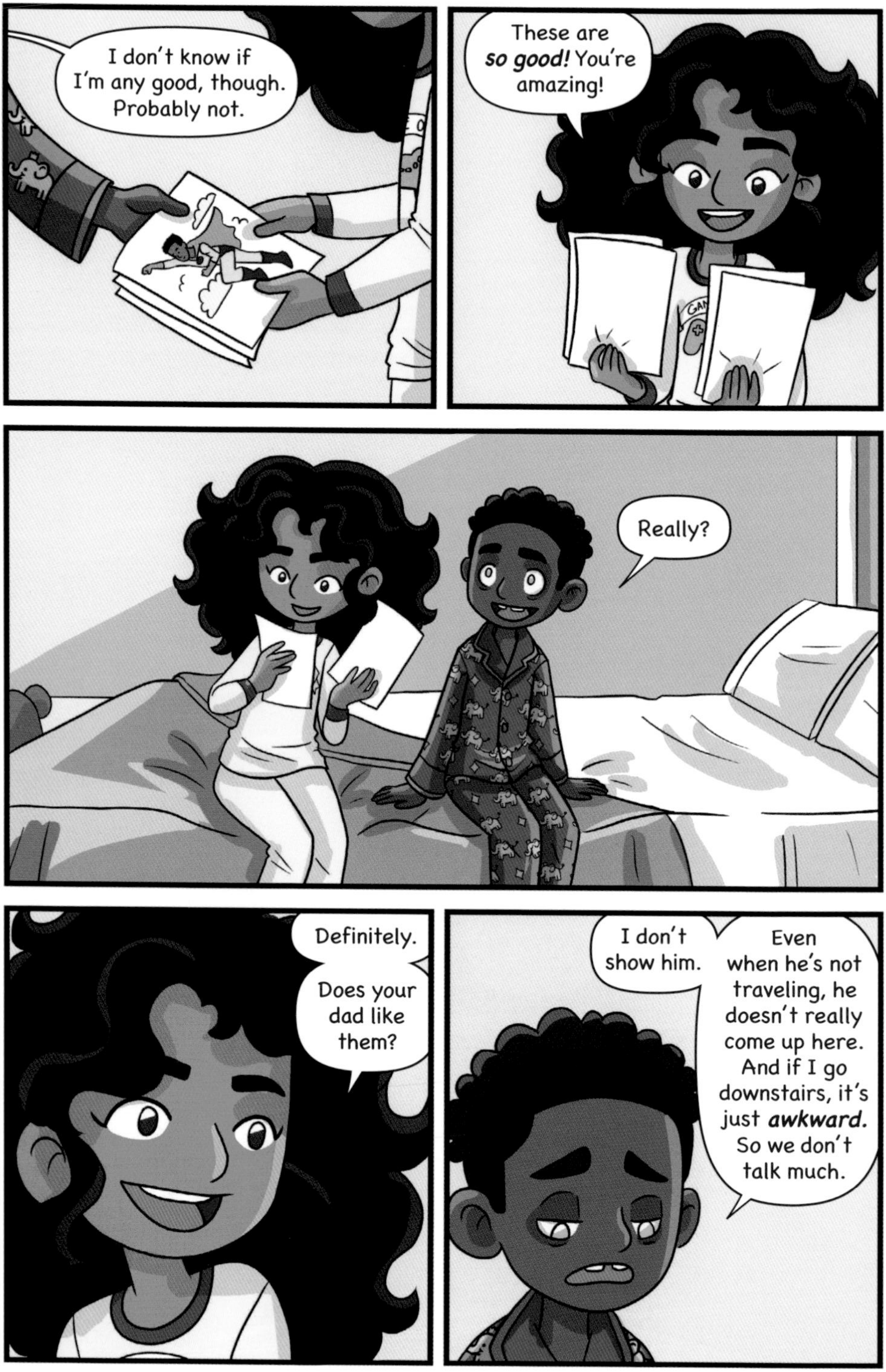
I don't know if I'm any good, though. Probably not.
These are *so good!* You're amazing!
Really?
Definitely.
Does your dad like them?
I don't show him.
Even when he's not traveling, he doesn't really come up here. And if I go downstairs, it's just *awkward.* So we don't talk much.

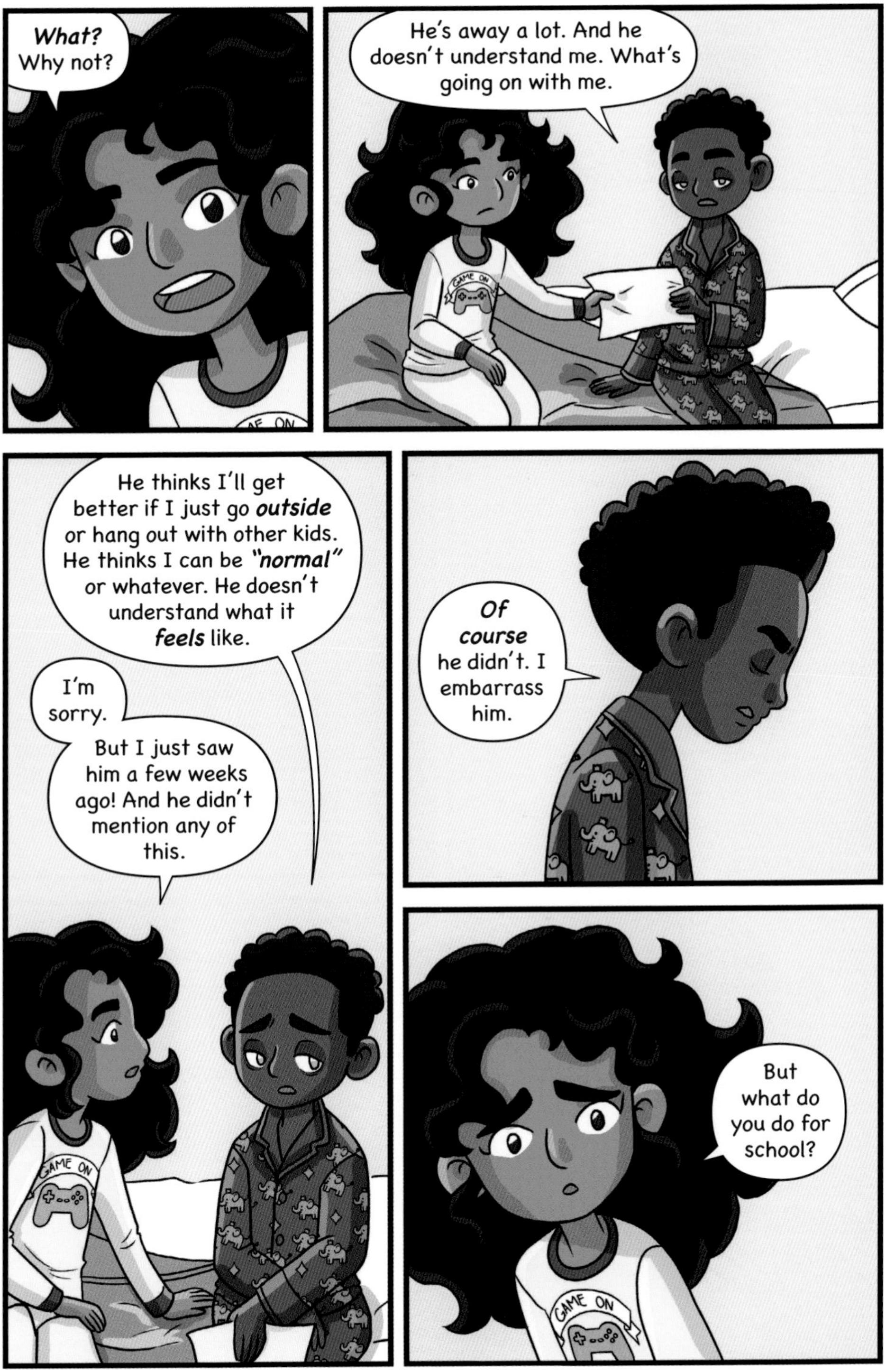
What? Why not?
He's away a lot. And he doesn't understand me. What's going on with me.
He thinks I'll get better if I just go ***outside*** or hang out with other kids. He thinks I can be ***"normal"*** or whatever. He doesn't understand what it ***feels*** like.
I'm sorry.
But I just saw him a few weeks ago! And he didn't mention any of this.
Of course he didn't. I embarrass him.
But what do you do for school?

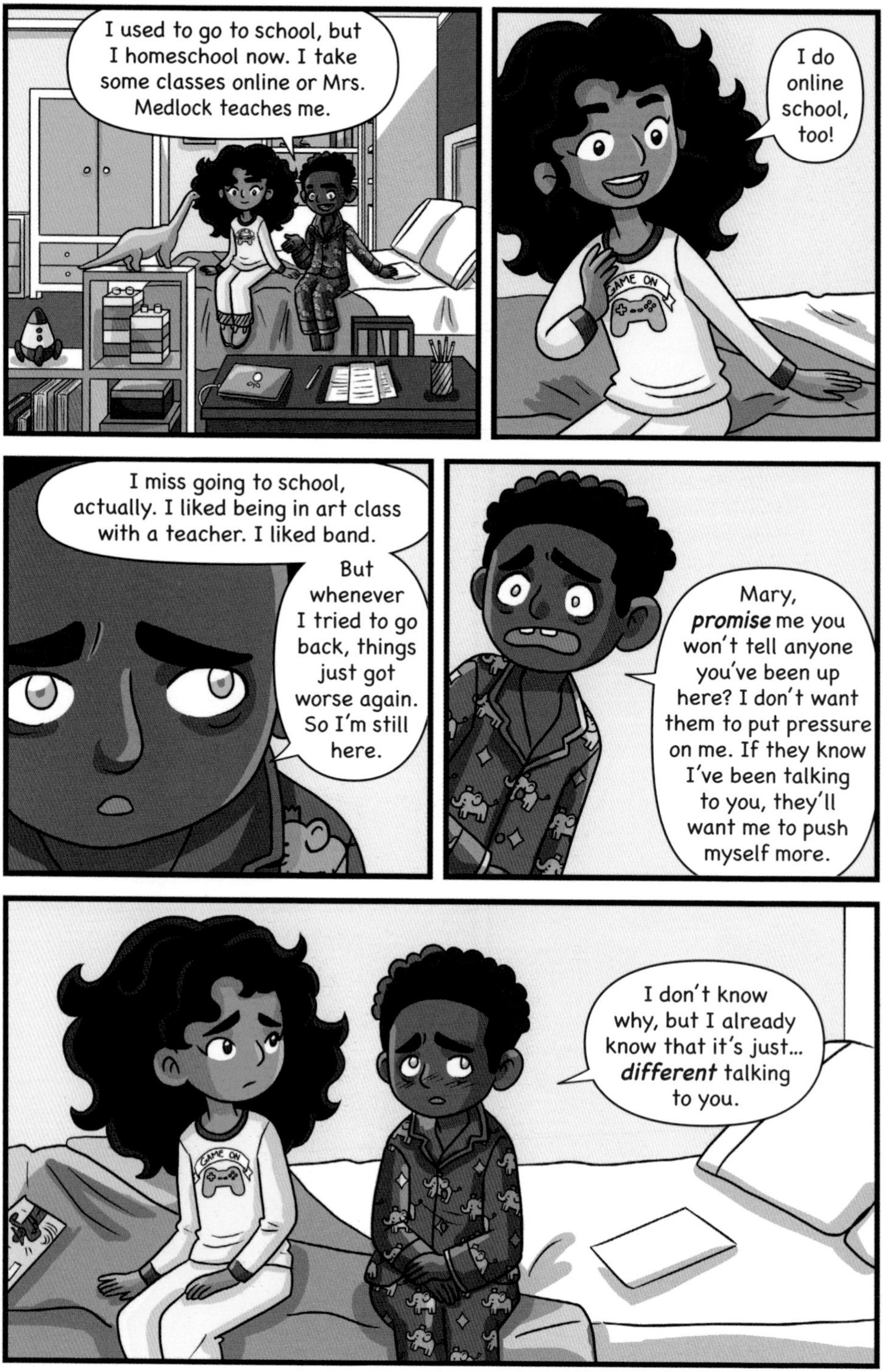
I used to go to school, but I homeschool now. I take some classes online or Mrs. Medlock teaches me.
I do online school, too!
GAME ON
I miss going to school, actually. I liked being in art class with a teacher. I liked band.
But whenever I tried to go back, things just got worse again. So I'm still here.
Mary, ***promise*** me you won't tell anyone you've been up here? I don't want them to put pressure on me. If they know I've been talking to you, they'll want me to push myself more.
I don't know why, but I already know that it's just... ***different*** talking to you.
GAME ON

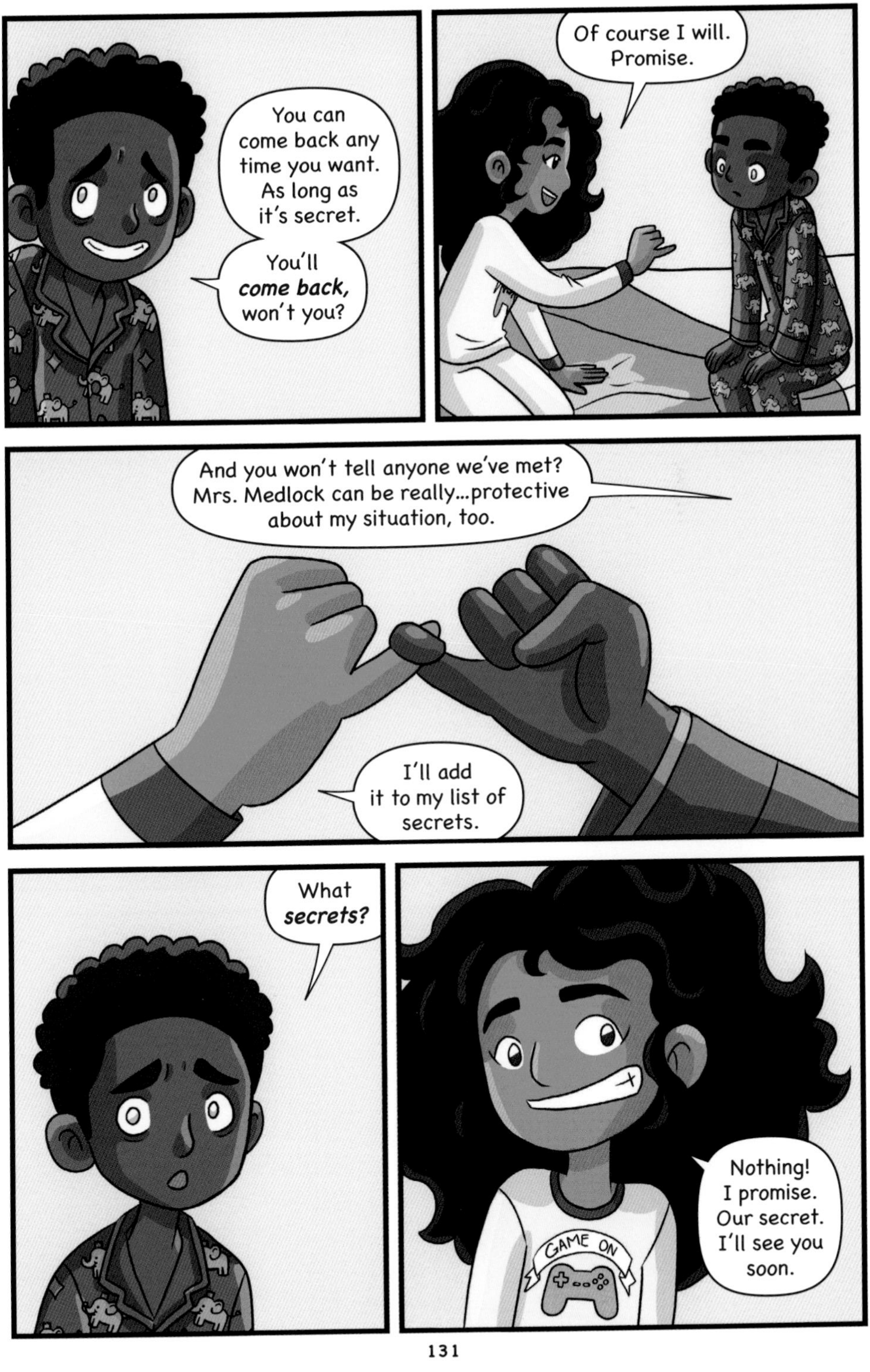
You can come back any time you want. As long as it's secret.
You'll ***come back,*** won't you?
Of course I will. Promise.
And you won't tell anyone we've met? Mrs. Medlock can be really...protective about my situation, too.
I'll add it to my list of secrets.
What ***secrets?***
Nothing! I promise. Our secret. I'll see you soon.
GAME ON

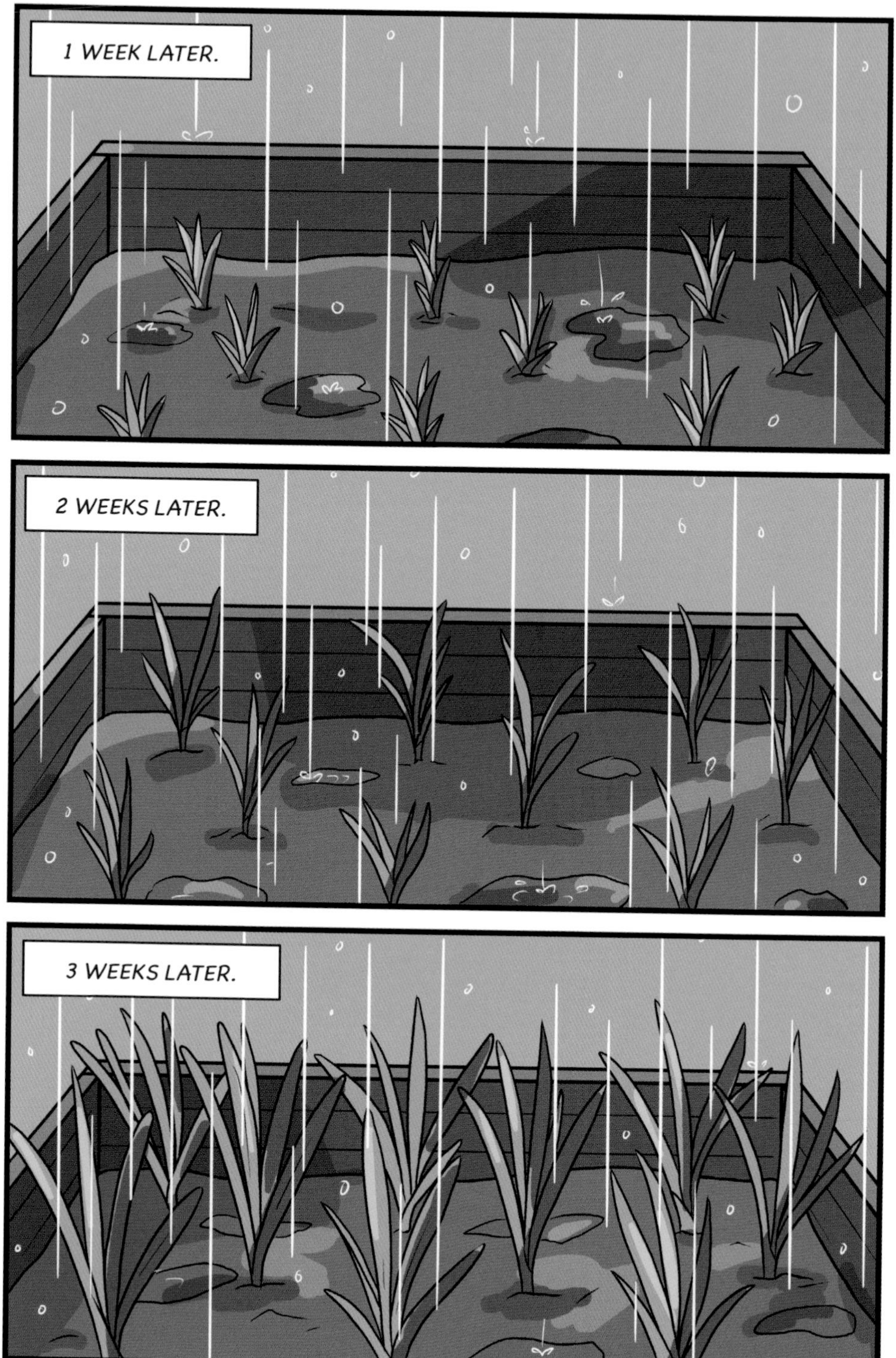
1 WEEK LATER.
2 WEEKS LATER.
3 WEEKS LATER.

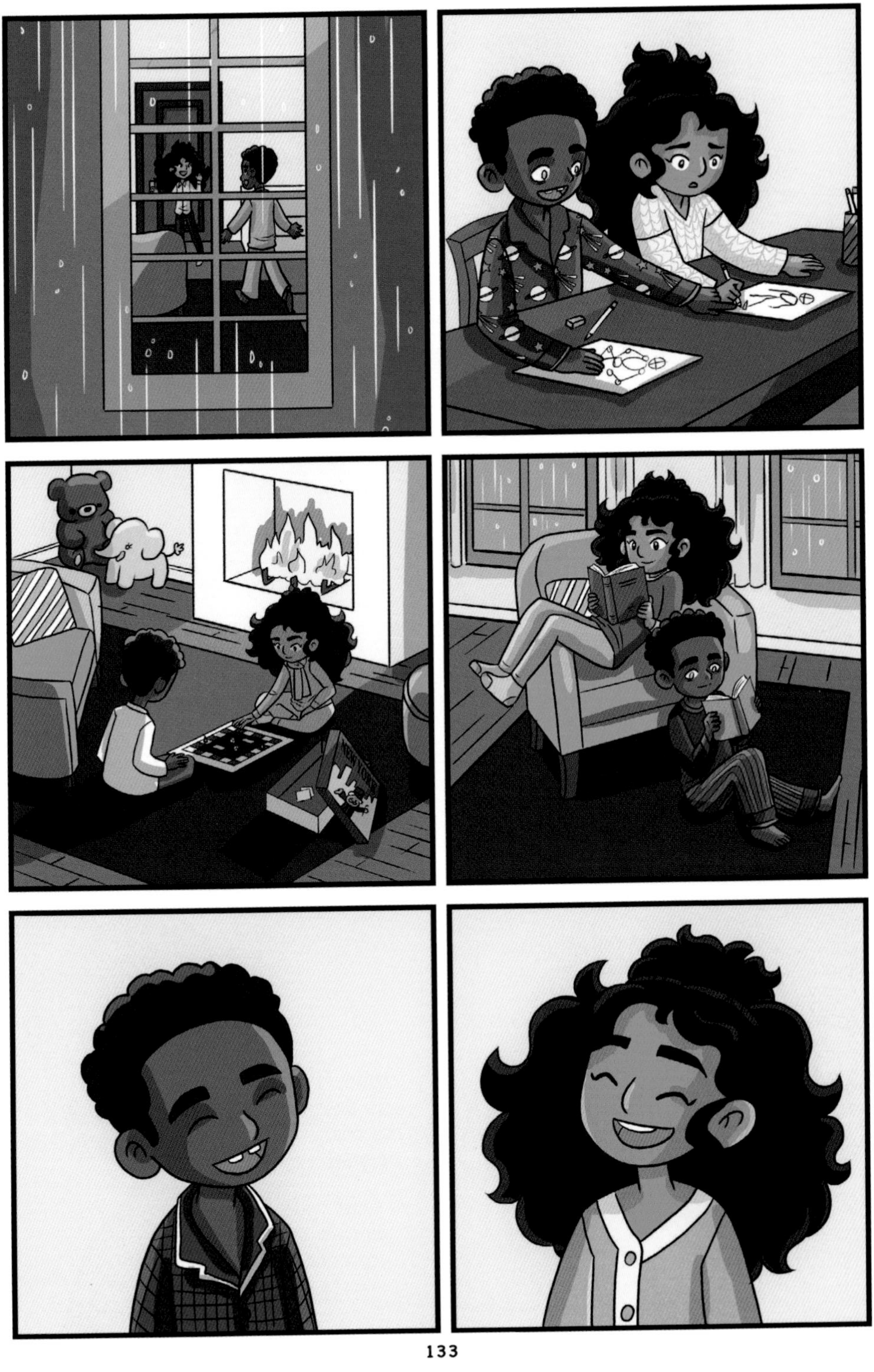
NEW YORK

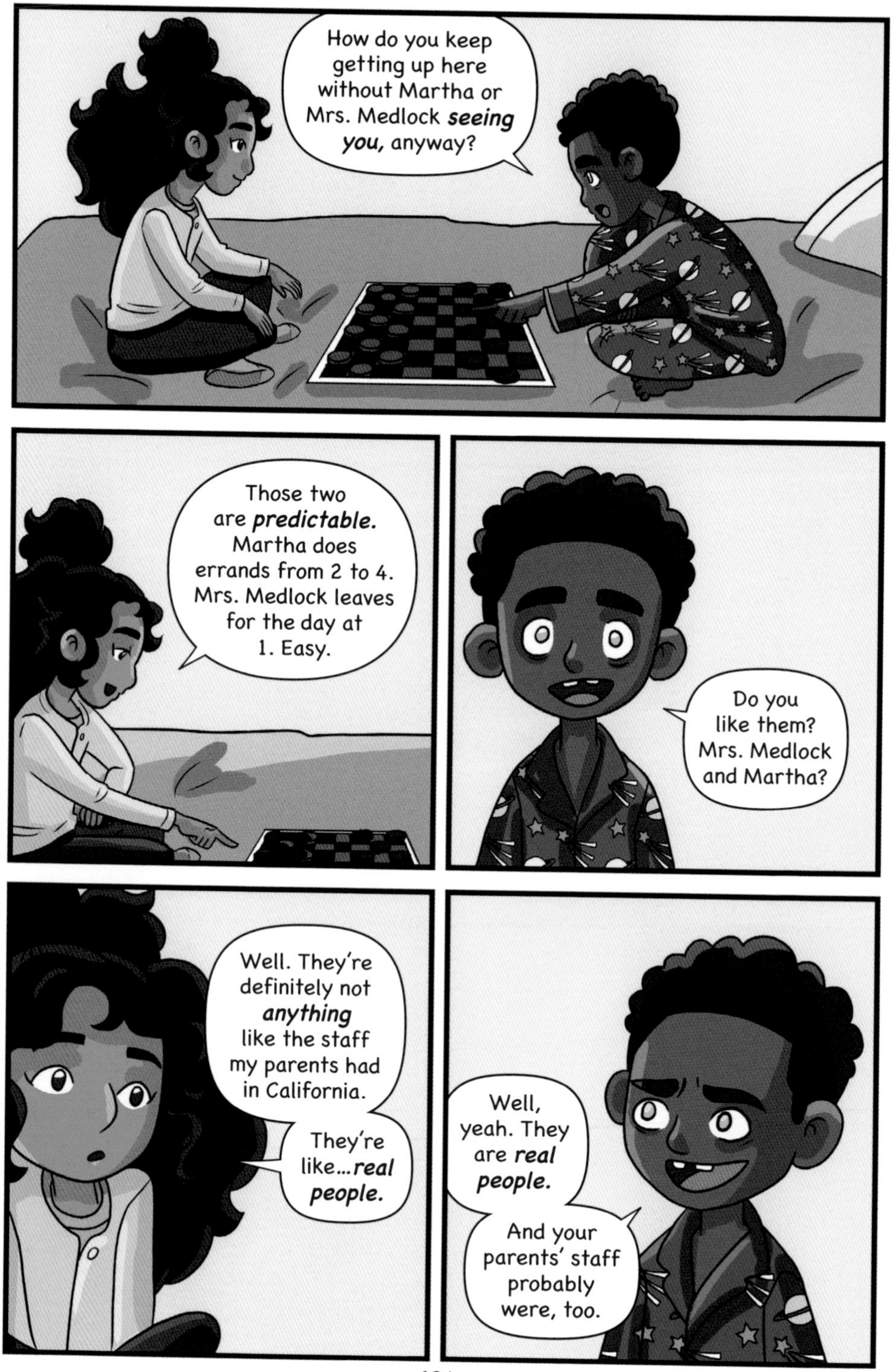
How do you keep getting up here without Martha or Mrs. Medlock *seeing you,* anyway?
Those two are *predictable.* Martha does errands from 2 to 4. Mrs. Medlock leaves for the day at 1. Easy.
Do you like them? Mrs. Medlock and Martha?
Well. They're definitely not *anything* like the staff my parents had in California.
They're like...*real people.*
Well, yeah. They are *real people.*
And your parents' staff probably were, too.

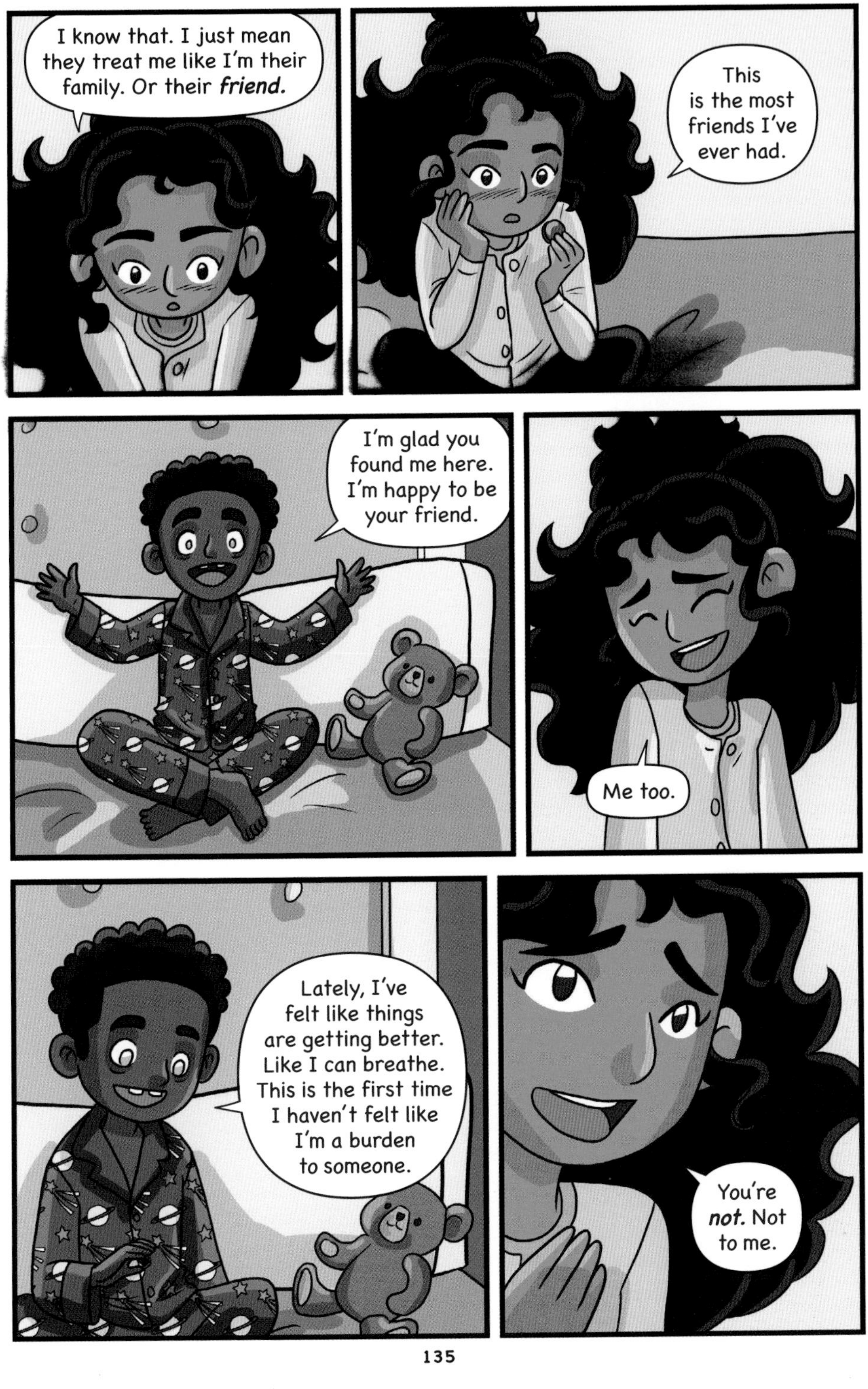
I know that. I just mean they treat me like I'm their family. Or their ***friend.***
This is the most friends I've ever had.
I'm glad you found me here. I'm happy to be your friend.
Me too.
Lately, I've felt like things are getting better. Like I can breathe. This is the first time I haven't felt like I'm a burden to someone.
You're ***not.*** Not to me.

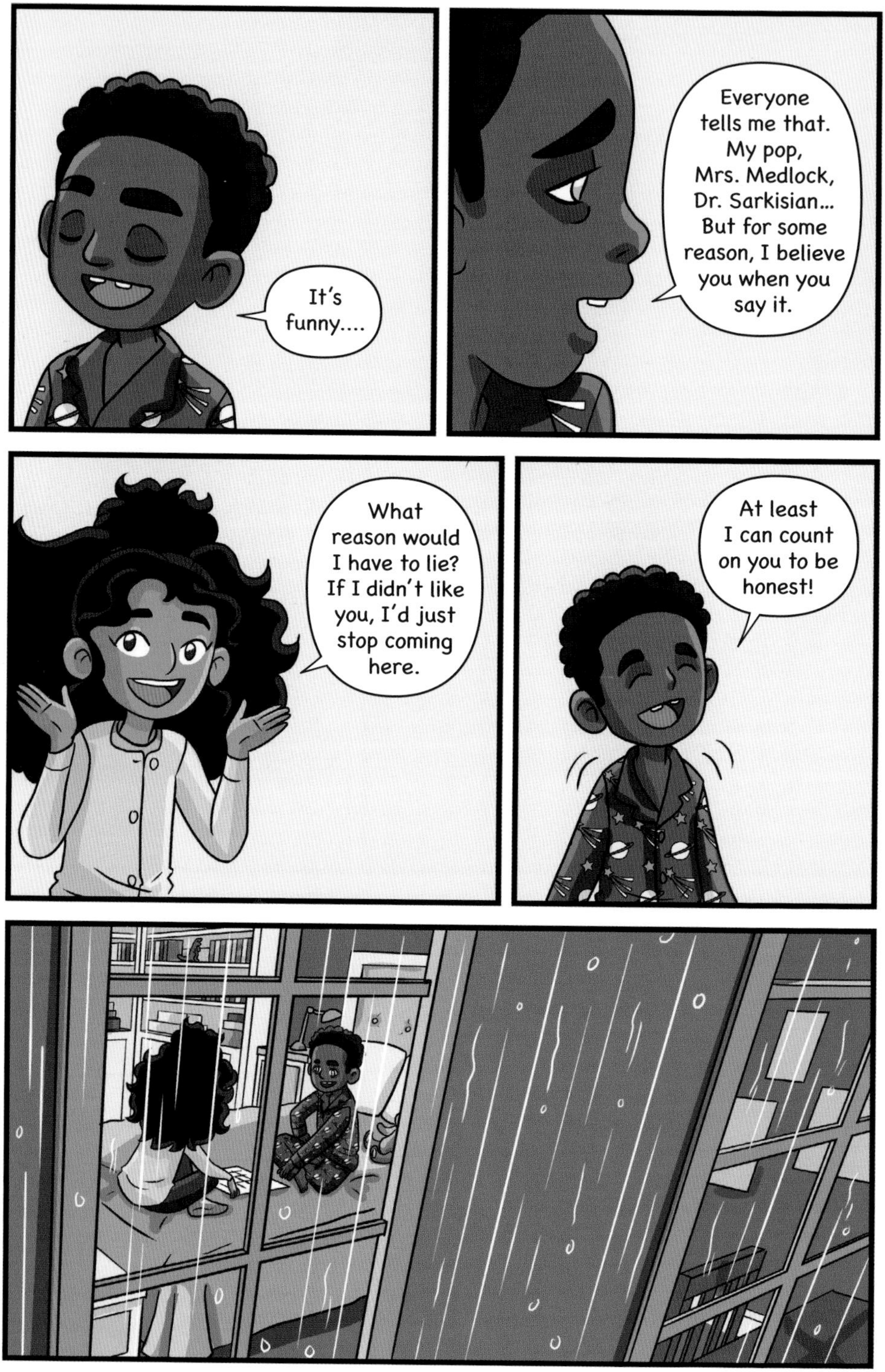
It's funny....
Everyone tells me that. My pop, Mrs. Medlock, Dr. Sarkisian... But for some reason, I believe you when you say it.
What reason would I have to lie? If I didn't like you, I'd just stop coming here.
At least I can count on you to be honest!

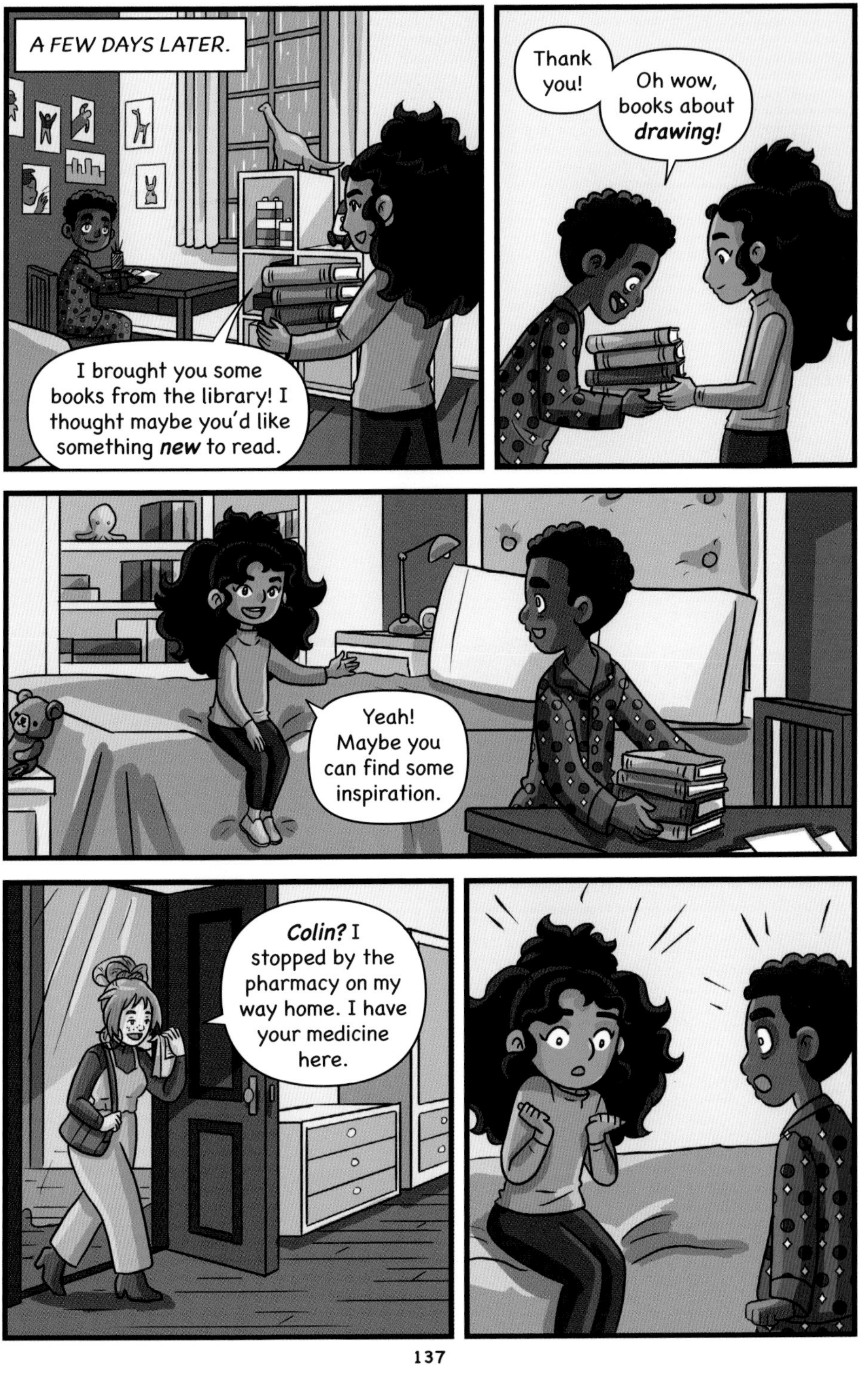
A FEW DAYS LATER.
I brought you some books from the library! I thought maybe you'd like something *new* to read.
Thank you!
Oh wow, books about *drawing!*
Yeah! Maybe you can find some inspiration.
Colin? I stopped by the pharmacy on my way home. I have your medicine here.

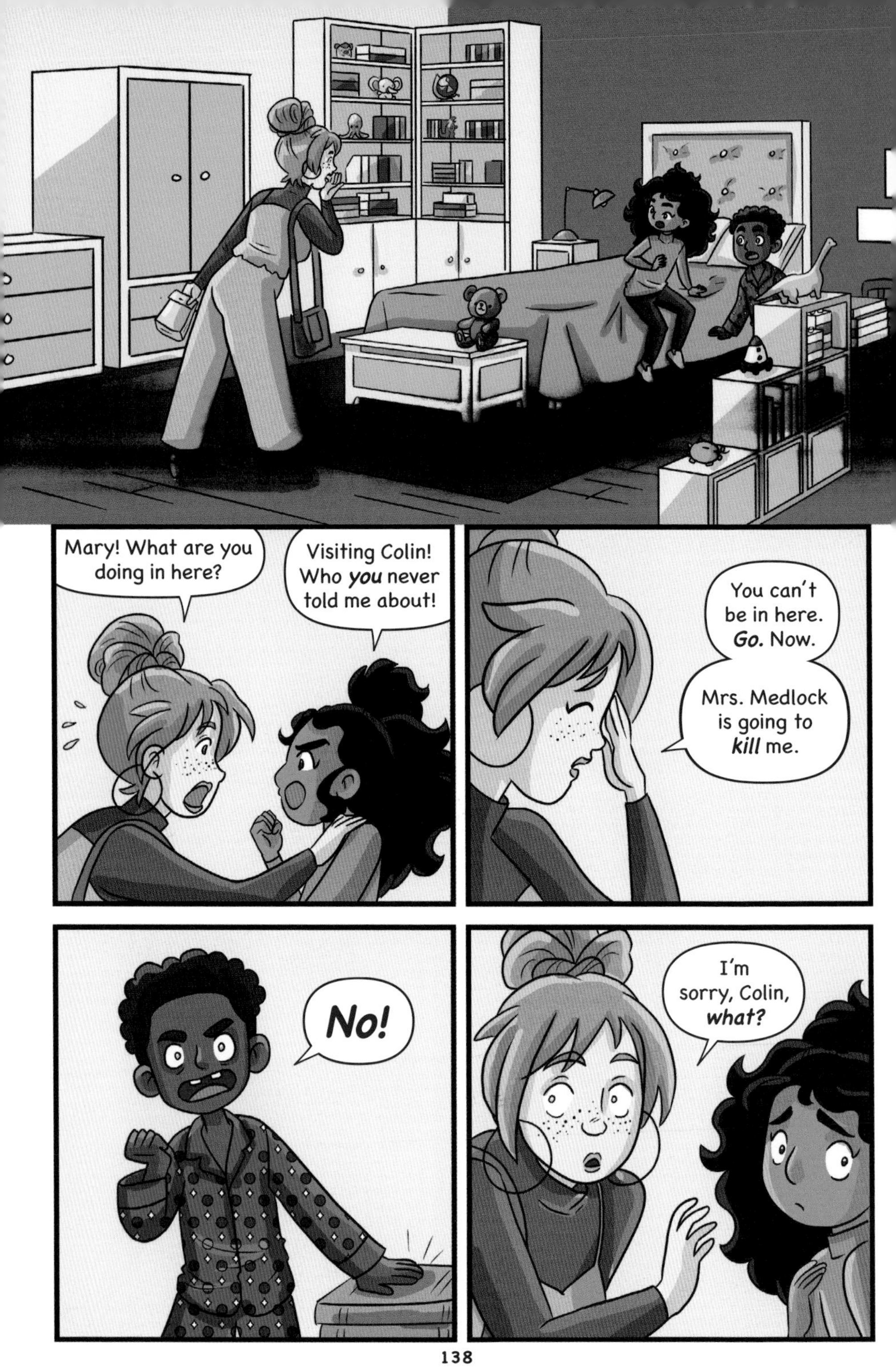

Mary! What are you doing in here?
Visiting Colin! Who *you* never told me about!
You can't be in here. **Go.** Now.
Mrs. Medlock is going to ***kill*** me.
No!
I'm sorry, Colin, ***what?***

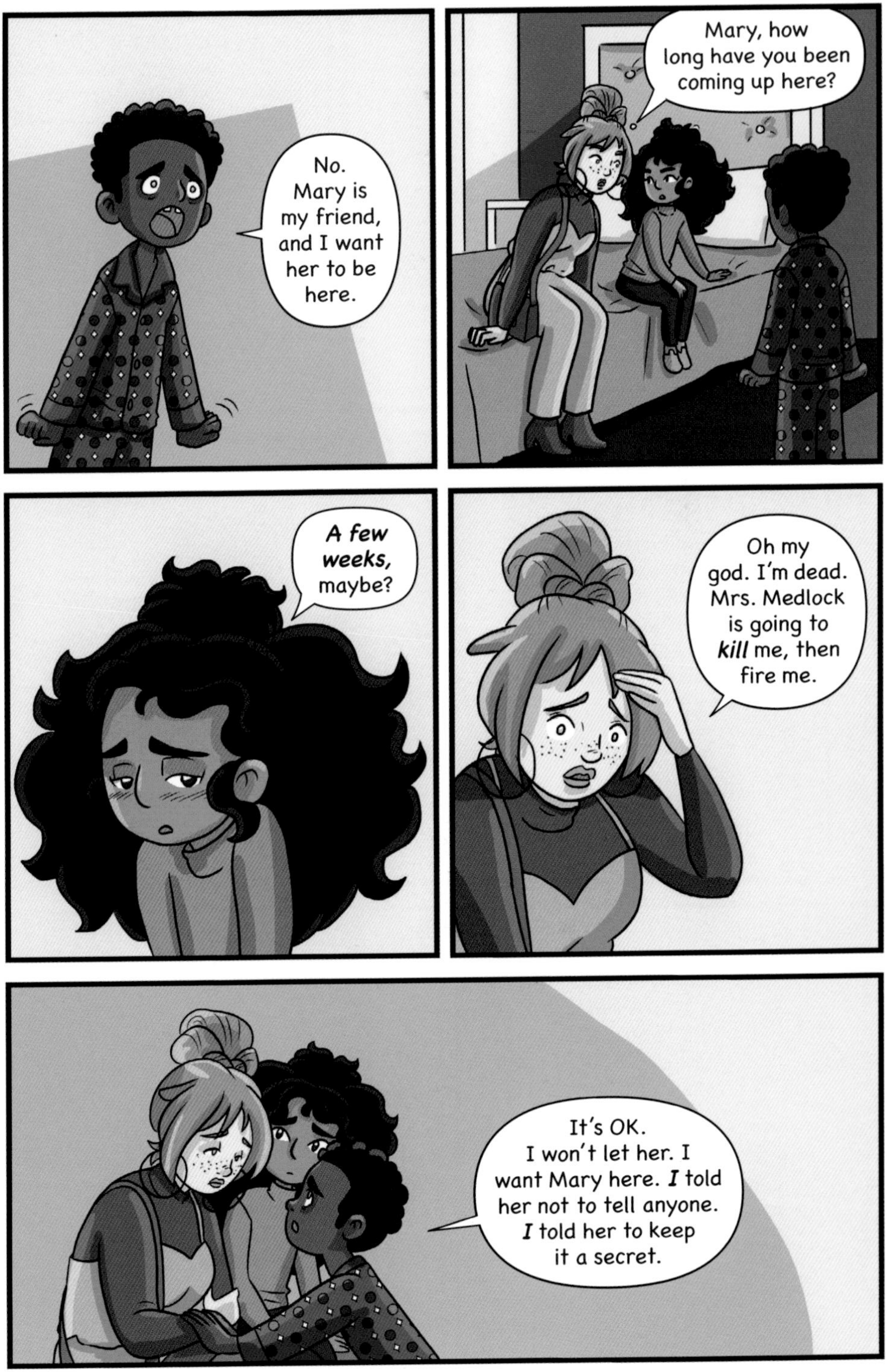
No.
Mary is my friend, and I want her to be here.
Mary, how long have you been coming up here?
A few weeks, maybe?
Oh my god. I'm dead. Mrs. Medlock is going to ***kill*** me, then fire me.
It's OK. I won't let her. I want Mary here. ***I*** told her not to tell anyone. ***I*** told her to keep it a secret.

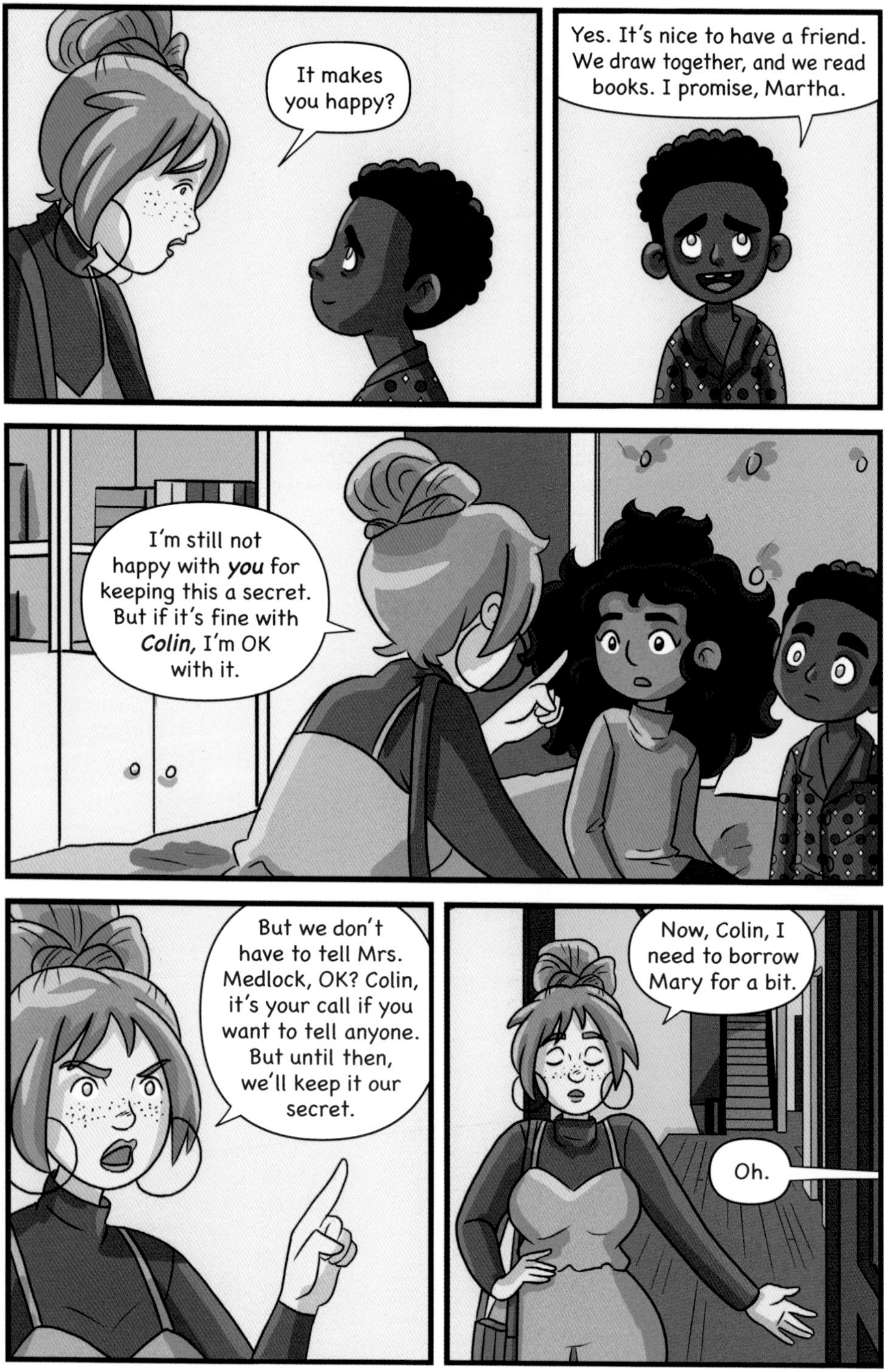

It makes you happy?
Yes. It's nice to have a friend. We draw together, and we read books. I promise, Martha.
I'm still not happy with *you* for keeping this a secret. But if it's fine with *Colin,* I'm OK with it.
But we don't have to tell Mrs. Medlock, OK? Colin, it's your call if you want to tell anyone. But until then, we'll keep it our secret.
Now, Colin, I need to borrow Mary for a bit.
Oh.

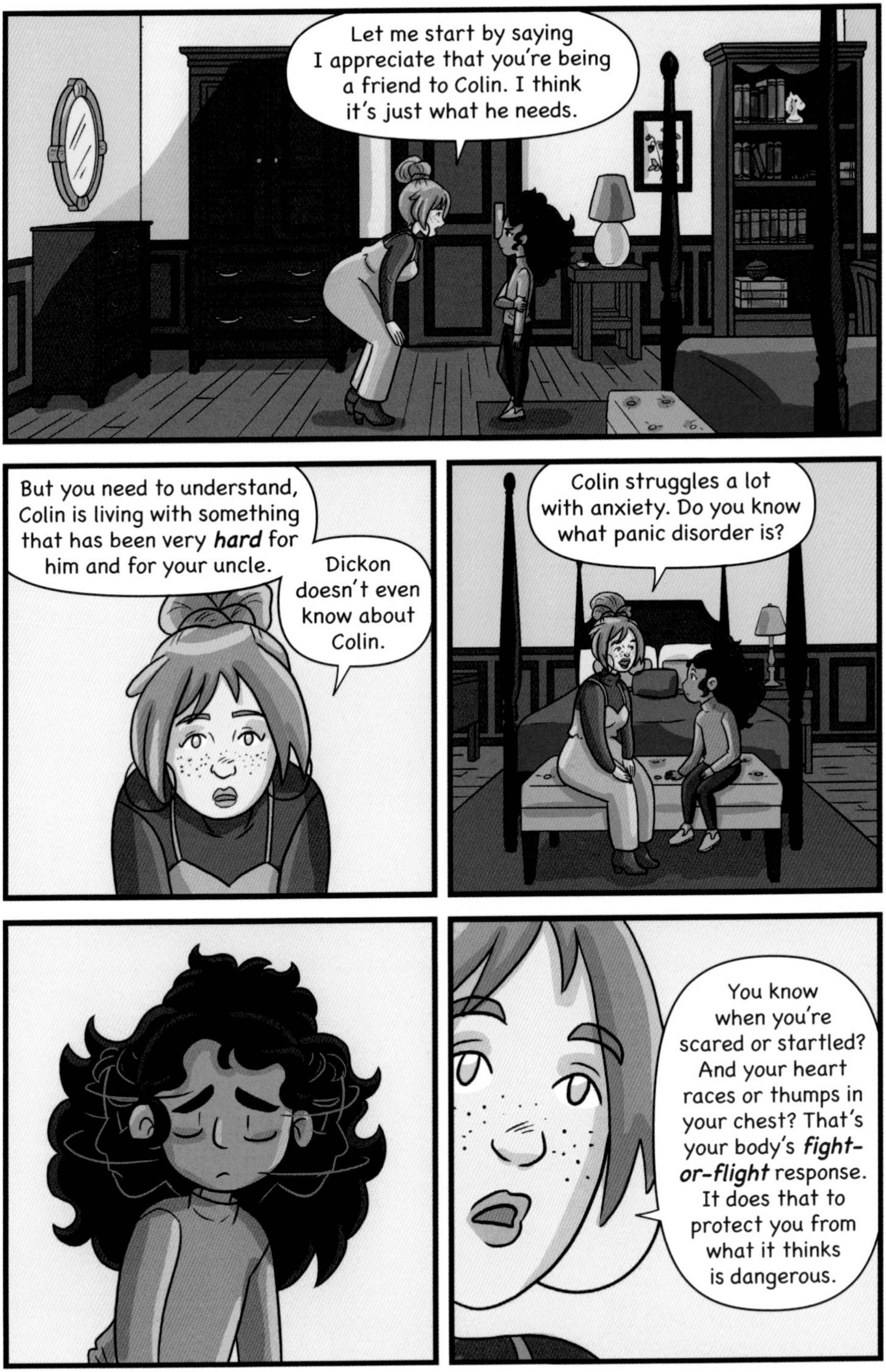
Let me start by saying I appreciate that you're being a friend to Colin. I think it's just what he needs.
But you need to understand, Colin is living with something that has been very ***hard*** for him and for your uncle.
Dickon doesn't even know about Colin.
Colin struggles a lot with anxiety. Do you know what panic disorder is?
You know when you're scared or startled? And your heart races or thumps in your chest? That's your body's ***fight-or-flight*** response. It does that to protect you from what it thinks is dangerous.

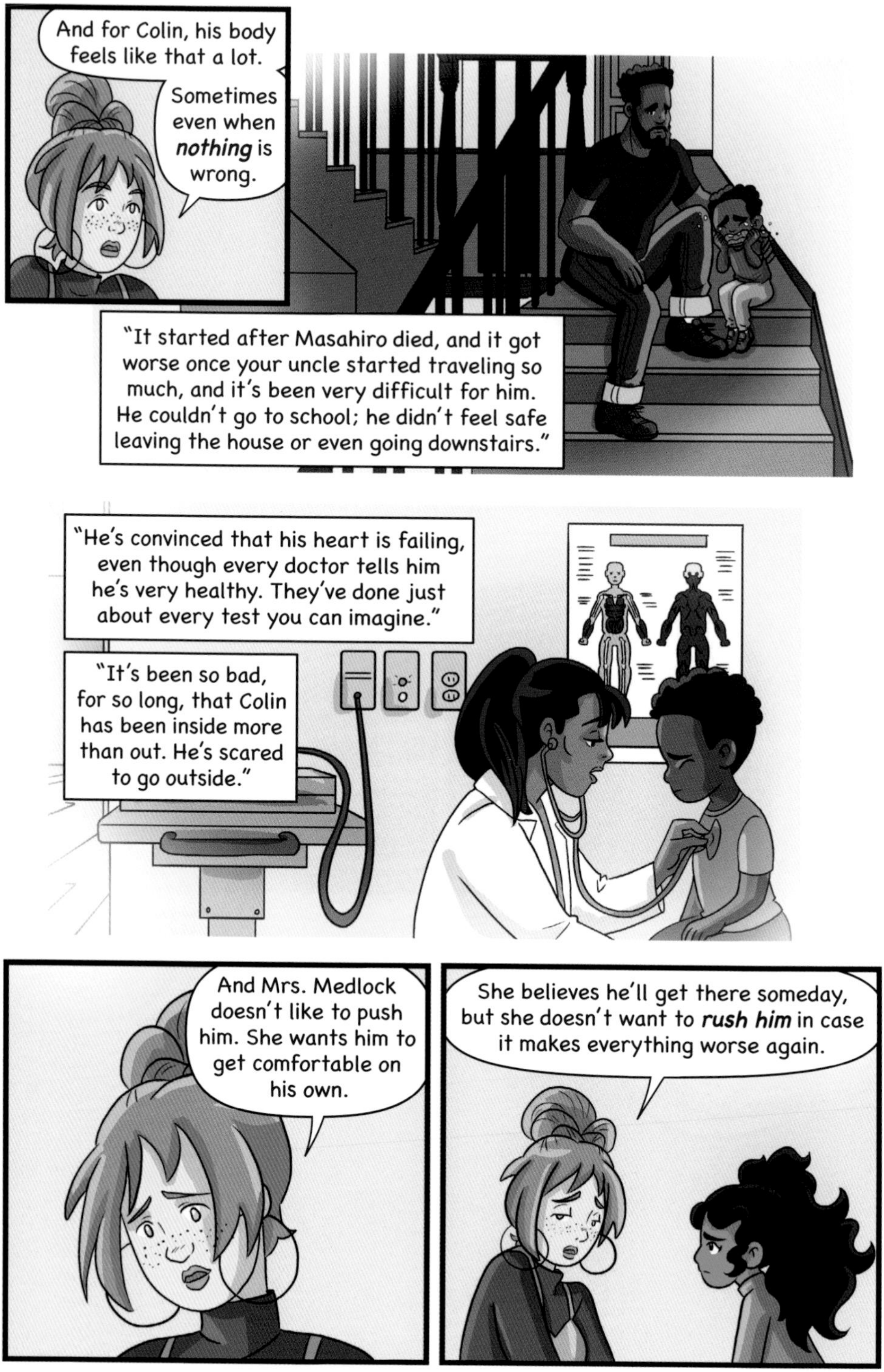
And for Colin, his body feels like that a lot.
Sometimes even when *nothing* is wrong.
"It started after Masahiro died, and it got worse once your uncle started traveling so much, and it's been very difficult for him. He couldn't go to school; he didn't feel safe leaving the house or even going downstairs."
"He's convinced that his heart is failing, even though every doctor tells him he's very healthy. They've done just about every test you can imagine."
"It's been so bad, for so long, that Colin has been inside more than out. He's scared to go outside."
And Mrs. Medlock doesn't like to push him. She wants him to get comfortable on his own.
She believes he'll get there someday, but she doesn't want to ***rush him*** in case it makes everything worse again.

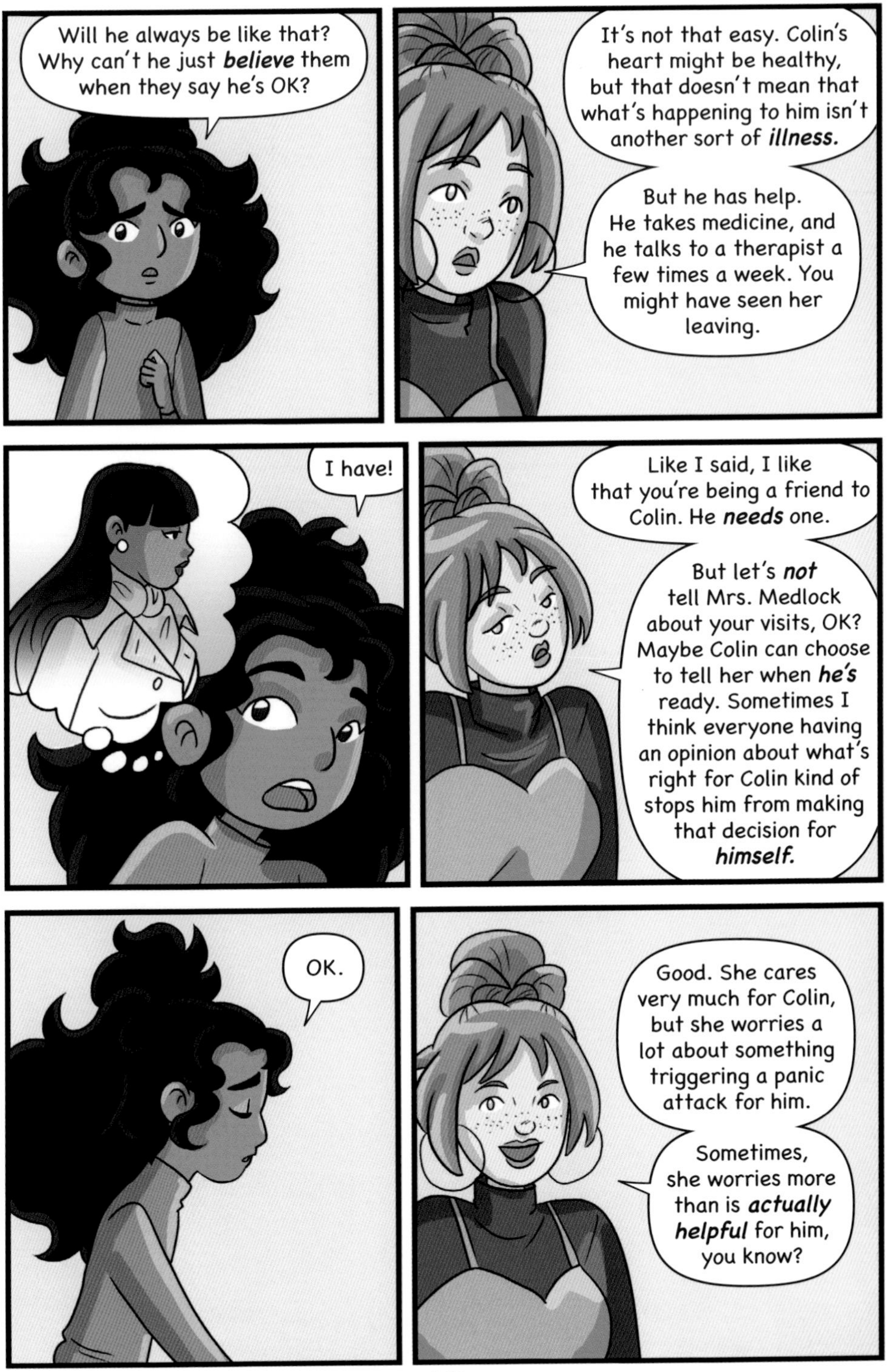
Will he always be like that? Why can't he just ***believe*** them when they say he's OK?
It's not that easy. Colin's heart might be healthy, but that doesn't mean that what's happening to him isn't another sort of ***illness.***
But he has help. He takes medicine, and he talks to a therapist a few times a week. You might have seen her leaving.
I have!
Like I said, I like that you're being a friend to Colin. He ***needs*** one.
But let's ***not*** tell Mrs. Medlock about your visits, OK? Maybe Colin can choose to tell her when ***he's*** ready. Sometimes I think everyone having an opinion about what's right for Colin kind of stops him from making that decision for ***himself.***
OK.
Good. She cares very much for Colin, but she worries a lot about something triggering a panic attack for him.
Sometimes, she worries more than is ***actually helpful*** for him, you know?

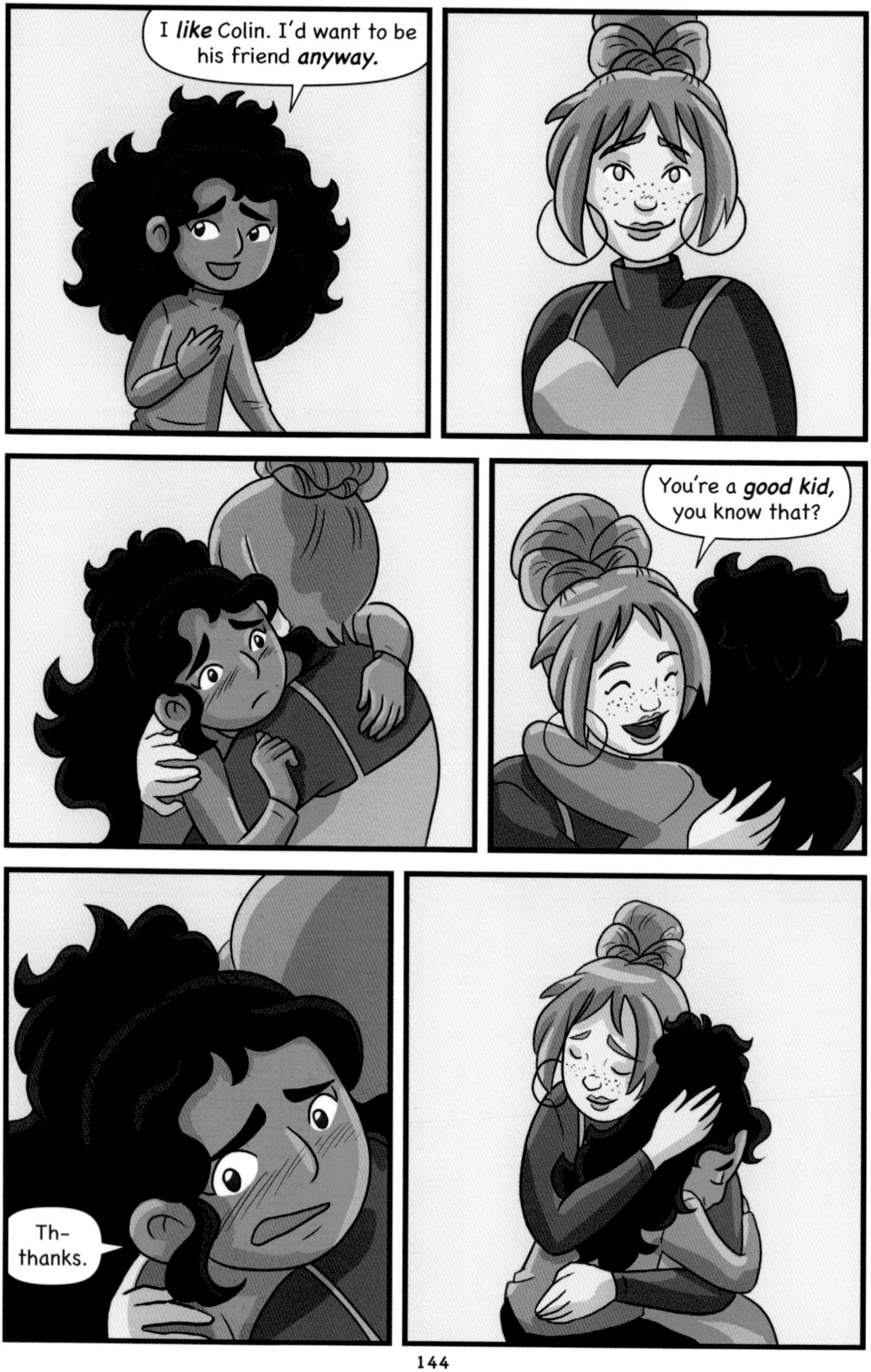
I *like* Colin. I'd want to be his friend ***anyway.***
You're a ***good kid,*** you know that?
Th-thanks.

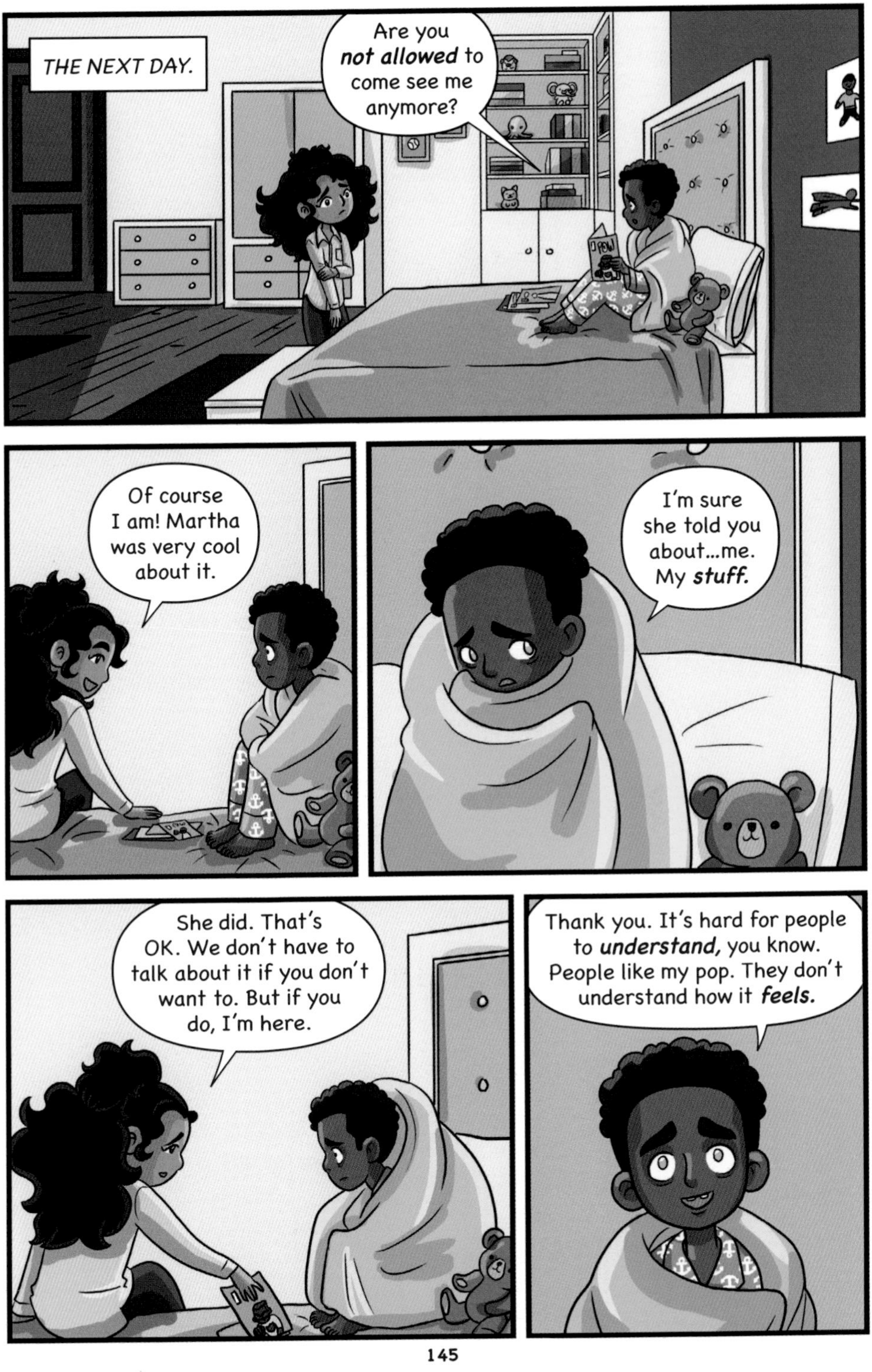
THE NEXT DAY.
Are you ***not allowed*** to come see me anymore?
Of course I am! Martha was very cool about it.
I'm sure she told you about...me. My ***stuff.***
She did. That's OK. We don't have to talk about it if you don't want to. But if you do, I'm here.
Thank you. It's hard for people to ***understand,*** you know. People like my pop. They don't understand how it ***feels.***

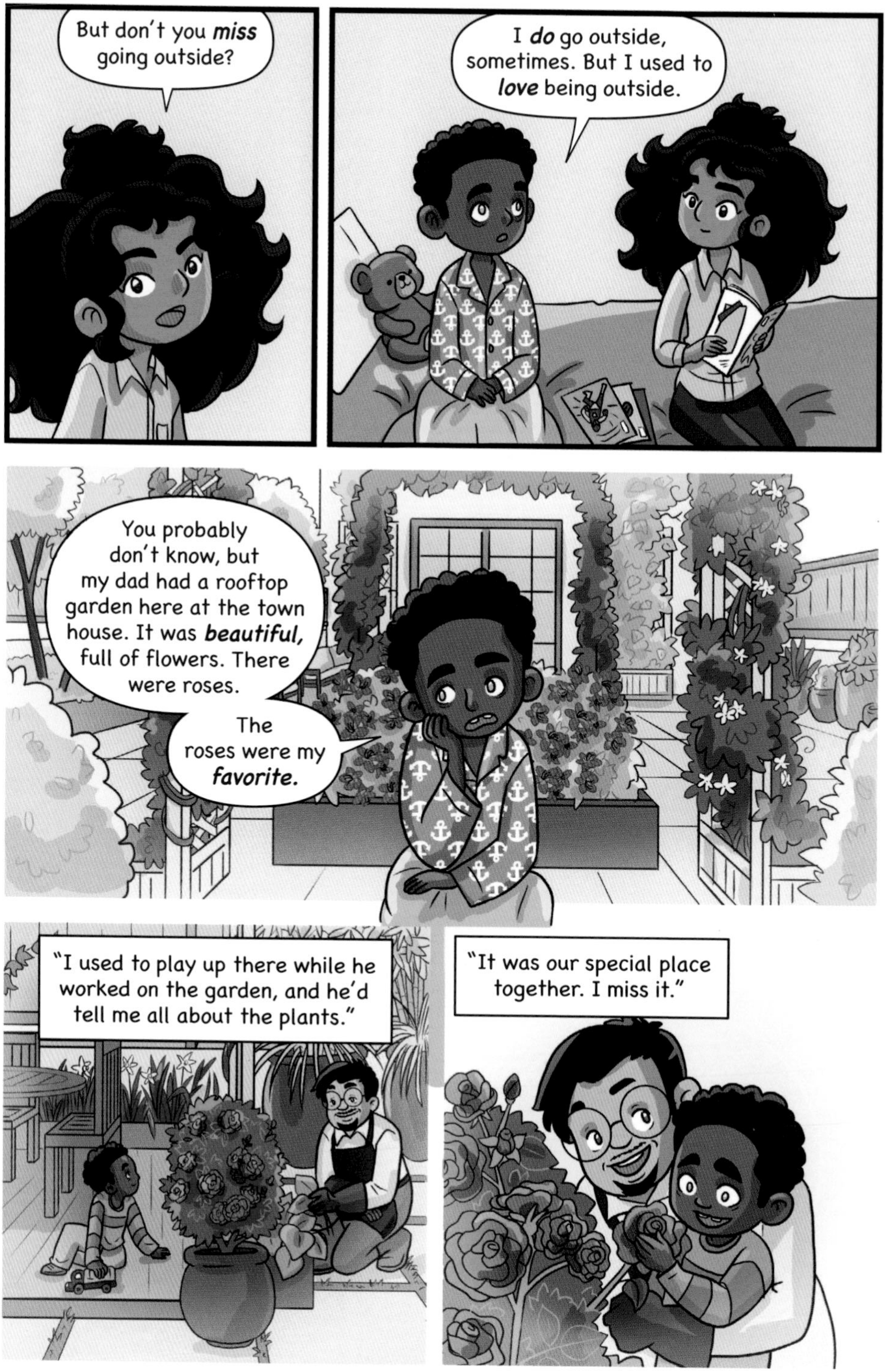

But don't you *miss* going outside?
I *do* go outside, sometimes. But I used to *love* being outside.
You probably don't know, but my dad had a rooftop garden here at the town house. It was *beautiful,* full of flowers. There were roses.
The roses were my *favorite.*
"I used to play up there while he worked on the garden, and he'd tell me all about the plants."
"It was our special place together. I miss it."

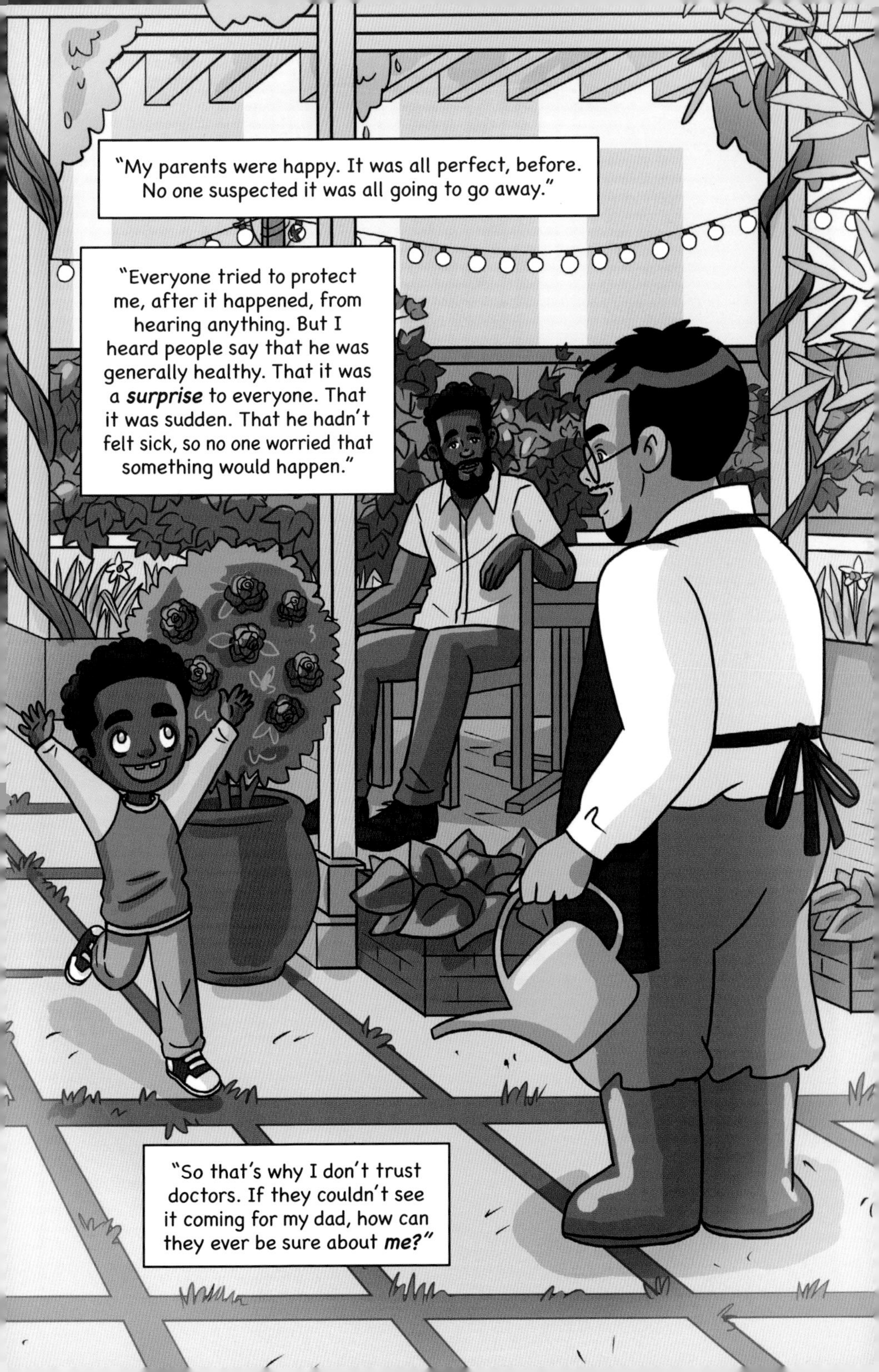
"My parents were happy. It was all perfect, before. No one suspected it was all going to go away."
"Everyone tried to protect me, after it happened, from hearing anything. But I heard people say that he was generally healthy. That it was a ***surprise*** to everyone. That it was sudden. That he hadn't felt sick, so no one worried that something would happen."
"So that's why I don't trust doctors. If they couldn't see it coming for my dad, how can they ever be sure about ***me?***"

After...after it happened, my pop locked the garden away. And now it's probably all dead and gone forever.

Colin...I have to tell you something.

I've **been there.** To the garden. I found the key and I've been going up there with a boy who lives next door. His name is Dickon.

We're not **hurting** it—we're bringing it back to life! It just made me so sad, to think of it up there, wasting away.

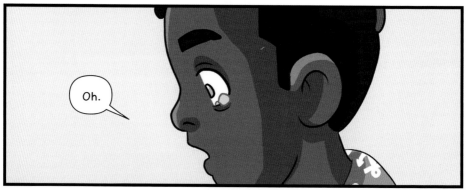

Oh.

Please don't be upset! I would have told you sooner, but I've been keeping it a secret from everyone. I can't let Martha or Mrs. Medlock find out, or they'll tell Uncle Archie, and he'll stop us!

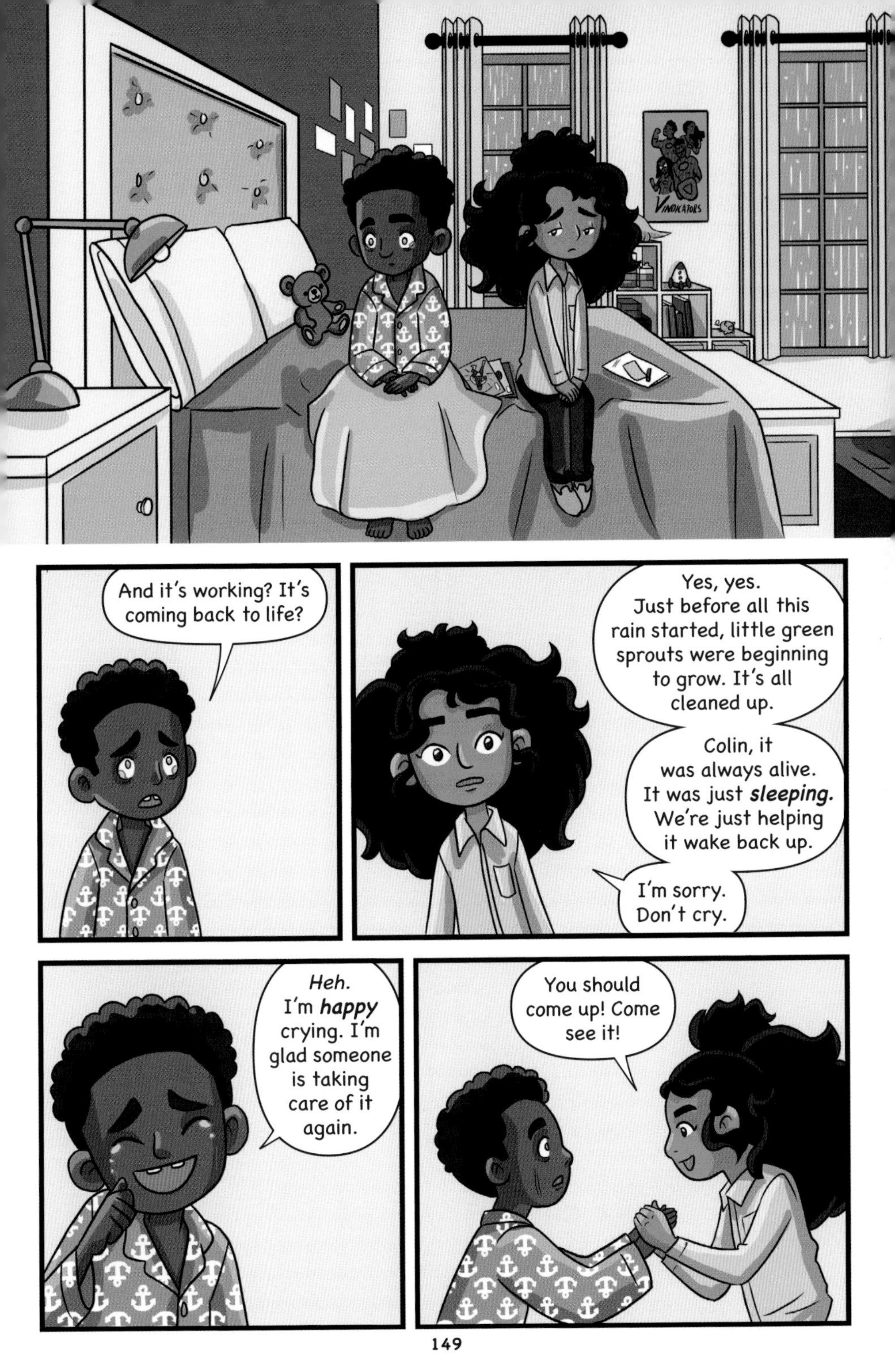
VINDICATORS
And it's working? It's coming back to life?
Yes, yes. Just before all this rain started, little green sprouts were beginning to grow. It's all cleaned up.
Colin, it was always alive. It was just *sleeping.* We're just helping it wake back up.
I'm sorry. Don't cry.
Heh. I'm ***happy*** crying. I'm glad someone is taking care of it again.
You should come up! Come see it!

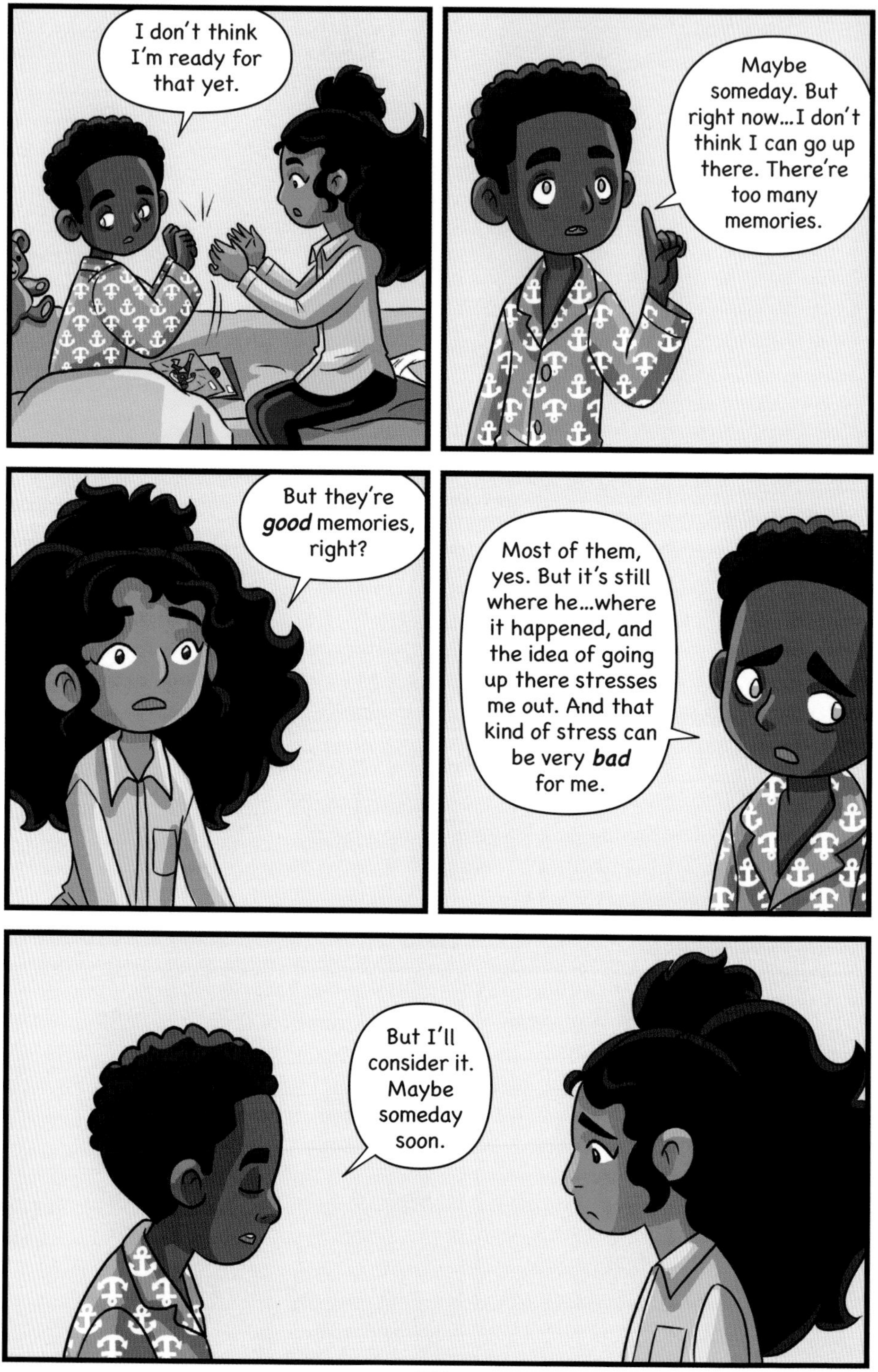
I don't think I'm ready for that yet.
Maybe someday. But right now...I don't think I can go up there. There're too many memories.
But they're *good* memories, right?
Most of them, yes. But it's still where he...where it happened, and the idea of going up there stresses me out. And that kind of stress can be very *bad* for me.
But I'll consider it. Maybe someday soon.

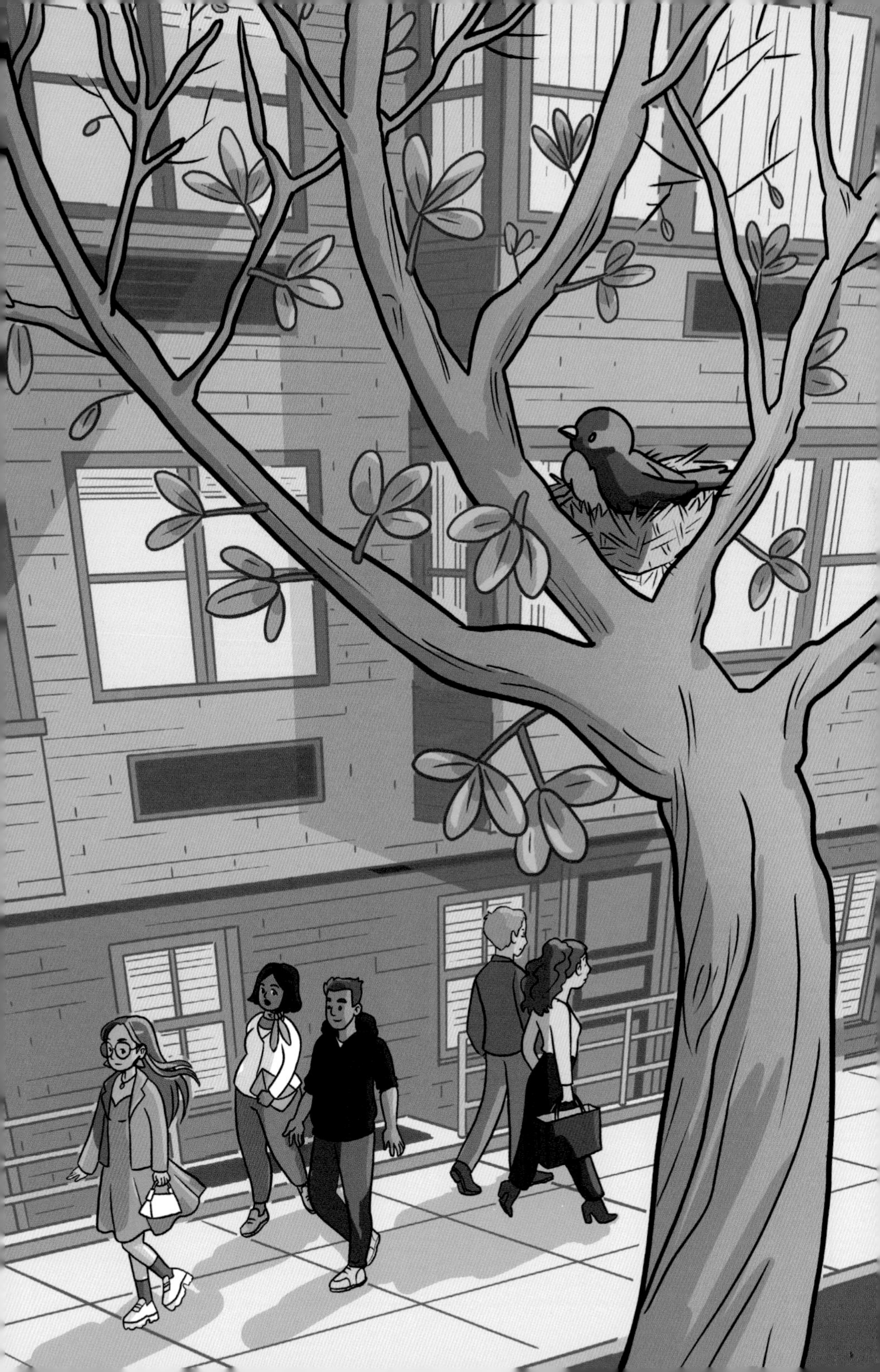

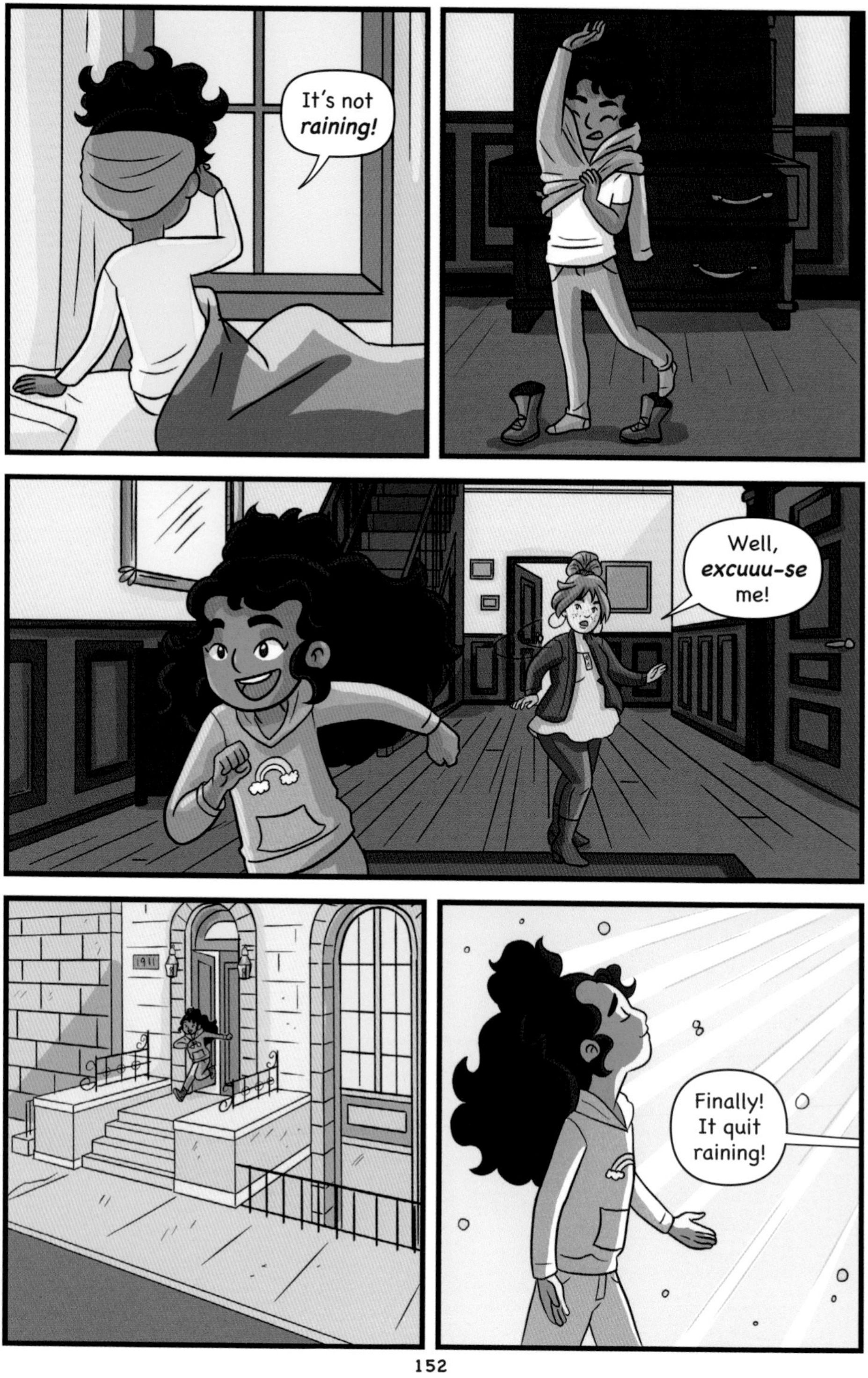
It's not *raining!*
Well, *excuuu-se* me!
1911
Finally! It quit raining!

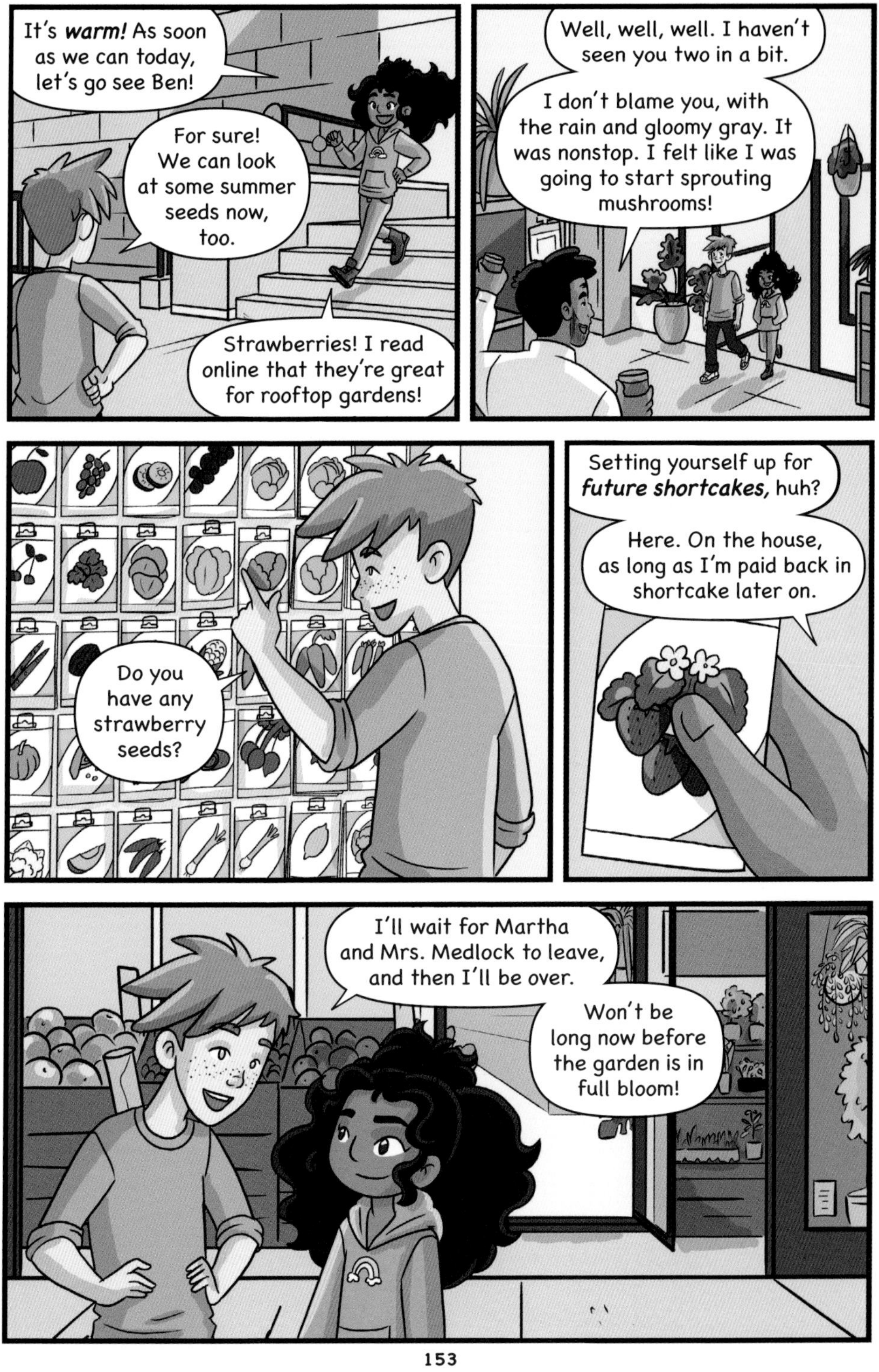
It's ***warm!*** As soon as we can today, let's go see Ben!
For sure! We can look at some summer seeds now, too.
Strawberries! I read online that they're great for rooftop gardens!
Well, well, well. I haven't seen you two in a bit.
I don't blame you, with the rain and gloomy gray. It was nonstop. I felt like I was going to start sprouting mushrooms!
Do you have any strawberry seeds?
Setting yourself up for ***future shortcakes,*** huh?
Here. On the house, as long as I'm paid back in shortcake later on.
I'll wait for Martha and Mrs. Medlock to leave, and then I'll be over.
Won't be long now before the garden is in full bloom!

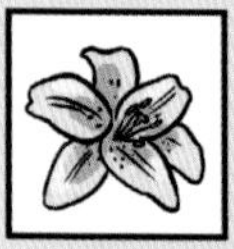

The_Secret_Garden

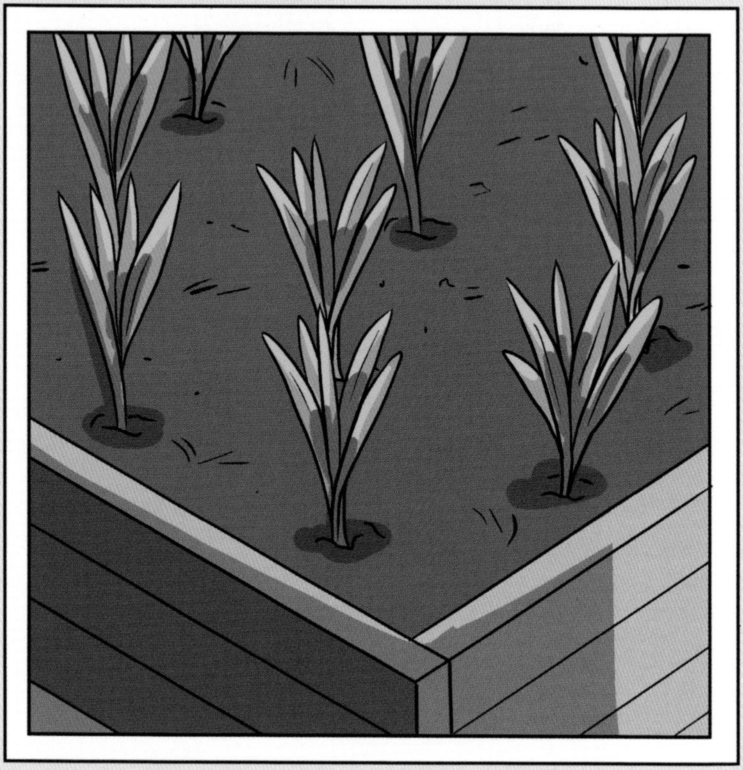

The_Secret_Garden Coming soon!!! 🌱🌱🌱🌱🌱🌱🌱🌱🌱

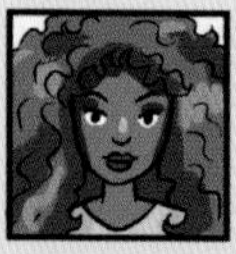

Pot_It_Like_Its_Hottt

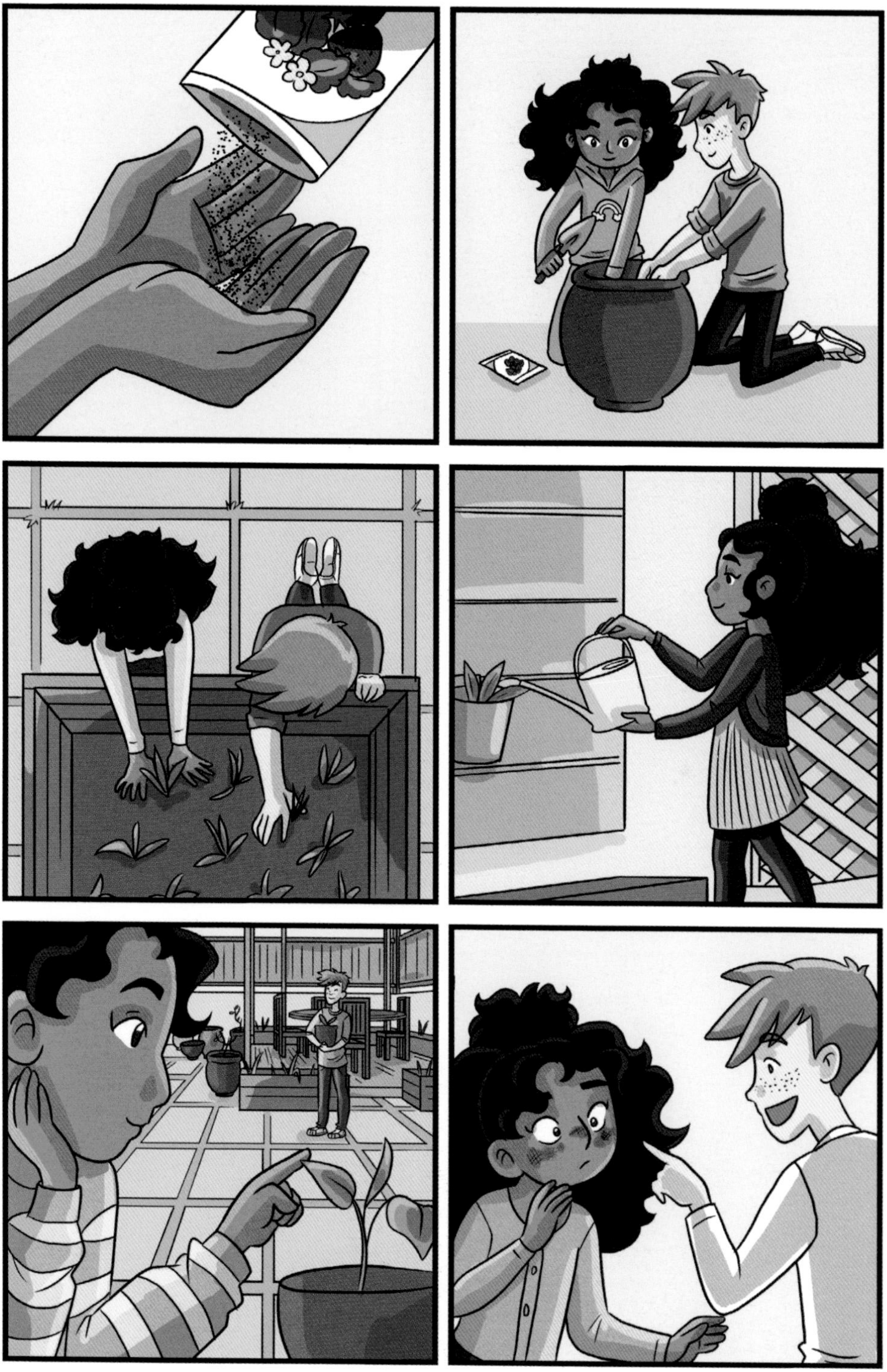

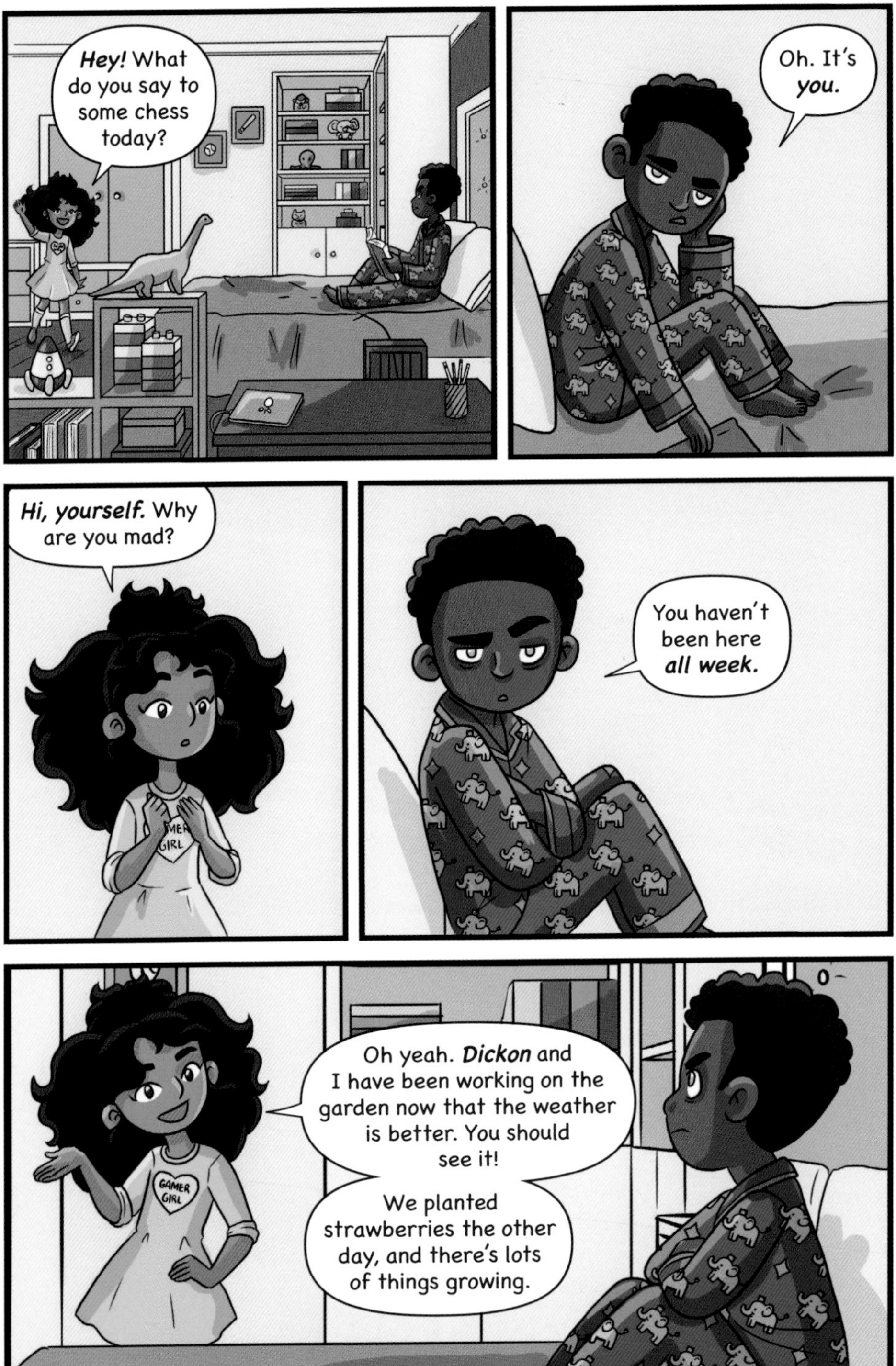
Hey! What do you say to some chess today?
Oh. It's you.
Hi, yourself. Why are you mad?
You haven't been here all week.
Oh yeah. Dickon and I have been working on the garden now that the weather is better. You should see it!
We planted strawberries the other day, and there's lots of things growing.
GAMER GIRL
O-

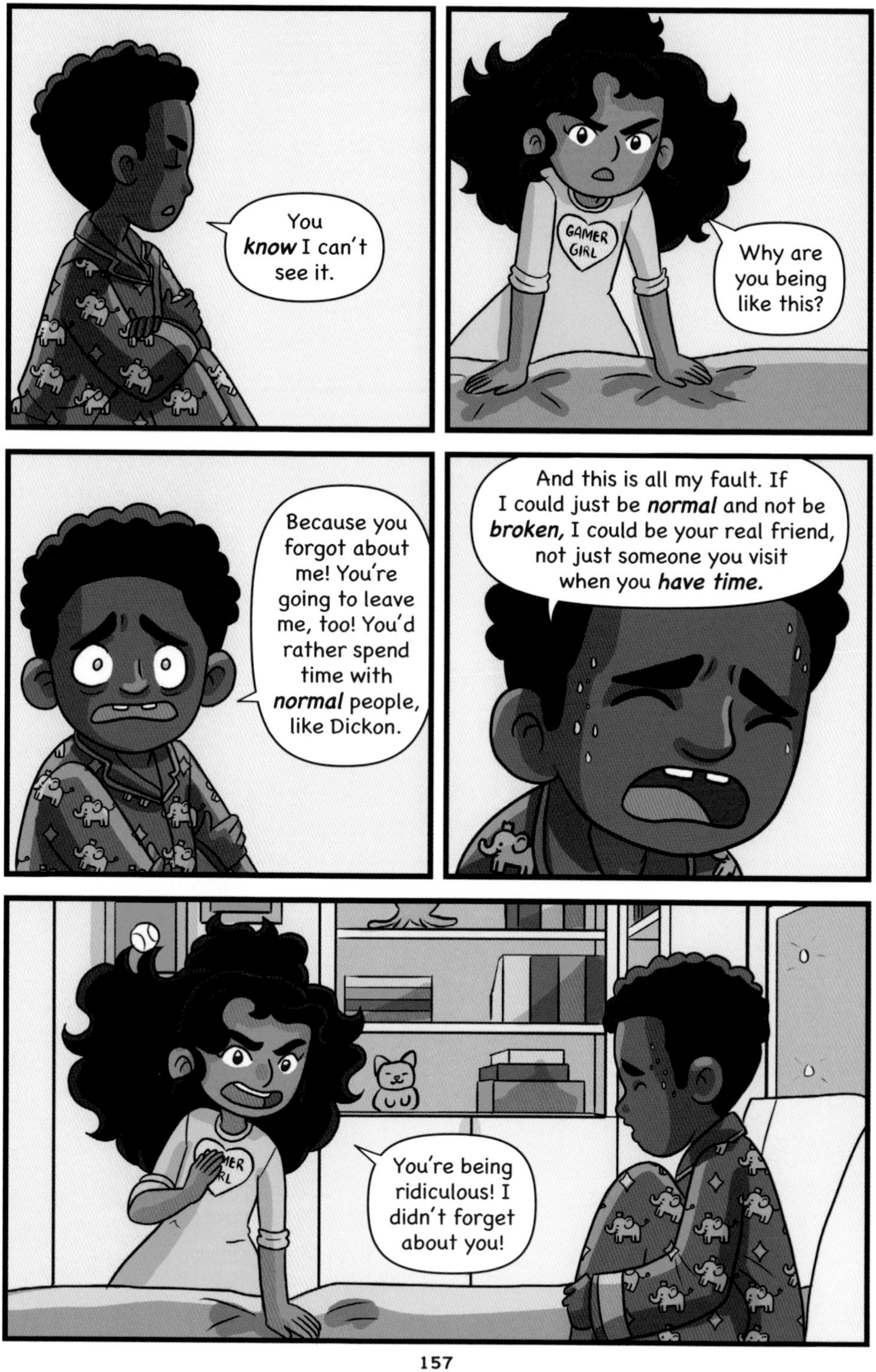
You *know* I can't see it.
Why are you being like this?
Because you forgot about me! You're going to leave me, too! You'd rather spend time with *normal* people, like Dickon.
And this is all my fault. If I could just be *normal* and not be *broken,* I could be your real friend, not just someone you visit when you *have time.*
You're being ridiculous! I didn't forget about you!

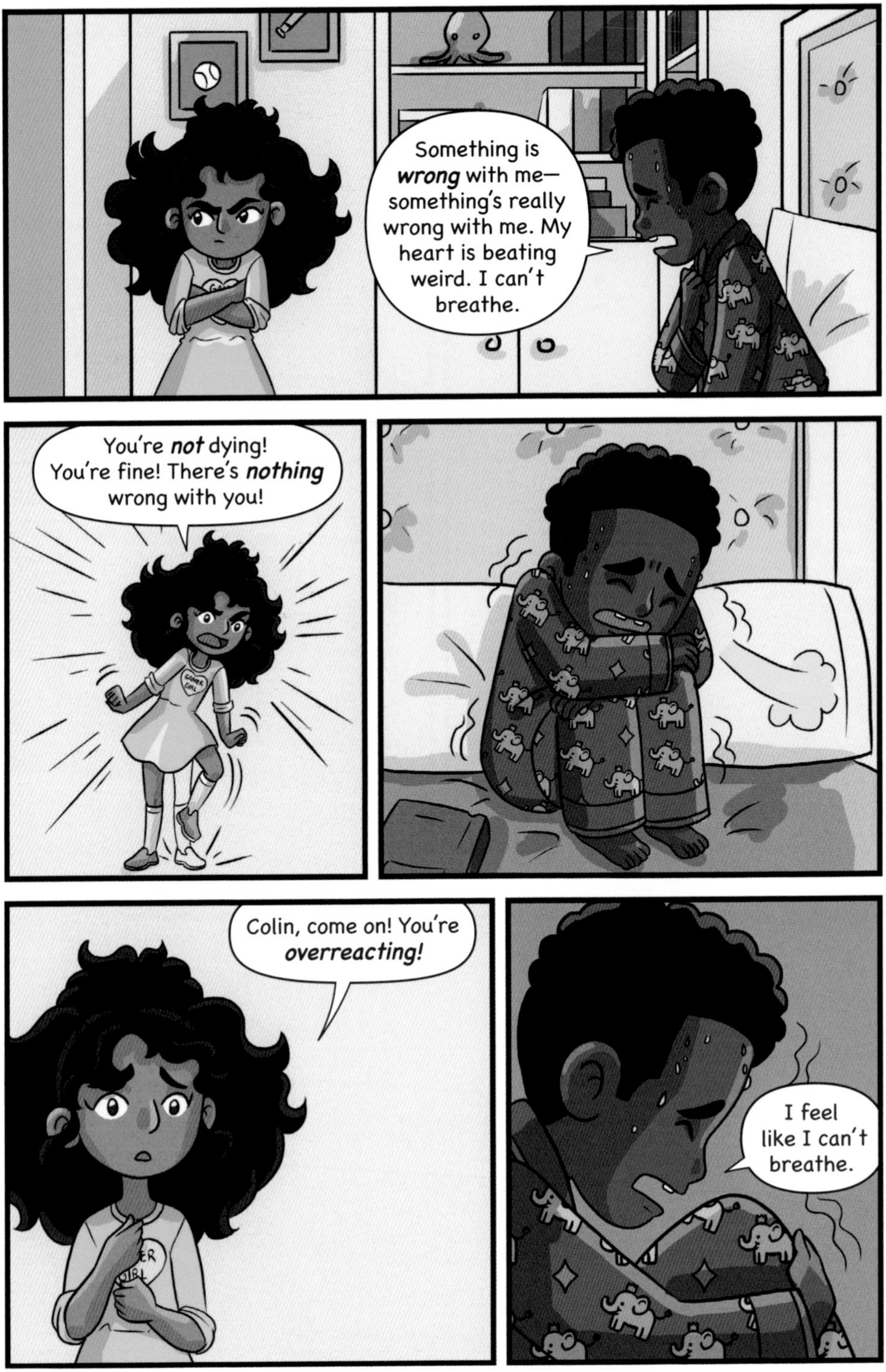
Something is *wrong* with me—something's really wrong with me. My heart is beating weird. I can't breathe.
You're *not* dying! You're fine! There's *nothing* wrong with you!
Colin, come on! You're *overreacting!*
I feel like I can't breathe.

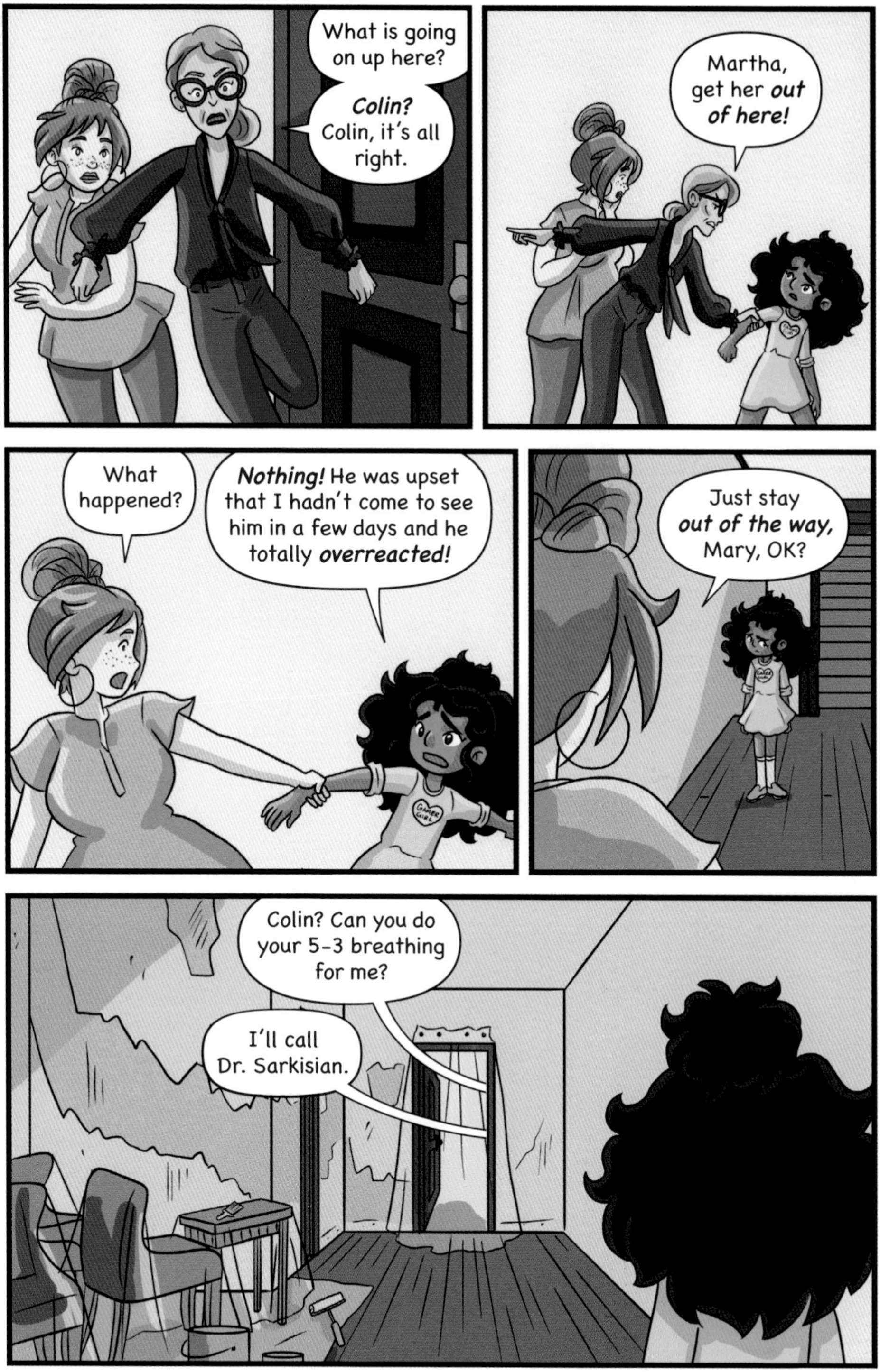
What is going on up here?
Colin? Colin, it's all right.
Martha, get her ***out of here!***
What happened?
Nothing! He was upset that I hadn't come to see him in a few days and he totally ***overreacted!***
Just stay ***out of the way,*** Mary, OK?
Colin? Can you do your 5-3 breathing for me?
I'll call Dr. Sarkisian.

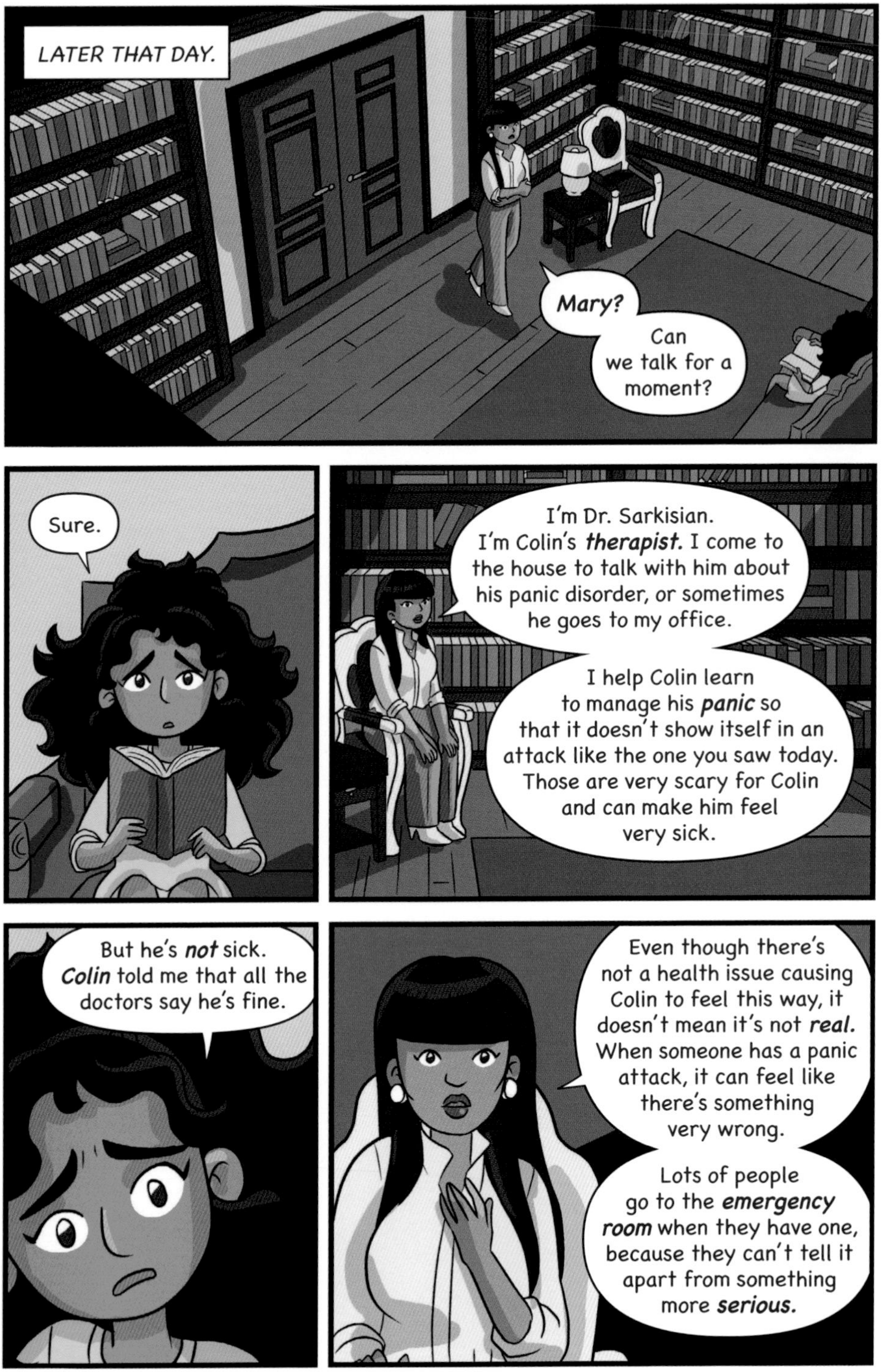
LATER THAT DAY.
Mary?
Can we talk for a moment?
Sure.
I'm Dr. Sarkisian. I'm Colin's therapist. I come to the house to talk with him about his panic disorder, or sometimes he goes to my office.
I help Colin learn to manage his panic so that it doesn't show itself in an attack like the one you saw today. Those are very scary for Colin and can make him feel very sick.
But he's not sick. Colin told me that all the doctors say he's fine.
Even though there's not a health issue causing Colin to feel this way, it doesn't mean it's not real. When someone has a panic attack, it can feel like there's something very wrong.
Lots of people go to the emergency room when they have one, because they can't tell it apart from something more serious.

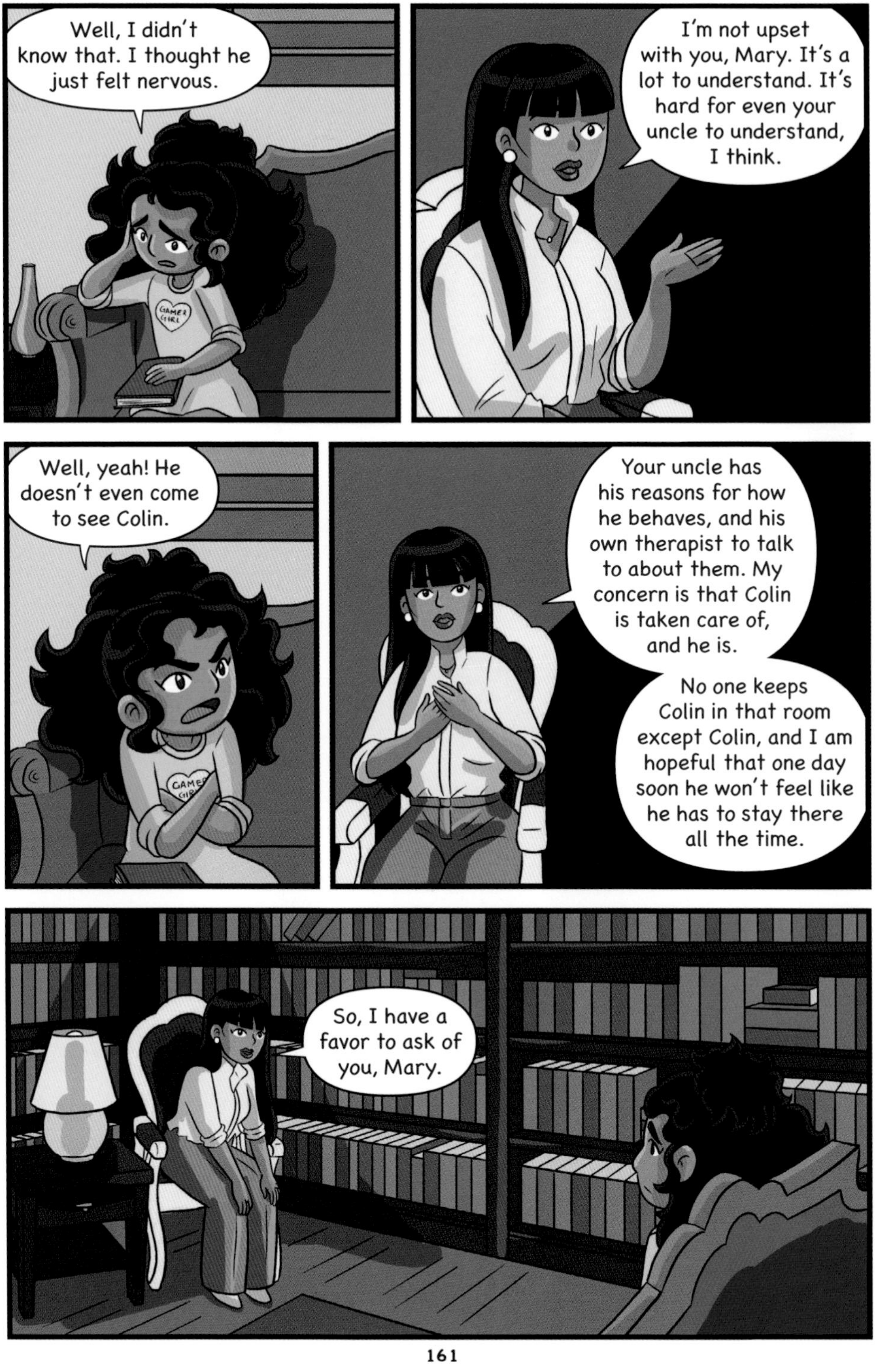
Well, I didn't know that. I thought he just felt nervous.
I'm not upset with you, Mary. It's a lot to understand. It's hard for even your uncle to understand, I think.
GAMER GIRL
Well, yeah! He doesn't even come to see Colin.
Your uncle has his reasons for how he behaves, and his own therapist to talk to about them. My concern is that Colin is taken care of, and he is.
No one keeps Colin in that room except Colin, and I am hopeful that one day soon he won't feel like he has to stay there all the time.
So, I have a favor to ask of you, Mary.

Colin let me know that you've been up working in his *dad's garden.*

Don't worry. I won't tell Mrs. Medlock or Martha. Colin stressed the secrecy of the situation to me.

I think it could be a nice thing for Colin to **help** you and your friend out in the garden. Would you be open to that?

I invited him to! That's what set this whole thing off! He says he *can't* do it.

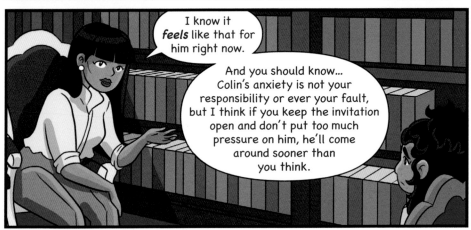

I know it **feels** like that for him right now.

And you should know... Colin's anxiety is not your responsibility or ever your fault, but I think if you keep the invitation open and don't put too much pressure on him, he'll come around sooner than you think.

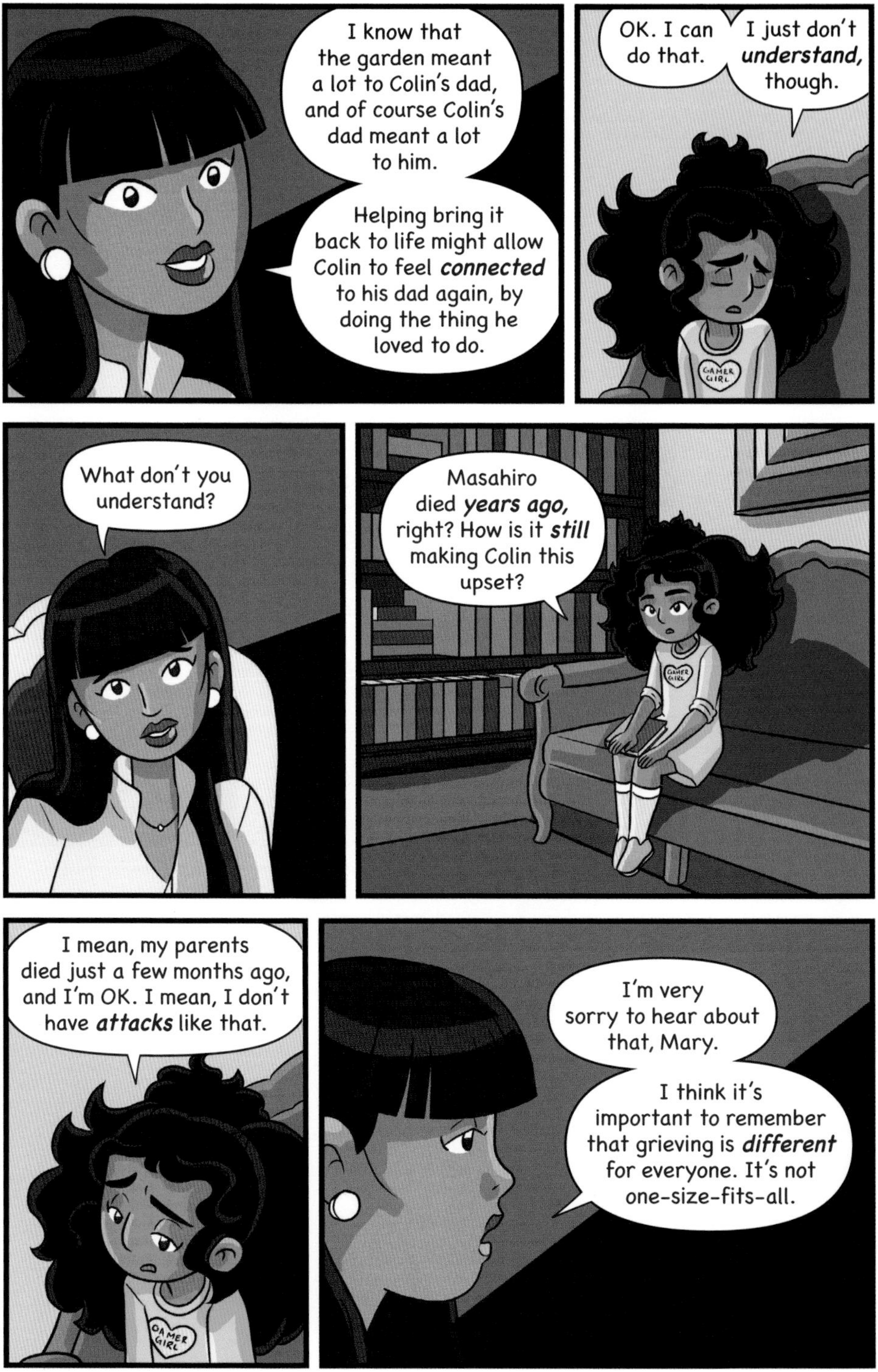
I know that the garden meant a lot to Colin's dad, and of course Colin's dad meant a lot to him.
Helping bring it back to life might allow Colin to feel *connected* to his dad again, by doing the thing he loved to do.
OK. I can do that.
I just don't *understand,* though.
What don't you understand?
Masahiro died *years ago,* right? How is it *still* making Colin this upset?
GAMER GIRL
I mean, my parents died just a few months ago, and I'm OK. I mean, I don't have *attacks* like that.
I'm very sorry to hear about that, Mary.
I think it's important to remember that grieving is *different* for everyone. It's not one-size-fits-all.

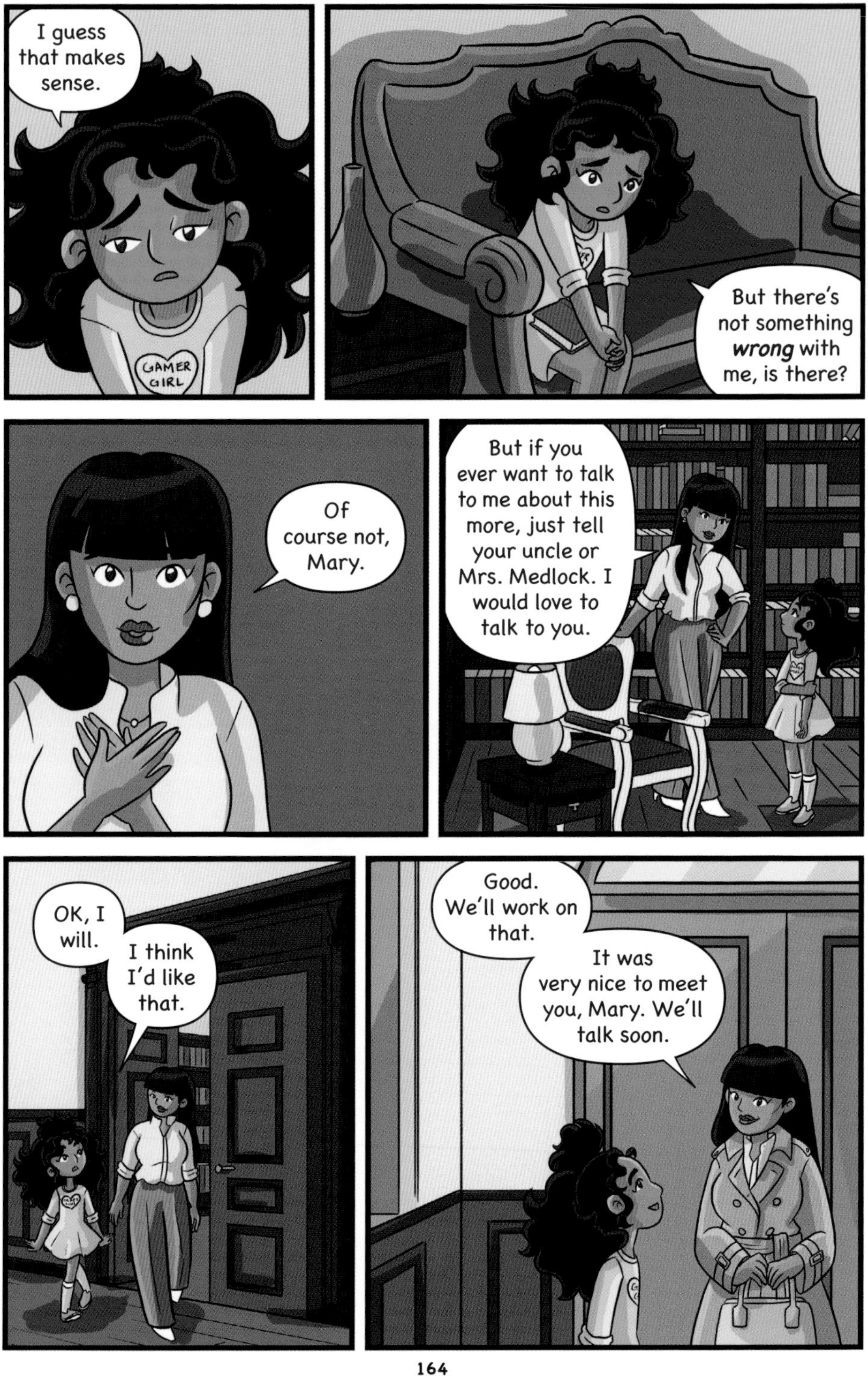
I guess that makes sense.
GAMER GIRL
But there's not something **wrong** with me, is there?
Of course not, Mary.
But if you ever want to talk to me about this more, just tell your uncle or Mrs. Medlock. I would love to talk to you.
OK, I will.
I think I'd like that.
Good. We'll work on that.
It was very nice to meet you, Mary. We'll talk soon.

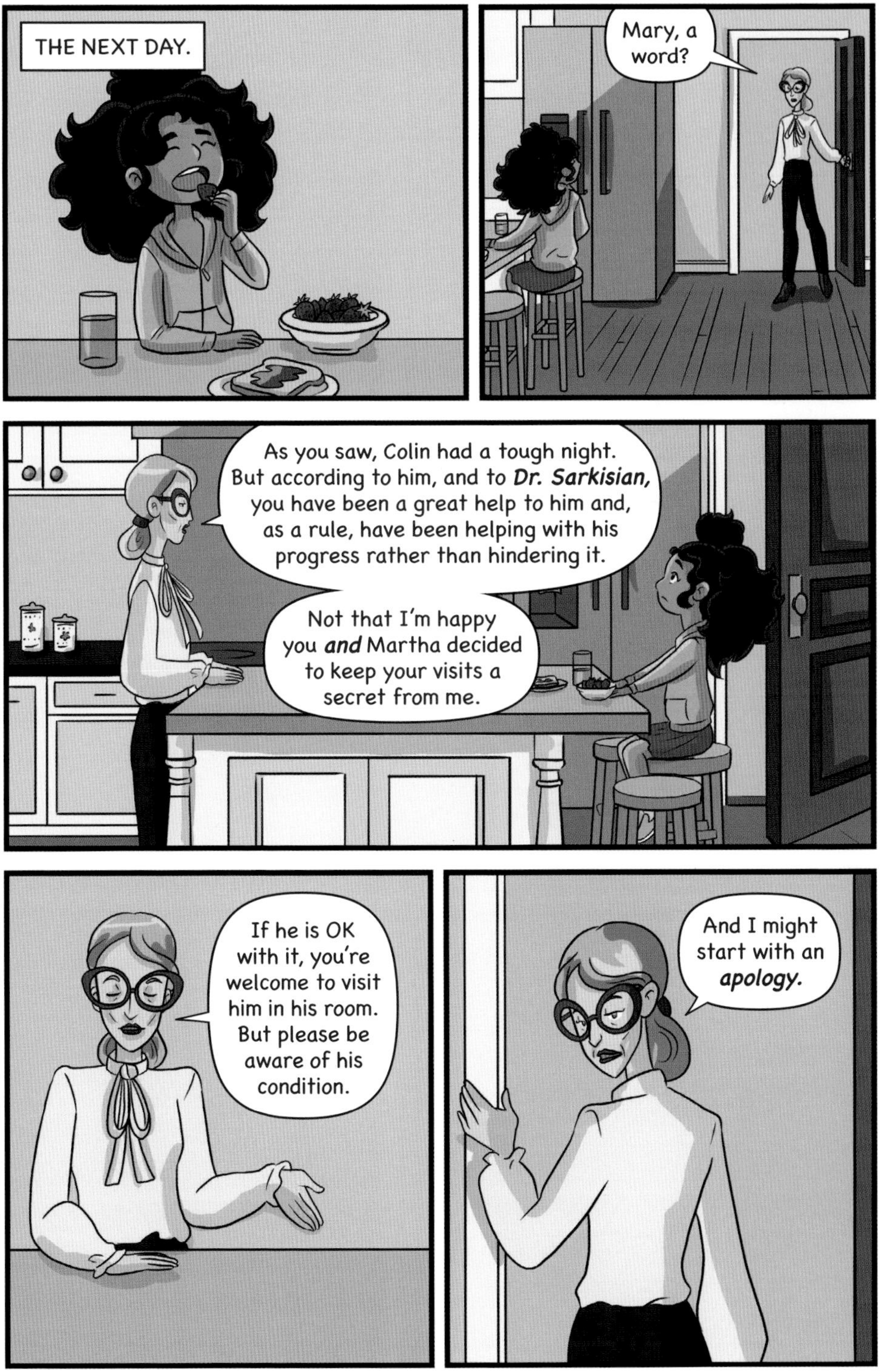
THE NEXT DAY.
Mary, a word?
As you saw, Colin had a tough night. But according to him, and to ***Dr. Sarkisian,*** you have been a great help to him and, as a rule, have been helping with his progress rather than hindering it.
Not that I'm happy you ***and*** Martha decided to keep your visits a secret from me.
If he is OK with it, you're welcome to visit him in his room. But please be aware of his condition.
And I might start with an ***apology.***

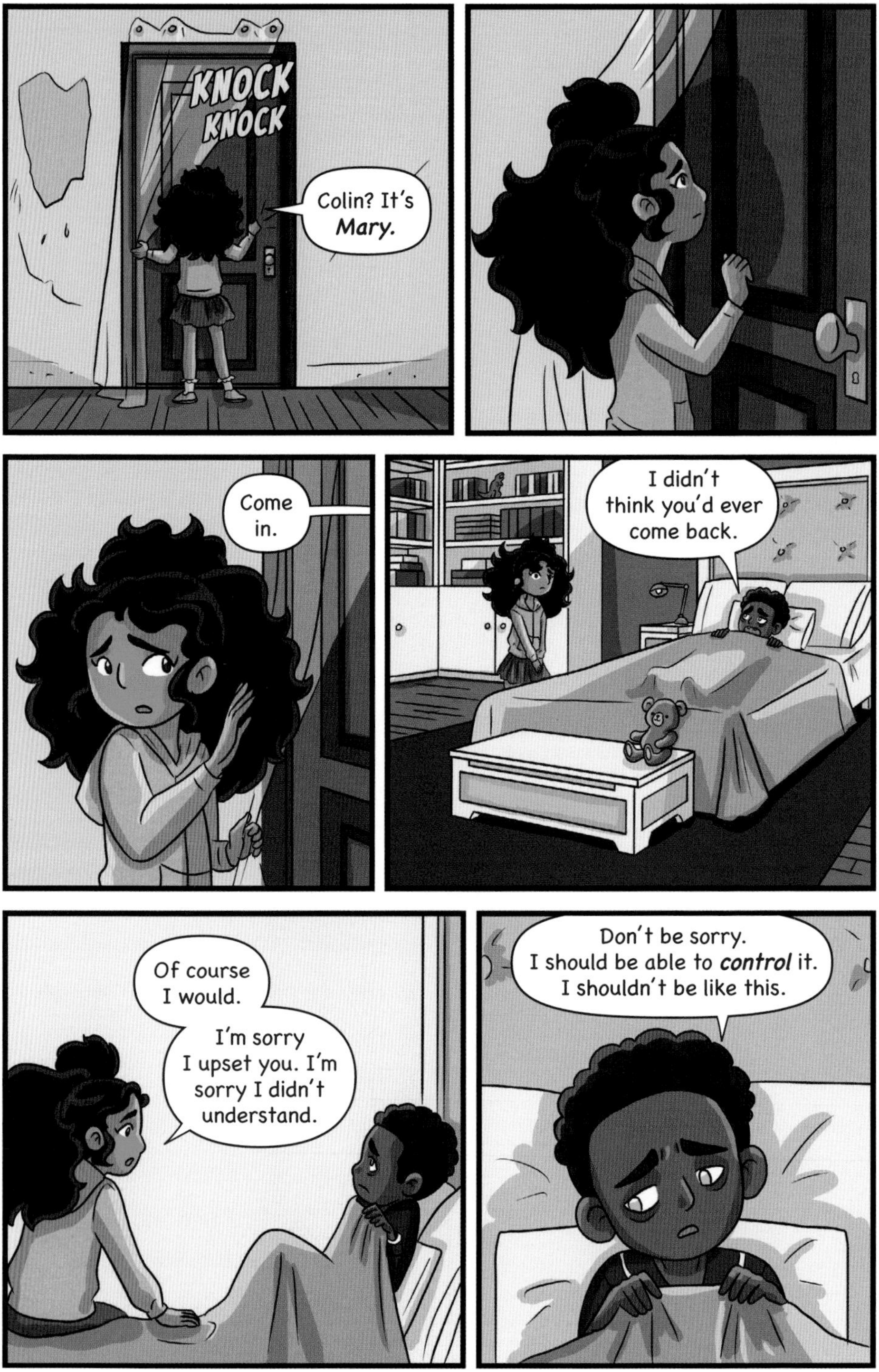
KNOCK
KNOCK
Colin? It's *Mary.*
Come in.
I didn't think you'd ever come back.
Of course I would.
I'm sorry I upset you. I'm sorry I didn't understand.
Don't be sorry. I should be able to *control* it. I shouldn't be like this.

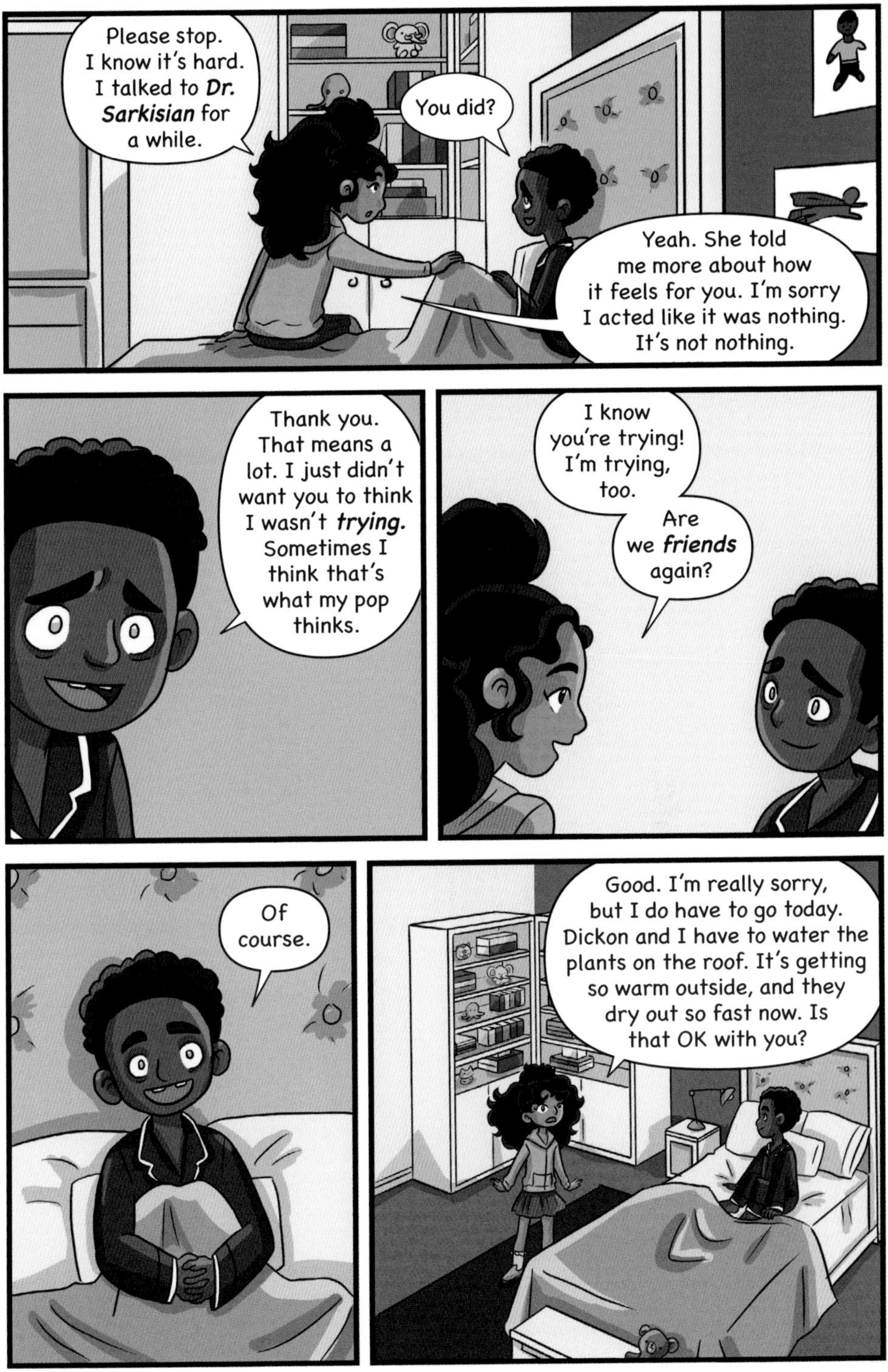
Please stop. I know it's hard. I talked to ***Dr. Sarkisian*** for a while.
You did?
Yeah. She told me more about how it feels for you. I'm sorry I acted like it was nothing. It's not nothing.
Thank you. That means a lot. I just didn't want you to think I wasn't ***trying.*** Sometimes I think that's what my pop thinks.
I know you're trying! I'm trying, too.
Are we ***friends*** again?
Of course.
Good. I'm really sorry, but I do have to go today. Dickon and I have to water the plants on the roof. It's getting so warm outside, and they dry out so fast now. Is that OK with you?

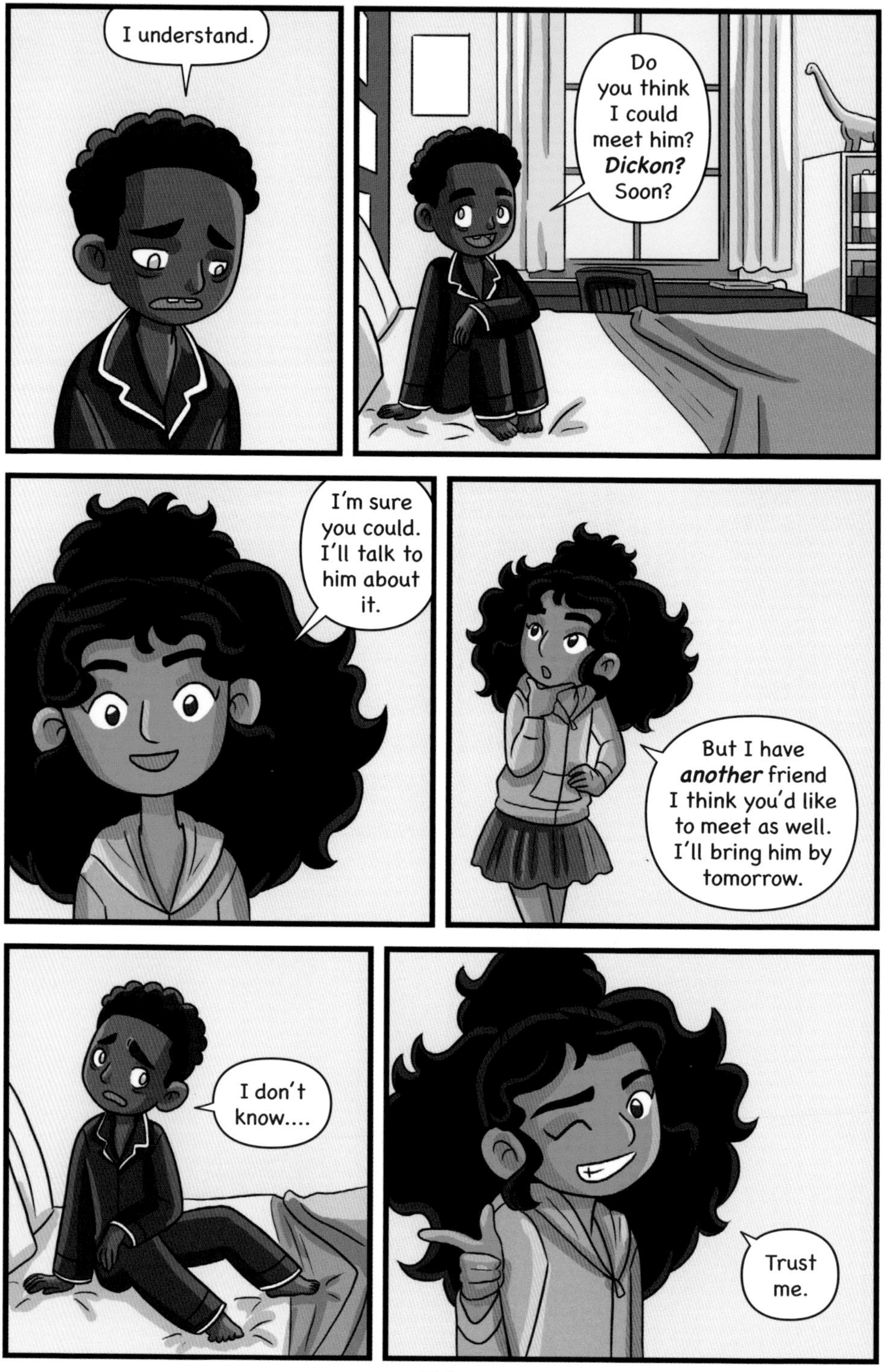
I understand.
Do you think I could meet him? **Dickon?** Soon?
I'm sure you could. I'll talk to him about it.
But I have ***another*** friend I think you'd like to meet as well. I'll bring him by tomorrow.
I don't know....
Trust me.

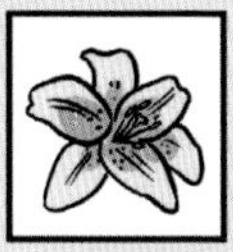

The_Secret_Garden

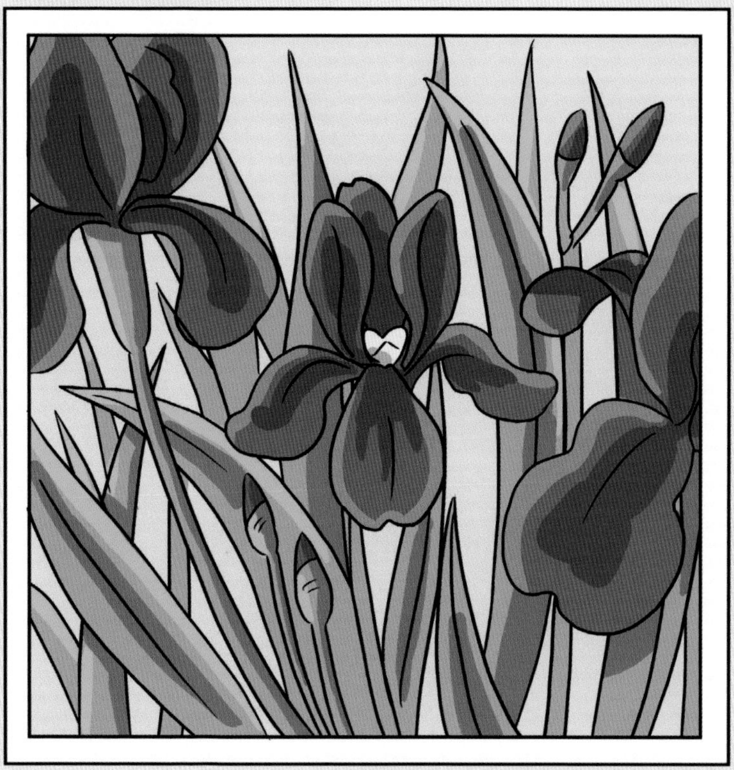

The_Secret_Garden Did you know that irises are one of the earliest flowers to bloom? We're sure happy to see them up here after all this gray weather. After they're done blooming, you can separate out the clumps, save them, and have even more irises next year!

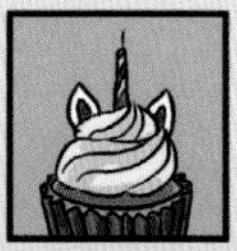

UnicornBaker4Life

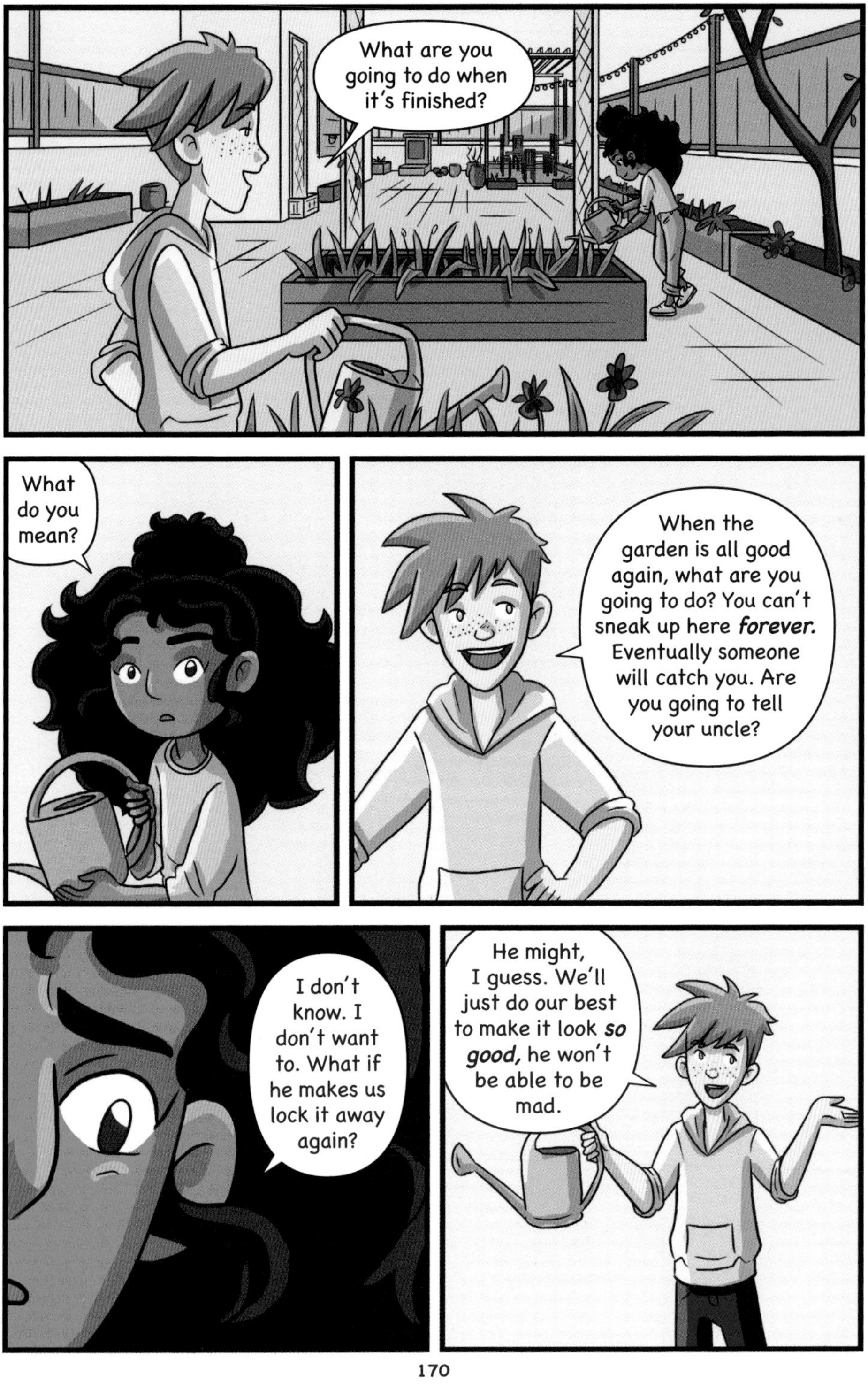
What are you going to do when it's finished?
What do you mean?
When the garden is all good again, what are you going to do? You can't sneak up here *forever.* Eventually someone will catch you. Are you going to tell your uncle?
I don't know. I don't want to. What if he makes us lock it away again?
He might, I guess. We'll just do our best to make it look *so good,* he won't be able to be mad.

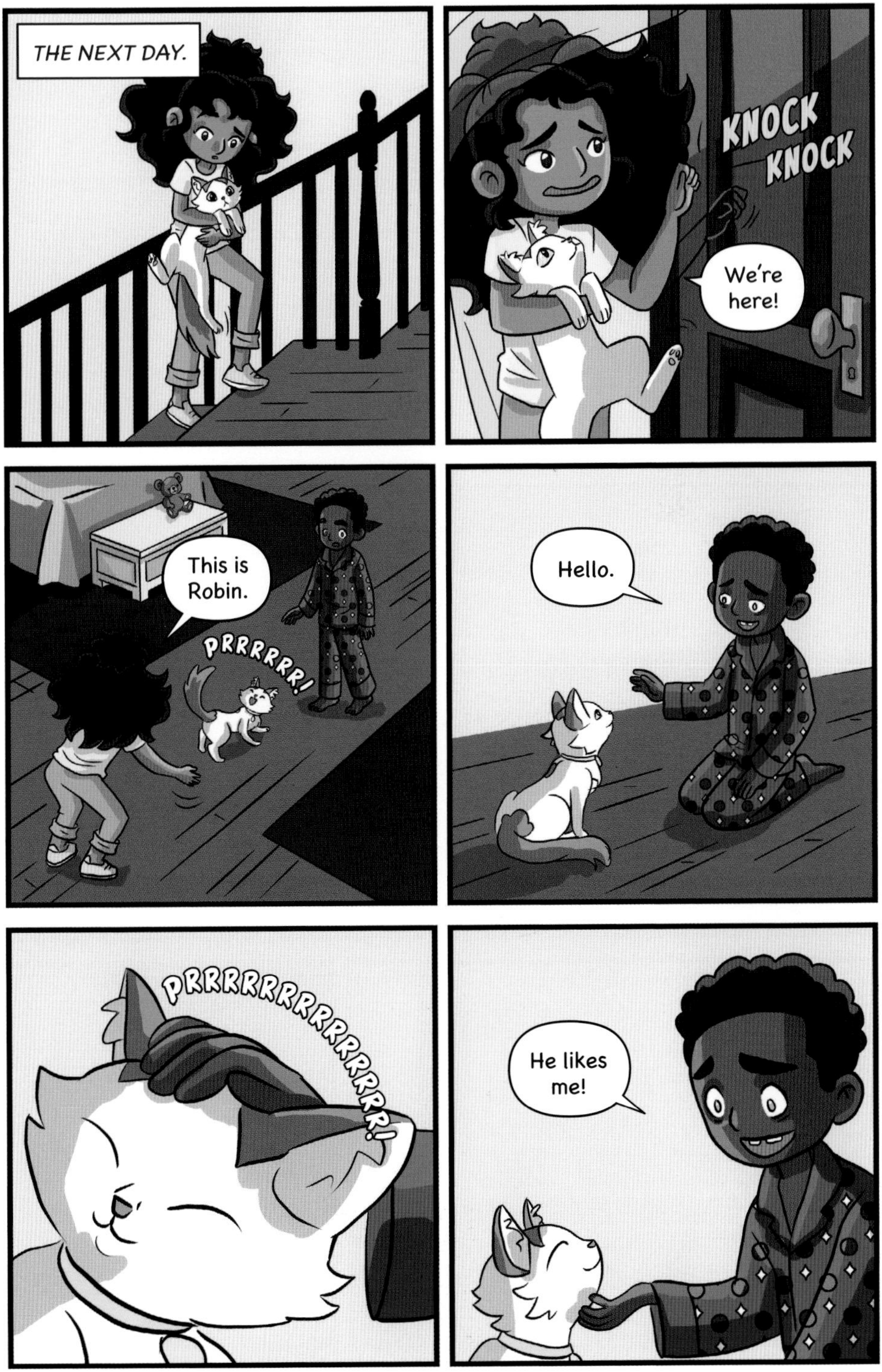
THE NEXT DAY.
KNOCK KNOCK
We're here!
This is Robin.
PRRRRRR!
Hello.
PRRRRRRRRRRRRRRR!
He likes me!

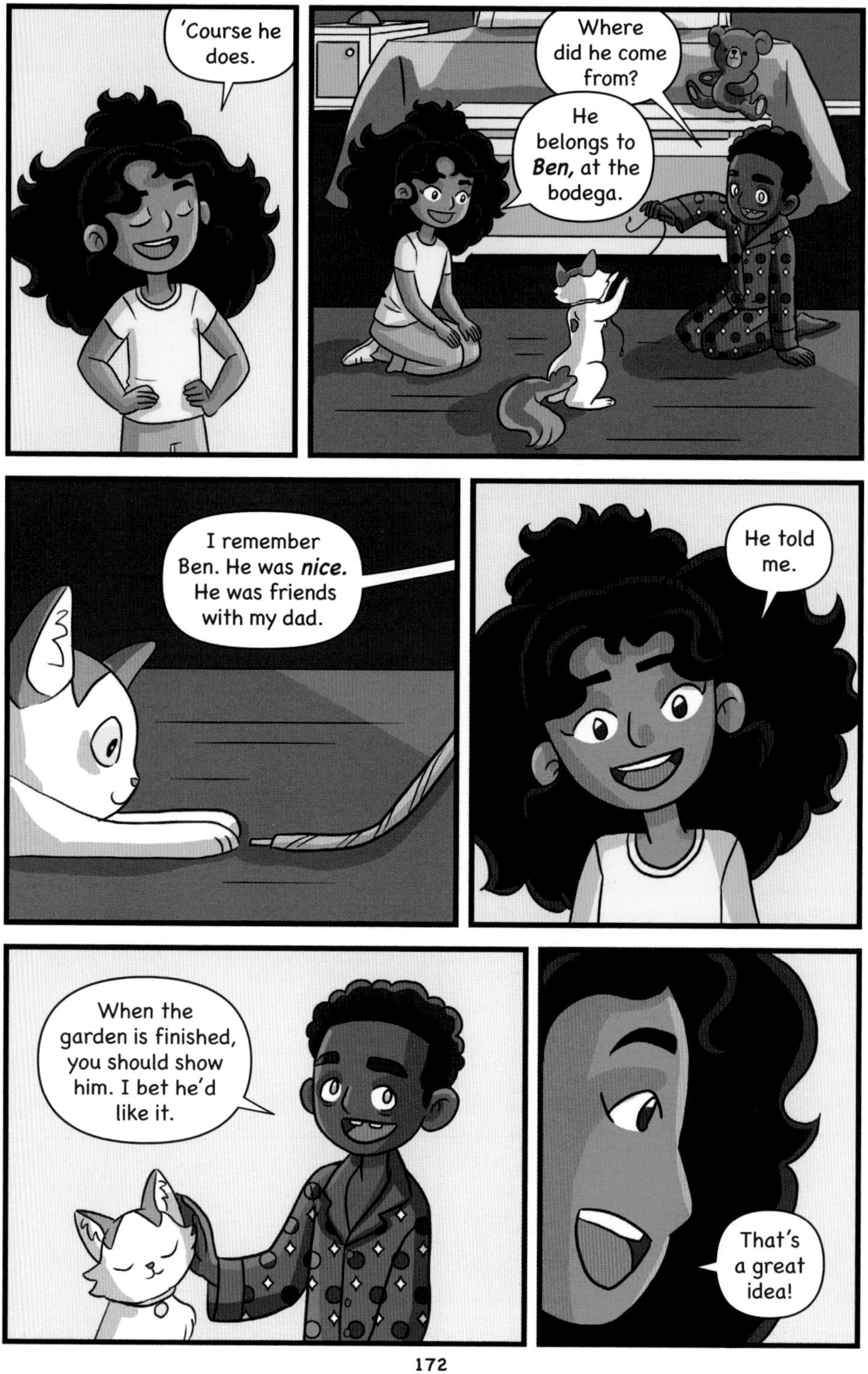
'Course he does.
Where did he come from?
He belongs to *Ben,* at the bodega.
I remember Ben. He was *nice.* He was friends with my dad.
He told me.
When the garden is finished, you should show him. I bet he'd like it.
That's a great idea!

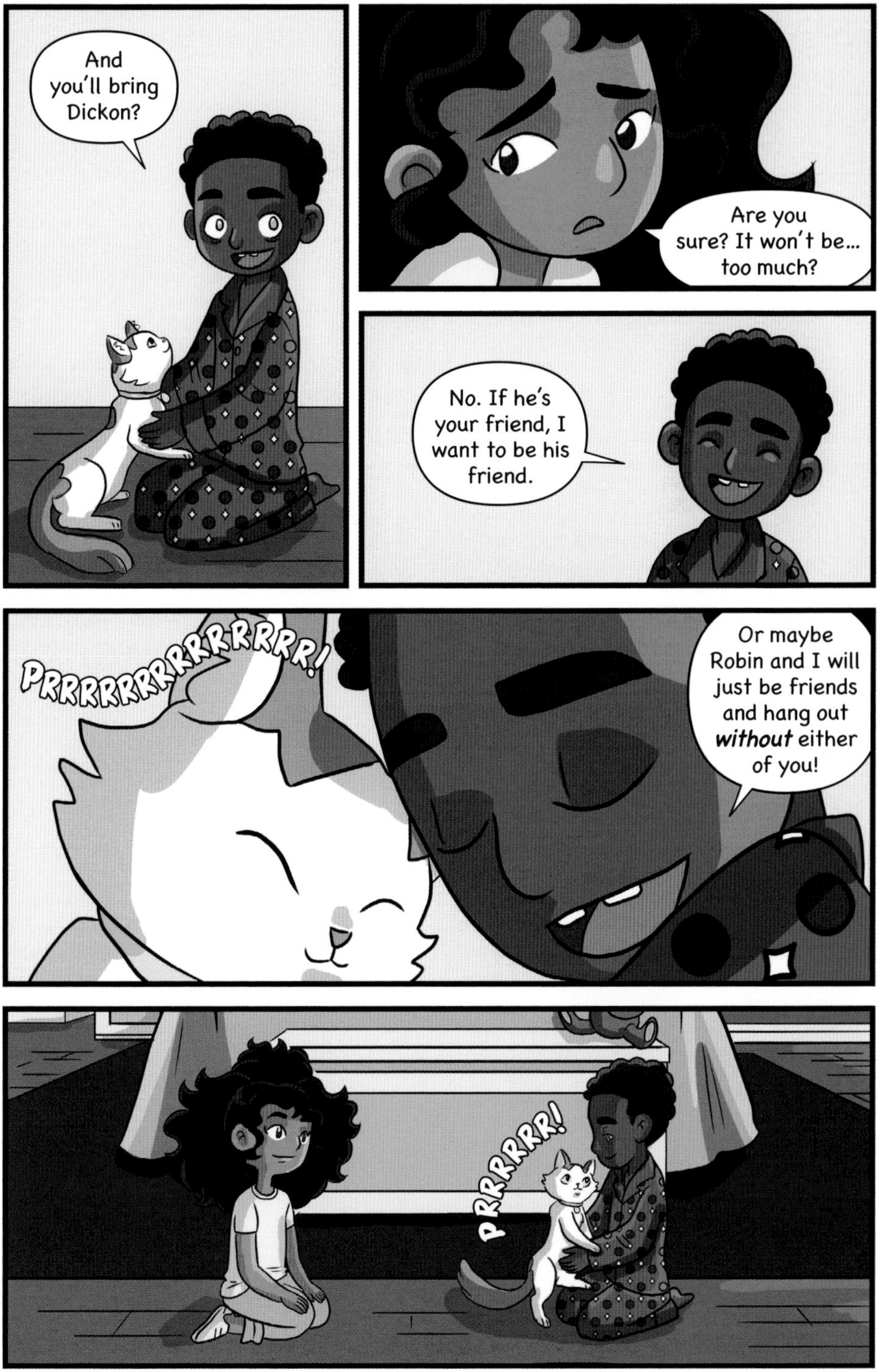
And you'll bring Dickon?
Are you sure? It won't be... too much?
No. If he's your friend, I want to be his friend.
PRRRRRRRRRRRRRR!
Or maybe Robin and I will just be friends and hang out *without* either of you!
PRRRRRR!

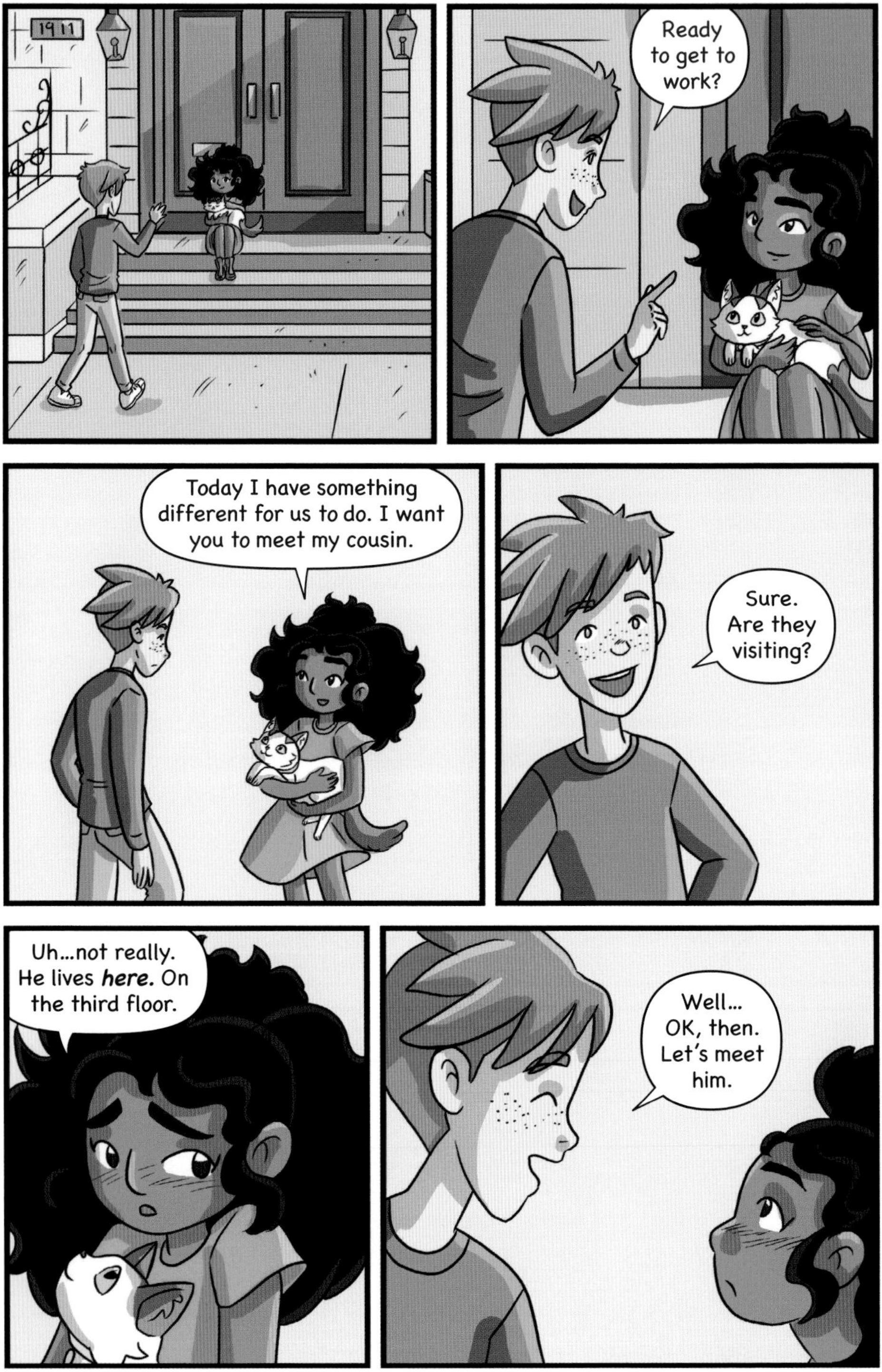
1911
Ready to get to work?
Today I have something different for us to do. I want you to meet my cousin.
Sure. Are they visiting?
Uh...not really. He lives ***here.*** On the third floor.
Well... OK, then. Let's meet him.

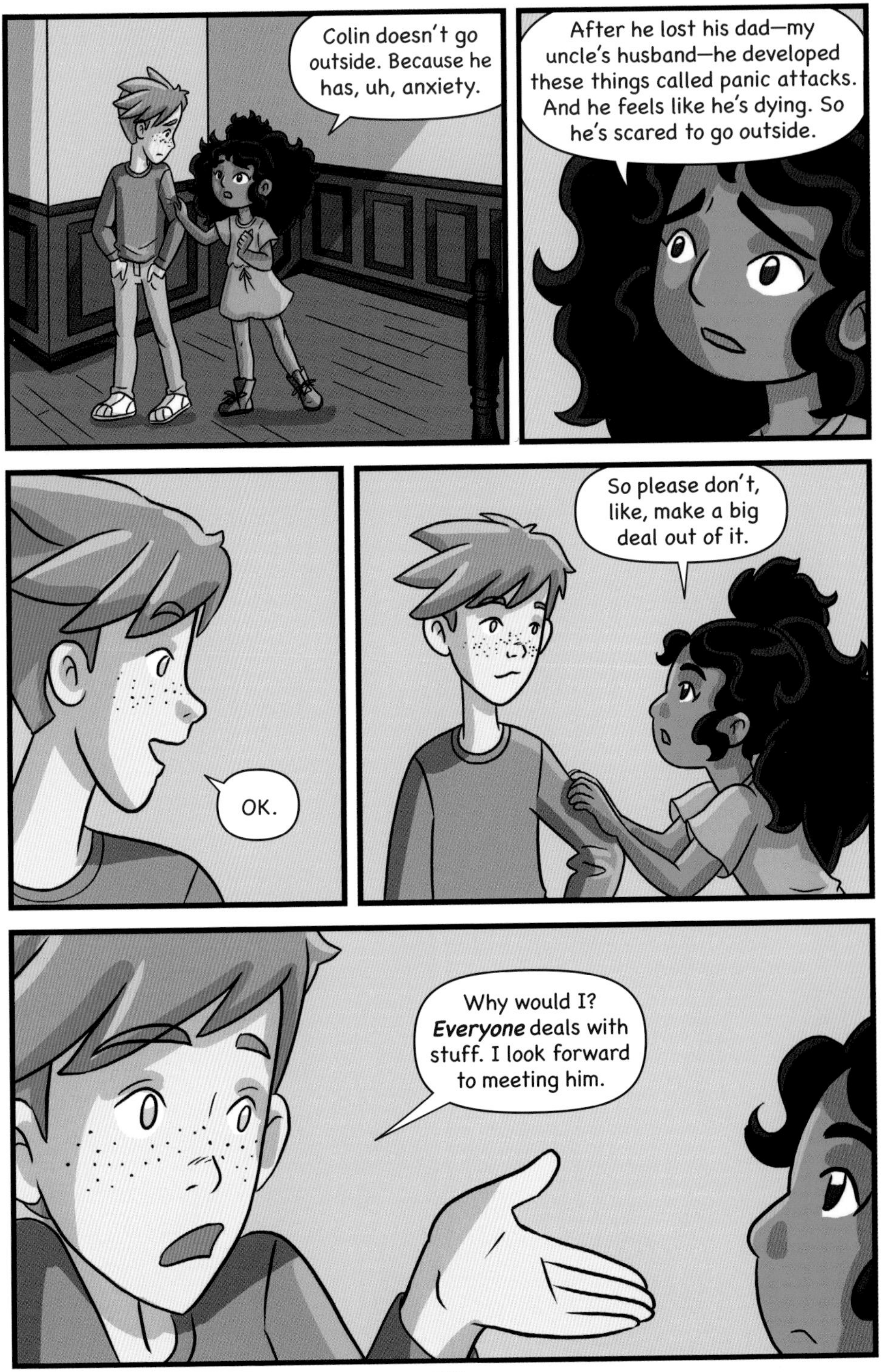
Colin doesn't go outside. Because he has, uh, anxiety.
After he lost his dad—my uncle's husband—he developed these things called panic attacks. And he feels like he's dying. So he's scared to go outside.
OK.
So please don't, like, make a big deal out of it.
Why would I? *Everyone* deals with stuff. I look forward to meeting him.

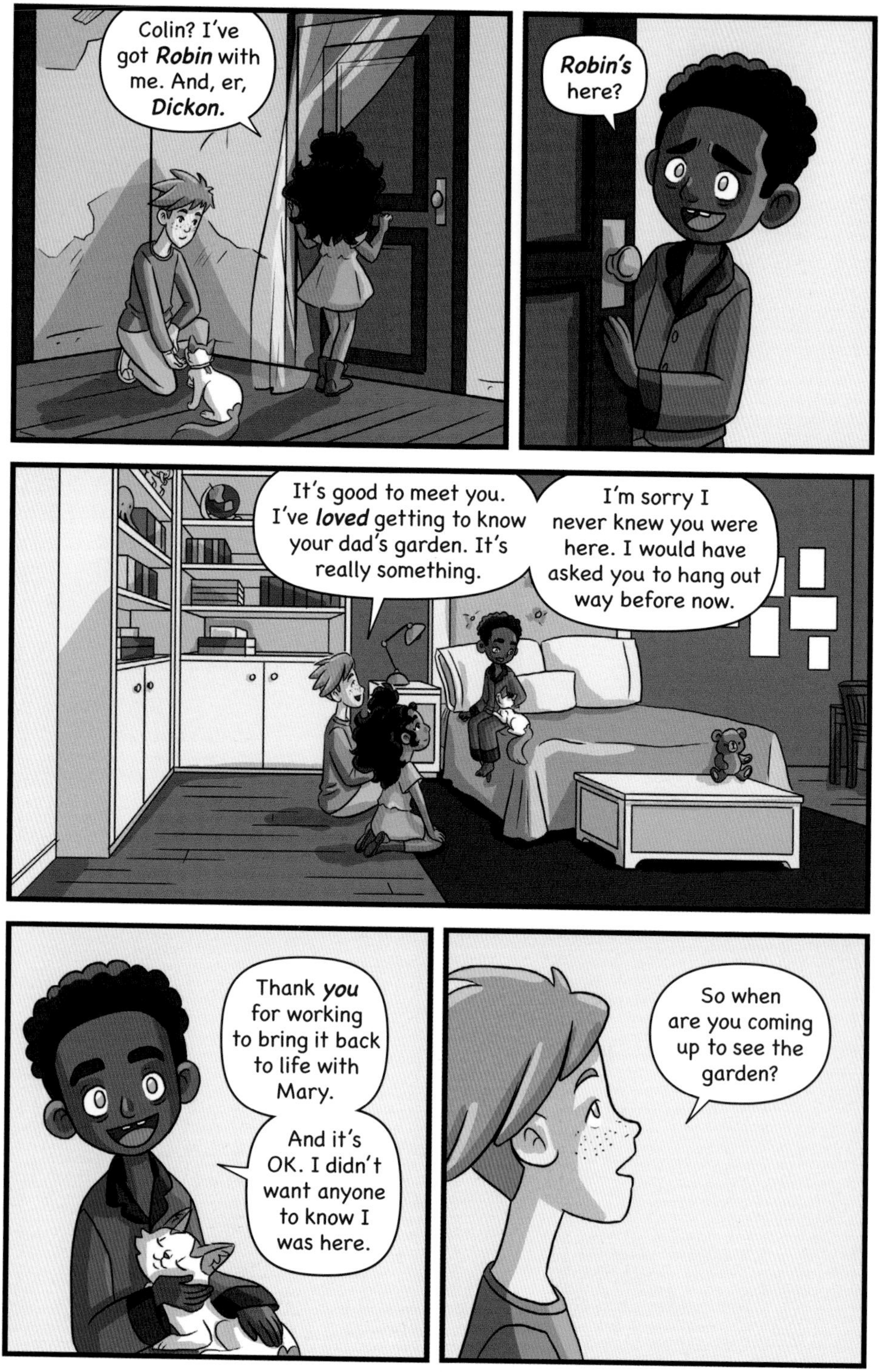
Colin? I've got *Robin* with me. And, er, *Dickon.*
Robin's here?
It's good to meet you. I've *loved* getting to know your dad's garden. It's really something.
I'm sorry I never knew you were here. I would have asked you to hang out way before now.
Thank *you* for working to bring it back to life with Mary.
And it's OK. I didn't want anyone to know I was here.
So when are you coming up to see the garden?

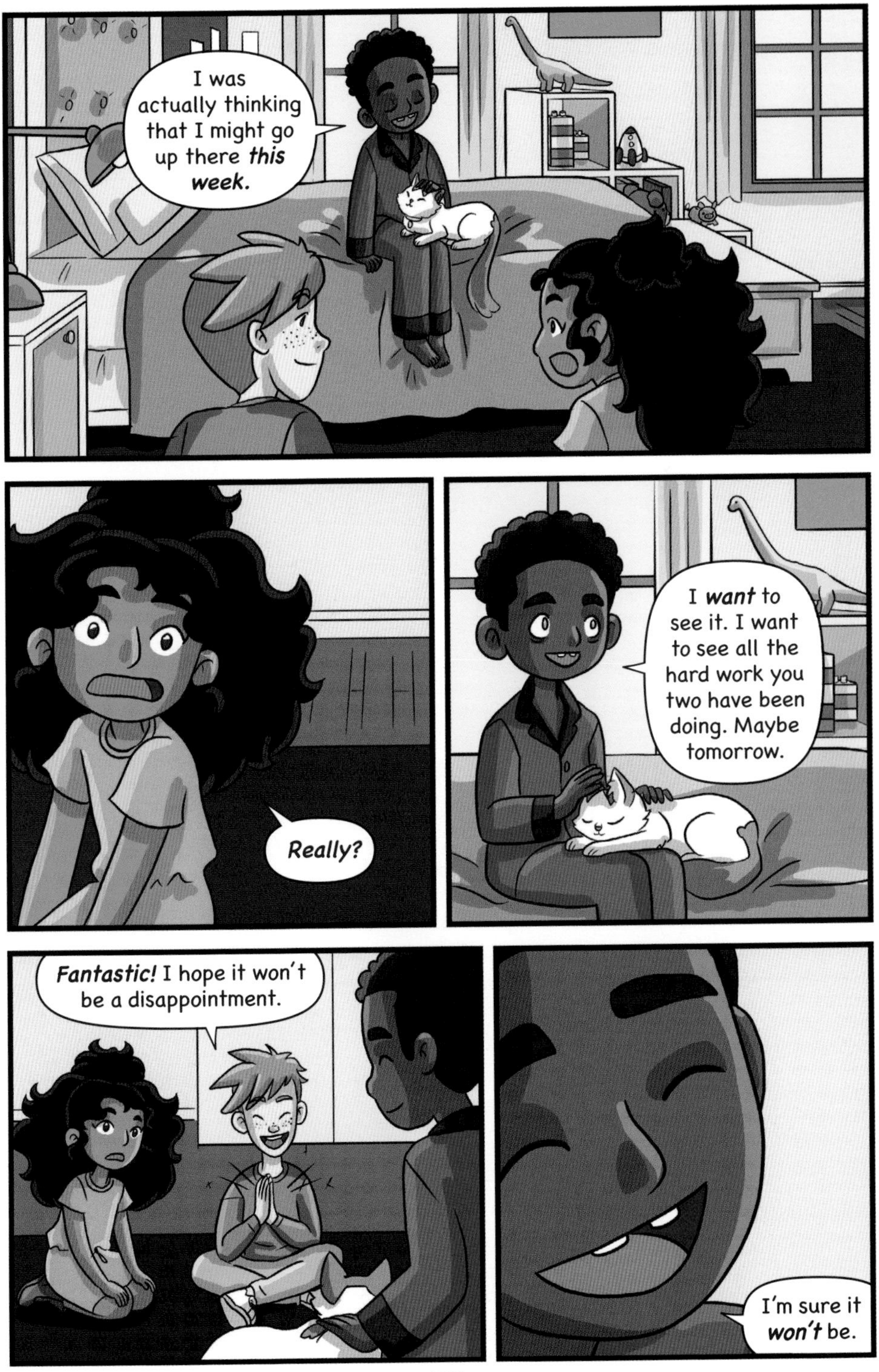
I was actually thinking that I might go up there *this week.*
Really?
I *want* to see it. I want to see all the hard work you two have been doing. Maybe tomorrow.
Fantastic! I hope it won't be a disappointment.
I'm sure it *won't* be.

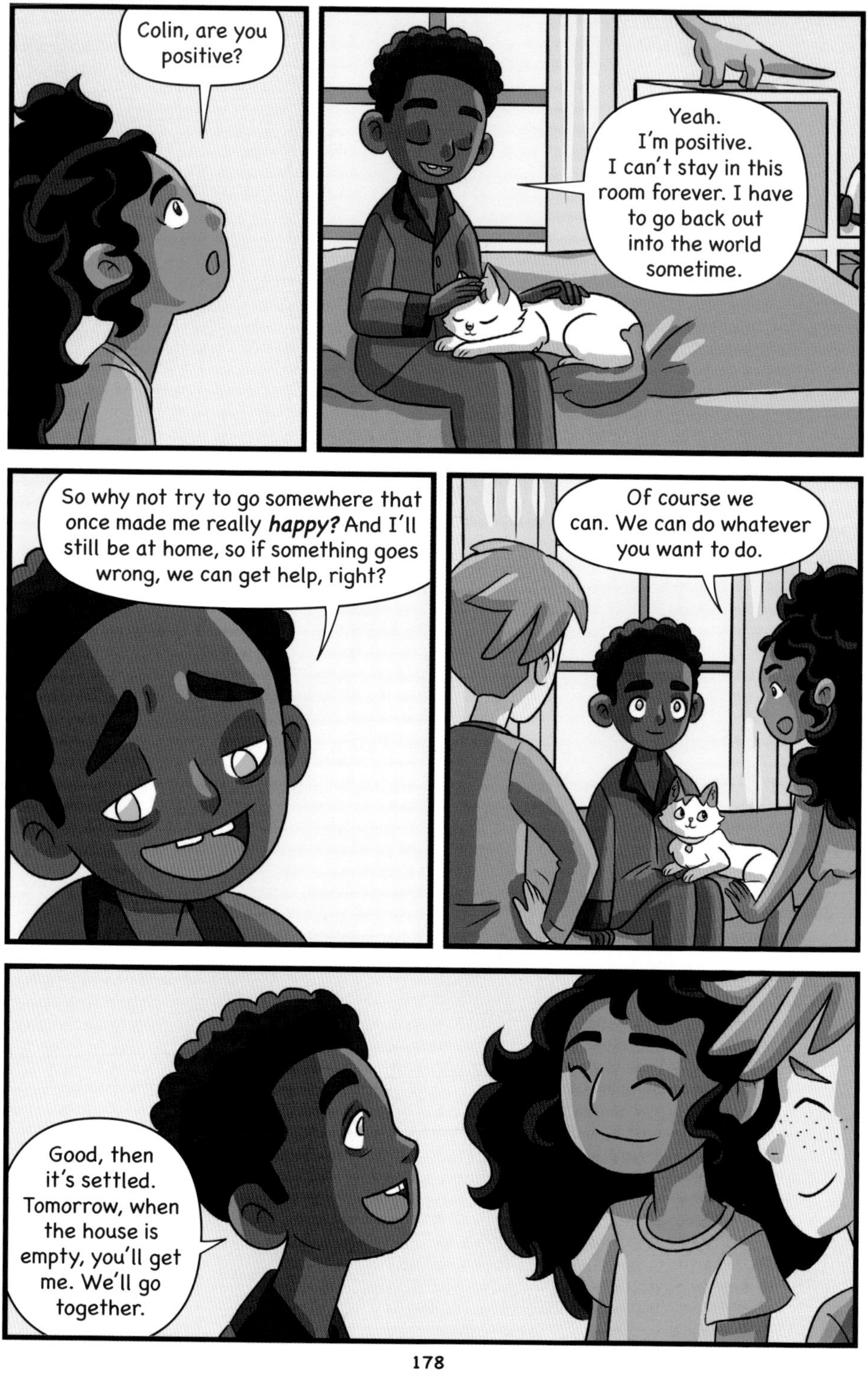
Colin, are you positive?
Yeah. I'm positive. I can't stay in this room forever. I have to go back out into the world sometime.
So why not try to go somewhere that once made me really ***happy?*** And I'll still be at home, so if something goes wrong, we can get help, right?
Of course we can. We can do whatever you want to do.
Good, then it's settled. Tomorrow, when the house is empty, you'll get me. We'll go together.

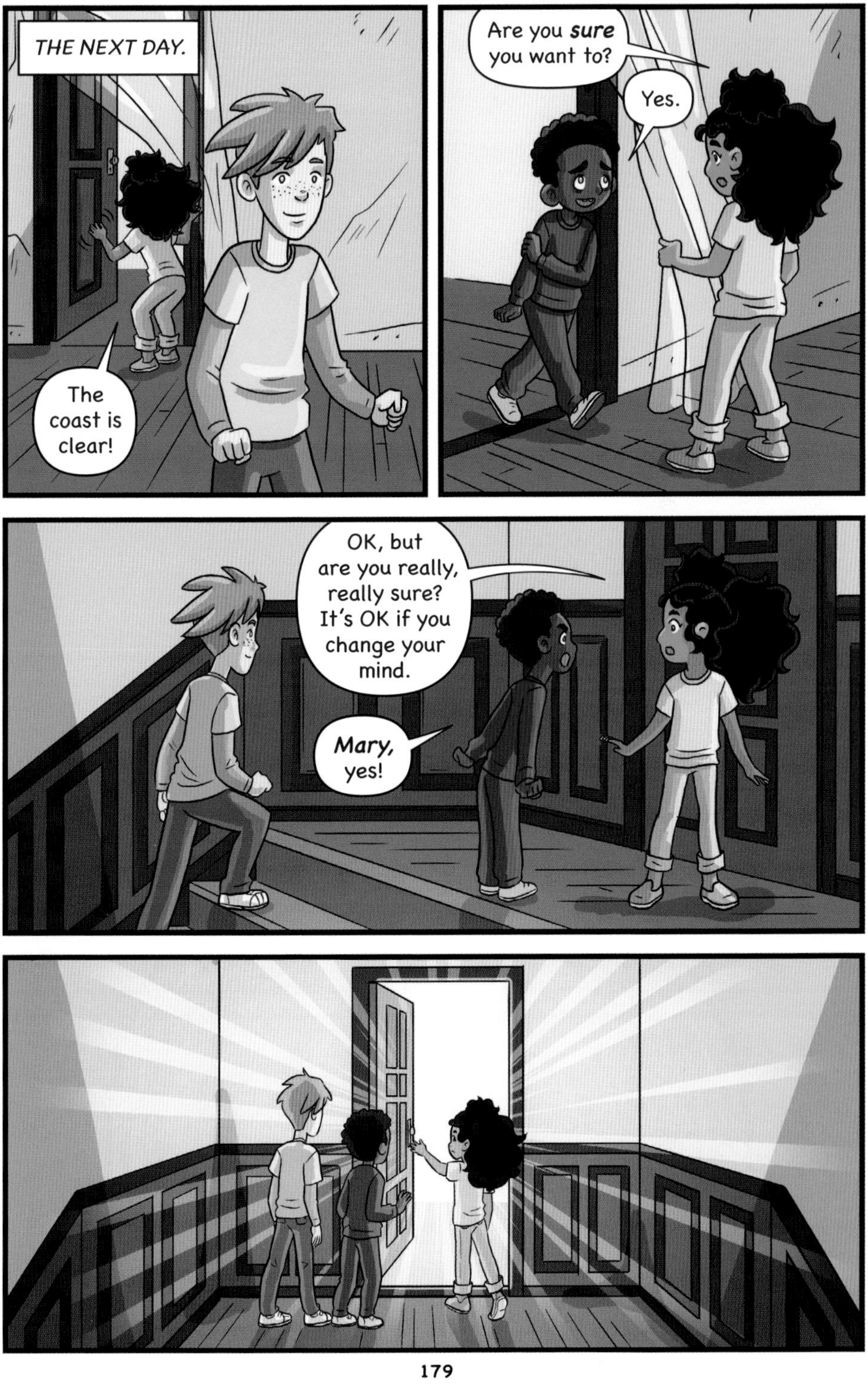
THE NEXT DAY.
The coast is clear!
Are you **sure** you want to?
Yes.
OK, but are you really, really sure? It's OK if you change your mind.
Mary, yes!

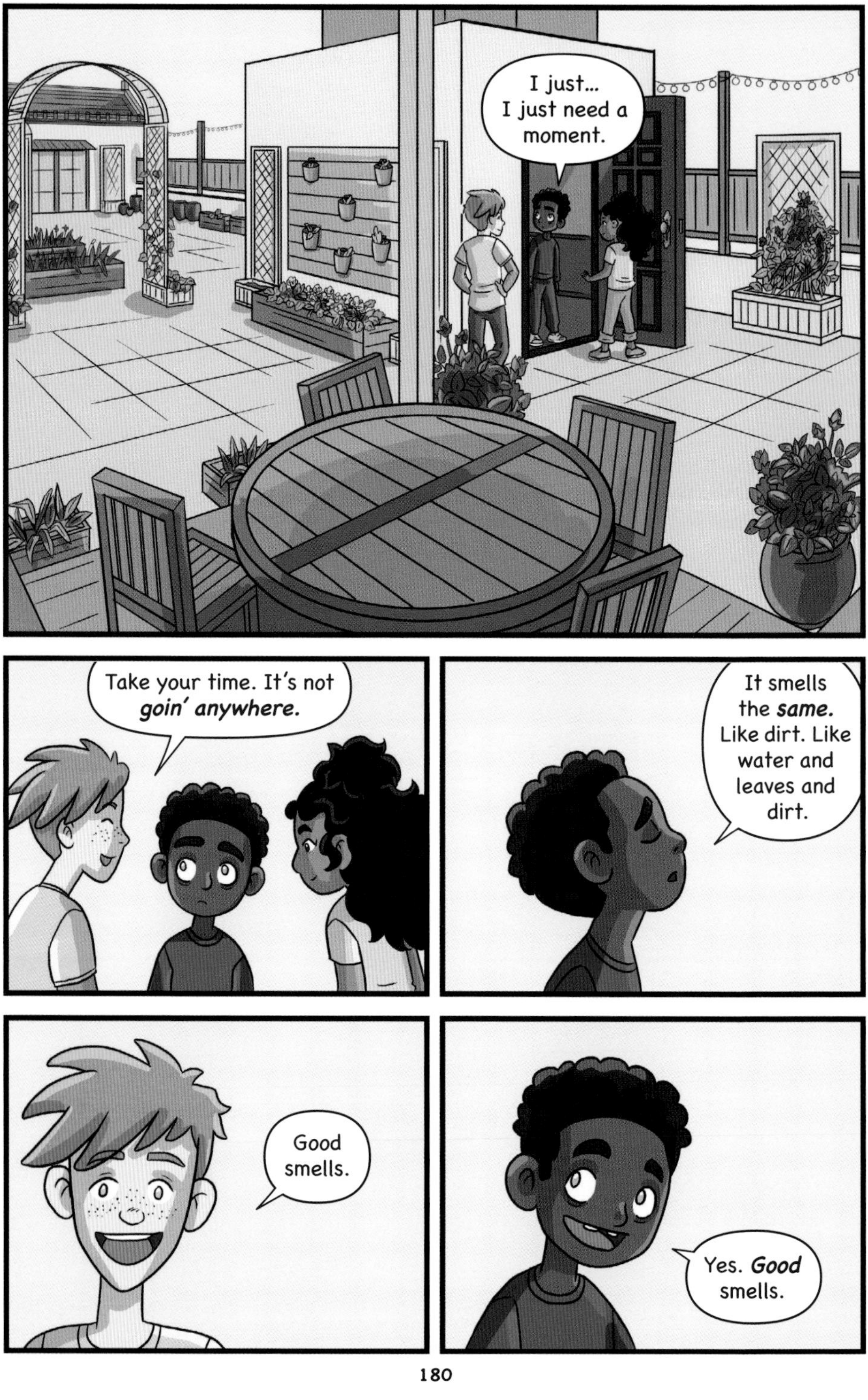
I just... I just need a moment.
Take your time. It's not *goin' anywhere.*
It smells the *same.* Like dirt. Like water and leaves and dirt.
Good smells.
Yes. *Good* smells.

I'm OK. I just need to breathe.

The roses came back to life.

They were never really gone.

When my dad was alive, he came up here almost every day. He always had some small task to do. He said it helped him feel centered. Helped him escape everything happening in the city around him.

I forgot how good it feels to be up here. It's almost like not being in the city at all.

I have to go back inside. I'm sorry. I can't.

Colin! I'm sorry. We shouldn't have let you come.

No, no. I wanted to come.

It was just...a lot. And when I feel a lot of emotions, my chest feels tight, and then I get scared.

But I want to come back again. I want to. I just need some time today.

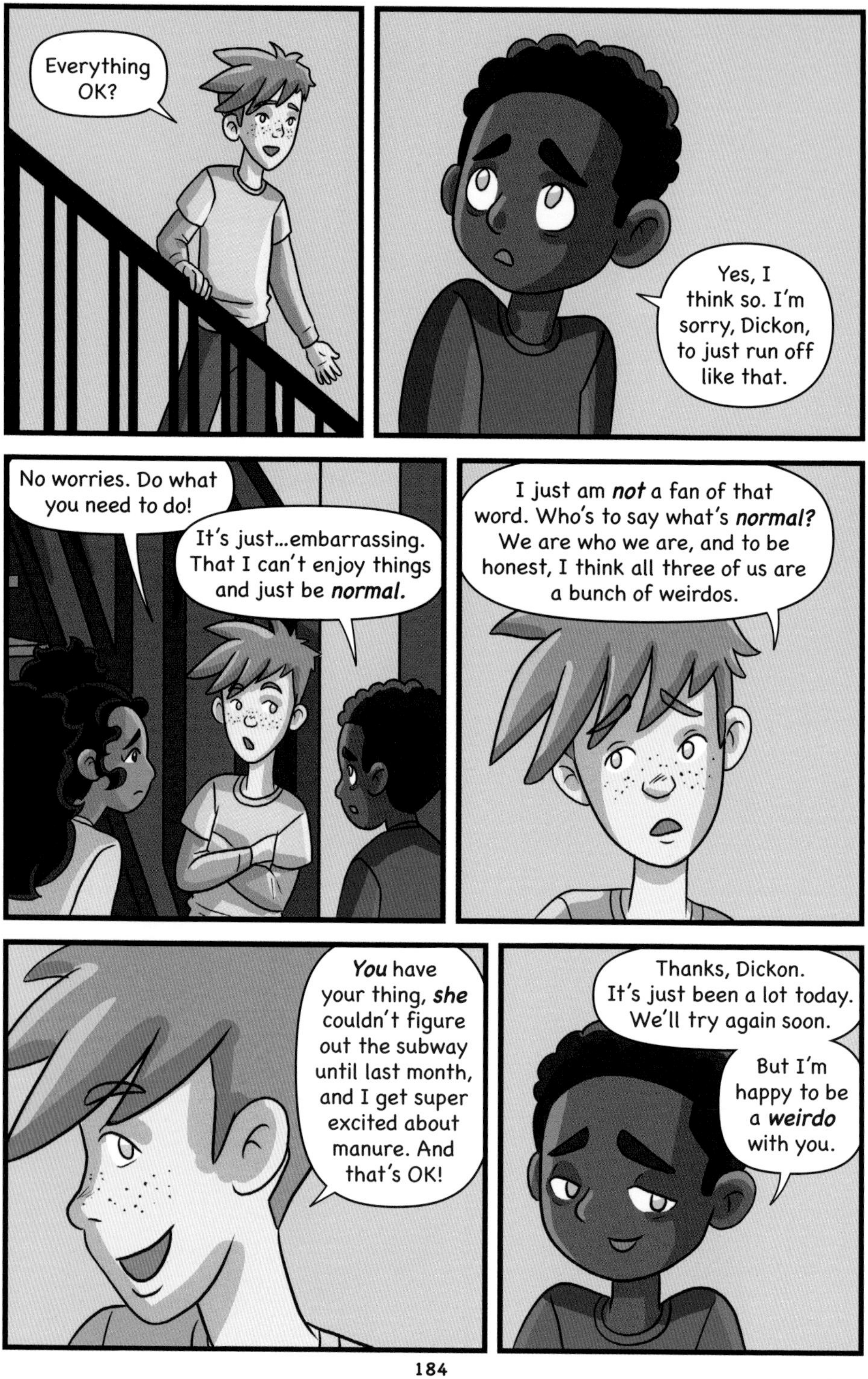

Everything OK?
Yes, I think so. I'm sorry, Dickon, to just run off like that.
No worries. Do what you need to do!
It's just...embarrassing. That I can't enjoy things and just be *normal.*
I just am *not* a fan of that word. Who's to say what's *normal?* We are who we are, and to be honest, I think all three of us are a bunch of weirdos.
You have your thing, *she* couldn't figure out the subway until last month, and I get super excited about manure. And that's OK!
Thanks, Dickon. It's just been a lot today. We'll try again soon.
But I'm happy to be a *weirdo* with you.

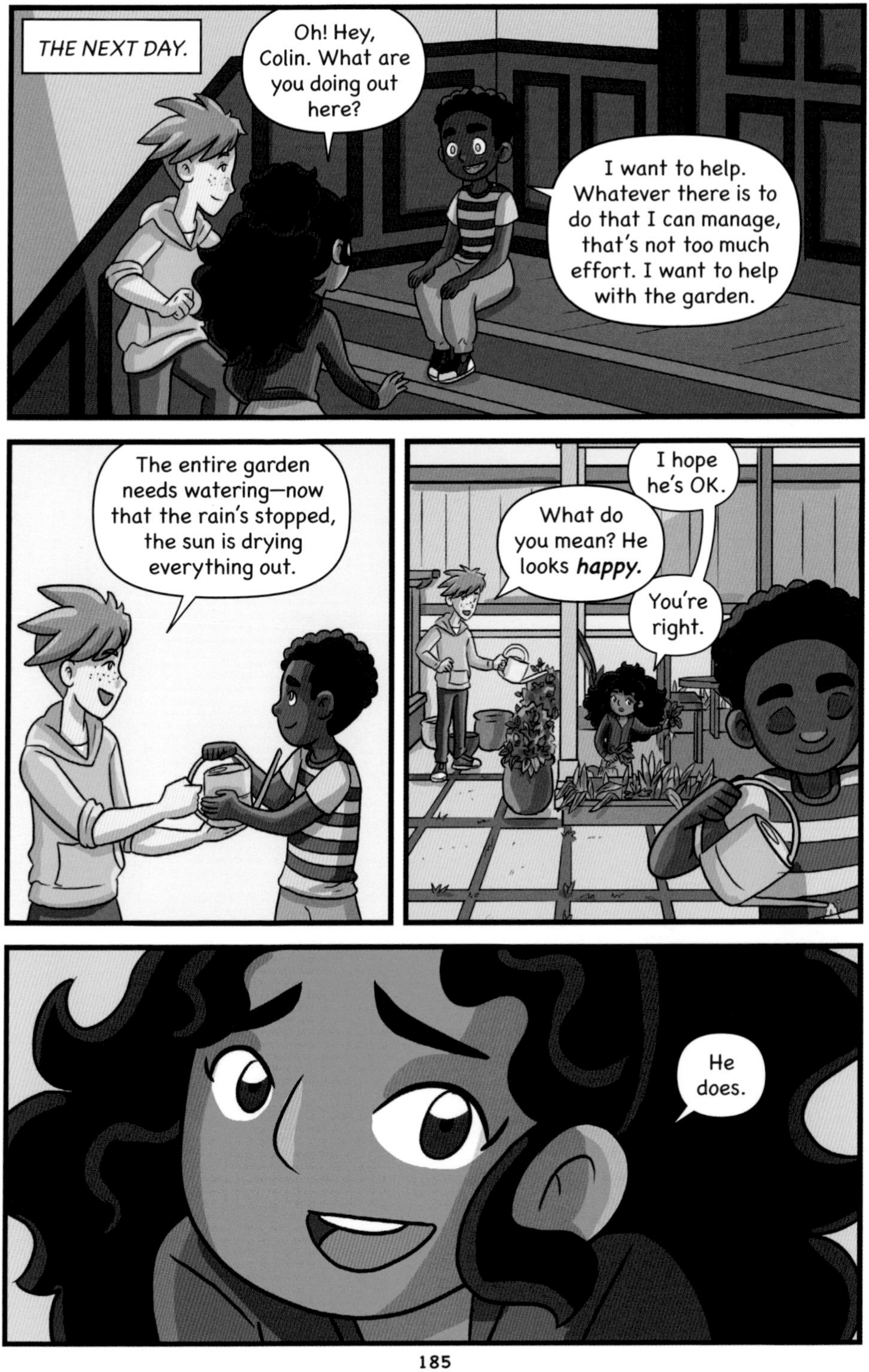
THE NEXT DAY.
Oh! Hey, Colin. What are you doing out here?
I want to help. Whatever there is to do that I can manage, that's not too much effort. I want to help with the garden.
The entire garden needs watering—now that the rain's stopped, the sun is drying everything out.
I hope he's OK.
What do you mean? He looks **happy.**
You're right.
He does.

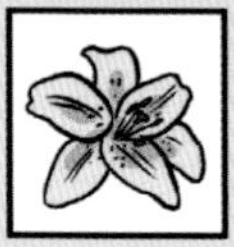

The_Secret_Garden

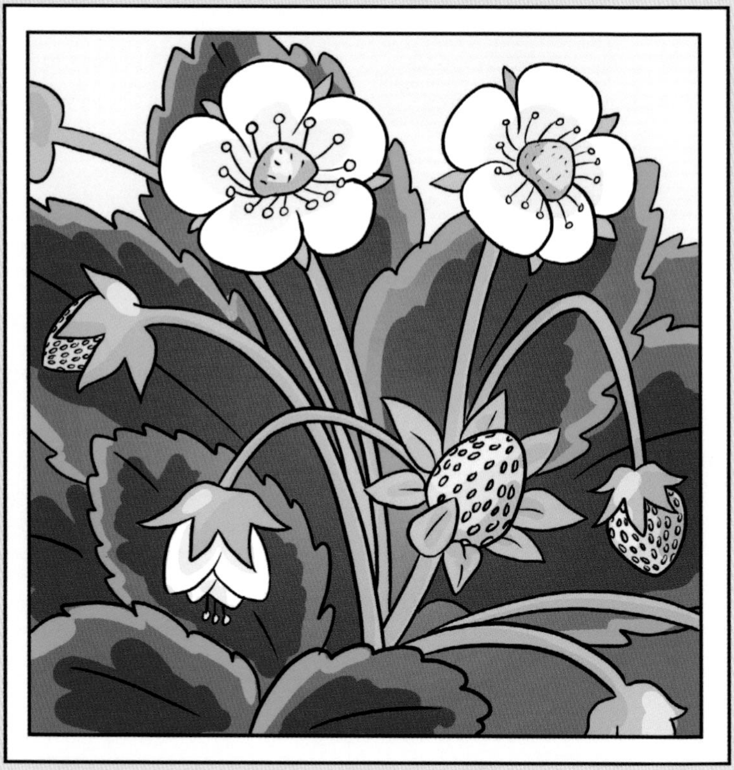

The_Secret_Garden These baby strawberries were just little white flowers a few days ago! They'll be super tasty soon… if the birds don't get them first. We're going to put up some mesh netting around them to help keep them safe! 🐦

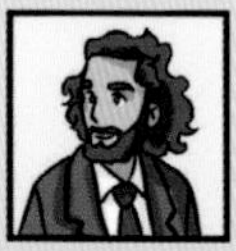

Plant_Prof

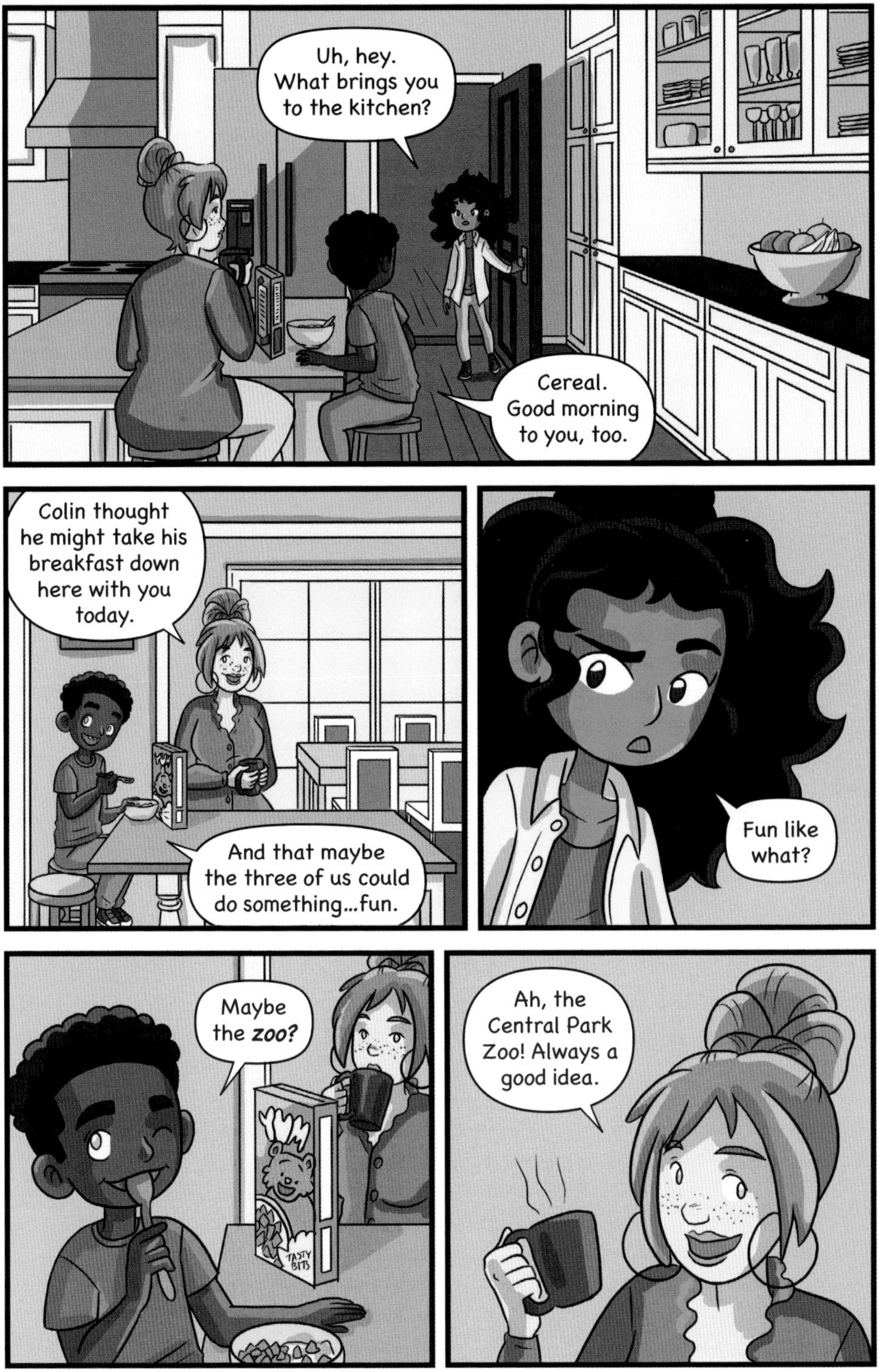
Uh, hey.
What brings you
to the kitchen?
Cereal.
Good morning
to you, too.
Colin thought
he might take his
breakfast down
here with you
today.
And that maybe
the three of us could
do something...fun.
Fun like
what?
Maybe
the *zoo?*
TASTY BITS
Ah, the
Central Park
Zoo! Always a
good idea.

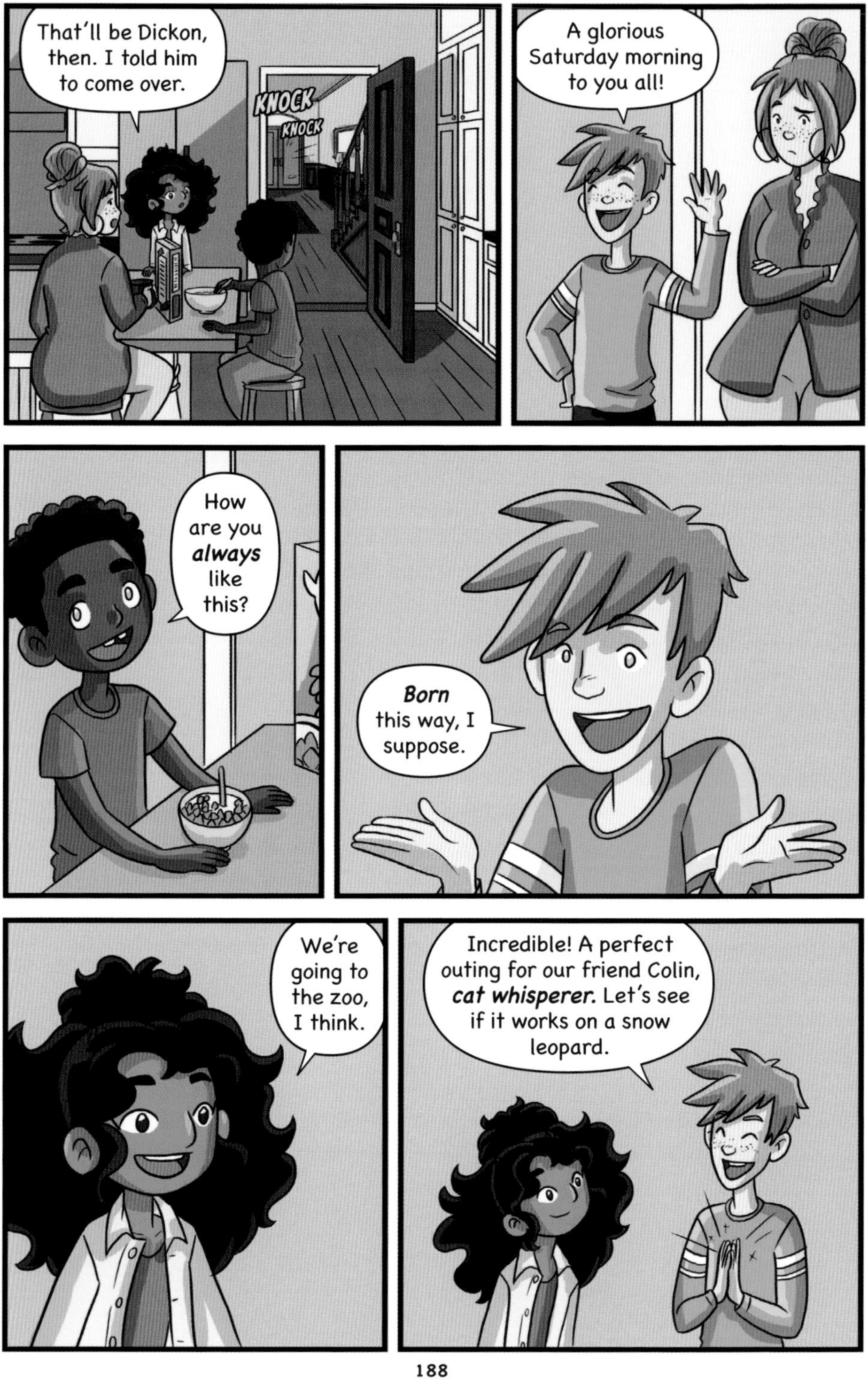
That'll be Dickon, then. I told him to come over.
KNOCK KNOCK
A glorious Saturday morning to you all!
How are you *always* like this?
Born this way, I suppose.
We're going to the zoo, I think.
Incredible! A perfect outing for our friend Colin, *cat whisperer.* Let's see if it works on a snow leopard.

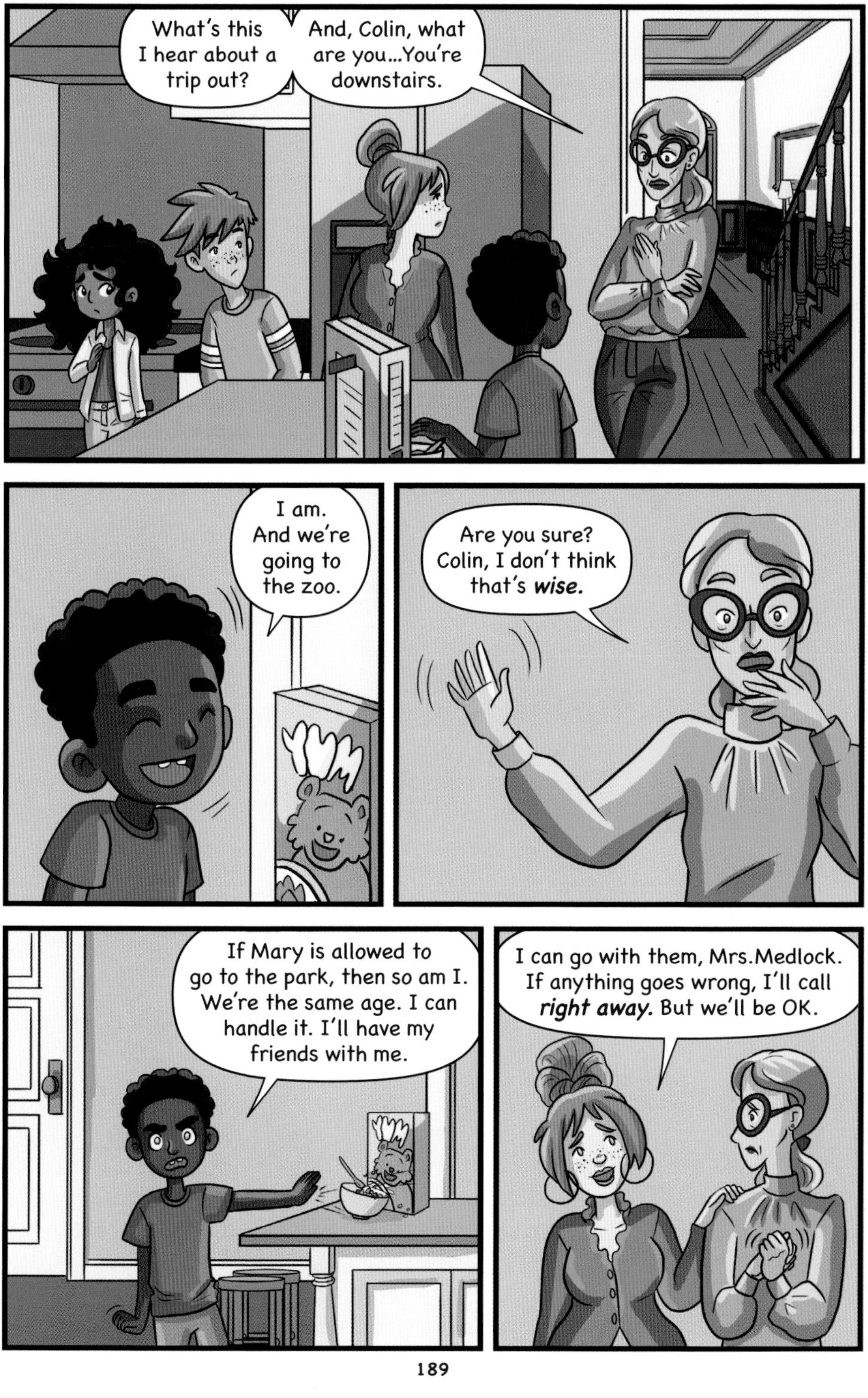
What's this I hear about a trip out?
And, Colin, what are you...You're downstairs.
I am. And we're going to the zoo.
Are you sure? Colin, I don't think that's ***wise.***
If Mary is allowed to go to the park, then so am I. We're the same age. I can handle it. I'll have my friends with me.
I can go with them, Mrs.Medlock. If anything goes wrong, I'll call ***right away.*** But we'll be OK.
YUM

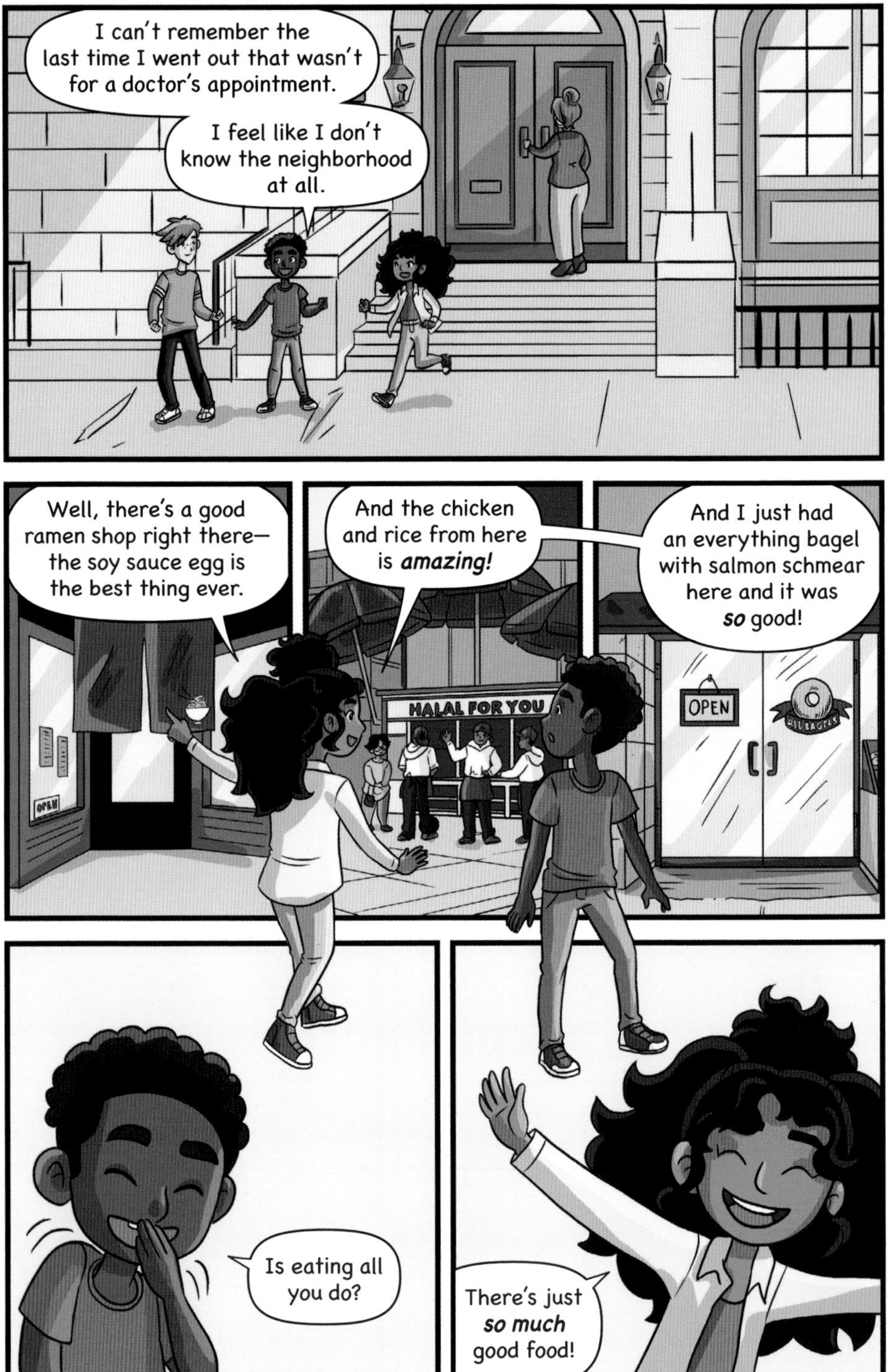

I can't remember the last time I went out that wasn't for a doctor's appointment.
I feel like I don't know the neighborhood at all.
Well, there's a good ramen shop right there—the soy sauce egg is the best thing ever.
OPEN
And the chicken and rice from here is *amazing!*
HALAL FOR YOU
And I just had an everything bagel with salmon schmear here and it was *so* good!
OPEN
Is eating all you do?
There's just *so much* good food!

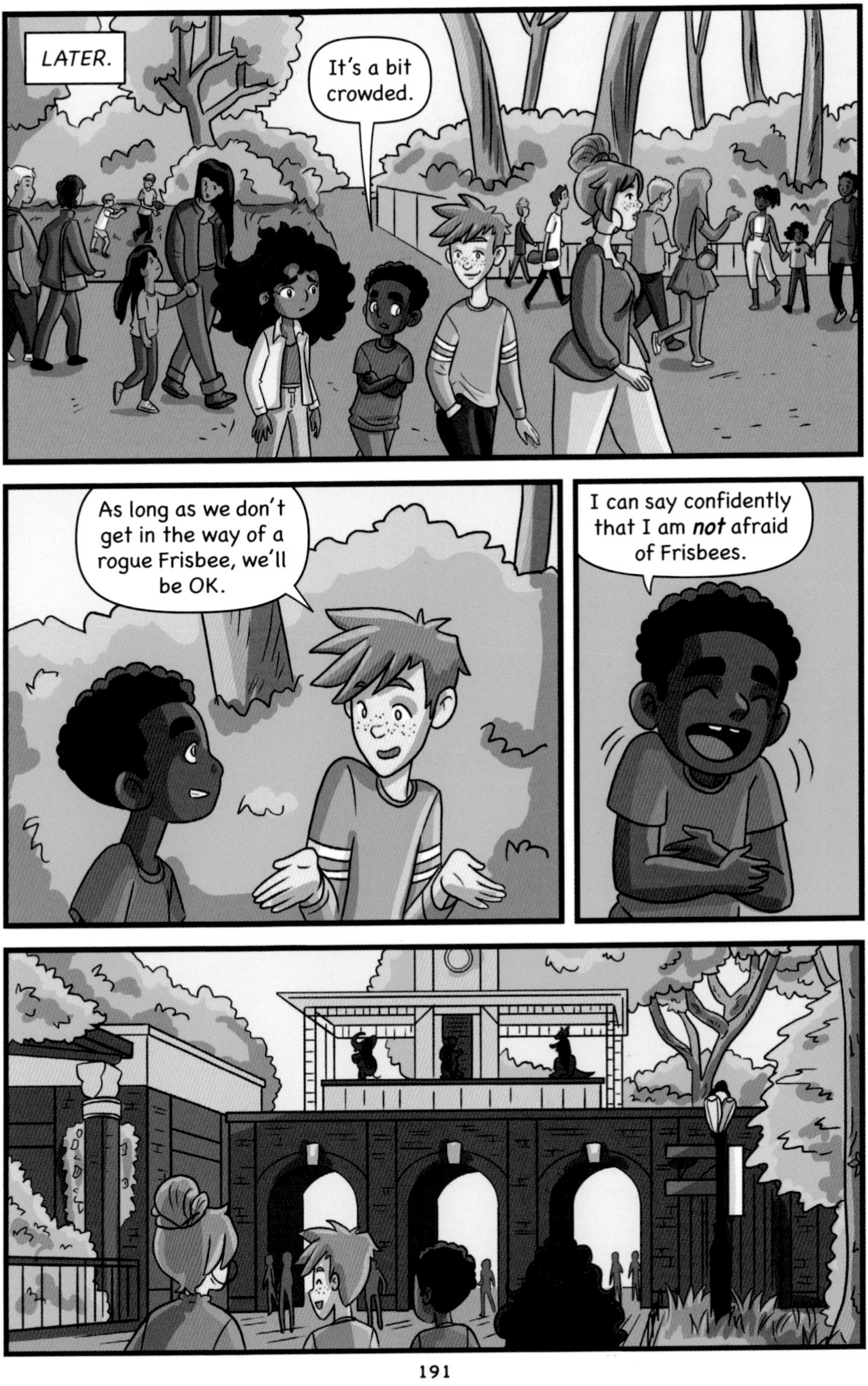
LATER.
It's a bit crowded.
As long as we don't get in the way of a rogue Frisbee, we'll be OK.
I can say confidently that I am *not* afraid of Frisbees.

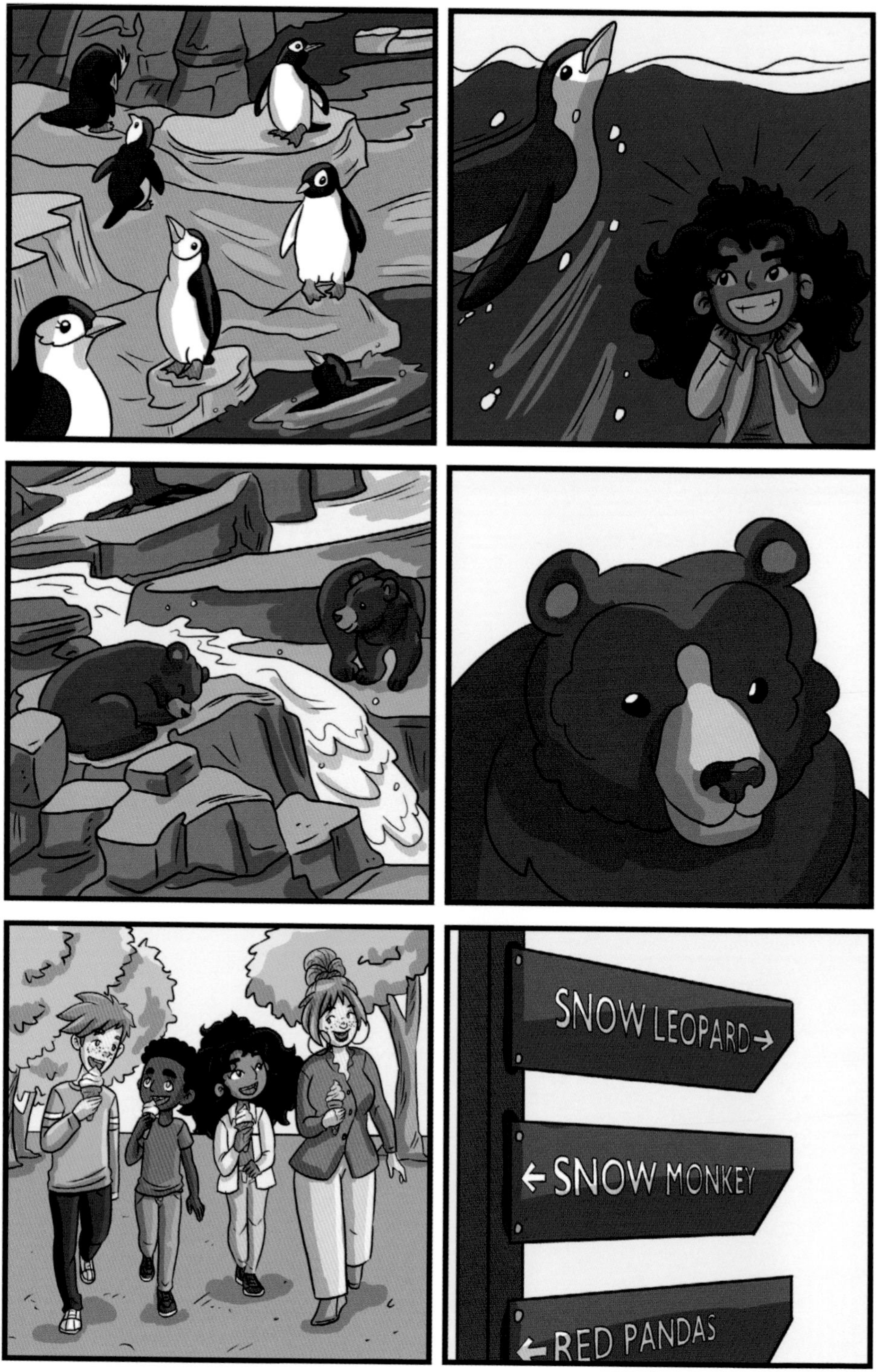
SNOW LEOPARD →
← SNOW MONKEY
← RED PANDAS

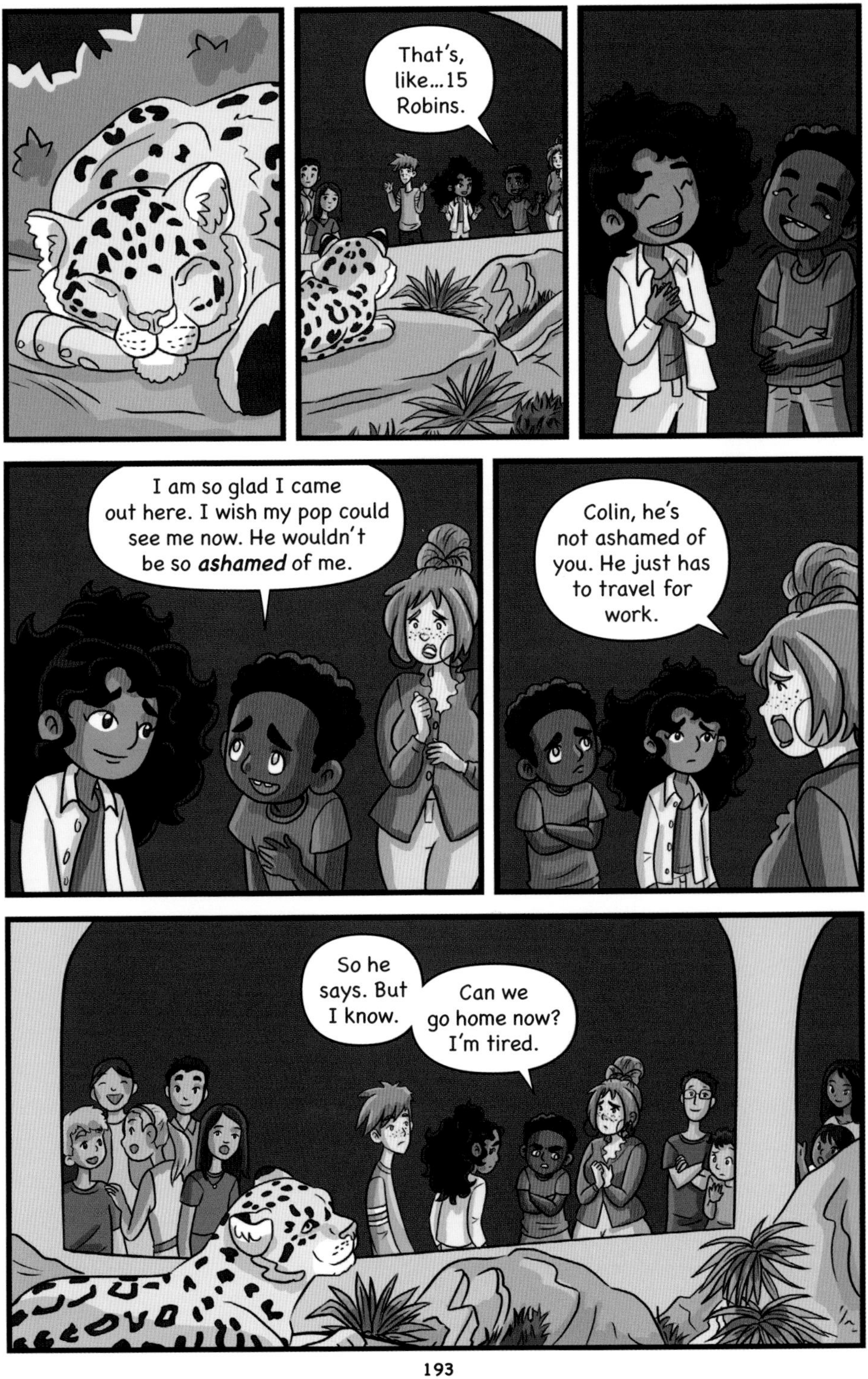
That's, like...15 Robins.
I am so glad I came out here. I wish my pop could see me now. He wouldn't be so *ashamed* of me.
Colin, he's not ashamed of you. He just has to travel for work.
So he says. But I know.
Can we go home now? I'm tired.

Martha

eMAIL

INBOX | Starred | Sent | Drafts | Spam

NEW MESSAGE

TO: archibald_craven@craveninc.com

FROM: martha_cravenhousehold@craveninc.com

SUBJECT: Mary Update

Mr. Craven,

I hope you're having a good time in Asia and not working too hard! Spring has finally truly sprung here in NYC and I wanted to just give you an update on the house. I've gotten to know Mary, and even though she started out a little prickly, she's turned out to be a great girl. She and Dickon have become fast friends! Colin is doing well, really well, in fact. He was asking about you just today. Maybe we can set up a time for you to have a video call with him? Just a thought.

Best,
Martha

SEND

Personal

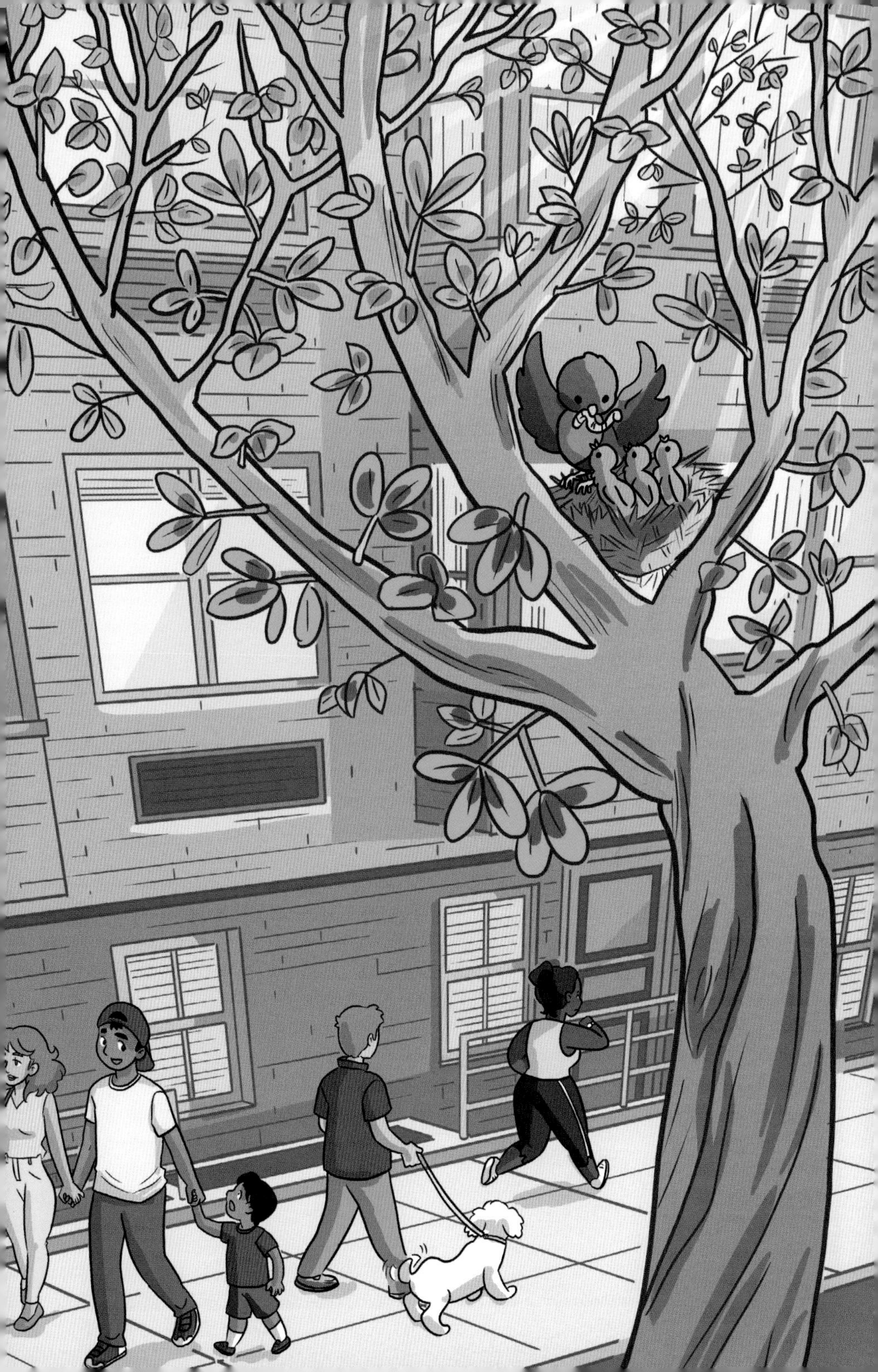

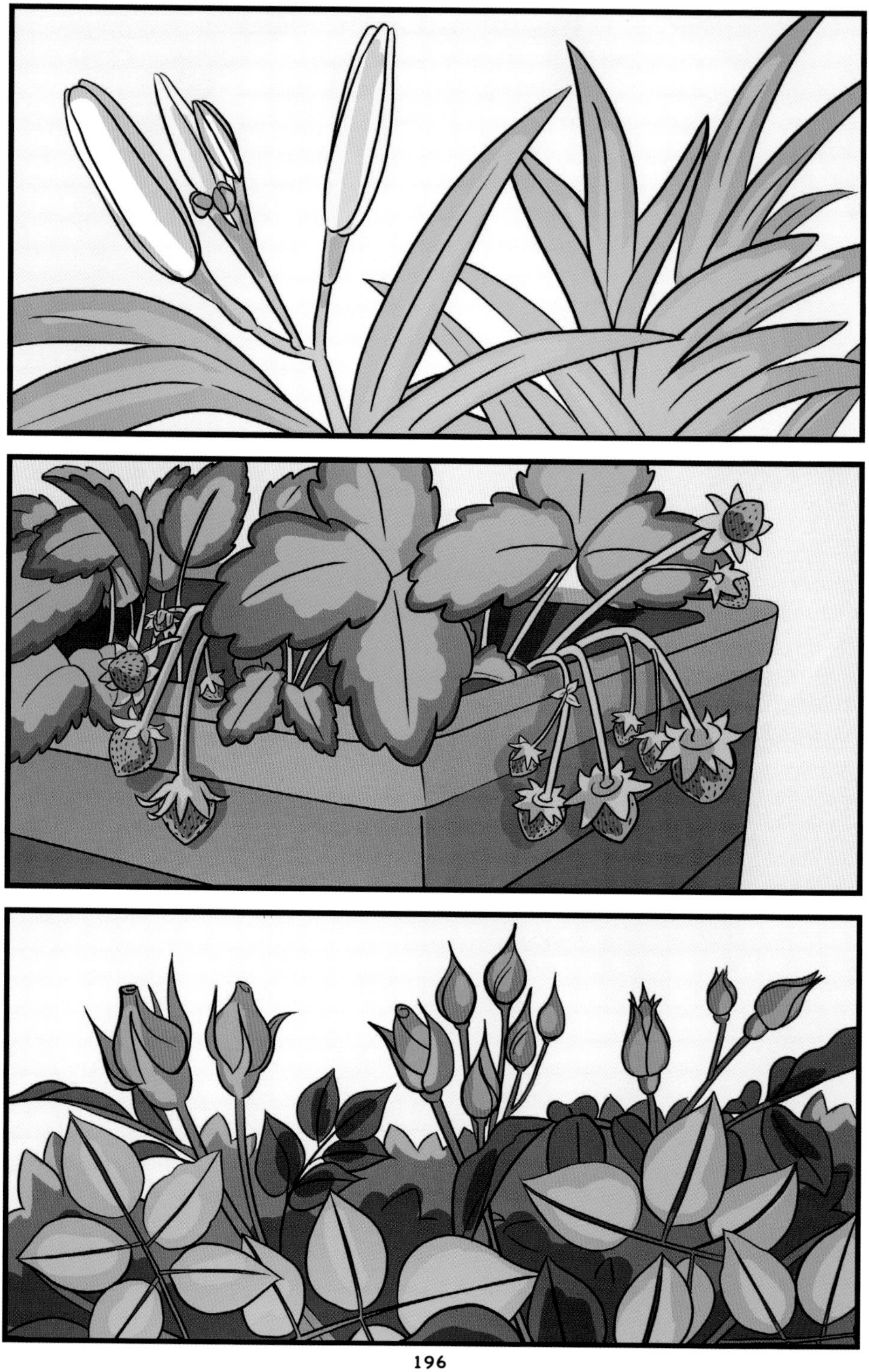

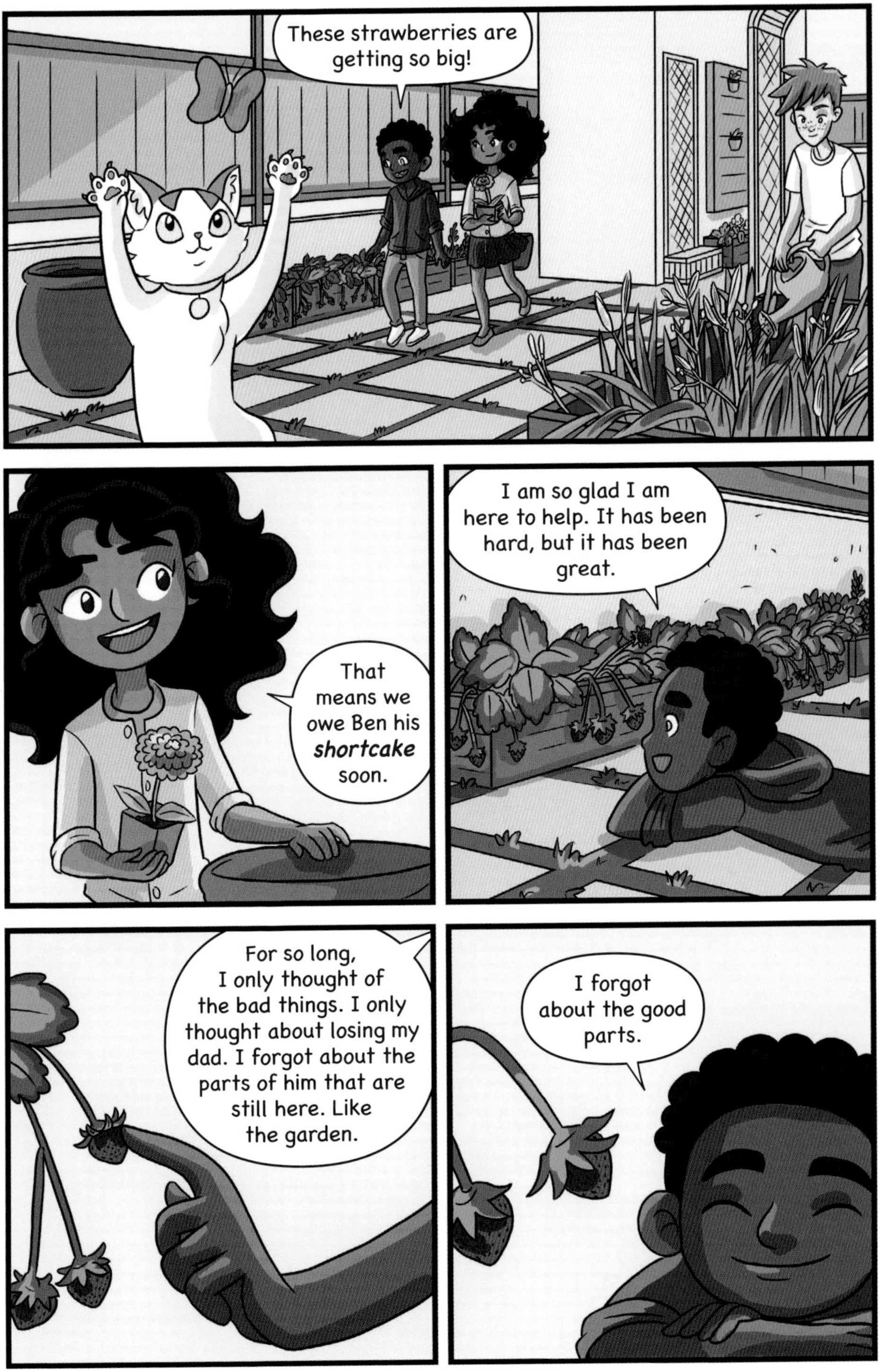
These strawberries are getting so big!
That means we owe Ben his ***shortcake*** soon.
I am so glad I am here to help. It has been hard, but it has been great.
For so long, I only thought of the bad things. I only thought about losing my dad. I forgot about the parts of him that are still here. Like the garden.
I forgot about the good parts.

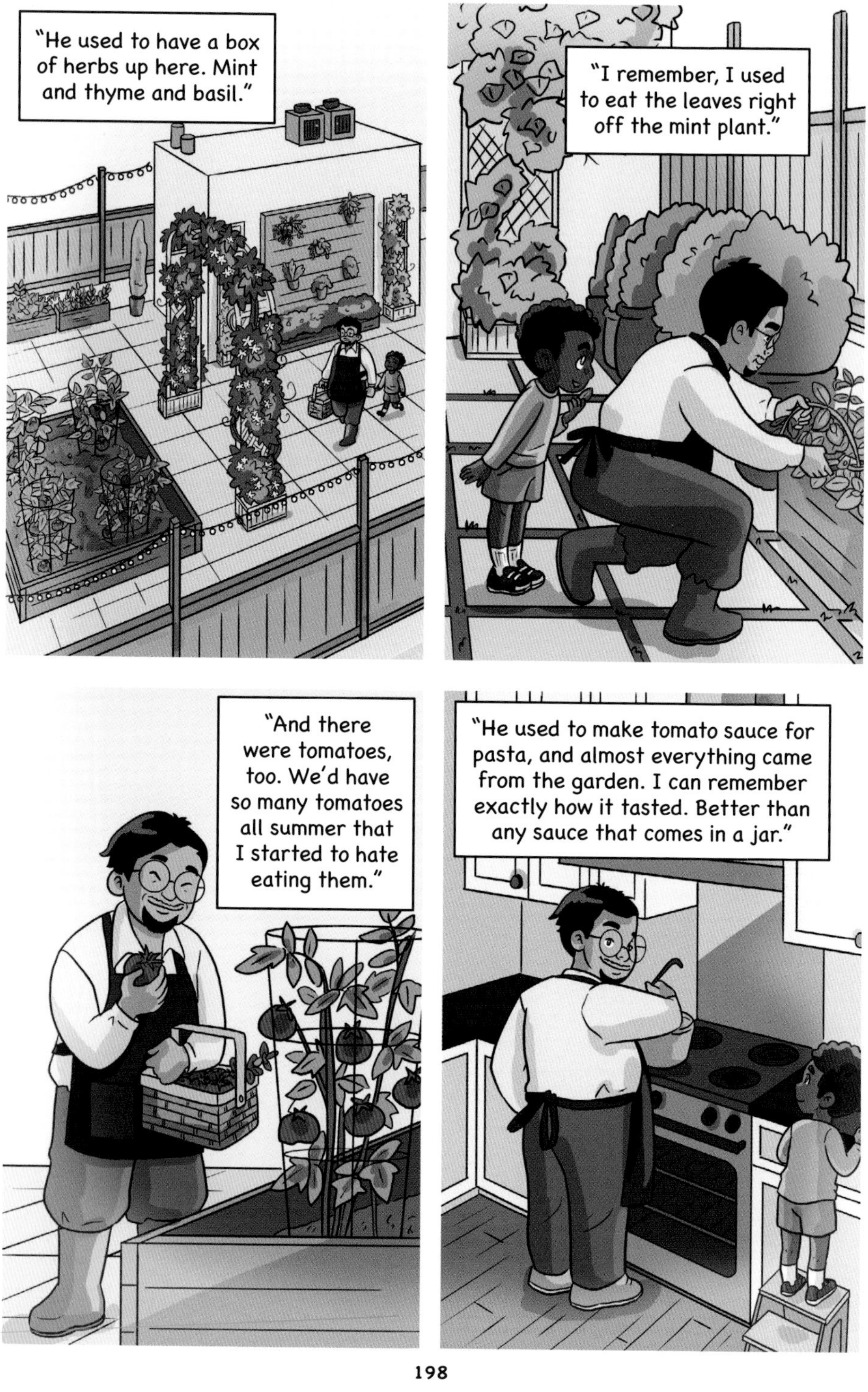
"He used to have a box of herbs up here. Mint and thyme and basil."
"I remember, I used to eat the leaves right off the mint plant."
"And there were tomatoes, too. We'd have so many tomatoes all summer that I started to hate eating them."
"He used to make tomato sauce for pasta, and almost everything came from the garden. I can remember exactly how it tasted. Better than any sauce that comes in a jar."

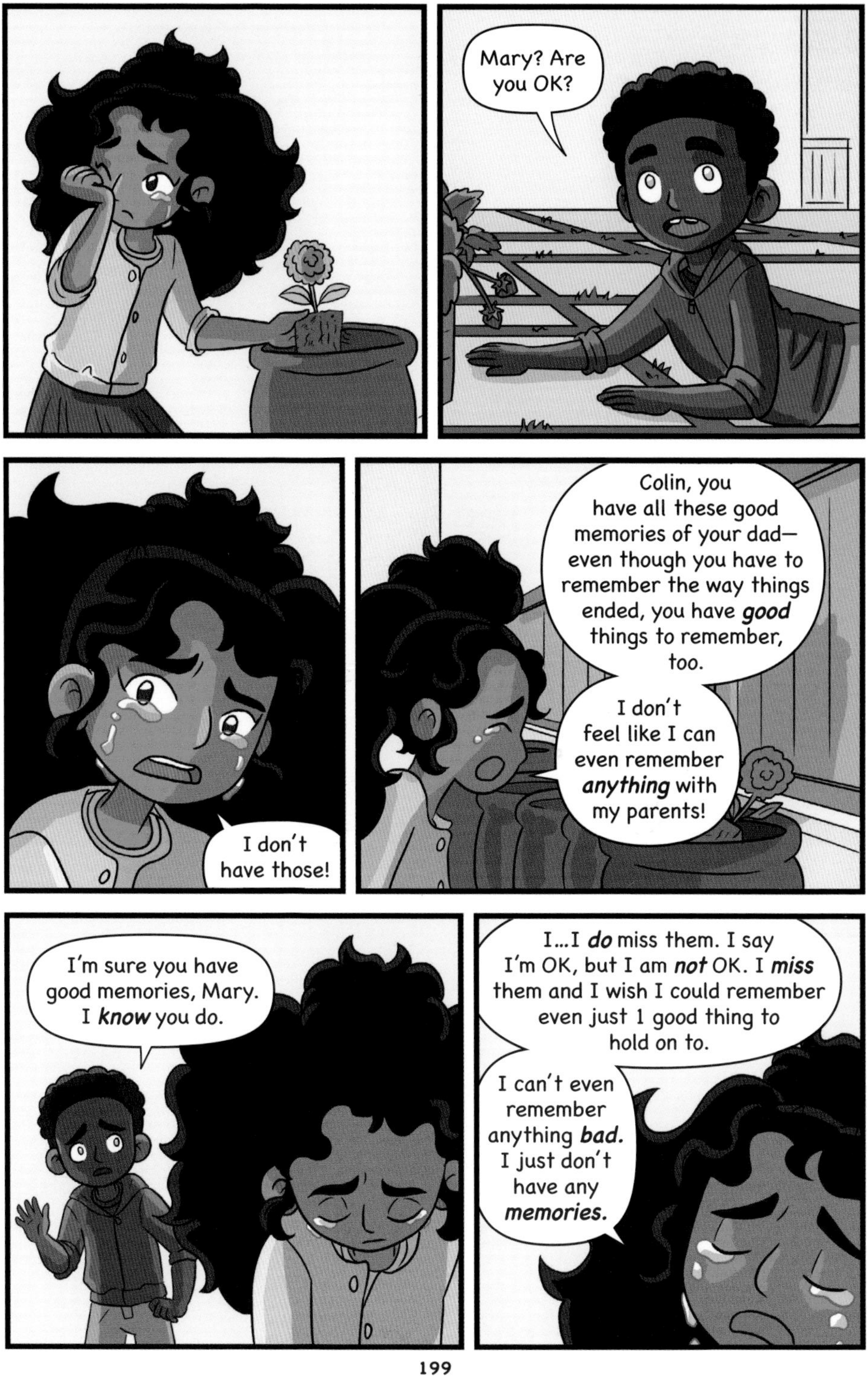
Mary? Are you OK?
Colin, you have all these good memories of your dad—even though you have to remember the way things ended, you have *good* things to remember, too.
I don't have those!
I don't feel like I can even remember *anything* with my parents!
I'm sure you have good memories, Mary. I *know* you do.
I...I *do* miss them. I say I'm OK, but I am *not* OK. I *miss* them and I wish I could remember even just 1 good thing to hold on to.
I can't even remember anything *bad.* I just don't have any *memories.*

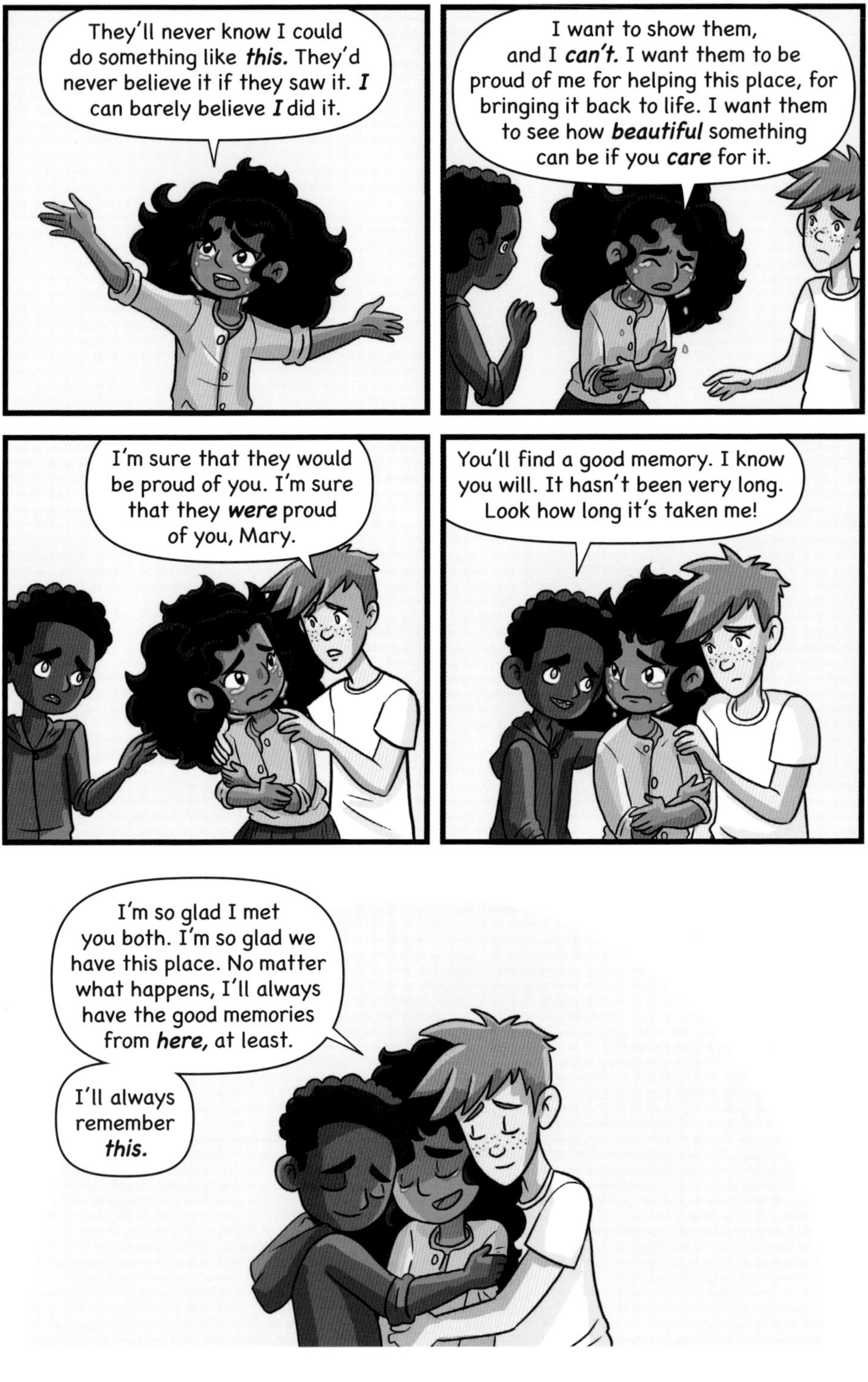
They'll never know I could do something like *this.* They'd never believe it if they saw it. *I* can barely believe *I* did it.
I want to show them, and I *can't.* I want them to be proud of me for helping this place, for bringing it back to life. I want them to see how *beautiful* something can be if you *care* for it.
I'm sure that they would be proud of you. I'm sure that they *were* proud of you, Mary.
You'll find a good memory. I know you will. It hasn't been very long. Look how long it's taken me!
I'm so glad I met you both. I'm so glad we have this place. No matter what happens, I'll always have the good memories from *here,* at least.
I'll always remember *this.*

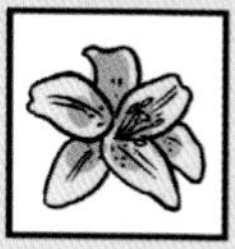

The_Secret_Garden

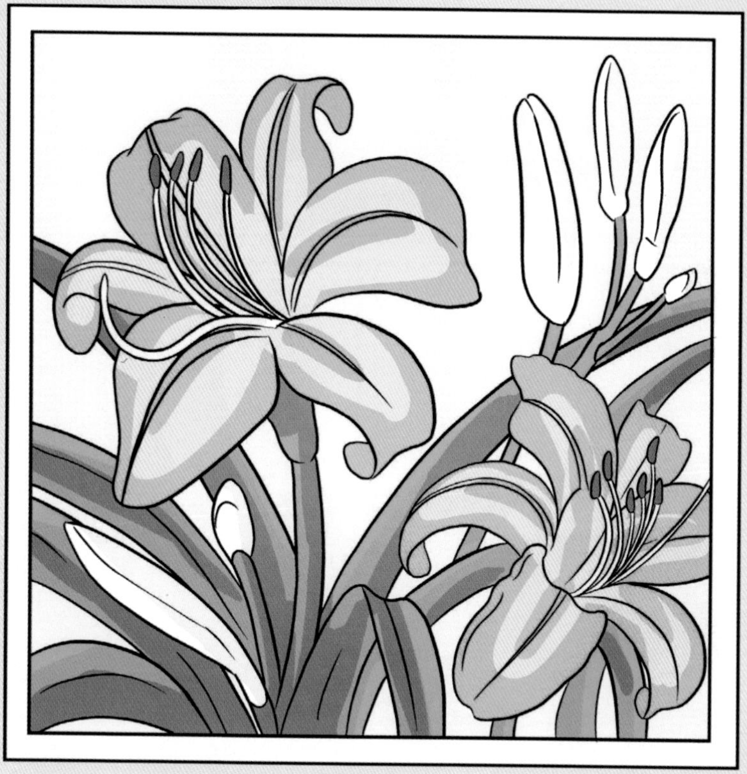

The_Secret_Garden Remember that ugly little bulb? It's a beautiful lily now! We were worried that it wouldn't grow in the raised beds, but now it's rocking this giant bloom. :) We also read online that daylily buds are edible—would you ever try one?

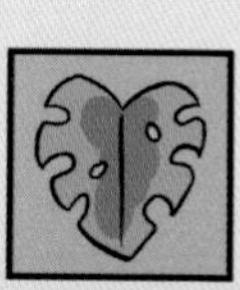

Plant-tasticPlants

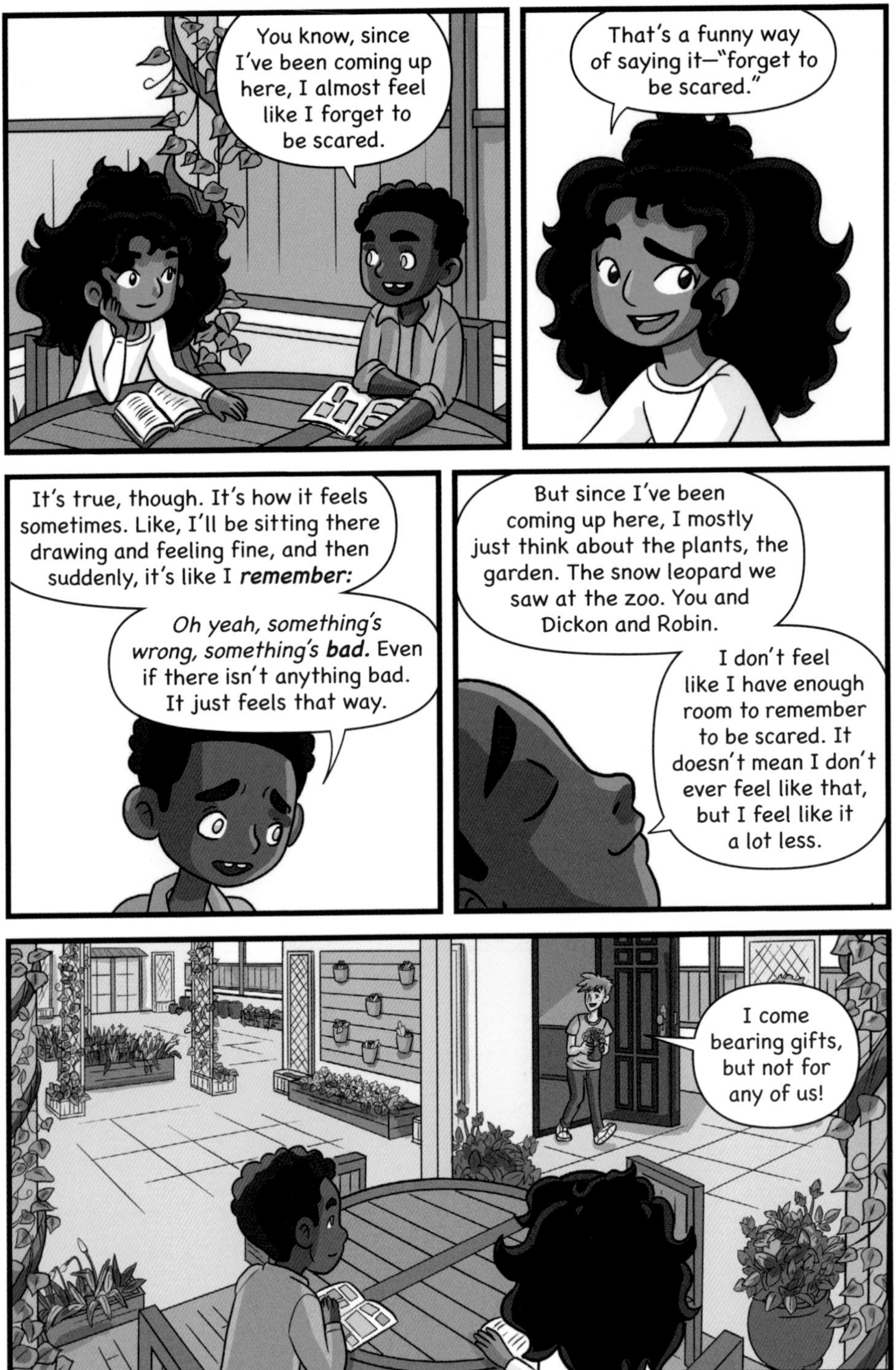
You know, since I've been coming up here, I almost feel like I forget to be scared.
That's a funny way of saying it—"forget to be scared."
It's true, though. It's how it feels sometimes. Like, I'll be sitting there drawing and feeling fine, and then suddenly, it's like I ***remember:***
Oh yeah, something's wrong, something's ***bad.*** Even if there isn't anything bad. It just feels that way.
But since I've been coming up here, I mostly just think about the plants, the garden. The snow leopard we saw at the zoo. You and Dickon and Robin.
I don't feel like I have enough room to remember to be scared. It doesn't mean I don't ever feel like that, but I feel like it a lot less.
I come bearing gifts, but not for any of us!

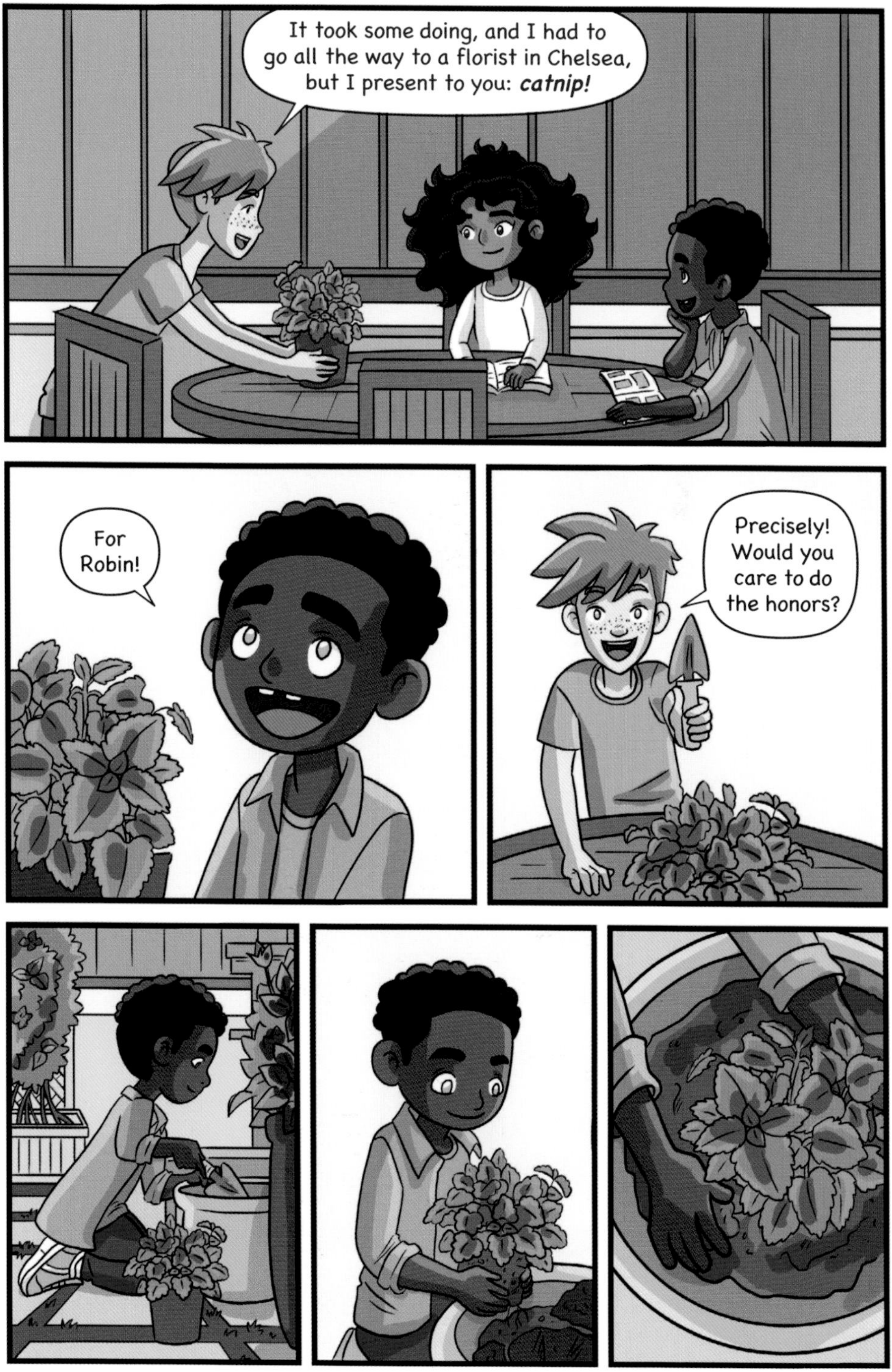
It took some doing, and I had to go all the way to a florist in Chelsea, but I present to you: *catnip!*
For Robin!
Precisely! Would you care to do the honors?

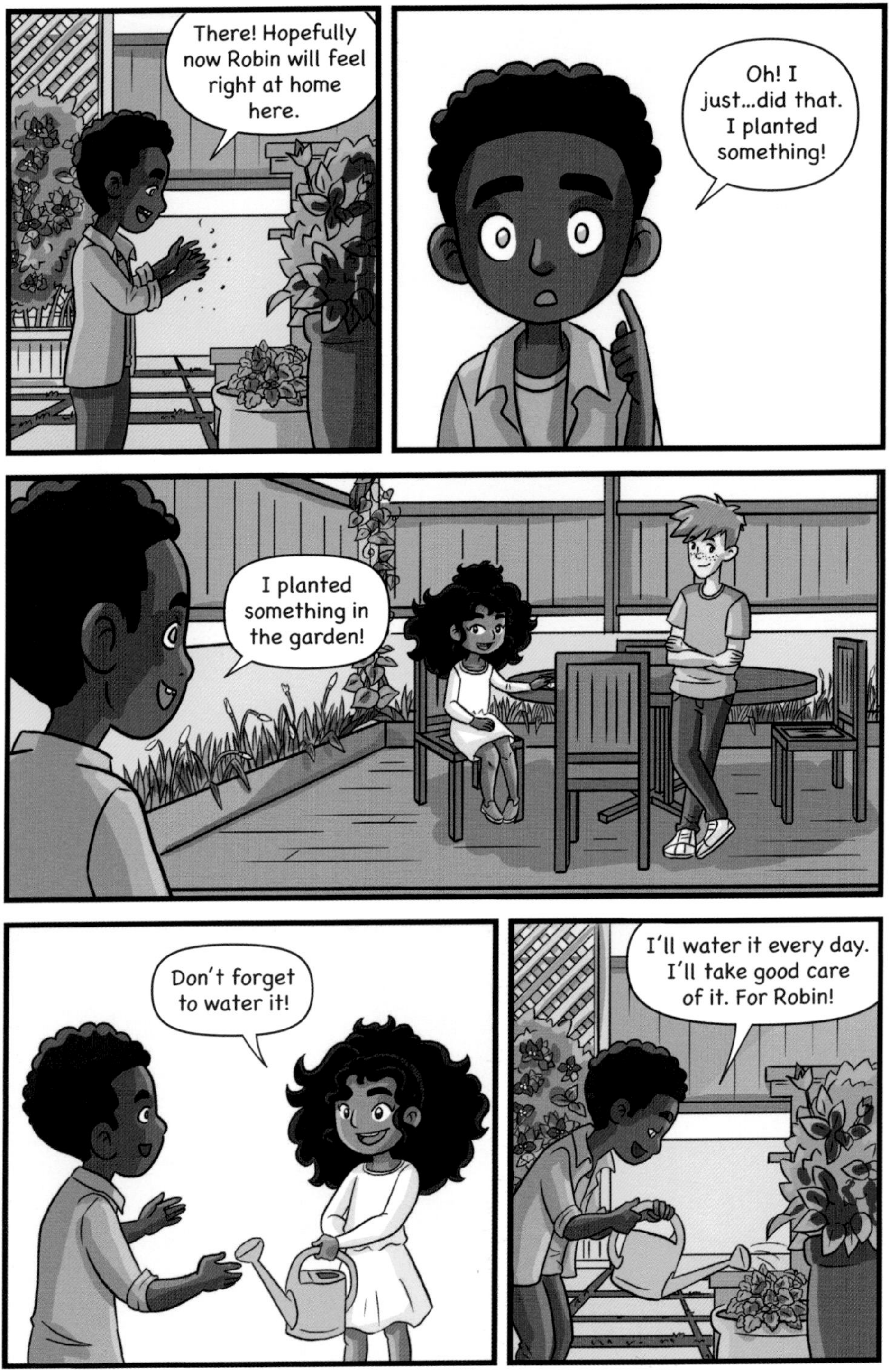
There! Hopefully now Robin will feel right at home here.
Oh! I just...did that. I planted something!
I planted something in the garden!
Don't forget to water it!
I'll water it every day. I'll take good care of it. For Robin!

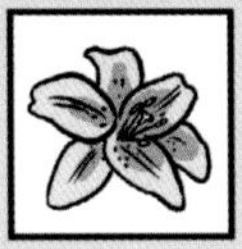

The_Secret_Garden

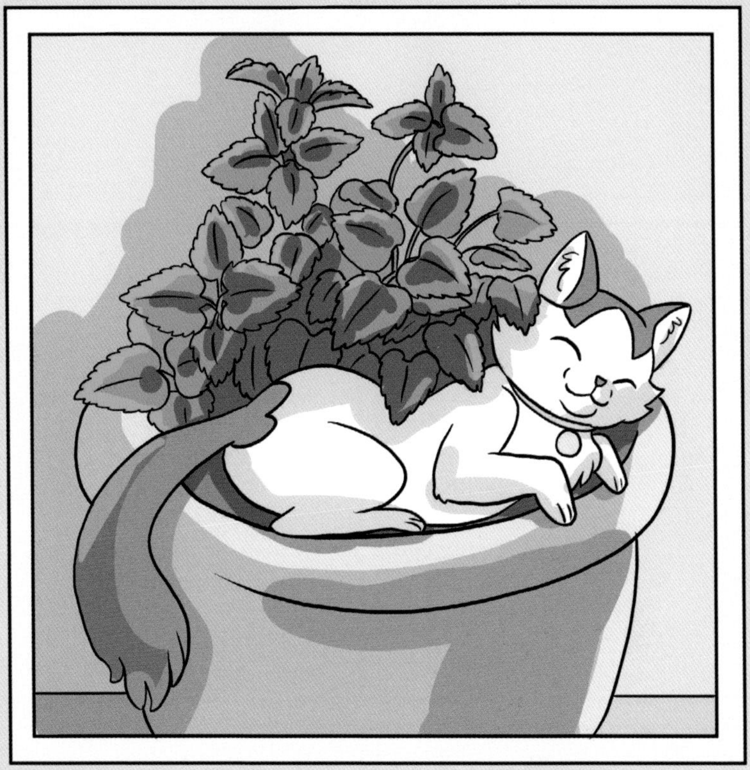

The_Secret_Garden Happy #Caturday! Did you know that both catnip plants and cats love a hot, sunny spot?

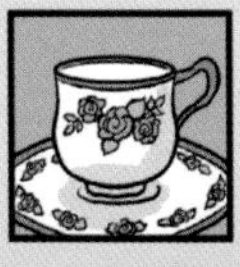

therealcupoftea

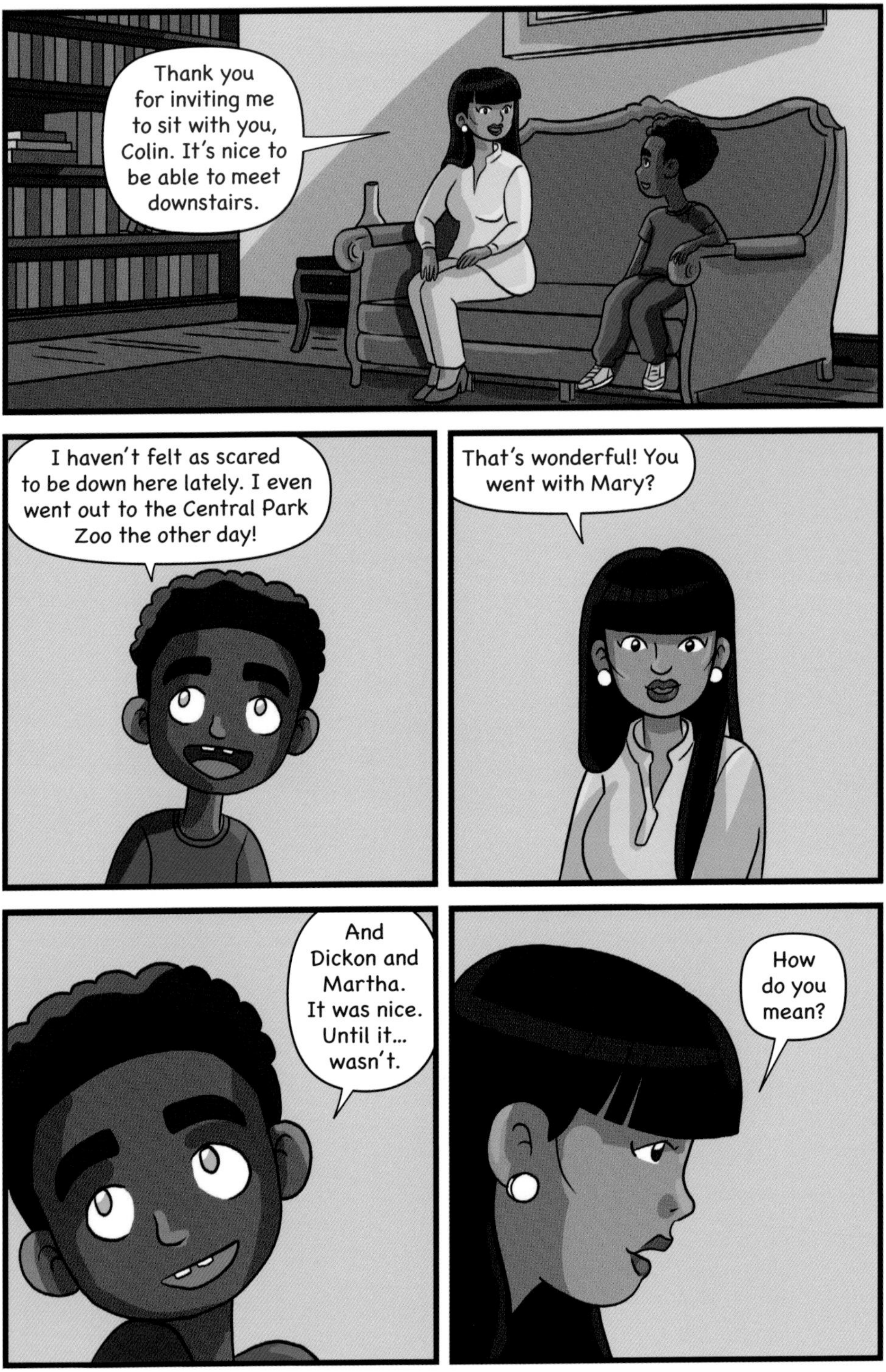
Thank you for inviting me to sit with you, Colin. It's nice to be able to meet downstairs.
I haven't felt as scared to be down here lately. I even went out to the Central Park Zoo the other day!
That's wonderful! You went with Mary?
And Dickon and Martha. It was nice. Until it... wasn't.
How do you mean?

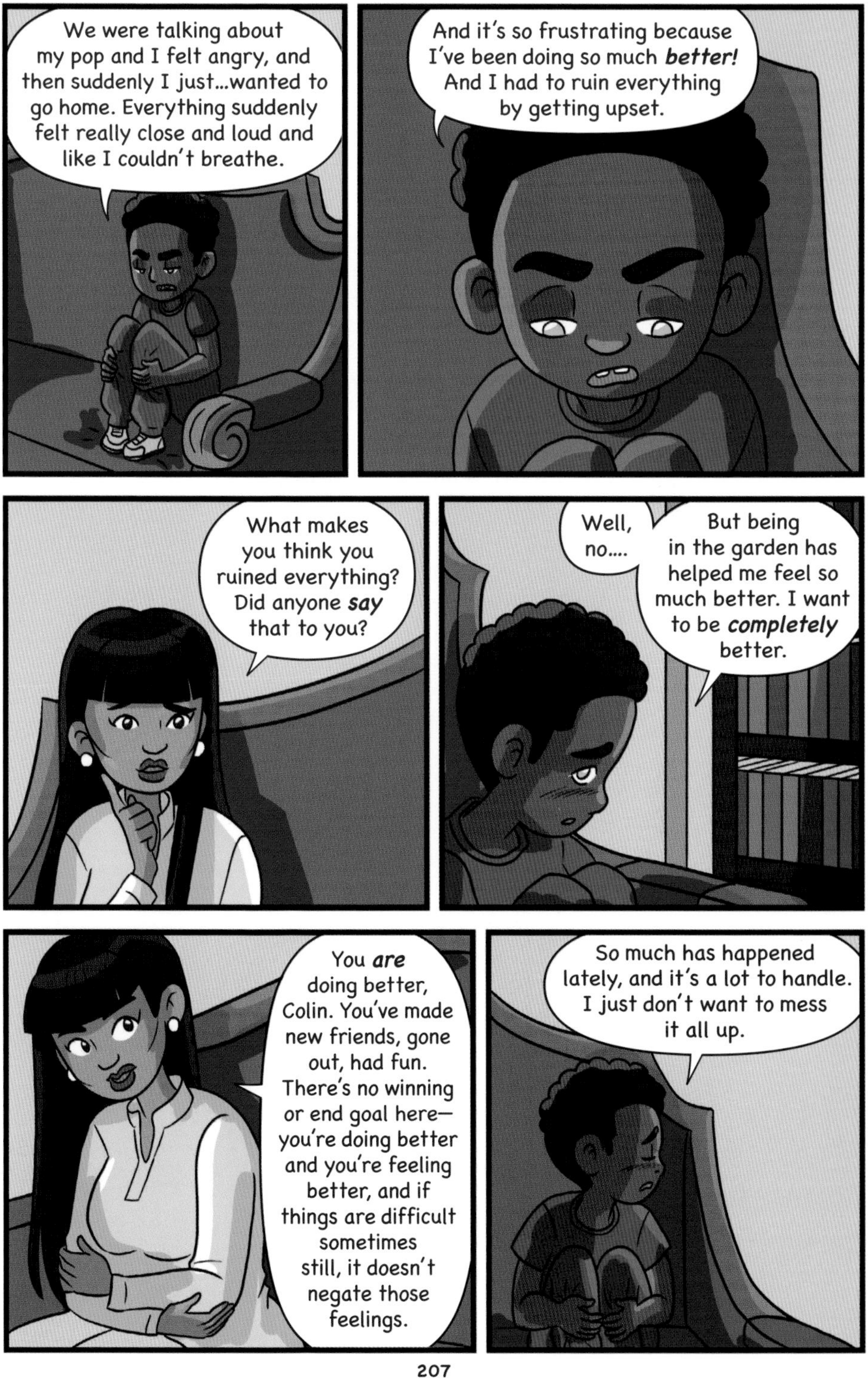
We were talking about my pop and I felt angry, and then suddenly I just...wanted to go home. Everything suddenly felt really close and loud and like I couldn't breathe.
And it's so frustrating because I've been doing so much ***better!*** And I had to ruin everything by getting upset.
What makes you think you ruined everything? Did anyone ***say*** that to you?
Well, no....
But being in the garden has helped me feel so much better. I want to be ***completely*** better.
You ***are*** doing better, Colin. You've made new friends, gone out, had fun. There's no winning or end goal here—you're doing better and you're feeling better, and if things are difficult sometimes still, it doesn't negate those feelings.
So much has happened lately, and it's a lot to handle. I just don't want to mess it all up.

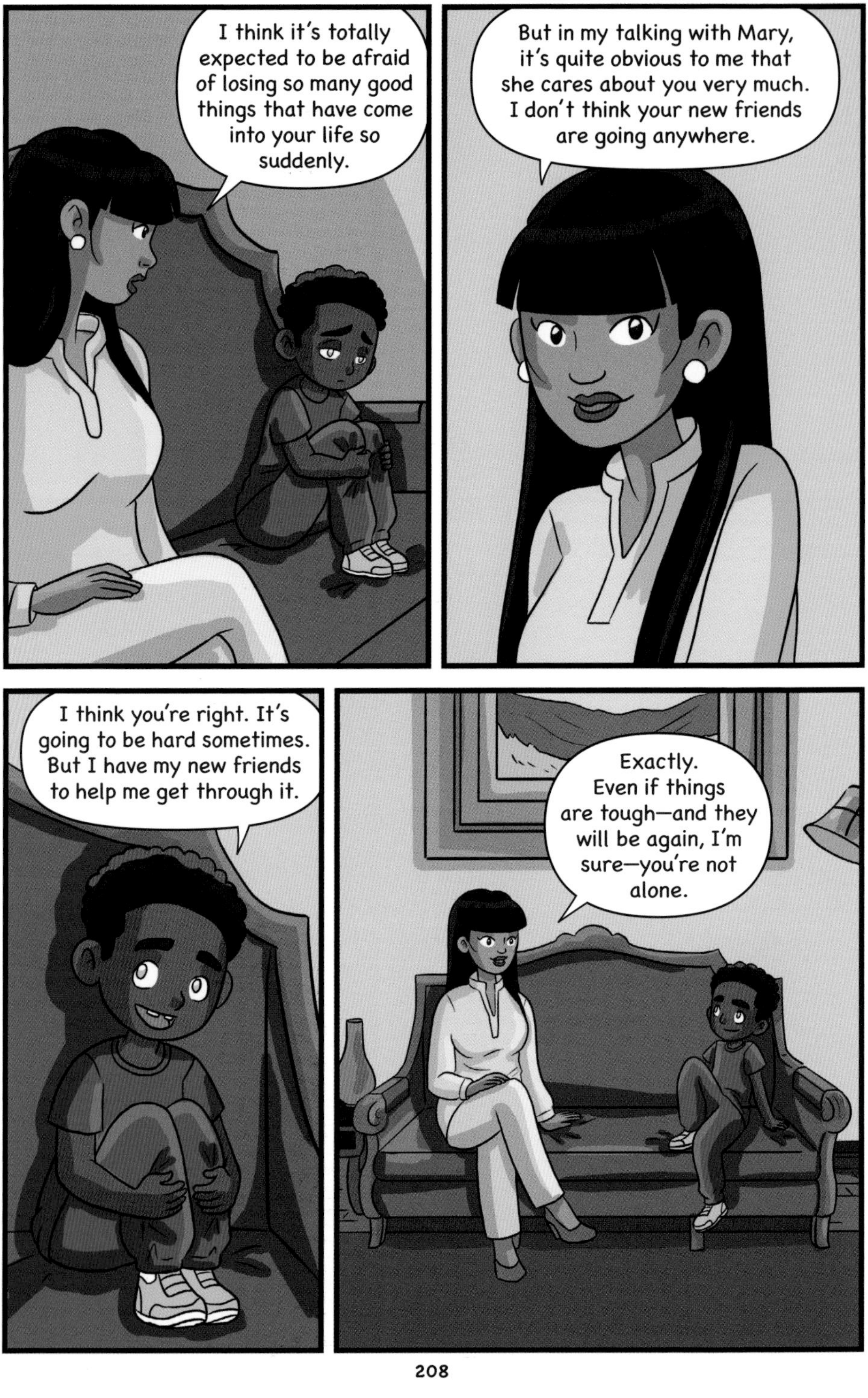
I think it's totally expected to be afraid of losing so many good things that have come into your life so suddenly.
But in my talking with Mary, it's quite obvious to me that she cares about you very much. I don't think your new friends are going anywhere.
I think you're right. It's going to be hard sometimes. But I have my new friends to help me get through it.
Exactly. Even if things are tough—and they will be again, I'm sure—you're not alone.

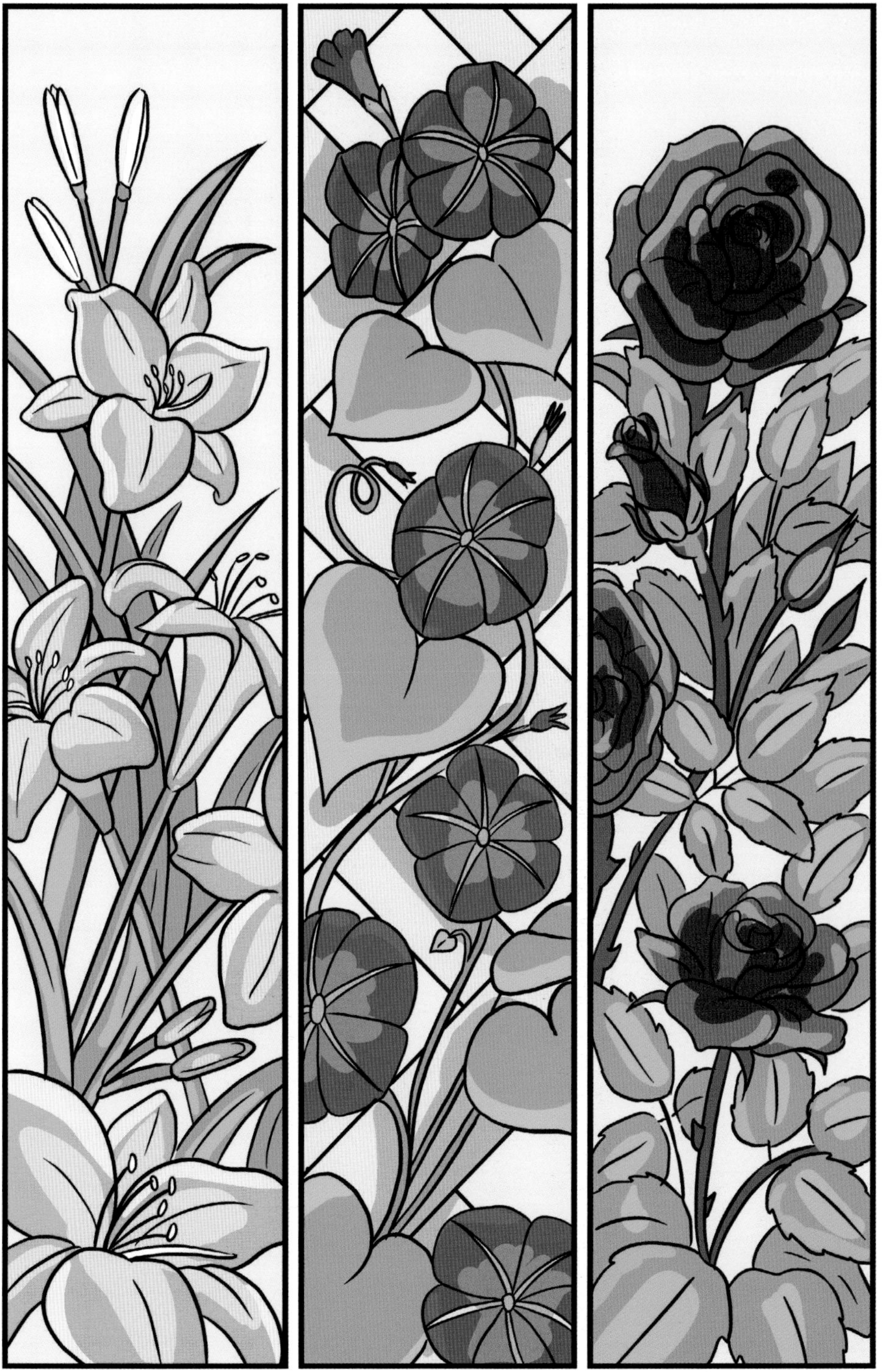

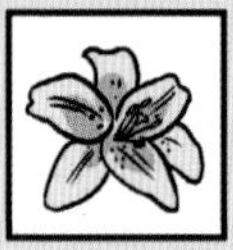

The_Secret_Garden

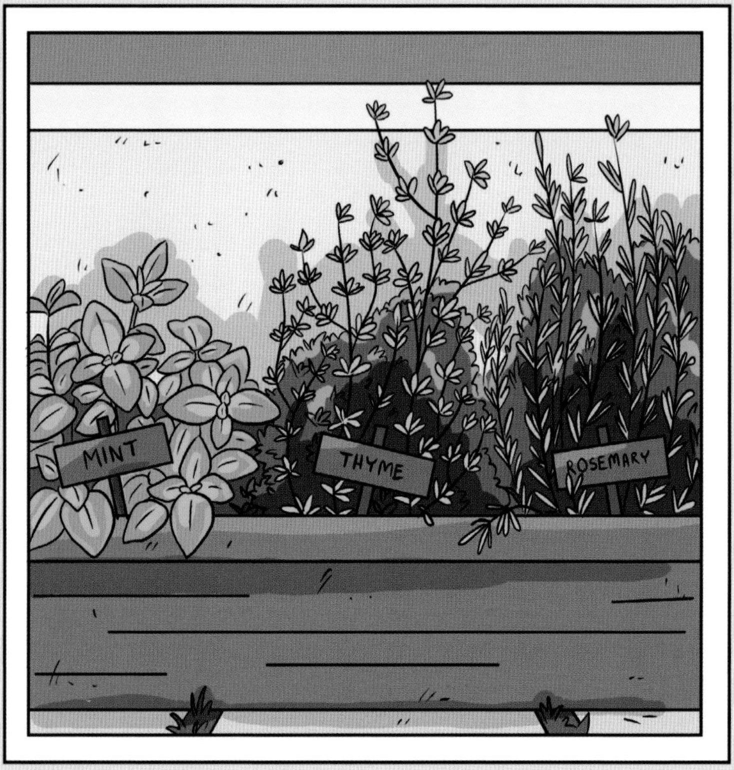
MINT
THYME
ROSEMARY

The_Secret_Garden We planted all the herbs where we'd brush past them while watering, pruning, and mulching…they smell amazing!

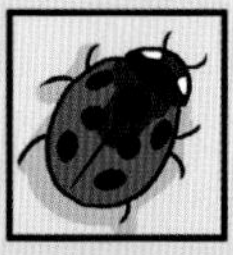

Bugs_And_Hugs

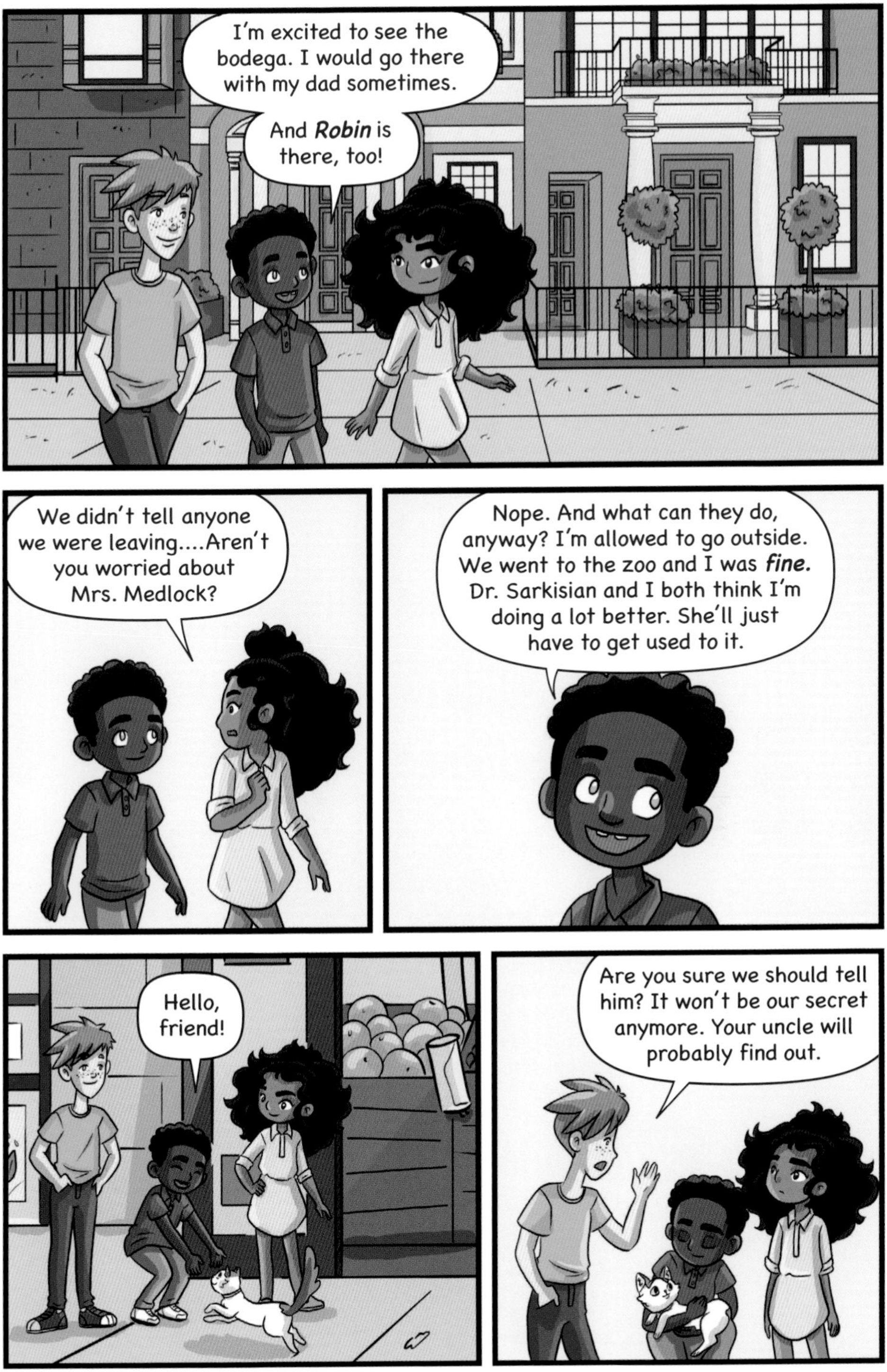
I'm excited to see the bodega. I would go there with my dad sometimes.
And *Robin* is there, too!
We didn't tell anyone we were leaving....Aren't you worried about Mrs. Medlock?
Nope. And what can they do, anyway? I'm allowed to go outside. We went to the zoo and I was *fine.* Dr. Sarkisian and I both think I'm doing a lot better. She'll just have to get used to it.
Hello, friend!
Are you sure we should tell him? It won't be our secret anymore. Your uncle will probably find out.

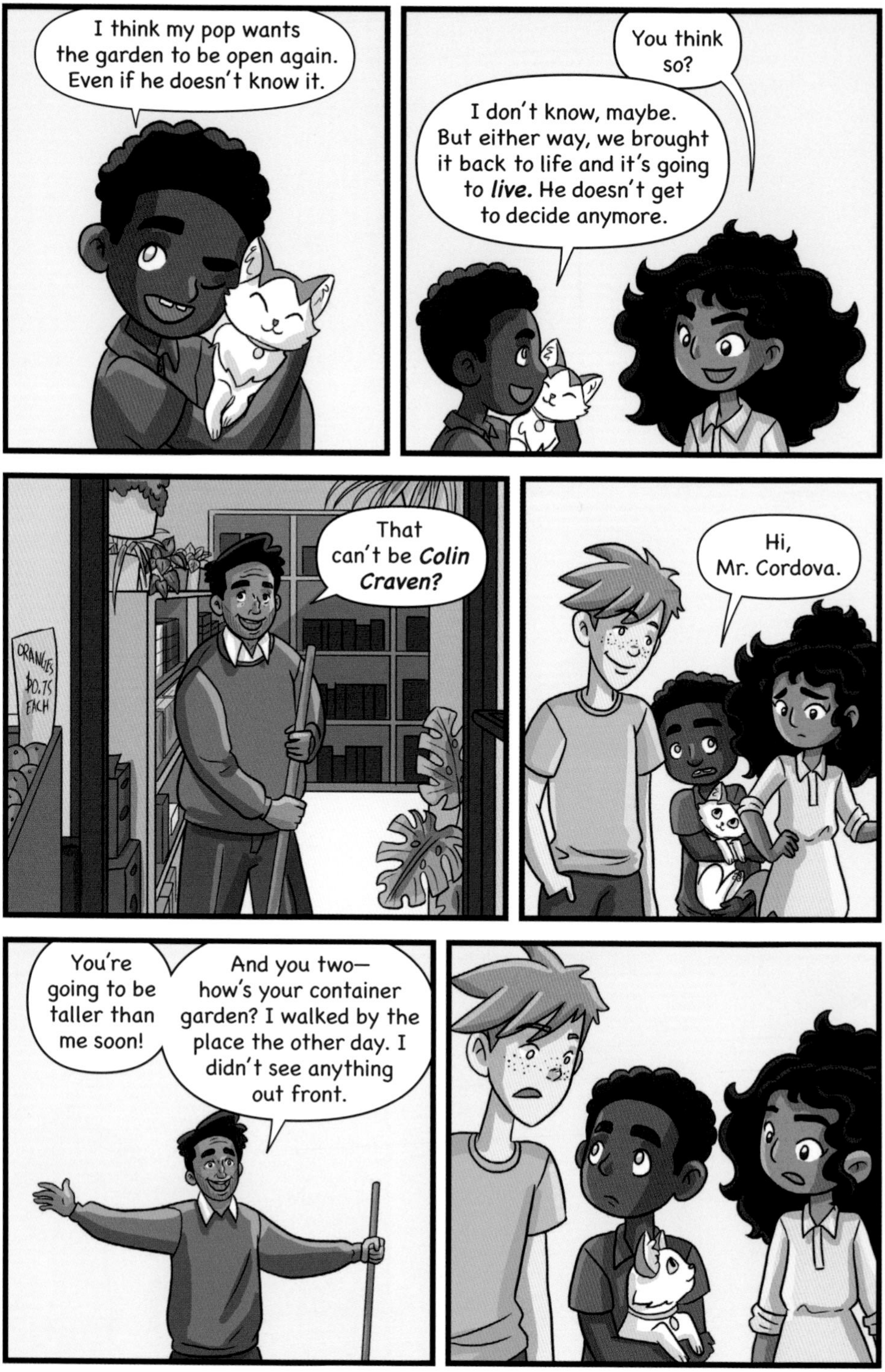
I think my pop wants the garden to be open again. Even if he doesn't know it.
You think so?
I don't know, maybe. But either way, we brought it back to life and it's going to *live.* He doesn't get to decide anymore.
ORANGES $0.75 EACH
That can't be ***Colin Craven?***
Hi, Mr. Cordova.
You're going to be taller than me soon!
And you two— how's your container garden? I walked by the place the other day. I didn't see anything out front.

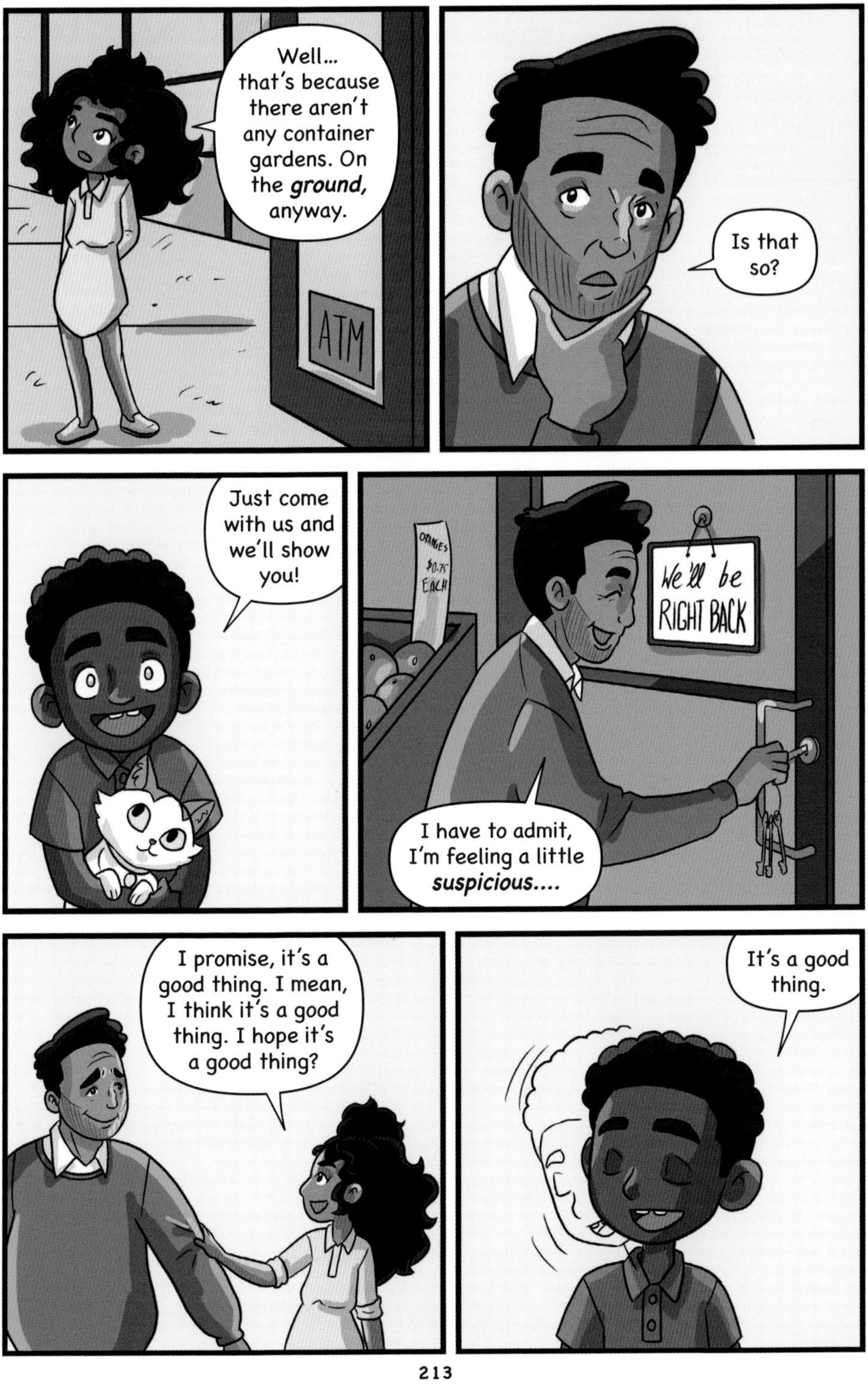
Well... that's because there aren't any container gardens. On the *ground,* anyway.
Is that so?
Just come with us and we'll show you!
ORANGES $0.75 EACH
We'll be RIGHT BACK
I have to admit, I'm feeling a little *suspicious....*
ATM
I promise, it's a good thing. I mean, I think it's a good thing. I hope it's a good thing?
It's a good thing.

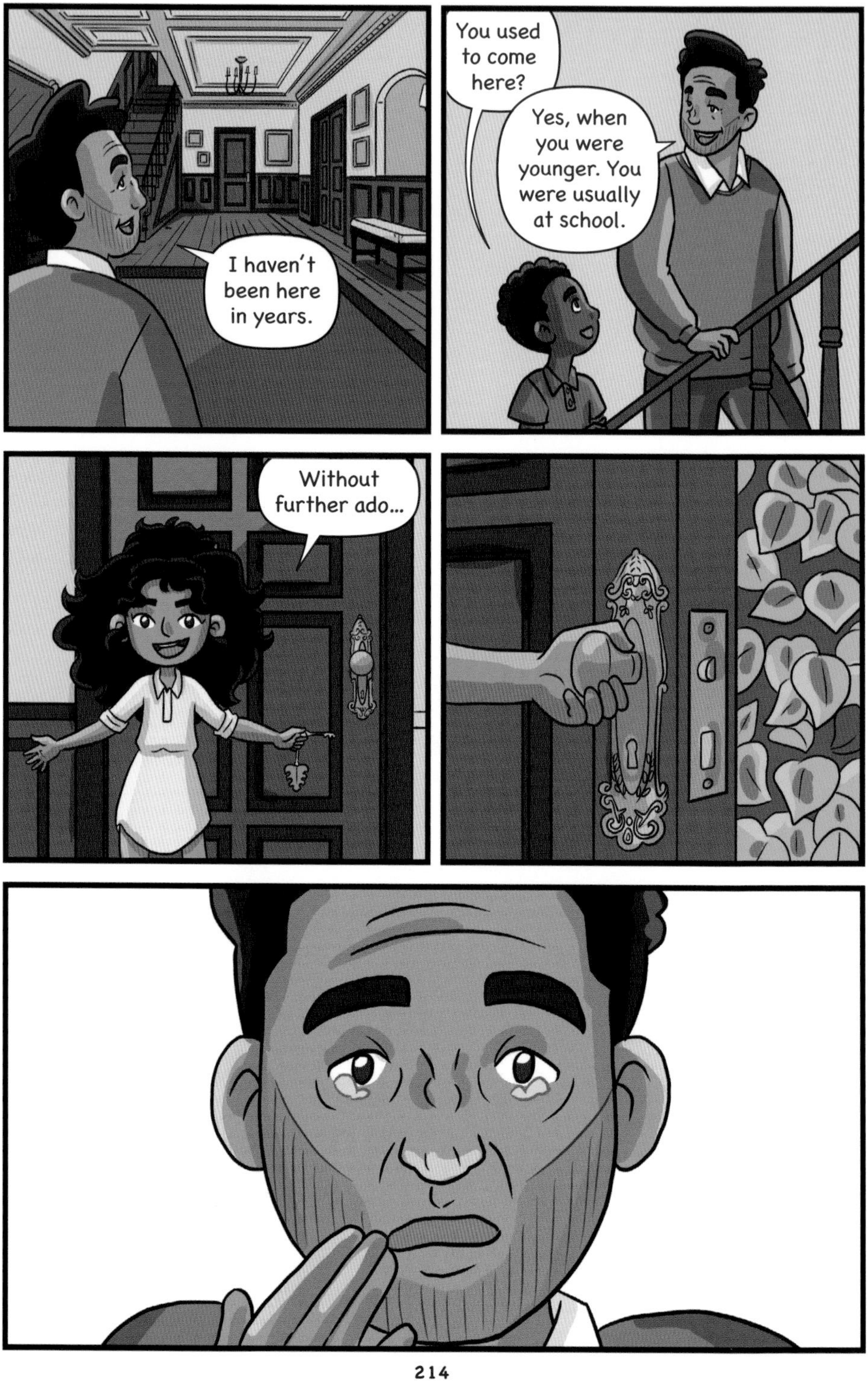
I haven't been here in years.
You used to come here?
Yes, when you were younger. You were usually at school.
Without further ado...

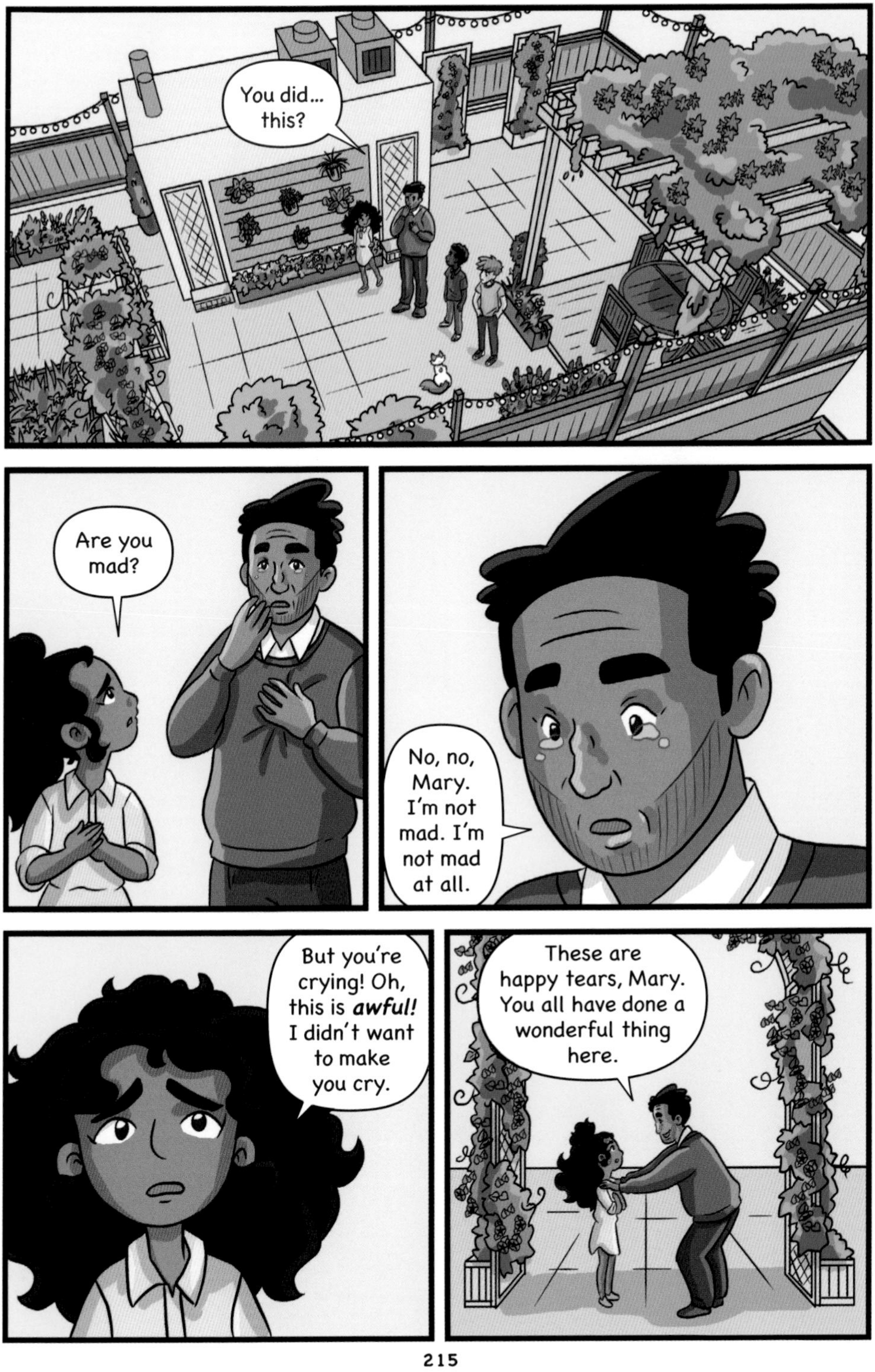
You did... this?
Are you mad?
No, no, Mary. I'm not mad. I'm not mad at all.
But you're crying! Oh, this is *awful!* I didn't want to make you cry.
These are happy tears, Mary. You all have done a wonderful thing here.

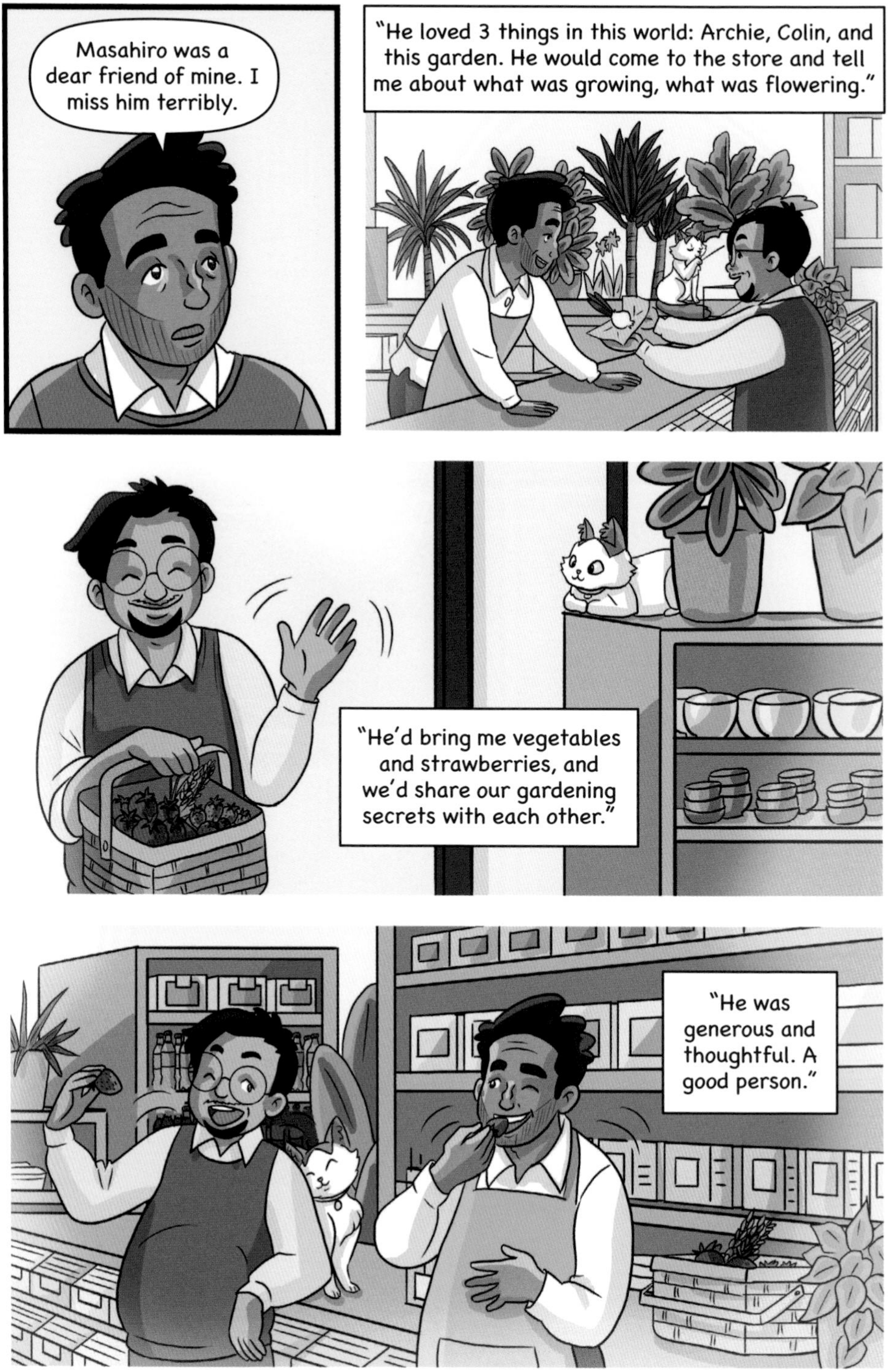
Masahiro was a dear friend of mine. I miss him terribly.
"He loved 3 things in this world: Archie, Colin, and this garden. He would come to the store and tell me about what was growing, what was flowering."
"He'd bring me vegetables and strawberries, and we'd share our gardening secrets with each other."
"He was generous and thoughtful. A good person."

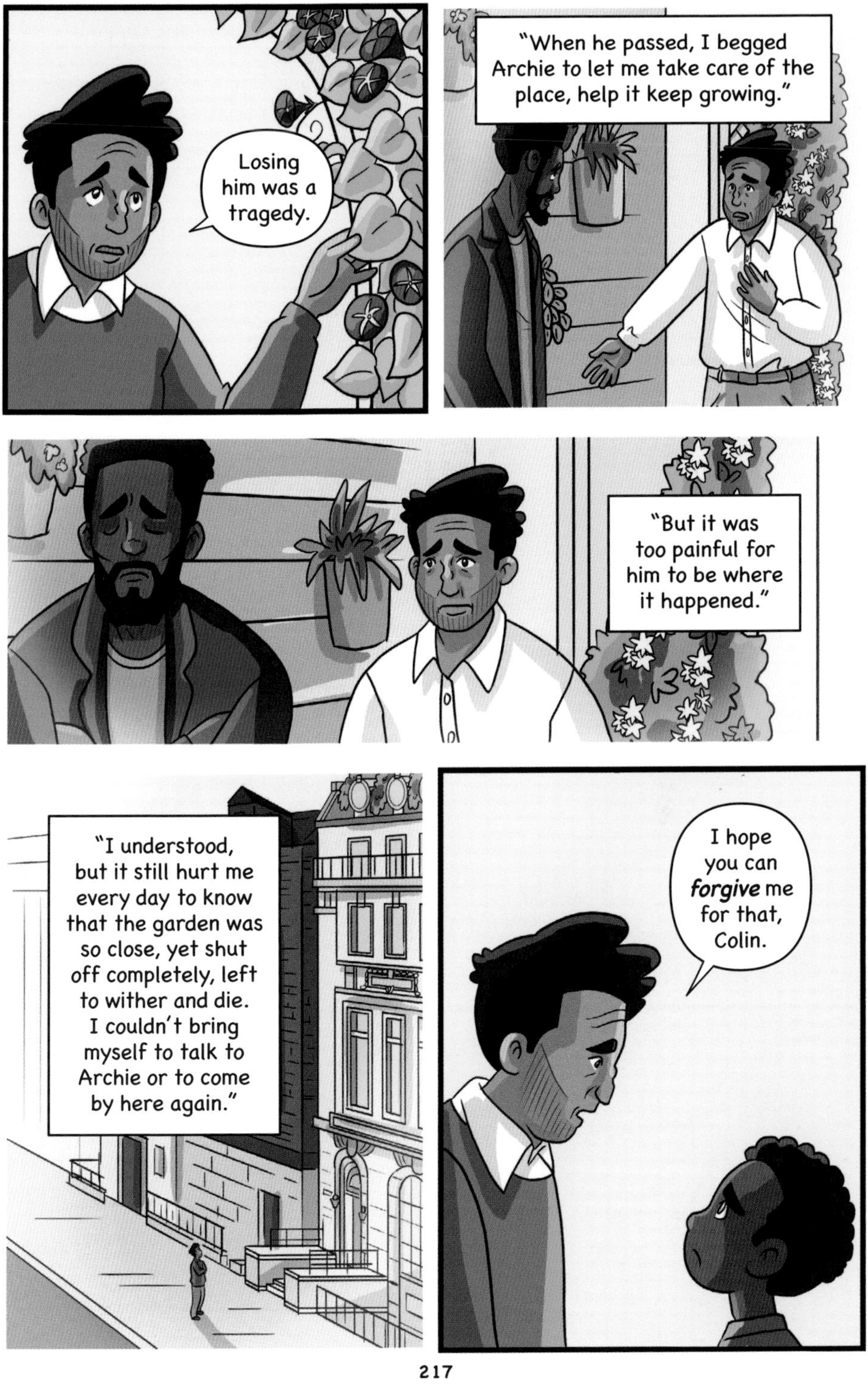
Losing him was a tragedy.
"When he passed, I begged Archie to let me take care of the place, help it keep growing."
"But it was too painful for him to be where it happened."
"I understood, but it still hurt me every day to know that the garden was so close, yet shut off completely, left to wither and die. I couldn't bring myself to talk to Archie or to come by here again."
I hope you can *forgive* me for that, Colin.

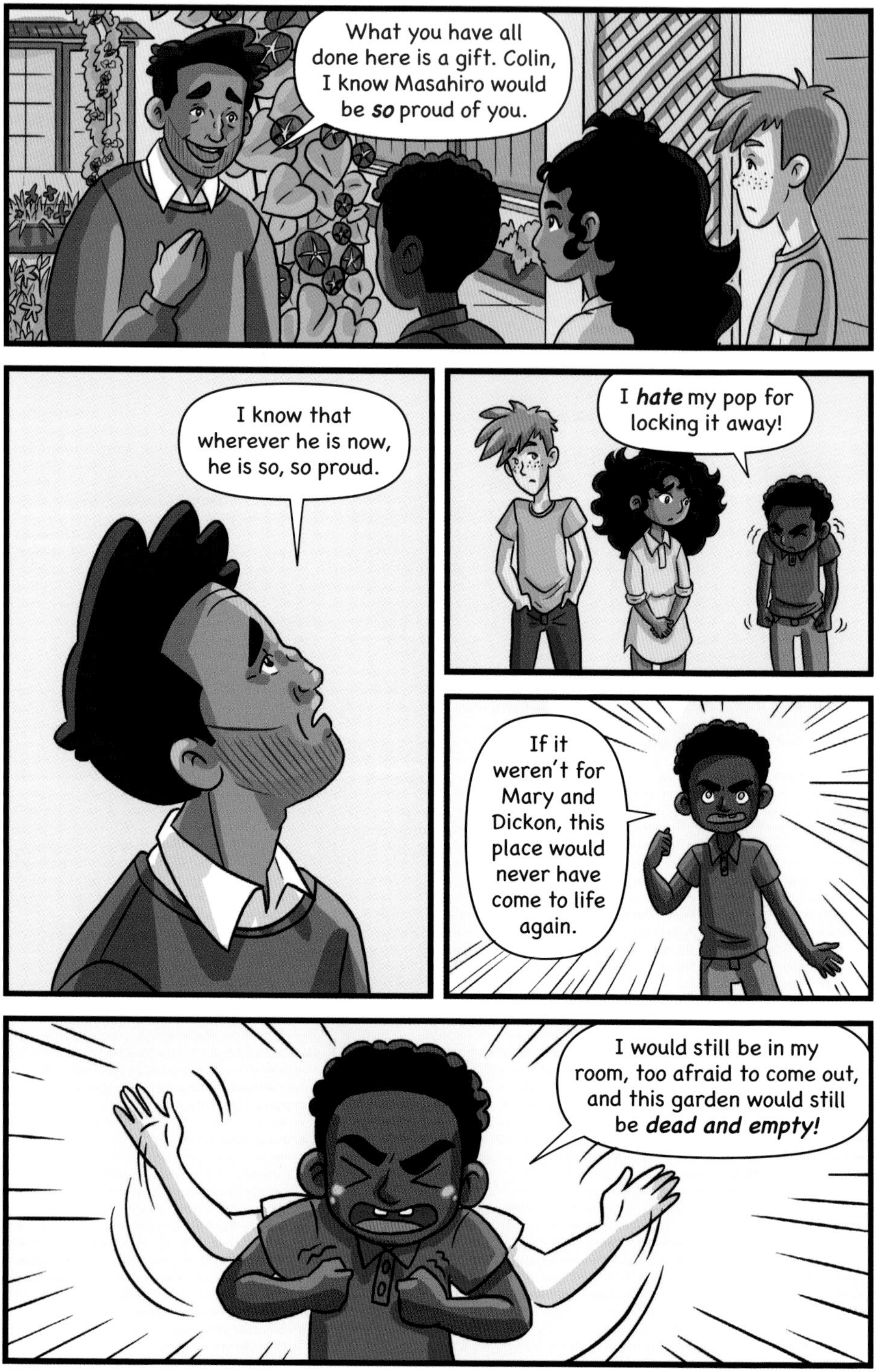

What you have all done here is a gift. Colin, I know Masahiro would be *so* proud of you.
I know that wherever he is now, he is so, so proud.
I *hate* my pop for locking it away!
If it weren't for Mary and Dickon, this place would never have come to life again.
I would still be in my room, too afraid to come out, and this garden would still be *dead and empty!*

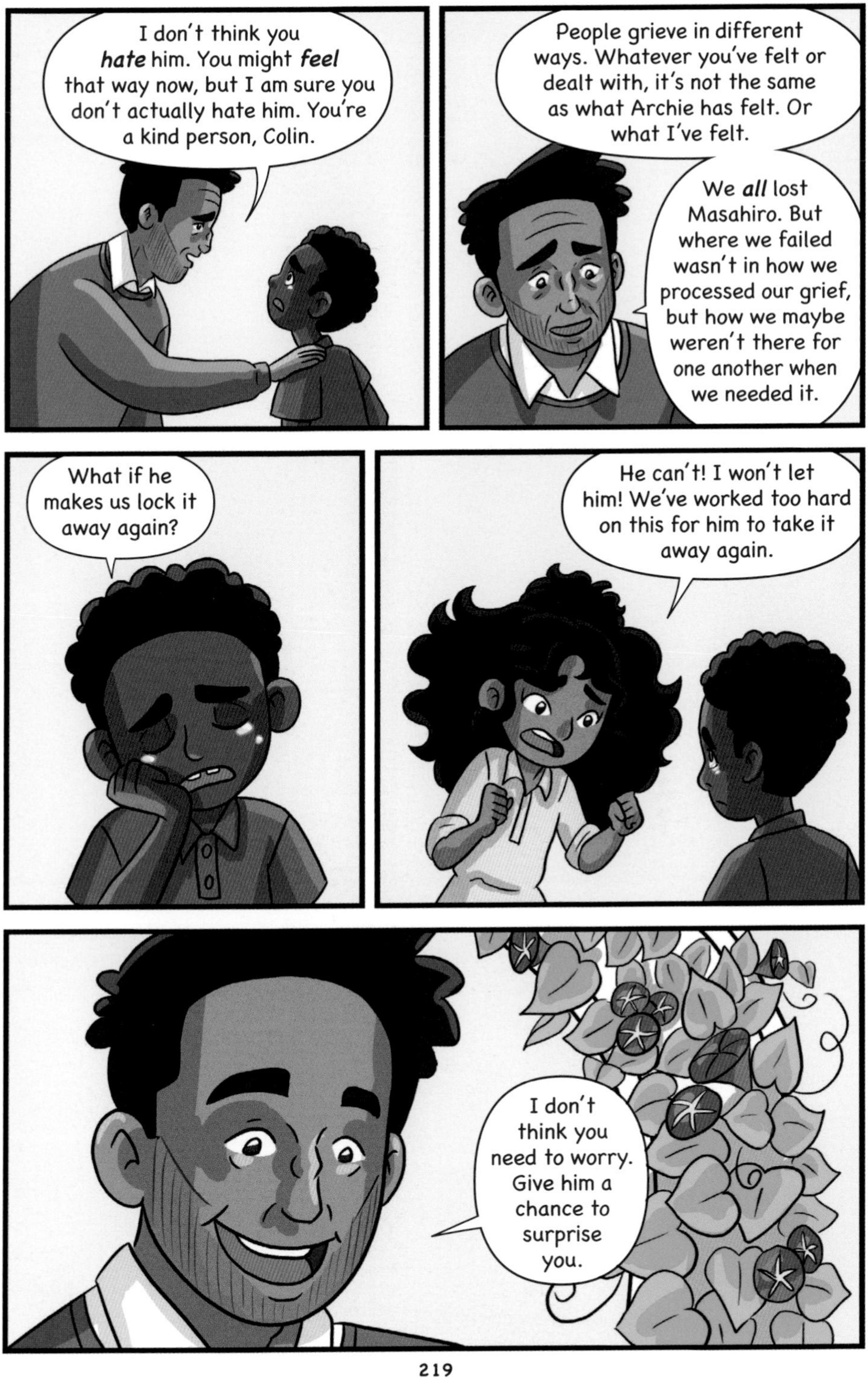
I don't think you *hate* him. You might *feel* that way now, but I am sure you don't actually hate him. You're a kind person, Colin.
People grieve in different ways. Whatever you've felt or dealt with, it's not the same as what Archie has felt. Or what I've felt.
We *all* lost Masahiro. But where we failed wasn't in how we processed our grief, but how we maybe weren't there for one another when we needed it.
What if he makes us lock it away again?
He can't! I won't let him! We've worked too hard on this for him to take it away again.
I don't think you need to worry. Give him a chance to surprise you.

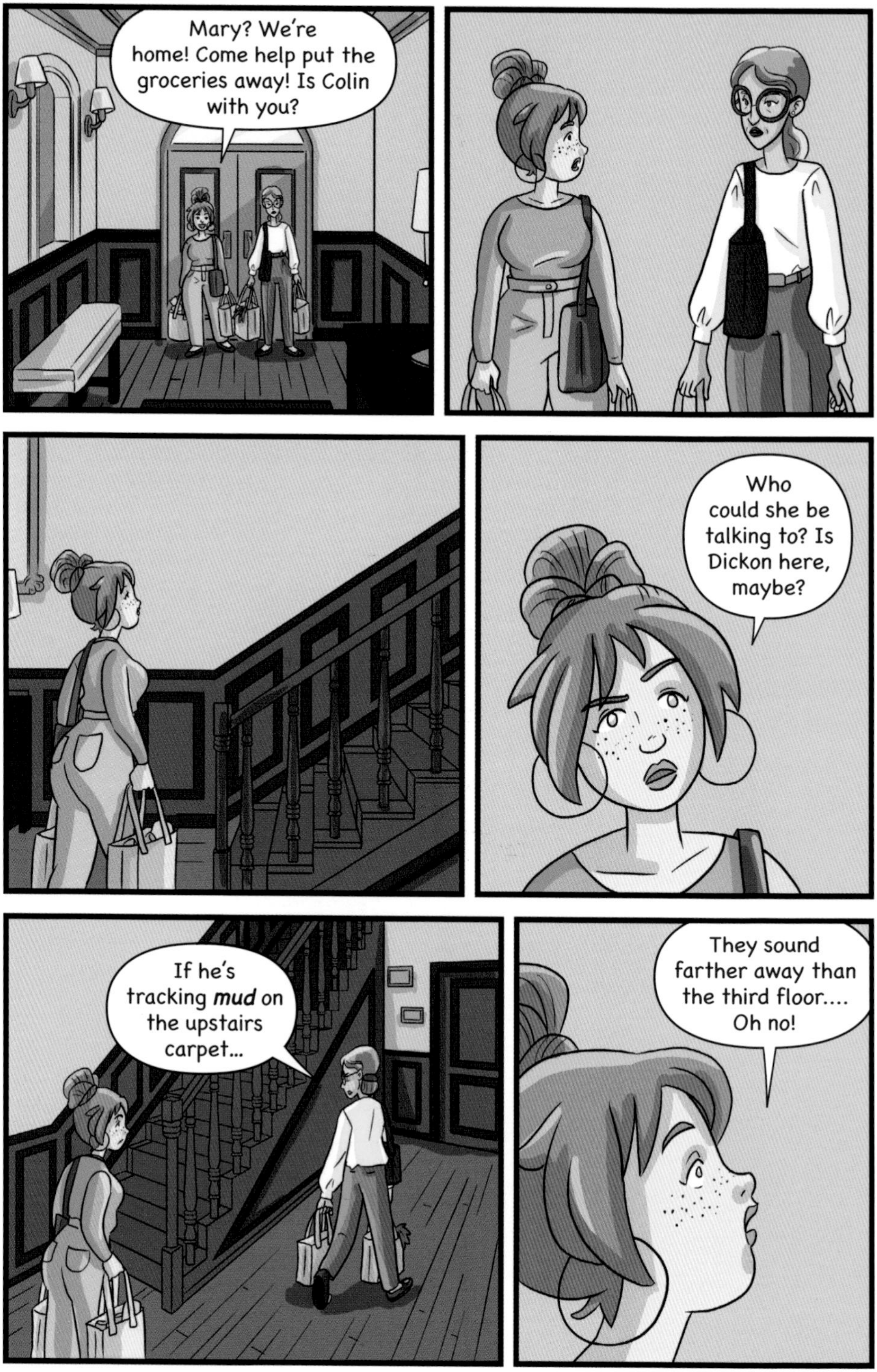
Mary? We're home! Come help put the groceries away! Is Colin with you?
Who could she be talking to? Is Dickon here, maybe?
If he's tracking *mud* on the upstairs carpet...
They sound farther away than the third floor.... Oh no!

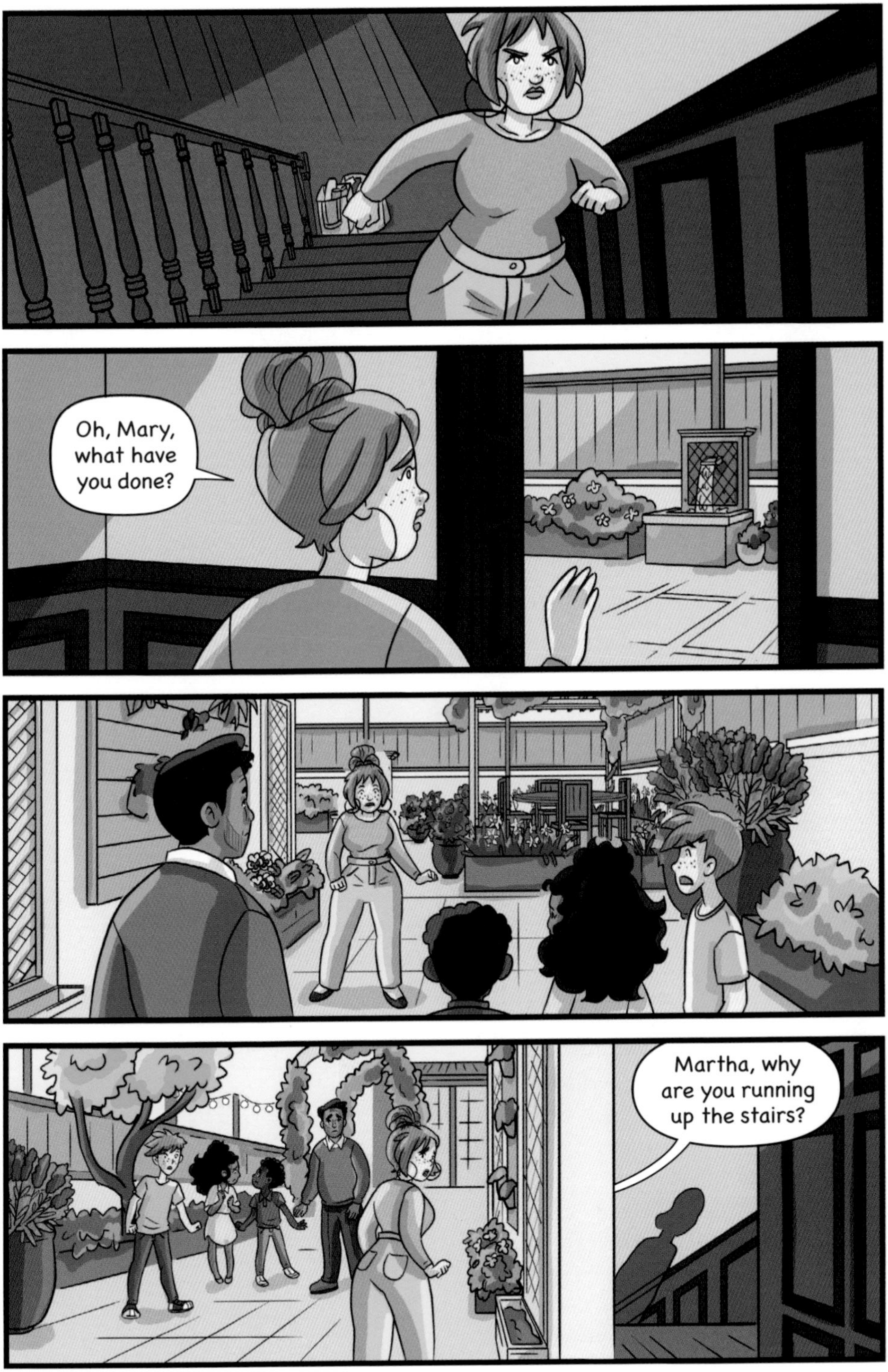
Oh, Mary, what have you done?
Martha, why are you running up the stairs?

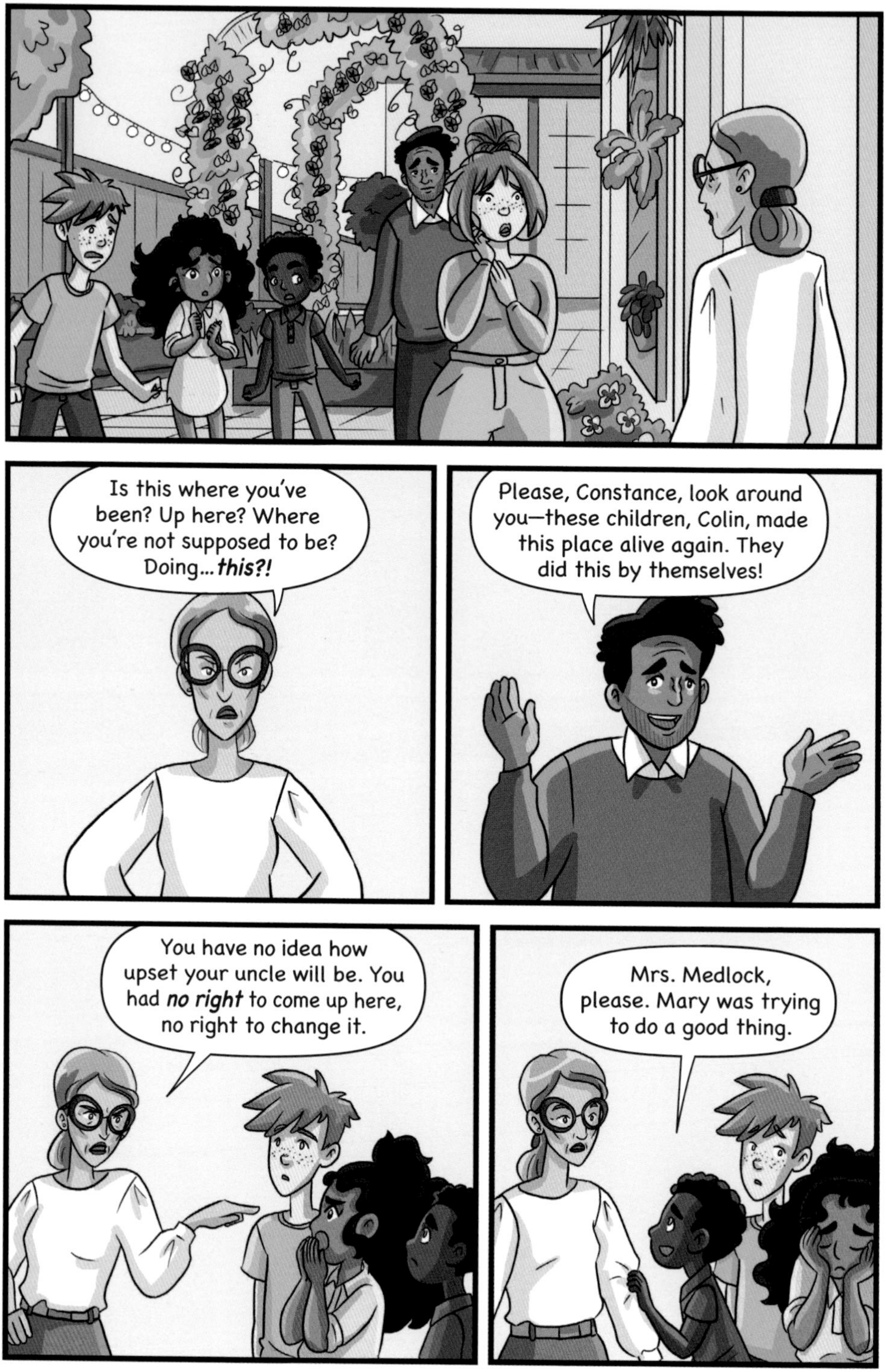
Is this where you've been? Up here? Where you're not supposed to be? Doing... *this?!*
Please, Constance, look around you—these children, Colin, made this place alive again. They did this by themselves!
You have no idea how upset your uncle will be. You had *no right* to come up here, no right to change it.
Mrs. Medlock, please. Mary was trying to do a good thing.

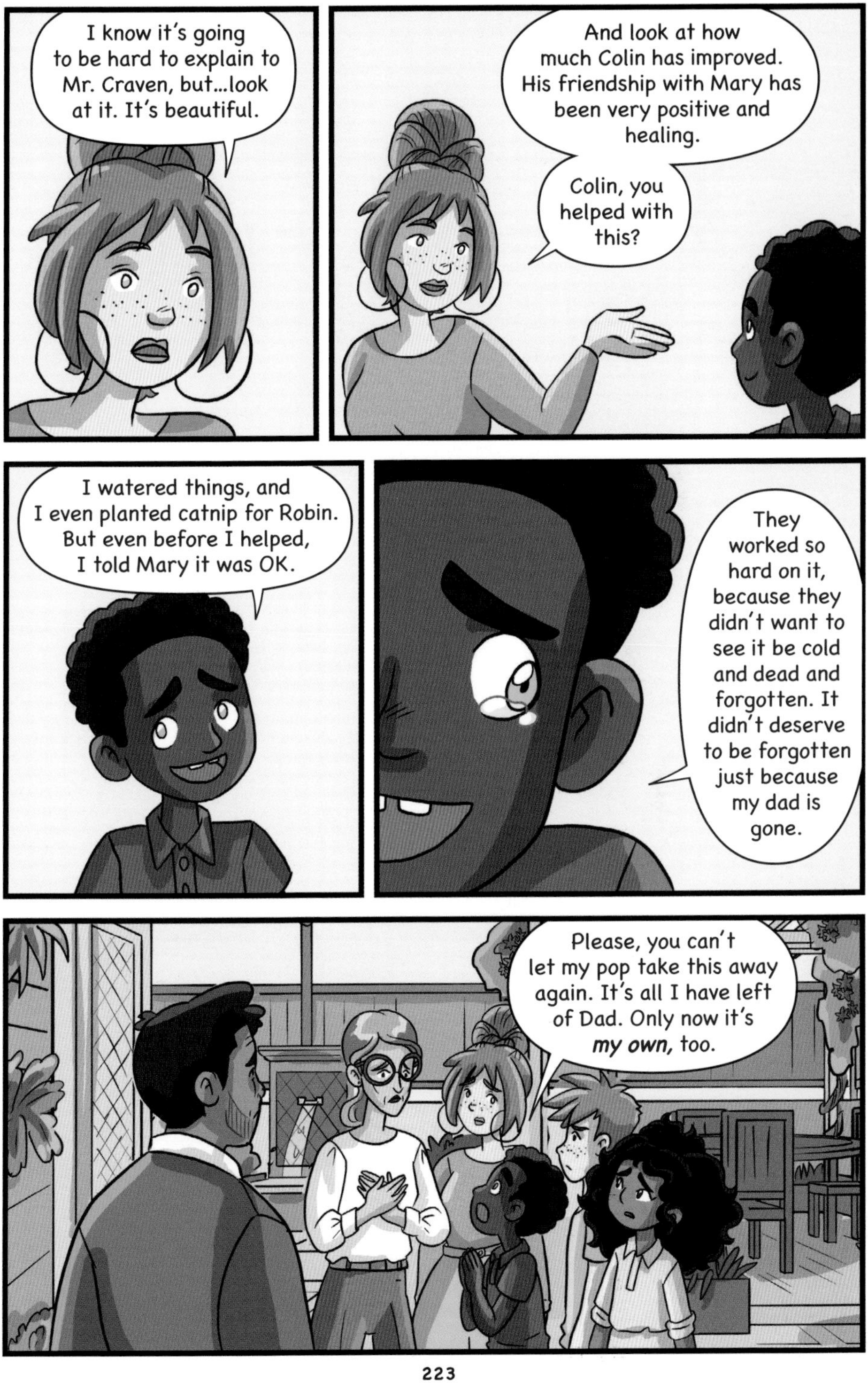
I know it's going to be hard to explain to Mr. Craven, but...look at it. It's beautiful.
And look at how much Colin has improved. His friendship with Mary has been very positive and healing.
Colin, you helped with this?
I watered things, and I even planted catnip for Robin. But even before I helped, I told Mary it was OK.
They worked so hard on it, because they didn't want to see it be cold and dead and forgotten. It didn't deserve to be forgotten just because my dad is gone.
Please, you can't let my pop take this away again. It's all I have left of Dad. Only now it's *my own,* too.

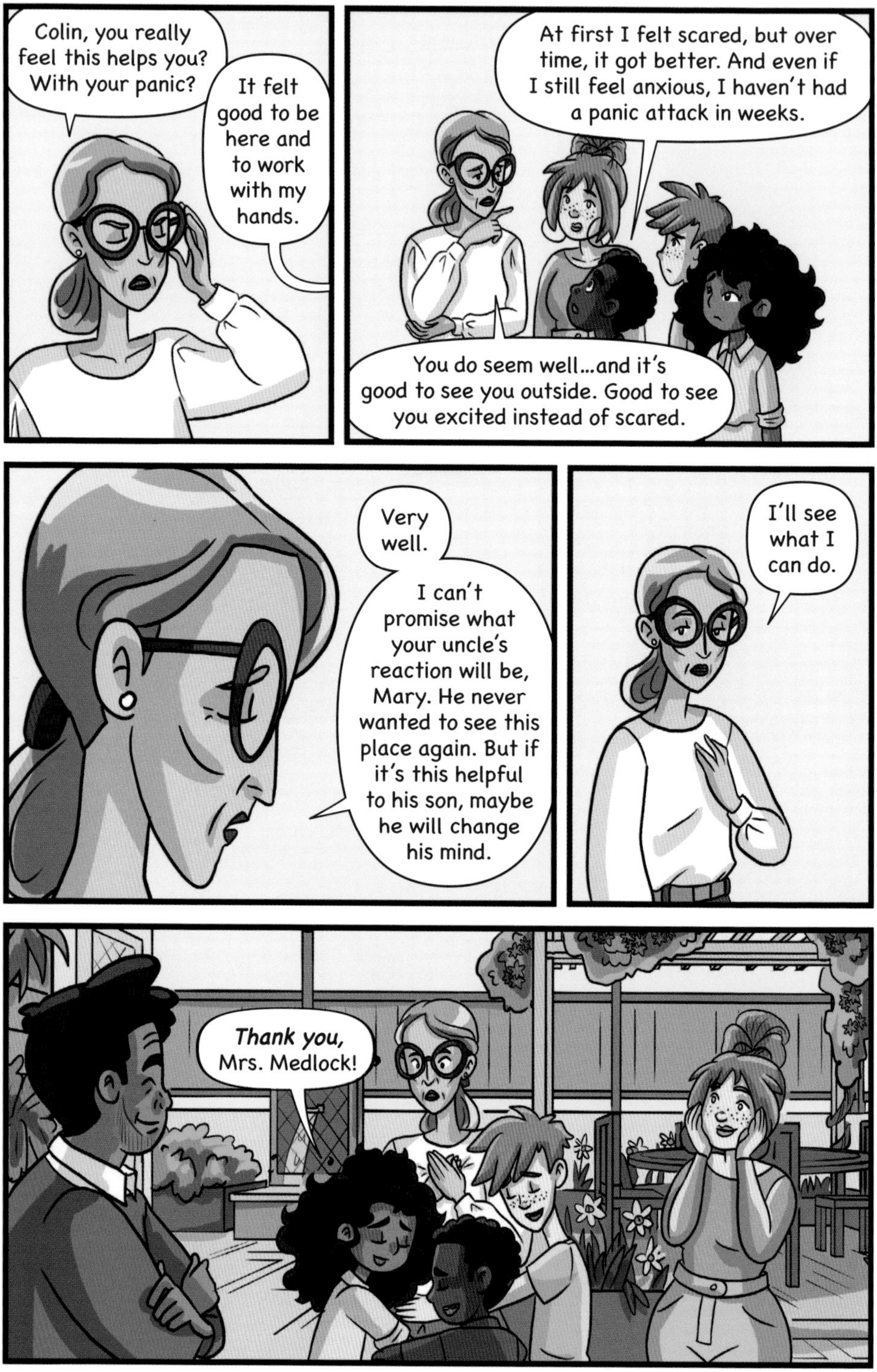
Colin, you really feel this helps you? With your panic?
It felt good to be here and to work with my hands.
At first I felt scared, but over time, it got better. And even if I still feel anxious, I haven't had a panic attack in weeks.
You do seem well...and it's good to see you outside. Good to see you excited instead of scared.
Very well.
I can't promise what your uncle's reaction will be, Mary. He never wanted to see this place again. But if it's this helpful to his son, maybe he will change his mind.
I'll see what I can do.
Thank you, Mrs. Medlock!

Medlock

eMAIL

INBOX | Starred | Sent | Drafts | Spam

NEW MESSAGE

TO: archibald_craven@craveninc.com
FROM: medlock_cravenhousehold@craveninc.com

SUBJECT: Colin

Archie,

I hope things are well in Hong Kong. The purpose of this letter concerns Colin. Don't worry, he is well—he is more than well. He and your niece have found each other and, despite my worries that the girl would be too much for him, they seem to have bonded quite quickly.

I know you had planned to stay in Asia an additional month. But I feel like now would be a good time for you and Colin to talk. I may be overstepping my role here, but I hope you will at least consider coming to see him.

Best wishes,
Constance

SEND

Household finance

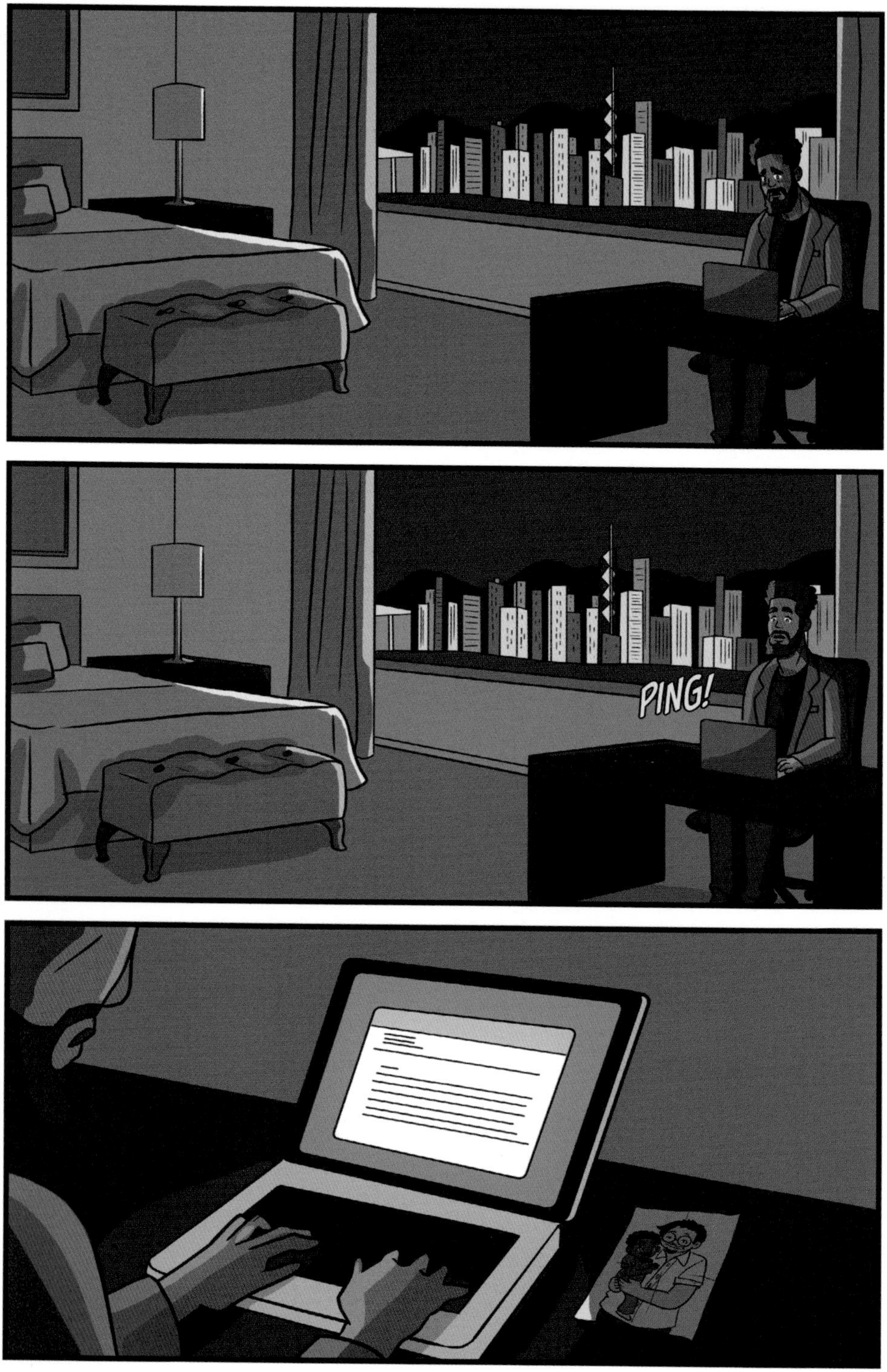
PING!

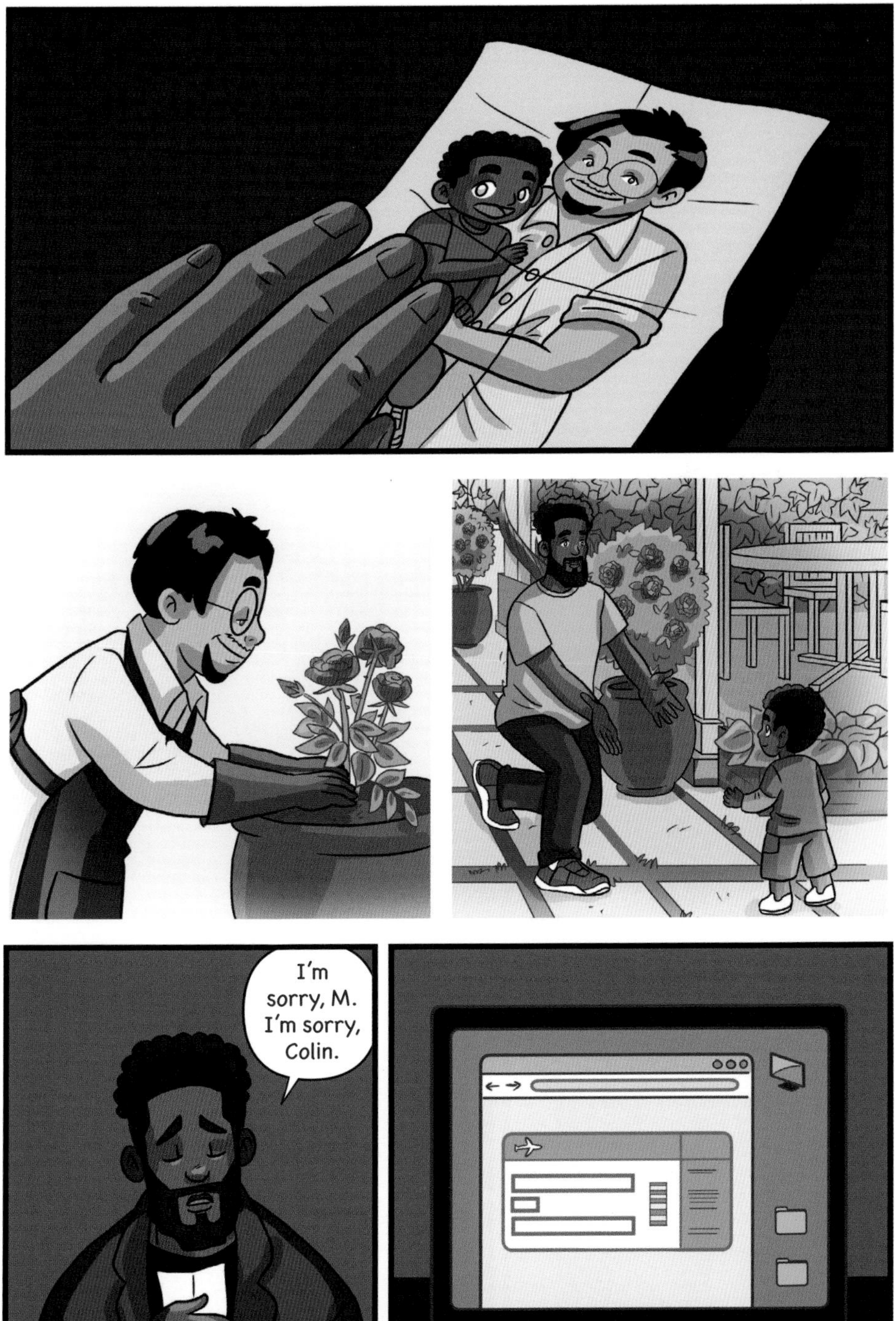
I'm sorry, M. I'm sorry, Colin.

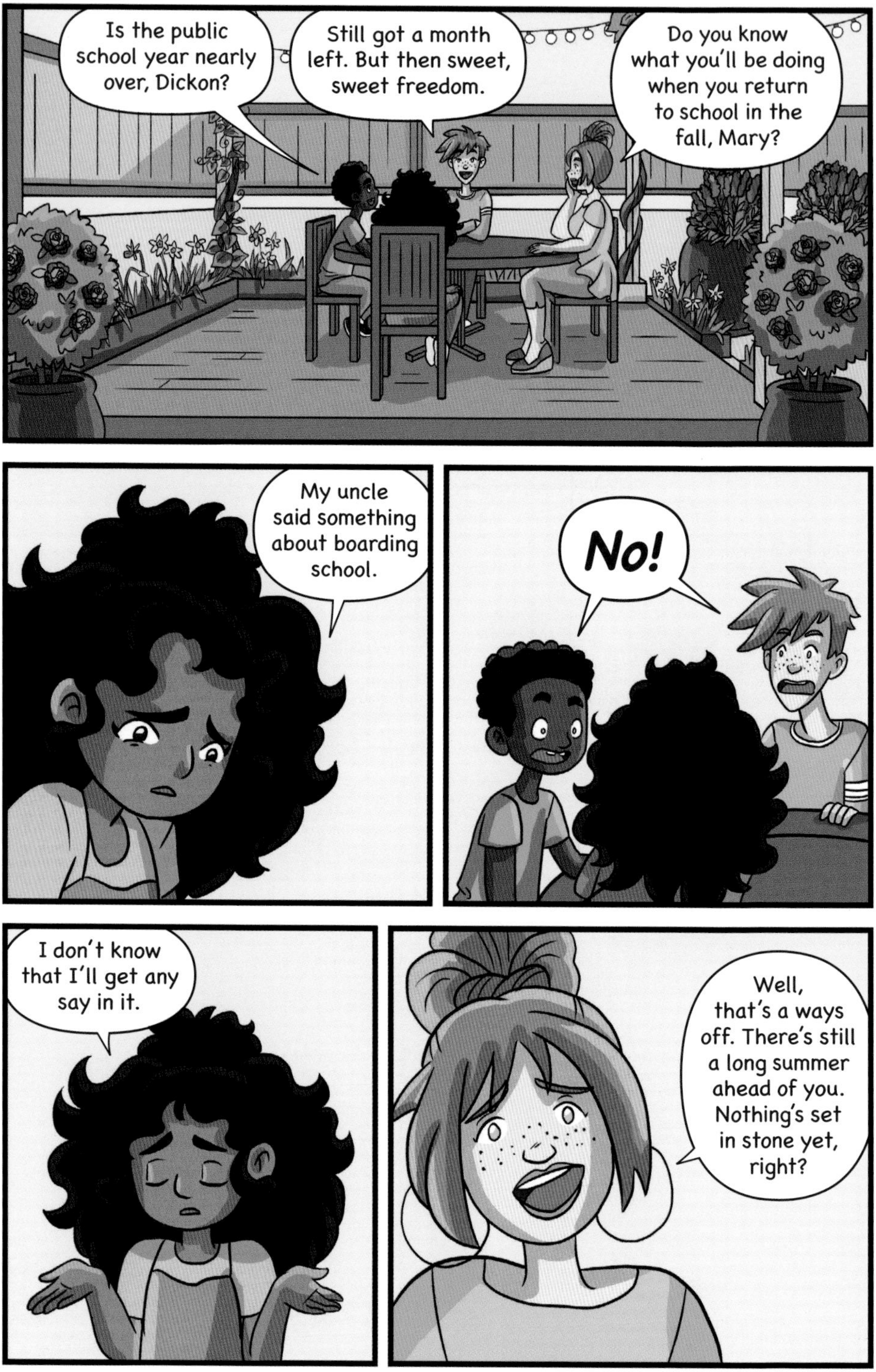
Is the public school year nearly over, Dickon?
Still got a month left. But then sweet, sweet freedom.
Do you know what you'll be doing when you return to school in the fall, Mary?
My uncle said something about boarding school.
No!
I don't know that I'll get any say in it.
Well, that's a ways off. There's still a long summer ahead of you. Nothing's set in stone yet, right?

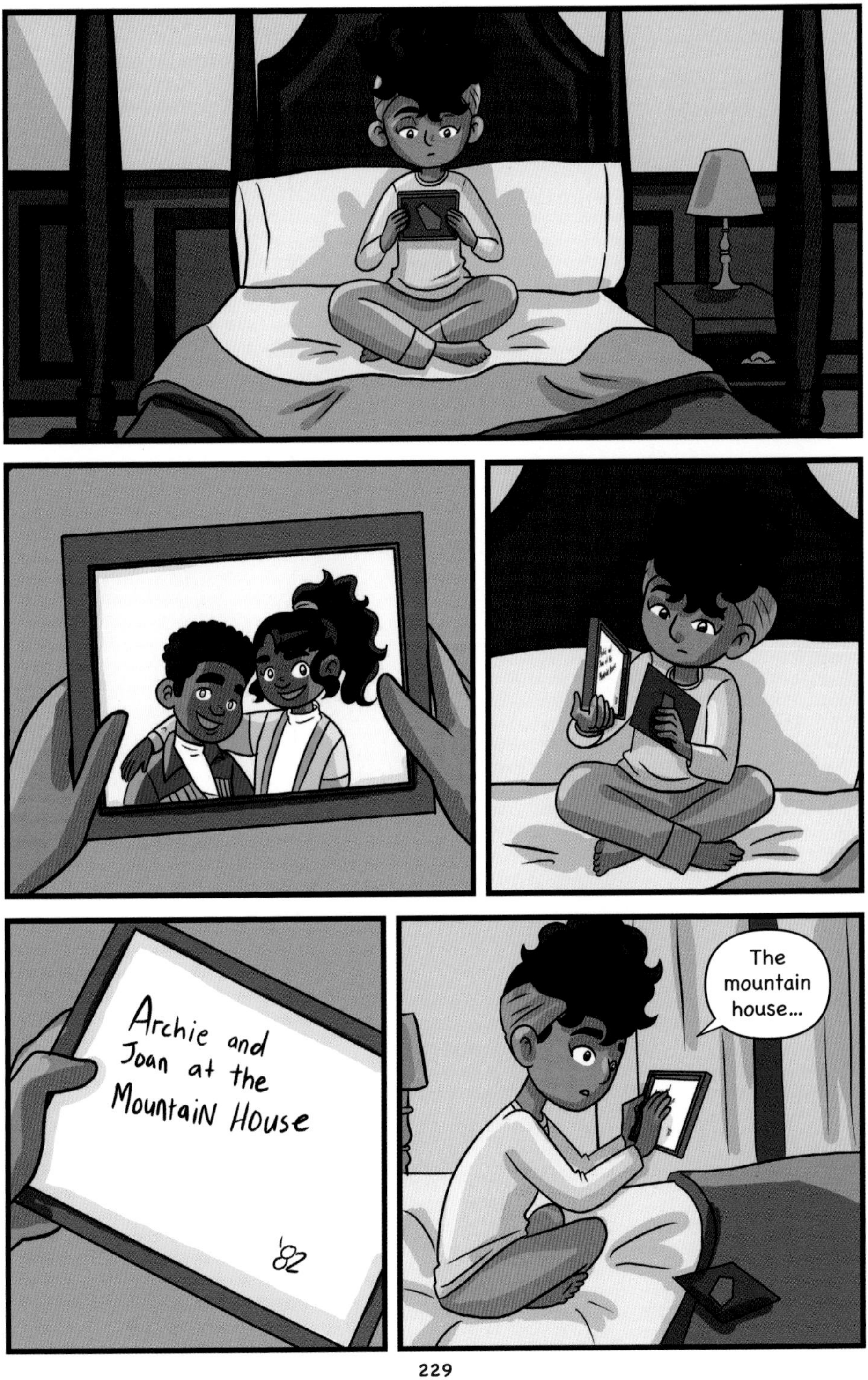

Archie and Joan at the Mountain House
'82
The mountain house...

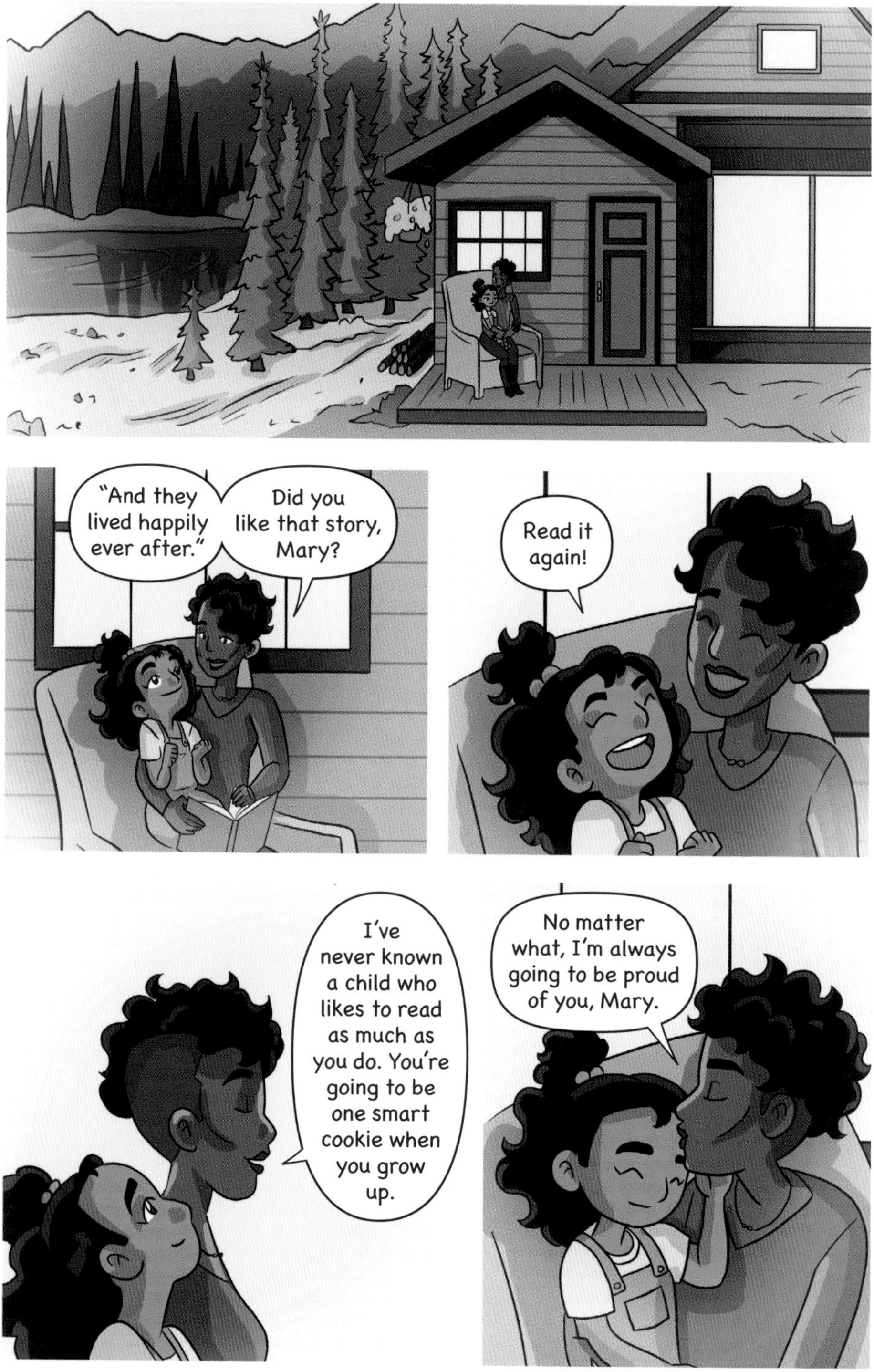
"And they lived happily ever after."
Did you like that story, Mary?
Read it again!
I've never known a child who likes to read as much as you do. You're going to be one smart cookie when you grow up.
No matter what, I'm always going to be proud of you, Mary.

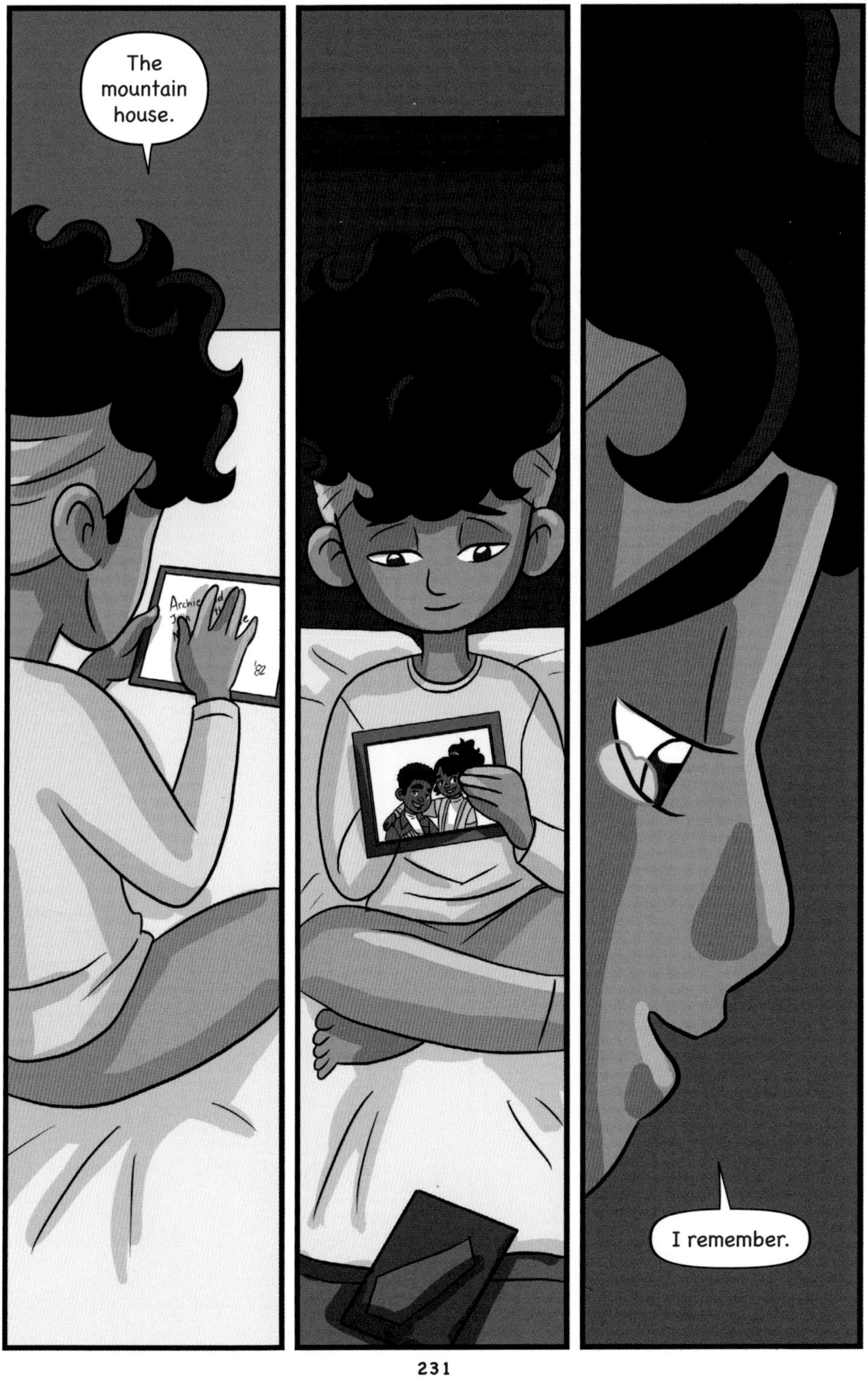
The mountain house.
I remember.

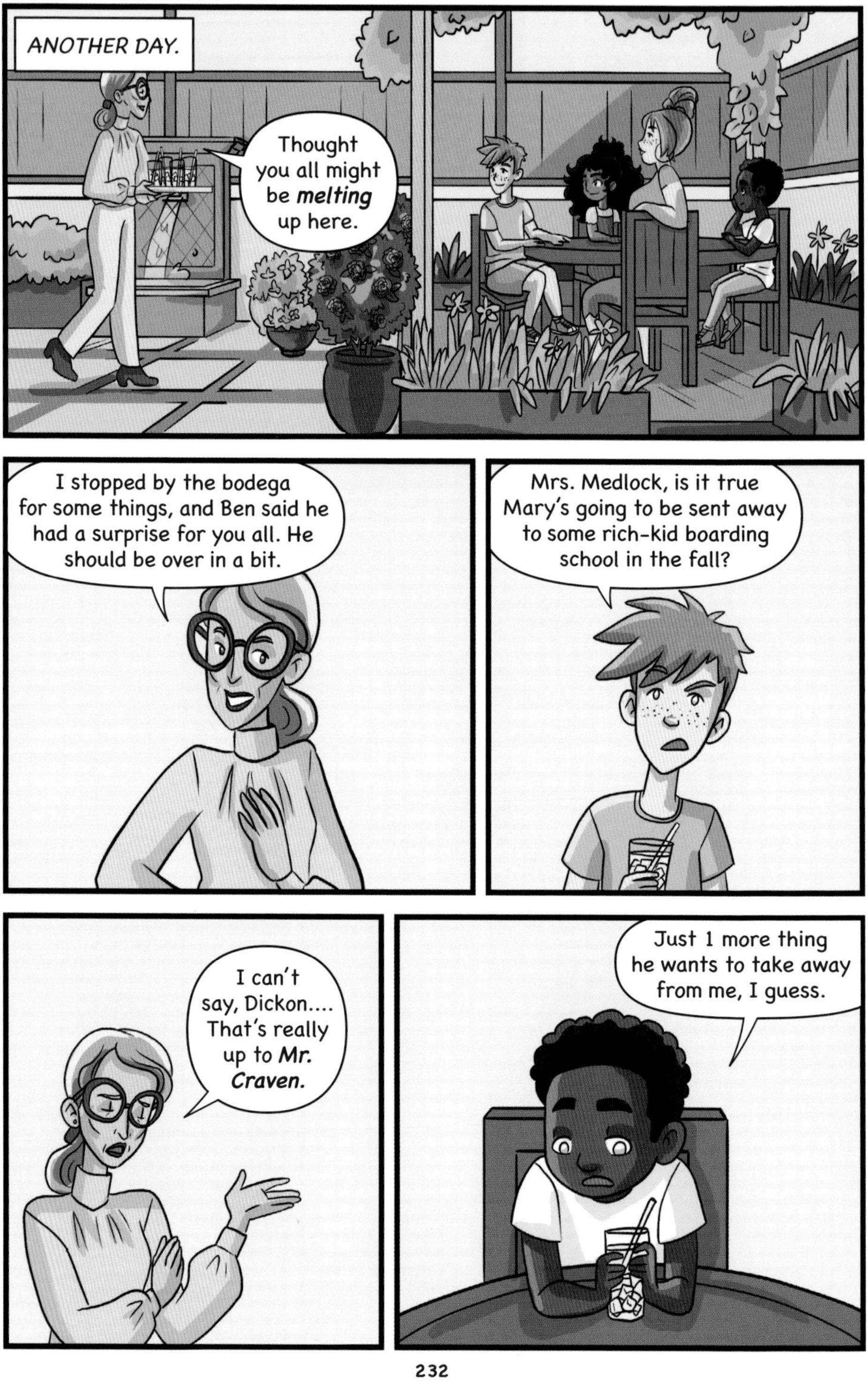
ANOTHER DAY.
Thought you all might be *melting* up here.
I stopped by the bodega for some things, and Ben said he had a surprise for you all. He should be over in a bit.
Mrs. Medlock, is it true Mary's going to be sent away to some rich-kid boarding school in the fall?
I can't say, Dickon.... That's really up to *Mr. Craven.*
Just 1 more thing he wants to take away from me, I guess.

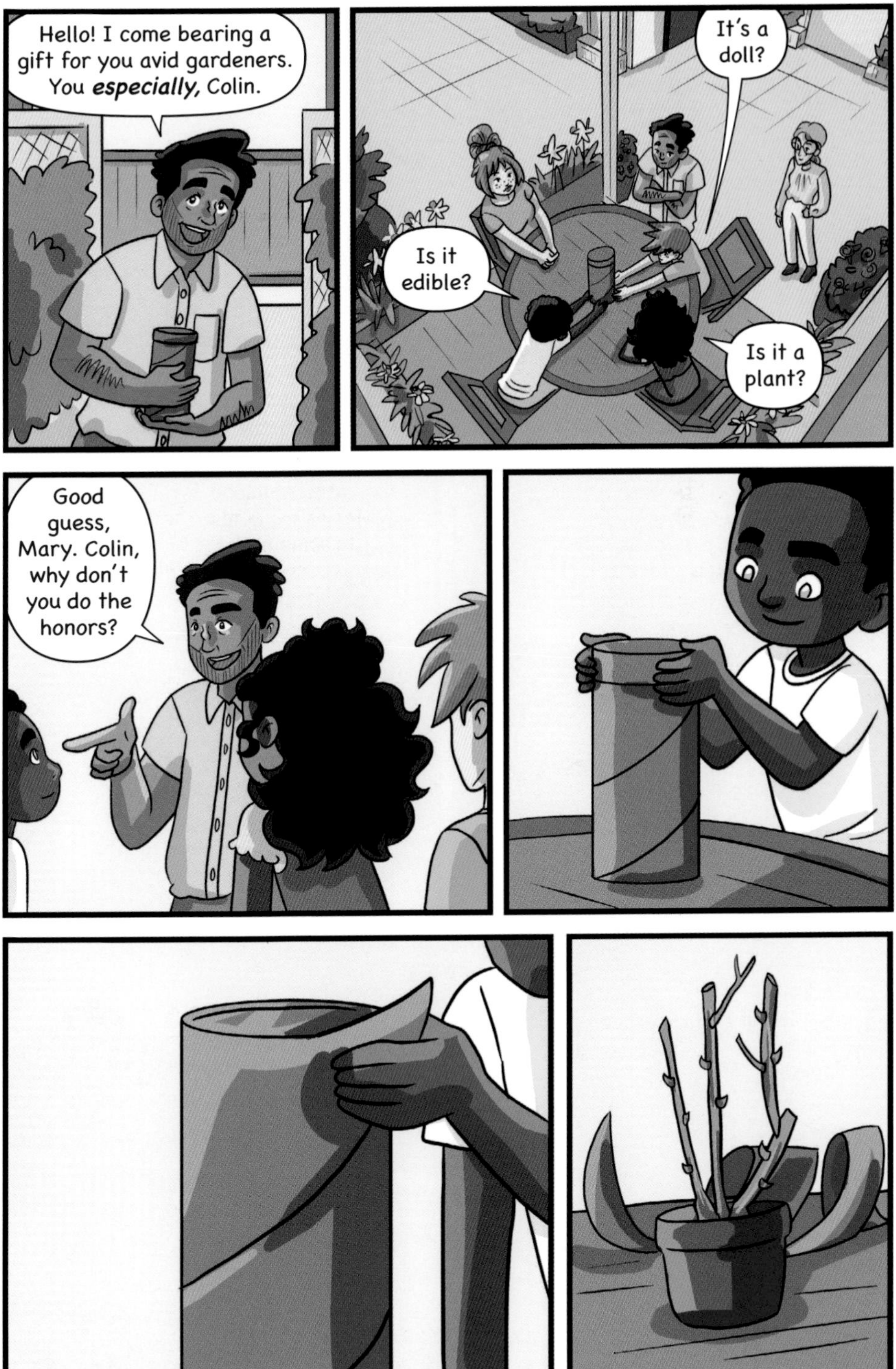
Hello! I come bearing a gift for you avid gardeners. You *especially,* Colin.
It's a doll?
Is it edible?
Is it a plant?
Good guess, Mary. Colin, why don't you do the honors?

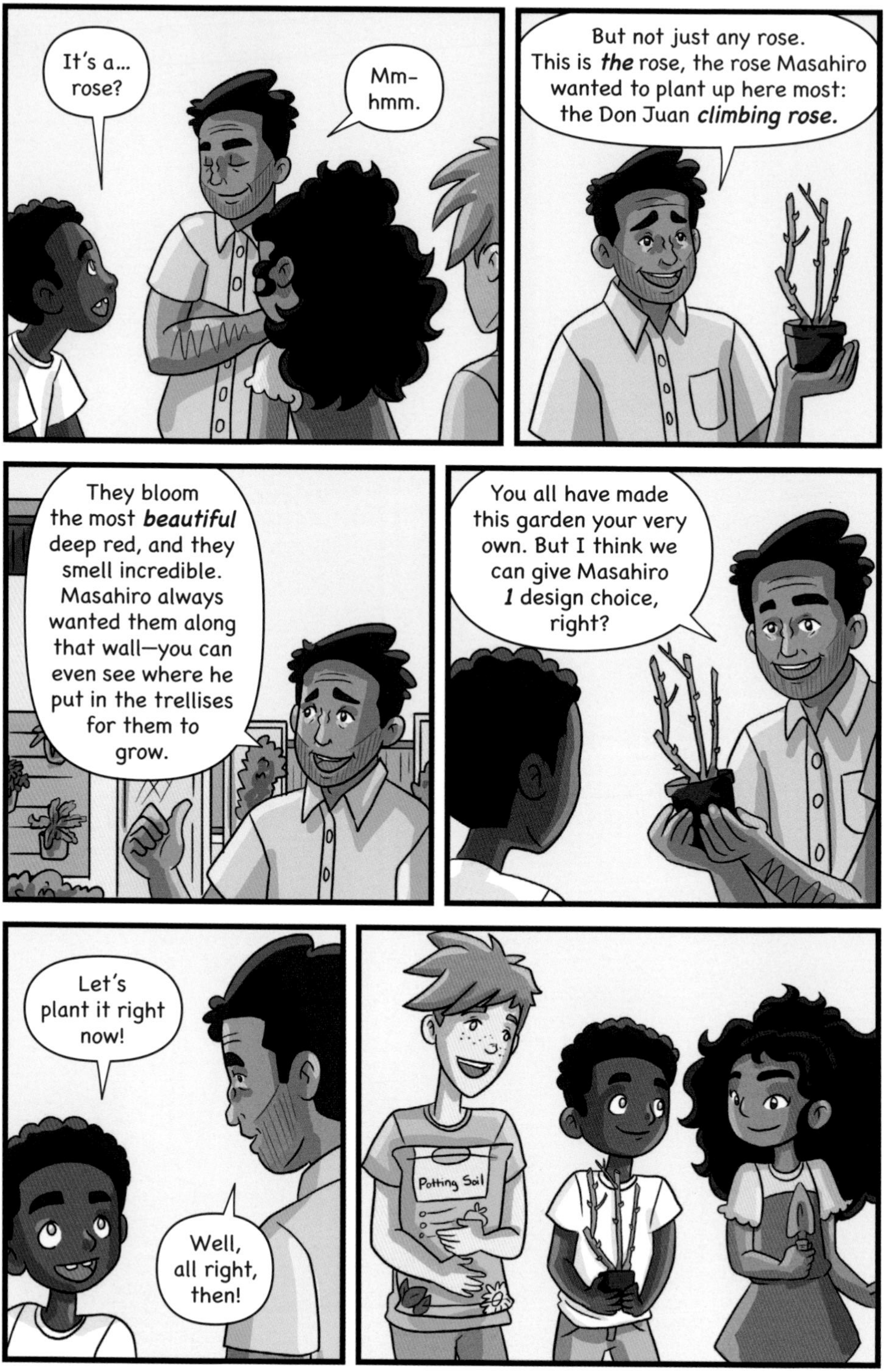
It's a... rose?
Mm-hmm.
But not just any rose. This is *the* rose, the rose Masahiro wanted to plant up here most: the Don Juan *climbing rose.*
They bloom the most *beautiful* deep red, and they smell incredible. Masahiro always wanted them along that wall—you can even see where he put in the trellises for them to grow.
You all have made this garden your very own. But I think we can give Masahiro *1* design choice, right?
Let's plant it right now!
Well, all right, then!
Potting Soil

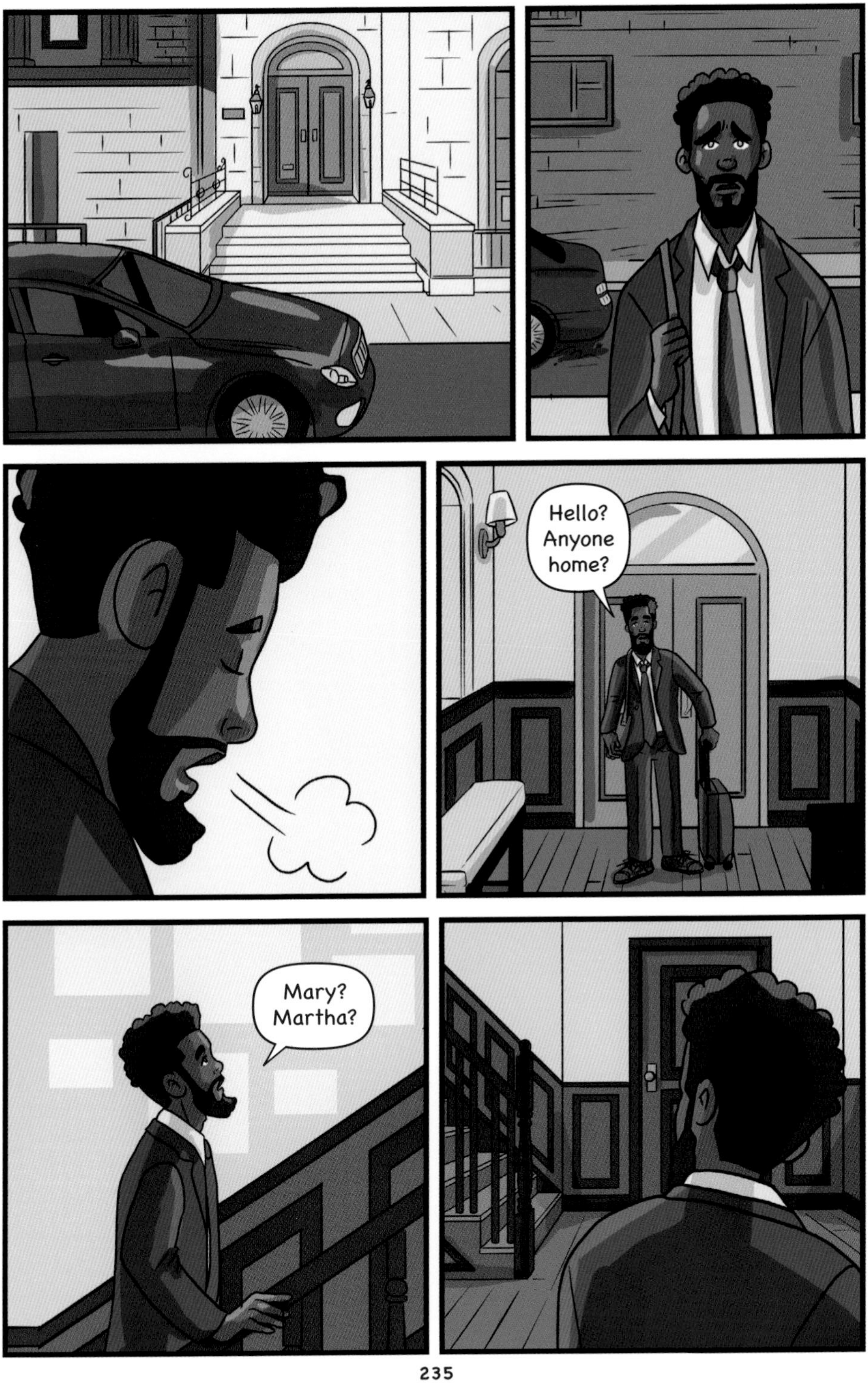
Hello?
Anyone
home?
Mary?
Martha?

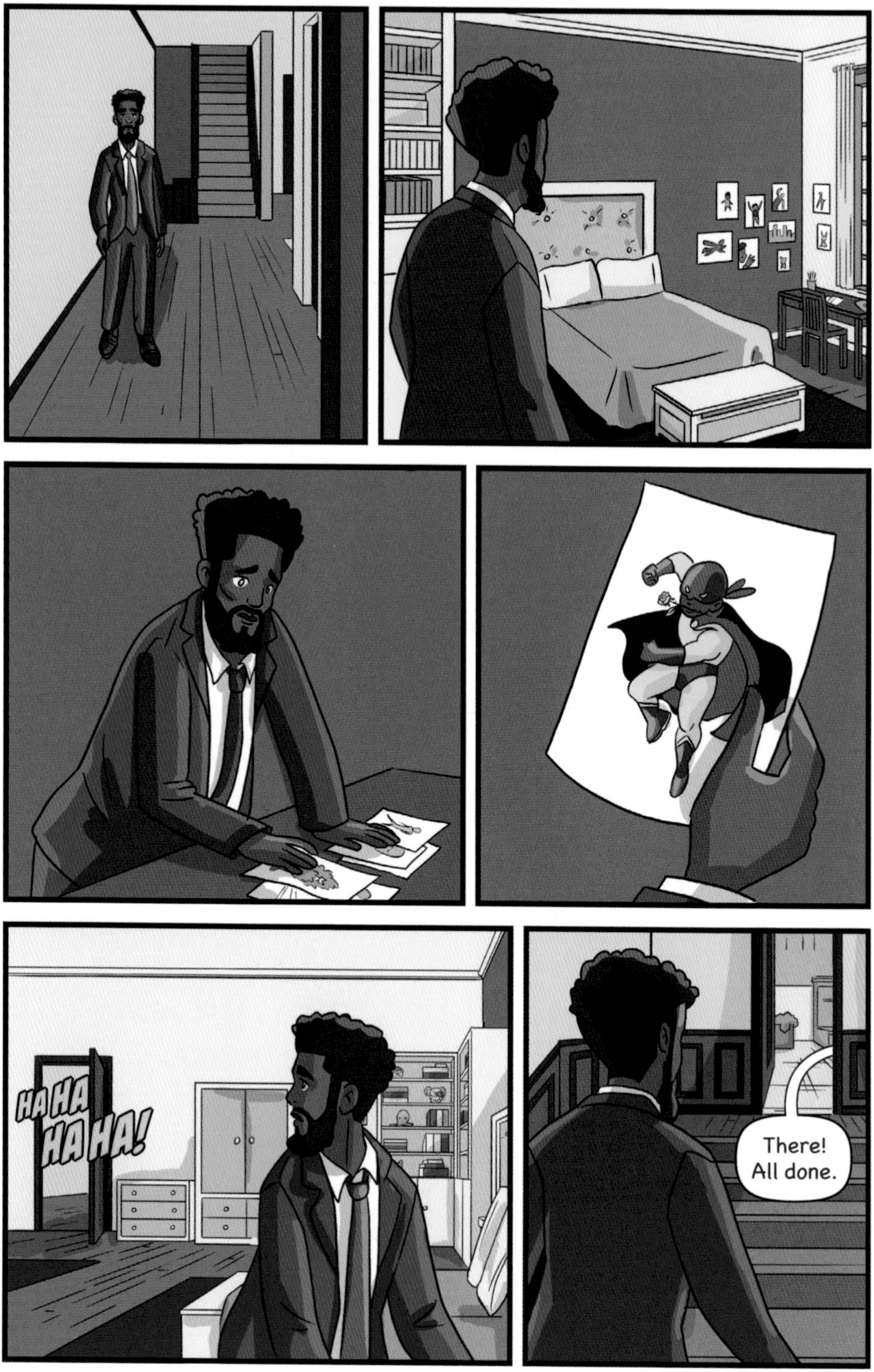
HA HA
HA HA!
There!
All done.

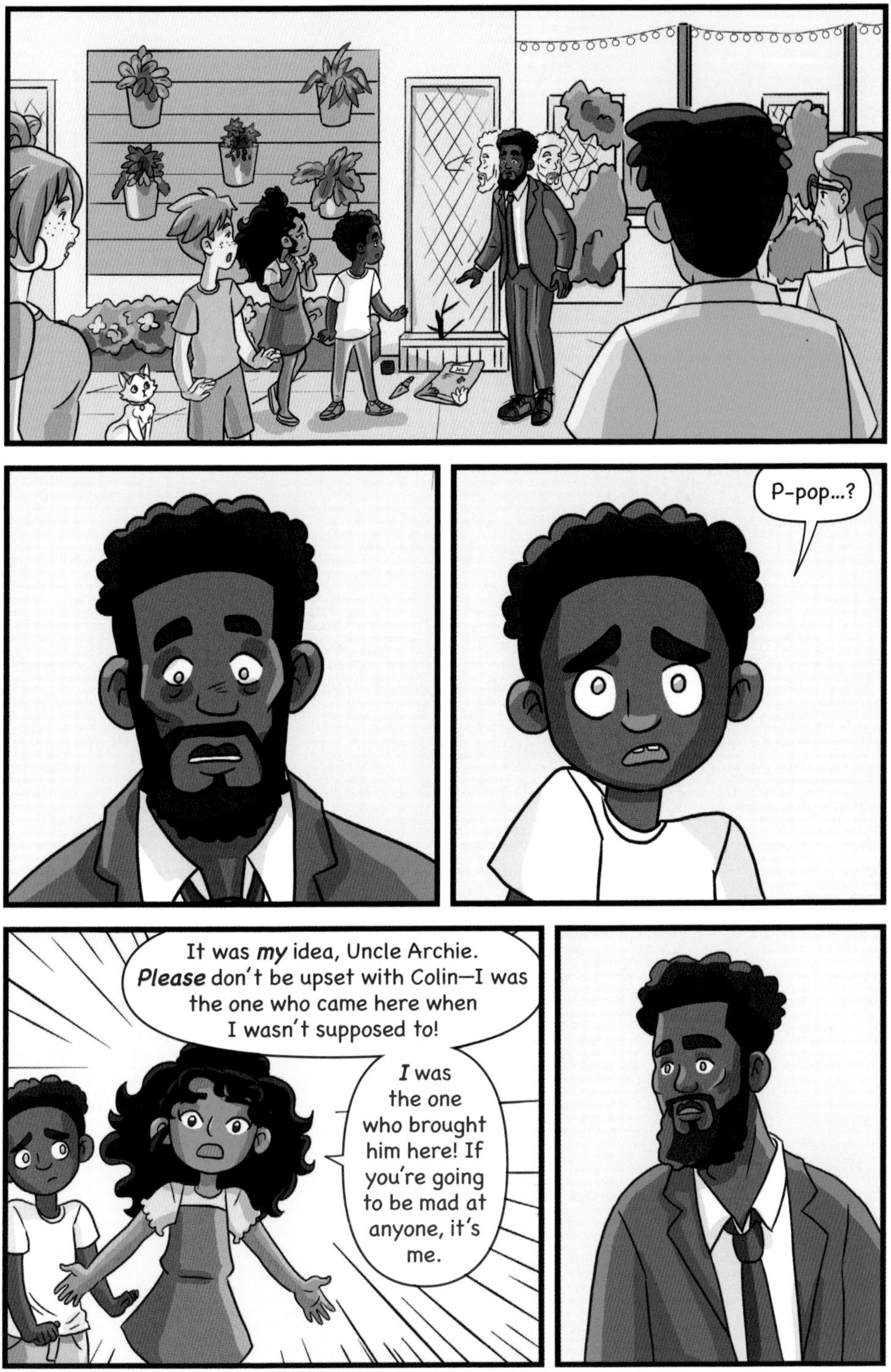
P-pop...?
It was *my* idea, Uncle Archie. *Please* don't be upset with Colin—I was the one who came here when I wasn't supposed to!
I was the one who brought him here! If you're going to be mad at anyone, it's me.

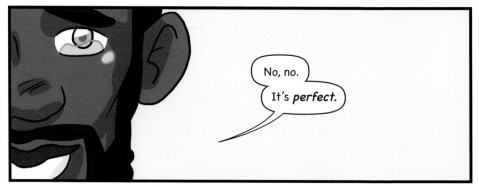

No, no.

It's *perfect.*

This place was Masahiro's passion, his dream.

From the moment we first saw the house, he knew he wanted to put a garden on the roof.

It took years for him to create it, to make it what it once was. What it is now, again.

And he would *love* this. Colin, he would love what you've done here. *I* love what you've done here.

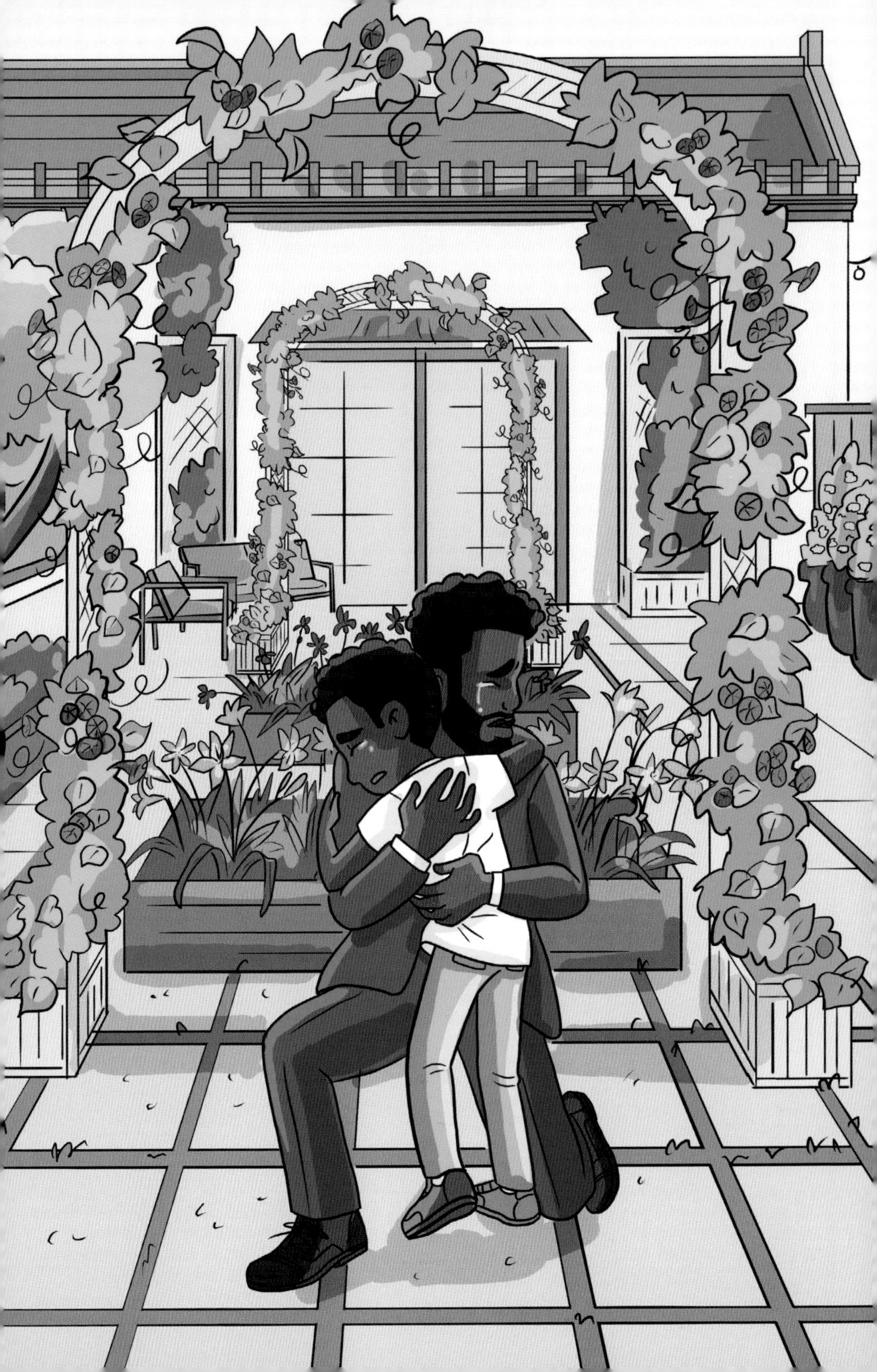

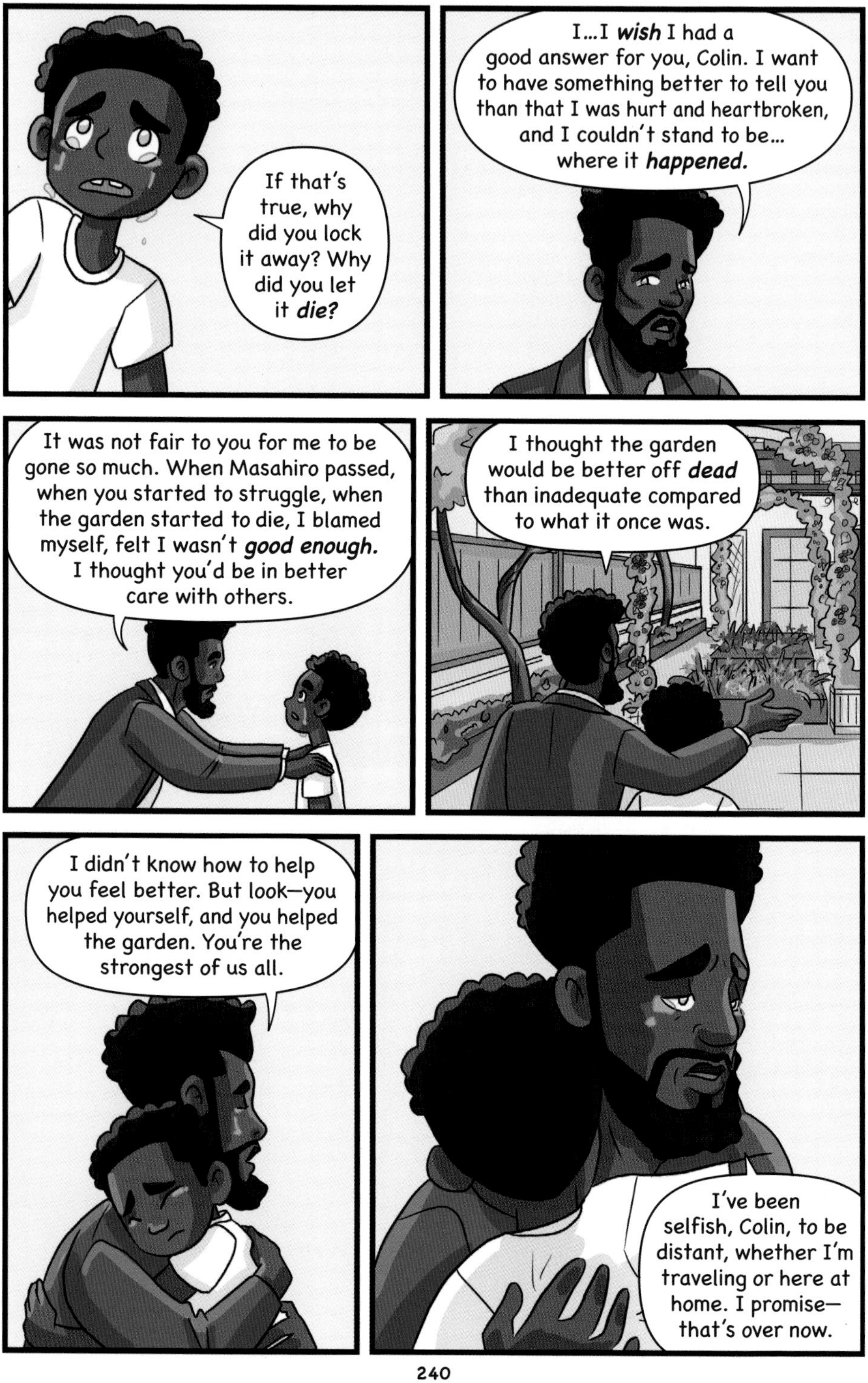
If that's true, why did you lock it away? Why did you let it *die?*
I...I *wish* I had a good answer for you, Colin. I want to have something better to tell you than that I was hurt and heartbroken, and I couldn't stand to be... where it *happened.*
It was not fair to you for me to be gone so much. When Masahiro passed, when you started to struggle, when the garden started to die, I blamed myself, felt I wasn't *good enough.* I thought you'd be in better care with others.
I thought the garden would be better off *dead* than inadequate compared to what it once was.
I didn't know how to help you feel better. But look—you helped yourself, and you helped the garden. You're the strongest of us all.
I've been selfish, Colin, to be distant, whether I'm traveling or here at home. I promise—that's over now.

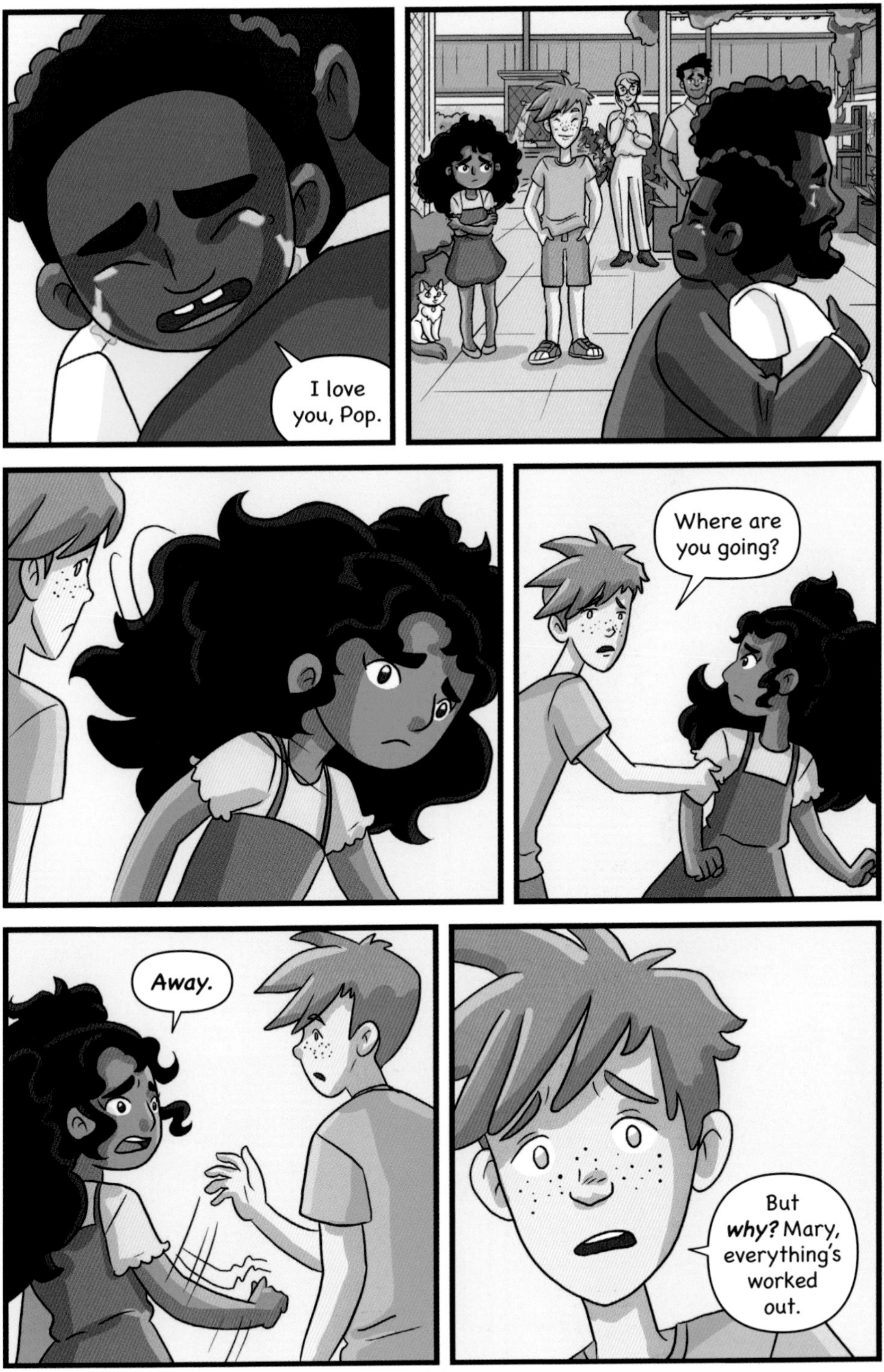
I love you, Pop.
Where are you going?
Away.
But why? Mary, everything's worked out.

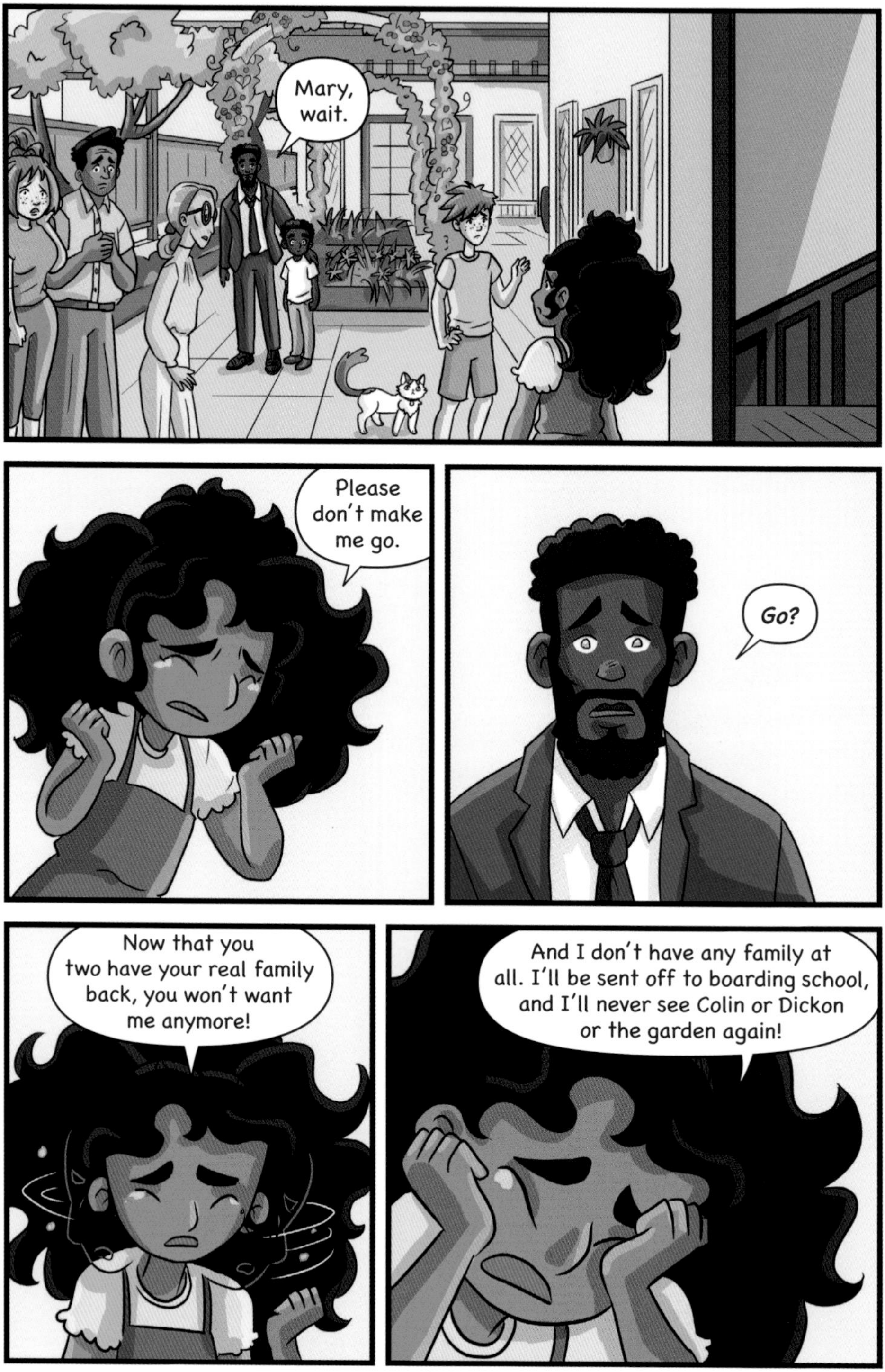
Mary,
wait.
Please don't make me go.
Go?
Now that you two have your real family back, you won't want me anymore!
And I don't have any family at all. I'll be sent off to boarding school, and I'll never see Colin or Dickon or the garden again!

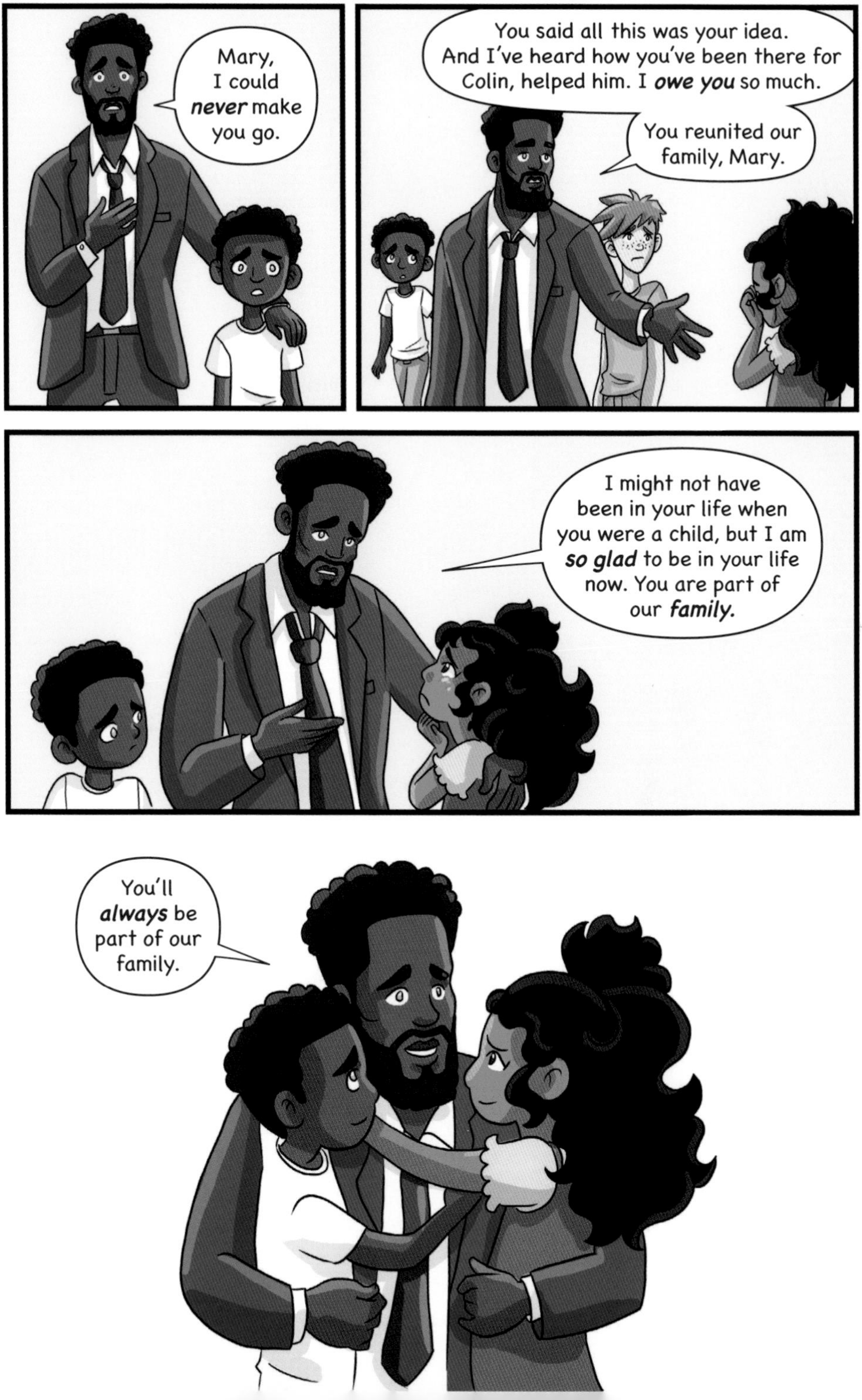
Mary, I could *never* make you go.
You said all this was your idea. And I've heard how you've been there for Colin, helped him. I *owe you* so much.
You reunited our family, Mary.
I might not have been in your life when you were a child, but I am *so glad* to be in your life now. You are part of our *family.*
You'll *always* be part of our family.

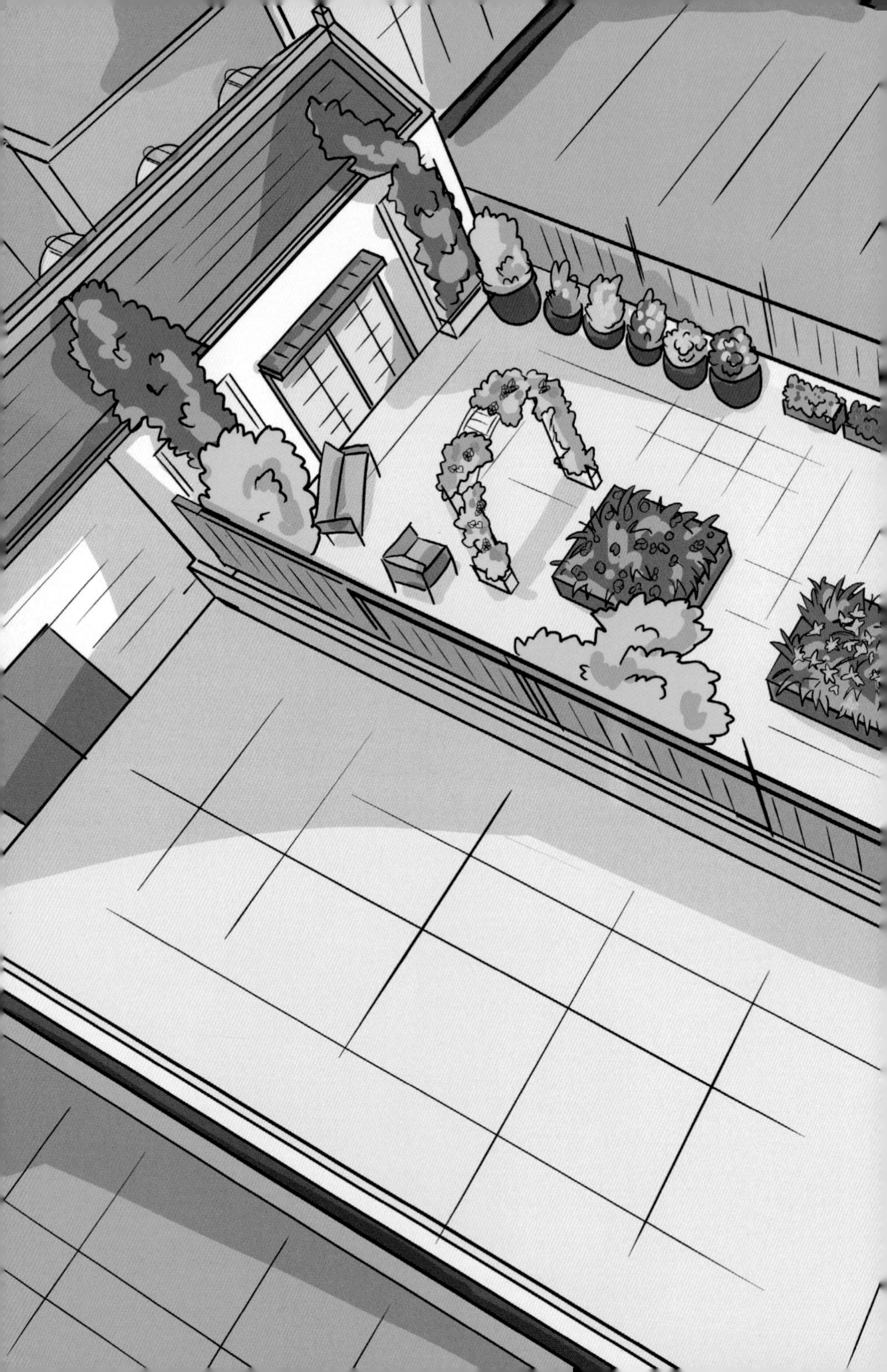

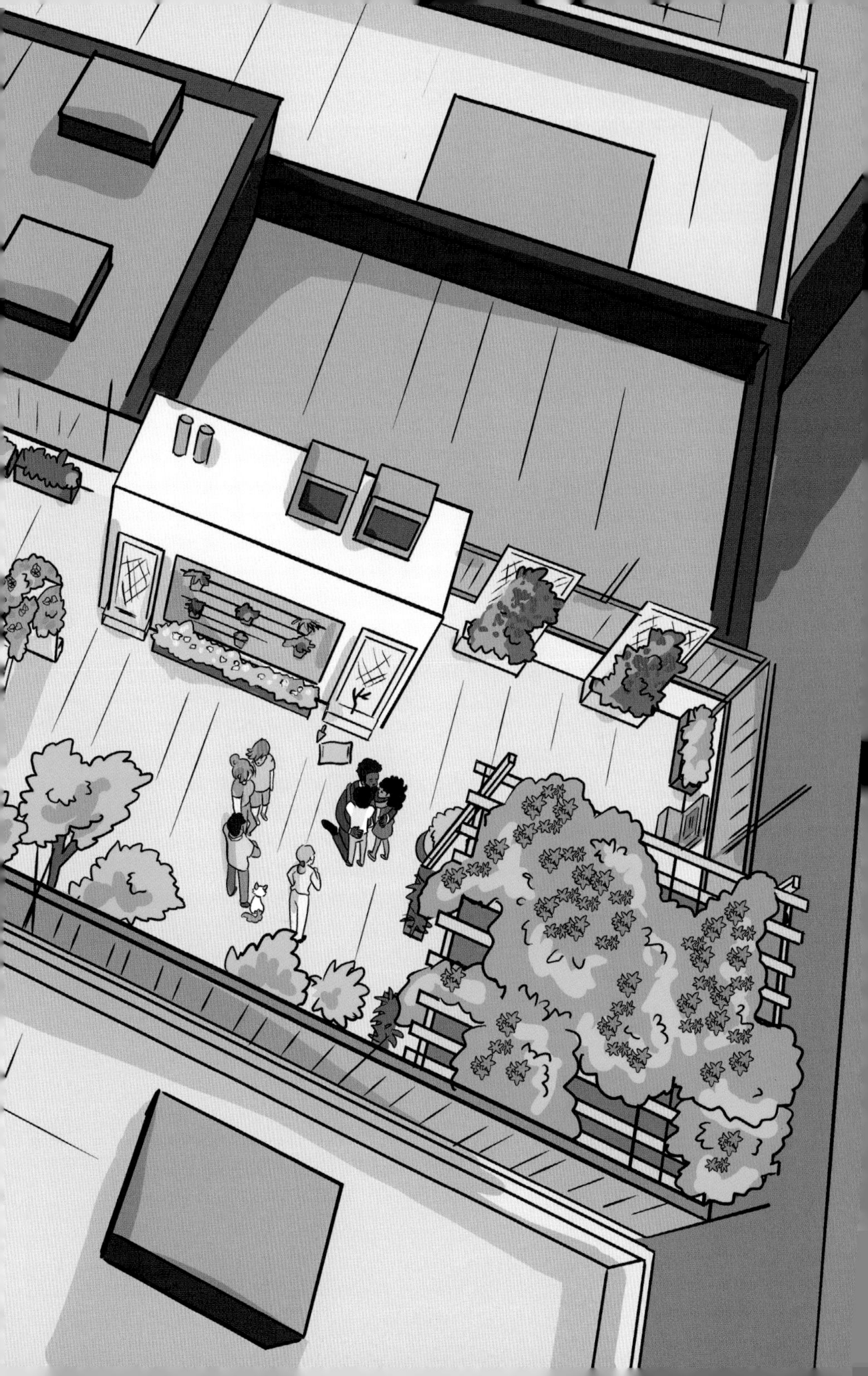

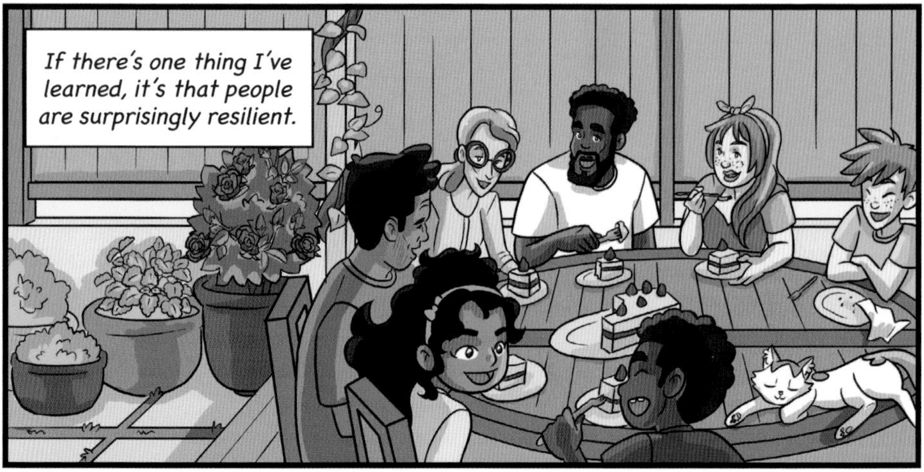
If there's one thing I've learned, it's that people are surprisingly resilient.

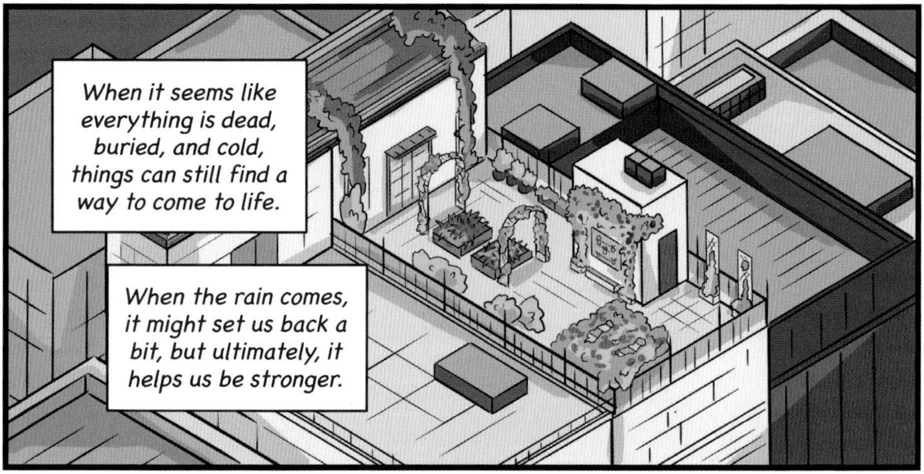
When it seems like everything is dead, buried, and cold, things can still find a way to come to life.
When the rain comes, it might set us back a bit, but ultimately, it helps us be stronger.

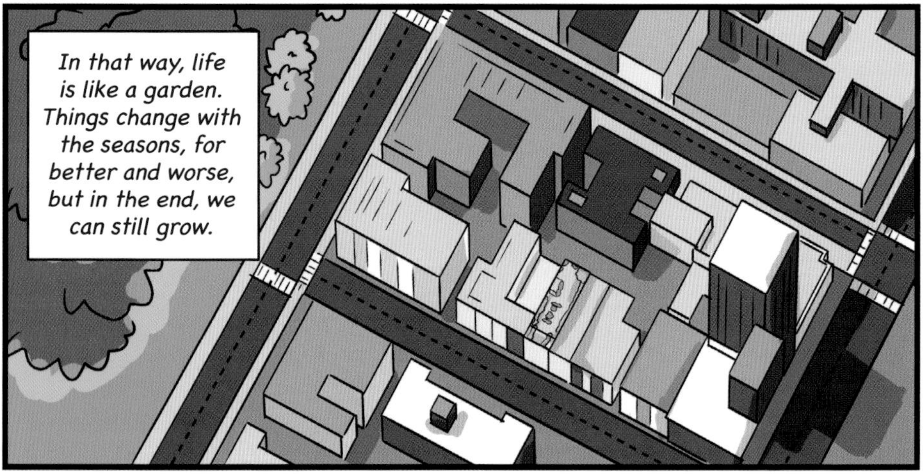
In that way, life is like a garden. Things change with the seasons, for better and worse, but in the end, we can still grow.

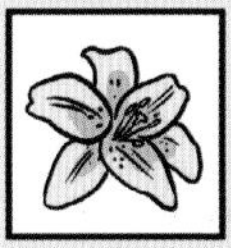

The_Secret_Garden

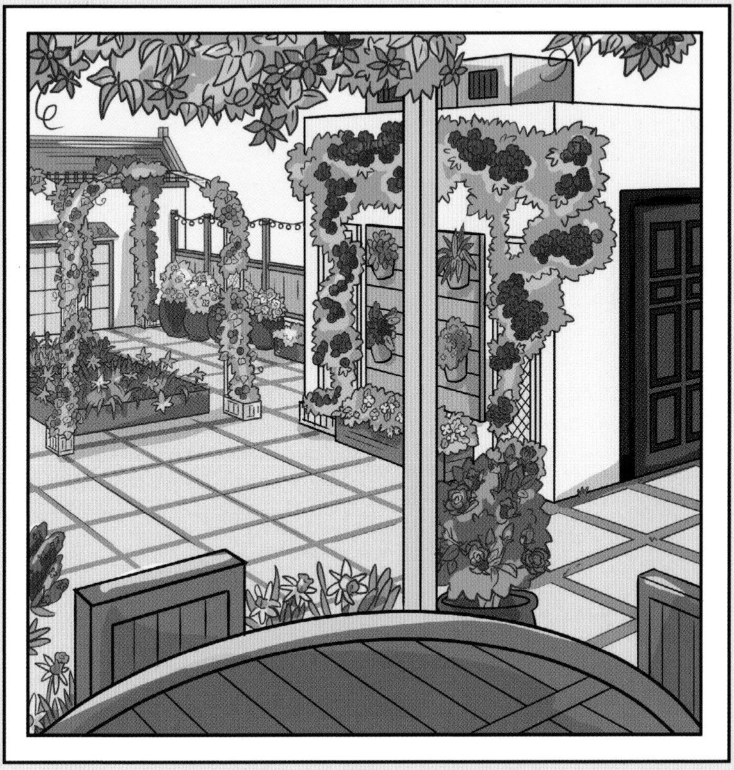

The_Secret_Garden Since the garden is in the sun all day, these plants are pretty much always thirsty. All this beauty means hours of watering!

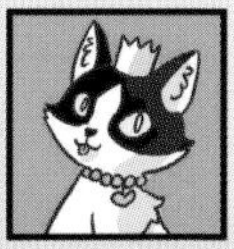

The_Cultured_Cat

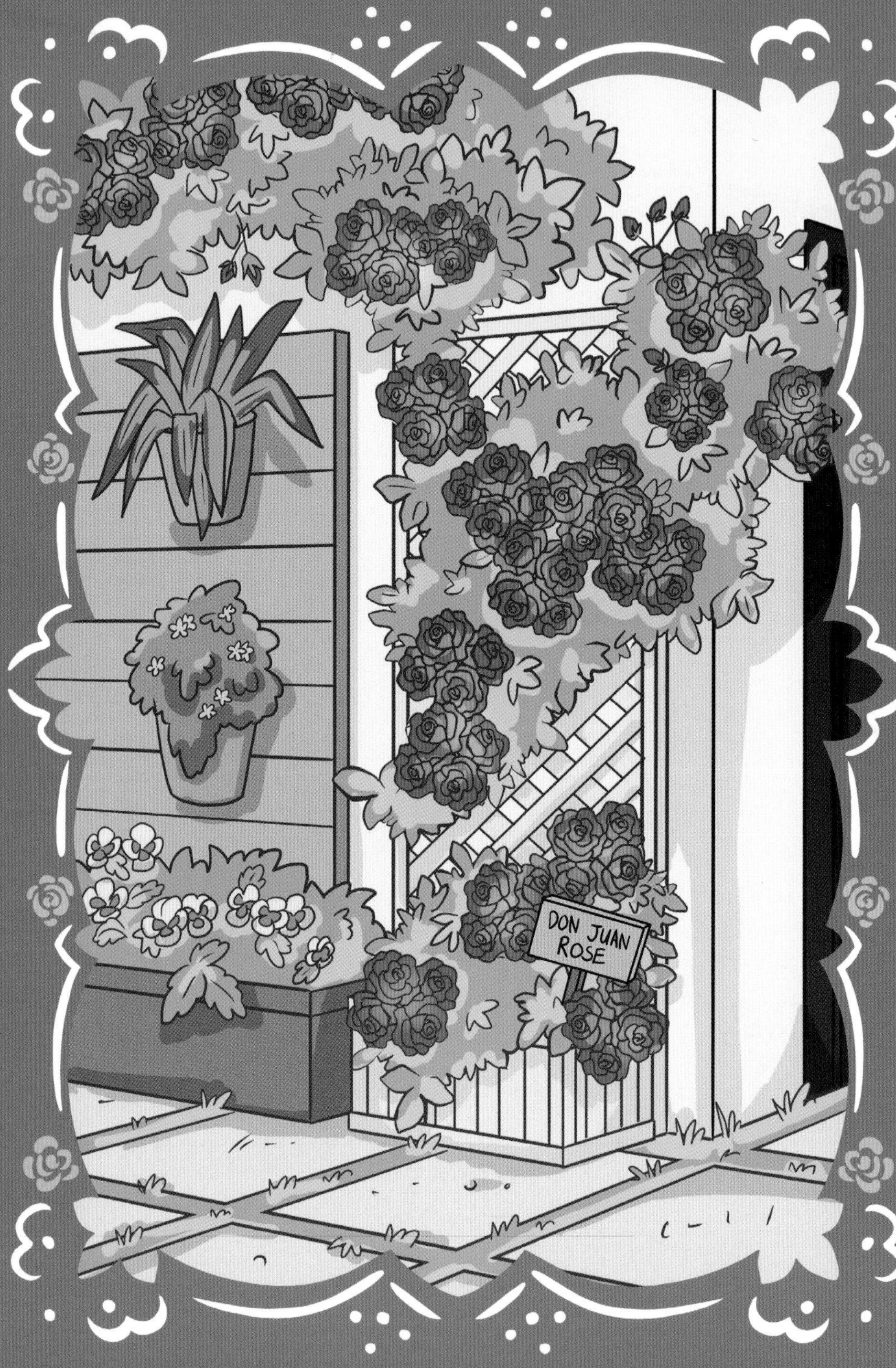
DON JUAN
ROSE

Acknowledgments

Endless thanks to my agent, Anjali Singh, for her wisdom and guidance, and my editor, Rachel Poloski, for her insight, for her encouragement, and for the opportunity to tell Mary's story. Forever love to my husband, Eugene, for his support and his frozen-pizza-baking skills on deadline nights. Eternal gratitude to Steenz, my best friend, creative sounding board, and hype man. -Weir

Thank you to my husband, Ioannis, who did more than just support me while I ventured through the biggest project in my life thus far. Thank you to the BlamKatz, who gave me all the pointers, tips, and encouragement a newbie could ask for. Thank you to my family, who gave me unconditional support in my art aspirations so that I never doubted what was possible. Thank you to every art teacher, college professor, work colleague, and friend who knew I could do this. And lastly thanks to Nicky Rodriguez and K. Novack, who made sure I could get to that finish line. -Padilla

Eugene K. Ahn

Ivy Noelle Weir

is a writer of comics and prose. She is the cocreator of the Dwayne McDuffie Award-winning graphic novel *Archival Quality*, and her writing has appeared in anthologies such as *Princeless: Girls Rock* and *Dead Beats*. She lives in the greater Boston area with her husband and their two tiny, weird dogs.

Amber Padilla

Amber Padilla

is a cartoonist and illustrator based in Oakland, CA, and holds an MFA in Comics from California College of the Arts. *The Secret Garden on 81st Street* is Amber's debut graphic novel. Originally from Santa Ana, CA, she was raised on a healthy diet of animation, science fiction, soap operas, and Japanese anime and manga. When she's not drawing or crafting, she enjoys snuggling with her cat and spending time with her husband, family, and friends.